CONTENTS

Copyright	
Dedication	
Act 1 – She's So High	4
One	5
Two	17
Three	36
Four	46
Five	66
Six	91
Seven	110
Eight	134
Nine	154
Ten	171
Act 2 – This is a Low	187
Eleven	188
Twelve	200
Thirteen	221
Fourteen	241
Fifteen	263
Sixteen	289

Seventeen	310
Eighteen	338
Nineteen	362
Twenty	381
Act 2 – Sunday Sunday	397
Twenty-one	398
Twenty-two	418
Twenty-three	434
Twenty-four	456
Twenty-five	477
Twenty-six	498
Twenty-seven	519
Twenty-eight	542
Twenty-nine	563
Thirty	587
Epilogue – Bank Holiday	620
Afterword	634

Copyright © 2021 Ciarán West

All rights reserved

For all those 70s kids who made the 90s the new 60s

BREAKING INTO HEAVEN

BY CIARÁN WEST

The year after I lost my sister and my boyfriend should have been hell, but it wasn't. The boys from Jon's band were so good to me. Bríd too, and Ciara. Then, somehow, I was part of that band, and our band hit the big time – in Ireland, at least. By the time we were booked to play Féile '95 it was like I hadn't taken a breath in eleven months. They say the past catches up with everyone, eventually, but I wasn't ready to be caught yet. Back then, I thought I could keep running forever. That insane, beautiful weekend in Cork City changed everything. There was sex, drugs, and we even found time to fit in a little rock and roll. I laughed a lot, and I cried a little. I got high, I got low, I found out so much – about my friends, about love, and about who I was meant to be.

ACT 1 – SHE'S SO HIGH

ONE

"Look sharp, lads - and ladette, sorry." Brian was driving us down. He'd not only managed to borrow the minibus from Ardscoil (the one they'd won on Blackboard Jungle) he'd convinced Eddie the caretaker to take out most of the seats, so we could fit our gear in there, and so we could all sit on the hard metal floor, apparently. My arse was already numb, and we were still in Limerick. It was Friday, the 4th of August, and it was sweltering already at half eight in the morning.

"What's that now, Brillo?" Niall, our bass player, was in the back, with Ian and me. Tim was up front in the passenger seat, poor bastard.

"It's Boxer, you big ginger Chewbacca," said Brian, or Brillo, as they called him. Or Boxer, as he called himself (no one else did, despite him always telling us to.)

"What do you mean, look sharp?" Ian had a soft pack of Lucky Strikes. He was always buying weird new fags whenever he saw them in a shop. It was like his hobby. I couldn't do that. I only smoked my Marlboro Lights, now. Unless I didn't have any. Then I'd smoke fucking anything; I was a demon for them.

"Coming into the badlands, squire. The Wild West, or is it the Wild North? I've no compass on me, like. Bandit country, anyway. Home of Mr. South," Brian said. He meant Richie, our drummer. My chest felt funny, like I'd had a fright. We were in Thomondgate, was what he was saying. Crossroads, where Jon lived, or where he used to live. I didn't know why I was getting anxious, I'd been here before, lots of times. Back when they were still using Richie's shed to practice and I tagged along to watch. When I stopped just tagging along and started being part of the practice, and then part of the band. When I'd gone to visit Jon's family after everything that had happened, too. It had been a while, though. Brian pulled into the alley behind Richie's. His back gate was open. Someone came out, but it wasn't him.

"It's Señor South, the Senior South!" Brian said, in that way he had of, well, saying things.

"Morning, rock stars," said Mick, Richie's dad. They were the head off each other, although Richie looked a bit like his mum too, with her high cheekbones. I nodded out the window at him. Niall waved like an eejit, joint still in his hand, cool as a breeze. Richie's dad would think it was a rollie, probably. A very big rollie, that stunk of hash. Or he wouldn't give a shit.

"Where's young Ringo, Mr. S? I'm on a tight schedule here, like. Don't want to be stuck on the road to Cork behind every other muppet that's going to this yoke," Brian said, pointing at his Tag Heuer. I only knew it was called a Tag Heuer because he never shut up about it. A watch was a watch to me, I didn't get the hype.

"He's just finishing up his Weetabix, Brian," Mick said.

I fucking amn't!" said a voice behind him.

"Hoh! Here he is."

"You didn't finish them? Shur that's an awful waste, says you." Mick had the exact same icy blue eyes as Richie. You could see it now they were standing together, especially in the sunshine.

"I don't eat Weetabix, you gowl." Richie had a sports bag with him. It'd just be clothes or whatever. He didn't need to bring any gear, there'd be plenty of drum kits at this thing, Brian said.

"Oh right, too good for cereal are you now, is it? Just because you've been on 2TV, like? Amazing how fame changes people, all the same."

"I've never eaten Weetabix in my life, like," Richie said, throwing eyes at Mick, but I found that hard to believe. You couldn't live your whole life without experiencing the Bix at least once.

"Can we stop talking about Weetabix please and hurry up?" Tim said, as if we were in a rush or something. We weren't due on stage until after midday. On Sunday.

"You heard the maestro, Souths. Wrap it up," said Brian. There was an awful looking Holy Mary magnet thing, like you'd buy at a Novena, on the dashboard in front of him. I wondered if it was there when he picked up the minibus or if he'd brought it himself. Both were equally possible.

"Who's that, Tim, is it?", Mick said, squinting in the passenger side window. He could only see out of one of his icy blue eyes, I couldn't remember which.

"It is, Mick. Want me to give him a dead leg?"

"Nah, you're all right, Brian. Can't be harming the talent, now."

"All the talent is back here, Mick. He's just the eye candy," said Niall, sticking his head between the front seats. He'd passed the joint over to me. Tim played the keyboards, he was probably more talented than any of us, but you couldn't say that, especially not in front of Ian.

"Oh right, are ye all present and correct back there then, yeah?"

"Hi, Mick!" said Ian. I said nothing. I wasn't being rude; I was trying to hold in a massive toke.

*****

About an hour later we were well on the way to Cork, and everyone in the back was well on the way to being wrecked. The joints were getting passed and the cans were getting sunk. *Rock and roll*, as much as you could be rock and roll in a school minibus that some kids won on a TV quiz show for massive nerds. I could never get on our Blackboard Jungle team. I hadn't ever tried, and I wasn't exactly thick, but it was Laurel Hill Coláiste. Our nerds were a cut above your normal sort of nerd. Our team was like three Marie Curies. On brain steroids.

We'd all finished our Leaving Certs this summer (except Richie, who did his last year), so it was a very *school's out forever* sort of vibe, as well as the buzz of playing at our first real festival. Not just any festival either. The biggest one in Ireland, and probably the best lineup they had ever had. Blur, The Prodigy, and the Stone fucking Roses, among others. The tickets were like gold dust, Brian said, even though none of us needed one, obviously. The only bad part was it wasn't in Thurles anymore, and in the new place (Páirc Uí Chaoimh), the camping was gonna be a good bit away from the actual music venue. Wasn't gonna matter to us, since they'd put us up in Jury's hotel, but if you were just a normal person going to it, it'd probably be a bit shit.

Someone had a stereo ghetto blaster thing, but I hadn't brought any CDs with me, so I had to listen to whatever anyone else was putting on. Didn't matter, really. Music was music, if you were getting wrecked. You didn't get to choose what they played in pubs and clubs when you were out on the tear, and it hardly ever mattered. Well, unless you meant to go to Termights, but you went in the wrong door and ended up in the other club, I couldn't remember what it was called, now. But it was all pure chart music Europop shite. At least if you went into Strictly Riddim they'd play proper rave music that you could take drugs to. You couldn't take drugs to Snap!

8

or Whigfield, that would be shite. Or to the Scatman song. Listening to the Scatman song on speed would probably kill you. Green Day was what someone had on now, and that was grand. I knew that album off by heart, and it reminded me of more good times than bad ones.

"Mad, isn't it, though?" Ian said, out of the blue. His eyes looked a bit watery, from one thing or another.

"What's mad?" Niall was trying to open a can of Scrumpy, but he wasn't doing very well at it.

"Just like, all of it, like. I mean, remember this time last year?"

"No, sorry. Refresh my memory," Niall said, joking. He shook his head at the can and handed it to me to open. I had good nails, I did it in two seconds, and it made a massive psss-sssshhhh sound. Must've been bouncing around in the cooler thing while we were driving.

"Fuck off, you know what I mean. Like, the Battle of the Bands, the Cranberries the next day, and then-"

"And then, yeah, anyway-" Niall tried to cut him off, or hurry him past that bit, so's not to upset me. It was sweet of him, but he needn't have bothered. I gave him a look to let him know as much.

"Er, yeah. Sorry, Caoimhe, sorry," Ian said. I did some gesture with my hand to tell him he was grand, and to carry on. I could feel my face going red, so I took out my fags to distract myself.

"Anyway, after everything that... happened, it was like we'd lost everything. Not just like, well, not just the important things, but you know, the band. The future... of... us."

"Brillo, write that down, will you? *The Future of Us*. That's the name of our *difficult second album*, like!" Niall shouted up to the front. Brian didn't hear him, or he did, and just ignored him. Both were equally possible.

"Haha, no. But what I'm saying is…" Ian stopped mid-sentence and stared into space. I didn't know if he was trying to think of the right words, or if all the hash had short circuited his brain. Both were equally possible.

"Well, I'm glad we had this talk," said Niall, leaning across and taking the joint from his fingers. It was probably for the best.

*****

"Right, listen up, children! Whisht a while there, *agas cúineas!*" Brian had stopped at a petrol garage that had a café and some shops, and hopefully some toilets, since I was about to burst.

"Yes, teacher?" Niall said. He'd already pissed into an empty 7up bottle a few miles back. I was glad it was a 7up one, since the green plastic meant I couldn't see his disgusting wee, even if I had accidentally seen his penis.

"Get anything ye want in the shop there, food, fags, booze, whatever. I've the magic credit card with me, so it's all on Crabtree Records' tab, kids."

"Wahey! Fags and booze!" said Ian, even though what he really needed was a strong coffee.

"No limits, like?" Niall asked. Our record company was tiny, so I didn't think they'd be happy with us maxing out their American Express, but we weren't getting paid a lot by Féile for our slot, so it made sense to make the most of the perks. I'd definitely be making the most of my room in Jury's (paid for by MCD), especially the minibar, cos our record company wasn't rich, but Denis Desmond definitely was, if you believed what you read in the papers.

"No limits as far as I know, squire. That said, if you come back here with a high-class hooker and a schoolbag full of heroin, we might have to have words," said Brian, turning off the engine.

"If he can manage to get whores and drugs on tick at half nine in the morning on the road to Cork, I think he's entitled to them. Fair is fair, Brillo," said Richie, who hadn't been much company since we picked him up earlier, but also hadn't pissed in a bottle or showed me his willy, so he was ahead on points as far as I was concerned.

*****

I was queuing in the shop for some fags and a bottle of wine. Brian had said to just tell them that we were at pump number 4 and that he'd come in and pay for everything when we were all done, but that didn't sound like it was gonna work. If I was working there and a bunch of teenagers said that to me, I'd tell them to feck off. Hopefully he'd come back in before I got to the till, though. I looked around for the rest of them. Ian was over by the crisps, picking up as many six packs of Frisps as he could carry. The munchies had struck, clearly. Niall was talking to a girl over by the chocolates. She was pretty, in a rock chick sort of way. Probably not a high-class prostitute, though, and no schoolbag full of smack. Richie was looking through a magazine. FHM, it looked like. Or Loaded. One of those ones, definitely. The ones that were full of boobs but weren't actual porn.

"Hi! Sorry! Sorry to bother you!" Some youngwan appeared out of nowhere in front of me.

"Yes?"

"Sorry like, I was just, am, my friend over there said-she's after telling me that you, that you're, am..." She stopped and looked across at some other girls over by the door.

"Uhuh?" I looked at her, trying to figure out her game.

"Are you Kweeva Shox, off that band, like?"

"Oh. Am, yeah. Yeah, I guess I am." It didn't happen a lot, but when it did, it always took me by surprise, and I was always mortified. Especially if they wanted an autograph or something. Like go away, will you? I'm no one.

"Aw, mad out! I mean, I don't like yeer music or anything. I'm into more like real music, like grunge and stuff, no offence."

"Heh. None taken." So much taken, like. So much offence taken.

"But like my friend Sinéad is pure into ye- pure into you, like. I swear, she's nearly lesbian for you or something, no offence."

"None taken!" Genuinely none taken, like. I apparently enjoyed making teenage girls sexually confused.

"Could you come over and say hi or something, like? Please, Kweeva Shox, it'd make her whole life, like." I liked the way she called me the whole name, like we were in Demolition Man. Not that it was my actual name. It was a record company decision, because apparently Caoimhe O'Shaughnessy was way too difficult for Brits or Yanks to pronounce. Shocks was my nickname in school, so I was fine with it.

"Can she not come over to me, hon? I'm kind of in this queue, like." I gestured at the queue I was standing in, in case for some reason this child had never heard of or seen a queue before.

"I'll go ask her now, so, yeah?" said the girl who didn't like our band or me, skipping over to my biggest fan, Sinéad, who would hopefully simultaneously burst into tears and wet her knickers at the thought of touching the hem of my garments. *Real music, like grunge and stuff.* The fucking cheek, like.

*****

"We all present and accounted for, yeah? No stragglers? No one sneak off to buy hashish or anything, no?" said Brian, back in the minibus. Everyone muttered something back at him. We were all here. Niall was up front with him now; Tim had come back with us. I wasn't sure why they'd swapped, but Niall and Brian got on well sometimes, in a weird way. Usually by slagging each other off, where they both thought they were getting the better of each other because neither of them got the other one's jokes.

"Hashish…" said Ian, through mouthfuls of Frisps. He hadn't offered any around yet.

"The reefer," said Richie.

"Reefer madness," I said.

Brian didn't smoke gear. He didn't do any drugs at all, so of course he thought he knew all about them, based on no experience whatsoever. Like he was your dad. He was our real manager nowadays though, not just someone who pretended to be, so he had an excuse to be all straight and sober. Apart from pints. Or spirits. One time he sniffed some poppers. He'd be telling that one to the grandkids. *Mayonaise* came on the stereo; I loved that one. Ian had put on Siamese Dream after Dookie was finished. Would have put it on sooner except Niall wanted us to wait and hear a hidden track at the end, one about wanking. It hadn't been worth it.

"What was going on with those little girls?" Tim said, asking me.

"Oh, that was a meet and greet with the fans," said Richie, smirking.

"How come I never get any fans coming over to me in public and stuff?" Ian said, not to me specifically or anything.

"Cos you're not a gorgeous bird with fantastic tits and an arse you could bounce pennies off. No offence, Kweev," Niall said, leaning back into us.

"None taken!" None taken at all. Facts were facts.

"Pfffff. That's sexist!" Ian said, reaching for one of the new lot of cans they'd bought. I didn't even know if it was too early to buy drink when we bought it, but Brian had enough charm to wangle it for us at the till, especially since our bill had come to so much. Thanks, Crabtree.

"Ah, it's not," I said.

"Sexist against me, I meant!"

"You not getting asked for autographs has nothing to do with you being a boy, man," Richie told him. I nodded. I was drinking my wine straight from the bottle. Partly because I was someone Hot Press magazine described as "A raw, ethereal mix of Stevie Nicks and Janis Joplin for the Indie-minded generation," but mainly because we'd forgotten to bring any glasses.

"What's it to do with, then?" Ian said. He'd brought three guitar cases with him. For the Gibson, the Fender, and his twelve-string acoustic that no one was allowed to touch. I'd looked at it for too long once, just with my eyes, and I was pretty certain he'd put a hex on me for it.

"It's cos you're called *Ian*, and your hair isn't rock and roll enough," Brian said. I looked out the window to see where we were, but I'd no idea. We were on a big road. That was the breadth of my understanding when it came to intercity driving. I'd leave that stuff to him, poor bastard.

"Ian Curtis didn't have rock and roll hair, you twat."

"Maybe that's why he hung himself," Richie said, and Niall laughed one of his too-loud, too-long laughs. I didn't really get it, but then I did. I was thinking of the *Hit Me with Your Rhythm Stick* guy first, but he was a different Ian. Ian Curtis was the *Love Will Tear Us Apart* guy, with all the moodiness and the twitching and the suicide. Grim.

"Hanged himself," said Tim.

"That's what I said, like."

"No, you said hung himself."

"Yeah, what's the difference, like?" Richie did the face he always did when he thought they were taking the piss out of him for not being posh like them. It wasn't as if he was stupid, either. He was going to remind, us any second now, of his academic achievements.

"Pictures are hung, people are hanged," Tim said, looking very matter of fact, as he often did.

"Well at least we don't have to wonder why no one wants your autograph anyway, Timbo," said Richie, and everyone laughed.

"So next time I'm chatting up a bird I should tell her that I'm well hanged, then, yeah?" Niall asked.

"Niall, that's just wrong!" I said, after a good gulp of the Pinot Grigio. I was glad I'd got one from the fridge and not the shelf, in this heat.

"You being a prude now, Caoimhe? Not like you, love." Brian was talking to me through the rearview mirror, like my dad used to when I was small.

"No, I just meant him telling women he has a big langer would be wrong. We all saw it earlier, like. False advertising is a crime."

"Hey!" Niall looked hurt but I wasn't sure if it was put on. I was only pulling his leg. I'd not seen it long enough to make a proper judgement.

"That was below the belt, Shox," Brian said, delighted with himself.

"Boom boom!" I said, holding in a smirk. Ian broke into song:

"Boom boom boom! Let me hear you say way-oh!" and everyone replied with the compulsory:

"WAY-OH!"

"BOOM! Shake shake the- oh Jesus fuck no!"

"Whoa!!!" said probably everyone.

Brian slammed the brakes, and everyone got thrown around in their seat or in their lack of seat. I fell forward, my heart jumped into my throat, but thankfully I didn't spill any of the Pinot. The screeching sound was so loud it made my ears ring after.

"Brillo, for fuck's sake!" Ian was on his back, like an upside-down woodlouse, his belly covered in bits of Frisp.

"Sorry chaps! And chapess! Fecking Alsatian it was. Ran across the dual carriageway, there. He'd a death wish or something!" He was gasping for breath and the back of his neck was scarlet. We were still moving, so he must have managed to just swerve it, instead of stopping properly. Could have been a pile-up or something. We could've all been killed. Very rock and roll. Like Lynyrd Skynyrd, although they were in a plane. Still, at least it had stopped that potentially fatal sing-along of awful pop songs with the word 'boom' in their title. Small mercies.

TWO

"Hold up, who's this?" Brian said, looking out the side window. We'd recovered from nearly dying horribly earlier and we were a fair bit more along the road. I'd no idea how long it took to drive to Cork. It didn't look that far away on a map; not as far as Dublin anyway, but there was a lot of traffic, so.

"Someone thumbing a lift," Niall said.

"I can see that, you muppet."

"Well, I hope you're not thinking of picking them up," I said. My wine was finished. I'd necked the last third of it, cos it was getting warm; my bladder was already regretting it. I looked at the communal 7up bottle and started wondering how accurate my aim was.

"Why not, shur? Plenty of room," Ian said.

"The more the merrier," said Drunk Tim, which was what I was calling him now, in my head. He was different from normal Tim. He smiled more, and he was all touchy-feely when he talked to you. I knew him well, by now. Harmless, mind. And not a vomiter, thankfully.

"What does the sign say?" Niall said.

"Probably says: I Can't Believe None of You People Have Ever Seen the Texas Chainsaw Massacre," I said, but no one got it. Philistines.

"It says Féile 95," said Brian. He'd slowed down now. We were on a normal road, quieter than the big one with the two lanes. I looked out the back window, the next car behind us was ages away, we were grand.

"That's the thing we're playing at!" said Drunk Tim, all excited. They had all been drinking and having smokes already this morning by the time they picked me up in Castletroy. They must have started at about half seven. What a life we led.

"Is it?" said Niall, doing a stupid voice.

"Hang on a second, ye." Brian slowed down. He was actually going to pick the guy up. We'd already cheated death once today, that boy was pushing his luck. We all looked at each other in stupid, drunk, stoned silence for a minute, then the door opened.

"Well look who it is!" Ian said, beaming.

"Uncle Frank!" said Drunk Tim, and he wasn't wrong. It was Jon's uncle, Frank. The one from Cork. On his way to Cork, apparently. He lived in Limerick now though, so it wasn't that strange. Still crazy that we'd managed to run into him, though. Or vice versa. Must have been fate. My stomach felt funny for a second, and I thought about Jon, miles away in that place, all alone. I hadn't gone there in ages. There was no point. He couldn't hear me now, no matter what I wanted to tell him. He'd never be able to hear me again. He was gone. I shook it off and came back to reality again.

"How's the lads?" Frank said, saluting everyone. Then, looking just at me, "How's tricks, Kweev?"

"Ah, I'm grand, shur. Fancy meeting you here, like. Hop in there, plenty of room." I loved the bones of Frank. Out of all of Jon's family, he was the one who'd been the soundest to me after everything that happened. It felt like he was *my* uncle sometimes. The sort of uncle who'd get hash for you, not the sort who tried to get you to sit on his lap at parties after he had one Jameson too many, thanks be to God.

*****

"To be honest I can't believe ye're not farther up the bill, boys. And girls, sorry Caoimhe," Frank said, a bit later on. People were always doing that, apologising for calling me one of the boys or the lads or whatever. Nice of them, but I didn't give a fuck. I was used to this sausage festival of a life, which today had included a bonus glimpse of actual sausage.

"Further," said Drunk Tim.

"Huh?" Frank looked at him funny.

"It's further if you're talking figuratively. It's only farther if you're travelling an actual distance."

"I'll make you travel an actual distance out the fucking back door onto the road in a minute, boy. Is he always like this, lads? How d'ye not kill him?" We nodded at the first question and shrugged at the second one. Drunk Tim didn't care, he was smiling away like a slow child on a bouncy castle. He was lovely, really. You could tolerate the pedantry once you were used to him.

"Why do you think that? About the bill, I mean?" I thought we were incredibly lucky to be asked to play at all, and it wasn't like I was modest or anything. Well, about some things, anyhow. Frank nicked a fag off me before he answered.

"Sound. Well, like I know ye haven't been around long or anything, and ye've only the one EP out,"

"Album coming soon, though," Ian said. How soon was still anyone's guess. It was all recorded and mixed, they just hadn't given us a date yet, Crabtree.

"Exactly. And like, ye've been all over the radio, ye've been on Dave Fanning for an interview, Eclectic Ballroom as well, ye did 2TV on the telly. The only thing ye haven't done is the Late Late Show."

"Gay Byrne has it in for me, to be fair, since the incident with his prize goat," Niall said, but everyone ignored him, he was only talking shite.

"Ye got into the charts here, and ye supported the Cranberries a few times in England. Oh, and ye're really big in Cork, boy."

"We are?" said Ian. His hair really wasn't rock and roll. Fair play to him, though. At least he wasn't a try-hard.

"Well, bigger than ye'd be in Dublin, like." Frank dressed like he was our age, but like he was our age in the 80s. Probably because the 80s was when he was our age. I was dead clever, sometimes.

"That's cos we've hardly done any gigs up there, though," I said. I wasn't being defensive, just stating a fact.

"Exactly, Kweev. Whereas ye've played Cork loads of times."

"True," I said. Crabtree was based in Cork City, even though they'd a small office in Limerick, on Glentworth Street. Seamus, who owned the label, had loads of contacts in the Cork scene, so we played there as much as we did in Limerick. Which would make you think I'd know how long it took to get from Limerick to Cork, but you'd be wrong.

"And lads, most important of all, Féile isn't on in Dublin. It's on in…?"

"CORK!" shouted Drunk Tim, looking around like he was trying to see what prize he'd won.

"Well, when you put it that way, yeah, fuck Féile, like. Stop the car, Brian, I'm gonna phone up Denis Desmond and tell him we want the closing spot on Sunday," I said, opening a can of cider from the cooler. Wine and cider mixed okay, it was wine and beer you had to be careful of. The grape and the grain, or something like that, they always said.

"Instead of the Stone Roses?" said Drunk Tim, who had probably memorised the whole three-day lineup after looking at the poster once, he was such a little Rainman sometimes, bless.

"Fuck the Stone Roses!" I said. The cider tasted like balls, and not in a good way either. Old balls. Old sailor's balls. I gagged a little. I was my own worst enemy, sometimes.

"Fuck the Stone Roses!" everyone else said, together. Even though we all loved The Stone Roses, and we couldn't wait to see them live. Except maybe Niall, but that was just Niall for you. Wasn't his fault he was such a contrary bastard when it came to musical taste. That sort of thing was probably genetic, in fairness.

*****

"So, is anyone else going ye know, like? Any support from the Motherland gonna be in the crowd for ye?" Frank had taken over both rolling the joints and supplying what went in them. He had proper *maryjoanna* on him. The fancy, scary-looking alien plant stuff, not the Oxo cubes we normally smoked. You didn't mix it with tobacco, when you made it properly. That made it strong as fuck. I was slightly worried, but you had to try everything at least once. Unless you were Richie, and it was Weetabix.

"Ciara and Bríd are coming, yeah," Ian said.

"They are? That's grand, so. Why aren't they here with ye today then, are they only going Sunday?"

"Nah, they have tickets for the whole weekend; they bought 'em before they even knew we were playing, like," Ian said. I hadn't known that bit. What a pair of traitors, possibly.

"Yeah, but did they not need a lift?"

"No, like. Bríd has a new fella and he's driving them down. We said we'd see them down there, like," I said, because I felt like I hadn't spoken in ages, even if I probably had.

The joint was lit now, and it smelled… interesting.

"A new fella, hah? And who's he belong to, like? One of them Quin's heads, is it?"

"No, he's like this mad posh hippy. Way older than her. Doesn't even drink or nothing," Richie said.

"Doesn't even drink??? What is he, pregnant or something?" Frank was beside me and the joint was going clockwise, so I got it next after him. Or anticlockwise, maybe. I'd forgotten which one was which. Both were equally possible.

"Nah, he just smokes, really. And he does pills. And LSD. And mushrooms. And speed. And-"

"Jaysus, he sounds like no fun at all, lads," Brian said, back at us. I wondered if we were in Cork yet. The city, or the county. Either would do me at this stage.

"Fuck off Brillo, you narc!" said Drunk Tim, and everyone laughed, because it was such an un-Tim-like thing to say. I took a long toke on the weed or whatever you called it. I held it in for a few seconds, just to be hardcore.

"Nice?" Frank said to me, I assumed he was asking me about the taste, or something. Real weed was supposed to have different tastes, hash all tasted the same.

"Mhmmmm, yeah. It tastes like… ummm."

It tasted like the smell of the rubber bits on the edges of bus windows when it's been raining out and there's lots of condensation inside, I thought. Pretty specific. I kept this information to myself, just to be on the safe side.

"It tastes like…?" Frank was looking at me with his eyes, which were probably the best organs for the job, in fairness. This stuff was STRONG. Oh boy.

"It tastes like stop Bogarting that spliff and pass it on," said the human beside me with all the hands and feet. At least two of each. I must have fallen asleep after that, because the next thing I knew we were at the hotel, and my head was full of sunlight, and the beeping of other people's cars.

*****

"Christ, I needed that." Me and Richie were inside the café part of the hotel, getting some coffee and some toast. I'd asked for a fried egg sandwich, but I'd been denied, like Wayne and Garth. We didn't have any gear to carry off the bus. He had two pairs of drumsticks and I hadn't even brought a mic, because the mics they had were going to be ten times better than my poor little £300 Shure one. We had bags with clothes and stuff, but hopefully the lads would spot them and bring them for us.

"Was it that strong?" Richie said. I wondered if he was still with that girl, Dearbhla. I hadn't seen them together in a good while. I'd ask him in a minute.

"This?" I nodded at my cappuccino.

"No, you gimp, the hash." He threw a paper tube of sugar at me, and I'd normally have dodged it, but I didn't have any reflexes, so it just hit me on the forehead and plopped into the foam at the bottom of my giant cup. Oh dear.

"Weed it was, not hash." It definitely wasn't like any hash I'd ever smoked. I couldn't even describe what it was like, even now.

"Ah, potato tomato," he said, looking a bit guilty. Probably for twatting me on the head when I was defenceless.

"Tomayto, tomahto," I said, not sure if he'd got it wrong on purpose or not. I felt like Tim now.

"Potayto, potahto."

"Let's call the whole thing off!" said the chirpy little redhead waitress who'd appeared out of thin air to collect our cups, and also to give me a heart attack, apparently. Richie was already paying the bill for us; I didn't have a chance to offer. Didn't matter, anyway. It could be reparations, for the sugar-based assault a minute ago.

*****

"What's going on here, then?" I said, when we found the others, in the lobby. Some of the others, anyway. Brian wasn't with them. Or Tim, now that I looked again.

"What? Nothing!" Niall looked like I'd just caught him wanking off. Worse than that, even. He looked like I'd caught him wanking someone else off.

"All right, calm down, ginge," Richie said, looking past him to where Frank and Ian were. Frank's backpack was on a table, they'd all been looking at it. Something was up.

"Right, spill. Now!" I said, looking at him, and then at Frank.

"Okay, keep yeer voices down though, like, yeah?" said Uncle Frank, sitting down on the couch behind the table. Everyone else found a seat too. This was all very mysterious, or else I was still high from whatever strain of madness he'd let me smoke.

"What's the scala?" said Richie. That was like his catchphrase. Jon used to say it too, but not anymore, obviously.

"Well. You see, and I'm trusting ye here lads, and you, Kweev."

"Mhhhhhmmmm." Trusting us with what, exactly? I was literally about to find out.

"I have a proposition for ye, like. A good one."

"Well, colour me intrigued, Francis," I said, because I'd always wanted to say something like that in real life.

"Colour you… anyway, here's the thing. I need to leave some, eh, property of mine with ye."

"With us?" Richie said.

"Well not with ye exactly, just like, in yeer rooms maybe. Or in the van."

"Minibus," Niall said.

"What does that matter?" Ian asked him, annoyed.

"Those swotty lads didn't win Blackboard Jungle just so random fellas from Cork could go around calling the minibus a van, Ian."

"Stop acting the lala, Nailer," Richie said, thumping him on the arm.

"Yeah, Niall, cop on. Stop acting the Tim. Anyway, Caoimhe. The thing is, I've nowhere safe to keep it myself, see, and…" I realised just then that Frank hadn't brought a tent with him. What was he gonna do, sleep under the stars? Stay up for three-

"What is it that needs to be kept safe, Frank?" Richie said, eyeing the bag. I was eyeing it too, cos unless he'd been able to fit a tent and a sleeping bag in that little satchel, the thing must be in there.

"Okay, I'll just show ye. Hang on a sec." He looked around, almost theatrically, to see was anyone else paying attention to us, and when he was sure there wasn't, he opened the drawstrings on top and let us look upon the treasure. I felt like the lads in Pulp Fiction when they look inside yer man's briefcase. There were one or two oohs and several exhalations. Someone possibly whistled. It was pills. Ecstasy tablets. It was full up. There must have been hundreds in there. Thousands, maybe. It felt illegal just looking at them. A schoolbag full of drugs. Brian was basically Nostradamus.

*****

"We can't tell him."

"Tell who? Tim?" Richie said. We were on our way down to the underground car park to pick up our bags from the bus, because the lads hadn't bothered bringing them in for us. They were all checking into their rooms, Brian was gone with them, even though he wasn't staying in this hotel. He'd given me the keys. Frank had 'gone for a walk', he said, while we decided if we were gonna help him out.

"No, you idiot. Brian." I hadn't even thought about Tim. Tim wasn't gonna be a problem.

"Oh, right, yeah," Richie said. He got me. "Why's that then?" He did not get me.

"Because he's Brian! And he doesn't like, understand it. He's not into that whole scene. He'll go spare, he'll be going on about *killer rave drugs* and all that, he'll be like my Mum."

"I suppose, yeah. My Mam's the same, like. It's the newspapers, sham. Scare stories. Yokes aren't that dangerous, if you do 'em properly."

"Well, I dunno if they are or not, I've never done one, but that's not the point."

"You've never done a yoke? Are you sure? I thought you were well into drugs, like? You're always on something when we're out." *On something,* like. Now Richie was the one sounding like Mum.

"Huh? No, I, well I just do whizz- speed, like. I've never tried- I'm a bit-" Ecstasy was one of the things they'd found in Áine, when they did the autopsy. Ecstasy and something called *Gamma-hydroxybutyrate*. GBH, they called it. I'd never been offered that anywhere, but whenever people were doing Es, I'd just say no thanks and stick with my wrap. It wasn't that I thought speed was safe, or that it wouldn't be cut with all sorts, the same as Es are, it was just a mental thing. I couldn't think of Ecstasy without thinking of her, in the worst way, and thinking of her like that was no buzz at all.

"I swear someone told me before that you'd done yokes with them. I can't think who it was, now." He screwed up his face like he was trying to remember something from before. "Nah, it's gone. But yokes are rapid, like. They're mellow, but they're like speed a bit too. Like you get the energy you get off speed, but it's more smarter, like. You do more thinking. And you love everyone," Richie said. I couldn't see the minibus yet. The strip lights down here made everything look weird. My skin looked a bit green, so did his face.

"Yeah, I've had the sales pitch before, Rich, I just- oh, here we are." Brian had parked down the very end of the place, next to someone's amazing looking Ferrari. I looked around and spotted a few more sports cars. There must have been lots of famous people staying in our hotel. I wondered if we'd see Kylie around, she was playing tonight. I didn't think my heart could take that. She was too gorgeous, and she was cool now, as well. All her new songs were so good you could put them on the stereo in the car and no one would slag you off for it. Well, not too much, anyway. I'd always thought she was cool, anyway, even when she was still in Neighbours and singing *The Locomotion*. Always ahead of the trends, that was me. A trailblazer.

*****

"*Dooobie, dah. Dooobie dah.* Like that, yeah, and I'll sing it in a different key. Like, *dooobie dah. Doobie dah.* See?" We were upstairs on the second floor, in one of our rooms. Richie's, it was. We had these doors joining the three rooms in the middle, so you could wander through, but you could lock them if you didn't want that, yer one downstairs had said. Mine wasn't one of those three anyway, thank God. If Jury's had put me in a room with a door adjoining the room of some big smelly boy I'd have gone down to reception and complained.

"*Dooobie dah. Dooobie dah.*" Niall's voice was lovely, you wouldn't think it to look at him. I'd recruited him to be my backing singer, since he didn't have an acoustic bass. I didn't even know if they existed. Either way, he didn't have one, so he could be the Supreme to my Diana Ross, instead.

"That's perfect, yeah. Are we right, so?" I looked around at the rest of them. Ian had his twelve-string out, Richie had bongos. He hadn't *brought* bongos. They were just in his room when he got in. No one knew why. There weren't any bongos in *our* rooms when we checked in. Or any guitars, or saxophones, either. There wasn't even soap or shampoo in my *en suite*, for fuck's sake. Priorities were all over the shop in this place, clearly.

"Good to go, boss," Ian said, and he hit a string to give us the note. I looked at Niall to make sure we started it together. I loved this song, but it made me sad too, cos of what it was about. Maybe I needed a bit of a cry, though. I hadn't had a good one in ages.

We'd supported the Cranberries last Christmas at the Brixton Academy in London, and in a couple of other places after that. It was absolutely surreal, I spent most of the time pinching myself. Everything had just gone so fast for us, like supersonic fast. It was a fluke that we'd got the gigs at all, because the old version of the band were supposed to have some unwritten thing to maybe support them in the future sometime, but that went out the window after what happened to Jon that night. They'd kept onto Brian's phone number for some reason though, and in the winter, when the band supporting them in London had to drop out at the last minute, some lackey rang a bunch of numbers in a notebook or a Filofax to get a replacement, and Brian happened to be the first one they got through to. He just bluffed his way through the call, and next thing we knew we were on a plane to England.

The lads and Dolores were a bit confused when they saw us, with the new lineup, but it worked out great, because we had me, so their fans were grand with a rock band who had a girl singer. That night was the first time I heard them do this song, *When You're Gone*, and it had me in floods, for a few reasons. I eventually got the balls to ask herself for the chords to it. It wasn't on any of their albums, but it'd probably be on the next one they did. It was way too good not to be, like.

*****

"Can we smoke spliffs in here?" Niall said, later, not waiting for the answer before he sparked it up anyway.

"Can you smoke spliffs anywhere, really, Niall? Is there any place where it's actually kosher?" I said, because even though we'd asked for all our rooms to be Smoking, this definitely wasn't what they meant. We'd be all right though, unless one of the chambermaids was an undercover narc.

"You can smoke spliffs in a Garda station, it's legal there," Richie said. I gave him a look, because you absolutely could not do that, and he was gonna make his tongue go black from the lying. I wanted some Black Jacks now, picturing that in my head. I missed that taste; I hadn't had it in yonks. Maybe we could put them on our rider. Or just cut out the middleman and get some Pernod. That was like liquid Black Jacks, that got you drunk -and very horny, for some unknown scientific reason.

I made a mental note and then took the joint Niall was passing me, knowing full well that I'd have forgotten all about it in about a half an hour. The Black Jacks, the Pernod, and my libido. Sounded like a good title for an autobiography. The joint was just hash this time. No need for me to put my pyjamas on before smoking it.

"In the Garda station, how's that?" Ian said, taking the hash off me.

"Cos like, if they confiscate it off you, they'd be technically, uh, they could get done themselves for possession, like. So, the Garda station is this special zone where you're allowed to have hash and not get done for it, or else the Gardai would all have to be arresting each other, see?"

"So, the station is like an embassy or something, but like instead of it being sovereign, um, instead of the immunity of-" Niall was struggling.

"What about when they take hash off you in the street, Rich? Do they arrest themselves then?" I said. I was getting hungry. I wondered if the minibar had Taytos, and if they were 25 quid a bag or something. Not that I'd be the one paying.

"What? No, like, that's different."

"Why is it different?" I said. I had a Snickers in my bag, I wondered how melted it would be.

"Never mind all that, what are we gonna do about the Frank thing, lads?" said Ian. Damn it, anyway. I had Richie on the ropes here and all.

"What Frank thing?" said Tim, who I didn't even know was in the room until then. Not-Drunk-Anymore Tim was a much quieter beast than his alter-ego.

"They'll explain," I said, heading out the door to the hall, cos that was the only way to get to my room, since Jury's hadn't put me in one of the ones with the adjoining doors. I'd half a mind to go down to reception and complain.

*****

By the time I came back, after a quick wee and an even quicker Snickers, Brian was there, so the whole Frank conversation would have ended, thank God. I had no interest in any of it. Like I'd said to Rich, I didn't even take pills, so Frank offering to sort us all out with free ones in return for stashing the stash in our rooms wasn't exactly a good deal for me. I'd let them sort it out, I wasn't fussed.

"There she is," Brian said, giving me one of his smiles that he probably thought were charming.

"Where were you?" I said. He'd disappeared with Tim earlier, and only one of them had come back.

"Ah, you know, show business. There's no business like it, says you." There wasn't a joint going around anymore. I wasn't sure if that was deliberate, because of him being here, but that was stupid. We were always puffing away around him, and he was our manager anyway, not our dad.

"How's that working out for you?" I said, but I didn't know what I meant by it. Sometimes I opened my mouth and words tumbled out. Sometimes I even put a tune to them.

"Grand, shur. I ran into your arch nemeses downstairs."

"Our arch what now?" Richie said. He was smoking a fag and he hadn't tipped it. I was getting nervous looking at the big spear of ash on it.

"The Downpatrick lads."

"Come again?" Niall was lying on the bed, you couldn't see his head, the pillow was so soft.

"The ones who've an *Uncle Pat*."

"You've lost me." Rich still hadn't tipped it; it was going to fall on the carpet in a second.

"Ash!" said Brian, reading my mind, clearly.

"Yeah, Richie! Watch what you're doing there!" I said, suddenly finding an ashtray by some sort of Divine Providence and throwing it over to him. It was only plastic, no chance of me killing him.

"What? No, Ash the band," said Brian, looking at me like I was remedial.

"Oh! Those pricks," Ian said, clearly apathetic on the

subject.

"Ah, I see. Are they playing this thing?" I said, even though of course they were. They'd hardly have time to come to a festival as punters, what with their busy jet-set rock and roll lives, like.

"Yeah, they're doing a full hour, Tim said to me," said Brian.

"Who, me?" said Tim, looking confused.

"No, you twunt. Tim Wheeler," said what used to be Niall, from somewhere deep in the pillow.

"Oh. Yeah, that makes more sense, yeah," said our Tim, who was not and never had been the lead singer of Ash.

"Do you think he's a ride?" Ian said, looking at me.

"Who?"

"Tim, obviously."

"Which Tim?" I said, messing.

"Tim Wheeler, you gowl."

"Nah," I said, truthfully too.

"No? Why not?" Ian said. I was starting to think he fancied Tim Wheeler now, to be honest.

"Well, I know this sounds stupid, but bear with me, yeah?"

"Sure." Ian cracked open a can of something green. Heineken or Carlsberg, I couldn't see it properly. Didn't matter, they were both rank.

"Well, you know Barry Sullivan from Quin's?"

"I do, yeah. Goes to Clement's? Or he used to anyway," Ian said. It was still hard to get used to being finished school, we'd probably be calling people "so and so from Laurel Hill" or "yer man from Ardscoil" for a while now.

"Yeah, that guy. Anyway, I dunno if anyone else sees it, but to me he's the head off Tim Wheeler, like. Especially when he has his hair the same as him." I looked around to see if anyone agreed with me. Couldn't tell.

"Anyway, so, I can't think of Tim, from Ash, without thinking of Barry Sullivan, so it just ruins it for me, you know?"

"What's wrong with Barry, like?" Tim said, looking lost.

"Well, his name's Barry, like," I said.

"And?" Brian had found a chair to sit in. He'd his arms and legs crossed, he looked like an uncle at a Christmas party.

"Well…you can't think about someone that way if they're called Barry. Not… sexually. I'm sure he's lovely and everything, but he's a Barry. You don't have sex with a Barry. You couldn't! You'd be lying there in bed, and he'd be slapping it up you, and all you'd be thinking to yourself would be: that's Barry's penis in me. There it is. There it is again. Hmmm. Take your penis out of me now, Barry. Take your penis out of me and call a taxi." I stopped, because it was obvious that everyone in the room thought I was mental now. Niall had even sat up from his sunken pillow to give me a strange look.

"Well now," said Brian, getting up out of his uncle chair.

"So, what day are Ash playing, anyway?" Tim said to him.

"Today, about an hour from now, I think." The Tag Heuer made a brief appearance from under his shirt sleeve.

"I'm going for a slash," Niall said, charming as ever.

"Have one for me too," I said, thinking we'd better get a move on soon. I didn't care about any of the earlier bands (until whenever Kylie was on, obviously), but I wanted to see the stage, and the backstage, and the VIP area. It was gonna be, as my English cousin Tara would put it, *absolutely mint* (mate).

*****

"Richie says you're not taking any pills tonight," Niall said to me, on our way to the stadium. We were walking, because getting a taxi would have taken ages, and no one had laid on a limousine for us, much to my chagrin, or however you pronounced it.

"Yeah, that's right." I wasn't and I didn't need to. *Just say no,* as Nancy Reagan used to say. When she was on Grange Hill. But I'd only say it to that particular drug, obviously. Not to hash, or to speed. I had two wraps in my bag, hidden under the nine bras I'd brought for three days, and one in the bra I was wearing now. There was clearly some sort of theme occurring.

"Ah here! But the Prodigy are on, like. The actual Prodigy. Tricky as well." He had a four pack of Budweiser with him, the small, 330ml ones. It was gonna be a long three days: for us, and for our livers.

"So?" Cork looked like a sort of cleaner Limerick. I'd been here before loads, but never really in the daytime.

"So, they'll be so much better on yokes, like. And Kylie, too."

"Kylie?" Sure, her new stuff was very clubby, like *Confide in Me* and some other ones, but I was picturing a load of E-heads gurning to *I Should Be So Lucky*.

"Yeah! She's the gorgeousest bird on the planet but imagine how more gorgeous she'd be if you were on a yoke."

"I don't follow." I was trying to concentrate on getting across the zebra crossing without dying. I didn't know Ecstasy had some sort of magical beer goggle properties, and I didn't think I'd need them to find Kylie gorgeous, either. That deal was already done, by God and nature.

"Everyone looks better on Es."

"I'm gonna have to disagree with you there, Nailer." I'd seen plenty of pillheads when I was out clubbing. Aesthetically pleasing they were not. They looked like they were trying to chew their own faces off.

"No, no, like. I mean when you're on E, everyone is beautiful. It's like… it's like you can see all the goodness inside someone. It's hard to explain, but it's true. You're just so… loved up. You love everyone."

"Will I love Paul Robinson off Neighbours?" I hated that guy.

"I dunno who he is, but maybe."

"Ugh, I'll pass."

"Aw, come on!"

"This is peer pressure, Niall." We were outside Páirc Uí Chaoimh now. I could see a big marquee tent. That was the Groove Stage, where all the dance acts were on -and where all the people chewing off their faces would be, naturally.

"Okay, okay. I'll leave it, for now. Here, have one of these." He pulled me off a can of Bud from the plastic ring thingy.

"This is beer pressure, Niall," I said, because I was hilarious.

THREE

"Who are they, then?" I was looking up at a bunch of skinny looking fellas on the stage. I didn't know the song.

"Who are they? Are you mad?" Ian said, looking like I'd just called his mother a whore, or kicked his dog.

"I'm quite sane." Relatively speaking, anyway.

"That's the Verve!" He said it like I should know who that was. Like I'd been looking at the Beatles playing *She Loves Me* and I'd asked him why those four men looked like their Mums had cut their hair with a pudding bowl.

"It's not ringing a bell, sorry." We were closer to the stage now. Yer man singing had some fierce cheekbones altogether, but he wasn't good looking with it. He was gaunt, and not in a sexy, Jarvis Cocker way. He looked like the last days of Freddie Mercury, but less toothy.

"The Verve? Used to be called Verve but they had to change it because of some copyright thing, I think. They've been around for ages; can't believe you don't know them. *Voyager*? *A Storm in Heaven*? Richard Ashcroft?"

"Is that him there?" I pointed up at the guy singing. He walked like a monkey. So did Liam Gallagher. Must've been an English thing.

"Yes!"

"He could do with a few hot dinners, like."

"Ah here, he's a legend. They're one of the best bands in England. They had a sort of psychedelic sound for the first few years, very trippy stuff. *A Storm in Heaven* was produced by John Leckie, you know, who did The Stone Roses' first album? They're great pals with Noel from Oasis, he even got the name *Slide Away* off one of their songs. They supported Smashing Pumpkins a couple of years ago when I went to-"

"Ian, none of these things you're saying are interesting. Please stop talking." We were at the fence to get backstage, thank God.

"I-I..." He gave up.

"Can I help youse there, folks?" The security guy was English – Northern English, maybe, and very huge.

"You could let us in, that'd be a big help," I said. We'd lost Niall, but he was probably in there already.

"Fraid it's not that simple, luv. Restricted area, talent and press only. Can't come back here unless you work for the papers, or you're in one of the bands. Off you pop now, chook. Enjoy the show." He sounded annoyed, but maybe people had been trying it on all day with him. That, or he might just be a twat. Both were equally possible.

"We *are* in one of the bands!" Ian said, taking a break from gawking up at his musical hero who I'd never heard of before.

"Yeah? Where's ya passes, then? Come on, let the dog see the rabbit." His eyes were hidden behind the mirror shades, so I couldn't tell if he was flirting with me, or he just wanted me to show his dog a rabbit. I took the *Access All Areas* card/ribbon things out of my handbag, trying to hide the bottle of Malibu that was in there. Not that he'd have minded, since we were the talent, and the talent doesn't live by the rules of mere mortal festival goers. Everyone knew that.

"Oh, I see. Crane is it, yeah? Like Frasier Crane?"

"That's the one," I said, because that's what we always said. It was quicker.

"*I don't know what to do with those tossed salads and scrambled eggs!*" He wasn't a bad singer, for someone whose head was 70% neck.

"Very good," I said, and practically leapt through the gap when he opened it up for us. Ian was right behind me. If he hurried, he might even be able to meet his malnourished monkey god backstage.

*****

"Caoimhe, isn't it?" He had a Northern Ireland accent. No idea why that surprised me, I knew he was from Northern Ireland. Maybe it was cos he didn't sing any of their songs in it.

"Um. Yes, that's what they call me, yeah." Smooth, Caoimhe. Real smooth.

"That's what who calls youse?" He was smiling. He was incredibly pretty. Didn't look anything like Barry Sullivan. I'd been a fool to ever doubt him.

"Um, people. Cos it's my name." I was doing well with the flirting here, definitely. A natural at it, I was.

"Haha! Yeah, that makes sense, I suppose. Youse are playing Sunday, is it?"

"What?" My mind had run out of brain.

"Your band - Crane. Youse are on early, Sunday, aren't yis?" He was the same age as us, seventeen or eighteen, they all were. But he didn't seem it. I'd watched the video for *Girl from Mars* on MTV the other day. They were like superstars. They waxed their chests.

"Ah! Yeah, we are. Sunday. Early." I'd been wandering around, taking in the sights, when I'd nearly tripped over the three Ash boys on the grass, and he'd hopped up and started talking to me.

"Looking forward to it? Nervous? Ahhhh, youse'll be fine. We used to shit ourselves at things like this, but it's just like any other gig, you know? Youse'll get used t'it, so y'will." He said it like they'd been on the scene for yonks, but then again, they had. Compared to us, anyway. Probably doing Glastonbury when they were eleven or something.

"Ah, yeah. I suppose. Lots of people, though." This was mental. Why did Ash know who we were and when we were playing? Why did Tim Wheeler know my name? Why do birds suddenly appear, every-

"Aw sure they're the best bit, like." His smile was absolutely gorgeous, and he had this rare mix of confidence, star quality, and down to earthness that was already making me a bit in love with him. He was quite little, standing face to face with me, but he was perfectly formed. Rock stars weren't supposed to be tall, anyway. Brian always said that.

"Yeah. Yeah, you're right. Need a crowd, don't you? Wouldn't be a gig without one, like. I remember-"

"ASH? ASH! TWO MINUTES, GUYS!" screamed some bitch about two feet from my poor ear.

"Shit, that's us," he said, like he was apologising to me for it.

"Yep. You're definitely Ash all right." I looked at the other two for a second as they got up. I didn't know their names. Boy who plays drums and boy who plays bass, was all I knew about them.

"We definitely are. Right then, give us a wee kiss, will youse?"

"Sorry?" I was clearly still unconscious in the minibus after Frank's joint. Or I'd died and gone to a really specific version of Heaven.

"Aye, for luck!" He was smiling again. Those pretty eyes, those long lashes, the eyeliner that I'd only just noticed, those shoulders, that tight, retro t-shirt with the fitted sleeves that hugged the tops of his lovely arms instead of just flapping around them. My knickers were like a sauna.

"Oh, okay." I didn't close my eyes or pucker up. I didn't know what I was supposed to do. I'd forgotten how kissing worked.

"ASH! ASH TO THE STAGE, PLEASE!" Fuck off, bitch, I'm trying to work here!

"Good luck on Sunday too, yeah? We won't see you, we're playing *T in the Park* tomorrow, flying up to Scotland tonight." He leaned into me and put his lips on my lips. Not a proper shift, just a bit of a smacker, but slightly longer and harder than your average smacker. He smelled great, too.

Like a mix of shower gel and raw sex appeal. Eventually it had to end, though.

"Um, break a leg!" I said, as the three of them ran away up the steps, thankfully without breaking any of their legs.

"Caoimhe!" someone shouted behind me. I didn't turn around; I was still a bit shell shocked from The Timmening.

"CAOIMHE!" Right in my fucking earhole this time.

"WHAT?" I spun around, it was Niall, blocking the sun with his massive body.

"Stop shifting Ash, will you? They're our nemesises, like."

"I have stopped," I said, even though I hadn't really started yet. I walked over to the steps. We were allowed go up onto the side stage, probably. It was an area, and we could access all of them. *Girl From Mars* started up, and I moved a little faster, flashing my newly acquired VIP wristband at the security fella standing by the big curtain.

*****

"Here, I got that contact number for you anyway there, love." We were out the back area again, after Ash's set finished. They'd been brilliant. Played a load of songs I hadn't heard before, and a few that we all knew. They'd come off the stage the opposite side from us after, so I didn't get to see lovely Tim again. They were probably in a helicopter over the River Lee by now, quaffing champagne and getting blowjobs off wanton sluts. Lousy.

"Whose number would that be, Brian?" I said. I didn't remember asking him to get me anything. I hadn't seen him since Jury's. There was some lot called Pop Will Eat Itself playing now. Not my scene, by the sound of them.

"Tim Wheeler, of course. Your new fella. I was talking to their manager there," He handed me a bit of paper with a number on it in biro. Started with 073. I didn't know what area code that was, but maybe they were different in the North, cos it was kind of in England.

"The fuck did you do that for?" I was mortified. A bit,

anyway.

"Good PR, like."

"Good what, now?" Ian said. He was cross with me, possibly, over the whole shifting one of Ash thing. I didn't care.

"Public Relations, you ignoramus," Brian said. He had a pint of Guinness in a plastic cup. It looked all wrong to me, like when you see a dog wearing a little human jacket.

"What are you on about?" I said. I'd lit one cigarette straight after the other, and this one tasted like air.

"Well, you going out with the singer from Ash, like. No publicity is bad publicity, says you. Imagine how much it'll raise your profile, Kweeva Shox." He took a sip of the Guinness and made a face. A dog in a jacket probably would've tasted better.

"Pffft, like her profile needs any more raising," Ian said, like I wasn't even there. He hated the way the press people made everything about me sometimes, instead of the whole band. He'd said it plenty of times before though, so at least he wasn't keeping it bottled up, the poor misfortune.

"Will you fuck off, Ian. Shur that's just life. Ye can't name anyone out of Blondie except Debbie Harry, but they all still get paid, like," said Brian.

"Hang on, do I get any say in this?" I said.

"Any say in what?" Niall was back from the loos. I'd have to ask him where they were, my bladder felt like a baby was sitting on it. I looked around for some wood to touch, but there wasn't any.

"Brian's pimping me out, like."

"Brillo, you can't be a pimp. You don't have the style for it. You don't even own a cane," he said.

"I'm doing nothing of the sort you fecking bollix. I'm just doing my job. And my job is making ye famous." He said it like he really believed it, probably because he did.

"And what if I don't want to shag Tim Wheeler, Brian? What then, eh?" I opened a can of Budweiser. A bigger one, this time. There was so much free booze backstage that I felt if I didn't drink it'd be like losing money.

"Do you?"

"Do I what?" The beer was gorgeous and cold, thank God. I was on my way to getting a good tan already, too.

"Want to shag him?" Brian was resting his chin on his fingers and leaning into me. He looked like one of those old statues.

"Well, yeah," I said, stubbing out the fag, as it was doing nothing for me.

"Well then. Hardly a sacrifice, is it?" He leaned back like he'd played Checkmate on me, the smug prick.

"There's such a thing as consent you know, Brian."

"You literally just consented there, though," Tim said. I looked at him and mouthed "fuck off". He wasn't Drunk Tim again, yet, but the day was young.

"What else have you planned then? For me, like? What other ways of exploiting me have you dreamed up, Brian?"

"Am, well you're doing a photoshoot after your 18th, hopefully." He said it in a much quieter voice this time, but still loud enough for everyone to hear.

"What like, in Playboy?" Niall's eyes lit up with imagined perversions.

"WHAT?" I said, picturing myself in the nip on a sunny beach, with my legs akimbo.

"For fuck's sake, stop it, Nailer," Brian said, rolling his eyes.

"Thanks, Brian," I said. I wasn't getting my bits and pieces out to sell a few records, like. Fuck off.

"Imagine thinking I had the pull to swing Playboy, you eejit. No, it was Loaded magazine the lad I was talking to works for. D'you know that one, Caoimhe? It's classy, like. No smut. Black and white, he was saying. Can't be porn if it's black and white." He looked at me, all earnest, like.

"Okay," I said, and all their jaws dropped at once.

"Okay?" said Brian, picking up his rotten pint again.

"Okay?" Niall said, shifting a little uncomfortably where he was sitting. I didn't want to guess why.

"Really?" Ian said. He looked funny too. I couldn't wait for Ciara and Bríd to come along, I'd already had my fill of only hanging around with boys for the day, and it wasn't even two o'clock. I needed a proper girly talk, especially about the shift.

"Yeah, I don't see why not. As long as…"

"As long as?"

"As long as the rest of ye are going to be in the photos with me. In your underwear. Or less than your underwear, maybe."

"What?" Ian sounded like he was gonna puke.

"Ah now," Tim said, looking fierce worried.

"What's the matter, Ian? I thought you were always complaining that they made everything about me and not about the rest of ye, like?" I was simultaneously delighted with myself and about to explode from holding in a piss.

"She's a point all right, lads. Better start the diets, it'll be November before ye know it," said Brian, smiling his head off. November, he said. I probably would do it, in fairness. Might be cool. Might be dead glamorous. Mightn't even have to get my nipples out. Pop Will Eat Itself had stopped playing now. Pop Can Go Fuck Themselves - that was what Niall called them, earlier.

*****

When I was finished in the loo, I suddenly came over all exhausted, and had to sit back down on the seat. They had real toilets for us, not portaloos. Permanent ones, inside an actual building. Made sense, since there were always gigs and events on here, it wasn't just a GAA ground. I got the Malibu out of my bag and took a big swig out of it, as if that was going to wake me up. Then I remembered I had the wrap. I used the tiny spoon on my necklace to get a good bump, and then another one – a treat for each of my nostrils; they'd earned it. Niall gave me the spoon necklace as a present when he came back from Amsterdam last year. My Mum was full of questions about it, but she wouldn't have a clue what it was for. She was a square, maaaan.

I remembered Frank then, I wondered where he was. Still walking around with a bag of drugs on him? He was going to get *so* arrested if he wasn't careful. The lads had decided they were going to hide the stash for him, they said. I was keeping out of it. The less I knew the better, especially if I ended up down the cop shop, with a rake of detectives trying to grind me for information. What a life we led.

I flushed the loo again, just in case someone had come in after I did it the first time. Couldn't have the gossip rags getting hold of a scoop about me being a dirty non-flusher. That publicity *would* be bad publicity, no matter what Brian said. I sniffed a bit and wiped my nose with the back of my hand. I thought about lovely Tim Wheeler, with his lovely accent and his lovely everything else, for a second, and I smiled like an idiot. He was already gone, but hey – I had his number. The game might still be afoot, Watson. Or at the very least, it might be a hand. Tim Wheeler's hand. Down my knickers. Mmmmm. Maybe I'd stay here for a little while. There was no hurry, after all. I had another small bump of the good stuff, in case I needed the extra energy, like.

*****

"Where did you disappear to?" Tim said, when I eventually got back.

"I went for a wank," I said, grabbing a beer. I was gasping, suddenly. It had been boiling in there, and it was boiling out here, too.

"Pffffft. Girls don't do that!" he said. He looked somewhere between shocked and disgusted.

"Why not?" I said. My fags were somewhere in the handbag, but they were doing a good job of hiding from me now.

"Cos ye don't have willies," said Niall. He was wearing a cardigan now, despite the sun splitting the rocks.

"You've got me there, yeah," I said, rolling my eyes. Boys who went to Christian Brothers schools were so ignorant about women, and about sex in general. We'd to teach them everything, like.

"When girls wank, do ye finger yerselves or is it more rubbing the clitoris, like?" Ian said, like I'd volunteered to take questions from the audience, or something.

"The clitoris," Tim said, giggling.

"What do you call a bag full of fannies in a sweet shop?" said Niall.

"Clitoris Allsorts!" Brian said. I hadn't noticed him being there until then, maybe he wasn't.

"You guys are such fucking children, you know that?" I said, not pissed off with them really, just tired of them.

"No we're not!" Niall said.

"Nuh-uh!" Tim said, hardly making a case for himself.

"I'm older than you are," said Ian.

"I'm more mature than all of ye, lads," said Brian.

"Wah, wah, wah! I'm a big boy! Change my nappy! Change my nappy!" said someone who wasn't any of us. I looked around and saw Ciara, and I nearly jumped into her arms, I was so glad she was here. Bríd too, just behind her. The weekend had officially started.

FOUR

"Any tongue action?"

"Ciara!" Bríd threw a matchbox at her. The girls had stolen me away for a natter and a catch-up. Some band called The James Taylor Quartet were playing, but it wasn't the actual James Taylor, so I didn't care.

"What? Inquiring minds need to know, honey." We were still in the backstage area, I'd given them passes the other day, and one for Bríd's fella. We'd had six extra altogether, I gave one to Niall when he went off to find Frank earlier, so that left two.

"No tongues, no."

"So, just a peck, no passion?" Ciara wasn't impressed. We were over by the free bar, on some benches, by a table.

"Well, I wouldn't say that, no." I remembered the kiss again, it was pretty good stuff, even without the tongue action, as she called it.

"Like blood from a stone, with you. Anyway, were they any good?"

"Were what any good?"

"His testicles."

"CIARA!" Bríd didn't have anything left to throw.

"I'm messing! No, I mean Ash. What were they like?"

"Oh, they were great. Played loads of songs, lots of good ones."

"Did they do *Kung Fu? Uncle Pat? Girl From Mars?*"

"Yup. And another one, a new one. Hadn't heard it before, but it was definitely their best one. Um, angel something?"

"*Angel Interceptor*," Bríd said. She was an Ash megafan. She must've hated me for getting a snog off Tim, but if she did, she was hiding it well.

"I'll have to have a listen out for that one. Anyway, so, what's the plan for tonight, like?" Ciara had really pretty eyes, a kind of grey blue that looked purple sometimes. Beautiful, but they made her look like a witch as well, especially when she went overboard with her eye makeup.

"I think we're attending a music festival," I said, lighting up one of my fags.

"Shut up, you gowl. I meant, well, drugs. Are there drugs? Where are the drugs? I wish to see the drugs." To say Ciara was fond of Class As would be like saying Michael Jackson was partial to the odd nose job.

"Well, I've speed, and they've shitloads of gear, but wait til you hear this…" I started telling her the story about Uncle Frank, the bag, and the dodgy deal. A black guy walked past our table and gave Bríd a smile. Might have been the fella from Black Grape, or maybe it was Tricky. Both were equally possible.

*****

"You're definitely having a pill tonight, by the way. I'm not taking no for an answer." Me and Ciara were in the good toilets, sharing a cubicle, so we could have some of my stuff.

"I already said to the lads that I don't want to, Ceer." I was sick of telling people at this stage. I couldn't explain why to them without bringing up the Áine stuff, and I didn't want to do that, cos they'd all be doing sympathetic faces at me and saying comforting things and that would drive me bananas. And as well as that, I knew my reason was kind of stupid and didn't make sense, so I didn't want to say it out loud and have them all tell me exactly that to my face.

"Yeah, but I'm not the lads, am I? I'm Ciara! And you'll have Bríd with you as well, like. Double your pleasure, like the chewing gums. Oh! Remind me to get chewing gums later, will you?" Bríd had gone off to find her crusty hippy boy, she'd be back in a while. I hadn't ever talked to him properly; I'd just seen him around with her a few times.

"So?"

"So, you'll be doing pills with Bríd and me, and I'm wonderful and nice and clever and gorgeous, and I'll mind you all night, and we'll go dancing, and I'll give you amazing massages, and-"

"Massages?" I absolutely heaped a load of speed onto the spoon for her, since she had some catching up to do.

"Thanks! Yeah, massages. Like, Es are brilliant, but if you forget to get up dancing, or if you're just happy sitting around, sometimes your muscles get stiff, like." She walloped the powder up her schnozz like a pro, God love her.

"That doesn't sound good." I was already afraid of dying from pills, I didn't want to get cramps off them as well. I loaded up a spoon of it for myself, just not as loaded as her one had been. I was pacing myself, like a good girl.

"Yeah, no. But if you've someone who can give good massages, the relief is amazing. It's like, orgasmic."

"Orgasmic, you say?" I definitely liked orgasms. I'd already had one today, and I was always open to the idea of more.

"Absolutely. Oh, and speaking of which, when you have an actual orgasm on those things – when you, you know, come – it's sooooooo intense. Like setting off a volcano in your-"

"I dunno if I'd be riding any fella tonight though, Ceer. Not if it's my first time taking a new drug, like." I'd no idea what the experience would be like. If I was gonna be out of control, lads would be a no-no. Especially lads who were strangers.

"Well, now. One - no one said you have to be riding a fella when you come. Two - how many fellas can make you come anyway, honestly? And three - you just practically admitted you're going to do pills tonight there, so hah! Jinx, no backs, times a thousand infinities."

"Ah, feck it. You've got me there. I suppose I have to now. Law of the jungle and all that." I was warming to the idea though, since I knew Ciara would be minding me. I trusted her one hundred percent, we loved each other. Maybe it'd be grand. Maybe it'd be more than grand. Maybe it'd be amazing.

"Yay!!!! Oh, we're gonna have such an amazing time, Kweev. You're gonna pop your yoke cherry with me! I'm SO EXCITED! You're gonna have the best night of your life!" She was giddy as a puppy; it was great to see.

"I hope so. And Ciara?"

"Uhuh?"

"When you said I didn't have to be riding a fella when I came, did you mean I could just do it myself, or-"

"Did I mean you could lez up with me in the hotel later on?" Ciara gave me a wicked smile, while opening the lock on the door.

"Uh, yeah?"

"That's for me to know and you to find out, sugartits," she said. I'd no idea if she was serious or not. I got a bit funny thinking about it. Then we were out in the sunshine again, and Bríd was there, with her fella, who was called something I couldn't remember.

*****

Benson, he was called, that's why I couldn't remember it - cos it was so stupid. It wasn't even his first name either. It was his surname. His friends all called him it, like they were still in school, despite him clearly being at least 25. When you asked him his first name he treated it like this ridiculous game, where he would never ever tell, no matter how much someone begged. Luckily, I didn't give a fuck what it was, so with me the game was over very quickly.

"Oh, you're gonna love buzzing, Caoimhe," Bríd was saying to me, over at the catering table. All the food was free for the acts, and they didn't seem to care if we took loads, or if we brought someone over who only had a normal AAA pass, and no special VIP wristband. I guessed it was cos the food was gonna be thrown away later if people didn't avail of it, so the non-VIP plebs eating it was less lousy than it going to waste.

"Yeah, I hope so." I was still a little nervous, because of the whole "dying" thing, but the booze and the speed was helping me. It occurred to me that taking an E on top of a load of speed and liquor would probably increase the chances of me dying, but I quickly made that thought go out of my head by eating the largest burger I'd ever seen, and enough chips to make Sir Walter Raleigh feel guilty for ever going to America.

"There's no need to worry, honest. They're really safe. When you hear about people dying, it isn't from the Es themselves, like." Bríd was still persisting with the whole vegetarian lifestyle, so she had less of a choice than me. She'd found a sliced veggie pizza and basically taken the whole thing. Benson wasn't with us. He'd gone off to do something. Maybe to be an African American butler on an Eighties sitcom.

"It isn't?" I said. Surely tabloid newspapers hadn't lied to me.

"No. They die of stuff like heat exhaustion, from dancing all night without drinking enough water." *Note to self, drink plenty of water tonight.*

"Yeah?"

"Yeah. Or some of them die because they were told to drink lots of water by everyone, but they don't realise that Ecstasy is an anti-diuretic."

"A what now?" I was talking with my mouth full; my mother would have been appalled.

"It stops you from weeing."

"It does? How?" Nothing could stop me from weeing when I needed to go. An elephant with a machine gun couldn't stop me.

"Dunno, just the opposite of how a diuretic makes you want to wee."

"And what's a diuretic?" It sounded like a diabetic. They'd never made me want to wee. They were just people who had a fit if they ate a Twix.

"Like coffee, or beer. You know the way you don't have to go for the first couple of beers, but then after the third one you have to go after every drink for the whole night?"

"Definitely."

"Well, that's cos alcohol is a diuretic, I think. Same with caffeine."

"Jesus, you're like a scientist, Bríd. And tell me again, what's wrong with the anti-ummm"

"Anti-diuretic. Well, cos you can't wee, basically you end up sweating out all your excess fluid."

"Ugh, what, your piss comes out as sweat?" I pushed the rest of my chips away.

"Not exactly, but what I'm saying is, you're dancing, and you get thirsty, you drink water, it cools you down, the water comes out as sweat, and you get thirsty again. But-"

"There's always a but." I came away from the food bit to spark up a Marlboro Light.

"But… say if you're not dancing, if you're just sitting on the couch? Then you're not going to be thirsty. Not really thirsty, like you would be from dancing. And cos you're not dancing, you're not sweating, so you're not losing fluids. Are you following me?"

"Just about." I should have brought my dad's Dictaphone.

"So, if you're just chilling in your chair, enjoying the E, not moving or sweating, but you read in a newspaper or on some leaflet that you should drink litres and litres of water… and remember now, you still can't wee,"

"Cos of the anti-diarrhoea," I said, but I was just acting the lala.

"Haha! Anti-diuretic. Well anyway, the water has nowhere to go, and you get something called Water Toxicity, which means your body, that was already about 70% water to begin with, now has way more water than that, and well..."

"And well, what?" She couldn't leave me hanging like that!

"All your organs fail, and you die," said Bríd.

"Oh." *Note to self, don't drink any water tonight.*

*****

"Well, they're a bit like the Happy Mondays, right? Because they've still some of the same people in them."

"Right..." I was making Tim explain Black Grape to me, since they were on next, and I hadn't even been in the crowd once yet.

"But you know the way the Happy Mondays have some good songs, and they're really... melodic, but then you have Shaun Ryder being obnoxious, and Bez just sort of standing on the stage, doing drugs, and shaking a tambourine, and dancing all weird?"

"Yep." I could picture all that in my head, definitely.

"Well, Black Grape are like that-"

"Oh, good." I'd go out and see them in a minute, so. Maybe bring the girls.

"Except without the good songs, or the being melodic." Tim was drinking a bottle of water. Imagine being at a festival and drinking water, like.

"Oh."

"And Shaun's less good at singing now, he just shouts a lot. And Bez is worse at dancing, somehow."

"Oh."

"The wanderers return, look," said Ciara, beside us. I looked to see who she meant. It was Frank and Niall.

I wondered what time it was, I'd ask Richie in a sec, he always had a watch. Frank didn't have his bag with him; I didn't know if that was a good sign or a bad sign.

"Fancy meeting all ye here," he said. We were all here, too. Less one Brian. He'd gone on a schmooze cruise, looking for *important people,* to *connect with,* he'd said.

"Welcome back, Uncle Frank!" I said, raising my bottle of rum to salute him, which made me feel like I was a pirate. Yaaaar!

He was wearing a Thin Lizzy t-shirt, black combats, and oxblood Doc Martens. I looked down at my Docs – the blue, suedey-looking ones I'd got at Christmas. They were class. I'd a brilliant dress on too – black and white, knee-length, flowery summer one, with the cinched waist, half-length sleeves, and a scoop neck, to make the most of the new Wonderbra.

I never wore necklines like that in real life, but I wasn't me this weekend, I was being Kweeva Shox. She was a bit more whorish than me, which was great. She'd wear fishnet tights, or studded collars, or tiny jeans shorts. I liked being her. Especially cos I could take her off, like a wet raincoat, when I got home and go back to being just Caoimhe.

"Thanks lads, listen now. Who wants a mint?" Frank said. No one said anything. Most of them weren't paying any attention to him.

"I'm grand, Frank, thanks," I said. I probably wasn't. I could smell the stale fags and rancid, fermented coconuts off my own breath, despite my speedy nostrils. Or maybe because of them. I wasn't sure how it worked. I wasn't a drugs scientist like Bríd.

"No, lads. I mean, who wants a *mint*?" Frank said, shaking a little blue box really loudly. It was those new Smint ones. You could get them in the loos in nightclub toilets, next to the condoms. All the emergency tools you needed if you'd just pulled.

"What's that? A *mint*, you say, Frank?" Niall said, sounding strange, like he was in a play or something.

"Yes, Niall. A delicious, fresh, *absolutely legal* breath mint. I've plenty of them here, and I've lots more back in the hotel!" I had no idea what either of them were on about, but I was quite drunk and full of amphetamines and hamburgers. They reminded me of Paul McCartney and Michael Jackson in the video for that song they did together. Selling the dodgy medicine off the cart, in the old days.

I ran my hand through my hair, it was all right, not too sweaty. I thought about putting it up, but that was what Caoimhe would do. Kweeva Shox wore hers down, wild and sometimes tousled. I got the tousled look by using shitloads of mousse and a Babyliss diffuser thing that you clipped onto the end of the dryer. It looked rapid but it took a bit of time to do. Dolly Parton used to say, "It takes a lot of money to look this cheap." I was more like, "It takes a lot of effort to look like I've done fuck all."

I'd bleached the brown and dyed it pillar box red a few months ago, like Miki Berenyi, from Lush. They were playing here tomorrow afternoon; I couldn't wait to see them. I might even get to meet her. What a life we led.

"Frank, is the Smint box full of Es, or something?" Ciara said, next to me.

"Why would you think that, Ciara?" said Niall, still talking funny.

"Forget about it, Nailer. We're wasted on them. C'mere all of ye and get yeer drugs, like," Frank said, so we did. The Smint box was like an arseways Pez dispenser – you pushed a button on top and one little mint came out the bottom, so we took turns with our hands out to catch a pill (or two pills).

It reminded me of when you went up for Communion and there'd be the weird people who didn't let the priest put it on their tongue, they held out their hands for it instead.

*****

"Right, who do we have here, boys and girls? From the band, I mean." Brian was back. It'd been about 20 minutes since I took my E, I wasn't feeling anything yet. I didn't have a clue what feeling to look out for, but Ciara and Bríd said I'd know it when it happened.

"All of us, I think," I said, looking around the terrace thing we were all scattered around, up the top left of the stadium, still behind the backstage fence, though. The main stadium had seats under a big shelter on one side, and terraces on the other side. Most people were on the pitch now instead, cos that was where the stage was. It was only half full out there, from what I'd been told. I hadn't gone out yet, I would when I came up on this thing, definitely. Maybe.

"Cool beans. I need two of ye – the two soberest, please. And not anyone on drugs, either." Good luck with that pal, I thought.

"For what?" Ian said, putting his hand over his eyes to block the sun. He'd taken a pill same time as me. Everyone had, even Tim. We'd done a sort of cheesy hands-in huddle first, like we were in the NFL, or the Captain Planet gang.

"Féile TV want an interview, lads. I said I'd come grab two of ye." Brian had been doing his actual job after all, not just wandering around chatting up women.

"Why only two of us?" Niall said. He'd taken off the cardigan now, smart boy. It was even hotter than it had been around midday – crazy, since it was supposed to rain at festivals, so everyone could get muddy, or catch pneumonia.

"Cos it's on this couch yoke, and there's only room for Pat himself and two people. Stop asking questions, you muppet."

"Pat who?" Tim said. He was still on water, but now he was after taking Ecstasy, so it was no longer uncool to be drinking water at a festival.

"Pat O'Mahoney."

"Pat O'Mahoney off Head 2 Toe, like?" I said. Was he gonna be interviewing us about fashion? I'd be grand, so. I was a style icon, according to the Clare Echo.

"That's the one. He doesn't just do that though," said Brian, getting impatient.

"What else does he do?" I said.

"He fills in for Dave Fanning on the radio, like. He's doing all the RTE coverage this year, shur."

"What, this thing is on TV? The whole festival?" I said. How had I missed that information?

"Yeah, it's highlight shows, they show them the next day, I think," Ian said. "Not live or anything."

"Oh. And this interview will be on the telly, will it, Brian?" I asked, checking my hair without a mirror. Nobody would be looking at it anyway, not with this dress on.

"Yeah, hopefully. Anyway, which of ye fucking *gets* is sober enough and not too high on drugs to come do this thing with Caoimhe?"

"What do you mean, *with Caoimhe*? She's not sober, and she's on more drugs than all of us!" Ian said. What a little fucking snitch! I went to punch him on the arm, but he was too far away.

"I mean that they want two of ye, and she's obviously a shoo-in, since she's the face of the band, she's the most photogenic out of all you ugly scuts, and she writes most of yeer songs." He'd completely ignored the thing about me being on drugs, no idea why.

"No she doesn't!" Ian said, squeezing his water bottle so hard it made a cracking noise. *Here we go*, I thought.

"Fine, she writes most of the lyrics, then," said Brian.

"All of the lyrics," I reminded him. I obviously should have left it or tried to diffuse the situation, but Ian was annoying me now, the little narc.

"WhatEVER! I'm assuming you don't want to volunteer, Ian, since you're having such a hissy fit about it, so who else wants to? Hands?"

"Hang the fuck on, I never said I didn't want to do it, Brillo." Ian stood up all angry, got a bit dizzy, and sat down again before he fainted.

"Oh, just pick him, Brian, it'll be quicker", I said. I didn't give a shit who was doing it with me, I was ready for my close-up, Mr. O'Mahoney.

*****

"Wait, no, here they are. Welcome, um, Limerick band, Crane!" said Pat O'Mahoney when he spotted us running over to where the cameras were, in front of a tattered looking couch. I'd needed the toilet, cos apparently the anti-diuretic thing hadn't kicked in just yet. I'd pissed like a horse, and more besides. Ciara had said to expect that- a small while after dropping the first E, your body just sort of *evacuated* itself, she said. Manky.

He was in the middle of the couch, and he didn't seem to be about to scooch over, so me and Ian just plopped ourselves down either side of him.

"Hello!" I said to him, and then I looked at the camera, and gave a stupid wave.

"Hello, Kweeva Shox. And…" Poor Pat looked a bit lost for Ian's name. I wasn't gloating about that, of course. Definitely not.

"Um, Ian Hurley, lead guitar," he said, like he was answering a teacher.

"Of course, of course. Anyway, like I said, welcome to Féile TV, both of you. You're playing on the Sunday, right?"

"Right, yeah." Ian answered him, I was just trying to stop myself staring at the camera, especially when it wasn't pointing it me. Otherwise, I'd look like a gombeen to the people watching at home.

"Opening the show, as well. Kicking off the last day. That's a cool little Irish line-up at the start all right. Yourselves, Schtum, The Devlins, Revelino. You know any of them from gigging around?" He was looking at me, now. He'd probably go back and forth between us with the questions, for balance. My heartbeat was going ninety miles an hour. Might have been from the run over. Might just be the nerves, I thought.

"Ah, no. I don't think so. We don't know a lot of bands, we're kind of new."

"*You* know Ash," Ian said. Pat looked confused.

"As in, Ash, the band from Downpatrick, who played tod- who played Friday, yeah?" He'd stopped himself saying "today", maybe because the interview would be going out tomorrow, I thought. I was dead clever sometimes.

"Yeah, I mean I don't know any of them, but Caoimhe *knows* Tim, definitely, if you catch my drift, Pat." He was such a little fucker, I was gonna kill him.

"Oh, you do, do you? Anything you want to share, Caoimhe? Are we getting a Féile TV exclusive here? Young love between Ireland's two top teenage bands?"

"Ah, what? No! No, shur I only met him the once, like. For a minute or two. Wasn't long enough to-"

"Was long enough for you to ATE the face off him,"

Ian said, grinning like a chimp. I was mortified now. Pat O'Mahoney had said we were one of Ireland's top two bands, though. Well, top two of the teenage ones, but it was still rapid. I was swelling with pride. Or with... I wasn't sure.

"The plot thickens, hahaha! Anyway, moving on, what kind of a set list have you planned, guys? Or, guy and gal, sorry, Kweeva. Will we be hearing your version of *Season of the Witch* on Sunday?"

"Yes!" said Ian.

"No!" I said, at the exact same time. There was a big pause before either of us tried to speak again. I felt a wave of... *feelings* roll over my chest, go up my neck, and rush into my head. Oh boy.

"Which is it?" Pat said, looking like he was very much regretting ever agreeing to this interview.

"Witch, is it? Witch. Season of the Witch. *Must be the Season of the Witch! Two rabbits running in a ditch!*" Those weren't even the proper lyrics. I was going slightly mad, as Freddie Mercury would say, when he was still alive. I couldn't cope with all the rushing warmth and feel-good feelings that were coming at me and running through me. I held onto the arm of the couch, really tight, and squeezed my thigh with my other hand.

"Indeed," said Pat, probably looking desperately for the floor manager or whoever it was who made the hand signal at you to wind things up. We were on a couch in a field, though. There wasn't even a floor, let alone someone to manage it. I took in a big deep breath and looked at Ian. He was smiling like the people in the video for *Black Hole Sun*, and his pupils were so big and black they were making his blue eyes look brown.

"*Doooooon't it make your brown eyes bluuuuuuue?*" I was singing again. Singing on the TV! Childhood dream, achieved. We'd been on 2TV once, with Dave Fanning, but it was only an interview, we didn't play live, or even *mime* live. They just talked to us for a bit, then they played the video for *Deep Breaths*. Pat looked at me like I'd five heads. Ian laughed, but he didn't know about his blue eyes going brown, so he was probably laughing at something else. We were still on TV, they were still recording us, at least. I'd been planning on ringing Mum to make sure she tuned in tomorrow night to see us. Probably wouldn't, now.

"Crystal Gayle. My Mammy at home loves her, fair play," Pat said. I looked at him really closely. His skin looked nice. Like he moisturised. Did men moisturise? He probably did. He was the guy off Head 2 Toe.

"Are you the guy off Head 2 Toe?" I said, looking at him without blinking. I'd forgotten how to blink. There was too much stuff to see now, and I didn't want to miss any of it; that's how it felt to me

"Uh, I am, yes. Why, do you watch it?" I caught him looking at my tits, but who'd blame him? Not me. They were looking glorious altogether today, Ciara said, earlier. I looked down, and I was inclined to agree with her. My eyes jittered for a second, and I swallowed all the spit that was left in my mouth. I needed a drink of water. I looked around for a bottle, and the eyes jittered again. No idea what that was. Probably just me dying. I looked at the cameraman and asked him to get me some Ballygowan, but I only asked him in my head, so he mightn't have heard me.

"Aren't we supposed to be talking about the band?" Ian said, but I didn't find it annoying. I didn't find him annoying now, I actually liked him. I had great understanding of his-

"Yes! Yes, we are. Sorry, this has been very surreal, even for Féile TV, hehehe."

"My mum loves Head 2 Toe," I said, touching Pat on the arm. He was wearing a t-shirt, so I got to feel skin, and all

his little hairs. I was liking this drug, so far. It made the most normal things feel amazing. I licked my lips; my tongue still had a taste of chemicals on it. Where was that water?

"She does, does she?"

"Oh, yeah definitely. Loves it, like. Loves you as well, even though she thinks you might be a gay, but I said to her that you're not, you're just in touch with your feminine side and anyway, even if you were, what would it matter, you know? Where's the harm in it? Love is love. My friend Ciara is bi, like, well not officially, but I mean, she definitely is, we've all heard the rumours, but anyway, earlier, she was all like, kind of flirting with me, but not really, but kind of. And I was all like, hang on there, I'm not that way inclined, or at least I don't think I am, but maybe I've just never met the right woman or something? Who knows, Pat? Who ever really knows, until they try it? Anyway, I didn't say that to her face, but I definitely said it in my head like, but hold on now, Ciara love, if you're watching this, babe, I'm sorry. You can absolutely ride me any night of the week, and twice on Sundays, yeah? I lllllllllovvvve you. I really do, like. *Sexually*." Just saying the words made my chest fill up with something really nice. It was like a liquid, but it wasn't making me drown. It was liquid joy. Mmmmmmm.

"I think it's safe to say she won't be watching this," Pat said, with a look on his face that was either terror or just incredible admiration for my bravery and my candour, and I chose to believe it was the second one. I looked over at Ian, but he was just flicking a lighter and staring at the flame. I could hear Tricky over on the stage, I needed to get up and dance.

"Okay then, ahhhh, thank you very much, Kweeva Shox and..."

"Ian Hurley!" I whispered very loudly into his ear, or possibly his neck.

"- and Ian Hurley, from Crane! Catch them if you can on Sunday afternoon, and we'll catch *you* after this short break!"

"I think that went well," I said to Brian, after we left, but he mustn't have heard me, cos he didn't say anything back. Didn't hear me when I asked him to give me a piggy-back, either. Must have gone a bit deaf, from being around all those big speakers.

******

"Here, get that into you, before your jaw turns into powder, babe." Ciara put something into my hand, discreetly. Another E? I wasn't ready, I'd only just come up. On my first ever one, too. She must've forgot.

"I don't think I'm ready, hon." The bass from the speakers up onstage felt like it was inside me, vibrating my whole skeleton, in a good way.

"Ready for what? A Wrigley's Extra?" She looked amazing. She always did, but it was like I was seeing her differently now. Like I'd put on magic 3D glasses that let me see more beauty on top of the beauty that was already there. Or maybe it was beauty from underneath. Beauty from the inside, where all the real beauty was supposed to be.

"What?" I looked at my palm and saw the little rectangular pellet of chewing gum, and I understood. I popped it in my gob and bit down, and the mintyness sort of sprayed out all over my tongue and my taste buds, it felt like. I *had* been grinding my teeth, she was right. I just hadn't noticed until she pointed it out.

"Good girl. How you feeling? You okay? You enjoying it?" She was in really close to my face, so I could hear her over the sound of Tricky, or over the sound of Tricky's band – Tricky himself wasn't that loud, he was just mumbling something I couldn't make out.

"Good. Sooooo good. This is- you were- nnnnnnngh!" I

had to stop talking when another wave of loveliness washed over me. I squeezed the tops of her arms and smiled so hard the muscles in my face hurt.

"Told you, didn't I?" She was smiling too. I'd seen her smile a million times before, but it was like I was seeing it for the first time again, now. I looked over her shoulder to see where the rest of us were, but the crowd was moving and rotating and we were moving and rotating with it, so it was like we were the little plastic discs on that safe-cracking game we used to play when I was small- passing by each other every so often and then moving away again. *Downfall*, that was what it was called, the game. I was dead clever sometimes.

"Excellent! And it's only gonna get better, trust me." I found that hard to believe. How could anything be better than this? This was the BEST.

We were in a crowd of strangers now, but it didn't matter. It was like we were locked into our own plastic bubble; when she looked in my eyes, everyone else just went out of focus. She was dancing all sexy and slow, like a belly dancer, maybe. All wiggly and jiggly. I felt hands on my hips from behind and I jumped a little. Someone's warm face was against my cold neck, but Bríd didn't have to say anything for me to know it was her. She had a smell that was instantly recognisable – or, at least, it was now. Coconut shampoo and caramel lip balm, with a hint of something else that I couldn't quite describe. I moved my hips side to side, and she moved her arms with me.

"Miss me, lover?" Her words felt hot in my ear. I didn't turn around, but I raised my hand and put it back to find her cheek and run my fingers through her lovely curly hair. It felt soft and scratchy at the same time, like something else I couldn't remember right now. I loved my girls - this weekend would have been shite without them. Or, not as good, anyway.

"Always, babe," I said, because nothing sounded silly right now. Everything sounded perfect, to me at least. I took another deep breath, because taking deep breaths was brilliant now. *Deep Breaths,* that was the name of our first single. I was in the video for it. Wearing a gorgeous vintage corset, with real whale's bones in it. You couldn't drink fizzy drinks in a corset, the costume woman said to me. Couldn't remember why, now. It looked great, though. I felt very glam in it, that day, like a little sexpot, or something.

"Give us a kiss!" I said, to Ciara, when Bríd moseyed away.

"Huh?" We were standing too close to the front; it was getting deafening. I took her wrists and walked backwards with her.

"A kiss!" I really wanted a kiss, not a shift, but just to touch my lips off someone's. Like I had with Tim Wheeler. I got the shivers. Good shivers.

"A kiss?" She had on a tight T-Shirt, a Throwing Muses one, cos she was cooler than the average bear. Her boobs looked massive. Swollen. She wasn't wearing a bra. Mine felt uncomfortable all of a sudden, looking at hers being all free. Wonderbras weren't comfortable anyway, but they weren't designed with comfort in mind. Couldn't take it off, though, not in this dress. This dress *demanded* a Wonderbra, unfortunately. It *insisted* on one.

"Yes!!!" I couldn't stop looking at her big, pretty, purple, witchy eyes, and her lovely cartoon lips. Betty Boop lips. I was so... whatever it was called when you were on Ecstasy. *Ecstatic*, maybe. She smelled like vanilla ice cream, but she always did.

"Am, okay. If you're su-" I didn't let her finish, I smashed my mouth into hers. Her lips were soft and spongey, like tiny pillows. A little wet too, probably the gloss. My head was straight, I wasn't doing that tilt you did when you wanted to turn a kiss into a shift, with a boy. I had a little thought about what'd happen if she slipped me the tongue, but it wasn't a bad thought. It wasn't scary or nervous. I hadn't had a bad thought since back on the couch, with Tim, and yer man off Head 2 Toe. There were no bad thoughts, or bad feelings. The kiss was even better than I'd thought it would be. My lips were tingling, my scalp was tingling, my, well, everything was tingling, really. She was all soft and squishy to press against. There were like, boobs, *everywhere*. It was sooooooo nice. We came away from each other, after what felt like ages. I wasn't sure which of us had pulled back first, but it didn't matter.

"Wooooo!" said someone male and unfamiliar.

"Whahey!" said someone else.

"Go for tit!" said another boy's voice, behind me now. I spun around and saw we'd a ring of leering lads surrounding us. They'd clearly enjoyed the show, the pervs. I gave them all my middle finger, and collapsed, laughing, into Ciara. She didn't say anything, she'd already started dancing again, so I did too. I saw Ian Brown in the crowd and I saluted him, as if I knew him or something.

"Is that…" Ciara said, noticing him too. He was tiny. Smaller than my new husband Tim Wheeler, even. Very *striking* looking, though. Most of him was cheekbones and haircut. I was in awe.

"Ian, boy!" shouted one of the lads in front, possibly one of our audience of perverts, and then it all went crazy, with people coming away from the crash barriers up front to run over and mob poor little Ian Brown, the King Monkey, who'd only come out for a dance and a listen to *Hell is Round the Corner.* I pulled Ciara out of harm's way and grabbed Bríd too, cos it was time to go backstage for Kylie now. Or it would be, soon enough. I was so high, I never wanted to come down from this. Never, ever, ever.

FIVE

"All right, all right, part the Red Sea there, guys. Coming through, coming through!" The man's voice was behind us. We were all side stage- me, the two girls, the lads from Crane, and a few others who we didn't know.

"Who's this, now?" Niall said, in between chews. Everyone was absolutely flying now, it was brilliant.

"Sorry, guys," said a woman's voice. Her accent was familiar. Sounded like someone off Neighbours. Everyone moved to either side, like the traffic when an ambulance is coming, and so did I.

"Thanks, people!" said the (very short) woman, passing through us, onto the stage. She had red hair - not red like mine, actual ginger - I didn't see her face, but I knew that bottom. Two guys and a girl followed her out.

"Wowzers," said Ciara, squeezing my arm.

"Jaysus," said Tim, his eyes glued to yer wan.

"I nearly touched her! She nearly touched me, I mean!" someone else said, but I was just gawking at Kylie now. She'd on a pair of purple trousers and an aquamarine silky blouse thing – no little clubby dress, or hotpants, but she still looked like the sexiest woman in the whole world to me. I felt like I was gonna faint.

"Kylie Minogue," I said, and again, "Kylie… Minogue," like I was from some lost tribe in the Amazon rainforest, and those were the only two words of English I'd been taught. Her band started up a song, and it took me a few seconds to recognise it was *Confide in Me*. I liked that one. I liked them all, though. Especially right now, with my big loved-up head.

"Oh my God, I think I'm gonna actually die, like," Ciara said. I said nothing back, I was watching Kylie do her little dance and move her little bum. She was doing that dancing thing where you squat down slowly til your arse is nearly on the floor, and then come back up slowly again. Like strippers did. Or like I did, after too many vodkas, on a Saturday night in Doc's. Richie had been right about seeing her when you were on a yoke. It was too much to take, nearly. I squeezed Ciara's hand and she squeezed mine back.

*****

A few songs later, I had a brainwave. I came out of the side stage bit, paying no attention to the people asking me where I was off to. I made my way around the back of the stage, all the way, over to the other side entrance. There was no one there at all. She'd probably come off on this side, and I'd be the only one around. I'd definitely meet her, now. I was a genius. She had just finished *Automatic Love*, and the band were starting the next one. I didn't recognise it at first, she wasn't singing any words yet.

"How ya goin'? Room for a small one?" said someone behind me. A man, deep voice, Australian. Probably one of Kylie's entourage or crew or whatever, coming to tell me to clear off. Damn it, anyway. So close. The guy stood up beside me. He was massive. In a tall way, not a fat way. He definitely wasn't fat. He was casting a shadow across me; he was that lanky.

"Hi," I said, not really looking at him, cos there was an actual Kylie Minogue to look at instead.

"Been great so far, hasn't she?" said Mister Whoever. He wasn't telling me to leave, though, so that was good.

"Yeah, she's rapid altogether," I said, sounding like the Limerickest person on Earth, suddenly.

"*Rapid altogether*," he said, chuckling. I didn't mind him laughing at me or taking the piss out of me. I was high as a kite, and I was bulletproof, and I was five yards away from Kylie Minogue. He could chortle away, so he could.

"Yeah-" I started to say something, then I looked at him properly. He had grey suit trousers on, a short sleeved white shirt with little black designs on it, and he'd long, jet black hair. Then I saw his face.

"You're Nick Cave!" I said, in a slight daze.

"Well, I should hope so, mate. If I'm not, this next bit's gonna be awkward." He gave me a big Nick Cave grin and sauntered on to sing his bit of *Where the Wild Roses Grow*. What a life we led.

Unfortunately, the next guy who came along *was* actually one of Kylie's entourage (or crew, or whatever) and I had to go back to the other side to watch the rest of the set, with the lesser mortals. It was grand though, cos she did *Put Yourself in My Place* next (without any of the Barbarella striptease, mind), she did *Shocked*, and they finished with *Better the Devil You Know*. Thirteen-year-old me would've been over the moon. Seventeen and four fifths years old me was probably even more happy, but she was off her face, in fairness.

*****

"Jesus, that was so good!" Ciara said. She was in the cubicle next to mine, we'd come in for the normal reasons this time, not to snort things. I was gonna give snorting things a break for tonight, just to be safe. Or *safe-er*, at least.

"It was amazing! She was amazing! She's so beautiful, like. Really great voice as well." That part had surprised me. You only ever heard her miming to the CDs on telly. I'd never heard her sing live before.

"Yeah, especially on the one with Nick." I heard her pull the toilet roll thing, then she blew her nose. I checked my own to make sure it had paper in it.

"Ah, yes. Nick. Good old Nick." I'd met him, at least, even if I'd missed out on herself. I could tell the grandchildren about that. They probably wouldn't know who he was, like, but still. I was obsessed with *Let Love In*, I knew every song on it, inside out and back to front.

"He's gorgeous in person, isn't he, like? So… iconic looking, or something," she said. We were gonna go sit backstage on the big step/seat things for a while after we were done here. Smoke a joint, maybe. Get some Ballygowans from the bar. Moby was on now, with his big shiny vegetarian head, but we'd be able to hear him from there, and it wouldn't be as eardrum-bursting.

"A massive ride, he is. Literally, like, cos he's literally massive. And that voice. Jaysus. It's so deep!" I said. His singing voice was even deeper than his speaking voice, I'd experienced both of them now, up close and personal.

"And the way he had his arms around her when they were singing, too. Looking into each other's eyes. Definitely riding."

"Oh, absolutely, like," I said. The chemistry between them had been almost crackling loud enough for the microphones to pick up.

"Abso-fucking-lutely shagging each other, chalk it down. *Allegedly*. Anyway, Caoimhe, sweetie?"

"Yes, darling?" I felt another mini come-up from the Ecstasy. It was the gift that kept on giving. Bríd told me earlier that you came up all intensely first, then you had lots of smaller waves for about two or three hours, until you hit a peak, and after that you got more, less intense, waves until either you came down, or you decided to neck another one and come back up to another peak.

"Why are we here?"

"That's a bit of a heavy question for today, Ceer." I sparked up a ciggie. Those were something else that felt better while you were on yokes. I'd been chain-smoking them for the last hour, I'd have bronchitis by bedtime, probably. And lung cancer by Monday.

"No, not in a philosophical way, dear. I mean, why are we *here*. In this building. Right now."

"To go for a piss!" I said, not really understanding. I was pretty sure I hadn't reached the peak Bríd was talking about yet. I'd no idea what that was gonna feel like, but I was dying to find out.

"And have you?"

"Have I what?"

"Gone for one? A piss, I mean."

"Uh, no. No, I haven't, actually."

"Because what's the one thing we can't do when we're on these things, eh? The thing we've both forgotten we can't do?"

"Ahhhh!" I said, the penny finally dropping, even if nothing else had.

"Yup. So, pull your knickers up, then, unless you've some other reason to have 'em around your ankles." I looked up at where her voice was coming from now - she was leaning over the top of my stall.

"I told you before, Slattery. You've to at least buy me dinner first," I said, pushing the flusher, in case the paparazzi were lurking.

"Well, I would, but I don't think you can eat when you're on yokes. I don't think you have an appetite. I never do, anyway," she said, which was news to me, sort of, but then most drugs put you off eating. Well, apart from hash. I came out my door and squinted at myself in the big mirror on the wall opposite. I looked grand. I'd be fine. I'd do, for now.

"Fine, just take me for breakfast afterwards then, ya hoor," I said, linking arms with her, and then the two of us started skipping, like we were off to see the Wizard, or something.

*****

"Ahhhh, Shox. Ye're just in time," Ian said, giving me a hug, when we found the rest of them. It felt weird, because it was probably the first time he'd ever touched me in either of our lives. But only weird for a few seconds, then it just felt… new. New, and okay. Maybe even nice? I wasn't sure, yet.

"Just in time for what? Oh, refreshments! Sound," said Ciara, seeing the pile of water bottles sitting in an ice bucket. It was one of the black Guinness ones from behind the bar. I put my hand out and she passed me one. The freezing cold felt amazing in my sweaty hand.

"Nailer is gonna tell us how he lost his virginity, sham," Richie said. He sounded extra-Thomondgatey. They were all sitting on the grass. The plan to go up on the steps must had been forgotten, I thought. This was better, though. Grass was comfier, and no one was higher up or lower down than anyone else, so we could see each other's faces.

"You lost your virginity?" I said, looking at Niall.

"Christ, we were only gone for like fifteen minutes. You're a fast worker, Niall," said Ciara, and everyone laughed.

"Hey, Bríd. Hi… *Benson*," I said. I'd remembered his name; I was doing well.

"Hey, chickee," she said. He nodded at me and did a sort of Elvis Presley lip curl. He was kinda sleazy. Way too old for her. But it was her life, and I didn't feel like being judgey now.

I didn't feel like being negative at all. I was full of love, and peace, and unregulated narcotics. I made a space for myself in the circle that had formed around the bucket.

"Caoimhe!" said Drug Tim, who was making his debut with us tonight. He looked very happy, and kind of serene. Like a Kung Fu Monk, or something.

"Timothy," I said, nodding. I had an unlit cigarette in my hand, but no matches. Bríd's Benson leaned over to me and flicked open a gold-coloured Zippo, the big charmer. I bent down and took a light and gave him a thumbs up. The gas in it smelled like petrol, but in a nice way.

"Where's Brian?" I said to Richie, who was beside me in the ring.

"His missus is here, they're up at the stage, watching yer man." Aisling was all right; I knew her from school. She wouldn't be into all this though, the drugs, so I wouldn't talk to her much tonight. Or I would, and I'd freak her out with my mad yapping and my big saucer eyes. I could hear Moby, but I didn't know any of his songs, so it was just sounds. Sounds were good, though. I'd noticed that the E worked much better if there was some sort of beat you could listen to. When there was silence, you didn't feel it as much.

"And Frank?" I hadn't seen him since the Smints incident. *The Smintsident.* I was hilarious; to me, anyway.

"Oh, I dunno. He's off doing business, I think. Out there?" Richie pointed past the fence.

"Ah. Grand, so." Frank's new career as a big-time dealer had taken me by surprise, but I was very glad of it now. It'd come in handy, to put it mildly.

"So, I was out on a Saturday, with Bobby Clancy," Niall said, starting his story. He had a joint in his hand, but it wasn't lit.

"Bobby who used to go to Ardscoil?" Ian said.

"Bobby Clancy from the North Circular?" said Tim.

"Yep, same fella," Niall said. He lit the joint and took a big pull. I'd be glad of it when it got to me, it'd be nice to have something to mellow me out. It'd been all rushes and highs for the past two hours. I was one of those people who could smoke gear without getting anything off it except chilled out and slightly giggly. Unless it was that stuff Frank had earlier, obviously. That stuff was on another level, I wouldn't be trying it again in a hurry. Richie was the opposite to me. He got a whitener every time, without fail, so he just didn't touch the stuff anymore.

"What's he like?" Bríd said. I'd no idea who they were talking about, the name didn't ring a bell.

"Ah, he's all right, like," said Niall. His skin looked really nice, the skin on his face. It was all uniform and flawless, like he had on good foundation. Maybe he did. Tim Wheeler wore eyeliner. So did Nicky Wire from the Manics. It was the 20th Century, after all. Nearly the 21st. Imagine that? We'd have flying cars, soon. And hoverboards.

"I heard he's doing burglaries now," Ian said.

"Yeah, no, he's broke into a few places, but not like people's houses or anything. Just shops and stuff, in town. When he was drunk or on something, he says." Still sounded a bit like burglary to me, but I wasn't a solicitor.

"What? Bobby Clancy, Carol Clancy's big brother, like? With the glasses and the red cheeks? Fuck off will ye, he's not a burglar. He looks like an altar boy," said Ciara. Carol Clancy's name did ring a bell. She was a friend of Ciara's from Salesian's. I'd met her once or twice. Quiet girl, til she was langered. Like a female Tim.

"No, he definitely is. He's gone wild since he left school. Always taking yokes, and selling them too, as well. That's why my brother doesn't like me palling around with him, like, but anyway!" Niall stretched his arms up over his head and something made a satisfying cracking noise. I felt a little stiff, too. I remembered what Ciara had said about massages. I'd have to get one off her later. Or sooner. Orgasmic, she'd said. My forehead must have been sweaty, because the breeze was making it feel cold. Cold in a nice way, though.

"Yes, anyway. Carry on, Niall," Bríd said. She passed the joint to her fella without having a hit off it. She didn't smoke anything, she had bad asthma, poor love. Benson looked like he was scientifically examining it before he had a pull off it, the gowl. Bríd was already infatuated with him, you could tell, so we'd have to leave any criticism until after they broke up, which they definitely would. Otherwise, we'd be wasting our time; that was always the way when one of us had a fella who was a dick.

"Yes, no more questions about Bobby, like. Anyway, we were a bit skint that night, so we got some 20/20 in Fine Wines. The big bottle of it."

"Ugh!" I said. That stuff was rank.

"What flavour?" asked Richie, as if that mattered. It all tasted like chemicals and vomit. I drank some water to wash the memory out of my mouth.

"Tequila Sunrise," Niall said. The joint still hadn't found its way to me.

"Classy," Ciara said.

"Yeah, so anyway we were drinking it down in the alley on Denmark Street, or Ellen Street, I can't remember now," Niall went on. Denmark Street was where I'd met Jon for the first time. I put him out of my mind, or I tried to, anyway. No thinking about him and no thinking about Áine tonight please, brain. Thanks in advance.

"Even classier," Richie said.

"Yeah, yeah, yeah, so to cut a long story short…"

"Ah, don't!" I said.

"Don't what?"

"Don't cut a long story short, like. I love long stories." Moby's music was either getting louder or my hearing was getting better. Both were equally possible.

"Yeah, cut a short story long!" said Ian. He was the one who had the joint. I looked at it, wondering if I could use The Force to bring it over here, like Luke Skywalker's lightsaber. The sun was gone down, almost, but it was still light out. It'd be dark by the time the Prodigy were on, which was good. They felt like the sort of band you should see in the dark, for some reason. They were nightclub music, even though they'd a full band when they were live, with electric guitars and everything, Richie had said.

"There's um, anyway, we end up in Doc's, eventually," said Niall. The joint came to me, since Richie wasn't having some. I got a Christmas morning feeling when he handed it over. I had my knees up in a kind of triangle shape, but my dress wasn't long enough to go over my legs, so I'd all my wares on show, down below, well not all of them- I still had knickers on, last time I checked. I wouldn't have realised except I caught Tim gawking at my crotch, eyes on stalks.

"Timothy can you at least be a bit more subtle when you're *perusing* my vulva, please?" I said, letting out a massive cloud of smoke. The gear hit me straight away and mixed up with all the E feelings like a perfect cocktail of something or other.

"*Vulva!*" Bríd said, nearly falling backwards from laughing.

"I don't know what that is," said Drug Tim, looking very lost, but still a bit Kung Fu Monkish.

"Explains a lot," I said, but I was only messing with him. Tim was lovely and harmless. I put my ankles together anyway though, because now I'd alerted everyone to my uncovered gusset, and I didn't want someone like Benson getting a free view, the dirty old perv.

"Focus, people!" Ciara said.

"Yeah, focus. Anyway, so, we're in Doc's,"

"The pub or the nightclub?" Drug Tim asked.

"Why does that matter?" said Ian.

"Because it does, okay? I need to set the scene. In my head." He had the joint, which would be weird normally, but since he was Drug Tim now, drugs were grand.

"Okay, well both, then."

"Both?" Benson said. His voice was very deep, but not in a sexy, Nick Cave way.

"Simultaneously? Were you in two places at once? Like Padre Pio?" I said. My water was finished already, I grabbed another and tried not to think about organ failure.

"No! We just… we went to Doc's pub first, and then the club after. But it was when we were in the pub that I met Lisa."

"Who's Lisa?" I said. I didn't know any Lisas. Except Lisa Flannery, maybe. And Lisa Carroll.

"Let him tell the story!" Ian said. I stuck my tongue out at him, and he gave me the finger. Some things never changed, Es or no Es.

"Lisa is the one who broke his tender maidenhead, probably," Ciara said, and I gagged a bit, because I remembered someone telling me once that maidenhead meant your hymen, and I couldn't ever forget that now.

"ALL RIGHT! All right. Anyway, so I was just having my pint, minding my own business, like," Niall said. He had a can of lager now. Could you drink booze on Ecstasy? I couldn't remember. He was, anyway.

"I find that hard to believe," Bríd said. Benson never looked at her when she was talking, the way a normal new boyfriend would. He was like his own thing, independent of her. I didn't like it. I loved Bríd, I didn't want her to end up-

"What do you mean?"

"She means that whenever we're out, you do the opposite of minding your own business, you slut. You spend the whole night circling the dancefloor, stalking your prey," said Ciara, and Bríd nodded at her like to say, "Spot on."

"Pfffffft. *Allegedly*," said Niall.

"Can I have a Budweiser too, Nailer?" I said, suddenly getting an urge to taste some.

"Ah, yeah look, there's a cold one below," Benson said, putting his hand into all the ice and pulling out one of the small sized Buds for me.

"Cheers, babe," I said. I loved him now, Bríd's Benson. I'd got him all wrong. A gentleman and a scholar, he was.

"So, Lisa came over, did she? While you were just trying to have your quiet pint?" Ciara said, helping out with the storytelling.

"Yeah, she asked me for a light, and we got chatting, like you do."

"Textbook stuff," said Ciara. "Whenever I'm on the prowl, looking to steal the virginities of hapless, innocent lads from Ashbrook, the old "Got a light?" routine always goes down a storm."

"He's never going to finish this story," said Drug Tim, sounding like normal Tim, for a second or two.

"He won't if you don't shush, you gowl," Ian said, throwing the cap off his water at him.

"ANYWAY, SO. So, I'm chatting away to her, working the charm, *shut up, Ciara*. Turns out it was her birthday that night. Or at least she was out celebrating it that night, cos maybe it was in the week or something, but you do that, don't you? Wait for the weekend, for a better night. We're getting on famously, I'm getting all the good vibes off her- she's touching me when she talks, lots of eye contact, all that stuff. And I think like, I'm in here, definitely."

"As you do," I said. In fairness, unless the story had a shocking twist, he was definitely in. *In her vagina, am I right?* I drank the end of my Bud, and held in a massive burp, cos I was a lady.

"But then, just when I'm planning on going in for the kill-"

"Oh, you shouldn't kill them, Niall. Killing women is a form of abuse," Ciara said. No one had the joint now, that I could see. Must've been finished.

"Whatever, so, like I said, I'm limbering up, like."

"Limbering up!" Bríd did a shriek of a laugh, and then had a bit of a coughing fit. Everyone stopped to make sure she wasn't having an asthma attack, but she was fine, after a bit.

"And I was just about to lean in for the kiss... when she says, out of nowhere: I'm sorry."

"Why was she sorry?" Tim said.

"Probably sorry she'd asked a big ginger murderer for a light in the first place," Richie said.

"No! She said... she said she was sorry, but she had a boyfriend."

"What?" I said. There was a twist, after all. A big wave of pleasure came over me, unrelated to that revelation, and I had to steady myself a second.

"Yeah. So, like, it was awkward after that, and eventually she just went off to the rest of her friends."

"That was the weirdest sex story ever," said Ciara, and we all laughed, except Niall.

"Shush, that's not the end of it. Anyway so, I'd lost Bobby, but I found him again, and there was no reason for me to hang around there anymore, so we went into the nightclub."

"And was yer wan in there?" said Richie.

"No."

"What a cunt," I said, and Bríd flinched, because she was one of *those* girls. I forgot that about her sometimes. She was all right otherwise, though. Nobody's perfect.

"So, you went home, pulled your mickey thinking of her, and you counted it as a shag, yeah?" said Ian.

"Fuck off, you. No, when the nightclub was over, we went outside. And like, ye know Doc's, you've to go back out through the beer garden if you want to go through the big arch thing, yeah?"

"Yeah," I said. I hadn't many memories of it, I was normally polluted at that stage, or speeding like Sonic the Hedgehog and on my way to some party.

"Well, I'd lost himself again, or he'd just fucked off home – he does that a lot. So, I'm out by those round benches, and who do I fucking run into?"

"Was it Salman Rushdie?" Ciara said, and immediately got a matchbox in the forehead for it.

"Lisa!" said Drug Tim, beaming.

"Yup. So, I'm not really fussed, cos she's already rejected me once, and I'm a bit cold, and I'd no jacket."

"The poor babba," I said, sparking up a fag. My boob was itchy inside the bra, and I didn't know why, but then I remembered the wrap of speed was in there.

"So, when did you- I'm not really sure where this story is going, sorry," Bríd said.

"I'm getting to it, calm down! Anyway, so, she's chatting away to me, getting all touchy-feely again, but this time I'm resisting it, cos-"

"Cos she's clearly some sort of flakey lunatic," I said. I knew plenty of ones like that one. Gave the rest of us a bad name, they did.

"Well yeah, but I just didn't want to get my hopes up for nothing. Anyway, she wasn't reading the signs I was giving off, cos eventually she asks me to walk her out."

"Oh, hello!" Ciara said.

"Yeah, and not only that, she starts asking me where I'm living, do I have my own place?"

"Ashbrook, and no you do not," Drug Tim said, helpfully.

"Yeah, I tell her as much, so then she's asking me is there any quiet place around town to take a girl for some… privacy." Niall was multitasking now – telling the story while rolling a new joint. Good man.

"The WHORE," Ciara said, laughing.

"Neh, anyway shur I had to think on my feet, and then I remembered that place where me and Bobby had drunk our 20/20, like. That was dead quiet, and out of the way of the main road. It's like an overnight car park, but they close at around ten."

"Ideal so, for lovemaking," I said, icking at the thought of riding down an alley in Limerick. I had a horrible image of Áine out of nowhere and tried to shake it. That joint had better be ready soon, I thought.

"Whatever, anyway, so we go down there, it's quiet. I

don't make the first move-"

"You FUCKING gentleman, boy," Ian said.

"Well, yeah. But she wasn't a gentleman-"

"I fucking hope not, or this is gonna be a very different story to the one I was expecting," I said. The horrible image of Áine was still in my head, and now one of Jon had joined it. *Come on, joint. Come on!*

"Haha. Anyway, she's eating the face off me, groping me every which way, and I'm doing the same to her."

"Why am I thinking about an orangutan now?" said Drug Tim.

"Why aren't the rest of us thinking about orangutans, Tim? That's the question you should really be asking," Ciara said, but they'd lost me now. Niall carried on.

"Eventually anyway it's getting really heavy. Her skirt is up, her knickers are off, my jeans are halfway down, there's been fingering, handjobs, blowjobs, lickouts, you name it, we were after doing it." He didn't look boastful, he was more like someone telling you about bargains he picked up at a jumble sale, I thought.

"Jaysus..." said Drug Tim, an innocent lamb compared to the rest of us. Or was he? We'd literally never know.

"So! So, she's basically trying to get me to put it inside her then, and-"

"Exsqueeze me?" said Bríd, looking shocked.

"I know! And I probably would have too-"

"Without a condom?" I said, doing a face of someone who had definitely never had unprotected sex while drunk or off her face, or at least I hoped that was what I looked like.

"Yeah, maybe. Anyway, I didn't have to."

"How so?" Bríd, again. Her Benson didn't say much at

all, but he was as interested in all this as the rest of us, from the look on his face.

"Well, first she asked me if I had anything."

"What, like the Clap, or AIDS?" I said, even though I knew exactly what he'd meant.

"Hah! No, like if I had a condom. Which I didn't. So, she's being all coy and saying that we can't do it then, but I'm getting a vibe off her like she wants me to *insist* that we do it anyway?"

"Oh no..." Ciara said, her mouth open now.

"Yeah. I definitely wasn't okay with that shit. I didn't even know her. Who knows what she could have said about me to other people, if like, she got pregnant off me or something?"

"Yeah, true," I said, though I didn't understand what he was saying. Everyone else seemed to though, so I went along with it

"Anyway, so I'm all like, shur we can still do everything else. But then she goes, hang on!"

"Hang on?" Ian said. He had the new joint. I'd forgotten it existed, in all the commotion.

"She says she has a condom, in her handbag."

"The fuck?" Ciara said, leaning towards him now, fully committed to the soap opera he was weaving for us.

"Yeah, turns out someone got her a jokey birthday card about sex, and it had a rubber johnny stuck to the front."

"Hopefully not pinned to it," I said, but no one got my joke, or they didn't hear me. Both were equally possible.

"Yes! Success!" Drug Tim said, and it made me laugh far too much for something that wasn't even funny. I was peaking, I had to be. I closed my eyes and took a deep breath, and my head went very light, and every bit of my skin tingled. Yep, this was it. Awesome.

"Well, yeah. Except…"

"Except?" someone asked. I had my eyes closed; I didn't see who.

"Except then she told me who had given her the card, like."

"Who had?" That was Ciara's voice. I was squirming now, pressing my bum and the rest into the ground underneath me. It felt like the only way to control the rush.

"Eh, her boyfriend."

"JESUS!" That was Bríd.

"Lousy!" said Richie, beside me.

"Harsh!" Ciara, again.

"Happy birthday to her, like…" said Drug Tim, very quietly, which made it even funnier, for some reason.

"So, you shagged her, yeah?" It'd been so long since Benson had said anything, he sounded like a stranger. Freaked me out a bit, but I was too busy having a full body nnnnnnngh to care for long. My toes were curling, I wondered if I should take my Docs off, but I couldn't handle opening laces with my head doing cartwheels like it was.

"I did. And it was good, as well."

"Ah, it's always good, for you men. And your first time doesn't involve pain or bleeding, so," Ciara said.

"No, it was good for her, too!"

"How do you know?" Ian said, looking all cynical. I was saying nothing, I was too high to make words come out properly, but at least my eyes were open.

"She told me! Honest, I wasn't doing anything special or nothing. I didn't know what I was doing, I'd never done it before. She was sitting up on a wall, right? Legs open. I was standing up, pushing into her, and I just popped it inside, and banged away-"

"Lovely," Bríd said, giggling.

"No, I was rubbing - I was doing circles on her clitoris at the same time, with my two fingers, you know? Using all the wetness from inside her to keep the tips of my fingers kind of slick?"

"It's wrong that this is arousing me, isn't it?" Ciara said. She had the joint now. There was a conspiracy against me, clearly.

"You're not the only one," said Drug Tim, and I burst into giggles again. I was so giddy I was going to have a heart attack in a minute.

"So did she have an orgasm or what?" Bríd said.

"Yes! I mean it was probably from my fingers-"

"More than probably," said someone. Took me a second to realise it had been me.

"But she came while I was still inside her, so it sort of counted, didn't it?" Niall looked all unsure and vulnerable. I wanted to give him a hug, but he was too far away, and I'd forgotten how walking worked.

"Oh, definitely. That counts. And on your first time, too. Take a bow, like. So, what happened then?" Ciara was having a mini stretch. I was still waiting for that massage. Later, definitely.

"Haha, that's the worst bit," he said, grinning like a loon.

"How do you mean?" That was me talking again. I was back down on earth with the rest of them, officially, although I was still peaking off my tits, and off all my other bits. I popped a fresh chewing gum in, cos my jaw was going into overdrive.

"Well, she was all gasping and out of breath and her heart was going ninety - she said - after we were finished."

"You absolute stallion," Ian said, getting another water. It was dark enough that they'd put some lights on above us. Moby was still Mobying away, behind us.

"Haha. So am, she says to me – and remember now she's no clue that it was my first time or anything – she says to me, "I know I shouldn't be saying this, but I've never, ever had sex like that with my fella. I've never come that hard, definitely not while having sex. I'm just blown away. You were amazing.""

"She did in her hole," Ian said.

"I think she did," Ciara said. "I can usually tell when someone is lying, can't I Bríd? And this one, I don't think he is."

"I'm honestly not, like." Niall looked innocent enough for me to believe him, too. My heart was thumping in my chest, and I could feel the sweat rolling down the lower half of my back. It all felt good, though. Incredibly fucking good.

"So, wait, why is that the worst bit, Niall? Or was the worst bit that the boyfriend gave her the card?" I said, "I'm a little confuzzled."

"No, it's not. I haven't got to that bit yet."

"Well, get a move on, we don't have all night," Richie said, finally passing me the joint from whoever had it last. I didn't even want it now, but I took a bang off it anyway. Might help to calm the fireworks that were going off in my brain and everywhere else.

"Okay, yeah. So, she says all that to me, and of course I have to say something back to her, don't I?"

"Of course!" said all of us girls, at the same time.

"Yep. And I remember thinking at the time that this was like a really important moment, lads. *Pivotal*, maybe, in deciding the sort of man I was going to be from then on. Cos, I could have- I should have – been honest, and humble, and told her it was actually my first time, and it must have been beginner's luck or something."

"Oh, she would have loved that, Niall! We all would, wouldn't we?" I looked around at the other two and they nodded, cos it was true.

"Oh. Really?" Niall looked a bit thrown.

"Really! It'd be sweet, and sincere, and it'd make us, well it would make *me* anyway, feel a lot more comfortable about what had just happened, like," Ciara said.

"Ah. Yeah, I can see that now, kind of." He was doing a face. No idea what it meant. Regret, maybe.

"What did you actually say to her then, Niall?" Bríd asked, sounding like she wasn't sure she wanted to hear the answer.

"Hah! Am, well, what actually happened, after she'd said all that to me about never having sex that good before, never coming that hard, and her fella not being able to make her orgasm like that… what I said was… "That's what they all say, love.""

"NIALL!!!" Bríd threw a full bottle of water at him, but he was too quick for her.

"Oh, and then I pulled the condom off and threw it against the wall beside us. *Snap! Thwack!*" he said, smiling a smile that was so big and genuine that it was contagious, like a yawn, or genital herpes.

*****

"I'm really, like – it's so, you know… I'm just so, uh, whoa. Whoa! God. Wow, like. Wow."

"Yeah, I know. Good, aren't they?" Ciara said. We were in the toilets again, because I hadn't fixed my makeup all day, and I'd been sweating like a child molester in a Barney costume, as Brian might say.

"Who is?" I was trying to focus on the mirror, but my eyes weren't cooperating, so far.

"The pills, you gimp." Ciara was a master of putting on slap. Or a mistress, maybe. She'd already done her eyes and her face; she was on the lip liner now.

"Oh! Oh yeah, I can't even – I mean, I've done – it's like-"

"Shhhhhh. Breathe." She put her finger on my lips.

"Breathing. Breathing, now. Definitely breathing," I said, trying to get the top off the Maybelline bottle.

"Good, good. That's a start. Breathing is always good. Want me to do that for you? Your face, I mean?"

"Please! Yes, if you don't mind, like?" I said. I took some of her water, just a small drop. It'd be fine, we were going dancing, I'd do a wee by sweating, or whatever Bríd had said. My organs weren't going to fall out or anything. Fingers crossed.

"Course I don't mind, silly. Hop up there, sit down, relax, and let Auntie Ciara give you a Ricki Lake makeover."

"A what?" I wanted to relax, like she said, but I had to stay still for her to do me, so I wasn't sure which I should do. She'd put perfume on, so she didn't smell so much like vanilla now. *CK One* was what she wore, usually. Or sometimes other Calvin Klein ones. *Dune*, by Dior, was my one. Bit expensive, but my family were always buying it for Christmas for me, so I never ran out of the stuff.

"Never mind, chick. Will I just do you like me?" Her hands were moving the sponge brush thing around my eyes like she was on fast forward, I was nearly dizzy from it. She apparently did eye stuff first, face stuff second. I'd thought it was the other way around. Felt like my whole life had been a lie.

"What's like you?"

"Nothing's like me, babe. I'm a one-off." She was doing liquid liner now - her own - I'd only brought pencils.

"You are. Will we – is this gonna last?" I said, a weird panic coming out of nowhere. I couldn't remember what Bríd had said now. Did you peak and then just come down straight after? I didn't want to come down now. I didn't want to come down at all. I still had my wrap, but...

"For me? Nah. I've done 'em too many times, I'll have another one in a bit." She dipped the wand thing into the mascara and took it back out slowly. That was the only thing she'd done slow so far.

"Yeah?" I had my back to the mirror, sitting up on the sink, so I couldn't see what she was doing. I trusted her though, I wasn't going to walk out looking like John Wayne Gacy or anything. She'd make me look fab.

"Yeah, but you and Tim will still be up for ages, honestly. First time is the best time. I'm jealous of ye, like." She had a great voice, like someone off the telly. She did lots of acting in drama groups, up in the Belltable theatre, but she was the least dramatic girl I knew.

"Me and Tim, yeah," I said, thinking of Tim from Ash.

"Not that Tim, you whore." Maybe Es gave you telepathic powers. It wouldn't have surprised me if they did.

"Ah, yeah. Tim the keyboard guy," I said. I'd forgotten he was doing his first one too, I'd have to talk to him about it in a bit, to compare notes.

"Glad you clarified that, thanks." She couldn't be finished doing my eyes already, could she? She was, though.

"Oh, right. Are you coming back to Jury's with me tonight, anyway?"

"Coming back with *you*?" She stopped putting the concealer under my eyes for a second and looked at me.

"With *us*, I mean. For a party, or a session, or a jam, or whatever they've planned." I didn't realise I'd said something wrong. *Had* I said something wrong?

"Aw. I thought I'd pulled for a second there, like." She went back to work. She dotted the liquid foundation around my face and blended it in like she was Bob Ross on speed. Her fingertips were barely on me, way lighter than I'd be if I was doing it to myself. She'd missed her calling as an MUA, definitely.

"Well, you can stay in my room if you like – I've a massive double bed. I'm a rubbish shag, but there's probably a minibar, and Sky Movies." I was messing with her, but I did want her to stay with me tonight, since she was supposed to be minding me.

"You really know how to show a girl a good time, Shaughnessy." She was done with my face, I turned around to see.

"Oh, that's brill, Ciara. Thanks so much. Look at that, like. You did the Cleopatra thing with the eyeliner and all! What's that called, properly?" I looked fantastic, and not just for someone who'd been awake since 7am and on drugs all day, either.

"Winged, I think. I call it Cat Eyes, though. Look at the two of us, like." She put her face beside mine and made a pouty face into the mirror, so I did too.

"Féile 95 won't know what hit it," I said.

"*Better than mortal man deserves*," she said.

"What's that from again? Beaches, is it?" I hadn't seen that in ages, I preferred decent, proper films, not all that girly sleepover shite.

"Close enough, babe. It's from The Terminator."

"Mortified, I am!" I grabbed my handbag before I forgot it. Ciara linked arms with me and pointed us towards the door.

"Shhhhh, don't be silly. Now, come with me if you want to live." She took out two fags, lit them both in her mouth, and passed one over to me. It was dark outside now, and I felt like the night was only starting.

SIX

"Did you know they've a funfair here?" Drug Tim was leaning against the fence, outside the dressing room area. The dressing rooms were just a couple of rows of portacabins or prefabs; I hadn't been in one yet, we wouldn't be let use one until Sunday probably, anyway.

"A funfair? Like a carnival?" The music had stopped, up on the stage. They were changing over, cos we'd seen Moby fuck off a minute ago. The noise of the crowd just chatting, laughing, and singing, was the only thing in the air now. It was kind of electric, being so near to thousands of people all having a great time. You could feel the vibes, Ciara said.

I wondered should we stroll out onto the stage and give them a wave, but we probably couldn't. Roadies were seriously cranky bastards at the best of times, but roadies trying to set up for the Prodigy in fifteen minutes in front of tens of thousands of impatient drunks would probably box you in the face if you got in their way, I thought.

"Yeah, only a small one, but they have rides."

"You've all the rides you need here, honey," Ciara said, beside him, putting her arm around his waist. I looked around to do a head count. It was properly night time, but it didn't feel too cold out. We'd be dancing in a minute anyway, so we'd be grand.

"But I want to go on the Waltzers," he said, sounding a bit wounded.

"We'll go tomorrow, okay? Mammy promises you, yeah?" Bríd told him, messing his hair. She had her nice jacket on, the navy moleskin one with the fag burn on the sleeve that definitely hadn't been done by me on the dancefloor in Termights last summer.

"Oof! You look... nice," Ian said, looking down at my cleaveage and not at my newly made-up face. I didn't care. I looked great all over, shur.

"Thanks. And you..." I looked him up and down, slowly. "You, have a *great* personality." I was only messing with him; he was a ride and he knew it. If anything, his personality was the worst part of him, the prick.

"Hahaaaaa," Niall said, appearing beside him, and also having a gawk at my tits. I felt like a one-woman Madame Tussaud's. They'd all seen them earlier, like. I hadn't grown new ones in the toilet.

"Anyone else want a good look at my knockers?" I said, a bit *too* loud, probably, cos people who weren't in our group stopped and looked over at me. Thankfully, none of them took me up on the offer.

"Nah. Seen one, you've seen 'em all, sham," Richie said, putting his arm around my shoulder, then kissing my cheek. Both of those things felt nice, especially since it was Richie, who was hardly the most affectionate youngfella on a normal day. He was a new Richie tonight, though. A sweeter, lovelier Richie. In touch with all his feelings, and his purer, inner self.

"Seen one? Who've you been riding that only has one boob?" I said, turning my head to face him. His eyes were massive, like a Japanese cartoon.

"Your Ma," he said, then he pinched my arse and walked off to catch up with the rest of the chauvinist pigs.

*****

"All right, guys? Having it tonight, eh? Laaaaavely. Nice one." An English guy with orange hair and lots of face piercings walked through the middle of us at the side of the stage, but he was already gone before I copped on he was Keith Flint, the main guy out of the Prodigy. He normally had green hair, I thought.

"Scuzi there, mates," said another English voice. I looked around and saw a beautiful looking black guy, with no shirt on. He had tight black trousers on, and some sort of sunglasses or goggles pushed up over his forehead. His eyes were freaky. I thought he was some sort of demon, until I realised it was just red contact lenses. It was the other singer guy – I didn't know his name - who was in the Prodigy too.

"Sorry!" I said. His chest was all shiny, there was no hair on it, and he was kind of built. Not all disgusting and veiny like a bodybuilder. More like a boxer. He stopped a second, looked me up and down in a way that felt very deliberate, then he pointed at my face.

"Hellooooo, mama. What's going on here, eh?" Someone on the stage was hitting drums, or it might have been a machine. The Prodigy would definitely have a drum machine, even if they had real drums, too.

"What's going on where?" I said, not sure what was going on anywhere, anymore.

"Hehehe. You're a funny girl. Funny and..." He looked at everyone else, who were all standing there, watching us and saying nothing. "How you guys doing?"

Everyone mumbled stuff like "Good", "Good, thanks," or "All right", at him, like they were Perry off Harry Enfield. *Yes, Mrs. Patterson!*

"Nice. You all *'aving it* tonight, yeah?" He was very English altogether.

"Are we having what?" Drug Tim said. I looked at him

to see how he was coping. Seemed grand to me.

"Havin' it large, mate," said Mr. Prodigy Guy. He'd a lovely smile, and a lovely face too, even with the devil eyes.

"We're having it extra-large," Niall said, offering the fella his joint.

"Nah, I'm good thanks, geez. Gotta go'ta work. Have a good one though, bruvva!" Then, to me, "And you, baby girl. Stay gorgeous yeah, Red? Niiiiiice." He gave me a wink, and literally jumped up the last few steps, landed on the stage, and started sprinting, whooping into his cordless mic.

"That was Leeroy, lads! *Leeroy Thornhill*," someone said, possibly Bríd, I wasn't looking.

"He can put his thorn in my hill anytime he likes," I said, fanning myself with my hand, all dramatic.

"No, that's Maxim. Leeroy is the other black fella. The one who plays keyboards and does dancing. Maxim is the rapper one, you eejit," Ian said. Always ruining my brilliant jokes with his pesky facts, that guy.

"He can put his max in my im anytime he likes?" I said, trying again, but that one was shit.

"He can put it in your *quim*, more like," Niall said, which was slightly better, even though that word was rank. *Cunt* was like poetry compared to quim.

The music started up properly, and we headed towards the gate bit, because this was one we definitely had to be in the crowd for.

*****

"I think I finally understand it." We were miles back from the stage, since we'd come out so late and all the spots up front were already filled, but Niall still had to lean quite close to me so I could hear him.

"Understand what?" I felt like I was riding on waves –

waves of mad, intense pleasure, and waves of bass, as well. The stage looked great from back here. Well, the big screens on each side did anyway, I couldn't see the actual stage with all these people in my way, I was only five six and I was wearing Docs, not heels.

"Well, everything, like. But I mean, I get it now. The music?"

"You get the music?" I could see on the screen that Keith was crowd surfing, and the security guards weren't happy about it. A black guy with bleached hair, wearing a sparkly top, was dancing all crazy on the stage. The real Leeroy, no doubt.

"I mean I get this sort of music, like. Dance Music, or Rave, or whatever it's called, you know?" He had to lean down as well as in, cos he was such a big, towering lump of a yoke. Six three, or six four. He might have still been growing, I didn't know when boys stopped, but it was after we did, definitely.

"Oh right, yeah. Yeah, it's good, isn't it?" I wasn't normally into this sort of stuff either, to be honest, but I liked some of it. Tonight though, it sounded amazing. Especially live like this, on a stage, with a band. There were so many things going on at once. Sounds, visuals, relentless, loud beats. Some other time it might have felt like too much, but now it felt just right. It felt perfect.

"Yeah, it's like – you know me, I'm really picky about music, like. I just like what I like and nothing else."

"Yeah, I know, I'm in a band with you," I said, a bit too loud, but he didn't seem to mind me screaming into his ear.

"Hahaha, yeah. Sorry about that."

"Sorry you're in a band with me?" I did a pretend pout at him.

"No! I mean I'm sorry I'm so picky when ye want to do

covers and stuff. I'm-"

"BRILLIANT, ISNT IT?" someone screamed into my other ear, nearly deafening me. It was Drug Tim.

"YES! YES, IT IS!" I screamed back at him. My chewing gum fell out of my mouth into the grass. Fuck's sake. I went into my bag for another one. I'd stolen the pack off Ciara.

"Anyway, what I'm saying is, I get it now. Like, it's cos of the drugs that I get it. This stuff was *written* for drugs. It was written by people *on* drugs. On *this* drug. It's – this kind of music, it's got all these like layers, and different levels, and you don't realise it when it's just on the radio, or if it's on in Tropics when you're pissed. But like, now, tonight, it's like I'm on this other plane of understanding, it's like-"

"Sorry, what? When were you on a plane? To Amsterdam, was it? I thought ye got the ferry or a coach or something?" Found the chewing gums, finally. I offered him one, and Tim too, except Tim was already gone. I looked to see where Ciara was, cos she was the one I definitely couldn't lose. It was grand, I could see her dancing with Bríd, behind Niall. Benson was there too, and maybe Ian.

"What? No, not that kind of - it's just like – I remember that one *Out of Space* came out and I thought it was shit, cos it was raver music and all that. But when they played it there a few minutes ago it was like… like better than the Beatles, do you get me?" He was squatting down on his haunches to talk face to face with me, but his body was still instinctively swaying to the music, so he looked like he was doing the squat dance Kylie was doing earlier. I let out a big, throw-your-head-back laugh.

"What's so funny?"

"Everything is funny, babe. Everything is brilliant. Hey! Can I get up on you?"

"Pardon?" He looked half shocked and half excited,

poor guy.

"Can you put me on your shoulders, so I can see the stage, properly, like? And don't drop me, please?" I wanted to see if I could see Keith on top of the crowd and give him a wave or something. It'd be cool to be up that high, anyway, and look the whole way around at all the thousands of people.

"Oh! Oh, right, I thought- put you up on my shoulders, like, yeah. Like they do at music festivals."

"We *are* at a music festival, Nailer," I said, wondering how we were gonna manage this now without killing one of us, but still wanting to give it a go.

"Oh, yeah. We are too, like." He crouched down like he was gonna start a game of Leapfrog with me. Hop up there now, and hang on tight to me, yeah."

"Brace yourself, Brigid!" I said, and got up on him like he was a donkey on the beach in Tramore.

*****

"Fancy meeting you here!" said a voice, beside me, up in the sky, a little while later. Niall was surprisingly good at giving shoulder rides, I'd barely had one wobble so far.

"Hello!" I said, as if Bríd being up here too was totally normal. I looked down and saw it was Benson she was mounting. Maybe he was a good boyfriend after all.

"This is AMAZING, isn't it?" She put her hand out and moved it across our view of the crowd. *Poison* had just finished; everyone had gone mental for it. It was like being at a heavy metal concert, just with less moshing, and more glow sticks and whistles.

"It's like... epic," I said, cos I couldn't think of a better word. Maybe there wasn't one. It felt pretty epic to me.

"Yeah, he's really working this crowd, isn't he?" She

was right. Every time Maxim said "BOOM!" or "COME ON!" everyone pumped their fists in the air at him. It was like Live Aid, when Freddie got the crowd clapping to *Radio Ga Ga*.

"He's brilliant altogether, shur. You still up?" I said. I was obsessing a little about the E, and about the comedown. I was nowhere near feeling like I was coming down, but I was still para about what'd happen if I did. You couldn't get back up after you came down, they'd said, earlier. You had to take another one before your eyes went all the way back to normal. I tried to look at her pupils, but I couldn't see shit in this kind of light.

"Up here?" Brid said, patting Benson's head like he was her horse.

"No like, up on your yoke." I wondered if she'd call him "Ben" if his first name was *actually* Benson. I would, definitely. It'd be less stupid sounding. Or "Benny". But then you'd be thinking of Benny Hill, which would ruin the sex.

"Ah, yeah. So far, anyway." She said, crossing her fingers. She had lovely hands; played the piano, or she used to, at least. The Prodigy were playing a song I didn't really recognise, but from what yer man was shouting, it had something to do with "the funky shit", anyway.

"Cool. Cool," I said. The song finished, and now there was a different noise coming from the stage. A man's voice, like on the radio. Like a newscaster. I listened a bit harder.

"Oh! This one is brilliant; do you know it?" Brid said, leaning a bit too far into me and nearly falling out of her saddle. She held onto my shoulder to steady herself.

"I don't think so, no?" I didn't own their albums, but I'd heard a lot of the new one, the Jilted Generation one, because everyone seemed to love it, no matter what they were into. The radio man was a weather forecaster – an English one, like Michael Fish, maybe.

"It's off *Experience*", said Bríd, which didn't help me much. "The song's called *Weather Experience.*"

"Oh right," I said, smiling at her like an idiot. I'd been smiling like an idiot for hours now though, so she probably didn't notice. The weatherman's voice got quieter, and some orchestral synths kicked in, like something Tim did with his keyboard sometimes. All of a sudden, I could feel the music inside my chest, and going up the back of my neck. It was glorious. Uplifting was the word I was thinking of. Uplifting, while me and Bríd were being lifted up by the two poor lads.

"Whoa," I said, reaching out to take her hand and squeeze it.

"Hahaaaa, I know! This is BLISS, like," she said. I realised then that I'd been running my fingers through Niall's hair and massaging his scalp with my nails, without thinking about it. He hadn't complained though, so it was grand. Maxim was pacing the stage again, Keith was down at the crash barriers, getting some love. They were probably all on Es, they must have been. They were on them, I was on them, we were on them. Thousands of this crowd were probably on them. Made the whole thing feel like a shared, well, *experience*.

"I WANNA SEE EVERYBODY-" Maxim screamed. Then the song went quieter, sort of low and hummy. Didn't sound right, at all. The lights on stage flashed and flickered. They went off completely. The music stopped, and for a second all you could hear was the bass pedal on the live drum kit. Then nothing. It was over already. I was very confused; they hadn't even been on for that long.

"The hell?" Niall said, below me. I was hoping he wasn't gonna put me down, since I was in the ideal place to see what the fuck was happening up there.

"Is that it, like?" someone said. It was pitch black in Páirc Uí Chaoimh, except for a few green glows from the crowd. It wasn't silent, though. There was chatter, and people blowing whistles, and then they started chanting: "WE WANT MORE! WE WANT MORE!"

"PRO-DI-GY! PRO-DI-GY!" They were all at it, now. I felt swindled. I'd been loving it, I thought they'd barely started. My calf felt crampy all of a sudden. I panicked.

"Here, Niall! Let us down, yeah?" I patted his head, and he didn't say anything, but he lowered me to the floor without either of us toppling over. I smelled *CK One* and vanilla.

"Hey!" Ciara sat down next to me on the grass. The chanting was getting louder and spreading all around the park, now.

"WE WANT MORE! WE WANT MORE!"

"PRO-DI-GY! PRO-DI-GY!"

"Hello, you," I said, feeling for her arm in the dark. I'd no idea why they'd turned off all the lights, instead of just the music. Or why the Prodigy had fucked off without saying goodnight. In the middle of a song, too.

"What's wrong with your leg, honeybun?" I felt her hand on my thigh. I'd my right leg stretched the whole way out in front of me on the ground, pointing my toes back at me, but it wasn't working, so far.

"Craaaaaamp!"

"Oh. You want me to–"

"Please! Yes," I said, wiggling my Doc boot at her.

"Okey doke. Relax and let Nurse Ki-Ki look after you," she said, opening my laces, quick as a flash, sliding off the boot, and taking my foot in her hand.

"Oh, God, thank you!" I thought for a second that my feet probably stunk, cos of the heat we'd had all day, and me wearing socks inside heavy boots, but I forgot about all that once *Nurse Ki-Ki* pushed my toes back, and the bad feeling went out of my leg. She was a girl of so many talents.

"My pleasure, dear. Here, what about all this, eh? What's happened? Is it over now? Where are the lights? They're supposed to turn on the floodlights at the end, so everyone can find each other. That's what they did in Thurles, anyway. This is just... bizarre." She'd started massaging the ball of my foot now, and the archy bit between the ball and the heel. It felt incredible. I didn't want it to stop. I wondered if she was gonna do the other foot next, but I didn't want to be cheeky and ask her. It just felt so nice, someone touching me.

"Mmmmmmm, that's lovely, don't stop. Am, yeah, I know, like. They just... stopped. Rude! Oooooh, yeah, keep doing that," I said. She was scraping her nail across the ridges on my big toe now. I didn't know why, but I wasn't gonna query it. It didn't feel like part of a massage, it felt...*erogenous*. Feet weren't supposed to be erogenous. Feet were supposed to be... feet.

"WE WANT MORE! WE WANT MORE!"

"PRO-DI-GY! PRO-DI-GY!"

"Haha! You're grand, I owed you a massage anyway, might as well be a foot one, shur. Will I take off the other shoe?"

"*Take it off! Take it all off!*" I said, which was from some weird song with a video where a guy was getting his hair cut, so the lyrics weren't as filthy as you thought they were. Or maybe that was a dream I'd had once, no idea.

"Okey dokey," she said, and undid the bow on my laces with one pull. Niall and Benson were talking to each other up above us, but I couldn't hear what they were saying, and I didn't really care, anyway.

"Hey. Not interrupting anything, am I?"

"Huh?" I'd had my eyes closed while I was enjoying

Ciara doing my other foot. It was Bríd, down on the grass with us now.

"Nope, just giving Caoimhe a bit of TLC," Ciara said. Her fingers were like magic, it was making my whole body feel tingly, not just the bits she was touching. A little wave of niceness rolled up my thighs and over my belly, and the muscles there got all tight.

"Lucky her, haha."

"Lucky me," I said, grinding through what was left of my chewing gum.

"WE WANT MORE! WE WANT MORE!"

"PRO-DI-GY! PRO-DI-GY!" They were still at it, and the whistles as well, which seemed to get louder and louder. No one was stamping on us or anything, even though it was too dark to see us down there. They just walked around us, if they were walking. Most people were just standing, though.

"Can I borrow your water?" Ciara said to Bríd. I didn't know where mine was gone.

"Yup. You dropping another yoke?" Bríd handed the bottle to me, and I passed it over.

"Think I might have to, yeah. I've been on the way down, and like, the music's over now-"

"*When the muuuuuusic's over,*" Bríd sang.

"*Turn out the liiiiights,*" I finished it off for her. They had turned them out, too, when the music was over. We were living in a Doors song.

"Haha, yeah. But really, I'll drop a half, or… I'll do a full one, but that'll be it then, for the night. I'll be back up properly by the time we get to Jury's, and shur there's gonna be music on there, we'll put something on."

"Yeah, or find a good radio station, Bríd said. Ciara was still molesting my feet. I was loving it but listening to them talking about all this was making me panic that I was coming down. Or that I'd already come down, maybe.

"Can I- will I take another one too, then?" I said, trying to make out Ciara's face in the dark.

"WE WANT MORE! WE WANT MORE!"

"PRO-DI-GY! PRO-DI-GY!" Niall and Benson had joined in the chanting now. Neither of them owned a whistle though, so that was something at least.

"Oh honey, I'm not sure that's a good idea." She squeezed my foot as she said it, as if she was squeezing my hand, in a comforting way.

"Yeah, Kweev, it's your first time. You should pace yourself, babe," Bríd said. I didn't like this. They were talking to me like I was Tim. I wasn't that green. I did drugs all the time. I was-

"Are you not still buzzing, anyway?" Ciara said, going back to pushing her thumbs into my arch. I wasn't sure if she was doing it to distract me or not, but it was pretty distracting, in a good way.

"I- I don't know. I'm not sure. How do I know?" At that precise moment, I didn't feel up at all, anymore. I didn't feel anything. I was down. It could've been my imagination, but it felt real. I felt panicky.

"Eh, you'd know." She popped something in her mouth and took a swig of the water.

"I think I'm down, Ciara. Or, heading there. Have you another one of those for me?" I'd only taken one from the Smint box. I didn't think I needed to take more, at the time.

"I do, but..." I couldn't see her face, but her tone of voice was enough for me to know she was hesitating about it.

"Ah, shur she'll be grand, Ciara. Won't we be minding her, anyway, like? We'll see you come to no harm, Shox," said

Bríd, swallowing one herself, so now I was the odd one out for sure.

"Okay. Majority rules, then," Ciara said, passing the pill into my hand, and I didn't even have to swallow it before I felt up again. *Placebo effect.* The lights came on again exactly at the moment the yoke went down my neck, like a miracle. We looked at each other's faces like it was the first time we'd ever laid eyes on each other, and then the three of us burst out laughing. A voice came over the PA, it was our old pal, Maxim.

"Yeah."

"What the hell?" Niall said. I was standing up now, next to him.

"Uhuh!" Maxim said.

"We're back in business," Ciara said, putting her arm around my waist. I hadn't put my boots back on, and my feet felt amazing on the soft ground. I was gonna take my socks off too, in a second. Feel the damp grass against my tingly skin. Nnnnngh.

"We don't let, no POWER CUT, spoil, our buzz," Maxim said, and everyone cheered. The screens were back on, and I could see him striding around like a big, shiny, brown peacock of a man. He was brilliant altogether.

"When we come, we come ROUGH," he said, which made me feel all funny in my tummy, and elsewhere. I took a chewing gum off Niall, chomped it, and breathed in the minty goodness. My airways opened up, and the night smelled like Heaven.

"Jaysus, the Prodigy are so heavy they broke Páirc Uí Chaoimh," Bríd said. Someone hit the strings on a bass guitar. The lights on the stage went off, came on again, red. Went off, came on again, blue. The person strumming the bass got faster, but it wasn't a song, or the start of one. Just the one note, over again.

"And when we come back… we come TWICE as HARD!" The crowd went mad again. The atmosphere was even better now than it had been before the power went out. I felt like I was coming up on the second E, but I couldn't be. It was way too soon. Or was it? I heard a bass drum pedal getting kicked, up on stage. I wondered where Richie was.

"We're gonna leave this one with ya…" said Maxim, and the whole crowd seemed to make the same disappointed noise, in my head anyway, cos that sounded like they were gonna finish soon. A voice came out of the speakers, it wasn't his. It was the sample bit, from *Their Law*. I knew this one, it was about some new thing in England where they were trying to make raves illegal, I'd read in Select or NME, maybe. Keith was on the big screens, miming the words of it:

What we're dealing with here, is a total lack of respect for the law.

The guitars started up on their own, for a few bars, then the other instruments joined in. Maxim was still striding, Keith was behind him, waving his arms and going mental.

"Do you understand?" Maxim asked us. "DO YOU UNDERSTAND?" We all shouted, "YEAH!" although I wasn't sure what he was asking.

"We come TWICE AS HARD!" Ye certainly do, I thought. The song was still building up to the first big breakdown - it was like, crescendoing, or something. The anticipation would have been palpable enough if it was just me listening, but in a field with like 30,000 people, probably all off our faces, it was almost too much to take.

"And TWICE AS ROUGH!!!" His face was on the screens now, all shiny and handsome and with those evil red eyes. We were all bouncing on the spot, holding each other's shoulders, getting ready for the good bit, so we could jump around and go mental.

"Everybody in Cork tonight…" That got the biggest cheer so far. The camera went on Keith for a second, he was messing about, running away from the spotlight that someone was pointing at him. They went back to Maxim. He did the "YEEEOWWW!" thing, we were seconds away now. "Ugh!" and another, "UGH!" Then, "Yeeeow!" and at last: *"Fuck 'em, and THEIR LAW!"* The whole stadium exploded with noise and lights and colours and joy and love and drugs. I took the deepest, longest breath of my life, and it felt like I was inhaling all of Páirc Uí Chaoimh – the people, the music, the whole fucking *vibe* of it. What a life we led.

*****

Thankfully, it hadn't been the last song. They'd played for a good while after, and we even had another power cut at some point. When it was all over and we were traipsing through the muddy, floodlit pitch, rounding up the stragglers and making small talk with equally chewy-faced Féile people, I was rushing like a mad rushing thing.

"We getting a taxi to the hotel, then?" Drug Tim said. He was still on his first one, as far as I knew, and I'd leave off telling him I'd taken another one, cos he was new to all this – proper drugs, I mean – so the one would do him. I was devouring a one-skinner I'd got Niall to roll me, to steady the ship, so to speak. It tasted gorgeous, but then everything did. Except food, maybe. I'd no desire for a garlic cheese chip now. Or for anything.

"How are you planning on doing that, Timothy?" Ciara said. She'd her shoes and socks off too, so had Bríd. We were like three hippy Earth Mothers, squelching through the muck at Woodstock. It was great.

"I was gonna put my hand up and say, TAXI!" he said.

"We're not in New York, man," Ian said. I hadn't talked to him in ages, but I didn't want to either, so it was grand.

"We're not even in New Cork, man," said Bríd, and we all laughed. *Fashion crisis hits New Cork, I saw a blind man, he was eating his fork.*

"We missed Massive Attack, did we? Or are they on now?" I said. We hadn't gone near the tent thing all day. We'd barely gone near the main crowd bit either, until the end, though.

"Ah, no, that's all over. They were finished before the Prodigy came on, even, so they wouldn't clash," Ian said, knowing a lot more about all of it than I did.

"Ah, that's lousy," Ciara said. She was linking me again. Half for the niceness of it, and half to hold each other steady so we didn't fall over.

"Ah, it wouldn't have been a proper gig anyway." Ian somehow still had a beer, in a plastic cup. They had glass ones in the VIP bar, so I did have to wonder how Brian had managed to end up with his Guinness in a beaker, way back earlier.

"What do you mean?" Richie said. All the boys still had their shoes on, the cowards.

"Like it'd just be 3D or whoever, from the band, DJing, like," Benson, who was still with us, said.

"Is that right? 3D, and… who else is in them? Tricky?" Bríd said, gazing at him in awe, or maybe it just looked like that, cos of the off-her-faceness.

"No, Tricky left them, I think. That's why he was playing on his own today," Ian said. I was learning all sorts of things tonight.

"Anyway, so are we walking to the hotel then?" I said, trying to get all their attentions, and only half succeeding. "If we are, ye need to tell me, cos…" I pointed at my bare feet, then at my Docs and socks, to clarify. I'd have made a great air hostess.

"No, I'll drive us," Benson said.

"You'll drive us?" I said. "Drive us in what?" Then I remembered he was the one who brought Bríd and Ciara to Cork this morning, so he must have a car.

"The van," said Bríd, smiling.

"What van?" said Tim. I hadn't seen him chewing all night. Did he not know you had to chew gum? Should I tell him? Then, as if he was reading my mind with the E-telepathy, he started chewing away.

"I've a VW Camper, like. Parked a bit down the road there."

"A Volkswagen?" Tim said, chewing like a mad chewing thing.

"That's what the letters stand for, yeah," said Benson, a bit smugly. Smugly was a good word. Rhymed with "ugly". And with "snuggly". I looked at Ciara. She definitely wasn't ugly. She had such a lovely figure, all curvy and soft and sticky-outy in the right places. I'd be getting snuggly with her later, in my room, and I'd have all that curvy softness to myself, I thought. Then I stopped thinking that cos maybe it was a weird thing to think.

"You can't drive, though?" I said. He was wrecked, like the rest of us.

"I can, too. Wanna see my licence, do ya?"

"No, I mean... I mean you're not in the right *condition* to drive, like." I looked around for a bit of support, but they were all looking at him to hear what he was gonna say.

"Why not? I haven't been drinking, like. Not since the afternoon, and I only had one or two, anyway. I'm sober as a judge. I don't even drink, normally." I'd forgotten the thing about how he didn't drink, but it was grand, since it had clearly been a filthy lie.

"It's true!" Bríd said, but she *would* say that.

"You're on pills though!" I said. I couldn't believe no one was backing me up.

"They don't breathalyse you for pills, like," Niall said, shrugging.

"I can drive fine on a pill, and anyway it's like ten minutes to the hotel. We'll be fine. I'm not forcing you though, Caoimhe. I'm not gonna hold a gun to any of your heads, like. But there's plenty of room for all of you, so who is coming? Show of hands?"

They all put their hands up, so I was outnumbered. I wasn't walking to Jury's on my own either, not with that crowd out there. I'd be raped five times before I had a chance to shout "FIRE!" once. I put my hand up as well, and that was that. Ciara gave me a squeeze, and that cheered me up, at least.

"Is it one of the old VW Campers, from the Sixties, like?" Ian said, after a few minutes of walking and slightly awkward silence.

"Yeah, it's the 1967 model," Benson said, smirking.

"Bought it new then, did you?" I said, and everyone laughed, cos I was hilarious.

SEVEN

"I've got the poison! I've got the poison!" Drug Tim was being a bit too loud when we finally got to the hotel. We'd given Benson the four-digit code for the car park, hopefully he'd have no problems finding a space and also hopefully he'd be grand leaving it there, even though he wasn't a guest. Bríd had stayed down with him instead of coming up with us. They knew what floor we were on, they'd be up in a minute, unless they were gonna have a crafty van-shag on the sly. It had a pull-down bed; I'd seen it when we were driving over. Cool, in one way; a bit rapey, in another.

"What's that you've got, Tim?" Ian said.

"Don't encourage him, you," Ciara said, rolling her eyes towards me. There was no one in the lobby now apart from the two girls behind reception. The lights were dimmed, and it was very quiet. Well, it had been, anyway.

"I'VE GOT THE POISON!"

"Shhhhhh, will you?" I said, slapping him on the arm hard enough to make him flinch.

"But I've got the poison!" He looked like I'd genuinely hurt him. Physically, and emotionally.

"Yes, Tim love. And we've got the remedy, okay? But it's upstairs, so go and wait for the lift, like a good boy," Ciara said, in her best Mammy voice.

"Excuse me?" One of the reception girls was talking

now, oh dear. We were in trouble. I pretended not to have heard her.

"EXCUSE ME!" She wasn't gonna give up, clearly. I turned around and gave her a big smile.

"Yeah?"

"Are you Kweeva? Kweeva from the band, Crane?" she said, scrutinising me. She had a pen in her hand, and a sheet of paper. Another fan, obviously. What a life we led.

"Guilty as charged! Who am I making this out to, yourself, is it?" Probably her younger sister. She looked a bit old to be into us, but we got all sorts, really

"What?" Her face was a blank.

"Ummmm..." My face was now also a blank. The rest of them were by the lift.

"You're Kweeva, yes?"

"Yes." I felt like I was being accused of a crime. The lift opened with a ding. They'd better hold it for me, I wasn't doing stairs at this hour of the night, or morning, whichever it was.

"Right, well two things. One, you dropped your room key."

"I did not!" I said.

"Well, I have it, someone handed it in, so you must have dropped it. Room 211, yeah?"

"Oh. Yeah, 211." Mortified. I looked over at the lift again, Ciara was jamming the doors open. I loved her.

"Okay, here you go, and look after it this time, yeah?"

"I will, sorry." *Sorry, Mrs. Patterson!*

"Good stuff. And, the other thing was, a guy called Brian Collins left a message for you. For all of you, actually, but he said to give it to you. So, here." She gave me the piece of paper and I took it without looking at it.

"Thank you!" *Thanks, Mrs. Patterson!*

"Okay then." She stood there, looking at me.

"Okay then."

"Did you not do the autograph in the end, then?" Ian said, when I got in the lift.

"Suck my dick, Hurley," I said, because I was still too mortified to come up with something clever.

*****

"All right, Caoimhe?

I'm assuming if you're reading this, you're still alive, and you haven't shuffled off your mortal coil in some sort of tragic, 27 Club overdose situation. You've at least 9 good years left in you, for me to "exploit"! I'm having an early night with the old ball & chain, so I won't be seeing you til tomorrow. Gotta get my conjugal rights, and by that, I mean a leg-over. Moby was good, we didn't stick around for the other lot – not my scene, or the bird's. Moby's not my scene either, but don't be telling her that now, haha.

I'm under strict orders from HQ, to order you and your minions to leave the fecking minibar intact tonight, so I've left some presents for ye upstairs. Enjoy your night, be good, and if ye can't be good, be careful.

Stay lucky,

Boxer."

He had nice writing, all the same, he'd never be a doctor. I wondered what he meant by "some presents", but I'd find out in a second, cos I was at my door.

"See ye in a minute, lads, I've to..." No one was listening to me, anyway. I put the key in and headed straight for the toilet.

There was a bar of soap and a bottle of Wash & Go in the shower, now. Hopefully they weren't the presents. Must've been someone from the hotel that put them there, although I didn't remember complaining. I still couldn't wee. I'd thought it worth a try, though. It was a good sign, mind, cos on the way over, Ciara told me that needing a wee was one of the first signs that you'd come down, and I definitely didn't want that.

Out in the room, I couldn't see any presents, so God only knew what he was on about. I thought about changing my clothes, but I was grand. The dress was light enough and airy enough that I wasn't minging with sweat or BO. I'd rubbed a damp facecloth on my pits and put on a bit of roll-on. The smell of it was something mighty, like sticking my head in a bouquet of flowers. Someone was knocking on wood. I heard it again, and panicked a little, until I remembered how doors worked.

"Are you decent, chickee?" Bríd, it sounded like. Benson must be the wham, bam, thank you, Ma'am type, I thought. Poor girl.

"I'm never decent, love. But shur don't let that stop you. Come in, it's open. OW!" I stubbed my toe on something hard under the bed. I'd not put my boots back on, even walking to and from Benson's Shag Wagon. I probably had a rake of splinters that I wouldn't feel until the morning.

"Ow?" Bríd came through, and I realised I hadn't turned on the light in the room. Must have had night vision. Maybe Es were like carrots.

"I hurt my – hit the switch there, will you?"

"Okay." The room filled up with light, it felt a bit biblical. I got down to see what was under there. Hopefully it wasn't a monster.

"What are you up to down there? You mad thing, ya,"

Bríd said.

"Looking for treasure. Hang on, what's this now?"

"Need a hand?"

"No, I've already got two of them. Hhhhhhnnnn-numph!" I dragged the big hard, heavy thing out from underneath. It was a slab of Budweiser. The cans felt cold, too, they must have come from a fridge. Brian's present!

"Ooh! Does that come with the room, like?" Bríd said, squatting down next to me.

"No, it's Brian. He must have left these here earlier for me. For us, I think." I was the only one who drank Bud out of all of them, so there'd been a bit of favouritism going on, all right.

"Good old Brillo, like. He's finally useful for something."

"Ah, he's all right," I said, trying to decide if I wanted a beer or not. Bríd had said alcohol was one of those diuretic things, so maybe it'd make me want to wee? Or maybe it'd just produce the wee and the E would have a fight with the beer inside my bladder and I'd just-

"He is, yeah. But everyone's all right tonight, like."

"Even Ian," I said.

"Well I wouldn't go that far, now," she said, but she was messing. She got on really well with him, even when no one was on drugs.

"Why are you back so soon? I thought you'd be having a shag down there," I said, remembering.

"A shag? Ah no, chance would be a fine thing, says you."

"What do you mean? Did ye fall out?" He wasn't here with her, maybe he was gone.

"Nooooo! I just meant that I'd love to have a shag, but

we – he, he can't, obviously." She looked disappointed. I decided on having a beer, and I offered one to her, too.

"Can't he? Is it his old age, yeah? No lead in the pencil anymore, like?" I took a sip of the Bud, it tasted cool and refreshing, and smelled like the skins of red apples, for some reason.

"Hahahah! You gowl. No, he has the *pilly willy*," she said, opening her can and smelling it first, like she was Jilly Goolden.

"The whatty what?" I sparked up a fag, they were my second ten box of the day and I'd only three left. Bríd did her usual *ewwww don't smoke on me, I have asthma* face, but it was my room, my rules, so, tough.

"You know… when boys take Es, they can't, am…"

"Spit it out, Bríd."

"They're not able to… perform."

"Perform…" I was picturing Benson on a stage, in front of a microphone, with his willy sticking out of his zipper.

"They can't get it up!"

"Oh! They can't?" News to me, but a lot of things had been, today. The beer was too nice, I had to put it down. Only so much room inside me for liquids.

"Most of them can't, anyway. You hear them talking about it all the time when ye're all buzzing at a party or whatever."

"That's a shame. How's that all going anyway, you and Benny-Ben-Ben, the Benster?" I'd never had a proper old natter with her about him, she was a very private person, but tonight she was being way more open, so.

"The relationship?"

"No, the sex." Fuck the relationship, like.

"Hah! Oh, it's like, so good, Caoimhe. So good." Her eyes did the thing eyes do when you're picturing something or remembering something, and her smile went ear-to-ear.

"That good, yeah? Why's that?" I hadn't had good sex in a long time. Or any sex in a while.

"Older guys, Caoimhe. They just... they know what they're doing, you know? There's no fumbling. They've been around long enough to know what works and what doesn't. They know what goes where."

"The penis goes in the vagina, that's about as far as I've got up to in the manual," I said, and we both lay back on the quilt, giggling stupidly.

"No though, honestly, it's like – it's hard to describe it," she said, looking at the ceiling now, all dreamy. I'd have been a little jealous of her, but I was on Ecstasy, and that emotion didn't seem to be available to me right now. So I was just delighted for her instead.

"Ah, give it a try," I said. I didn't care too much either way, but it was nice talking to someone while I was up and rushing like this. Chats were nearly as good as music, I'd noticed.

"Well, and you'll like this example, remember Kylie was going out with Jason, in real life, not just on Neighbours?"

"I do, I do." Poor Jason Donovan and his tragic mullet. What *had* we been thinking, way back when?

"Right, and she was all squeaky clean, and bubblegum pop, and all her videos were so cute, and your little sister and your Mum could both be into her?"

"Uhuh." I'd need an ashtray in a second, but it was nice lying down here, I didn't wanna get up.

"But then she met Michael Hutchence, right? And like

overnight she changed her image. Cut the hair short, started wearing leather pants. All her songs and videos got sexier, and sexier. And now like it was your Dad showing an interest, cos she was wild altogether."

"Mmmmhmmm." I remembered it well, but I remembered everything relating to Kylie. I was a one-woman *EncyKyliepedia*, me. I pictured the video for Step Back in Time, which came out around then, and she'd definitely been all sexed up. The outfits were absolutely... *absolutely*.

"Well, that was no coincidence, like. Jason Donovan was like her first big love, and everything. But Michael Hutchence, he was eight years older than her, he was mad into drinking and drugs, and you knew just looking at him that he'd be absolutely filthy in bed."

"Oh, definitely, yeah." He looked like a walking erection, that fella.

"Like, poor Jason was probably reading the Joy of Sex and finding out how to make sweet, tender love to his quiet little delicate fiancée," Bríd handed me over a clean ashtray from the bedside locker, just in time too.

"Sound! Yeah, yeah, I think you're right there."

"Whereas Michael was more like, "Oi! Minogue! You're coming with me, now!" and she probably couldn't help herself. It's that sort of dominant thing. It's... it's intoxicating, right?" She had her face turned to me on the bed now, so I did the same. She was seriously pretty, Bríd was, in her own, scrubbed, fresh faced, natural curls, sort of way. All my friends were rides.

"Yeah, I think it would be," I said, trying to remember if any man had ever got me drunk on the mere thought of him riding me. Nope. Not that I could recall.

"Like, with him, you know there's gonna be cocaine, and handcuffs, and a bit of spanking, like."

"Ooh!" No one had spanked me since I was a child, and that wasn't a sexual experience (thank Christ). I liked the sound of it right now, though. I liked the sound of it a lot.

"He basically *fucked* the girl-next-doorness out of her, like."

"BRÍD!"

"What!?" she said, looking fierce naughty altogether.

"The language out of you, like."

"Hahahah, leave me alone." She was smiling so hard it was making my face hurt, just looking at her, but I was doing the same, so that was probably why my face hurt, in fairness. This was rapid altogether, as Nick Cave would say.

"So what you're saying is that Benson handcuffs you to the bed and then he takes off his belt and whips your arse with it, yeah? And then what, slaps you across the face? Pisses in your mouth, is it?" I said, sitting up to stretch out my back.

"CIARA!" Bríd said.

"She's not even here!" I said, collapsing back on the bed, laughing.

"Oh yeah! Sorry, force of habit, like. It's usually her, in fairness."

"It is, you're right. Will we go find her?" I said, and we would too, after I'd stopped picturing Michael Hutchence weeing in poor Benson's mouth.

*****

"Where are the menfolk?" I said to Ciara when we found her in one of the joined up rooms. She was fiddling with the CD player, going through radio stations on it.

"Oh, hi. They're, uh, in the bathroom." She pointed at the door behind her.

"That's not the bathroom, that's the way into next door," Bríd said.

"Yeah, they're in that bathroom, cos it's the biggest one out of all of them," she said, finally settling on a particular station that was playing some dance music song I didn't recognise.

"Turn that up, that's good," Bríd said. I noticed an opened slab of Heineken on the bed behind Ciara. Maybe we'd all got one each? Of course we had. I wasn't the special favourite after all. Lousy.

"Sorry, can we rewind a second and go back to all the boys going to the toilet together?" I said. I thought about another ciggie, but I wouldn't have one yet. Not until I found out how many others were around, or where the fag machine was.

"No, they're not going to the toilet, you eejit. They're in the shower."

"That… does not sound better, Ciara," I said, wondering what kind of shenanigans had happened in the 20 minutes I was gone that had led to this apparent mass gayness.

"Go in and see for yourselves, like." Ciara took out a new box of B&H, unwrapped the plastic, and slid one out. That was good. I'd scobe a few off her for the meantime.

"Right so, we will," I said, opening the middle door and already hearing the shouts and screams from inside the echoey bathroom.

"What in God's name are ye up to?" I asked Tim, when we got inside. Him and Ian were standing by the loo. The other two were inside the glass shower cubicle, I could see the vague outlines of them. There was no water running, and they had all their clothes on.

"Benson is teaching us how to shotgun beers," Ian said,

as if that explained anything. I was gonna ask him something else, when there was a massive explosion behind the glass, and Richie screamed like a girl. There was a spraying sound, then a glugging sound, and finally Benson stuck his head out. His face was wet, mainly around his mouth and nose.

"Ladies! Wanna have a go?" This night just got stranger and stranger.

*****

"So what film did you say you got that from?" I asked Benson, a little later, when we'd all done at least one shotgunned Heineken, and after we'd towelled ourselves dry. For a man who didn't drink, he had some suspect hobbies. Including drinking.

"Ah, The Sure Thing."

"I don't know that one," Bríd said.

"I do. John Cusack and Daphne Zuniga, Tim Robbins is in it too, being young." I remembered the shotgunning part too now, thinking back on it.

"You know your stuff, girl. See, Bríd? Caoimhe knows who Daphne Zuniga is," he said, and I tried to hide on my face how proud I was of myself, but it probably didn't work.

"Of course I do! She's been in loads of things, like. Spaceballs, Vision Quest. She's in Melrose Place now – she's still around, like," I said, amused at how his face was lighting up.

"See?" he said to Bríd. She rolled her eyes, and I got worried I'd done something wrong, somehow.

"Please! Don't start him off about Daphne Zuniga, we'll never get him off the subject, like. Or his other one – Linda Florentine, is it?"

"Linda Fiorentino?" I said. She was the other one in Vision Quest, the main girl in it. She'd been in a few recent ones too. The Last Seduction was good. Very sexy.

"See?" Benson said, again. Loved me now, he did. We were best buds.

"For fuck's sake, how am I supposed to know these people? Those films came out yonks ago, I'm not old enough to know about them," Bríd said, drinking some water, and pussing.

"You're the same age as me!" I said. She was older, actually. She was eighteen next month.

"Yeah, well," she said, taking the puss off her face now and going back to smiling, thank God.

"So, what age are you then, Benson?" Drug Tim knew no conversational taboos. Drug Tim had no boundaries.

"Ah, I'm 27." He didn't say it like he was proud of it, but he didn't look too ashamed, either. Bríd looked… Bríd looked like she didn't want us to be having this conversation.

"So you were born in…" Ian was struggling with the maths.

"1968!" I said, after working it out.

"Jaysus!" Tim said.

"Fuck me!" Richie was shocked, clearly. He had a fag in his hand. I was sure he'd given up. Maybe I wasn't sure, though.

"You were born in the Sixties, dude," Ian said.

"Your van is only a year older than you are," I said, remembering my joke from earlier.

"Did you know the Beatles?" said Drug Tim.

"Fucking hell, you're nearly as old as me, boy!" said someone with a Cork accent, which was strange, because none of us had a-

"UNCLE FRANK!" shouted Bríd, and everyone turned around, delighted to see him. None of us were as delighted as *Old Man Benson* though, since the thing about his age was forgotten straight away once everyone started firing questions at Frank about where he'd been, who he'd met, and which famous people he'd sold drugs to, earlier on. 1968, though! Bríd was basically riding her Dad.

*****

"Did you mean what you said, then?" Ian was sitting next to me on one of the beds.

"What I said, when?" I'd said a lot of things today.

"In the interview. With yer man, Pat." He looked good, Ian did. Bit big-eyed, bit chewy-jawed, but still looking well. He was very good looking, but he was one of those boys who didn't have a clue about his own hotness until he started going out with girls regularly. That was what Bríd told me anyway, she'd known him for years. By the time I met him he was already well up his own arse.

"About Ciara?" I'd forgotten that. Hopefully they wouldn't put it out on TV tomorrow. I'd be morta, Ciara would be very confused, and my Mum would think I'd gone gay overnight. They wouldn't put it on, though. We'd been off our faces, RTÉ wouldn't want to be promoting that sort of behaviour, or the Bishops would be phoning them up to give out.

"What?" Maybe he'd forgotten too. Fingers crossed. "No, I mean about not doing *Season of the Witch*, like." He was smoking an orange coloured cigarette that looked like a crayon. It smelled appalling.

"Oh, that? Um, yeah. I don't fancy it." I was tired of that song, even if I was the one who'd suggested we do it originally.

"But it's like a big crowd-pleaser, Kweev."

"I don't think we'll have a big crowd to please," I said, being a smartarse. I was still very high. I wasn't sure if there was another peak to come, off the second pill, or if you only peaked once in a night. Didn't matter, I was good.

"Even more reason to do it, then. Get however many of them that do turn up to pay attention to us. Get them up dancing and jumping around, like." He had a point.

"Yeah, but I just don't want people to associate us with some song I didn't even – that *we* didn't even write, you know what I mean, Ian?" I made sure to correct myself mid-sentence there, in case I caused another hissy fit.

"They don't, though!" He stubbed out his crayon fag. It had a shiny gold butt that reminded me of the metal bit of those pencils with the rubber on top. I kind of wanted one now, just to see if they tasted like crayons, too. Or like pencils with a rubber on top.

"The article they did on us in the Sunday World literally had the title: Must Be The Season Of The Witch, like." They'd used a photo of me in my bikini top, from some outdoor gig we did in May. The Sunday World always found a way to make a story about boobs, it was a classy publication all right.

"Well, yeah. I'll give you that. But we've loads of originals. We're an originals band, not some Fat Tuesday or something. So, like, when we *do* do a cover, it's just cool. Like when Oasis do *I Am the Walrus* at the end of their gigs."

"I suppose." I didn't know if it was just the drugs, but he wasn't rubbing me up the wrong way like he usually did. He was making sense, too.

"We'll be doing all our own ones otherwise, like. All the really good ones, that *you* wrote. Like *Deep Breaths*, or *Future Ex*, or *Goodtime Grrrl*, and…" He was just licking my arse now, but it was working, fair play.

"Can we not do *White Rabbit* as our one cover, though? Or *Somebody to Love*?" I loved Grace Slick, I'd a big photo poster of her on my bedroom wall – one from the 60s, where she's got straight black hair and she's wearing a really cool army jacket with patches on the sleeves. I wasn't into the whole "Starship" version of them, with all the cheesy 80s power ballads. That stuff was embarrassing.

"Well, I like both of them too, Kweev. And you're rapid altogether at singing both of them, honest you are. But…, could you not just do those another time and do *Season of the Witch* this time?" he said, smiling and offering me one of his Crayola fags. There were lots of different colours in the box, like real crayons. "I'll be your best friend!" He was offering me his hand now too, to shake. Drug Ian was a new Ian altogether, but I wasn't complaining. I'd enjoy him while he lasted.

"Okay then, but only cos you asked so nicely, Hurlo," I said, and gave him a hug instead of a handshake. I lit up the fag; I'd gone for a violet coloured one, like Ciara's eyes were. *Sobranie Cocktail*, it said on the box. To both my disappointment and relief, it just tasted like tobacco.

*****

"So when are you gonna get yourself a fella?" Bríd said, to Ciara, when we were sitting in my room after another unsuccessful trip to the loo.

"Eh, I've gone off fellas," she said. I raised an eyebrow at her.

"Ah, you always say that, like. It's like saying "I'm never drinking again!" You don't mean it, really."

"Maybe she does, this time," I said. I was going to make a joint, but I wasn't very good at it, and when I wasn't good at things, I usually didn't bother. That's what my teachers used to say in primary school, anyway.

"Thank you, Caoimhe. Just because this one's all in love and coupled up, she thinks the rest of us should find ourselves a sexy pensioner with his own transport too."

"He's not that old!" Bríd said, laughing.

"He is, though," I said.

"You remember that song, Summer of 69?" Ciara said.

"Of course."

"Benson remembers the actual summer of 69. He was there."

"Fuck off! Anyway, what about Mark?" said Bríd. She had one of my Buds. She hadn't asked, but it wasn't like I'd paid for them, so fuck it.

"What about him?" Mark was one of Ciara's exes. Long haired guy, did the sound in the Theatre Royal.

"What was he, 33? When you were 16? Youuuuuu hypocrite!"

"I was going through a PHASE!" Ciara said. Her laugh was as gorgeous as her smile. Another little ripple of pleasure went through me, and I took a big breath.

"A phase of munching on elderly foreskins," I said, immediately disgusting myself. That happened a lot.

"Oh God, speaking of which, did I ever tell ye- no, wait, that's lousy. I can't say," Ciara said. She leaned into me to get a light while I lit my own fag.

"Well now you definitely have to!" said Bríd. She was right, too.

"Really? Okay then. But let's let this person remain nameless."

"Which person?" I said. My fag tasted weird. I took it out of my mouth and looked at it. Benson & Hedges. No idea where I'd got that

"Mark!" Bríd said. She must have had the tolerance of a saint to always be around the two of us, breathing filthy fumes on her every day. Still though, what else was she gonna do, get new friends?

"I didn't say it was Mark!"

"Fine then, for the purposes of your story, Mark will remain nameless. Now please, tell us about his weird dick," I said, because it was 100% gonna be an Unusual Penis Story. We all had at least one. They came with the territory. Sometimes they came too much, or they didn't come at all. But those ones were more Strange Spunk Tales. The theme song off Duck Tales was in my head now. I took out a nodge and some Rizlas and started rolling what was sure to be a very disappointing joint.

*****

"… apparently it's a medical condition. The skin is too tight to pull back when you're hard, so it just kind of stays there. Phimosis, I think he called it." I was telling them about Dan, who I was seeing over the Christmas last year.

"Yeeouch. Sounds painful," Bríd said. She'd already told her story, about Stephen Melling and his very short but incredibly girthy penis. Like a Babybel, were her words. I'd never look at him the same again.

"Yeah, apparently so. But it was just the look of it, I couldn't get over. Every time I had it in my hand, or I was thinking about popping it in my mouth, all I could think of was the battered sausages from the Lobster Pot," I said, and they screamed, laughing. I felt a weird feeling, like I was being watched, and they must have too, because we all looked towards the doorway at the same time, to see a very shocked Niall.

"Nailer!" I said, delighted to see him, but I was delighted to see everyone tonight.

"Big man!" said Ciara, raising her can at him. We seemed to have given up on water for now. Wasn't sure if that was wise or not.

"How long have you been standing there?" Bríd asked, looking worried but smiling at the same time.

"Long enough. Is this normal?" He came in and stood in front of the bed we were all on. He had a joint burning in his hands, but he'd forgotten about it, clearly. I took it off him, so it didn't go out.

"Is what normal?" I said, taking a drag. Just hash, no crazy weed, good.

"You lot, talking about our langers."

"Eh, no. Not really," I said, half-lying.

"Only if they warrant discussion, Niall," Ciara said. I loved how she talked. She had a way of putting things that was nice to listen to. She gave good diction.

"Exactly," said Bríd.

"And what would – I mean, how…"

"Well," Ciara said, not waiting for the end of the question. "If they're painfully big, we have to talk about that. Even if it's just to warn the flock." Those were quite rare, but they did exist. You usually found out about them from the guy himself, though. Big dick guys always found a way during a conversation to shoehorn it in - so to speak.

"Or if they're so tiny that it's basically a disability," I said. Those were even rarer. I'd only ever seen the one.

"Okay," Niall said, looking relieved that he wasn't in the latter group, but probably disappointed he wasn't in the former. Boys were like that. They'd have an eight-foot dick if they could, they didn't care that it might rip the girl asunder, as long as they could show it off to the lads in the showers, I thought. Straight lads were kind of gay.

"All sizes in between that - BORING!" Ciara said. "But, you know, boring in a good way, cos we can work with them." Bríd nodded at her wisdom, so did I. Most dicks were pretty much the same size. When they were hard, anyway. Not that I'd seen millions of them or anything. I'd only seen about twenty in real life. Give or take maybe ten.

"But obviously if he's got some weird deformity, like he pees sideways out of a slit in his foreskin," I said, remembering Simon.

"Or he has three balls," said Ciara, making us all look at her. Hopefully she was messing. If she wasn't, I wanted more details, later.

"Or anything strange at all, then we're gonna talk, Niall. It's only natural. Do you guys not talk about our vajayjays?" said Bríd, opening yet another can.

"Vajayjays!" I said. She was brilliant.

"No!" he said, looking like he was telling the truth. I felt slightly relieved, although my vajayjay was immaculate, so the only tales boys would be telling about it would be ones of praise and wonderment. Hopefully, anyway.

"Awwww. Well maybe I've misjudged your whole gender, then," Ciara said, passing him back the joint.

"Maybe," he said, looking her in the eyes without blinking. He sat down on the bed, and we all scooched over, because he was sound out, and we'd finished talking about willies for now.

After a while, Ciara took my hand and pulled me up. I went with her; my bare feet had forgotten how nice the carpet was. She took me into the little bathroom. I was intrigued, and a bit...excited? But she probably just wanted some speed. She could have asked me for that out there though, so maybe she wanted something else.

*****

"So, Niall. What would you think about a blowjob competition, eh?" Ciara said, a little later, when we were all a bit more relaxed after the second joint (Bríd the asthmatic excluded). She winked at me slyly as she said it, to let me know that this was it. Bríd looked shocked.

"A what?" Niall looked like someone had just told him the meaning of life. He sat up a bit straighter than he had been.

"Oh, just, for fun. Not with Bríd, obviously. She's taken, like. But, well… myself and Caoimhe are always joking about which of us gives the better, you know, *service*. And since we've never gone out with the same guy, it's really impossible to compare, do you know what I mean?" She looked at him, and then at me.

"I suppose so," Niall said, trying desperately to hide the enormous grin forming on his face.

"So, since it's a special weekend, and since we're all buzzing and there's no inhibitions or anything - You don't have any inhibitions tonight do you, Caoimhe?"

"Nope," I said, taking out a tube of lip balm from my bag, because I'd just remembered it was in there. I was a genius.

"Excellent. So basically, what we'll do is each of us will have a turn giving you a good, slow, long, wet suck, right?" She had locked eyes with him, it was making things extra tense. I had to remember to breathe.

"Okay!" He was fully on board. No inhibitions there, definitely not.

"You aren't allowed to come, though," I said, thinking quickly. I moved my newly balmed lips over each other, slowly and sexily, when I was sure he was looking at them.

"Why not???" He was devastated by this new development, poor fella.

"Well because if you *come* in my *mouth*, Niall - like if you absolutely spray your jizz all over the insides of my cheeks, and down the back of my throat, before Caoimhe has had her turn…" She was brilliant at this. I didn't even have a penis and I was getting an erection.

"Yeah?" Niall's voice was wobbling like he was doing a reading at the School Mass.

"Well then I'll have to wait ages like, until you're ready again, and I don't want to have to wait, Niall," I said, doing a mock sad face.

"You don't?" Niall said. I hadn't looked at Bríd for a bit, cos I didn't want her appalled face to make me burst out laughing and ruin the whole thing.

"No! I want to get that big thing all the way down me, give it a nice, hot, sticky tongue bath. Maybe give your balls a little lick or two? Wouldn't want them to feel left out, would we?"

"Lads!" Bríd finally broke her silence, in the background, but we ignored her.

"Oh yeah, the balls! Mmmmm, I bet you have nice balls, don't you? Do you trim down there? Shave?" Ciara said, touching his knee. I was going to explode laughing in a second if she didn't slow down.

"I, um…" he was lost for words for the first time since I'd met him. It was a Christmas miracle.

"We'll soon find out," I said. "Hey, Ciara. I have an idea!"

"What is it, babe?"

"How about like, since we're being lousy on him and not letting him come, right?"

"*In our mouths*."

"In our hot, wet little mouths, yeah. Anyway, how about when the contest is over…"

"Yeah?" She reached across and gave my right tit what could only be described as *a caress*. I didn't remember that being in the plan, but still. I threw in a little moan for good measure, ever the professional.

"And we like know who the winner is, for definite," I went on.

"Yes?" said Ciara.

"Yes???" Niall said. His face was almost purple.

"Well, how about the two of us finish him off together, like two of us sucking him off at the same time? Swapping his dick back and forth between our mouths?" I was a genius. A filthy, disgusting genius.

"OOH! Good idea!" Ciara said, somehow keeping a straight face, still.

"Brilliant. Right, so! Get it out then, Nailer," I said.

"What?" He looked confused.

"Your penis, Niall," Ciara said. "Chop, chop. It's not going to blow itself."

"Let the dog see the rabbit!" I said, and if I'd been technically able to urinate, that might have been when I pissed myself. Niall just looked lost.

"Fuck's sake, do I have to do everything myself around here?" I said. I went to open the top button on his combats.

"What are you-" He was only slightly protesting, I noticed.

"Oh, I do apologise, love. Is it okay if I put my hand inside here, yeah?" I said.

"Yes. Consent is important, guys." Ciara was so good at not laughing it was practically an art form.

"Okay, yeah," he said. *Okay, Mrs. Patterson!*

"Gooood. Hold on and I find this chap then," I said,

rooting around down there. It was a bit hairy, and I almost stopped, since the reality of doing this was a bit grimmer than when we'd been planning the whole thing in the toilet a while ago, Ciara and me. I finally found it.

"Theeeere we are…"

"The Eagle has landed!" Ciara said. Poor Bríd, though. God only knew what she thought was happening, I was amazed she hadn't fled the room in terror.

"It's eh… it's not very stiff, Niall. I can't even find a pulse, Ciara love. This thing is D.O.A. Dead on Arrival. What's wrong, Nailer? Do you not like us, then? Do oo not wuvvv us anymwo-re?" I said, frowning at him. It felt like one of those marshmallow Flumps you got in a bag of mixed-up sweets. I was gonna have to let go in a second, before I vomited. There was only so much I was willing to suffer for our art.

"Yeah, Niall. Are we not sexy enough for you? Do you not want to put it in our mouths, then?" said Ciara, crossing her arms.

"No! I do, I do! I dunno what's wrong with me, like. It must be the drugs! Can ye not – could one of ye not…" I felt sorry for him now, a bit, even though it was still very funny.

"Can we what? Niall, I can't work with this floppy material. What do you want me to do, pop it in my gob and see if it wakes up?" I said, taking my hand out of his awful, clammy jocks.

"It's no use to us, Niall. How are we gonna pass that from my mouth to hers without dropping it? It's like wet spaghetti."

"We'd be like Lady and the Tramp!" I said, and that was it. Couldn't hold in the laugh any longer. I went into convulsions for about ten minutes. Ciara joined me. Bríd eventually got it. Even poor Nailer laughed in the end, but only after me and Ciara said sorry a million times and covered his face in big sloppy kisses to make it up to him. What a life we led.

EIGHT

I was alone now, for the first time in what felt like yonks. The other three had gone in next door, to listen to music, and chat with everyone else. It was only after they left that I spotted the radio that came with the room. I turned it on to a station with dance stuff on, for a beat. It was probably the same one they had on in the other room. There couldn't be that many ones like that in the area, or in the country.

I'd told them I wanted to change my clothes, which was half-true. What I really wanted was to take my clothes *off* for a bit. Feel the air on my skin, because I'd noticed from walking around that any little breeze on my arms and legs felt amazing. There was a desk fan, over by the tea and coffee stuff. I popped it on, and made it do the oscillating thing. Bliss.

I looked at myself in the big, long wall mirror, in my bra and knickers. I'd a strange relationship with my body, all the same. I was full of confidence about it half the time, and the other half I'd be obsessing over the tiniest flaws. The skinny thing was obviously a big help – every girl I knew was always going on about wanting to be a Size 10 or whatever, and I was a Size 8, so I could wear anything I liked, and it usually fit me. *Wwwwhat a bitch.* It was what I was used to though – I'd been a skinny child, growing up - so I took it for granted, and on the days when I was having a self-esteem crisis, I didn't even see the skinny. I'd be looking at my stupid Sam the Eagle nose and wishing it was one of those little baby noses – a little perfect ski-jump of a thing, like Ciara's. Her face was perfect, now that her acne had cleared up for good. She was the exact same on both sides, too. Like a cat, or Christy Turlington. Both were equally symmetrical.

One of my boobs was slightly bigger than the other. You'd have to look at them, braless, for about ten minutes to notice it, but *I'd* looked at them for way longer in my life, so *I* always noticed it. My thighs were oddly big for a skinny girl, too. They didn't rub off each other or anything, not even in tight jeans, but they still looked enormous and flabby to me. I unsnapped my bra and pushed down my knickers, kicking all of it into the corner by the wardrobe. The boobs looked the same size now. They'd probably heard me slagging them off in my head. My hair down below was fair, probably cos I'd been a natural blonde until I was around twelve. Maybe it migrated down there during puberty. Kylie came on the radio – a different mix of Confide in Me. It didn't have the big orchestral bits that sounded like that other song, the "*it's going to be a fine night tonight*" one. Couldn't remember now who did that one. A bald woman with a crab on her head. She was no Kylie. I put on my navy blue La Perla and the matching knicks. I always wore matching sets, if I could help it. You never knew when you might be rushed to hospital and some George Clooney type doctor might see you half-naked. I suddenly came over with a major case of the horn and decided lying down would be more comfortable.

I thought about Ciara for a minute. Something was going on there, but I didn't know what. We were always thick as thieves, but today was more... intense. I didn't like girls, in that way. I didn't think so, anyway. I'd never been with one, never even considered it. There had been times, though, in my head at least. When we were younger there was this girl, Marian. Her parents were friends with mine. With ours, really, cos Áine was still – I moved on from the thought. Marian was a couple of years older than me, and three older than Áine. It didn't matter when we were all little, but somewhere around the time when I was twelve and she was fourteen, the way I looked at her changed. She was suddenly all full of boobs and bum, and I was still a few months away from getting my first period, and it was like we weren't equals anymore. She was like a little woman, and she was going with boys, and I was in awe of her. And a bit more. Like a girl crush, or something. We used to have baths together when we were small, but once she turned into grown-up Marian, that time seemed like a million years ago. She eventually stopped coming around, it would have been silly, her having to hang around with two kids, when she had a social life, and a boyfriend, and all that. But I thought about her a lot. Sometimes the thoughts were a little… graphic? But never *porno*graphic, like. They were just… nice. She moved away in 91, anyway. Never saw her again, and that was yonks ago. A new song came on. I didn't know it, but I was enjoying it anyway.

I had only been messing around, asking Ciara for the kiss, but it was so good. If we had been on our own, not in the middle of a concert surrounded by people – especially the fuckers leering at us – I might have… No idea what I might have done, really. But it would definitely have been more than we had done then. I realised my hand was between my legs. Not *doing anything* or anything, just *there*. I remembered I had an electric toothbrush in the bathroom. Tempting, but my head was too confused about stuff to do anything now. Very confused, indeed. I sat up, a bit too quickly and it gave me a head rush. Woo! Anyway, back to business. My blue Bikini Kill t-shirt that I got in America, and my good Dunnes leggings. That'd do me.

*****

"Hello, Nick Cave!" I said to the guy outside in the hallway, carrying a bucket of ice with a bottle of Smirnoff in it, who was quite clearly Nick Cave.

"G'day! We uh, have to stop meeting like this!" He was very smiley, but he only looked pissed, not all *hepped up on goofballs* like me.

"I'll stop if you stop," I said, walking with him, even though I'd only to go as far as next door to get to my own destination.

"It's Caoimhe, isn't it?" Nick Cave knew my actual name. I could quite literally die on the spot now and it still would have been a full life lived.

"Yes… who told you that?" My heart was thumping, and I wasn't sure it was the drugs anymore.

"Oh, I asked someone: *who's the chick with the cool red hair?* earlier, when you were at the bar, and they told me ya story, that's all." He was very tall, he seemed even taller in an indoor setting. I had to bend my neck funny to look at him.

"My story?" What story was this, I wondered? And who had told it?

"Naaaaah, not a real story. Just… *what's ya name, why ya here,* all that. She's Kweeva Shox, she's the singer from Crane, they're from Limerick, that's all we can tell ya, Nicholas." He looked very mischievous. His image was so serious, and so were all his songs, but he was a mad laugh in real life.

"They told you no lies, Nicholas," I said, wondering if this had been before or after I'd met him on the stage.

"Anyway, they put you lot up here as well, yeah? A room each, I hope. No sharing, no bunk beds. No slumming it for Kweeva and her merry band of Limerick men," he said. He was definitely a good bit drunk, but a nice sort of drunk. The ice and the bottle were making a clinky sound as he walked.

"Yeah, nothing but the best for us," I said. Being on drugs made you able to make small talk with international superstars, apparently. I wondered if I was being as cool as I thought, or was he actually talking to a gurning, chewy-faced half-wit, but I was probably grand. He'd been asking around about me and everything. He loved me, Nick Cave, did.

"True. Well, this is me." He meant the lift, his room wasn't on our floor, it seemed. The ice machine was, though. I'd learned this valuable info at least.

"You off to see Kylie?" I robbed a cube out of his bucket and rubbed it on the back of my neck. Heaven!

"Kylie? Kylie who?" he said, making a silly face. The lift wasn't here yet, but I could hear it coming down.

"How many Kylies do you know, like?" I said.

"You'd be surprised, mate." He was Australian though, maybe everyone was called Kylie over there.

"Pffffft, I'm only talking about the one that matters, Nicholas," I said, giving him a wink. "The One True Kylie. The Minogue. The Minogue Who isn't Dannii, I mean, obviously." The carriage stopped on our floor and the doors dinged open. The cold water was rolling down my back and making me shiver, in a nice way.

"Obviously, hehe. Yeah, she's great. She's not here though, sorry to disappoint you, 3AM girls." I didn't know what that bit meant, but I nodded anyway.

"She's not?" I wasn't sure I believed this Nick Cave fella, now. He seemed a crafty devil.

"Nope. Off on another plane to another gig. How the other half live, eh?" He rolled his eyes, as if he wasn't also a globetrotting musical god.

"Who's the booze for then?"

"Never you mind, Ms. Shox. Anyway, *hooroo*, catch you later. You have a good night, yeah? Don't do anything I wouldn't do!" He leaned over and kissed me on the cheek in an adorable, non-sleazy way.

"Thanks, I will! And you enjoy your vodka! And your ice! And your Kylie!" I said, standing on my tippy toes so I could look him right in the eye and see if he gave anything away. The lift doors started to close.

"I should be so lucky, mate," said my new pal Nick Cave, because he was hilarious.

*****

"Oh my God, where did you go, I missed you!" Ciara said, when I came through the adjoining door to where they'd all gathered, in 213, the middle room of the five.

"You were literally just in my room with me five seconds ago. I told you I was getting dressed and stuff, you fool!" I hugged her tight and aimed a big sloppy kiss at her mouth that ended up on her cheek.

"Who you calling fool, chump?" she said, latching onto me, post-hug. She was practically fizzing with the uppy-uppness. The radio was loud, and so was the noise of everyone chatting in their little groups. I opened my mouth to say something, but before I could, Ciara womanhandled a stick of gum in there.

"Urmmmnghthanks!" I said, looking at Bríd and Benson, sitting on the floor together. They looked like a real couple now, almost. They were in a world of their own, only looking at one another. Sweet.

"Am I in with you, later?" Ciara said, pushing my hair back out of my face in a way that was somewhere in the middle between how your Mum would do it and how your boyfriend would.

"In my bed?" I said. "-droom?" I added, quite unnecessarily.

"Yeah, in your bed." She paused, taking the piss, "DROOM."

"Yes. In my bed, and also in my DROOM, and if you play your cards right…" What was this? Flirting?

"Pffffft, promises, promises, Shox." She was standing close to me; my back was against the door. Her eyes were somehow even more gorgeous with all the giant pupil stuff going on. She smelled of mint and Calvin Klein and possibly Black Jacks.

"Were you drinking Pernod?" I said. I was doing the hair-fixy thing to *her* face now. I was leaning more towards boyfriend than mother with mine, or at least that was the intention, anyway. If you could call it an intention. In my head I pictured Ciara's mum, the English one, saying, "What are your intentions with my daughter?!" That was freaky. *Less of that please, Mr. Brain.*

"I was, yeah. Why, do I smell?" She put her hand over her mouth and her violet eyes went all flashy and dramatic. Everything seemed a bit more dramatic tonight, though.

"No! I mean, I can smell it, but it's nice. Where did you get it?" I remembered Brian's note about not touching the minibars. What was that about, anyway? Also, I hadn't seen any minibars yet, so.

"Oh! Did you not see the bag, like?"

"The bag?"

"Yeah, there's a bag!"

"Frank's bag, you mean?" I'd seen that one, definitely. It was under Richie's bed now, in the other room that wasn't adjoining. Room 215.

"Noooooo, silly! The bag of spirits! Brillo left it here for us. Well, for ye. There's vodka, Bacardi, Jameson, um…"

"Pernod," I said. I didn't have the appetite for any more drink tonight, but tomorrow was another day.

"Yes! And gin, for you!"

"Hooray!" I loved gin, all the same. It didn't make me sad like everyone said it did. It just made me, well, *drunk*. "Wait, what kind of gin?" If it was Cork Dry it probably *would* be gin that made me sad, but only because it was fucking rank.

"Fancy blue bottle gin!" Ciara was nearly pinning me against the door, with her thigh wedged in-between the two of mine. It would have been weird any other time, but it felt normal now. We fit each other really well, even though she was shorter. We were like a lovely, soft jigsaw. I liked how close her face was to mine. I liked feeling her breath on me. I liked the way she was absentmindedly fiddling with my hair, again. I liked… all of this. I was really hot now. I wondered had anyone bothered to bring the leftover water with them after we'd left the gig.

"Yay! Bombay Sapphire!!!" I said. You could say what you liked about Brian, but he never forgot what you drank. Not that I drank Bombay Sapphire much – you couldn't buy it down the pub or in Dunnes. It was imported stuff, from England, which made it even more impressive that he'd got me some.

"Everybody wins!" That smile again – she had really *attractive* teeth, I thought, looking at her. It wasn't just the straightness or the whiteness or even how clean they always were. It was the *size* of them. They were a perfect size for smiling – you never got too much gum, and the top set didn't overcrowd the ones below. It was like the Golden Ratio of smiles. I wanted to tell her now, I just needed to figure out how to articulate it properly, so she'd understand what I meant.

"Penny for them?" Ciara said.

"You got a purrrrrrdy mouth, lady," I said, finally spotting some water on the table beyond her.

"Haha! All the better to eat you with, dearie," she said,

rolling her thumb over the bit between the elastic of my leggings and my hipbone. Good lord.

"Promises, promises, Slattery," I said, moving her out of the way so I could go grab the Ballygowan before anyone else claimed it. Frank was standing up on the bed, for some reason.

"Okay, okay! People? Can I have everyone's attention, like? Can ye shush a minute? Turn off that radio there, Timbo, for me. Lads! LADS!" The second time he said "lads" sounded extra loud, because the music stopped at that exact moment. Everyone looked at him, with expressions ranging from surprise to *fuck off*. Ciara was still over at the door. I'd go back to her in a sec, after this.

"Speech! Speech! Speech!" Ian said, but in an incredibly sarcastic way, like he was Gene Wilder in Willy Wonka. Frank gave him the finger.

"Listen, will ye? I'll only be a second, like. I just… I just wanted to say-"

"BOOOORING!" someone shouted. Bríd, it was, the little brat.

"Yeah, yeah, yeah, Bríd. Very funny. Anyway, what I wanted to say was – FIRSTLY, well done all of ye for playing yeer first proper festival!"

"Yayyyy!" I said, but no one joined in with me.

"We haven't played it yet!" That was Ian.

"Well yeah, but ye will, like, unless something absolutely mental happens in the meantime, please God it won't, but touch wood anyway." Frank tapped the top of Drug Tim's head and we all laughed, except Drug Tim. He smiled, though, so it was grand.

"What was the second thing?" someone - someone who was definitely Ciara - shouted from behind me.

"I'm getting to it!" Frank shouted back.

"Get to it faster!" Niall, this time. He looked like he'd recovered from the trauma we put him through earlier, thank God.

"SECONDLY… well, it might just be the pills talking…" Frank went on.

"No, it's you talking. A pill can't talk," Drug Tim said to him, like none of the rest of us were even here.

"Shhhhh, Tim. Anyway, regardless of who's saying it, I just want ye to know how grateful I am for ye helping me out today, like. I love ye all, and I want ye to know it, and shur, here's to another few nights of this, and ah, sláinte!" He raised up his can of cider, and we all raised our waters, our beers, our unidentified spirits and mixers, or just our hands.

"Sláinte" said everyone, almost in unison.

"Cheers!" said a voice very close behind me, and I felt Ciara's arms around my middle, her breath on my neck, and her softness pressing into my back. *It doesn't get better than this*, I thought. But maybe it could. I hoped it would. I found her hands with my hands and linked her fingers into mine. I wondered what time it was, but if I was honest, I didn't really care.

*****

"Frank, what the *hell* is in these things anyway?" Ciara said, a little later. I'd changed my mind about having a drink, once I knew I had the fancy gin. There was Schweppes as well. No lemon, but I'd gone out and found the ice machine and brought a bucket in for us, after I told them all about meeting himself in the hallway.

"What d'you mean, what's in them, girl? Ecstasy is what's in them. MDMA, nothing else. They're Doves, shur. Pure as the driven snow." Frank looked mildly offended at the idea his illegal, unregulated drugs might be cut with some unknown substance, even though they probably (definitely) were.

"Nah, there's something. Something else, honestly," she said. The two of us were sitting on the floor, near the ashtray. Everyone else was scattered around, but mostly in this one room. No one had snuck off for some privacy, although the only couple here were Brídand Benson. The only official couple anyway, I thought. Shush, brain.

"Something else like what?" Ian said.

"I dunno, what drug makes you really, really horny, like?" Ciara said. I took a long, deep breath, which was my new favourite hobby.

"Horny?" Niall said. I remembered his Flump and my stomach clenched, involuntarily.

"Yeah!" said Bríd, making Benson look at her funny.

"Who's horny?" Richie said, coming in from outside, because his room wasn't attached.

"Ciara is," Niall said, laughing.

"And me!" said Bríd. Another look from her man. It was news to him, clearly.

"Caoimhe?" It was Ciara, turning to me.

"Yes?" I felt everyone looking at me.

"How's your, am, *situation*?" she said, unnecessarily coy, for her.

"How's my fanny, do you mean?" I said.

"In so many words, yes." She was so beautiful. I wanted to eat her up.

"Um, it's been pretty vocal, yeah," I said, not knowing why I'd put it that way, but giggling at the idea of it talking. Or singing, maybe.

"Well, it must just be ye then, cos I've a bad case of the

flops," Benson said. Bríd gave him a patronising hug, and he shook it off, but in a cute way, not a wankerish way.

"Yeah, I've no movement below deck either, like," Richie said, not looking fussed about it though. His girlfriend wasn't here, if she still was his girlfriend. I'd ask him later, if I remembered.

"Same here," Ian said. I loved the way everyone was being so frank, and no one was embarrassed. It wouldn't last, but it was a cool thing to be part of for a while, anyway. It made you realise how silly and irrational we were in normal life, with all our hangups and our taboos. I took another belter of a breath, and held it in my lungs for a few seconds, as if I was after taking a toke off the air itself. Mental.

"Well, there's no need to ask *me*, ye shower of bastards," Niall said, looking at us girls, and we all laughed, and then gave him apologetic nods. Well, I did, anyway.

"Must just be a woman thing then, girls. Fair play to ye, but the rest of us have the pilly willy, boy." Frank slapped his hands together and rubbed them like he was a dad signalling that it was time to go, but he didn't get up or make any sort of movement after it.

"I don't have a pilly willy," said someone. Everyone turned towards the voice. It was Tim.

"You don't?" I asked, cos no one else was saying anything.

"No. I've been fine all night, like. I mean, I don't mean – I haven't been walking around on the horn all the time. But ah, no – no, there's no problems there, I don't think." Tim was always an enigma, but this was a new level of... Timness.

"Prove it!" Niall said. Everyone giggled.

"Prove it how? I'm not gay!" Tim said, confusingly.

"Is it gay to have an erection?" Bríd said, wafting the

smoke from Benson's fag away from her face.

"Just show us, you bender," Ian said, even more confusingly.

"I'm not on the horn NOW!" protested poor Drug Tim, who was now *Stiff Tim* in my head, temporarily at least.

"Well then get on the horn, like. Ciara, show him your tits!" Niall said. I gave him the finger on her behalf.

"You show him yours," she said, well able for him.

"Why don't all the girls show him their tits, and then it'd be more fair, like," said Richie – ever the diplomat.

"No one's showing anyone anyone's tits, guys," Bríd said. Benson looked mildly disappointed at that, I thought.

"Shut up all of ye, I think it's – I think it's there now," Stiff Tim said, then without any warning at all, dropped his trousers to the knee, and showed us all his very pointy boxer shorts.

"Jesus Tim, that's a big one," Niall said. There were giggles going round the room, and the odd gasp.

"No it isn't," Ian said, being his usual Ian self again.

"It's the only one in this room that actually works, boy, so that makes my man Timbo the biggest stud here," Frank said, patting him on the back a bit too hard.

"In the land of the blind, the one-eyed man is king," Stiff Tim said, still standing proud, in every respect.

"Your one-eyed Jap is king now," Richie said, and everyone laughed, especially Tim, which made his little (or big, depending on who you believed) tent pole jiggle around in a hilarious, not sexy way. Penises were pretty hilarious in general, though. They were only sexy if they were attached to someone you wanted to shag. That was how I saw it.

"You can put away your weapon now, Tim. Thanks for

giving us all a look, though," said Ciara, squeezing my leg. I had a terrifying thought. What if it had been Niall instead of Tim who was the one that escaped the curse of the pilly willy? We'd have had egg on our faces, then. Or something that looked a bit like egg, anyway. I disgusted myself, sometimes.

"D'you know what would be brilliant?" Benson said. I turned around to look at him. Bríd had put her socks back on, I noticed.

"What would be brilliant, Benson?" I said, drinking the end of my G&T and wondering how much of what was left was just melted ice.

"Well, you know when it's someone's 21st, and you do the game where the birthday boy sits in a chair, and they put a blindfold on him, and then all the girls line up and give him 21 kisses?"

"What, EACH?" I said. I'd never heard of this game. Sounded like a recipe for cold sores, if you asked me.

"No! 21 altogether!" Benson said, looking at me like I was slow.

"Benson, we don't know any 21-year-olds, you old codger," Niall said.

"Yeah, old man. Make your references understandable to the younger generation," Ian added.

"I understood it!" Ciara said, but her sister was 21 last year, so she'd probably been to the party, but hopefully not joined in the snogging. A family could be *too* close, like.

"Anyway!" I said, taking charge, because someone had to. "What was your point, Benson? If that *is* your reeeeeal name…"

"Huh? Oh! Right, yeah. No, what I was saying was, wouldn't it be cool if we did that with Tim now, and his massive stonker, but instead of kisses, it was-"

"Blowjobs?" Ian said.

"Yes!" Benson said, looking around for everyone to high-five him with their eyes.

"Pffffft! You go first, then..." Ciara said, sparking up a B&H, which immediately made me want to.

"Hang on, Benson. Your girlfriend is here," I said, reaching down for Ciara's box (shut up, brain, you perv) There were only four fags left. I could wait a while.

"And?"

"And what you're saying is that you're grand with her participating in some sort of blindfolded blowjob gangbang with a boy you barely know, while everyone else watches?" I didn't like that the image in my head was actually a bit erotic, but I could blame Frank's tainted Sex-Es for that. Conscience clear.

"Uh, well," he looked at Brίd before he said anything else. She was looking at him too, and it didn't look like a green light look to me. "No, course not. It was only a mess. Course not, lads! Course not." The last one was for Brίd. I wasn't sure if it had convinced her though.

"I'm not wearing a blindfold," Stiff Tim said, as if the plan was still on.

"Why's that, honey?" Ciara said, offering me a fag herself now, so I couldn't say no, technically. That'd be bad manners.

"Well, I don't want to be having the best... *oral sex* of my life, and then take off my blindfold and find out it was Nailer doing it, all along," he said, and everyone laughed, but we nodded too, as they were wise words indeed.

*****

"Right then, you! Come with me. Sorry, Ian. She's mine,

tonight," Ciara said, dragging me out into the hall. I'd been talking to him about the lineup tomorrow. He said he'd heard that they were moving Orbital and The Orb from their middle slots on Saturday and Sunday to after the headline acts finished, since there had been such a massive crowd for the Prodigy, and since the dance tent had been a big success. He said MCD had underestimated how popular that sort of music was in Ireland now. I said they'd underestimated how many of us were taking drugs.

"Where are you stealing me to now?" I said, feeling half confused, half excited. Coming out from the room into the hall was like stepping into a vacuum, because the music had been so constant, and now it was gone.

"Your room," she said, pushing open my door, which I'd obviously neglected to lock. Nothing valuable in there anyway, I thought. I'd my bag with me, in the other place.

"My room," I said, wondering should I switch on the light, but then she did it anyway.

"That's where we are."

"What are we going to do in here?" I said, trying to sound... well, trying not to sound like an idiot, at least.

"Oh, I think you know exactly what we're going to do, Caoimhe," she said. I could feel my heart palpitating, in a good way, not in an *about to die* way, thankfully.

"Oh, I do, do I?" Did you flirt differently with a girl? Or did you just do the same as you would with a boy? I had no clue. I took another massive breath. I was still very up. All this was making me feel it even harder.

"Mmmhmmm. Okay, put your arms up for me." She had a look on her face that I couldn't decipher yet.

"My arms? Why?" I put them up anyway, though. She was the boss, in this situation at least.

"So I can do this," she said. In one smooth movement she grabbed the bottom of my top on both sides and lifted it up over my head, until I was standing there in my bra. The fan was still on, and the cold on my skin as the breeze hit me felt absolutely *scintillating*. That was the word that popped into my head, anyway. I looked at her, not sure if I should say anything. She stood closer to me and put her arm around my back, her fingers touching the strap of my bra. Fuck!

"Um..." was the best I could come up with.

"On or off?" She had her finger and thumb around the clasp bit behind me.

"Sorry?"

"Your bra. Do you want it on or off, while I'm doing this to you? I don't mind, either way. But it might be easier off." This was the strangest preamble to a sexual encounter I'd ever experienced. Maybe Joe Jackson was right, and it really was *Different for Girls*. Or maybe I was still unconscious in the minibus, after Frank's weed.

"While you're... doing this to me?" I said, leaning my head back so I could look at her properly.

"Yes, the massage, silly! Oh! Have you baby oil with you?" she said. She was 100% unaware that there had been any sort of Three's Company style misunderstanding here. I was very glad of that. I was such an eejit all the same.

"I do, yeah. It's in the bathroom, I use it for my legs after I shave them. I'll get it, shur," I said, pushing past her with my bra very much still on. I wondered did you blush all over your body when you were blushing, or was it just the face?

*****

"Christ, that was good," I said, lying on my back, after Ciara had finished giving me a good, thorough going over, *so to speak*. That thing of her being so light fingered and gentle doing my makeup didn't translate to her massage skills. Nurse Ki-Ki was a lot rougher when she had her baby oil-covered hands on your shoulders, back, and thighs. Touching someone's skin was amazing on this stuff, so touching that much skin, with all that lubrication, must have felt incredible. I'd almost done her as much of a favour as she'd done me. Almost. Possibly.

"You sounded like you enjoyed it, yeah. Even the thing I did to those muscles at the top of your bum, like? I wasn't sure you were gonna be able to take that, in fairness." She was sitting up, having a smoke, on the edge of the bed, but still close to me.

"The fisty-knuckly thing? No, that was AMAZING." It had hurt while she did it, but whenever she stopped, I got this incredible feeling of relief and lightness, like I was floating. So, so good, it was. She was brilliant at everything, this one.

"Yeah, haha. Although I hope these walls aren't too thin, because there might be a few questions when we go back in, about you shouting "Harder! Harder!" at me!" The perfect smile was back. I felt like I'd been put through a mangle, lying there, but in a good way. Like when you were sore the next day after a shag, but you were only sore because you'd had the *best* time.

"Oh God, I didn't, did I?" I vaguely remembered thinking it, but I wasn't sure if I'd been saying the words out loud or not. Until now, anyway. Oh dear.

"Just a little bit," she said, and then out of nowhere she leaned down and kissed my cheek. My whole face went hot. I was afraid to make eye contact, but I didn't know why.

"Sorry, was I not meant to do that?" she said, stubbing out her fag, and then swinging her hips and the rest of her around so she could look at me better. I felt strangely vulnerable now, and it wasn't because I had no top on and she was fully dressed. It was more... the everything else.

"What? No, you're grand, shur. You're my – we're all..." I couldn't find the right words.

"How about this?" she said, in a quieter voice, and leaned down to me again. This time it was a kiss on my lips. My whole body sort of tightened, but not in a bad, anxious way. She was sideways on my face, so the kiss was sideways too, but it still felt good. What was going on? I had given up trying to understand a good while ago.

"That... that is also okay," I said. I realised I'd put my arm across my chest now, covering myself. It wasn't a conscious thing – I hadn't done it on purpose.

"Good. I'm glad." She had her finger on my temple, doing little circles. Felt nice. What was happening? What was *going* to happen?

"Me too," I said, because I couldn't think of anything else to say. I wasn't sure if I should sit up, or if I should move over so she could lie down. I wanted her to kiss me again, I knew that for sure. I wondered if the E-telepathy was still working.

"Hey," she said, looking a bit serious all of a sudden. Was something wrong? Had I done something wrong? I hadn't done anything, though.

"Hi," I said, feeling like I was after meeting this person for the first time today, somehow. Or for the first time again, if that made sense. Nothing made sense though, really. I was just going with the flow, as the kids would say.

"How abooooouuuut... we go back in there for a while, have a bit more fun, and chats, and listen to music? Slag off Ian, talk to Tim about his anomalously turgid willy. And then, after that, we can just come in here, chill, lie down, have nice soft, comfy, lovely, Ciara and Caoimhe times, and come down off this stuff together, instead of being around a bunch of other people?" She flashed me an extra-gorgeous version of her normal smile. She had said a lot of things at once, I had to rewind it all in my head to get the details.

"Okay, that sounds cool," I said, even though a part of me thought it sounded rubbish compared to us just staying in here together for the rest of the night. Why didn't she just want to do that, instead? I was starting to get why fellas always complained about us being complicated. Maybe we only seemed complicated to people who were trying to ride us? Not that I…

"You sure, now?" Ciara said, taking my hand and linking her fingers into mine.

"I'm happy if you're happy, chick," I said, pulling myself up using her hand, until we were face to face. It was dead quiet for a bit, and I didn't know if I was supposed to be doing or saying something. She put her hand up to my face, and gently pushed my bottom lip down with her thumb. My eyes were locked into hers; I couldn't look away now. The silence between us, and in the room – it felt like time stopping. I moved my jaw a tiny bit, so my bottom teeth were scraping on the skin of her thumb. She slid her fingers under my chin, still looking me in the eyes. Neither of us were breathing at all, now. It was like we'd forgotten how. Then she smiled at me, and I smiled at her, and we both inhaled deep enough to catch up on all the missed breaths from before. It was like something from a sexy movie, except in sexy movies, Richie South doesn't start banging the door down and absolutely ruin the moment. What a cunt.

NINE

"Hello, Caoimhe O'Shaughnessy, how are you?"

"Oh hi, Stiff Tim." Whoops.

"Stiff what?"

"Never mind. How are youuuuu, babe? You still up, yeah?" He hadn't taken another one. No one had, since we'd come back. At least I didn't think anyone had.

"On the *E tablet*? Yes, I think so." He had such a way of speaking. Like he was in school, reading aloud for the class. There was a touch of *out the country* off his voice, even though he was from Caherdavin. Probably had culchie parents, although I'd met his mum – the massive ride – and she didn't sound too huffmuckerish.

"That's good, what are you doing standing by the door? Are you our new security guard, yeah?"

"No. I was going to go to my room," he said, as deadpan as a pan that was… dead.

"Why? Have you been bold?" This conversation wasn't exactly flowing, maybe I should let him off, I thought.

"No. I'm just feeling a little strange, Caoimhe. I was already in my room, I just came out, but I'm going back, now." He had the most earnest face in the world. When everyone was telling me about only seeing the good in people when you're on yokes, I kept thinking about poor Tim, who didn't have anything in him except good. What would I see in him?

Maybe I'd see all the hidden bad in him. Like that he secretly liked to stamp baby pigeons to death.

"Weird in what way, babe? Do you need someone to mind you, or to talk to you? I'm here if you want me, okay?" I meant it as well. I was feeling quite charitable with all this extra love inside me. And I wanted to take my mind off the whole thing where I'd nearly made a fucking eejit of myself with Ciara.

"Nah, I'm just – I just want to go and think about some stuff, and I can't think with all these people talking, and all the music, you know?" Sounded like he might be coming down. But then, what did I know about it? He'd only taken one though, and that had been... an unspecified amount of hours ago.

"Do you need a wee?" That was the only symptom I knew.

"What?"

"Have you been able to – can you go to the toilet, yet?" I couldn't see Ciara anywhere, but people were spread out over the three rooms now, she'd be somewhere around. It was her Richie had been looking for, banging on my door. He wanted her to come and back him up about something he'd said to Benson, because Benson wouldn't believe him, so it was basically a National Emergency, him breaking up our incredibly tense almost-proper-snog.

"I've been able to go to the toilet all night, Caoimhe." He looked confused.

"Tim! Your willy is MAGIC, you know that?" It truly was. It defied the laws of, well, biology.

"Thanks. So, what's going on with you and Ciara, then?"

"What? Nothing! Why, what have you heard?" I got a little panicky again.

"I heard you shouting "Harder, harder!" when ye were in your room together. I was just wondering what you were asking her to do harder?" He wasn't even smirking. He was asking a sincere question. I loved him, and his mystical mickey.

"Ah! No, she was giving me a massage, cos of all the stiffness, and I was really, really stiff," I tried not to look at his crotch, but I failed. "So, I was just letting her know she could be a bit firmer, you know what I mean? To get out all the… knots. That make sense?"

"I think so, yeah. So, Ciara knows how to give massages, does she? Where did she learn that?"

"Dunno. Massage School? Anyway, speaking of Ciara, I have to go find her now. You gonna be okay?" I gave his arm a squeeze.

"I'll be okay, Caoimhe. Enjoy the rest of yeer night, yeah?"

"Yeah, heheh. What's left of it, anyway, says you! Look after yourself now, love."

"I will. Night night, Kweev. Don't let the bed bugs bite you." He turned around and went into his room, the one next to mine, 212.

"I won't," I said, smiling a silly smile to myself. It had been such a great day, all the same.

"Don't let the Ciaras bite you either," he said - quieter, from behind the closed door, the cheeky fucker.

*****

I ran into an invisible wall of paranoia before going into Room 213. Had Tim only heard us because he was right next to us, in his room? Or had everyone in this one heard us, too? Had they all been in his room? Had he called them in to listen? No, Tim wasn't that sort of boy. He wasn't a

LAD lad. None of them were, really. They were all kind of quiet, except maybe Niall. He had a bit of rugby jock in him, although he couldn't play it anymore, since he hurt his back that time. He had charisma, Niall did. You couldn't miss the fucker. Brian liked to act the big man, and he was in with the rugger crowd, but he had a strange fatherly vibe to him. He wasn't some lech. You couldn't imagine him being sexual, or I couldn't, anyway. Richie was very quiet; in that way you can be very quiet and still always get the girls. I still hadn't asked him about the Dearbhla situation. He was one of those quiet boys who actually had a lot to say, but you only knew that about him if he was your friend, or if he liked you. He was really charming, once you got through his force field, and were close to him. Only people he hated thought he was *shy*, because he didn't say much to those people. That was how he put it to me one time, anyway.

Mum explained it all to me, one time – the difference between charisma and charm. Charismatic people were the ones you noticed in a crowded room. They were all big laughs and dramatic hand gestures. They were always surrounded by a little crowd, hanging on their every word. Underneath all that though, they were usually shallow, boring people. Mum said charmers were the opposite. You'd go the whole night not realising they were even at the party, but if they managed to break the ice with you and get you chatting, they'd hook you in, and you'd be smitten, and you'd probably end up going home with them. You might end up going home with the charisma guy too, of course. That guy always pulled. But out of the two of them, only the charm guy would be someone you'd want to see again. She'd told me all this one night when she'd had a few too many gins with me and I was asking her why she didn't like Dad's brother Anthony, the really handsome one. Turned out, both brothers had made a play for her back in ye olden days, and though she'd gone on a couple of dates with the flashy, Billy Big Bollocks brother first, it was the quieter, more interesting one (Dad) she'd married. Dad being an incredibly successful young corporate solicitor with a mortgage and a BMW and Uncle Tony being a wannabe nightclub promoter who hung around with gangsters and lived in a one bed flat, might have had something to do with it too, but I didn't say that to her at the time. I was stalling now. I had to go in. I steeled myself for the inevitable mocking cries of "Harder! Harder!" and went through the door, but no one said anything, so it was grand.

*****

"Am I charismatic?" I said to Ciara, once I'd found her. It hadn't been a long search. She'd been right there, by the bed, with the rest of them.

"You're a superstar, babe," she said, not exactly answering my question, but I wasn't gonna argue with her point, either.

"But am I charming, then?" I didn't think I was. I wasn't great at manipulating people or getting them to do stuff for me. I liked doing things for myself, though. I hated feeling like I owed someone.

"You're... hang on, where has all this come out of?" She spun around on her bum, so she was facing me properly. I looked down at her thighs and thought how cool it would be if she put her legs over mine and scooched in really close. That was a boy and girl thing to do though – a boy and girl *coupley* thing. People would look at us funny if we did that now, I thought, even though I sort of wouldn't care

"It's come out of my tiny little brain," I said, smiling at her, in an attempt to get that concerned look off her face. It worked, as well.

"Haha, sush, will you? Your brain is enormous. You're absolutely packing, in the brain department, Kweev. You've brains to burn." She was pushing my hair back again, giving me the warm shivers. Everyone else's chatting had turned into white noise, now I had her full attention. They might as well not be there, I thought, wishing that they genuinely weren't.

"Please don't burn my bwain, Nurse Ki-Ki. I'm be a good girl, I pwomise!" The baby voice was out, now. Put it back in! Put it back in!

"Heheh, I'm gonna be Nurse Ki-Ki forever now, aren't I?" She trailed her fingers from my shoulder, down past the crook of my elbow, over my wrist, all tickly, and left her fingers in my palm. I loved all of this, whatever the fuck it was.

"Oh, I dunno. Do you have the uniform?" I said, definitely not picturing it in my head.

"Fffffffssss, do you want me to get one?" Her eyes fascinated me. They were never the same colour any time you looked. Maybe she really was a witch.

"I'd like that. You're definitely going to have to check my heartbeat, so you'd better bring a stethoscope too." Was I being charming now?

"I think Nurse Ki-Ki might have to give you a full check-up, Caoimhe. You're long overdue one, from what I can tell, in my professional, Nursey opinion." Her lips made an O shape when she slowly blew out the smoke, like she was a French girl, in a black and white movie.

"That might be nice," I said. I was doing my seducey voice now. The one that never failed to work on boys. Well, on the ones who were very obviously already interested in me, anyway.

"Mmmmm, it might be." A smile again, a wink, and a squeeze of my hand. The radio was still on in the background. Niall was the only one talking. Maybe he was telling them another story about riding adultresses in car parks.

"Will there be an oral inspection?" I said, pushing it a

bit, cos why not.

"Oh, I'll be inspecting everything, honey. No stone left unturned..." Jesus Christ.

"Can you throw in a smear test while you're at it?" WHY WOULD YOU SAY THAT, CAOIMHE? WHY????

"Uh? Ha- Hahahaha! Awww, I love you, Caoimhe. You're hilarious, like. You're brilliant. I love you. C'mere to me," she said, pulling me in for a big hug. The smell of her hair was so overwhelmingly great I almost forgot that I was an idiot. The I love yous helped too, even if she only meant them in an *as a friend* way. Or did she? Shhhhh, brain. Be quiet for a bit.

*****

"So, did ye all fancy yer man, then?" Richie said, perched on the arm of the big comfy chair where Benson was sitting - Bríd on his lap

"Which man?" I said, coming through the door from the hall. I had gone down to reception, to the fag machine. Hadn't met a single rockstar on the way there or back. I was losing my touch.

"The coloured guy, on stage, in the Prodigy," he said, and one or three of us gasped.

"Richard South!" Ciara said, tutting at him.

"What is this, 1956?" Bríd said. She was on the water again, after several Jameson's & red lemonades. I was on nothing, cos I wasn't thirsty anymore. I was probably coming down, even though I didn't want to. Damn it, anyway.

"What did I say?" Richie looked confused.

"COLOURED!" almost everyone said, together at him.

"And what am I supposed to say? *African-American*, is it?"

"He's not American, though," Ian said. I'd forgotten he existed.

"African-English?"

"Just say *black*," Ciara said. Couldn't argue with that. She moved over to let me back into my seat, then moved back closer to me when I was settled.

"Okay, okay. Did ye fancy the black guy, on stage, who was in the Prodigy?" Richie said, carefully and slowly, in case he offended someone again, poor sod.

"Which one?" I said. There were two such people in The Prodigy. My brain was still half-working, at least.

"Ah, the rapper guy, like. Or the other guy, doesn't matter."

"Why doesn't it matter? They're two completely different fellas, you tool," Ciara said. She was sitting beside me on the bed, with our backs against the wall. Every so often she'd lean her head into the crook of my neck, like we were on a date at the cinema, or something. I was blissed out, just being next to her like this. It was so… *something*. Whatever it was, I didn't want it to stop.

"What he's really asking us, girls, is if we'd ever shag a black man. Am I right, Richie? Which is not only a bit racist, but also a bit *none of your business*," said Bríd.

"Well, yeah." Richie was drinking cider, still. I didn't know how many yokes he'd had. Probably the same as me. Maybe more.

"Well, it depends," I said, making Ciara turn her head to look at me.

"Depends on what?" Bríd said, giving me the suspicious eyes.

"Depends on which black man you're talking about," I said. I lit a new fag off the end of my last one, because it felt like I was being interrogated here. All it needed was for someone to start swinging the lampshade.

"This is true," Ciara said, thankfully.

"Oh right, yeah. I get you now," Bríd said.

"I don't." Richie stepped down off the armrest and started stretching his bones. Everyone had been doing it, in the last hour or so. Except me, cos I'd been serviced by Madame – sorry, *Nurse* Ki-Ki. How the other half lived, indeed.

"Well," I said. "Denzel Washington, okay. He's handsome, sexy, great voice, very talented. I'm in. Whereas Arnold from Diff'rent Strokes… not so much."

"I concur," said Bríd.

"Ah lads, don't be lousy. Little Arnold might surprise us all," Ciara said, making everyone laugh. There was no music on. Someone had turned it off, the idiots. No wonder I was on the way down. I'd have to fix that. I stood up. Little head spin. Still up then, thank God.

"Where are you off, senorita?" Ciara said, her voice sounding extra small. Her fingers grabbed onto the back of the elastic on my leggings, almost making me fall back on top of her.

"Music!" I said, in between mad chewing sounds and quick breaths. I bet I looked like a state now. I'd stay away from any mirrors, just in case. The gum had no flavour left in it, either.

"He probably has a massive langer though. Most of them do," Richie said, carrying on a conversation I'd assumed was finito.

"How do you know they do?" Ian said, once again manifesting himself into my reality without so much as a *pardon me*. I'd forgotten why I was standing up, now.

"I dunno, I just heard, like," Richie said.

"Richie, why are you thinking about the penises of random black men in such detail on this, the day of my daughter's wedding?" Niall said, taking the heart out of me, because he hadn't said a thing in ages.

"Your daughter's what?" Richie said, clearly having never seen it, the philistine.

"Here, have a fresh one, honey," said Ciara, shoving a stick of Doublemint into my hand. Now there was an offer I couldn't refuse. I popped it in my gob gratefully, and practically skipped over to resurrect dem beatz.

*****

My room felt weird, but then it was still a completely new place to me – I hadn't spent a night in it, yet – there was still something *eerie* about the look of it when I came in and turned on the light, though. I shook off the thought and got on with doing what I'd come in to do. I was getting good at shaking off thoughts, now. I'd barely had any about the stuff I'd been afraid of thinking about. Him, her – practically nothing, for the whole, long day. Such a long day.

I got down on the floor and rooted through my thrown-off underwear from earlier. Found it!

I'd decided to have a bump, just to stretch out the high, until we were going to bed. It was a good idea. It was also a bad idea. I couldn't just come down now though, not before I – before we – before whatever was going on reached its (un?) natural conclusion.

I unfolded the wrap and scraped a bit onto the dressing table thing, avoiding looking in the mirror, of course. I'd decided to do a line, apparently. That was what was happening, according to my hands, so I might as well go with it. I made it short and thick, I couldn't be arsed doing a perfect, nice looking one. It didn't need to look fancy; it was going up my nose, not out to a posh restaurant. I giggled. Giggling at my own jokes, alone in a hotel room, snorting drugs. If only Mother could see me now, eh? The rolled-up tenner was so new and crisp that it nicked the inside of my nostril, but I forgot about it the second all the dusty amphetaminey goodness hit the inside of my skull. Oof! A bit strong. But maybe that was good.

I was nervous, and I didn't think it was the excited kind of nervous. It was more like the *shitting yourself* kind. I'd been talking the talk all day, but in a small while, I was going to have to walk the walk, and I was a wreck, thinking about it. I didn't even know if any of it was real. Maybe it was all just a drug thing? I had nothing to compare it with.

Ciara and me were always messing about, when people were around, but that was just it – today, most of the stuff we'd said to each other had been when it was only the two of us. There had been no one to put on a show for, like. Still, it might be the drugs. They seemed to amplify every feeling, so maybe that was all that had gone on. And they'd all been going on about these ones making you horny, too. Maybe our mess-flirting just got a little more heated, because everything else was a little more heated? Maybe it was all just fake, and Ciara knew it was fake, and she thought I thought it was fake too? I just didn't know. I didn't know anything. I lit up a delicious Marlboro Light.

I didn't know what to do with a girl, in that way. I was clueless. I'd never even shifted a friend, as a mess, or in a game of dares. I was a total virgin at it. And Ciara, well, she wasn't? People said, anyway. I didn't know if it was true, I'd never asked her. What if I was terrible at it? I mean, I could definitely shift a girl – it'd be the same as shifting a boy, just with less scratchiness. What if there was more, though? You'd hear women in pornos – fake porno lesbians, probably – saying shit like "A girl knows what girls like..." and even though that was true, it wasn't true as well. Girls liked all sorts of different things – we weren't all the same person. I'd talked to enough of us to know that, especially when it came to sex stuff. Some girls would run a mile if a fella wanted to spank their arse, and other girls couldn't enjoy the night unless they went home with bruises. How was I supposed to know what Ciara liked? Should I ask her? How? When?

It was all very well thinking we've the same bits and bobs, and don't we touch ourselves all the time, and wouldn't you just... *apply* that knowledge to someone else. But what if I like being stroked somewhere and they prefer being pinched and pulled there, and I do what I like to them but it's not what they like at all? It was a nightmare, when you really thought about it.

Then there were vaginas. *Vajayjays*, if you were Bríd. Like, I had my own one and I knew how to work it, but what if I was trying to work someone else's, and it didn't work the same as mine? What if it worked all backwards, cos it was the other way around on someone else? Like how you can tie your own school tie, but if someone asks you to tie theirs for them, it's all mirrored, so your hands get confused and you make a hames of it? I was no good at tying other people's ties! I had to go behind them and put my arms around their front and tie it as if I was tying my own, then it was grand. Hang on... Oooh! I was dead clever sometimes, even when I was hepped up on goofballs. I put the speed away and headed back to the rest of them, before my head exploded with any more stupid thoughts.

*****

"Ah! There she is, Bríd. Just in time, quick!" Ciara patted the bed and I scooted over to jump up next to her. Literally every stupid worry that had been plaguing me in the room next door fell right out of my head the minute I saw her lovely face, with its perfect nose, and her lavender eyes, and her mouth that had all the right sized teeth.

"What's the scala?" I said, pretending I didn't see Richie

scowl at me for infringing on his copyright.

"Brínd is going to tell us a spooky story," she said, gripping my hand in her lovely, squeezy fingers.

"Ooh, cool. Like that time on Hallowe'en, in Niall's gaff," I said, squeezing her back, even harder. Everything was going to be fine. I'd just had a silly few minutes. We'd be grand.

"Well, yeah, except my story isn't stupid. And it's true," said Brínd.

"Everyone's a critic, all of a sudden," said Niall, from somewhere on the floor. The speed was already working. It was liked I'd slapped some defibrillator pads on my dying Ecstasy high and shouted "CLEAR!" I sniffed a bit too loud, but none of them looked at me over it, so maybe it was only loud in my head.

"Anyway, so. Everyone knows my dad is dead, yeah?" said Brínd, immediately getting all of our attentions. This would have been the *worst* possible time to make a "Well I hope he is, cos we buried him last week!" joke, so I didn't.

"Anyway, I was only six when it happened. We were on holiday down in Tramore at the time, and Dad had to work – they wouldn't give him the whole week off - so he was gonna drive down to us on the weekend." Benson was finally doing the *looking adoringly at her while she talked* thing.

"Do you know this story already?" I whispered to Ciara, but people shushed us before she could answer me.

"So, on the Friday, I'm at the beach with mum and Steven." That was Brínd's older brother. "You know the way it is, making sandcastles, going for a swim, eating ice cream, eating Taytos, eating sticks of rock."

"All the major food groups," Niall said, and no one shushed him. Unfair!

"Quite. So, anyway, Mum is snoozing in her deckchair after too much sunbathing," Bríd went on. "Steven wanders off down to the rock pools with his fishing net, trying to catch some crabs."

"He's catching a different sort of crabs these days, out in UL," Ciara whispered in my ear. No one shushed her either.

"So, I'm kind of on my own, even though Mum is technically still there. She's not exactly minding me, though. I wasn't safe."

"Jesus, did you get kidnapped?" I said, shocked.

"Shhhhh, let her tell the story, like," said Ian. I couldn't win with these people.

"No, Caoimhe, love. Nothing as bad as that," Bríd said, and I felt better then. "No, someone did come along, but it was Dad."

"But wasn't he supposed to come the next day?" Tim said. He must have come back in while I was out. I gave him a small wave; it was good to see him again.

"Nah, Friday is the weekend, isn't it?" said Niall. We were all allowed to talk now, apparently. Unless we were me.

"No, the weekend starts on Saturday", Ian said.

"We're literally at a festival weekend right now, and it's Friday today," I said.

"No, it's not, it's Saturday now," Richie said, looking at his watch. He had me there, but that wasn't my point. I looked at Bríd.

"He was supposed to come on the Friday, in the evening, so he was only a couple of hours early, like." That was that settled, anyway.

"So, what happened next?" Benson said. He was definitely allowed to talk; I'd leave him off.

"Well, I mean remember this was nearly twelve years ago, so my memory of it isn't perfect, but I remember he picked me up off the sand, and he gave me a big, long hug. And I thought he'd wake Mum, or ask about Steven, but he didn't. He asked me was I hungry, and shur when you're a kid you're always hungry, as long as you know that someone is gonna offer you something nice. Like sweets, or chips, or whatever. So, I says I am, and he says grand, we'll go to that takeaway place up on the main street where we went for lovely burgers the last time he was down with us."

"Awwww, he sounds nice, Bríd," I said, and everyone else made little agreeing noises, instead of shushing me. I was winning them over, clearly.

"He was a lovely, lovely man," she said, a few tears visible now, poor thing. I wanted to hug her, but she was miles away, so I hugged Ciara instead. "Anyway, we went for our burger, and we got chips, and we took them over to some benches, that were looking over the beach. The sun was really bright, I remember. And he sat there for what could have been – well, it must have been, hours. Just chatting away to me, asking me about school, my friends, all the usual. But really, really listening to me – like I was the most important person in the world, and he wanted to hear everything. Cos, he was always working, Dad. He'd never normally be around to hear what I'd got up to in school or in the day. He was either out at his job, or he was jacked tired after getting home, and Mum would tell us not to be annoying him too much. That's why I think I remember him listening to me on that bench. Why it's so clear."

"Yeah, my dad was the same as that, when I was small," I said. He owned his own law practice now, of course, so all the hard work had paid off, but I often wondered if he regretted missing out on so much of our lives. Even a year or so ago, when he took 12 months off from running the practice – a hiatus, as the Yanks called it - he was only home four weeks before he took a job lecturing in Law out in UL. A workaholic, basically. He always seemed to be trying to make it up to me, I thought. Of course, with Áine, he'd never be able to...

"And did your Mam not wake up and think you'd disappeared, like?" Richie asked. It was a very good question. We all looked at Bríd for the answer.

"Well, this is the thing. She did, and she went absolutely spare. Got everyone looking for me on the beach. People she knew, people she didn't know. She found two Gards on their lunches and dragged them along too. And you know how big the beach is there, like."

Most of us nodded or said yeah. Trá Mór literally meant "Big beach" in Irish. It was somewhere on the East coast. Wexford? I couldn't remember.

"And did they find ye in the end, like? Well of course they did, obviously, ye're here now. But did your Ma give out stink to your Da, like, for giving her a fright like that?" Richie said. He was really on the ball; I'd thought of none of these things.

"Well," Bríd said. "They did find *me*, eventually. On that bench, looking down over the beach."

"What about your dad? Where was he?" I said, gripped now with the story.

"My Dad died in a car crash earlier that day, Kweev. Between Limerick Junction and Tipperary Town. He never made it anywhere near Tramore, they told me. Except I know he did, somehow. For me."

"WHAT???" A chill went through me like I was *in* a horror movie, not just like I was watching one.

"Jaaaaaaney Mack!" Richie said.

"Yep. We worked out later, by educated guesses and stuff, that the time I said he came to the beach and collected me, was the exact same time he'd been killed, instantly thank God, in a head-on collision with this big milk lorry." Bríd looked like she was going to cry, but so did most of us.

"That's... mental. In a... in a nice way, kind of? Like cos it's so sad that he died, but it's just... wow. He came to spend one last special time with you."

"He did. And I mean, that's why I'm so spiritual and stuff – not like, Hail Mary and Our Father religious, but I definitely believe there's something else, other than just this, you know? Something bigger than all of us. Something... *vast*, that we can't comprehend, until we become part of it too, maybe. Like Dad did."

"Yeah," I said. I didn't believe in anything, really, but her story had given me something. Hope, maybe? Whatever it was, it was a good feeling.

"Thanks for sharing that with us, honey, that was beautiful." Ciara got up and gave her a hug, so then we all did. We were still all in a big mass loved-up huddle with her when Frank, still hugging, said, "Lousy that he didn't take poor little Steven for the burger and chips with ye too, though. No wonder that youngfella grew up so warped."

There was the tiniest of awkward silences, and then everyone laughed - especially Bríd - and we stayed in our big love-melee for a minute or two, silently soaking up each other's good vibes. What a life we led, honestly.

TEN

It was *fuck knows o'clock* when we got to my bedroom, although it was still dark, so at least it wasn't dawn yet. I'd planned on saying and doing all sorts of things when we were finally alone, but they all seemed silly in the cold light of day. Even if it was actually more the warm dark of night.

"You okay?" Ciara said, looking at me in the half-light. No one had gone for the switch when we came in, but the streetlights outside were enough to see each other.

"Couldn't be okayer," I said, not sure if that was true.

"Good. I'm glad. I'm just gonna go, um..." She nodded at the en suite.

"Oh, of course, yeah. Carry on, I'll be..."

"Here when I get back?" She touched me on my side and smiled as she passed me.

"Yep. Unless I get a better offer," I said, moving the quilt back a bit and sitting down.

"I'll be quick then, so!" She turned the bathroom light on, and it made everything in its path go yellow, me included. Then she shut the door and it was gone again. I wondered what to do about my clothes. Should I take them off? Should I wait for her to take them off me, like in a movie? Would she freak out if she came back and I was only in my underwear? I was thinking too much, again. I was still very up, on one thing or the other. I couldn't see if my pupils were big, I couldn't look in the mirror in the dark, and the dark made your pupils big anyway. I left the clothes on, for now. The toilet flushed, and Ciara came out. Light again, then no light.

"So…" she said, standing in front of me. I wondered should I touch her. Maybe not yet.

"Here we are," I said, as if that was useful information.

"Here we are, indeed," she said, in her lovely, velvety voice that was mostly Irish, with a twang of England in it. She was born in England, but she'd moved over here so young that all the London in her voice probably came from being around her Mum growing up. Her Dad wasn't on the scene, she rarely mentioned him.

"Hold on, there's been something I've wanted to do all evening, Kweev." *You and me both, love.*

"Yeah?" I said, smiling at her. I felt nervous again.

"Oh, yes." She unbuttoned her trousers, undid the zipper, and pushed everything down to her ankles - stepping out of them without tripping up and breaking her neck. It was like how taking off trousers happened in the movies. "That's been cutting into me all night, like. They're the right size and everything, it's just the bloating, from all the not-weeing," she said, smiling again. The trousers had left little red marks across the bottom of her tummy. That never happened in the movies.

"Did you go just now?" I said, wondering if her being able to would magically make me able to.

"Yes, amazingly. Otherwise, we'd have had to get these off me with the Jaws of Life!" She still had her t-shirt on, and obviously her knickers. I wondered was all her stuff still in Benson's van, and how was she going to get dressed in the morning, but none of that was important now.

"I did well, I wore elastic," I said, shoving my thumb

under my waistband and letting it snap back at my skin, for dramatic effect.

"Clever lady. Did you want to go try too, like? Before we…" Before we what? That was the six-million-dollar question.

"Uh, I don't feel like I need to. But yeah shur. Might be a different story when I'm in there," I said. I got up, and we were standing face to face again, give or take a couple of inches in height. She smelled different.

"Oh, I scobed some of your roll-on, was that okay?" E-telepathy again.

"What? No, of course it's grand. Shur now you smell of Caoimhe, you lucky girl," I said. I still hadn't moved.

"And isn't that the best thing in the world to smell of?" She put her hand up the front of her t-shirt to scratch something, and I saw her bellybutton piercing glint in the light from the street. I'd never had the courage to get one done, but I thought there were sexy as anything.

"You like it?" She rolled up the front of her top and held it so we could look at the thing properly. It was a bar, not a ring, and it had a sparkly jewel in it.

"It's gorgeous. What's the stone?"

"It's garnet. Purple garnet, like you all claim my eyes to be."

"Well, they are, kind of. Sometimes. Sometimes they're blue, sometimes they're greenish. They're amazing." I wished I could look at them properly now, but that would mean turning on the light, and that was a big nope from me.

"Awww, shucks. Your eyes aren't too bad yourself, like."

"I'm more of a Great Arse girl, I'll leave the pretty eyes department to you," I said, sounding confident in myself for the first time since coming into the room. More of that, please, Mr. Brain!

"It is a fantastic arse, all the same," she said, "especially for a skinny cow like you." I was about to get offended at that, but she reached behind me and gave me a hard squeeze, and I'd been so longing for physical contact without realising it, that all I could say was:

"I'm more *thin* than skinny."

"You're *thinny*," she said, running two of her fingers up my flank, now. Was something going to happen?

"Thinny. I like it," I said, wondering should I be touching her too, or should I just go with whatever happened. I put my hand on her hip, my fingers feeling soft skin, and the lacy side bit of knickers. I was still looking at her face.

"Go on then. Your mission, if you choose to accept it, is to have a wee-wee. Then you can come back and share this bad boy with me." She held up a smallish joint, just the right size for two people. That might be nice. I didn't really want to do any more procrastinating but having a joint would be relaxing for both of us, and being relaxed was never a bad thing.

"Okay, wish me luck!" I said.

"Break a leg," she said, planting a big smoochy smacker on my very closed mouth, but I was no more or less sure what the fuck was happening than I had been a few seconds before it.

*****

"Ah, Jesus he didn't, did he?"

"He did! The fucking cheek, like." The joint had been a good idea, I was well relaxed after a few pulls. We were sitting cross-legged on the big bed, both of us *sans pantalons* now, as I'd taken mine off before my highly successful wee, and not bothered putting them back on. It was better like this, anyway. We matched, now.

"I'd have fucking brained him, all the same," Ciara said. We were talking about James, an ex of mine, who had once tried to dry-bum me without so much as a "Brace yourself!", let alone some lubrication, and afterwards claimed that he didn't know he was aiming it in there, he just thought I was "really tight" in the vajayjay region. Men!

"I know! And the thing is, I was such an eejit for him back then, I think I believed him." Or maybe I'd just wanted to believe him, but it had the same outcome, really.

"James Doyle. Originator of the phrase: *it's easier to ask for forgiveness than for permission*," Ciara said. The joint was nearly finished, but it was grand. I'd had enough. I was *sorrrrteeeed*.

"He didn't even ask for forgiveness, though!"

"What a cunt," she said, and I almost looked around to see if Bríd was looking daggers at her, but Bríd was probably in the van now, or conked out on the floor.

"Right, what's next?" my brain said, although it came out of mouth as well.

"What's next?" She stubbed the roach out in the plastic ashtray, then turned her gaze back on me. So pretty. So perfect. So alone, with me. Yikes! But good yikes.

"Well, yeah. I dunno – here!" I said, scooching forward, legs still crossed. I got up as close as I could to her.

"Hello…"

"Hi." I unknotted my legs and carefully put them over her hips, like I'd wanted to do earlier. One at a time, mind. I wasn't a contortionist. The light was still very low, but we'd been sitting here long enough that my eyes were accustomed to it. *I've grown accustomed to her face.*

"Oh. This is new," she said, but not in a bad way.

"Lots of things are new, today," I said. "Would it work better with your legs over mine, instead?" I was thinking it might, since I was the taller one.

"Would what work better?" I couldn't tell anything from her tone. My brain was very tired, though, even if the rest of me wasn't.

"Um, this." I moved myself even closer now, if it were possible, til we were almost bumping into each other, downstairs - like a pair of new neighbours.

"I'm none the wiser, she said, putting her hand on the top of my arm, then moving it slowly down to the back of my wrist. Was that a good signal?

"I dunno. I just wanted to-" I stopped to take another deep, deep breath. The air near her was a mix of my Impulse roll-on, her vanilla conditioner, and another smell that I couldn't place.

"Get closer?"

"Yes! Closer. Close is good, don't you think?" I caught myself staring at her chest, like I was a twelve-year-old boy. I dropped my hand onto the top of her thigh, and just sort of left it there, for now. It was softer than any skin I could ever remember touching before.

"I didn't have much of an opinion on it, either way, but uh, you give a good sales pitch, Shox." She lifted her knee a little bit, and my hand fell down and landed in the space between us. Centimetres away from, well, everything. My heartbeat was loud enough for me to hear it now, I wondered if she could, too.

"I can be very convincing, or so I'm told," I said. How was I being so cool? It wouldn't last.

"I can be very convinced, apparently," she said. She

looked down at my hand, but it didn't make her move herself back, away from it. She didn't move forward either, though, so it probably didn't mean anything.

"You say that like I've been doing all the running," I said, moving her fringe with my fingers, so I had more of her face to enjoy.

"There was running?"

"Maybe *chasing* is a better word," I said, smiling.

"I see," she said, regarding me. That was what she was doing now – it wasn't looking. It was *regarding*.

"What is it you seeeee?" I said, smiling at her again. This flirting with a girl thing was actually quite easy after all.

"Hmmmmm. I spy, with my little eye… my very, very, very pretty friend Caoimhe."

"Oh, I'm your friend now, is it?" I said, laughing to cover up the panic. Where was this conversation about to go?

"Well, you are, aren't you?" A small frown, but not a cross one. Then back to the regarding.

"Absolutely. You might even say, best friends?" I was losing my coolness. That was a silly thing to say – Bríd was her best friend. I was a total rookie at Ciara-friending compared to her.

"Haha! You might, yeah."

"Let's just say *very close* friends, yeah?" I pushed myself nearer to her as I said the words "very close". I was back to being an absolute smoothie with the ladies.

"I think I can live with that." Both her hands were resting on my hips now. Thumbs on the sides of my knickers, fingers underneath my shirt. I put my arms up like I was going to yawn, linked my fingers in the air, and brought my hands down behind her neck, like I was a boy putting the moves on her at the cinema.

"Is this okay?" I said. I wanted her to be okay. With everything. But I had no idea how I'd react if she said she wasn't, either.

"I'm liking it so far," lovely Ciara Slattery said, walking her fingers up the sides of my spine, underneath my shirt. I had goosebumps everywhere.

"How about this?" I said, kissing her very softly on the forehead." I was boiling hot, like it was still the daytime, or like someone had put the rads on.

"Yuhuh."

"This? And *this*?" I kissed her with the same amount of softness - on one cheek, then the other. I opened my eyes, and now it was my turn to regard her. She looked okay. I mean, she looked fucking amazing and beautiful and perfect, but she also looked *okay*. That was the important thing.

"My turn," she said, moving her face up to mine, and kissing me on the mouth. It was different from before. There was more… pressure. Her top lip broke through both of mine and touched my teeth. I didn't know what to do next. It didn't matter, anyway. She pulled back just as it was about to get interesting.

"We still friends?" she said, back to regarding.

"Very close friends," I said, and this time it was me who kissed her. I did what she had done, I didn't want to rush it. Her balm was making things quite slippery, in a very nice way. I pulled away after a bit, and I swore I felt her tongue flick against my lips for the teeniest millisecond, which was somehow hotter than if she had just gone for it and shoved the whole thing down my throat.

"Tssk, naughty!" I said, absolutely wanting her to carry on being naughty.

"Who me?" She was smiling a new smile now. New to me, anyway. Maybe it was her sex smile. Not that we were having sex, or anything. We'd barely kissed each other, so far.

"Yeah... I've got my eyes on you, missy." I touched her collarbone through the t-shirt, and slowly let my fingers trail down her boob, stopping before I got anywhere *too* sexual, cos it wasn't like I'd asked her if *that* would be okay.

"Not just your eyes, apparently," she said, gently taking my fingers off her, and bringing them back up to her neck. Ten-Four. Message received. I'd leave that, for now.

"Sorry!" I really hoped I wasn't fucking everything up.

"Shhhhh, no need to be sorry. Come here." She lifted my chin with the edge of her finger and gave me another closed-mouth kiss that went on so long we both had to breathe through our noses to keep it going. It was so weird. Doing this with a fella I was shifting would have been hilariously rubbish. I'd have thought he was an altar boy, or a closeted homosexual. Doing it with her was *fucking hot,* though, somehow. Probably because, in this scenario, I was the closeted homosexual. Or bisexual. Or whatever the fuck you called this. I smiled at her again. I never got tired of looking at that face.

"Happy then, yeah?" said Ciara, thumbing the clasp at the back of me, but not trying to open it.

"Ffffffffffff, just a little bit." I looked down for a second. We were nearly smooshed together, knickers to knickers, like. But not quite. There was like a *Vernier calipers* amount of distance between her and me, and that was again somehow hotter than if we were actually touching. It was like the space between us, and how little of it there was, made it all incredibly tense and sexy. Like as if the gap between us was as important as the parts it was separating? Like the silences between the notes in Jazz. I wondered did she feel the same, or was I just mad? Both were equally possible.

"Hmmmmm, let's just see, yeah?" Ciara said. Her hand

was flat against the skin on my back now – her thumb doing little movements across my shoulder blade. It was like she'd read the manual that came with me – I couldn't imagine her touching me in a way that I didn't like, and I was looking forward to being proved right.

"What are we going to see?" I said, wondering if she'd meant something specific or if it was just one of those things people said.

"Just, well, ummm." I wasn't sure if she'd finished, but I kissed her again anyway. This time I was the one who put a little tongue into the mix, but it was still pretty innocent.

"Sorry, you were saying?" I hadn't taken my face away far, my big old eagle nose was side by side with her perfect baby ski-jump one – foreheads pressed, open lips overlapping, without touching. Inhaling and exhaling so close to each other it felt like we were both taking the same breath.

"It'll keep," said Ciara, taking in one more lungful of air, and then closing her mouth over my bottom lip. I relaxed my neck, tilting my head slightly so our almost-open mouths could slide into each other – tongues barely touching, just gliding over one another. She tasted like Doublemint, and Pernod, and bliss.

*****

"Fuuuuuuuck!" I said, when we eventually came up for air, after what seemed like a hundred thousand kisses. My mouth was all tingly, especially my bottom lip, which it turned out she had a real penchant for dragging through her teeth, mid-kiss. Not enough to hurt, or break skin, but definitely enough to send all sorts of signals to the bits of me she hadn't even got around to touching, yet.

"Woooo!" Ciara said, letting her face fall so that our foreheads did the tiniest bonk.

"That was… something," I said, putting my hand on

her jaw, to bring her face up where I could see her again. Her pupils were dilated, but I didn't know if it was cos she was still up, or because she was just very aroused, like I was. Both were equally possible.

"Hmmmmm. I always thought you'd be a great kisser," she said, giving me another little closed-mouth smooch. Everything was so wet and sloppy now that even those ones felt like utter filth. It was like fucking Monsoon season in my knickers, *excusez mon français.*

"Well, now! If you think I'm good at that, wait until you see how… utterly inexperienced I am at everything else," I said, and she let out a loud laugh. Her face changed then, I noticed.

"At everything else, yeah? I didn't know there was going to be an everything else," she said. We still had our tops on. I hadn't touched her anywhere *serious* yet, and she hadn't tried doing anything either. I was a little afraid to, despite the obvious party that had been going on in our mouths, to which we were the only ones invited.

"I'm – I was fine with all the nice kisses, to be honest. I don't really mind if – I would like-" I was babbling now. Cool Caoimhe had left the building.

"I would like to do everything else, Kweev, honest I would. I'm absolutely fucking, well, you know," she said. There was a change in her tone, and I looked at her face to see if it was there, too.

"Me too," I said, my head filling with all sorts of thoughts that weren't like pictures or movies. They were more like feelings – pure feelings, of niceness.

"But the thing is…" Uh oh.

"The thing is?" I didn't want there to be a thing! I wanted to kiss her again, so much. I wanted to do more than that. I didn't know how it all worked, but I wanted to find out.

I wanted her to show me. I listened up, though, even if I was dreading what she might say next.

"The thing is, today has been amazing. Not just this thing with us, all of it has been amazing. And... I'm very aware that this isn't something you normally do – be with a woman, I mean..." It wasn't something I ever did, but I didn't say that to her.

"Uhuh?"

"And I'm so flattered – that's not even the right word. Fuck's sake. I'm so... honoured? No. Look, I'm really happy that all of this happened today. And tonight, Jesus fucking Christ, especially tonight, or this morning, whatever it is now."

"Mhmmm?" I hadn't anything to say, and I didn't want to interrupt her, anyway. I was just hoping for her little speech to make a U-turn at some point, even though I knew it wouldn't.

"I'm sorry, I sound like such a dickhead, don't I?"

"No, you don't!" I squeezed her hand, but it felt like it was a different hand now. Colder, maybe. I wanted a ciggie, but they were probably on the floor somewhere, in the dark.

"I do, but thanks. You're too nice to me. Anyway, look, to cut a long story short instead of cutting a short story long, I'm worried."

"Worried about what?" She'd lost me now. I felt incredibly vulnerable all of a sudden, and the only person I wanted to fix that vulnerability seemed to be the same one who was causing it.

"About you."

"Me?" Why would she worry about me? I was grand.

"Well, about you, and about me, and about us."

"Us?" I liked the sound of there being an us, but I suspected that was not where she was going with this, unfortunately. I started to feel bad, in that awful way where you feel bad from not knowing things, rather than feeling it about actual facts. Turned out my fags were on the bed, next to the pillow, I grabbed them and lit one, pulling hard on it, like a man in front of a firing squad in a war film.

"Yeah. The us that *was* - before tonight, the us that *will be* – as in, after this, or after we do something really significant, I mean."

"Was this not really significant? It felt pretty significant to me, like," I said, feeling hurt, now. That was new. The us we were before tonight never made me feel like that. Maybe she had a point. But...

"Of course it was – is – sorry, I'm being stupid with my words, I'm kind of exhausted."

"Yeah," I said, feeling a sort of invisible barrier rising up between us now. I didn't like getting hurt. I normally avoided any chance of it. I felt sad. I didn't want to feel even sadder.

"Look, I like you. I love you, you're my friend. But I've fancied you for quite a while, now Caoimhe."

"You have?" No one had told me this. I didn't know what to – I didn't know how to –

"Yes! Yes, a million times yes, but it was like – back then, or even like, last week, I was under the distinct impression that you were *not* into women, in the slightest. You'd told me you weren't, like. On more than one occasion."

"I wasn't!" Or was I? Who the fuck knew anymore?

"Exactly, so... it was just fun and safe, and I knew I could flirt with you without worrying about you rejecting me or whatever, cos there was nothing to reject, cos you were very straight and I'm very not, and we could never *be*, so there was like... no risk." She took a fag off me and mouthed a thank you with her lovely mouth that was no longer on my mouth.

"I think I understand, yeah. But like now, you know I *do* like women. Or, that I do like you, at least. I haven't had a go on any of the others, like. So, isn't that better?" I did not understand how to lesbian correctly. It seemed like a minefield.

"You'd think so, wouldn't ya?" She smiled, but it wasn't a happy smile. "But what it actually means, is that now there *is* a risk."

"A risk of what?"

"A risk of losing you. You know? Either losing you as a friend cos we crossed some sort of line that we can't come back from – some sort of fucking sexual... rubicon - and it turned out to be a mistake..."

"I'm not a mis- this isn't a mistake!" I said, almost angry now. And what the fuck was a rubicon when it was at home?

"Well we don't think that now, but Caoimhe you have taken a lot of drugs today," she said, pausing to find the ashtray.

"So have you, like!" The cheek of her.

"Exactly! But the difference is, I *know* I like girls as well as boys – I've known it since I was eight years old. Whereas you, you've gone *from naught to Navratilova* in about three seconds flat today." I giggled at that, and immediately hated myself for doing it.

"And I'm worried that a) you might regret it, b) you might blame me, and resent me for it, or c) you won't regret it or blame me, but you'll just put it down to experimenting, or trying it out, and you won't want anything to do with me in that way ever again. Like, I was just a guinea pig, or a phase, or whatever. And if that happens, what happens to our actual friendship? Does that get broken, too?"

"Ciara, Ciara, Ciara... babe. I know what – I understand where you're coming from. And like, I can't make you do things you don't want to – I wouldn't ever dare, that would be shitty."

"Thank you."

"But on the other hand, I don't wanna just stop."

"Stop what, exactly?"

"This! All of this. All of... that. I want to go back to the bit before you started all your speeches and stuff. I'd like to start over! Can we start over? Please?" I had her wrists in my hands, now. I felt a little pathetic, but I was only saying what I felt. She had said *her* piece. I hated this. How had we managed to turn the hottest snogging session of all time into this overwrought melodrama?

"I don't know, babe. Why don't we just try to get some sleep, yeah? And talk tomorrow, with clear heads? I'm really coming down hard now, and this is all a bit much, I'm sorry." Her face was kind, still, but something had broken between us, and I didn't know how to fix it. I didn't know if I was genuinely this upset or if I was just coming down incredibly hard off all the drugs I'd taken. Both were, unfortunately, equally possible.

"Will you still stay here? To sleep, I mean?" I didn't want to be alone, and her not being here would be the worst kind of alone. It was all going so well, and then it went waaaaay downhill, because I – had it been me who ruined it? Or her? I was so confused. I didn't want her to go. I really, really, really wanted her to stay.

"Of course I will, Kweev. Just um, I'm gonna be really sweaty and clammy and all overheating and stuff, so don't think I'm being rude or awful if I don't want to cuddle or to spoon, okay? I don't want you thinking it's because of something else, I'd hate that, I really would."

"No, it's okay. I won't think that, I promise." It wasn't okay, I would definitely be thinking that, and I wasn't promising shit, sorry.

"Thank you. For everything. I mean it," she said, neglecting to add the one thing that might have made it all better – a kiss.

She blew out the last of her smoke through those lovely, O-shaped lips, and I watched it turn into little swirls of dusty grey, dancing on top of the sunbeams that were sneaking in through the gap in the curtains. It was the proper morning now. I needed sleep too, but I knew I wasn't going to get any. There was too much ouch inside my heart, and I couldn't make it go away.

ACT 2 – THIS IS A LOW

ELEVEN

I did get some sleep, after all. Well, I closed my eyes, and time went past, and every single event of the day replayed in my head, including all the stuff at the end, but it didn't feel like sleep. Must have been, though, because otherwise I would have noticed Ciara leaving.

Someone banging on the door woke me up from my non-sleep the first time. No idea who, I just ignored them. Didn't even open my eyes, so maybe she was still there, then. Maybe she got up and answered it. Maybe it had been Nick Cave, and she'd run off with him to Australia. Maybe she'd been kidnapped by a passing carnival. Whatever it was, she was gone, and I wasn't sure if I was sad about it, cos I felt mortified, and I hadn't been looking forward to having to look her in the eye in the morning. Not that I'd done anything wrong. Or had I? Fuuuuuck. It all came back again.

By the second time someone knocked, the sun was so bright, even with the curtains drawn, that I had to give in and come back to the world of the living and the awake.

"WAKE UP, BOOOOOO!" someone outside was singing.

"FUCK OFF, CUUUUUUNT!" I sang back. They knocked again. I was going to have to stand up, using my actual legs, and open it. One day we'd have robots for these things. Like in Rocky IV.

"Are you alive in there, chickee?" It was Bríd. I felt a bit guilty for using the C word, as she'd call it, now. But not too guilty, because she'd made me get out of bed when all

I wanted to do was crawl under the duvet forever until my sweet, inevitable death.

"Possibly. Do you have a fried egg sandwich?" I said, opening the door, which wasn't locked, and which I could easily have told her to push open by herself. I was dead not clever sometimes.

"A fried egg sandwich?" Bríd was loaded up with what looked like dry cleaning bags. Or the things dad kept his nice suits in. Either way, they had clothes hangers coming out the top.

"Yes, the breakfast of champions, Geoff Capes swears by them. The fuck are these? Where is Ciara? Why does my head feel like it's full of babies with hammers?"

"Ciara? Dunno. She was with you last time I saw her," said Bríd, helpfully. I looked around for my box of fags, and for a fried egg sandwich, but I knew in my heart of hearts that I'd only find one of those. Both were not equally possible, for once.

"Hmmmm, same. Can we get room service? Is there a..." I spotted the cream coloured telephone on the locker, answering my own question.

"Well, I can't. I'm not even a guest here." Bríd was laying down her weird suit bags all over my bed. Still didn't know why she was here, but it was okay. She was one of my least annoying friends.

"What do I do? Press nine?" I put the handset under my chin. Even the dial tone sounded like it had it in for me.

"I think nine is for an outside line. You have to press something else for reception. Try zero, or one." That sounded like too much choice for my brain to handle. I put the receiver down, with a *clack*.

"Changed my mind. I'll just *not* be hungry instead. Bríd? Why does my brain feel all wrong?"

"Ah that's the serotonin," she said, as if that meant something. I lit a fag. Fags were like food, kind of. They stopped the hunger anyway, with their delicious, cancery taste.

"Come again?" I was looking at the suit bags. Were they from Brian? Were we having an image change? Were we going to be the new Madness?

"Well, Es don't actually have anything in them that gives you good feelings or happiness, or pleasure. They're more like a key," she said.

"I see." I did not see. The fag wasn't strong enough, either. Maybe I should get a pack of *Marlboro Heavies* instead, I thought.

"Well, your brain has stores of something called serotonin, and that's the feelgood one. Dopamine is a feelgood one too, actually, I think. But serotonin is what controls your moods. When you have depression, it's cos your brain isn't producing enough of it."

"Okay." Being friends with Bríd was like watching 3,2,1 Contact. Every day was a school day.

"So, in a normal person, you have enough serotonin stored inside you for your brain to ration out a little every day, and keep you smiling and happy, yeah?"

"I get you." I did get her now, surprisingly. I was dead clever sometimes.

"But, if you can imagine that store of serotonin as a water tank in the attic, right?"

"Right…" What? Lost me again.

"Now imagine the pipe under it has a valve, to control the flow to the house downstairs?"

"Oh! Yes, okay. I'm with you now, again. Tea?" I was already up, I might as well make myself useful, as Mum would say.

"Could murder one, yes, thanks. Anyway, when you take the Ecstasy, it's like you spin that valve, until it's fully open."

"Lefty loosey, righty tighty," I said. I'd learned that once when I had to take the front wheel off my BMX. Not from Dad, from Mum. Solicitors didn't know how to use spanners.

"Zackly. So, all the water – the serotonin - comes flooding down into the house…"

"Aaagh, the carpets will be ruined!" I said, wondering when the kettle was going to hurry up and boil.

"Haha! Metaphor! So, me and you, on our pills, we get like a week's worth of feelgood hormones – the serotonin – in like a few hours. We get flooded, like the house. See?"

"So like, the happiness was inside us all along?" I said, finally hearing the click, and seeing steam rise out of the spout. I hadn't had a cuppa in ages.

"Yeah! But the reason you feel so… empty today, is - no sugar for me, please!" Brid said, making a gesture at me.

"Sweet enough, yeah?" I didn't take sugar either, I barely took milk. Wait, was there even any milk?

"Something like that. Anyway, what I'm saying is, cos we used up all the serotonin last night, there's none left this morning. So we like, can't feel… anything. For a little while, anyway. It wears off, don't worry, chickee. Where's the milk?"

*****

"Tá bainne againn!" Brid said, coming back from downstairs with a pint carton of Golden Vale. I'd just drank my tea black, cos I was hardcore.

"*Maith sibh, a ghrá.* What would we do without you, eh?" The tea was rank, but not because it had no bainne in it, more because I felt like dogshit.

"Be killed to death by foxes, probably."

"Probably. Anyway, come here and tell me – am I gonna be on this downer all day, then?" I had lots of speed left; I could take some of that. Cocktail of drugs, go out like Sid Vicious. Maybe stab my girlfriend to death, for good measure. Not that I had a girlfriend. Fuck's sake. Gah!

"You're on a downer?" She sounded surprised.

"Yes! I'm on the downiest of downers. Down Central. Welcome to Downsville, population: *Moi*."

"Hmmmm. You shouldn't be?" She held her teacup like a mum, or a teacher.

"Why shouldn't I?"

"Because like, the serotonin isn't just the happy – it's like the ups *and* the downs. Sooooooo, what you should be feeling like is just... nothing."

"Nothing," I repeated, definitely not feeling nothing. The tea was too horrible, I put it away.

"Yeah. Not up, or down. Just... in the middle. Apathy – that's the word, yeah? So, I dunno. Maybe it's cos like you're always so flying it and hyper and upbeat all the time, that to you, the middle feels like the bottom?"

"I'm not... *upbeat* all the time," I said, having a stretch, but stopping immediately as it felt like my spine was going to snap in half.

"Ah you are, Kweev. You're the life and soul of the party, like. Everyone loves you."

"Of the party, maybe, yeah. But like, that's me drunk or on speed, or sometimes both, Bríd." Sometimes? *All* times.

"Hmmmmm, I guess. But you're like, an extrovert, so-"

"I am fucking not!" I didn't know if that had offended

me as much as it felt like it had, or if it was just cos I'd fallen into an abyss of existential dread. Both were equally possible.

"You are! There's nothing shy about you, like. You're very outgoing, you'd talk the cross off the back of a donkey."

"Again, like, that's me when I'm wrecked, love. And I'm wrecked a lot, especially since… Anyway, that's not what extrovert means." I hated when people got this stuff wrong. I took it dead personally, even when I wasn't in a black pool of suicidal gunk.

"It isn't?" Looked like Bríd didn't know a science thing. Rare.

"No! I'm an introvert, definitely. It doesn't mean I'm shy or I don't like socialising."

"No? I thought it did, though?" She was leaning into me now, a captive audience of one.

"No, no. It's like, introverts are all about the world in here." I pointed at my temple. "Whereas extroverts – or extraverts? Doesn't matter. They're all into this stuff." I waved my hand around the room, but I didn't mean they were into the room, I meant something bigger.

"You've lost me, *sicín*." She was sitting on the bed with me now, we'd moved the suit bag things out of the way. Still didn't know what they were about. Didn't care, either

"Am, okay. Extroverts love things like sunny beach holidays - introverts want to go somewhere that has galleries or museums."

"So extroverts are thick?"

"No! Not necessarily, anyway. They just care more about the outer world than the one inside their minds, yeah? They're happy doing stuff like sunbathing or going to the gym. They don't need to be stimulated mentally, as long as they're being stimulated in some way. So, getting a bit of sun, or pounding the treadmill - they can do that for ages, but introverts would get bored really quickly. Does that make sense?"

"Mhmmm."

"Like, introverts never get lonely, cos we get recharged by being on our own. And we can play a video game, listen to an album, watch a good film-"

"Don't extroverts do that as well though?"

"They do, yeah. But they'd enjoy all those things more if they had someone to do them with, see? Doing them on their own is like a last resort for them. Because they recharge their batteries by being around other people. Doesn't even matter if it's friends or strangers."

"Ah. I see, now, kind of. So, the introvert thinks that doing those things alone is... better?"

"Much better. If someone else comes along, it's not as good for us."

"Why?" said Bríd, who was probably finding out for the first time in her life that she was an extrovert.

"Because even if we've made ourselves brilliant at chatting or socialising or flirting or whatever, it's not our natural state. So, we have to shift into this other gear, to act in a way that extroverts, or normal people, can just do naturally. And the easiest, laziest way to do that is to get shitfaced. Are you getting me?"

"I am, yeah. Jesus, I'd no idea, Caoimhe."

"Heh. Most people don't, shur. Look, here's a good example of the difference, right?"

"Shoot."

"If you ask an extrovert to come out with you on the weekend, the first thing they'll say to you is, "Who's gonna be there?"

"Right…"

"And if you ask an introvert the same question, the first thing they'll say to you, assuming they don't just refuse you flat out, like, will be, *"Who's gonna be there?"* I said it in a different tone this time to a few seconds ago, but I wasn't sure I'd done it enough, cos Bríd said:

"I don't get it," and shrugged at me. She looked remarkably fresh and not like the walking dead, but she'd probably had a shower already. I suddenly became acutely aware of the absolute pong of sweat off me, but I'd fix that later. I'd soap and shampoo now, thanks to the Toiletry Fairy.

"Well, the extrovert is asking because she wants to make sure there will be loads of people out, and hopefully some people she's never met before, so she can make new friends."

"But the introvert, she's asking because she hopes it'll just be a few of ye, and it'll be people they know already and they like, so they don't have to put in all the effort to… act like they're normal?" Bríd said, looking like she was after winning the spelling test in Junior Infants.

"By Jove, I think she's got it!" I said, and I'd have laughed too, if my entire capacity for joy hadn't been chewed up and spat out by filthy recreational pharmaceuticals.

"Yay! You learn something new every day, eh? Hang on, so if you're an introvert, does that mean you'd rather be alone now, chick? You want me to go? Give you some peace?" She was so nice, like. I was lucky to have her.

"I will literally slash my wrists if you even *think* about abandoning me right now," I said, not even sure how much of that was a joke. She opened her arms wide for the hug, and I sank into her like she was the world's most comfy bean bag.

*****

"Harta is over in Denmark, working in the factory that

boxes them up, like. He says he might be able to get me one wholesale, after he gets himself one." Frank was talking about the new Sony PlayStation that was coming out at the end of next month.

"And by wholesale he means he's gonna rob them, yeah?" Richie said. We were all in his room, drinking cans of Bulmer's. It was something to do, anyway. Better than moping about bloody Ciara, who had not only disappeared from my room, but she'd also taken my hotel towel as well, like a psychopath. I'd to borrow one off Tim, but luckily it was before my shower and not after it that I noticed it was gone. I hadn't washed my hair. I couldn't be arsed.

I'd borrowed one of Niall's big, long t-shirts and I was wearing it like it was a dress. I'd nothing else on except a pair of knickers and a bit of foundation and mascara. I must have looked fairly decent in it, anyway, judging by how many times I'd already caught Niall and Tim surreptitiously perving me.

"Maybe, like. Either way, it's a bargain," said Frank. He was a bit old for playing video games, but he was a bit old for lots of things he did. He never surreptitiously perved me though, thank God.

Bríd and Benson were gone off to get everyone some rolls for breakfast - and an egg sandwich for me, if possible. It wouldn't be possible, though, cos I was pretty sure everything was gonna go wrong for me today. I could feel it in my (very sore) bones.

"I've one pre-ordered in Smyth's," I said. I didn't even like the look of most of the launch games, except the fighting one, Tekken, but it was more a case of actually owning the actual console and seeing what it could do. I'd seen lots of demos of it, it was like something from the future. Tekken looked exactly like the one in the arcade, and the one in the arcade made Virtua Fighter look like it was on the Commodore 64.

"I'll be having sleepovers round yours every weekend after that, so," Richie said. He'd met me in the hallway earlier when I was looking for Ciara. We didn't find her. Ian wasn't answering our knocks, and I didn't want to go in through the middle door to disturb him, cos I didn't particularly want to talk to him anyway, other than to ask him if he knew where Ciara was - which he wouldn't, if he was asleep.

"We'll hide you out in the treehouse, so my Dad doesn't find you," I said. The cider was lukewarm. I could get ice from the hallway, but that would involve moving.

"I would live in that treehouse if ye let me," Richie said. "It's bigger than my house, like. I'd pay rent and everything." He was probably exaggerating, but it was pretty big.

Dad had built it for us two girls, when he was still the sort of Dad who did things like that, and when both of us were young enough to appreciate it. That was when there still was a both of us. Now Áine was gone, forever. I thought about the day I'd shown it to Jon, and all the mischief we got up to in there. That was the first time he'd been to my house. The last time, as well, actually. He was gone, too. Fuck. I didn't need to go to this place, emotionally, now. I had enough going on with the abyss and the lack of a will to live.

"Will I bring us in some ice, lads?" Frank said, looking at his can like it was after insulting him.

"Go on, shur. And a few pint glasses from down in the bar, please?" I said, cos I knew he'd get them if it was me asking, cos he loved me, Frank did. Loved me like I was family, he always said. Gah. Cold cider would be good. I thought of something else that would be good, too. I looked at Niall and did a pretend sad face. It didn't take much to fake one, the way I was feeling.

"What's wrong?" he said, in a nice way. Cos he *was* nice,

all the perving notwithstanding.

"It's my moooooouth," I said, in a voice like you'd do when you were trying to get a day off school sick.

"What's the matter with it, love?" He leaned over nearer to me, trying to see.

"It... doesn't... have... a joint... in it..."

"Hah! I'll see what I can do," he said, picking up the tin that had all the gear and rolling stuff in it.

"Hurrrrrrryyyyyy, I don't have much tiiiiiiiime," I said, cheering myself up a little bit, until I started thinking about the whole Ciara thing again. Fuck, EVERYTHING. At least it wasn't raining. Not yet, anyway.

*****

"Right! There's cheese and ham rolls, there's a ham on its own roll, there's chicken salad, there's a smoked salmon one – that's yours, B - there's a veggie one for me, no one touch that," Bríd said, putting a tray full of bready things down in front of the hungry and hungover. Benson - or B, as he was now known – had some takeaway coffees in a cardboard holder thing.

"Aw, sound!" said Richie, going straight for the ham-only roll, because he was a ridiculously fussy eater, despite his mum being the best cook I'd ever met. I saw nothing I wanted among the selection. I was extra-famished too, after the massive joint we'd just had. Just my luck, today. The universe hated me.

"And... for a very special girl," Bríd said, squatting down to me, "a very special sammidge."

"Huh?" I said.

"Bring it in, B!" she said, making eyes at Benson behind me. I smelled it before I saw it. Glorious!

"How did you get me a-" I cut my own sentence off because finishing it wasn't as urgent as chomping into the fried egg sandwich. It was still warm. The yolk was half runny, half solid. It tasted like all my dreams coming true.

"Hahah, you can thank B, like. They only had cold egg and cress ones down in the café, and I was like, will we get her that? But B said it was egg mayonnaise and that's not anything like a hot fried egg, so he went over to the woman in the kitchen bit and did a bit of charming the pants off her to get her to cook you up the real deal." She reached over to squeeze his calf and gazed up at him adoringly like the absolute fucking saint he was.

"THANKS, BEEEE!" I said, without waiting for my mouth to be empty. He'd got me TWO fried egg sandwiches, not one, on a PLATE - cut diagonally as well, which always made sandwiches taste better - that was just *science*.

"No problem, Queeeeee," he said, and I thought to myself that maybe this whole *going out with a fully grown adult* thing that Brídwas trying out had its benefits after all. Even if it did mean having to touch a willy from the 60s.

"I don't like fried eggs," Richie said, making a yuck face at my delicious breakfast of champions.

"You don't like anything, Richie! You're a fucking thief of joy," I said, wolfing down the second triangle, and pouring myself some more icy Bulmer's. The day had just got a million times better, but it probably wouldn't last.

TWELVE

"Any survivors left from last night? I see ye found the cans all right, no need to leave ye a map to them, was there?" Brian appeared in the doorway of Richie's room with his Brianness already turned up to eleven. He was dressed like someone who was going to a party on a yacht, I thought. Not very rock and roll.

"Ah, most of us are still alive, but you'll have to kick Hurley's door down, I think he might have done a Jimi Hendrix," Richie said. Frank and Niall had gone downstairs to stretch the legs, or that was what they'd told us, anyway. Tim said he needed another shower, so he'd gone to blag some more towels off the hotel people. He was gonna get me some too, cos he was a dote.

"Ah he's a few more lessons to go at the Savin's School of Music before he can die a proper guitar legend, Rich. What's with the puss on this one's face?" said Brian, talking about me like I wasn't in the room.

"Fuck off, Brillo," I said. I never called him that, ever, but it was a special occasion.

"Jesus! Okay, okay. Forget I asked, Janis fucking Stroplin." It was a good one, I'd give him that. I didn't give him a smile though, so I won, technically.

"Where's your ride of a Laurel Hill bird who's too good looking for you, Brillo? She finally see sense and leave you?" Richie said, studying a box of fags he'd found on the ground.

He chucked them over to me then, since they were mine.

"She's back in the B&B, squire. Recovering, she is." Brian never stood still when he talked, or even when he wasn't talking. He was always swaying a little at the shoulders or the hips or tapping his foot. Maybe he had ADD, or ADHD, or whatever it was called. Or maybe he was just fucking annoying. Both were equally possible.

"Recovering from the crushing disappointment of last night's bedroom antics," I said. She wasn't the only one.

"Yeah, yeah, yeah. Speaking of disappointments, ye better not feck up this interview like ye did the last one, yeah?"

"Which interview?" I said, having a big stretch of my legs, then putting them across Richie's lap, like he was the leather pouffe we had in the living room back home. He looked over at me for a second, but it was grand. I was very comfortable around Richie; I always had been. He never got the wrong idea when you were just being friendly with him. He was very respectful of women. It was either that, or he just didn't fancy me at all, which sounded a bit too farfetched to me.

"The one with Pat O'Mahoney and Féile TV, that I'm after bending over backwards to rearrange for ye, you ungrateful wretch."

"Oh right, yeah. The interview. I knew about that, yes." Did I know about it? I had no clue if I did or not, but I did now, so.

"Good. So are you going to go make yourself look presentable or are you going on the telly wearing a massive Sex Pistols t-shirt and a smile?"

"What? Oh, right. Yeah, no, I'll put something on now, so." I'd no idea what, and I honestly didn't care enough to even think of something in my head.

"Great stuff. Cos, Caoimhe love, we all know you could go out wearing a bin bag and you'd still be gorgeous," he said.

"Aw thanks, Brian!"

"But you can't actually do that, cos you've an image to maintain, like."

"Heh. An image to maintain, what are you like?" He always talked about us like we were already mega-famous, or something. We weren't even as famous as Ash – my estranged husband Tim Wheeler's band.

"Yes, an image. And, despite what ye degenerates might think, ye're not actually here for a holiday. Ye're here on the record company's dollarooos, so ye're technically at work." His face was *all business, no barbecue*, now, to borrow one of his own ridiculous sayings.

"We're at work?" Richie said. He moved himself around a bit, under my thighs, then he settled. He must have been uncomfortable. Hopefully it was that, and not a rogue boner. I wondered if their willies all worked again this morning, and then I stopped wondering, because bleurgh.

"Yes. It's not just the set on Sunday. It's the whole weekend. Walking around, meeting the fans, getting snapped by the paps. It's all part of the working day, lads. Seamus didn't put ye up in a hotel for three nights for the good of his health, like. Ye've to give something back."

"Seamus paid for these rooms?" Bríd said, before I had a chance to.

"He did, yeah."

"I thought it was Féile that pays for them?" I said.

"Pffffft! Maybe if ye were Blur, like, or even that Nick Cave fella ye all love, who I've never heard of in my life," Brian said.

"Oh," I said. We were definitely no Blur or Nick Cave.

We weren't even a Menswear or a The Wildhearts, whoever the fuck The Wildhearts were (I'd seen them on the poster last night).

"Féile only offered to put ye up on the Saturday night – tonight, I mean - cos of being on first tomorrow. And not in this place, either. In some two star shithole down the road that's basically a youth hostel. So, Seamie says to them, no you're grand so, leave it, and he just paid for the three nights here out of his own pocket, like."

"Jesus! That was sound of him." He must have really loved us, Seamus, I thought. We were pretty loveable, mind. Well, I was. And maybe Richie. And Tim. Niall, at a push.

"It was very sound of him, yeah. And he bought ye all that booze I left here last night, too. So you can pay him back now by going in and putting on something snazzy, and a bit more makeup to hide all the drugs you've been doing and the sleep you've been missing, and then go do a brilliant interview, yes?"

"I think I can manage that, yeah," I said, realising in that moment that Brian only pretended not to notice all the shenanigans we got up to. He knew it all, he just didn't give out to us. Which was kind of sound of him. Very non-judgmental.

"Where's your other half, by the way?" he said, looking at me.

"What?" I wasn't sure what he was on about, my *other half*. It wasn't as if he meant-

"Slattery! Your fecking Siamese twin. Why isn't she joined to your hip this morning like she has been all weekend?" he said. I felt Richie's little giggly laugh go through my legs, which felt strange. Bríd and Benson said nothing.

"Ah, she's AWOL, I think. I'm not her keeper, like." I got up to go and change, before anyone else asked me any more awkward questions. I wasn't worried about her, but if she didn't show up soon, I'd start to be. I hadn't a great track record with people I cared about going missing. Or with them coming back, safe. I put that thought out of my head and pushed in the door to my room. I'd have a quick fag first, then I'd turn this mess into movie magic. Or into Féile TV magic, at least.

*****

"Are you naked, or can I come in, chickee?" Bríd hadn't been long following me in.

"Well, I'm *half*-naked, but you can fully come in," I said. I had the radio on, tuned to some rock and roll oldies thing. *American Girl* by Tom Petty was on. I couldn't hear that one now without thinking of Buffalo Bill and lotions getting put in baskets.

"Grand so," she said, coming through, "I've been sent to give you a hand."

"Sent by who?" I had my makeup nearly done already. Just needed to take the towel off my head and do the blow dry and diffuse trick. I hadn't had a full shower again, I just did the hair and hopped out. The fan was on, so the rest of me was dry again before I put on my underwear.

"You look fierce glam, Caoimhe," she said, not answering my question.

"Do I?" I hadn't done much. The only thing different from normal was the lip gloss, which I'd got in London ages ago and never used. It did look great, though – all pink and shiny.

"Yeah, no – I'm talking about this whole - perching on a fancy chair in your posh bra and knickers, with a towel wrap on your head, doing your mascara into a mirror with lights all around it - situation." I looked around at her and she was making a frame shape with her fingers at me. "All we need is for you to be in black and white, now, Rita Hayworth. Click, click!"

"Hahah! I didn't even realise I was doing something special, like." I was just being myself. Clearly I had Old School Glamour flowing through my veins. It felt lovely, someone saying nice things to me, though. I needed it this morning.

"You're just a natural star, Caoimhe. Bottle some of it up and give it to me, yeah?"

"You don't need it, honey. You're a classic beauty, shur." I leaned down to plug in the hairdryer, and it made a loud *VOOOOOOO* noise, frightening the shit out of both of us. Must've left the switch on the last time I used it.

"Am I?" she said, after I'd shut off the racket for a second.

"Well you must be, if there's auld fellas from the 1960s after you," I said, turning the noise on again so I couldn't hear whatever she was gonna say back to that.

*****

"So what level of sluttiness are we talking about here?" Benson, or B, was driving us to the stadium. Brian seemed to have stolen the Ardscoil minibus to use as his personal automobile to ferry himself and Aisling around. I hadn't seen it since we'd arrived yesterday. I hadn't seen her at all, I didn't think.

"My outfits aren't slutty!" I said.

"You're the one who said they were!" Bríd said. Apparently the things in the bags were my stage clothes – Dad was supposed to have them delivered for me tomorrow morning, but he'd sent them a day early. I didn't know why, I hadn't talked to him since Thursday night, but maybe he thought it'd be smarter to get them there well before time, in case there was some delay with them on Sunday morning. He was dead clever, sometimes.

"I said they were vampish. And I may have said whorish." Definitely didn't say slutty.

"Potayto, tomahto," said Richie. He was coming to do the interview with me, since Ian was still asleep or dead, and Niall had disappeared with Frank. Tim was with us in the van too, but Brian wasn't very into the idea of putting him in front of a camera, for some reason. He could sit in on the one for Hot Press, though. That was only on a tape recorder.

"Anyway, can someone elucidate?" Benson said. We were nearly there already. It was still early; the first act wouldn't even be finished yet. The Kelly Family, whoever they were.

"The fuck does that mean?" I said. The elderly knew so many big words, it was almost intimidating.

"It means to make clearer, or to give more details," said Richie, who had apparently swallowed a dictionary recently.

"When did you get so articulated, South?" Tim asked him.

"I've literally got into Trinity College to do a degree in English, you snobby prick," Richie reminded him, and reminded me too, cos I'd forgot that. Or was it 'forgotten'? Richie would probably be able to tell me. He was great at the auld English, apparently.

"Well done, Richie, man!" Benson said, turning us into a parking space.

"Cheers, Mister B. Oh, and it's *articulate*, anyway, Tim. People are articulate, lorries are articulated," said Richie, delighted with himself, altogether.

"Anyway, just wait and see, or you'll spoil the surprise for yourself, lover." Bríd had been nosing through all my outfits back in the room, seeing all the new stuff I had, and she'd asked if she could try some on, and maybe borrow one of the ones that I wouldn't be wearing. It was very unlike her – she would have run a mile before from some of the stuff on that bed - but she'd changed a lot, recently. Especially since she'd met her own personal Mikey Hutchence.

"Exactly. Let's just say you're going to see a side of Bríd you've never seen before, Mister. And you can thank me, afterwards," I said, picturing his jaw on the floor if she came out wearing my latex minidress with the matching stockings. She was welcome to it, really. Any item of clothing that you had to cover yourself in talcum powder just to get on and off without injuring yourself was probably against God and against nature.

"There's lots of sides of Bríd I've never seen before," said Tim, but thankfully no one asked him to elucidate. The engine stopped, and I slid the door open to let in the air, the sunshine, and the absolute bang of hash smoke from someone across the carpark.

*****

"What in the name of all that is holy on Jesus Christ's green Earth is THAT?" I said, pointing up at the group on the stage, but also meaning the noise that they were making. It was a song about wishing you were an angel, from what I could make out. Listening to it was kind of making me wish I was an angel, because at least then I'd be dead.

"That's the Kelly Family," said Tim, helpfully. The stadium was pretty empty, except for a few early arrivers, and us, and what appeared to be the Kelly Family's hardcore fans, up by the barriers.

"I know that, you spanner, I just mean what are they... supposed to be?" There was a whole bunch of them up there. Nine or ten of them. They looked like no band I'd ever seen. There was so much hair, but not in a Heavy Metal way. It was more like they were... I couldn't think of the word now.

"Tinkers, are they?" Richie said.

"Richie!" Bríd said, smacking him on the arm.

"Ow! What did I say now?"

"We don't call them that anymore," I said. I was still gawking at the freaks up there. Their outfits were just mental. Like some sort of Oktoberfest/Leprechaun/First Holy Communion combination. And what the hell was this song? The child-sized being doing lead vocals had no gender, it was just a vessel to transport hair, as far as I could make out.

"What do we call them then? Itinerants, is it?" Benson asked. I didn't think that was right, either.

"Travellers," I said, because there was nothing bad sounding about that word. And also, it described what they liked doing. A descriptive noun, as Richie might call it, up there in Trinity. He'd deferred, so he wasn't actually there yet. We were all deferring this year, the rest of us, so he'd have to defer again. He might never actually get to do the course. Drummers in bands were always dying. I'd seen Spinal Tap enough times to know that.

"They're not Travellers, though. Or Itinerants, or anything like that," Tim said, and we all turned to hear his inside scoop.

"What are they, then?" I said, not even sure these things were of our world, and wishing someone would banish them back to whichever dark hell they'd slithered out from.

"Yanks!" he said, and suddenly it became clearer. They did look like what Americans who'd never been to Ireland thought Irish people looked like.

"Irish Americans, is it?" Benson said. We were almost at the gate. I looked at him for a second, thinking how was he gonna get in with us, but then I spotted his pass around his neck, which he'd obviously had all day yesterday as well, and I wondered why I'd forget that, but maybe I was dying of brain rot now, on top of everything else.

"I think so, yeah. They're very big in Germany, is all I know."

"So is David Hasselhoff," I said, and everyone nodded or grunted, because we all remembered that Berlin Wall concert, and the enormous crowd. The Germans were not to be trusted on matters of music. There were few things they'd done in World War 2 that compared with the atrocity of making Mitch Buchanan from Baywatch a multi-platinum-selling recording artist. At least the war crimes were punished. No one had been tried at Nuremberg for the success of *Looking For Freedom*.

*****

"Well, now! You scrub up nice, don't ya? You'll do, fair play. Nice one, Cyril." Brian looked me up and down like he was my Mum inspecting me before the first day of school. He was already backstage when we got there. The beautiful Aisling as well, looking like she'd had plenty of sleep last night, despite his lies about wearing her out. I had no idea why he was calling me Cyril, but with him it was often best not to ask.

"Shut up, Brian. She's a strong, independent, autonomous woman and she doesn't need your approval of what she wears."

"Thanks, Ash," I said, although I was pretty sure she'd just called me a robot.

"Ah, go'way with your Germaine Greer shite at this hour of the morning. I was giving her a compliment, shur. Can't say anything anymore these days, or ye'll bite our heads off," he said, suddenly looking about fifty.

"I don't read Greer, Brian. It's the 1990s – there's a new wave of feminist thinking. You'd have noticed that if you took your head out of your arse long enough to pay attention to anything other than the rugby scores." I liked this one. She could stay.

"Did she not write that yoke you've always got your head buried in, then?" said Brian to her, giving me a look for lighting up a fag, even though we were outside in the open air, and I was an independent cyborg female.

"You mean The Beauty Myth? By Naomi Wolf?" She gave him a look that would wither plastic flowers.

"Probably, I dunno, I was listening for the rugby scores," he said, smacking her on the bum, which didn't make her go mental at all, to my surprise. She just chuckled, and then she smacked his arse herself. True equality, in our time.

It wasn't as if I'd put on anything fancy. Just the Breeders t-shirt that I'd turned into a belly top with Mum's sewing machine, and my Miss Sixty bell-bottom jeans, which I'd also done a bit of customising to – they fit really well around the bum, but the front was too tight, so I took out the buttons from the fly and put a ribbon in the holes instead, like shoelaces, so I could loosen it or tighten it depending on how much I needed to. Looked really cool, as well as being comfortable, and it made them a one-off. A bit like me.

"Will we go get a drink?" I said, to no one in particular. Richie was the only one who heard me, anyway.

"What, for a change, like?" he said, sarcastically. We'd been drinking all morning, but in fairness it was only Bulmer's, and I'd had so much ice melting into mine it might as well have been shandy.

"Well, if we drink something that isn't cider, that's technically a change," I said. I fancied a gin and tonic, with an actual slice of lemon in it, if they had such an exotic, decadent thing here.

"Good thinking outta you," he said, then he put his arm around my waist, all friendly-like, and escorted me to the bar.

*****

"I wonder where Ciara is?" I said, a little later, trying to sound casual about it. They did indeed have sliced lemons behind the bar. They had Bombay Sapphire too, which made my mood shoot up so high I was almost in the promised land of *feeling nothing*, where Brídclaimed I should rightfully be.

"Dunno, her ex's place?" Richie was drinking a Bacardi and Diet Coke. He wasn't on a diet – he was skinny as a rake – he just didn't like *the red Coke*, as he called it.

"Her ex?" I scrunched up my face at him. *What you talkin' bout, Willis?*

"Yeah. She has some boyfriend – sorry, he used to be her boyfriend – who lives here, in Cork. That's where she was yesterday, like."

"Yesterday when?" This was all news to me. News I didn't like. I got a horrible feeling down in the pit of my stomach, and felt it start to move up to my chest.

"Umm, early on. That's why she didn't see Ash, yeah? Brídand Benson were here, out in the crowd – Brídis mad into Ash, like. Ciara didn't come along til after they were finished." He had a straw with his drink. He said it made you get drunk quicker, but I didn't know if that was true. I'd need to see the science.

"I see. And how do you know all this?" More importantly, how didn't I know all this? I was her *very close* friend. Or I used to be, anyway, fuck's sake.

"Ah, just from talking to Bríd, yesterday, like."

"Right. And who is he, this fella? When were they together, like? When did they break up? Why did they break up? Why would she-"

"Jesus, calm down, Kweev."

"Sorry," I said. Too many questions at once, and no answers yet. I drank some drink and lit up a fag.

"You're grand. Look, I don't know anything else, shur. You'd have to ask herself, like. When she shows up, I mean." He shrugged, and his face did the thing you did with your face while shrugging. What was that called? An *i dunno*?

"Ah, okay then. Maybe that's where she is. Doesn't matter, as long as she's okay." Okay absolutely RIDING some fella all morning and all day, I thought. The bad feeling was already up in my chest at this point. Or in my heart. Either way, it was shit.

*****

"Okay, good – I'm all set up here, guys, so it's up to you. Do you wanna wait a bit and see if this Tim guy shows, or... will we just go ahead with you two?" We were three or four drinks deep, as the Yanks would say, by the time Matt from Hot Press showed up to do our interview. We hadn't been planning on having that much booze, but as Richie said, "Fuck it, it's Christmas!"

"We don't need him, Matt. You have the real meat and veg of the band right here, shur. No other ingredients necessary. No need to put gravy on us. You can skip dessert," I said, letting that metaphor run away from me a bit. We were still sitting up at the bar, but Matt had brought over a stool to join us.

"Interesting... So, we've met before, yeah?" Matt had a proper Dublin 4 accent, he sounded somewhere between a cheesy nightclub DJ and someone who read the news on TV. Like a gowl, basically. He was probably grand, though.

"Yes!" I said, because we had.

"No!" Richie said, because they hadn't.

"Oh, that's right, the last interview was just with you, wasn't it?"

"Yeah, there was a photoshoot and stuff. They made me hold a cat." I'd hated that cat, but I didn't like any cats at all, so the little guy had been onto a loser from the start.

"A cat? Why was that again?" A radio DJ, that's what he sounded like. One of those breakfast show ones who were a bit too chirpy when you were trying to have a hangover in peace.

"Because of some tenuous link to a cover song we were doing at the time, and we occasionally still do, about a witch," I said, rolling my eyes at it all, but high-fiving myself on the inside for using such a fancy word.

"Hmmm, tenuous. Nice," Matt said, unable to ignore the eye-watering girth of my drunken vocabulary.

"Twas far from "tenuous" ye were raised," Richie said, sounding like his Dad, Mick, for a second.

"So, you've come for the whole weekend, even though you're not playing until Sunday?" Matt raised an inquisitive eyebrow, as journalists probably did a lot.

"Well, yes. We're very lucky that our incredible boss at Crabtree records-"

"Seamus Ryan, right?"

"The very man," I said, almost giving Seamus a wave at home before I remembered this wasn't the TV interview.

"Yeah, Seamie is sound as a pound, like. MCD were too stingy to put us up for the weekend, Matt. Can you imagine that, hah?" Richie said, looking cross in the way four double Bacardis on top of four cans of cider, with only a ham sandwich in between, might make you look cross.

"Scandalous. So, have you seen a lot of the bands, or…"

"We saw the Kelly Family, earlier today," I said, doing a yikes face.

"Not a fan, I take it?" Matt said, laughing. He'd weird

teeth. I didn't know why they were weird; I'd just made up my mind that they were, and that was that.

"They're not Tinkers, you know."

"RICHIE!" I instinctively slapped the back of his hand like I was his mum, and he was a bauld pup of a child.

"Ow! Fuck's sake, Kweev!" He rubbed himself way too dramatically for the lightness of the tap I'd given him, the big baby.

"Right, moving on. Um, Kweeva you and I covered a lot of stuff about the band and the songs, etcetera, in our last interview. But this is the first chance I have to ask one of the lads a question that's specific to them, yeah?"

"Okay," I said, picking up my G&T.

"So, Richie. You're, how can I put it, *different* from the rest of the band, yes?" Matt had his more serious journo face on now, looking at Rich. Weird question, considering I was the one who was actually different from all of them, on account of me having a vajayjay.

"How do you mean, like?" he said. He was still drinking with a straw, even in front of the world's media. No shame, that boy.

"Well... I mean, in terms of your socioeconomic background, and-"

"My what, now?" This might be about to get interesting, I thought, leaning in.

"Oh. It means that you-"

"I know what socioeconomic means, sham."

"Yeah, he knows what it means, Matt. He got an A1 in English in his Leaving Cert, you know." I suddenly felt really protective of Richie, not that he needed me to be.

"Oh, I'm sorry, I-" Hot Press Matt was all a-fluster now.

"I've a place in Trinity waiting for me an' all, only I'd to defer," Richie went on, getting more Limerick with every syllable.

"Oh, cool. Congratulations!" Matt said, looking a bit like he thought Rich might stab him, because all Dublin people thought they were in danger of getting stabbed by Limerick people, with no exceptions.

"Aw, thanks, man," Richie said, softening a bit, and relaxing back onto his stool. The storm had passed, or at the very least, we were in the eye of it.

"Anyway, will I go on to the next question?" Matt said, looking down at his notes, his hands shaking a bit. This was gas. I'd almost forgotten how down I felt. Well, until just now, when I remembered again. Fuck's sake.

"Please," I said, because I assumed it was the right move. Rich had other ideas though.

"No, hang on a minute, lemme explain, or expand, or-"

"Elucidate!" I said, looking around for my prize.

"Haha, shuddup you," said Richie, giving my hair a little ruffle that felt quite nice all the same.

"Okay, what was it you wanted to say?" Matt made sure his little microphone was near to Richie, and I lit up a fag, in case it was going to be a ripping yarn.

"You see, Matt, when I joined this band, it had a slightly different line-up, as you know yourself."

"Ah yes, Jon Musgrave – he was your original singer, up until-"

"Up until last year, yeah. Listen there's no need to get into all that stuff now, everyone knows what happened to Jon, and I don't wanna be causing herself any upset here, when-"

"No, I understand," Matt said to him, then he gave me

one of those sympathetic nods that I hated so much.

"I'm fine, lads. Ye can talk away, ye can. Don't mind me, I'll be grand." I wasn't gonna let anyone think I was this delicate little flower that had to be minded all the time, cos I bloody wasn't. Well, maybe I was today, but that was different. That had fuck all to do with Jon, or with Áine.

"No, it's not important, Caoimhe. The point I want to make is just that, when that was the lineup, I was okay joining the band. Cos even though it was a load of posh boys, I had Jon there, and he was not only from down my place – Thomondgate, Matt – but he was my friend as well. So I'd someone like me, and who I liked. In the band."

Richie looked genuinely sad when he mentioned Jon. They had drifted apart a bit in the years before Rich joined Crane, but back in the old days they used to be best friends. And they were starting to be best friends again, he'd told me, one time. He'd lost Jon too that night. And, worse, he was there, and he saw it happen.

"And that was very important, yeah?"

"Yeah, very." Richie finished his drink, still using a straw, and the resulting slurpy noise sort of took the gravitas out of the previous moment, but it took some of the tension away too, so I was glad of it.

"And can you tell us why?" Matt asked, but I wanted to know too, of course.

"Well because, and now Matt, I don't expect you to understand this, or to be able to empathise – you've a fair auld D4 accent on you there, where did you go to school, The Rock?"

"Heh. I did go to Blackrock College, yes. Well spotted. Why?" Matt looked bemused.

"Thought so. Well, the best way I can try to explain it is - after four double Bacardis anyway, sham – uhhhhh. What

I'm saying is that there's *haves* and there's *have nots* in the world. I'm a have not, Jon was a have not."

"Right..." Matt had really stupid hair, why was I only noticing this now?

"Whereas Ian, Tim, Nailer, and our manager, Brillo, wherever that fucker has got to – pardon my French, sorry – well, they're all haves. And see, Matt – this is the bit you won't really understand, and look, I'm not gonna blame you for it either, like." Richie paused so he could order us more drinks, which he did without a word. Just nodded at the barman, like we fucking lived here now, or something. What a life we led.

"I'm listening, carry on," Matt said.

"All I'm saying is, the haves don't believe that they're haves. The rich, well people richer than me anyway – they don't think they're rich. Don't get me wrong, they know they're richer than people like me, Matt. And they've often no problem telling me as much, the pricks, especially when you're younger, in school like. But they're always like, "Oh, we're just *comfortable*!" Or "Oh we're *well off*, but we're not *rich*!" And do you know why that is, Matt?"

"Ummm, no?"

"It's because when you've money, you only socialise with other people who have money. You're never down where I live, hanging around with random poor people. You stay in your posh area, and in your wealthy social set. You only know poor people if they work for you, and you only meet poor people when they're waiting on your table or whatever. You don't have any poor friends. Just other rich ones."

"And, because you're not *friends* with any poorer people, you never spend time with poorer people and hear how tough it is for them, so you don't appreciate how good you have it?" Matt said.

"YES! I underestimated you, Matty boy. Judged a book by its accent. But yeah, that's it. And, on top of that, if you're quite rich, you're definitely gonna have friends who are so rich, they nearly make you feel poor, do you get me?"

"I do, yes. That's very true, very interesting. So, when – and we'll speed past the details here – when Jon was no longer in Crane and it was just you, and these guys who although you got on with them fine, you felt apart from them-"

"Yeah, I didn't even explain why, properly, sorry man, I'm a bit langered. I felt like they just didn't understand why I sometimes didn't have the *readies* to chip in for things, right? Like for a demo tape, maybe. Or hiring a PA, for a gig. I couldn't just ask my Da for it. There was no bottomless pit of savings. There was no savings at all."

"And because of this, did you feel like leaving the band, after, well, after Jon was gone?"

"I did." Richie had never told me this before, I was gripped, even though I knew how this story ended, since he was literally still in the band.

"So, what changed your mind?" Matt said. What, indeed?

"This one here," Richie said, putting his arm around me.

"The one and only Kweeva Shox, yeah?" Matt said, chuckling, as if I somehow wasn't the one and only Kweeva Shox.

"What, little ol' me?" I said, delighted that someone had finally acknowledged my *worth* in this world, like.

"Yeah. Cos, I mean – you're brilliant at the singing, and your songs that you write are amazing as well, but it wasn't that." Richie paused like he was trying to fight the Bacardi and come up with something poignant.

"Ah it was, a little bit, though," I said. Our drinks arrived, as well as a bottle of Miller for Matt.

"Haha! Yeah, okay, a little bit."

"Was it that Kweeva was socioeconomically... no, wait. Your dad owns Shaughnessy & Partners International, doesn't he? You must be absolutely loaded!" Matt said, which felt a mite personal and intrusive, but I'd let him off, cos it was Christmas.

"Oh yeah, we're fucking minted, like!" I said, laughing.

"She's a treehouse out the back that's bigger than my Da's actual house, like. Her driveway is longer than our whole four house terrace," Richie said, still hugging my waist.

"We have a gardener, AND a fucking maid!" I said. "Her name is Dolores!" I was laughing my head off now, so was Richie.

Matt looked very confused.

"But surely that means you're more of a... *have*, than any of the other lot in Crane? Why is- why does-" We'd broken Matt, it seemed.

"Well, because of this, like. Here!" Richie said, although I didn't quite know what he meant, but then I did, once my stupid brain caught up.

"Because of ..." Matt said, still holding his little microphone.

"I think he's saying that he doesn't mind me being rich because I admit I'm rich and I know I'm really lucky to be rich and like, my privilege isn't invisible to me, so it doesn't wind him up the way it does with other posh or rich people. That's it, isn't it, Rich?"

"Pretty much, yeah, like. You're rich, but you're not a fucking cunt about it. Pardon my French again, Matt."

"Ah, now. I am, sometimes," I said, although I wasn't,

really.

"You're not, and here – come here and I tell you one last thing – on this subject anyway, Matt," Richie said, looking solemn now.

"What's that?"

"The other reason I stuck around and didn't leave – the other reason I love this youngone so much, no matter how many millions her Da has in the bank, yeah? It's cos she was good enough for my pal Jon, and she thought my pal Jon was good enough for her, and it didn't matter to her where he lived or what money his Ma and Da had, Matt. He was good enough for her, so she's good enough for me." I wasn't expecting Richie South to be the first person to make me cry today, but at least they were happy tears. Most of them, anyway.

THIRTEEN

"No, I honestly never did, Rich. Not before last night. You must be mixing me up with someone else." Richie and me had gone for a toke, away from the bar, because we were VIPs, but we weren't that cheeky. Well, I was having the toke. Richie never did, cos of his whiteners. Except sometimes he forgot about the whiteners, if he was already wrecked, and he had a puff or two. It never ended well.

"You definitely took yokes before," he insisted, as if he knew me more than I knew myself.

"When was that, so?" The hash was strong. I'd got it off some guy in the bar, after the interview was over. He didn't charge me anything, he just broke off a nodge and wrapped it in a skin for me. Sound, like. No idea who he was or who he belonged to. He didn't even invite himself along for a smoke, like most people would.

"Am, the night you first met Jon? He told me ye did, anyway, when he told me how ye met. Said ye met in the street, after the gig, and then you said you were getting a taxi home, so we all went to that party and he took a yoke, but then he met you again out on the roof, and then ye were both on yokes together? I remembered it last night, when I was falling asleep, like." He said all this so carefully it was like watching someone playing *Operation!* and trying to pull a liver out with tweezers without setting off the buzzer. There was no need, really, but he was just being sweet.

"Oh! Yeah, no, I see where you're getting that idea now. It's, well, it didn't quite happen like that, but maybe Jon thought it did."

I remembered that night so well. It had become weirdly significant, long after the fact. For one thing, it was the night of Crane's first proper gig together, before I even knew who they were. As well as that, even though I'd only talked to Jon all night, the rest of them had all been at the party – the whole band, plus Harta, and Bríd, and Ciara. But I didn't know any of them yet, so I wouldn't have recognised them if I'd bumped into them. But now, they were all my friends, and I was in that band. How freaky was that? Kismet, or something.

"What do you mean?" said Richie. There was a band on stage, I didn't know which one it was. Either Joyrider or Reef, going by the flyers, but I didn't know any Joyrider songs and only the one Reef one, so unless *Place Your Hands* came on, I'd no idea. Sleeper and Lush would be on in a bit, I was going out front for both of those, definitely.

"What do I mean, what?" The hash had made me temporarily forget what he was asking me about. The hash, or all the gin. Both were equally possible.

"You said I'm wrong about you taking yokes that night, like. Can I have a smoke off that, yeah?"

"Nope. You can't, Richie."

"Why not?" he looked annoyed. He shouldn't have been, he should've been glad I'd more sense than to be giving him hash.

"Cos you don't actually want it, you just think you do," I said, then I dropped it on the concrete and squashed it with my shoe, so there would be no more discussion about it.

"Lousy…" he said, but then he smiled, cos he knew I was only minding him.

"Tough love, baby," I said, and then we walked over to the toilets while I explained to him how I'd been on a bunch of speed and hash that night when Jon met me out on the roof at the party, and how he'd been going on and on about how he could only ever talk to other people who were on yokes when he was on yokes, so I'd told him a little white lie about being on one myself, cos I didn't want him to stop talking to me or to go away.

It wasn't a serious lie or anything. I was obviously off my face, so he never copped on that I was on something different from what he was. What he didn't know couldn't hurt him, and all that. Then, on the night of the Battle of the Bands, I was gonna do yokes with him for real, but of course Harta never came back with them for us. All of that seemed like such a long time ago now, even though it had barely been a year.

*****

"How did it go? You're not pissed, are you? Or on something else?" Brian was by the big trestle table of food when I came back. Richie was still in the toilets; I'd come back without him.

"Shut up, Dad. And yeah, it went grand, shur. Not a bother." Matt had asked us a few more questions to get a proper article together, and we'd given him some good answers, I thought. I'd asked him to be careful not to make Richie out to hate the lads in the band, cos he didn't hate them at all, like. He'd said he'd try and write a fair article, whatever that meant. We'd see.

"Right, right. So are ye ready for the next one?" He had his Guinness in an actual glass today. He was learning.

"Well I am, but Rich is still in the bogs, I think." I could hear other music that wasn't coming from the stage. I looked over beyond and saw they had a little shack thing, with a mostly acoustic band playing. Looked cool, I'd go over in a bit and listen to them.

"Is he? What's he doing in there?" Brian looked at his Tag Heuer, as was the custom.

"I'd imagine he's going to the toilet, Brian."

"Probably better not to imagine him doing anything else, like. Okay, well when he's ready, come and find me, and I'll give the RTÉ lads a shout on the auld Motorola, yeah?" Brian had a mobile phone now, courtesy of Seamus. No need for it, like. He looked like Zack Morris, lugging that thing around with him.

"Okay, you do that, I'm gonna stuff my face now until I pass out," I said, loading up my plate with chips, rice, and curry sauce. The old 3-in-1, like they used to eat in the Bible. Someone came up beside me.

"Save some for the rest of us, yeah, tubby?" It was Niall.

"I'm not fat, I'm just *retaining cider*," I said, elbowing him in the ribs - or it was probably in the hip - the fucking height of him.

"Hahahhh. You going outside to watch the bands?"

"In a while, when the good ones come on. Why, is that where you've been?" I thought about Ciara, and had she surfaced yet. I stopped thinking about her then, just because.

"Kind of. I've been helping Frank," said Niall, putting a rake of cocktail sausages on his plate, and some stir fry veg, as if they complemented each other in the slightest, the philistine.

"Helping him? Helping him with what? Did he fall over?" I poured myself a pint of iced water from the big jug they had. The sun was absolutely scorching already, but at least the food place was in the shade.

"Ah, just a bit of business, love, don't worry about it," he said, probably thinking he sounded like Tony Montana, instead of like a middle class kid from Ashbrook trying to be all *street*.

"Oh, Niall. Be careful now, okay? You're not Frank," I said. The last thing we needed was our bass player being arrested for dealing drugs, although Brian would probably end up saying it was "great PR", and turning Nailer into the new Liam Gallagher.

"I'm always careful, Booboo. I'm smarter than the average bear," he said, putting a scoop of mashed potato on top of the other stuff on his plate, and I turned away from it in case I vomited all over my chips.

*****

"Okay! Okay, we ready for Take 2, Crane?" said Pat O'Mahoney, even though we hadn't done a Take 1 yet. Then I copped on he was making a joke about this being the second time we'd tried to have an interview.

"Ready when you are, Patrick," Niall said. He'd stepped in at the last minute, as Richie was nowhere to be found. He was wearing a gorgeous Blur t-shirt, for the day that was in it. Navy blue, with white ring bands on the sleeves and neck. There was a name for that particular style – a really simple, obvious name - but I couldn't think of it, now. Mum would know, definitely. Mum's brain wasn't addled with last night's drugs and this afternoon's gin, mind. Hopefully not, anyway.

"Excellent, okay Charlie, roll camera," said Pat. He was sitting in the middle again, although I was on the opposite side to where I'd been in the last interview, which already made it feel strange. My mouth tasted like curry sauce and fags, so I'd try not to breathe on him too much if I could help it.

"Okay, we're backstage here with one of Ireland's most promising up and coming bands, Limerick's own Crane. How's the craic, guys and gals?"

"I'm grand, Pat. How's your own crack?" Niall said, getting us off to a flyer already.

"Heheh, it's good, Niall. Can't complain. How about you, Kweeva Shox? Been getting a bit of sun, I see?" Didn't hear him asking Niall about his tan - bit sexist. Although Niall was physically incapable of getting a tan, being ginger, so maybe it wasn't.

"Well, yeah. I mean it's up there in the sky, like. Hard to avoid it," I said. I gave him what I imagined was an enigmatic smile, but I probably just looked steamed to him. I was back on the G&Ts, post-nosh.

"True, true. So lads, what's been your experience of Féile so far? First time here, yeah?" He had a microphone in his hand, and we had one each as well. A recipe for interrupty disaster, I thought.

"It's everyone's first time here, isn't it?" said Niall. I wondered who he'd robbed the T-shirt off, since he didn't seem like the type to like Blur. Or to like any band that normal people enjoyed. They had merch stalls around the stadium though, maybe he'd treated himself.

"Yeah, like. It was on in Thurles for the last... five years," I said, doing the maths quickly in my head.

"Huh? Oh, right, yes. First time at a Féile in general though? Even as a fan?" Pat was looking at Niall, but I answered, making him have to swing his head around to me.

"Yeah, I was gonna go last year, but I was a bit too down, like. Couldn't shake off the blues, Pat."

"You were? Why was that? The usual, yeah? Exams? Hormones? Boys? The parents on your case all the time, is it?"

"Oh no, nothing like that, Pat. No, see my sister got murdered, and then my boyfriend got hit by a truck, like."

"Oh. Oh, wow. I'm so sorry," Pat said, looking like he

wanted the couch to swallow him up.

"Why, were you driving it?" I said, absolutely straight-faced.

"Huh???"

"What a plot twist!" Niall said, dropping his jaw in mock shock horror. Charlie who was working the camera had gone four shades whiter than normal in about five seconds. We let the two of them stew for another thirty seconds or so, then we burst out laughing and said sorry to poor Pat, and got on with the interview properly, on our best behaviour, cos Brian would have absolutely killed us if we ruined this one too.

*****

"Well now, that wasn't too hard, was it?" said Brian, after we'd finished up. He hadn't been there for the start, thank God, so he was none the wiser about all the earlier malarkey.

"Easy peasy, melon squeezey," I said, grabbing my boobs through the t-shirt. I was feeling quite silly now, which was better than being mired in a bottomless well of despair.

"Grapefruits, maybe," Niall said, the cheeky get. They actually looked much bigger than normal in this top, so he was incorrect as well as rude.

"Shut up, Mr. Flump," I said, but he didn't understand, so it was wasted on him.

"Speaking of your diddies, you nearly lost the rag with poor Pat O'Mahoney there, didn't you? Bit touchy today, yeah?" Brian said. *Diddies*, like. Who said things like that after the age of ten?

"I'm not touchy, you fucking prick," I said, not making a great case for myself. "When was I touchy?" We were nearly at the bar, I wondered had Richie reappeared or would he just join the missing list with the others.

"Calm down, Shaughnessy. Jaysus, I'm only teasing you, Maurice," Brian said. Calling people Maurice, that was another Brianism.

"Okay, but when did I – oh, do you mean when he was being a sexist pig, like?" I said. I lit a fag. Box was nearly empty, I needed to get change for the machine.

"He wasn't being a sexist pig," Niall said, as if anyone had asked him. I was surrounded by men here; I needed some reinforcements from the vajayjay community. Where was Bríd? Where was Ciara? I remembered where Ciara probably was then, so I stopped thinking about her whereabouts.

"Yeah, all he did was ask you about your stage clothes, like. It was just a question," Brian said. We were at the near end of the bar now, but I didn't fancy anything yet.

"Yeah, but he was talking about how... *revealing* they are." No one understood me. I looked around to see if Bríd was here.

"So?" said Brian, trying to get the barman's attention by waving a 20 pound note at him. Why he was doing that at a free bar was anyone's guess.

"Were you not listening? All I said to him was that he was only asking me because I'm a woman – and that Robert Plant used to go around wearing spray-on jeans, showing off his massive langer, and all those Hair Metal guys in their Spandex leggings, like – how if he was interviewing them, he wouldn't be bringing up shit like that, he'd be talking about the music, yeah?" I'd no idea why I had to repeat all this; both of them had been there.

"All right, all right, I get you. Give it a rest though, yeah? Jaysus, I get enough of that off Aisling," Brian said, finally catching the barman's eye.

"You get enough of what off me?" said Aisling, appearing beside him like she'd been beamed aboard by Scotty.

"Bloody hell, you'll give me a heart attack someday, woman!" he said, giving her a hug and a peck on the lips.

"In your dreams, maybe," she said, giving me a wink to say hi.

"Look who the cat's after dragging in, lads. What've they been up to, eh? Dirty bastards," said Niall. I turned to see who he meant, and my silly mood disappeared in an instant. It was Ciara. With Ian. They were laughing away together, standing over with Bríd and Benson. Ian had his arm around Ciara – around *my* Ciara. I got a horrible feeling in the middle of my chest, and it started spreading out, making it hard to breathe. I wanted to look away, but I couldn't. Ciara didn't even like him, really – as a friend, or as anything else. What the hell was going on? Was that where she'd been all this time? In his room? Was that why he wouldn't answer his door all morning? Were they – had they - it didn't make sense? I stopped looking, before either of them looked back at me. I wanted to cry again, but this time none of my tears would be happy ones.

"You okay, Kweev?" Niall said, beside me. I didn't look at him.

"I'm fine. I'm just – I'm going to the toilet. I've to go to the toilet. I'll be – I'm fine." I walked off, lighting a new fag off the old one before it was even finished. I didn't need to go to the loo, I just didn't want to be here anymore.

*****

"You're those Revelinos, aren't you?" I said to the guy sitting at the front of the acoustic shed thing, after I finished clapping for the last song they'd played.

"We're *Revelino*, but yeah, close enough," he said, smiling at me from behind his sunglasses.

"Ah, ye're great, ye are," I said. "*And it feels, LIIIIIIII-*

IIIKE!" I sang a bit from their big hit song at him, a bit too loud, judging by how much he flinched. I'd had an absolute rake of speed in the toilet to get my head straight, but it might have made my head a bit fucked instead. Oh dear.

"Heh. Yeah, that's the one," said Revelino Man, stepping down off his stool and putting his guitar in its stand.

"Sorry! Must be so annoying when people do that!" I said, not as mortified as I should have been. I wanted a drink, but I was avoiding the bar like the plague, because I didn't want to go anywhere near there while Ciara and Ian were around.

"Beer?" said yer man, like some sort of mind-reader angel.

"Oh God, yeah. Thanks!" I took the can of Carlsberg off him and snapped it open. It was icy cold, too.

"No probs, man. Caoimhe it is, isn't it?" Christ, everybody knew my name at this thing, it was like being in the theme song off Cheers.

"That's me, yes."

"Nice to meet ya, I'm Bren. Listen, I've to make a dash for a slash, do you wanna..." He made a gesture with his head that I didn't quite understand.

"Do I want to come to the toilet with you? Bren, darling - we've only just met!"

"Hahaaa! You're funny. No, do you wanna hop up there and play us a tune while I'm gone, like?"

"Ooh! Can I?" I'd been enjoying their little *seisún*, but it'd be amazing to have a go myself, definitely. Hopefully I wasn't too speed-wracked to be in tune, but even so, fuck it, it was Christmas.

"Be my guest – guitar is there, it's in tune, must dash, I'm booorstin'!" Bren the Revelino Man said, grabbing his undercarriage for dramatic effect, and then disappearing towards the loos. I gave the guys in his band a nod or two and sat down in front of the mic stand. The guitar had pick-ups, but the amps had been quiet, and their drummer was only using a little jazz kit with brushes instead of sticks.

"Kay, then. I'm just gonna…" I realised I was talking into the mic instead of to them, so I turned around on the stool. "Sorry. You might know this one – you definitely don't know it as an unplugged one, but it's really easy. I'll start it myself, but we're going A minor, C, D; A minor, C, D, A minor, looped around for the verses, until the last chord going into the chorus, change the A minor to a G there. Chorus is A minor, F, C G, A minor-"

"Caoimhe?" said their bass player, waving his fingers at me.

"Yes, babe?"

"Are you going to play *Hurt*? By Nine Inch Nails?" he said.

"Well, yeah. I am, actually." This guy must be some sort of musical genius, I thought.

"Lovely, I know it, and these two will be able to follow us easy, yeah?" he said, meaning the drummer and the other guitarist lad.

"Brilliant," I said, turning around to look at the people in front of us. It wasn't exactly a crowd, but it was an audience. I'd never played this song in front of people before – I hadn't even done it at practice with the boys. I usually just played it in my room, by myself, when I was feeling sad. I played the first three notes, and the people looked up from their chats and their drinks. I started singing, and it felt like all the badness of the day just spilled out of me into those angsty, cathartic lyrics, and with every line I sang I felt a little better and a little stronger. But then the chorus came, with the bit about everyone I know going away in the end, and I had to hold in the tears, in case I made a show of myself.

*****

"Cheers, Caoimhe. Yous were fantastic, fair play. Loved that last one, too," Bren said, when I handed him back the guitar. We'd played one more song, - *Both Sides Now*, by Joni Mitchell – and we'd made the little audience into a much bigger audience, so I was delighted with myself altogether. Also, I'd seen this tall, stunning looking Asian girl with mad purple hair in the crowd watching, and she'd been smiling her head off at me, like she knew me, or something. I definitely didn't know her, though. I wouldn't forget someone who looked like her in a hurry. She was like a sexy cartoon. Like one of those Manga ones, or whatever they were called. Niall had loads of them on video. He'd have loved her. I had a look around to see was she still here, but she wasn't. Here one minute, gone the next. Like the Lone Ranger, or that homeless Alsatian dog from Canada.

Sleeper were about to go on, cos I heard two girls talking about them and then heading for the gate out, so I headed that way too. Might as well, it could be fun being in the crowd with a load of strangers, and I wasn't going back to the bar to find anyone to come with me anyway. I didn't know what was going on and I didn't want to have to think about it right now. I'd had fun today, so far, despite the awful feelings inside my head and the ones in my heart, too. I didn't need to go back to the lads yet, I was at a music festival full of thousands of other people, and even if I felt dead on the inside I was whizzing with enough chemicals and booze to fuel me on a little adventure by myself for a couple of hours. I didn't owe anyone any explanation and I didn't owe them my company or my time. I was my own person, and I was a big girl. I'd be grand. I'd be more than grand, I'd be great. I was going through the fence when I heard someone calling my name.

"Caoimhe? Caoimhe, darling! Hey, over here!" I looked to where the voice was coming from. It was Miss Asian Cartoon Girl – she was back. The plot was thickening. I walked over. She had two very good-looking lads with her, one either side. When she saw I was coming, she told them to leave, and they immediately did. She didn't say anything. She just did a little dismissive gesture with her hands, and off they went. She was like a Dracula, or something.

"*Fuck me pink*, where did you GET that top? It's *ssss-sickening!*" She had a very distinctive voice. It didn't sound… Asian. It was like a cross between posh Dublin and maybe a bit of American. She touched the hem of my top, then she put her fingers under it and slid them from left to right, across my ribs. Her fingernails were long enough to scrape me, but not sharp enough to scratch.

"Um, well I got it in America, like - in California – as a t-shirt, but then I turned it into a crop top myself," I said, still wondering who this mysterious vampire girl was and why she knew my name. Everybody knew my name, though. And they were always glad I came.

"Hmmmmm, did it yourself? Wow. You're like double-talented; I wish I was talented. I heard you singing in there – you're amazing. Lush voice. How do you know Revelino then?"

"Oh, I had a beer with Bren once," I said, which was technically true. I looked at her clothes, because I'd only seen her from the neck up when she was watching me sing. She was beyond OTT. Long, fingerless fishnet gloves. Long, shiny fingernails with a mix of black varnish and white, French manicured tips. Spiked dog collar on her neck. Black leather halter neck top. PVC miniskirt the same shade of purple as her hair. Black opaque hold-ups, and ridiculous, Cyberpunk platform boots with spike heels that looked like needles, they were so thin. She didn't look like she belonged on Earth, let alone in Cork City.

"Cool. But I guess you know all the bands, since you're *in* a band," she said, rooting inside her tiny bag for something. I still didn't know her name. The band on stage were tuning up, but we weren't at the right angle to see them, the big side screen was in the way.

"Yeah, maybe. What band are *you* in, then?" I said, wondering if she'd be offended that I didn't just know who she was, outright. I didn't know many Irish groups, though. I preferred all-female bands, and we didn't have a lot of those, if any.

"Me? In a band? Hah, you're so adorable." She looked like she was about to pick her nose for a second, but she just did a cute little sniff instead, and went back into her bag again.

"I am?"

"I'm not in a band, no. I've never been in a band. A few bands have been in me, but that's a story for another day, baby. Are you cool?" She had her hand out, right in my face, now. Took me a second to notice the white powder in her extra-long baby fingernail.

"Oh! Yes, I'm cool, don't worry," I said, thinking about that scene in Dazed and Confused. I held her hand to keep it steady and then I inhaled the speed as discreetly as you could be discreet when standing in public with someone who drew people's stares as much as this woman did.

"What's the verdict? Nice?" She had the *deepest* green eye colour, with these golden, star-shaped bits around her pupils that reminded me of those photos of galaxies at the edge of the universe that the Hubble telescope took.

"Oof! Jesus Christ. Wow." That was *not* speed. Cocaine? Hopefully just cocaine, anyway. Really should have asked. My whole head was affected by that tiny little bump. Definitely coke, I could already feel the numbness. I still didn't know this chick's name. Insane!

"Yeah, it's *immense* shit, all right. Double-immense. It's like, fuck-expensive. Not that I paid for it or anything, darling. I absolutely *covet* your hair, by the way. It's even more lush, up close. Come on, let's go boogie with the hoi polloi. I'm *Porsche*, by the way…" She reached down and took my hand in hers, and I absolutely let her take it, and take me, too.

"What, like the sports car?" I said, dancing with her into the crowd, which seemed to just part and let us through like magic. I'd been expecting a more *oriental* name, if I was honest.

"Hah! You're double-adorable, Caoimhe O'Shaughnessy. No, it's *Portia*. Like that girl, in the play. Hey! Look up!" On the screens above us, Louise from Sleeper was at the mic, with her guitar. They started playing *Bedhead*, and everyone got a little moshy, me and Portia, the Asian vampire alien sex queen who knew my full real name, included.

*****

Although we'd spent the entire set by Sleeper dancing, shouting, jumping, and hugging, I'd still managed to get to know a few things about Portia during the quiet bits between the songs. Like her age – 21. What kind of Asian person she was – Chinese, with a quarter Korean on her mum's side. Who she was here with – a girl called Mazz who was around here somewhere, but who I apparently was going to love meeting, as she was going to blow my mind.

"Fuck, I'm exhausted now," I said, after Louise Wener had said her goodbyes and Sleeper were finished.

"Well, you know what to do about that, don't you?" Portia said, winking at me and then nodding at her tiny little handbag thing, which was black leather and covered in spikes, so it matched the thing around her neck. This girl put accessorising in a whole new universe.

"Ah, yeah. Tempting, but I'd just honked four big bumps of speed before you gave me what you gave me, and now I've been jumping around for 40 minutes and-" even saying words was tiring. I put my hand on my chest, like an auld fella after he's just tackled a few flights of stairs.

"*Fuck me pink*, four bumps?" She did a 1,2,3,4 thing with her fingers that made me notice how tiny her hands were. Tiny in a good way, not in a terrifying baby-hands-on-an-adult way. "You're gonna diiiiiiiie, baby. But you'll make a beautiful corpse."

"Hahah! Stop now, you'll make me para," I said, not particularly wanting to die, which was a step up from a few hours ago, I supposed.

"So… can you get me one of these, yeah? With all your fancy, music industry contacts?" she said, fingering the laminated badge on the ribbon around my neck.

"Well, I can't get you one of *those*, no." I looked at her differently now. Was that was this had been about? Was she a user? A schemer? I couldn't tell from her face. Inscrutable, as my racist Nana would say.

"Oh. That's a shame. No worries, though. I'll get one somewhere else. Portia always finds a way." She squeezed my hand again, and then held onto it. I'd misjudged her, obviously. She wasn't just here for the perks.

"No, I mean I can't get you one of THESE," I lifted it up to show her. "Cos these ones say "Artist" on them, see?"

"Ah! Yes. I am not *an artiste* like you, pudding. My gifts lie in other departments." She had a thing where she made her nose twitch, like a rabbit's nose, when she said certain things. It was very cute. It was double-cute, even.

"Pudding! Hah. No, am, I think I can find you a normal AAA badge though. In a bit." Once I'm double-sure I can trust you, and I'm double-certain you're not gonna just take it and double-fuck off, I thought. Lush were tuning up.

"Oh, excellent! Thanks, Caoimhe. You're like a saint – like a guardian angel, I swear. And mmmm, if you could, try make it two? Because Mazz needs one as well, and once you meet Mazz, you're definitely gonna want her with us, trust me you will."

"Uhuh? Okay, we'll see." I was back to not quite trusting her. "But hang on. Weren't you already backstage, first time I saw you?" I'd completely forgotten that. The drummer from Lush was doing a beat. Someone did a 1-2 on the PA, but it wasn't Miki. It was some man, probably a roadie.

"Oh, well, yeah. I was there in an unofficial capacity, dumpling." She was looking up at the screens now, not at me.

"Unofficial capacity?" I was looking up there now, too. Miki Berenyi was in front of the mic stand, guitar slung over her shoulder, hair looking a bit like mine, the cheeky cow.

"Yes. I think the lay-people call it *sneaking in*." Now she was looking at me. Smiling, as well. She didn't do much of that, I'd noticed. She was very hard not to look at. Every time you did, you saw something new about her to like.

"Oh. Well then, we'll have to get you sorted then, won't we?" I said, as they started up the first song.

"And the lovely Mazz, of course," she said, walking her fingers up my spine, to the nape of my neck, in a way that seemed equally nonchalant and deliberate. Oh boy.

"And the lovely Mazz, wherever she's got to," I said, wondering where all my own people were now, but not wondering too much, really.

*****

"Finally!" I said, later on, when Lush started up *Hypocrite*. I'd been waiting all set for it. It wasn't their actual best song – even though I loved the lyrics of it to death - but at gigs like these you didn't need the best. You needed ones that everyone knew, because it made the atmosphere brilliant when all the people were experiencing it in the same way, at the same time.

"Ooh. Love this one, yeah," said Portia, throwing her arm around my middle and squeezing me. We'd found out a bit more about each other in the last half hour or so. Well, not about each other, really. Just about the bands we liked, which turned out to be mostly the same. All the *Riot Grrrl* ones, and the Breeders of course. All the spin-offs, Belly, Throwing Muses. We both had Kristen Hersh's solo album, and we both liked *Your Ghost* the best off it. She knew a few bands I'd never heard of, too. One called No Doubt, who she'd seen a few times in the States. She was obsessed with the singer off them – Gwen something or other. She kept saying my top was like something *she* would wear, on stage, so whoever she was, this Gwen one, she was a woman of impeccable taste.

"Do you like muffs?" she said, over the noise of distorted guitars and deafening drumbeats.

"I *beg* your pardon?" Christ, was there a pamphlet going around about me, or something?

"The Muffs! The band, sweet pea. Do you like them?"

"OH! I thought you... Yes! I fucking love them. Like, my whole wardrobe two years ago was basically based on Kim's clothes in their videos, I'm not even exaggerating, like." So many knee socks, so much wearing ribbed white tops under smock dresses. A whole skirting board's worth of lined-up boots in my bedroom. I didn't have the hair like her, mind. I would have been kicked out of Laurel Hill for it.

"Yeah, she's shit-cool, isn't she?"

"She's double-awesome," I said, relaxing into my new role as a cult member, clearly. I loved Kim Shattuck, though.

I'd made myself hoarse many a time trying to imitate the way she screamed when she sang.

"Haha! Double-awesome. I double-like you, cupcake. So, what's going on with this, then?" she said. Lush were finishing up their set with one of those loud, crashy, rock and roll endings.

"What's going on with what?" I said, cupping my ears to keep out all the cacophony.

"With this thing – the little criss-cross bit?" She gestured downwards at my jeans. "Did you make that yourself, too? Another one of your many talents?" She slid two of her fingers down behind where the ribbon was tied in a bow, and then looked me straight in the eyes. For the tiniest, scariest second, I thought she was going to yoink it open there and then and let my jeans fall down, in front of all these strangers. Like a school bully would.

"Um, that's, eh…" The words were stuck inside my mouth. She pressed the backs of her long, very manicured nails against the front of my knickers and then dragged them up my stomach, until she got to the edge of the belly top. Definitely not something a school bully would do. My heart had already been racing, it really didn't need that extra push. I took a breath to try and slow everything down inside me.

"Sorry, am I being *atrocious*, cherry pie?" She took her same hand and put it where my neck and shoulder met, which was a bit more neutral and a lot less nerve-jangling, for me. Her eyes were full of fun, and promise, and danger. But I felt pretty safe, for now.

"You're being the absolute *worst*, apple crumble," I said, trying to remember what band was on next, but I couldn't.

"Well, would you look who's finally decided to show her gorgeous face!" Portia said then, looking at something or someone over my shoulder. I turned around to see.

"Helloooooo!" the new person said, to her, but maybe also to me.

"Look at the gift I got for you, Mazz," said Portia, putting her hands on my shoulders and sort of presenting me to the other one. "You liiiiike?"

I felt really strange, now. I looked at the Mazz girl. She wasn't dressed like I'd pictured she would be, in my head, anyway. She was wearing a baby blue, satin camisole thing that looked more like underwear than clothes – no bra under it, I could see her two piercings. She had incredibly tight white jeans that were so low-slung at the waist you could see her hip bones poking out. Every inch of her was tanned – it looked real as well, no manky fake tan smudges on her. Who *were* these goddesses? And how were us mere humans supposed to compete?

"Of course I like! What's the matter, Caoimhe? Don't you remember me, chick?" said the Mazz girl, and now I was very confused. Then I looked at her face, which was as tanned as the rest of her, and surrounded by an incredible mane of natural blonde curls. She was unbelievably pretty, and so, so familiar to me, now. I *knew* that face. I *loved* that face. I'd *missed* that face, so much.

"Marian?" I said, opening my arms as she rushed in for the hug. She smelled of perfume and deodorant, but she smelled like herself too, and so many memories from my childhood came rushing back at once.

"Yay! It's like Surprise, Surprise! And I'm Cilla!" said Portia, from somewhere outside the gorgeous hug that I was already lost in and never wanted to come out of. How many years was it since I'd seen Marian Collins, I wondered? Four? Five? Whatever it was, it'd been too many. What a day this was turning out to be, after all.

FOURTEEN

I spent the short walk from the crowd to the backstage bit catching up with Marian. Well, not really catching up, more just talking about Áine, which for once I didn't mind, since she'd actually known her. Known her as a child - not who she was when she died - but I did a good job filling her in about the wild, crazy minx my little sister had grown into in her absence. I asked her why she hadn't come to visit last year, when her Mum and Dad had come down, and she said she was really sorry she hadn't, but she'd been going through a really awful relationship with a really nasty guy, who was massively controlling, and he wouldn't let her go, because he said her life in Limerick was in the past, and she was with him now. He sounded like a bastard, and I was very relieved when she said he was out of her life for good. We didn't talk about my Jon, because she wouldn't have known who he was anyway, so it would just have been the sort of meaningless platitudes I usually tried to avoid from people who never knew Áine.

"Not a chance, love." The security guy at the gate put his palm up in front of Portia's face, and I stopped chatting with Mar, or Mazz, as she was these days, and gave him a filthy look.

"What's the matter here?" I said, folding my arms and giving him my best business face, with none of the barbecue.

"The matter is I've already thrown this one out today, she's not allowed in, sorry." The look on his face told me he wasn't sorry in the slightest.

"Well, number one, she has a pass now," I said, lifting it up from Portia's chest to make my point. "Number two, I'm an artist playing here this weekend, and these two are my guests. And... number three, my dad is Denis Desmond's fucking lawyer, as well as his friend, so you really don't want me picking up the phone to call him at home right now, pal. It'd be more than-"

"All right, all right! Jesus! She can go in. Go on, all of ye. Get out of my sight," said yer man.

"Charmed, I'm sure," said Marian, curtseying as we went past him, and we all burst out laughing and skipped over to the bar area, because I didn't care about seeing anyone in there now, I felt bulletproof now I had these two with me.

"Right, who's having what?" I said, once we were there. No sign of our lot, which was strange, but maybe they were out the front. We'd missed almost all the bands yesterday, made sense that they'd have gone out into the crowd. I had, after all.

"No, I'll get these, peach," Portia said, doing a wave-away with her hand.

"What? And pay for them?" I said.

"You get free drinks?" Marian said, impressed.

"Well I haven't paid for any yet," I said. I remembered Brian and his note-waving. Maybe it was only an open bar for us with our "Artist" passes? It didn't matter.

"How the other half live, eh?" said Portia. I'd have to tell her later about my close personal friendship with Nick Cave. I'd already told her about Tim Wheeler not-really kissing me, and she'd politely feigned being impressed, in a way that someone who has probably had actual sexual intercourse with rock stars might do.

"Barkeep!" I said, because I'd always wanted to say that in real life. The barkeep looked less than impressed, poor sod.

"What can I get you, Caoimhe?" he said. *Your troubles are all the saaaaaame.*

"Hello! I'll have one of your lovely Bombay Sapphire gins, with tonic. Make it a large one, as well, purleeeze." I was absolutely bouncing with good mood feelings now, and it was 100% down to the company I was keeping. Okay, maybe 20% speed and cocaine. But 80% the company.

"Ice and a slice?"

"Of course. Aaaaaand, this delectable China doll will have…"

"Can I just have a tall glass, with a triple shot of Jager in it, three cubes of ice, and give me a mixer bottle of Coke on the side, darling. That'd be lush." This bitch was hardcore, I loved her.

"Okay, coming right up. And yourself?" he said, looking at Mar.

"Oh, Mazz will just have water, yeah?" Portia said. "She's Straight Edge."

"What's a…Straight Edge when it's at home?" Barkeep asked, before I had a chance to.

"Oh it's like this Mormon, skateboarder thing. They make a commitment to not do any drugs, not even caffeine, like. And no eating meat or dairy or eggs. No booze either, and no sex of any kind. Not even a sly handjob behind the bicycle sheds. It's tragic, if you ask me, darling," Portia said, fixing her shiny plastic skirt, which had rode up a bit on the walk over.

"And you're that, are you?" I said to Mar. "You're one of these Straight Edge people?"

"I am…" she said.

"Really?" the barman said, coming back with my G&T. I gave him a wink and threw in some kissy mwah lips for good measure.

"... in my *HOLE*, like." She burst out laughing. "Can I just have a Southern Comfort, lime, and lemonade, please? Double as well, cos fuck it."

"... it's Christmas," I said, very relieved that it had only been a joke. I couldn't have handled being around a sober person today - even if it *was* my Marian, from the old days. We took our drinks and went to sit on the grass in the sun.

"He really had it in for you, that bouncer guy, didn't he?" I said, sitting my arse down nice and comfortable. I was a little hot in my jeans, but it was better than having a PVC skirt on, I imagined. Portia was trying her best to find a balance between being comfy and not showing off her whole uterus to anyone passing, but it hadn't quite worked. Marian would probably get grass stains on her white jeans, even though the ground was dry as a bone, but she didn't look too fussed about it.

"That guy? Yeah. Thanks for stepping in, by the way. Was that true, about your dad?"

"Well, he's definitely the solicitor for MCD, but I don't think he knows Denis personally or anything. I was just chancing my arm." Dad's status in the world had got me out of many a scrape in the past, bless him. It almost made up for all those 80 hour weeks when I was small and devoid of a father figure.

"Nice," said Marian. I noticed for the first time that none of us were smoking. Was I the only one? I remembered Mar used to smoke, years ago. I used to go with her when she snuck out, during visits to our house. It felt dead cool, hanging down an alley with this older girl, puffing away. She'd never offered me a drag or anything though, she wasn't a brat. I had to make my own way in the world of getting addicted to nicotine.

"I'm having a fag, anyone want one?" I said, because just thinking about smoking had made me gasping for one.

"I don't smoke, no," said Portia, but she didn't make an eww face, like a prick would.

"I um… well I'm supposed to be off them, but I'm very terrible at it," said Marian.

"So, you do want one, yeah?" I said, offering her the box.

"If that's okay, yeah?" Jesus, she was so pretty. She always had been – naturally, too, even without a scrap of slap on – but she'd grown up nice, as Frank would say. I was basically the ugliest one here, and I was almost definitely a massive ride, if you believed other people.

"Course it is. And shur, they're only Marlboro Lights, anyway," I said.

"One calorie, sugar free," said Portia, and we all giggled. I hadn't even noticed the music on the stage behind us yet. I didn't care about it. We'd seen the ones I wanted to see, and Blur wouldn't be on til ages later, after it got dark.

"When did you give up?" I said, lighting hers with my match before it burned my fingers.

"Most recently you mean, like?" She took a long, first pull that was satisfying even to look at. Awful things, fags. They'd be the death of me.

"Yeah." My gin was very good. He'd put a cherry in the glass, for some reason. I could kind of taste it, kind of.

"About two hours ago," Portia said, laughing. She was adding a tiny bit of mixer to her glass, taking a sip, then adding more. I didn't know why, but it made it look interesting.

"Fuck you, spring roll. It was at least four," said Marian.

"Three hours, at a stretch, bacon and cabbage." I'd got used to Portia calling me various foodstuffs as terms of endearment. Apparently when these two did it to each other, it got a bit racial.

"Anyway, tell her about why Mister Security Guy hates you, Portia."

"Wait, there's a story?" I said. I liked stories.

"It's not that long a story, honey. All it is, is that me and blondie here were at Guns 'n' Roses in Slane Castle a few years back…"

"In 1992," Marian said. A year after she'd moved away, then.

"Yeah, in 92. The Chinese year of the…" She waited until we were both looking at her. "How would I know, you racists? I'm from Ireland. Anyhoo…"

"Do you guys like Guns 'n' Roses, then?"

"Not particularly, darling. I just go where the fun is," said Portia. I didn't think she was the GNR type, to be honest, but I barely knew her.

"I like them," said Marian.

"You do?" I said.

"Yeah, a friend of mine gave me a CD of theirs, like a million years ago now. And they kind of grew on me." Her face looked like she was remembering something sad. I didn't ask her what, it was none of my beeswax.

"I don't mind them, really," I said. "Well except that *One in a Million* song."

"The *immigrants and faggots* one?" Marian said. Portia looked at her, surprised.

"Yeah, and worse," I said. I hated how catchy that song was, in fairness.

"Anyway!" said Portia, fixing her skirt situation again, but never quite getting to a point where she was sitting comfy without showing off something to the world.

"Anyway!" I said, remembering she was supposed to be telling us a story.

"Anyway, that security guard there was also working backstage at Guns 'n' Roses. And when I tried to get backstage, we had a difference of opinion."

"A difference of opinion?" I said, wondering what philosophical debates bouncers got involved in.

"Yeah. See, my opinion was that I deserved to go backstage…"

"And he disagreed?" I lit another fag, because I owed my lungs a few for depriving them during Sleeper and Lush.

"Oh, no. He agreed that I deserved to go backstage. He just thought that I should pay him for my pass, babe."

"Ah, I see," I said.

"I don't think you do," said Marian, then she mimed asking me for another fag. I mimed telling her to help herself.

"He thought I should pay him with a blowjob, and I disagreed," said Portia.

"WHAT?" I said, picturing yer man in my head and trying desperately not to picture him with his knob out.

"It happens, honey," she said, shrugging. The crowd outside was really loud, the last song must have been good, or something. Or maybe they'd had another power cut.

"And did you do it?" I said. Something hit me on the head. It was my own box of fags.

"CAOIMHE!" shouted Marian, the thrower of the box.

"Babe if that double-disgusting human toad had experienced the glory of putting his dick in my mouth that night, we wouldn't just have got backstage passes and a free bar this weekend, I'd be headlining all three nights," She raised her drinkless glass and jangled the ice cubes to let us know it was time to go to the bar again.

*****

We'd been there for quite some time before one of the band finally found me. I was just about to go to the bathroom when Richie almost walked straight into me.

"There you are!" he said, giving me a half a hug.

"Here I am!" I said. I realised the other two were still sitting on the grass, so I took him by the shoulder and turned him towards them.

"Richie, these are my new friends I found today, they're lovely. That's Portia, there. Like the girl in the play, not like the sports car." She gave Richie a small wave, but she didn't smile, because smiling wasn't her jam.

"And this one here, well she's not new at all, actually. I know her since-"

"Whoa, is this real or did someone spike me with acid, lads?" Richie's jaw was on the floor. He was staring down at Marian.

"Hello, *Richie Richard*. Long time no... anything," Marian said, and I didn't understand what was happening at all, but something was definitely happening.

"It's really you, isn't it?" Richie said, dropping down on his haunches so he could look across at Mar, face to face. She giggled, and nodded at him. She looked happy to see him. But why?

"Fuck me pink, I forgot about this bit!" said Portia, revealing absolutely nothing to me.

"Sorry, what's going on? Do you two know each other?" I said.

"YES!!" they said, both at the same time.

"How???" I said, looking at everyone, one by one.

"Remember when I used to come up to see you and Áine, years ago, Caoimhe? With my mum and dad?"

"Well, obviously I do," I said. That information was not helping me figure this out.

"Wait, you two knew each other years ago?" said Richie, looking lost.

"Shhhhh! One revelation at a time, little drummer boy," said Portia, sounding really Chinese, for some reason.

"Remember back then when I told you I had a boyfriend, Caoimhe? Like, a proper boyfriend, going with each other for good? When I was about thirteen, nearly fourteen?" said Marian, doing the swirly thing with her hand that means *come on, you'll get there.*

"Yeah, I do, I think. No, I do! You were mad about him. You were still with him last time I ever saw you, actually." I was a bit too tipsy to remember things any faster, but I was trying.

"I was, and that was about four years ago, in about 1991, yeah?"

"I think so, yeah." I saw the two of us, down the alley. Her smoking a fag, me keeping a lookout. I could even picture our clothes.

"Do you not remember my boyfriend's name?" Marian looked like she was trying to implant the answer in my brain telepathically, but we weren't on yokes, so she had no hope.

"Richie was the boyfriend's name. It's the same Richie who's standing there. The end," said Portia, who was clearly tired of this game of Charades now.

"That can't be right," I said, because it couldn't be. Even though Richie lived in Thomondgate and Thomondgate was where Marian's folks had moved after Kennedy Park and Caherdavin and when I thought about it really hard, I *could* remember her saying her boyfriend was a *Richie* or a *Richard* and they clearly knew each other, and now it all made sense except for one thing-

"But you're like 20 this year and Richie is 18 next month. How did that work in 1991? Or 1989, even?" I was doing maths frantically in my head, but to no avail.

"Oh, I was her toyboy, Caoimhe. But I was an *advanced* child. I did my leaving when I was sixteen, like. Got into Trinity college too," Richie said, looking at Portia when he said that last bit.

"Oh yeah, I totally *molested* him." Marian said, stubbing out her fag. "He'll probably need years of therapy when he finally stops blocking out the trauma. You got into Trinity? Well done, Rich! Prouda yous!" She scooched along the grass until she was nearer to him, and they had a spontaneous hug that made my heart melt a little. What a life we led.

*****

"Do you know anything about these things, Porsh? Like, I took two last night, will this one still work? Will it take ages for me to come up? Will the coke affect it?" Me and Portia had gone off to the toilets to give Mar and Rich some time together to catch up. I still couldn't get my head around it all, but it was brilliant, anyway.

"I dunno, I'm not a scientist, honeybuttons. But, like you said, last night was your first time ever taking them, so you should probably get something off this one. I don't think you've burned yourself out just yet. And anyway, we can plug the gap with this." She was chopping up two lines on the cistern of the toilet. We were both in the one cubicle.

"Okay, that's cool. I'd like to go back to that buzz; it was pretty amazing." I thought about how the night had ended, and I felt bad for being cross with Ciara. All she'd really done was be honest with me. The Ian thing was still worrying me though. If she had done that, then I had a right to be cross with her. Didn't I? I didn't know anymore.

"You're miles away there, pudding. Come back to Portia now." She snapped her fingers in front of my face, and it worked.

"Sorry, babe. I was just thinking." I was always thinking. I needed to cut out that habit.

"Who is he? Who broke your heart? Or was it a *she*?" she said, giving me a nice, caring look, that felt real.

"Um, no one. Why would it be a girl, anyway?" I said, not sure why I was asking.

"Why wouldn't it be? We're as bad as men, sometimes, chicken. Anyway, I just assumed – about you – was I wrong to assume about you?" She was looking me in a studious way, like she was trying to figure me out.

"You can assume what you like, lover. Doesn't mean it's true," I said, annoyed with myself now for being all evasive instead of admitting... well, I didn't even know what there was to admit.

"Doesn't mean it's untrue either though, yeah? Wanna go first?" She'd brought a drinking straw in with her, one she'd bitten and torn to snortable size, in the absence of scissors.

"Nah, you go," I said, glad that the subject had been changed.

"Okay. Age before beauty, it is," she said, which was silly, cos she was prettier than me as well as older than me. She *snoot*ed the whole line in one go. It was like seeing a child blow out all her birthday candles at the first try.

"Woo! *Excuse moi, mon cherie*," I said, wondering how hot she must be in that plastic skirt. My latex dress was like wearing a sauna, but we women suffered for our sexiness. It was like a rule. I tried matching her snorting skills, but I only managed three quarters on my first go. I had the second bit and leaned my head back to let the goodness get into me properly.

"Is Richard dealing then?" Portia said, inspecting the porcelain for any leftover powder with a wetted finger. I liked watching her do things, watching her move, or even just watching her stand still. She was the most aesthetically pleasing person I'd ever met, male or female. She had no bad angles. She'd probably look elegant while falling down a flight of stairs.

"Richie? Noooooo. Frank just gave him a few to bring to me when he found me. We were lucky he had enough for the three of us, really. Uncle Frank is the one with the actual stash," I said. I thought about Niall dealing for him today and wondered had he done it yesterday too. They'd been together a lot, earlier on. It was possible.

"Right, and Uncle Frank is... your uncle?"

"Eh, no. It's hard to explain. He's actually my ex-boyfriend's uncle."

"Well that's a strange connection to have with someone, but I won't judge, pumpkin. What does your ex think of you hanging around with his old uncle?" I realised then that Portia didn't know much about me at all. Which was fine, really. I didn't need everyone to know me inside out. It was nice to be a stranger to someone for once. It was nice to be new.

"Uh, he can't really say anything anymore. I'll explain it to you some other time, yeah?" Maybe when we were all loved-up later on. That would be easier, I thought.

"Absolutely. So, what will we do now, sausage?" she said. I was suddenly aware of how physically close to me she was, considering how big the cubicle was.

"I dunno. Go back outside? Or go to the dance tent?" That was where everyone else was, Richie had told us. They'd all dropped Es, which made me feel bad and feel left out, for a few seconds, until I remembered it was me who ran away from them earlier, not the other way around.

"Don't want to. Don't *feeeeel* like it," Portia said, doing a silly baby voice. She was playing with the bottom edge of my top again. I wasn't sure if she was more enamoured with it, or with what was underneath it. Both were equally possible, I hoped.

"Are you coming on to me, *my little Chinaaaa girl*?" I said, because the cocaine horn had suggested saying it, and my regular brain was unable to think of a reason not to.

"Do you want me to come on to you, *my little,* uhh, *Limeriiiick bird*?" Her Bowie impression was much better than mine, fair play. Her hand had moved up under my top, and I felt her nails brush against the underneath of my very braless boob. Oh boy.

"I honestly don't know, yet," I said, chickening out at the last hurdle. It was true, though. I didn't know anything – about this, about Ciara, about liking girls, about knowing myself. I knew nothing. I was from Barcelona.

"Well then, you let me know when you do know then, yeah?" She moved her face close, and I felt her warm breath on my cheek as she skimmed her mouth over my skin. The hot feeling moved across to my ear, filling up all the little channels, and then there was a different sensation that I didn't understand until it was already over – she had pulled on my stud earring with her teeth and then let it go again. Christ alive.

"I definitely, definitely will," I said, reaching across her to open the lock, and wondering what I'd done in a previous life to have earned this new status as a fanny magnet for very hot bisexual girls.

*****

"Yeah, I mean last year the lineup was very strange altogether. They'd the Beautiful South on before the Prodigy, House of Pain, Primal Scream, and then Crowded fecking House, boy. Twas like being at a nightclub where the DJ didn't know what crowd was in. Blur were very good – probably the best on the Sunday, as well as the Cranberries - but Féile had put Elvis Costello down as the headliner." Frank was talking to Marian and Richie when we got back to them. Niall was there too.

"Well, well, well, she's not dead at all, Frank, look!" he said. He looked like he'd sampled the merchandise a fair bit earlier than I had, going by his eyes, and the way he was dancing on the spot like an eejit.

"Aboy the kid, where've you been hiding, love? You've been missed!" Frank said, to me. Both him and Niall had definitely noticed Portia – how could anyone not - but they'd done nothing about it, so far.

"Hello Francis, hello Niall. This is Portia. Portia: Frank and Niall. Frank and Niall: Por- sorry I did that bit already." My head was whizzing, in a good way.

"*Uncle* Frank. Niall, the bass player. I've heard so *little* about you both," Portia said, offering neither a hug nor a hand to them. She was too cool for that.

"Porsche like the car?" Frank said. I didn't bother correcting him.

"That's not a Chinese name. But you look like you're Chinese," Niall said, but somehow it wasn't meant in a *rude* way? He was saying what he saw, like he was on Catchphrase.

"WHAT??? Do I? God, I must be really, really stoned." Portia started feeling her face, especially around her eyes.

"Guys! Guys! It's happened again. No more joints for me, pudding," she said to me, without cracking a smile.

"Of course, sherry trifle," I said, then I pointed at my face and swirled my hand around it dramatically. "What about me, am I okay? Still Irish?"

"I'm *not* sure, cupcake. You might want to take it easy for a bit. You're looking *slightly* Cambodian in the mouth, there," she said, frowning. The two lads standing up looked perplexed.

"Doesn't just affect the face either, like. I was in the jacks a while ago there, and my boobs were gone a bit Japanese, from all the gear I smoked earlier. Well, my left one was, definitely," said Marian, joining in. She was sitting right up into Richie, her arm draped over one of his knees. They were looking very cosy; it was so sweet.

"Yep, we've all been there," Portia said, nodding wisely at everyone in the circle.

"Sorry, *what?*" Niall said, not smiling or laughing now. Or dancing, either. Frank looked equally mystified. Richie just looked blissed out and content, cos he'd a Marian now. A long-lost Marian, found again. Kismet, all over the fucking shop.

"Worst one is when your fanny goes all Vietnamese," I said, trying to think of more ridiculous shit to say. I felt like I was coming up on my pill, but it was way too soon. Or was it?

"I haven't had that one yet, thank God," Mar said, actually blessing herself. I loved her. Richie put his hand over his mouth to stop a laugh getting out.

"Oh, it's terrifying, honestly. One minute you're walking around with a perfectly normal, Irish vagina, the next minute.... you've got a *Ho Chi Minge*," I said, because I was hilarious.

*****

We all walked down through the main field to get to the tent thing outside, because the lads had convinced us it was great in there, though I was a little sceptical. Someone was playing on stage, it might have been the Boo Radleys, it might not. Everyone was chatting away like old friends now, the ones already up on their Es providing adequate social lubrication for those of us who were just slumming it on free booze and expensive cocaine, so far. Marian making her left boob sing *Turning Japanese* was a particular highlight. Herself and Richie weren't exactly together yet, in a togethery way, but you'd have needed a crowbar to pry them apart, as well. Frank and Niall were all over Portia like a pair of cheap suits, and she was being remarkably tolerant of their loved-up drooling. She seemed like someone who didn't need attention or praise to thrive – she wasn't the slightest bit needy or insecure – but she didn't hate the limelight either. I was fascinated with her, so far, but that was probably down to how little she shared about herself, rather than any of the few things she did reveal.

"So did she try to get off with you?" Marian said, appearing next to me, with Richie at her other side.

"Pardon?"

"Portia – when she stole you away to the toilets or whatever. Did she try to lez you up?"

"Um…" I wasn't sure if I should be saying anything about it; I didn't want to betray someone's privacy or whatever.

"That's a yeah, then," Mar said, chuckling. "It's okay, you're not telling tales out of school, Kweev. She's got a bit of a thing for you, even before she met you, so it's no big shock or anything." Richie was listening to all this, but he wasn't saying anything, or even reacting, really. Too blissed out to care, more than likely.

"Well, no, we had a bit of a moment, all right. A nice

moment, but nothing happened. Well, nothing too scandalous, anyway." I got the good shivers, picturing it. Not scandalous enough for the newspapers to care, but probably scandalous enough to make my Mum faint, I thought.

"Oh right. I didn't know you were even into… I didn't, um – it's been ages since I've seen you, like." She was smiling. Either at me, or at some memory of us. Both were equally possible.

"Ah, I'm… it's complicated," I said, cos it was.

"You were always complicated, babe. In a good way, I mean."

"Haha, yeah. But not this kind of complicated, I don't think." I thought about me and my girl crush on Marian, and wondered how true what I was saying was.

"Ah, I dunno about that," said Mar.

"She's always been a bit lesbo," Richie said, suddenly finding his tongue.

"What do you mean?!" I said, giving him the evil eye, but only for a second.

"You're always going on about girls being rides, like. Talking about their arses and their tits, and all. And like, not just Kylie Minogue or other famous wans. You do be saying it about real people as well. You do be perving women more than Nailer, and he's the biggest perv I know, sham!" Richie said. He was holding Marian's hand. Had he been doing that all along? I hadn't noticed until just now.

"That doesn't mean anything, you fool. We're allowed to say other girls are beautiful. It doesn't automatically mean we're *gay* or something. We're not like *boys*," I said. We were outside the stadium already, next to the dance tent, but I couldn't see where you went in.

"Hmmmm. I suppose," Richie said, spotting the marquee too. I checked my wrist to make sure I had my band on.

"We can hold hands with them too, without it meaning something *sexual*," I said, nodding down at theirs and raising an eyebrow. They both did the same sheepish face, smiled dopily at one another, and the Spanish Inquisition into my sexuality went no further for now, thank Christ.

*****

"Did you notice the way Richie sounds way more Thomondgate when he's talking to Marian?" I was still outside the Groove Stage, having a fag. You could definitely have a fag inside there, it was basically a nightclub made out of tent, but I needed a moment to steady my nerves before I went in and *met* everyone.

"What is a thomond gate?" said Portia, who I'd convinced to stay with me, even though she didn't smoke.

"Oh, sorry, it's just the bit of Limerick, like a very working class area, where he lives. And where she used to live, when they were going out with each other." I was still getting used to this alternative history of theirs.

"Ah, okay. Why do you think he's doing that then, muffin? Trying to be her bit of rough is he, yeah?" She was getting so many looks from passing blokes, dressed like she was, but she never so much as acknowledged it happening. She was too cool for any school, this one.

"Maybe. Or maybe he's unconsciously trying to recreate the circumstances when they used to be an item, to make it easier for her to get it on with him again. Psychological warfare, or something." The fag tasted grand, but it felt like a little countdown timer in my fingers. An hourglass made of fire and ash, reminding me that I'd have to go in there when it was finished, and face the music. Figuratively and literally, like.

"A nostalgic trip back to the days when she used to

touch a child's penis," said Portia, making me laugh so hard I nearly swallowed the ciggie.

"Ah, stop!"

"She's the one who should have stopped, sugarplum. No one should be touching an eleven year old's willy, for any reason. That willy belongs to Christ."

"What would Christ want with an eleven year old's willy, like?" I slowed down on the fag, in an attempt to delay the inevitable.

"Judge not, lest ye be judged, O'Shaughnessy." Her saying my name reminded me of something I'd been meaning to ask.

"What's your real name, then?" I glanced at her shoulders, suddenly envying the absolute piteness of her. She was so *lean* everywhere she made skinny old me look like Giant Haystacks.

"This is my real name. Portia. Nice to meet you," she said, sounding cynical, which wasn't new, but it was new hearing it aimed at me.

"Yeah, but what's your surname, though?"

"Oh. My surname is Xû," she said, as if this was the first time anyone had ever asked her. Perhaps it was.

"Sorry?" I'd missed it, because some arseface going in the entrance had been shouting.

"H-soo!" she said, slower than the last time, so I would understand.

"H-sooo?"

"H-SOOO!!!" she said, much louder this time.

"Bless you!" said some random man walking past, and we both gave him a look.

"How do you spell that?"

"Ah, it's an X and then a U with a little hat on it that looks like a roof. Xû!"

"Ooh, that's cool. Xû!" I said it over and over in my head, to get used to it. "So, Portia Xû?"

"No. No, in Eastern culture – Asia, I mean, not Dublin - the surname comes first, so it would be Xû Portia."

"Interesting. But what's your real Christian, I mean, *first* name?" Thought I might as well go for it; this was as forthcoming as she'd ever been with personal stuff.

"Portia!" she said, not fooling anyone.

"It's definitely not Portia," I said. Unless of course it was. Both were equally possible.

"Why isn't it?" She did a grumpy pout at me, but it just made her even better looking. I *coveted* her face, as she would say.

"Because it's not a Chinese name, and even if you're gonna say it is, the Chinese language doesn't have a P in it."

"The Chinese language doesn't have any of your silly western letters in it, tater tot." That was a new one, what was she gonna call me next, *bag of chips*?

"You know what I mean. It doesn't sound right. I can't think of any Chinese things that start with P." I had no idea if I was right or not, but it was fun to argue with her, cos she was so feisty.

"Uhhh, Peking?"

"That's not real!" I said.

"Yes it is, it has its own duck!" I'd made her smile, so that was one thing off my list of things I wanted to do with her, at least.

"Hah! It's *Beijing*! Peking is a thing that white people called it, ages ago. We learned it in History. Why am I better at China than you are?" My fag was finished, but she hadn't noticed yet.

"Ffffffsssss! Foolish roundeye!" she said, in a Chinese accent so terrible that my attempt at one would probably have been better.

"Shut up and tell me your real name, you beautiful idiot," I said, taking both her hands in mine and joining all our fingers. No idea why, it just felt right.

"Okay, okay. It's Ling," she said, squeezing my hands in a way that made me realise that I was coming up massively on the pill. Especially the part when she released the pressure on them and they felt so light I thought they might just float off, and me with them.

"Lin?"

"No, Ling! With a G at the end, sweets." She looked double-double-gorgeous to me now, with all this blood rushing around my body. She was almost glowing. Looking at her face was like a drug in itself.

"Ah, I see. So it's Ling Xû, then?"

"Nearly, sausage," she said, mentally willing me to remember the trick.

"Xû Ling!" I said, delighted with myself. I pulled her in really close so I could look at her immense, double-pretty, distant-galaxy-eyes, and take a big deep breath of the air around her.

"That's me. The real me," she said, and now she looked different. Younger, more innocent, less vampirey. But, even more beautiful, somehow. It was getting very difficult not to just kiss her. I couldn't, though. Not yet. Not until I… ugh.

"What does it mean, then?" I said, snapping out of the trance for a second, so I could get my emotional bearings.

"What does Ling mean?"

"Yeah." I wondered if it was close to Linda, which was Spanish for "beautiful". I knew things!

"It means "the sound of Jade", actually."

"Jade who?" I said, and then immediately felt like an idiot.

"Hah! Foolish roundeye. No, you know the semi-precious stone, jade? – well, it makes this unique noise when a piece of it bangs off other pieces of it. Counterfeit stones don't make that noise, so that was how jewellers would know they were buying the real deal. Cos it made a *LING*! sound? You catch my drift? That's what I mean by *sound of jade*."

"Wow, so your real name kind of means that you're the proof that something precious and beautiful is real and not fake?" That was the best way I could put it.

"Yeah, *semi-precious*, but pretty much that."

"So why did you change it then, *Xû Ling*?" I loved it. She'd be Xû Ling now in my head forever.

"Because I get immense sexual pleasure from people confusing me with a German car. Let's go in, cupcake. Xû Ling is coming up double-hard, and Xû Ling needs to dance."

FIFTEEN

"Did you see Lush?!!" Bríd was dancing in a strange way – she wasn't normally a raver, so she was improvising. It was like her usual, indie dancing, but faster. I was probably doing the same. It didn't matter. No one was going to judge us here. *You got to let the muuuuusic, mooooove your feet*, and all that jazz.

"Yeah, and Sleeper, they were brilliant, like!" The tent was jam packed, it wasn't easy to find people, but she'd been moseying, so she'd bumped into me, quite literally. The music was incredible, even though I didn't recognise any of it. That didn't matter. It wasn't the time for sing-alongs and hits. It was time for beats and bass and strobes and lasers.

"Miki's dress was lovely. Was like something you'd wear!" Bríd said. She was very up, even more than she'd seemed yesterday, but I hadn't spent much time with her yesterday on these. Not one to one, anyway.

"The black one, yeah? It was cool." I didn't remember much about the dress, we were too far away to see her properly, but her hair had been incredibly bright red in the sunshine. The bass was thumping now, I could feel the drumbeats going from the floor, through my feet, up my legs, into my hips, higher and higher. It was like nothing I'd ever experienced. It was like someone had designed the whole place – the setup, the acoustics, the way the crowd was constantly rotating and mingling - with people on Es in mind, which they probably had. It was perfection.

"Hi! I'm Bríd!" she said, over the thumping beats, putting her hand out to Portia.

"Like the Nirvana song?" said Portia, but she was only messing. She took Bríd's fingers in her hand, held them for a second, then gave them back. That was a lot, for her, in fairness.

"She's very beautiful and like, *exotic*, isn't she?! Who does she belong to?" Bríd said, shouting into my ear, loud enough for Portia to hear every word, not that she'd mind any of it.

"She belongs to the girl Richie's hanging out of," I said, pointing at the newlyweds. And to me, I thought, but I kept it as a thought, for now.

"OH! Richie's got himself a woman? That was quick, like! The *dark horse*. I'll go say hi!!!"

"Do, shur. He'd love that," I said, letting her past me.

"Caoimhe?" Portia said, pressing her hips into mine and wrapping me around the waist. She smelled so good.

"Yes, corn on the cob?" I said, putting my arms over her shoulders, so it looked like we were having a slow dance to frantic rave music.

"Hah! *Corn on the cob*. Anyway, I'm going, now."

"WHAT???" *Everyone I know, goes away, iiiiiin the eeeeend.*

"Yes, I'm going… to get us some gum! Oh, and some water. Be right back, pop tart!" She kissed me on the cheek before I had time to get cross about her freaking me out. I watched her as she slinked across the floor, making pilled-up ravers instantly move out of her way without uttering a word to them. What a mysterious vampire of a ride of a woman she was.

"This place is full of druggies, boy." Frank was next to

me now. It was like a weird, sporadic meet-and-greet in here.

"So?" I said, looking around and having to agree with him. If there was a single person not on something in this tent, I hadn't seen them. And if they did actually exist, they were probably here by mistake. And fucking terrified.

"Oh, I'm not complaining, like. I've sold out already. I'm gonna head back to Jury's and stock up. You need anything from over there?" Frank's new business was thriving. Pity there wasn't a Féile every weekend, he'd be a millionaire in no time.

"I think I'm okay. Are we going back later, before we go to watch Blur?" I remembered promising I'd let Bríd try on outfits, and that she wanted to wear one tonight. Plans could change, though. Especially our plans.

"Going back where, to Jury's?" Portia was back already, with a chewy mouth, and a minty present for me. I gobbled it up, and then kissed her on the cheek to thank her, and she kissed me back. We were *très continentaux* today, chérie.

"Yeah, not now, though. Where are you two staying, anyway?" I hadn't asked her until now; it hadn't come up. The atmosphere in this place was *crazy* good. I didn't know who was playing the tunes. I couldn't see who was standing behind the sound equipment and decks, and even if I could, I didn't know what any of these superstar DJs looked like, except Carl Cox, but he wasn't on until tomorrow. Whoever it was though, they were doing everything right.

"Same as you, lemon drop. Jury's." Portia handed me a bottle of water - my own one - she'd brought two over. No way she'd had time to buy water and get chewing gum, she must have vampire-thralled some helpless boy into handing his ones over to her.

"Wow, thanks! So, what, you were in the same hotel as I was, all this time?" That was freaky.

"I knooooow! We were like ships that *didn't* pass in the night. Still though, you've got me now, dumpling." Her hand was cold and wet from holding the water, and it made me feel all sorts of sensations when she touched my bare stomach with it. My mouth was full of mint again, and my ears were full of bass and drums. I took in one of my trademark big breaths and surveyed the dancefloor. Everyone was off their tits, and the vibe was incredibly friendly. There were people on that floor who I'd cross the street to avoid in normal life, they were so terrifying and different, but now all I could see were sound-out faces and potential new pals. The music felt so very *deliberate*. That's what these guys got paid the big bucks for. The guy on the decks was taking everyone up to massive heights together, letting us feel a few seconds of pure, unadulterated chemical joy, and then carefully bringing us back down so we could get ready to fly again. It was like experiencing music on a different plane of existence – not a plane to Amsterdam. It was like, instead of just listening to it, I was absorbing it on a cellular, molecular level, and keeping it in me forever as a memory of an amazing time with amazing people. Or something.

"This is the life, right, sherbet?" Portia was behind me now, linking her fingers in front of my belly and resting her chin on my neck. I was still coming up in lovely, measured rushes – not as intense as my first time yesterday, but not particularly mild, either. I tilted my neck to the side so there was less space between us and we were sort of hugging with our faces.

"This isn't how I pictured heaven, to be honest. But that's what it feels like, *Ling*." I put my hand up and ran my fingers through her ridiculously double-cool hair. It felt like liquid silk.

"Does feel a little heavenly, doesn't it? And we haven't even started yet, darling." She unclasped her hands from around me, and in a second they'd moved up to my neck and shoulders, her fingers and thumbs going through my sore, knotted muscles as if they literally were the figurative putty I was gradually becoming in the hands of this strange, exquisitely beautiful girl.

It was Heaven, indeed. And not *just like* it, either, Mister Robert Smith. Not *close to* it either, er... Color Me Badd? We'd broken all the way into it, Ian Brown - and we were gonna stick around for a while. My eyes closed shut on their own, I took a massive breath, and everything looked an incredibly pretty shade of purple. Reminded me of-

"Not interrupting anything, am I?" said a familiar voice from somewhere in front of me. I opened my eyes, and Ciara was there, looking bemused and big-eyed and absolutely gorgeous.

"Oh, hello." I was suddenly very aware that there was a Chinese girl surgically attached to me, but before I could think about it any further, Portia broke away and took a step back.

"Hello, stranger. Where have you been hiding yourself?" She was regarding me again, but it was in a different way from last night. I felt... something. It was neither good nor bad, it was just something.

"Oh, here and there." I wanted to ask her why she'd disappeared in the night, why she took my towel, what she was-

"Ah, I see. Me too, we must have just been in different heres and theres." She hadn't acknowledged Portia yet; I didn't know if that was deliberate or not.

"I'm Portia. I thought I'd introduce myself, since no one else is going to."

"Portia. Like in The Merchant of Venice? That's beautiful. I'm Ciara," said Ciara, offering her hand. Portia took it, turned her palm so they linked fingers, then gave her a long, tight hug. That was new.

"Well, nice to meet you, too!" Ciara said, looking at me over Portia's shoulder with a look that said, well, I'd no clue what it said.

"Sorry, I'm not a big hugger, petal, but you're very embraceable." Petal? *You can't eat flowers!*

"Hahaaaah. You're grand. I liked it," Ciara said, looking into her eyes, which were probably still incredible, even in this shitty light.

"So!" I said, feeling left out, both because of their little hugfest, and because my normal brown eyes were rubbish compared to either of theirs.

"Yes! So! I... I have to go find a loo, cos you know, I've just come up, and well. So, I'll catch you both in a bit, don't go far, yeah?" She was looking at me when she said the last bit, which made me feel lovely inside. Lovely, but also a bit worried. I didn't know why.

"Smashing, pumpkin. And tell us where they are when you come back, please. Portia doesn't normally do porta-potties, but beggers can't be choosers, darling," said the Chinese one, putting her hand back around my waist, which I didn't really want her to do in front of the non-Chinese one, but I was way too full of good feelings for it to be an issue.

"Okay, will do. Laters, you." That was directed at me, again. Hopefully, anyway. I'd fucking missed her much more than I'd realised.

"So that's the one? That's her is it, pudding?" Portia said, once Ciara was out of sight and sound.

"Pardon?" I was dancing automatically now, it was brill. My body and the music were no longer two separate things, it felt like.

"That's the girl you're so hung up on, today. She's the one making you all... *reluctant*."

"I don't – how did you – ah…" This vampire lady was too much. She had psychic powers I could only dream of.

"Oh, come on… The tension between you two was ridiculous! I wouldn't blame you either, sausage. She's immense-looking. Incredible boobs, too. Not like the head of the Itty Bitty Titty Committee, here." She gestured at her chest.

"Hah! Don't be stupid, Ling. You're literally perfect."

"Oh, I know. I totally rock, and anyway, my arse more than makes up for the lack of frontage, chicken. I'm just saying *she* looks good, too."

"She does, yeah." She really did. Always, but even more, this weekend. I was rushing hard now. The green lasers coming from the stage were bouncing all over us, and it was hard to keep my jittery eyes from trying to follow them.

"But that's not why you like her, cupcake."

"It isn't?" A different song was on now, or at least I thought it was different. The mixing was so smooth that it was hard to tell.

"Nah, you're not the shallow type, Kweevy-weavy. You like what's going on in that girl's *brain*, not what's going on in her *brassiere*."

"Hah! Yeah, you're right. She's cool. She's very cool." Cool was way too simple a word to cover it, really.

"Oh, I'm aware, peach," said Portia, sounding a bit… resigned?"

"You're aware of…?"

"I'm aware that you're absolutely *Head Over Feet* for Ms. Witchy Eyes. Smitten like a kitten, you are. So much so that you can literally turn down *this* magnificent Cantonese buffet," she said, doing a sweeping hand gesture up and down her body to let me have a look at what I *could have* won, as the guy always said on Bullseye.

"Hah! You're amazing. And silly. And beautiful. And sexy." I pulled her in as close as possible so I could feel her skin against my own, while the drugs and the music and everything else ran through me.

"Hmmmm. Yes, I am. But you've still…" she paused, taking some of my stray hair out of her mouth. That never happened in the movies.

"I've still what?"

"You've still decided to *eschew* the *foo* of Xû," she said, leaning closer into me and doing the trick with my earring and her teeth again, except this time around – now I was rushing on a pill as well as horned up on coke - it felt like she'd lit a cherry bomb and dropped it down my knickers. Oh boy.

"Jaysus…" I said, holding onto her in case I fell over.

"Sorry. Just reminding you, in case you need reminding, jam tart." She pressed her face into the top of my head and took a big sniff of my hair. I didn't know what to say, so I put my head on her shoulder and sank into her for a bit, breathing in all the different scents of her and letting the blissed-out feelings take over. I thought about that song from when I was around ten, about heaven being a place on earth. She had really nice shoulders too, Belinda Carlisle. She had really nice everythings, I thought, picturing the video for it. Then the music started getting faster and we untangled ourselves so we could have a proper dance.

I had no idea what was going to happen tonight. I didn't know if things were okay with Ciara again, or if it was just the drugs that had made us seem okay. I didn't know if she still felt like she had at the end of last night, or if we could try again tonight. I didn't know if she thought I was *with* Portia now, but if she did, she'd been incredibly cool with it, just there. I didn't know if that was just the drugs too, either. I didn't know anything. But it didn't matter now, and it wouldn't matter, for ages yet. No need to overthink it, Caoimhe. Heaven is a place on Earth - in a tent, in Cork. Just go with it.

*****

"Is that brand new, darling?" Portia said to the man in the yellow hi-viz who was fiddling with the portaloo outside, when we'd finally tracked down where they were, from Ciara's directions.

"Sorry, what?" He'd a big Cork accent on him. Probably cos we were in Cork.

"That loo, is it a new loo? Has it never been used before, babe? Is this the unveiling?" Portia seemed normal to me, but yer man probably thought she was mental, with her large pupils and her wildly animated mandible.

"It's brand new, yeah. Why?" He had those glasses on that were normal ones, but they turned into tinted ones when it was sunny out.

"Well, because I'd like to christen it!" she said, still dancing on the spot, despite the music being a fair bit away. I was the same, though. We'd brought the music with us, in our molecules.

"You'd like to piss in it?" he said. He'd clearly gone deaf from working here all day, poor sod.

"That works too. So, can I?"

"You can of course, love. Fire away there, says you. Tis all ready." He was looking at her funny and I realised it was cos he'd been expecting her to speak like Bruce Lee or something, but a Portia voice had come out instead. It happened frequently.

"You're an absolute star, thanks! Wait here, jelly tot. I'll be quick as a flash."

"Enjoy," I said, taking a pull on the half a fag I had left.

Ciara had only talked to us for a second when she came back, but that wasn't her fault. Portia had dragged me off immediately, because she was bursting. I had to go as well, so it couldn't be helped. I'd talk to Ciara when we got back, and all would be right with the world then. Hopefully. The door opened, but Portia didn't come out.

"Pssst!" She said, doing the *come here* finger at me. "Come into my office, buttercup!"

"Why am I – what are you up to?" I said, closing the door behind me.

"You don't mind going while I'm here, do you? I can leave if you like?" She was looking at me strangely, but it wasn't a bad strange.

"Ah, no. I don't care," I said, very much hoping that the Number One I'd been planning didn't turn into something more serious. I liked her, but we weren't at the *shitting in each other's presence* stage of our relationship yet. If there even was such a stage.

"Cool, don't worry, I won't peek, honey." She turned her back to me, and then it was me doing the peeking, at what a tabloid journalist might describe as her shapely derriere. I yanked down my jeans without undoing the bow thing, knickers as well, and let nature take its course.

"Finished now, you can turn around, there's no fear of you," I said. She was smiling again. I still wasn't used to that.

"Excellent. It's almost nice in here, isn't it? Relatively speaking, I mean."

"Yes. It's nice, for a festival bog."

"So…" she said, in a tone that I recognised from some time before.

"Small bump?" I said, trying to read her mind with my E-telepathy.

"Oh. Yeah, I guess we could. There's nowhere to chop a line though, *chérie*, so we might have to use my special nail again."

"Or this," I said, taking my chain with the spoon on it out of my jeans pocket. Her eyes lit up.

"Oooh! Look at you with all your fancy drug paraphernalia, milky moo." That was my favourite one so far, definitely.

"What can I say? I'm a woman who carries miniature spoons about her person. Right then, let the dog see the… cocaine."

*****

"A game, yeah?" I said, wondering if I could light up in this thing and then remembering that Portia didn't smoke at all, so it would not only be rude, it would be attempted murder.

"Well yeah, a game. It's like, we invented it – as a means to a… no, that's not right - as a *solution* to a particular problem." We'd had one good spoon of coke each and then said we'd have no more. It was still early. We could change our minds later.

"And what was this problem?"

"Well, the problem was that I was seeing someone, and he was seeing someone, but our other halves weren't out with us, and we were very off our faces and terminally horny, but neither of us wanted to cheat." She stopped to take a breath. I took one too, it was contagious.

"Well that was nice of ye, like," I said, meaning it sincerely. I didn't do cheating either. I was a good girl, apart from all the times when I was a bad girl, obviously. Never because of cheating, though. Not my style.

"Yeah. Yeah, so, what we did was – me and this fella,

George his name was – what we did was we made up a game to amuse ourselves, but also to get rid of the frustration and whatnot."

"Right. And what did this game involve?"

"Well, I'll tell you now, peach. What it was, was we tried to come up with ways to do stuff with each other that technically wasn't cheating."

"Technically?" I was *très sceptique* already.

"Well, yeah. So, there was no kissing. Definitely no French kissing. No touching anyone's organs."

"Organs! Hah! Your liver must have been devastated."

"Hahah, shut up, you know what I meant. Anyway, no sexual touching that you'd ever do in a real sexy situation with your actual boyfriend."

"Or girlfriend," I said, sticking up for my new Sapphic sisterhood.

"Or girlfriend, yes. So no stroking of the boobs or the bum. No rubbing crotch areas or rubbing them against each other - definitely not that. I mean, dry humping is basically your whole sex life until you start having actual sex, there's no way you could consider that *not* sexually touching," she said.

"Ah, the memories. Dummy Riding, we used to call it."

"Hah! That sounds so bad, but it kind of makes sense, linguistically, so I'll add it to my enormous vocabulary now. *Dummy Riding*. Fancy coming round my house while the parents are at mass, Joshua? We can do some Dummy Riding!"

"Oh God, now I'm picturing you having sex with one of the mannequins from the window in Todd's," I said, wondering if there was a queue of angry people outside our little hideaway, dying for a slash. Then I remembered they were all on pills, so none of them had the ability to wee. Or to get angry, for that matter. We were probably grand, so.

"What's a Todd's?" Portia said, letting her Dublinness show.

"Oh, it's like Switzer's, for Limerick people," I said, hoping that explained it.

"Switzer's is Brown Thomas now, in Dublin anyway," Portia said.

"Brown Thomas?" I said, giggling. "That sounds like something you'd end up with if you didn't wear a condom while bumming someone."

"It'd probably be the least serious thing you'd end up with, in fairness, sausage," said Portia, and we both did a yuck face, thinking about the joys of urinary tract infections.

"So what's it called, this game?" I said, sniffing a little sniff and feeling the weird, anaesthetic liquid going into my throat. Cocaine was the same amount of disgusting as speed, but it had that extra ick of making you think you'd swallowed some Bonjella too.

"It's called Can't Do Me."

"Can't do me?" I sort of understood, but I didn't as well. It was getting very hot in here now. I didn't know if it was the drugs, the lack of new air, or the growing tension between us. Good tension, obviously.

"Yeah, because whatever you get up to, as long as you follow the rules, they can't do you for it, yeah? Oh, and also because the two people playing it aren't allowed to *do* each other, duh!" Portia wasn't tall at all; I'd finally figured out. The heels on her platform boots were at least five inches, maybe six. She was probably Kylie-sized in her socks. Obviously not something that would put me off her. Quite the opposite.

"Ah, I see. Why are you telling me about this anyway?

Do you have a boyfriend?"

"Nope."

"A girlfriend?" There was no way someone who looked like her was single.

"Not at the moment, chicken." She winked at me, but I didn't know what the wink was implying.

"Well neither do I. On both counts. So..." I didn't know where I was going with this, so I stopped.

"Yeah, but you're like *emotionally involved* with that Ciara girl, right?"

"Hmmmm. I really don't know how to explain, I just-"

"I don't need you to. All I'm saying is, if you want to play the game with me, you can. And you won't be doing anything wrong, and your conscience will be completely clear, and you can carry on with your... *pursuit* of the witchy one, or whatever it is you're up to. That's all, really. Or we can just go." She reached for the lock, but I put my hand on her arm to stop her, because fuck it, it was Christmas.

"Okay, okay. I'll bite," I said, filling up with something that was between drug-aided horniness and natural anticipation.

"Biting is allowed. You just can't leave any marks, cupcake." Her eyes flashed at me, and the little gold stars almost looked like they were spinning around her big black pupils. She was such a double-knockout.

"Cool. What else?" I was tense and relaxed at the same time now.

"Open your mouth, a little bit."

"Okay," I said, wondering what was coming next. My hands were a little shaky. I closed my fists to stop it. Portia leaned her face in to me. She opened her mouth the same amount as mine, and my heart got a lot faster in a very short space of time. Oh boy.

"Now," she said, stopping a few millimeters from my lips. "I'm not going to snog you. I'm just gonna put my bottom lip between your top and bottom lips, yeah? And then I'm just gonna do nothing at all, okay?" Her eyes were so close to mine that our lashes were almost touching, which made me blink without meaning to.

"Yuhuh."

"Okay, here we go. And Caoimhe?"

"Yeah?" I was so hot now. Roasting – everywhere - it was like a furnace between us.

"Don't forget to breathe." She pushed her mouth into mine, and then just left it there. I had no idea how this game was supposed to relieve frustration. Having her mouth so close to me – her tongue right there, half an inch from mine – this wasn't relieving anything. She was breathing now, heavy. Me, the same. Our breath in each other's mouths, mixing. I could almost taste her, just from swapping air with her. I made a noise that was somewhere between a breathy sigh and a mousey squeak. She finally pulled away, and we were eye to eye again, panting like we'd just come off a treadmill.

"Fucking hell…" I said, gripping onto her hips, pressing against the skin between her top and her skirt.

"Fucking hell good, or fucking hell bad?" she said, pushing my fringe off my forehead and leaving her fingers inside my hair.

"Oh definitely fucking hell good," I said, not sure how much of this game I was going to be able to play, if that had only been Level One.

"Good. I'm glad. And remember," she looked in my eyes again, "They can't do us for it…"

"They can't," I said. "What's next?" The vein in my temple was throbbing, hopefully not in a *going to die* way.

"Oh, there's no order to it or anything. There's no rhyme or reason to the game, pudding. You can improvise. That's what I do, anyway."

"You'll have to show me," I said, still breathless. "I'm new here." I put my hand up and touched her cheek. She leaned her face into my fingers, and then her mouth was on them. She nipped the knuckle of the middle one with her teeth, which gave me a little start, right in the heart. Then some small, firm kisses along the side of my finger. It was ridiculous how sexual it felt. It was the combination of the innocent act, the filth already in my mind, and then the love/sex drugs acting like a magical thread, sewing those two things together. That was the best way to describe it.

She put two of my fingers in her mouth, and it was an amazing mix of boiling heat and slippery wetness. I was involuntarily crossing my legs now. It was insanely intense.

"Jesus Christ," I said, although Jesus Christ would not have approved of this sort of carry-on.

"Want me to stop, *chérie*?" Portia said, taking the spit-covered fingers out of her mouth and pushing them towards my face. I didn't understand what she was up to, until I *did* understand. I opened my mouth and tasted her off myself. We were doing pretty much nothing, and it still somehow felt like we were *fucking*. Couldn't do us for it, though. That was the name of the game.

*****

"I love your eyes, you know that, sugarplum? They're such a deep shade of brown, they're like Cadbury chocolate buttons. Or more like Minstrels, even," said Portia, when we were outside again.

"Minstrels!" I said, beaming at her. Minstrels were made by Galaxy, so it was funny her saying that cos she was the one who had actual galaxies in her eyes.

"Yeah, they're absolutely sickening. They're lush as fuck," she said. Such a compliment, coming from her, I thought. It was like having the Mona Lisa sing *I Like Your Smile* at you.

"Well, thanks. Don't eat them, though. I need them, for all the seeing and stuff."

"Pfffft! Can't do me for it," she said, looking double-cute, sickening, and lush – all at once. We had kept going with the game for a while, until someone actually did knock on the door, and we had to leave. It was probably a good thing, because at that exact moment *Xû Ling* was blowing hot breaths through the criss-cross ribbons of my jeans, and that was veering into *probably can do us for it* territory.

"Hello, Caoimhe. Where have you been?" It was Tim, who I hadn't seen since he didn't do the Hot Press interview with us.

"She's been hanging around in toilets with strange women," Portia said, squeezing my hand, which she'd been holding for ages now.

"You're a new person. I don't know you," Tim said, sounding like he was in a video for teaching kids about Stranger Danger.

"Tim, this is Portia. She's from the Far East." No idea why I said that.

"The Far East. Cool," said Tim. He didn't look wrecked yet. He was in his serene, Kung Fu Monk mode again today.

"Dún Laoghaire, to be exact, buttercup," said Portia, because she lived in Dalkey, I remembered Marian saying. Her family must have been even more loaded than ours. Dalkey was very posh, I knew that, but only from reading about it in the papers. Bono and The Edge lived there. And Maeve Binchy, my favourite author. Oh, and Van Morrison, who wrote that fucking song everyone annoyed you with if you grew up being a girl with brown eyes that looked like Galaxy Minstrels, as I had.

"Ah. That's why you sound so Irish, I see. You're very good looking, you should be a pop star or a movie star, maybe. Caoimhe, this Ecstasy tablet I took isn't working yet. How do I make it work?" He was so funny, without actually being funny, this boy.

"You just have to belieeeeve, Tim," said Portia, squeezing his cheek like he was someone's new baby. "Wait, is this the Tim who has the willy that doesn't get floppy on pills, Caoimhe?"

"My reputation precedes me," Tim said, again with a completely straight face.

"So I've heard, big boy," Portia said.

"Yeah, he can wee as well, all the way through his buzz. His penis is like the Anti-Penis. I think they mention it in the Book of Revelations," I said, the two of us looking at poor Tim with a mixture of admiration and scientific interest, but no lust, thankfully.

"Jesus, cupcake. We might have to take him somewhere with a little more privacy later, yeah?" she said, winking at me, then giving Tim's shoulder a massagey squeeze. He immediately went from Kung Fu Monk to Kenneth Williams, facially.

"For what?" I said, cringing a little at the thought of Stiff Tim in the altogether, trying to poke us with his science-defying schlong.

"So we can take his blood and study it for the antidote," said Portia, and Tim gulped so loud I could hear it over the sound of the drums and bass.

*****

"So, will you be able to vote in the divorce referendum this year, shortcake? Will you be old enough in time?" Me and Portia were standing over at the edge of the floor, both of us having some water, and me a fag.

"When is it, November? Yeah, I guess so." I didn't really care about it – I didn't believe in marriage at all - but I was obviously gonna vote Yes, because it was embarrassing how backwards our country was sometimes. It was still illegal to be gay until a couple of years ago. You couldn't buy rubber Johnnies in a shop until about 1991. The *state* of us, like. Mortifying.

"Cool. I'm not sure how I'll vote." Portia was really good at chewing gum without it making a noise, I'd noticed. I needed her to teach me her ways. Lots of her ways.

"You're not?" This was new, but then everything was new with her, cos she was new, to me, even though I felt like I'd known her for yonks.

"Yeah, I mean I'm totally for divorce, and for all kinds of progress, honey. But, on the other hand, I don't want to give my dad the satisfaction of being able to legally dump my Mom."

"You what, now?"

"Oh, it's a long story. But basically, my dad went to the Ukraine six months ago – said it was for business, but it turned out it was for pleasure too, because he brought himself home a gold-digging Russian whore."

"Oh, Ling. I'm sorry." She was really opening up to me now. It was nice, but it also made the dilemma in my head a bit worse, because the more I got to know her and the more she seemed like a real person instead of this mysterious vampire cartoon girl, the harder it was to-

"Yeah, no it sucked, but mainly for Mom. That woman has supported him through everything. Emotionally, and when he went bankrupt that time, financially as well. Now she's basically getting thrown in the bin, for some perfect looking, long-legged, plastic-tits, Slavic slice. It's tragic, *mon amie*. It truly is." She looked sad now, I put my arms around her waist and pulled her into me close. The lovely scent of her went up my nose right at the same time as I got a little rush off the pill, almost as if one had caused the other. Perhaps it had.

"And what's she like?"

"My Mom? She's the greatest woman who ever lived. She's my hero, sweet pea. She's the best." She smiled in a brand new way, to me at least. It was so genuine and pure that it made my heart flutter.

"No, sorry, I meant what's the other one like? The new girlfriend. As a person, I mean?" I said. Portia looked at me, but she didn't speak for a few seconds. Then she cleared her throat, and said:

"Is there a word for someone who's *worse* than a cunt?" She was visibly cross and upset now, I didn't like it.

"A *double-cunt*?" I said, and thankfully she smiled again, and we disappeared into each other for another long hug, because long hugs were the best - and so was she.

*****

"How are these better than the ones from yesterday, like? How are they like… stronger? How is that possible?" Richie said, dancing next to me, which was strange. Not him being next to me. Him dancing. A dancer he was not.

"I don't know! I thought I wouldn't even come up on it. I thought nothing would happen!" I said. Portia had gone off talking to some people from Dublin she knew, so I'd danced into the crowd, smiling at complete strangers, and feeling amazing. No sign of Ciara, but it was really packed now, she could have been anywhere. Marian and Rich had danced past me, and I had to grab onto her to let her know I was here.

"I can't help ye, I wasn't on these yesterday," she said. She looked extra amazing now. Lucky Richie. It was hard not to stare at her, but she wouldn't have minded anyway. No one minded anything right now. It was all good.

"What were you on?" I said, putting my hand on her waist, because I couldn't stop touching everyone, it was addictive.

"Oh, I was just high on life," she said. "And cocaine, obviously." She smiled a big, pretty, white teeth smile. God, I'd missed her. I just hadn't realised until we met each other again. I thought about Áine, and how much she'd have enjoyed this weekend, but I didn't feel sad. It was very, very hard to have negative feelings right now. I wished I could keep that superpower forever, but I knew it would only last as long as the chemical high did.

"Portia said ye are in Jury's too?" I said. I hadn't much water left, and the bar out here wasn't free. I'd have to see if I had any money in my purse in a bit.

"Yeah, we've a room on the third floor!"

"Just one room?" I said, surprised.

"Yeah, we were saving money – well, I was, she's loaded. One room, one double bed. We just thought that if one of us pulled we could go stay with whoever we pulled, and the other one could have the room, you know? Better than fucking camping, anyway."

"And did either of ye? Pull, mean." I said, wondering then if I should be asking, with Richie here. Too late now, though.

"Nah, we just went back to the room together, high as a kite. And no."

"And no, what?" I said, puzzled. Richie was pretending

not to listen, but he definitely was.

"No we didn't get off with each other. I'm not into girls, yeah? Not even if they're Portia, hahaha!" Marian stopped and whispered something to Rich, he nodded at her, and then she took my wrist.

"You okay?" I was trying to remember the exact last time I'd seen her, and what ages we were. I couldn't pinpoint it, though. It hadn't been an important day at the time. We wouldn't have known it was going to be the last time ever. It wasn't though, anymore. We'd found each other again. Kismet.

"Yeah, can I be a fucker and scab a fag off you, Kweev?" She was definitely failing at giving them up, but you couldn't give up in the middle of taking Es. Smoking was one of the best parts of the whole experience, I'd found.

"Of course you can, you want me to come with?" I had like two left, might as well have them between us, then I'd go get some more. We danced our way off the floor and found a nice corner.

"There! Ooh, I was gasping, babe. Cheers." She was so bad at giving up fags she still had her own lighter. I could have sworn I'd lit hers with my matches earlier though. Maybe she'd found it down the bottom of her handbag. You could find literally anything in the bottom of your handbag if you looked for long enough. That's how they discovered the Rosetta Stone, probably.

"No probs. So, what's going on with you and himself?" I'd been watching them a bit. They were very close, but they hadn't shifted or anything. Or if they had, they'd done it when I wasn't looking.

"Ah, I dunno. He's single, I'm single, we'll see." She was devouring the fag altogether.

"Oh. He's single?" I'd never asked him about why

Dearbhla wasn't here. They'd broken up then, I supposed. Poor Richie. Although he'd fallen on his feet now, so he was grand.

"Yeah. Pretty recent, same as me, so we're both on the rebound, like. But that's kind of better, you know?"

"It is?" I noticed Niall had come along, over on the dancefloor, so Richie wasn't on his lonesome anymore. Not that it would have mattered. You were never alone if you were on a dancefloor full of people on yokes, it felt like.

"Yeah, cos we were honest about it, so we know the score, and whatever happens, we know not to be reading too much into it, like. Does that make sense?" Her top was dripping wet with sweat or water or whatever it was. It made her look like the Final Girl from a horror movie. She was pretty enough in the face and bouncy enough in the chest to be one, I reckoned.

"Yeah, totally. And ye can cheer each other up and keep each other company this weekend."

"Yeah, and like, I know him. It's like, really good on a weekend like this – especially taking yokes or coke or whatever – to have someone you trust. I haven't spoken to Richie in years, but I know he's not some rapey stranger guy. I used to be in love with him. We've lots of memories and stuff. It's been amazing doing yokes with him so far, I'm dead happy I met him here." She looked really glowy and warm and open and honest and loved up. I got a buzz just listening to her say all that.

"Yeah, that actually does sound ideal, ye'll probably have an amazing, loved-up time, definitely. Lots of memories and cuddles. He can mind you all night, like."

"And he can bang the living fuck out of me tomorrow morning, when the floppy willy thing wears off," said Marian, and I swore her pupils got even bigger than they already had been, from imagining it.

"That too, yeah, haha, you whore. I love you!" I said, giving her a big hug that felt lovely, but also a bit ouchy, as I'd forgotten she had bits of spiky metal in her nipples. Being a woman was a logistical fucking nightmare at times, but we persevered, regardless.

Portia had said earlier, when we were talking about Tim – that the upside of the pilly willy was it wore off the next day, and it was like your penis had a lot of catching up to do, so you got a tree trunk of a boner first thing in the morning. So Marian was in for a treat tomorrow, definitely.

I was wondering what I'd be doing in the morning, or in the night, and who it would be with. I wasn't anxious about it though. *Que sera, sera.*

"How are my two favourite white girls?" said Portia, materialising beside us, although without a puff of smoke.

"All the better for seeing you," I said, turning so I could lean back into her, sliding my face up next to hers. She kissed my cheek, and I turned my head quick enough to catch her lips with mine. Just a peck, mind. Couldn't do me for it. Marian gave us a little stern *I'm watching you two* look, but then she laughed and took one hand of ours each and dragged us back up to the lads.

*****

"Come!" Portia said, a little while later, dragging me a few feet away from the others.

"For what?" I said. I was peaking so hard already, everything felt either way too intense or incredibly blissful. I stood up, facing her, and my body started moving again, regardless of whether I wanted it to.

"I just want to have you to myself for a bit, cupcake," she said, taking my hand and putting it on her neck. Her skin felt like satin.

"I'm all yours then, Ling," I said. Nobody else was exactly offering. I hadn't seen Ciara since before we went to the toilets that time, and that felt like ages ago.

"Good. Ling likes you being all hers, Kweeva Shox." She looked unbelievable, like as if she'd taken her normal Portia Perfection and turned it up to eleven. Her *Porfection.*

"Does Ling like this?" I walked my fingers up behind her ear, and stroked the hair behind in small, gentle circles, the way I liked people to do to me.

"Oof... Ling likes!" she said.

"What Ling likes, Ling gets," I said. I loved that I called her by her real name now, when no one else was around. It was like our secret. Not even Mar called her it. It felt *intimate.*

The music was pounding, the strobes were flashing, the girls in the crowd were wearing next to nothing and writhing around us in a tangled, sweaty, fleshy mass. It was dark and bright at the same time. My eyes jittered again. I stopped playing with the hair behind her ears and moved over to the back of her neck to do more of the same. My other hand was on the skin between where stocking ended, and skirt begun. Not moving or stroking. Just touching her enough to let her know I was here.

Portia's fingers were behind the ribbons on my jeans now, she was using them to pull me closer to her. I looked at her face through the flashing lights and the darkness. Her eyes smiled before her mouth caught up. I felt her fingers slide up my top, but she didn't touch my boob. She used the back of her hand to lift the shirt away from my skin, letting in a little draught that gave me goosebumps, if they weren't there already. She kept her hand still, where it was, so her palm was millimeters above my nipple. Each breath I took moved me closer to her, then away again. I was going to explode in a minute, this was too much. She moved her mouth closer and did the not-kissing thing with her lips between mine. Both of us had gloss on, which made the sensation even more amazing this time around.

Everyone else in that place had disappeared, as far as I was concerned. Her hand stayed there, unmoving, under my top. I wanted to push myself against it, but then we would've broken the rules. The fingers of her other hand were still down my jeans, not touching anything either. Her breath in my mouth tasted of mints, and of Jagermeister, and of her. She didn't move a muscle. It was exquisite torture. I wanted it to stop now, and I didn't want it to end ever.

The whole thing probably lasted a minute – 90 seconds, tops - but when she finally broke away, whispering "Can't do me for it," into my ear, it felt like time had stopped, just for us, for hours. I pulled myself together and looked over her shoulder at Niall, Richie, and Marian, expecting them all to be looking at us, jaws on the floor. They hadn't seen anything. They couldn't give a shite what we were up to. They didn't even know we were gone.

SIXTEEN

"Where *is* Ciara, I haven't seen her since... ages," I said to Bríd, in the back of Benson's van, on the way to Jury's.

"Oh she's with that boy," she said, as if I should know what that meant. I felt like I should be feeling something bad. I couldn't, though. It didn't seem possible. Very strange.

"What boy is that?"

"Zachary? Zach, whatever he's called. He used to be her boyfriend, a good bit back. I don't really know him, he's all right, I guess. But like, everyone seems all right today, so, I mean, he could be a serial killer too. But he's probably not." Bríd was unable to sit still, it was funny, but not in a way that I was laughing at her. It was just amusing to watch.

"Hmmmm," I said. "Are they together again, or something?" I was being remarkably calm about this. I wouldn't have been, under normal circumstances. But then, under normal circumstances I wouldn't have had any reason to be jealous of Ciara being with a bloke, so there were no such thing as normal circumstances anymore. All bets were off.

"Doubt it," said Ian. Hadn't seen him in ages as well, but I hadn't wanted to either, so it didn't matter.

"Yeah, he seems gay, Ciara wouldn't go out with a gay guy," said Tim, who had finally come up on his pill, judging by his massive pupils and the way his knees were dancing to the beat of the engine.

"Maybe she's into the gays now," said Ian, looking at me, although I was probably imagining the implication. He could imply away, I didn't care. I was flying it.

"We still doing *Dress Up Bríd*?" Benson shouted back from the driver's seat.

"Yes, Benson. We are. Don't worry," I said. Portia was beside me, not saying much, but she was there, and that was enough. I didn't know what to think about Ciara, but I was fine. I was way, way too happied-up to have any sort of negative feelings. Not even for Ian, who I sort of suspected might have given *my* Ciara the benefit of his tree trunk penis this morning. Even thinking of that now didn't do much to me. I was double-bulletproof, for some reason.

"Frank, are these different pills?" Richie said, reading my mind before I even had the thought. E-telepathy with added E-clairvoyance.

"Yeah, they're still doves, but there's a different colour speckle on them. Why, do they feel different, boy?" Frank was up front with Benson. Niall was still back at the tent; I didn't know why.

"They feel a fuck lot stronger, Frank," I said. "In a good way, like. I feel like I'm made out of happy. You couldn't make me sad if you tried, like."

"Absolutely," said Bríd. "I'm way more off my tits than I was last night. Ciara said she is too. They're fucking deadly, like." That was a lot of swearing for Bríd. They really must be life-changing, these speckly doves, I thought. Benson would probably be allowed to do her up the bum later. Or tomorrow morning. When the Fat Dick Fairy visited.

"Well then, we'll keep those ones for us, and sell the other ones to the punters, yeah? Deal, boys and girls?" Frank said, smiling back at us with his big Cork head, while we drove through actual Cork.

"Deal!" said everyone, together. Portia pressed her very warm cheek against mine, and I turned to look at her.

"You okay?" I said, moving her hair out of her eyes so I could see them properly. Still galaxy-like, still gorgeous.

"Mmmmm, very." She gripped my thigh and squeezed it hard, taking in a big breath through her nostrils. Her forehead was pressed against mine, noses touching.

"Whatchu thinking 'bout?" I said, dreamily, moving my face back a few inches so I could take in all of hers.

"Ohhhh, lots of things, cherry pie." She bit her bottom lip in a way that could only be deliberate, and it made my everything tingle. My hearing seemed so acute now that I swore I could hear her teeth scrape over the skin. She opened her mouth a tiny bit, and I looked inside at where my fingers had been earlier, before she'd fed me the taste of her. Oh boy.

"Maybe you can tell me about them later, Ling. Tell me, or show me." I said the *Ling* part the quietest, because it was still our secret, and there were people around.

*****

"I went to National School with a girl called Aoife Cowman, and hardly anyone ever made fun of her name, but like, once the Simpsons started on TV, when she was going into Secondary, her life was nearly destroyed," Bríd said, arm-linking me up the hallway after we conquered the stairs. We were going to take the lift, all of us, but Frank said that walking up a couple of flights of steps would make the blood rush through you and get you whizzing, and we were all pretty suggestible right now, so that's what we did.

"Hah! I can imagine. Poor Aoife!" Bart barely even said it on the show, but I remembered there had been this ridiculous marketing campaign for about two years, with the slogans on t-shirts and Bermudas and socks and coasters and keyrings and basically anything you could print words or a picture on. The world went Simpsons crazy for a bit.

"Yeah. I mean, the surname was bad enough, but cos she was called Aoife too, every time you saw her name on the roll call, or on a list on the message board, it was down as "A. Cowman", so." Bríd stopped outside the door of 211, and studied it intensely for a few seconds, like it was hanging in the Louvre.

"We going into mine, is it?" I said. We didn't hang around in my room, usually, all of us. The middle room, Ian's one, made more sense.

"No, we're just getting the slutty clothes, babe," she said, with a massive, white-toothed smile that was like someone turning on their high beams without there even being any fog.

"Oh. Yes, indeed. My whore wardrobe. My *whoredrobe*." I fished the hotel keyring out of my bag at the first attempt. I looked around to see where Portia was, but she'd stalled a bit behind us, deep in chats with Frank. I thought about poor Niall again. I hoped he was being careful. He probably wasn't. I finally got the pointy bit of the key and the holey bit of the lock to make love together, and the door opened with a satisfying click-pop. I was expecting a smell of stale fags and sweaty sheets, but it looked like the maids had been in to change the bedding, and they'd left the window open as well, so it was lovely and fresh in here. What a life we led.

*****

"Right now, no laughing at me, yeah?" Bríd said, walking out Ian's en suite door in her knickers and bra. I didn't know why the sight of it shocked me. I knew she was going in there to put on clean ones, and I knew she was gonna come out again. Still though, it was very new. She wouldn't have got changed in front of me and Ciara normally, let alone a load of fellas. That was MDMA for you, though. *A whole new world*, as Aladdin would say.

"I don't think it's them *laughing* you have to worry about, Chupa Chup." Portia was beside me again, having disappeared with Frank somewhere for a few minutes, earlier. I hadn't asked her why. Didn't matter.

"Fucking hell, Bríd. When did you turn into a ride?" said Richie, getting a smack on the thigh off Marian for his troubles.

"She was always a ride, you goon," I said, although he was kind of right. She'd been hiding a lot of secrets under her normal, day to day clothes, or her manky Scoil Carmel uniform. She'd an incredible figure. Everyone I knew was a ride, it seemed. Especially tonight.

"Thanks, lover," Bríd said. There was nothing shy about her, it was brilliant. She was like a supermodel on the catwalk, except for the Snoopy socks, obviously. You wouldn't have seen Cindy or Claudia wearing those.

"The reason you look so sexy now is because we've never seen you without clothes on," Drug Tim said, helpfully.

"I have," Benson said, delighted with himself.

"So have I," Richie said, and we all swung our necks around to look at him.

"WHEN?" Bríd said, her hands on her hips, ready to strop. She'd a lovely flat stomach, even now, with the *can't wee* bloat.

"Yeah, Richie. When?" Benson said, not looking angry or anything, just looking like this was news to him. He probably didn't mind. He was old, old people probably didn't get jealous about your exes, since ye'd both have loads of exes, cos of being old. Bríd wasn't old, though, and she'd barely any exes, that I could remember anyway.

"In your house," Richie said. Bríd still looked mystified.

"What about my house? You've been in my house once,

like. And you definitely didn't-"

"There's a photo of you in your bedroom. Of you and Steven, in the bath, when ye were small," said Richie, and everyone seemed to do the one sigh of relief and understanding at the same time, like we were all sharing the same mind.

"Ah! Yes, there is, yeah." Bríd was smiling again. Benson nodded.

"What were you looking at photos of naked kids for, Rich?" Ian said, rolling something that looked like it was just a fag, unfortunately.

"Yeah, Richie, you child molester," Marian said.

"You can talk!" I said to her, and she stuck her tongue out at me.

"Anyway, what am I putting on first, then? Are we having a vote?" Bríd said, completely getting into this idea of an impromptu fashion show.

"Rubber dress!" Benson said, predictably enough.

"Short-shorts and fishnet top!" I said, because I'd already forgotten what was in the rest of the bags. Frank wasn't with us. He'd like, politely excused himself from all this when he'd heard the plan. Said he was a bit too auld to be looking at any of us without our clothes on, and he'd some stuff to take care of anyway. He was such a lovely man. Just the least skeezy guy you could ever meet. Best fake uncle ever.

*****

"We can see your panties in that skirt," said Tim. He wasn't wrong. It was my seven inch leather one, it was basically a belt. I usually wore fishnet tights with it as well, which did nothing to hide the gusset situation. Best thing to do was wear black knickers, so you didn't draw attention. Or red ones, if you wanted to draw attention. Depended on the occasion, really.

"Yeah, you're flashing your gash there a bit, Bríd," said Richie, as if he enjoyed getting thumped on the leg by his new wife.

"Don't be vile," Portia said. She was standing up, not sitting with me, because she'd got very involved in the sexy fashion show, and she'd been doing Bríd's makeup for her too, intermittently.

"Yeah, Richie," I said, even though I didn't really care. It was just a word. I said way worse ones all the time.

"Not Richie, pudding. Tim."

"What have I said that's wrong?" Drug Tim said, looking neither offended nor pleased, as usual.

"Panties!" said Portia, putting two fingers in her mouth and doing the universal mime for vomiting.

"What's wrong with panties?" Bríd said. You really could see her knickers. Everyone here had already seen them, obviously, but it felt different when you could see someone's underwear while they had clothes on. Like the way the bit of skin between Portia's stockings and her skirt looked sexier than if she hadn't been wearing either of those things – sexier than if she was naked, even. I didn't know *why* that was, I just knew that it *was*.

"I just hate it, peach. It's a horrible sounding word. Like *moist*, or *clump*." She was behind Bríd's head now, doing something with her hair. She had a bunch of hairpins between her fingers, and a couple in her mouth.

"Ugh... moist," I said, pretending to shudder.

"Exactly, possum. It's just not a sexy word, either. It gives me the gawks. I go to the States a lot, because my father does some work there, in California? Silicon Valley and all that stuff. Anyway, the Yanks, they think that word is normal. They're always saying it, despite my good advice, darling. It's double-tragic." She was really beavering away at

Bríd's hair now, while talking to us. I wondered what style she was doing for her, but we'd find out soon enough.

"What would you say then, like? Instead of panties?" I said, starting to agree with her now. It wasn't a nice word to say, let alone hear. Or maybe I was just going along with her cult teachings again.

"Knickers, of course!" She lifted some of Bríd's hair up, and I could see that she'd done it in a plait. French plaits, it looked like, the ones that you had at the back of your head, to show off your neck. Bríd had a lovely long neck, so it was a good idea, I thought.

"How is knickers any better?" Ian said. He looked really weird. It was cos he was smiling, I realised. His voice still sounded grumpy as usual, mind.

"Well, because you can't talk *dirty* about panties, pumpkin. You can't talk about wanting to rip off someone's panties, or making their panties wet, can you? No, you can't."

"Why not? *Ouch!* You're okay, I'm fine, carry on," said Bríd. Portia had pulled her hair a little too hard. I had a thought about Portia pulling *my* hair a little too hard and me quite liking it, but I told my brain to shush, cos I wanted to hear about the knickers and stuff.

"Sorry, honey blossom. I'll be more careful now, I promise. Anyway! What I'm saying is, knickers is the better word. Panties is what you call the underwear of a five-year-old. You can't find it sexy at all, unless you're some sort of paedo, my dears." She'd given Bríd's locks a break now and was giving her a shoulder massage that was making me want one too. All in good time.

"But see, with knickers," she went on, catching my eye for a second and giving me a little *hello* wink. "You can say stuff like - I'm gonna pull your knickers to the side and slide my hard *fucking* cock up you. Or maybe - I'm gonna rip those pretty little knickers off you and stuff them in your mouth to muffle the screams while I'm fucking you. Or like - I'm gonna cut those knickers off *with this knife* and use them to tie your wrists to the bed frame. Then I'm gonna fuckin' go down on you for *hours and hours*, until the sheets are *saturated* with my spit and your *come* - You know, that sort of thing, yeah?" She'd done a slightly different voice while she was giving us the examples – like she was an actor, playing a part – but it was still her saying it. She looked around at the room at us, seeing our reactions to her tirade of filth. It reminded me of Back to the Future, when Marty finishes his guitar solo in front of the 1955 audience, and they're not quite ready for it, but their kids are gonna love it. My mouth was suddenly very dry, *mais ma culotte ne l'était certainement pas,* pardon my French.

"Knickers it is, then - that settles it," said Tim, more deadpan than ever, and everyone burst out laughing, relieving all the tension in an instant. I loved these people; I never wanted to not be around them.

*****

"Oh, I must play you this one, sausage. Hang on a sec." Portia was looking through her zip-up CD wallet thing. We'd finally got Bríd sorted, in my Day-Glo pink latex dress and white latex hold-ups, which were always going to be the winner with this crowd, in fairness, the loved-up fools – me included. She looked fab in it, even if it was a bit uncomfortable, even with the talc and without any undies. Then again, she was absolutely off her box, so she was probably grand.

They'd only been pinning and braiding her hair to get her prepared for the *pièce de résistance* – a pastel blue, shoulder length wig, from Portia's personal wig stash, which was apparently a thing that existed. It was an incredible combo – she looked like she was from another dimension - like she was in a French cartoon, about spaceships and faraway galaxies. We were all knocked out by her. She was standing by the wall over, talking to Benson and Ian. Tim was sitting on the floor with us, Mar and Rich had popped to his room "to get something". A likely story.

"What's this one now?" I was wondering if I should change my own clothes, before we went back. I couldn't be arsed, but I'd probably change my mind once I saw what *Xû Ling* was gonna wear. Couldn't have the two of them making me look like a wallflower, like. I'd an image to maintain, as Brian said.

"It's the Clueless soundtrack, butter bean. Film's not even out yet, but I got this when I was across the pond, as you do. It's not *brilliant*, but there's an acoustic version of *Fake Plastic Trees* on it, and also, this…" She closed the lid on the CD player and pressed play. The start of the song sounded familiar, but new as well.

"*Kids in America*?" I said, recognising it from the opening line. Wasn't Kim Wilde though. It was a different Kim. "Wow, wait, is that-"

"The Muffs, yeah! Shhhh, listen to it a minute, it's lush." She reached over and touched my knee, moving her fingers over the material of my jeans in a little arc, not light enough to tickle or hard enough to be annoying. It was *just right*. Goldilocks would have approved.

Ciara hadn't come back yet, with or without the mysterious Zach. She probably wouldn't, either. It'd be time for us to head back there soon enough, anyway. I wasn't too fussed, as long as I didn't think about it, and there was enough going on here with everyone, and with Portia, that my thoughts rarely wandered off elsewhere. It was fine. It was grand. It was going to be okay, whatever happened. I was on an incredible buzz, I was just concentrating on that, for now. Other bridges could be crossed when they arrived. The song ended, and she pressed Stop on the thing, so the next one mustn't have been any good.

"That was brilliant, it's not on their new album though, or it's not on the version I have," I said.

"No, it's just on this. You can borrow it if you want, to tape it. I don't mind, sugarlump." She was playing with my hair, and she leaned in to kiss my cheek. I did the *turning quickly* trick again and caught her on the mouth with my lips. Just a quick peck. Couldn't do me for it.

"So are you a lesbian now, Caoimhe?" I'd forgotten Tim was right next to us.

"What? No…" I said, in my least convincing voice ever. I *wasn't* a lesbian though, so I was technically not lying. I noticed that the other three had stopped chatting and were looking over our way now, ears wide open.

"Oh. Okay, I just thought you might be, cos of all the stuff you two have been doing together. Doesn't matter to me, anyway, just be yeerselves, girls," said lovely, wonderful Tim, meaning it too. The door opened and Mar and Rich came in, not even slightly looking like they'd been having a mini-romp elsewhere. Her hair was still immaculate, and he didn't even have a crease in his t-shirt. Boring bastards.

"She's not an anything, Tim darling. She's just a Caoimhe, and like you say, she *is* being herself. And I think she's doing a great job of it," Portia said, fixing my hair again, but this time without any kisses.

"She's doing a terrible job of not acting like a lesbian, in fairness," Ian said, as if I wasn't in the room. I still didn't care, though. Maybe I would tomorrow. I'd save him a kick in the shins, just in case.

"Lesbian, schmesbian," Portia said, waving her hand at him, dismissively. "First off, we haven't even *done* anything – can't do us for it, pudding. Secondly, even if we had, so what? Doesn't mean anyone is one thing or another, does it?"

"Well..." Richie said, as if anyone had asked him. I put a kick in the shins on my list for him as well.

"Well, nothing. Look, *boys*, because that's what most of you are here – Benson excluded, obviously – life is complex, and so is love. And sex, and romance, and everything in between. The reason you're so bloody hung up on these labels and whatnot is because your sexuality is repressed, sausage." She said the word bloody in a strange way. It made her sound a bit foreign, but then she *was* foreign – *a bit*.

"What, my sexuality?" Ian said, still smiling that unnatural smile of his.

"All of yours. It's not your fault – it's the way society works. You can't express yourselves fully, because when you do, the world tells you that you're not manly. That you're *acting like a girl*, as if that's a bad thing to act like. Or that you're gay, and being thought of as gay then becomes like your worst fear, yeah? You'd rather someone thought you were a murderer than a little poofter, am I right?" She looked at them, but no one said anything back.

"I am right, trust me. We – we ladies have our own repressions and hangups, but we're allowed to express ourselves – both emotionally and physically. We can cry, we can need a hug, we can snuggle with someone, we can hold hands, we can do lots of stuff you guys can't or won't. And we're better for it, chicken. It's one of the few advantages of being a woman."

"But I don't want to hold hands with a fella, or cuddle with one," Ian said.

"Why not?" said Marian, joining in the fun.

"Because that would be gay!" Richie said.

"Would it though?" I said. I liked this conversation now, cos I was gradually understanding the point Portia was trying to make.

"Yes!!!" Ian, Richie, and Benson said, all together.

"So, if you held my hand now or gave me a cuddle, Ian, would it make you want to shift the face off me, or to touch my langer? Would you get *the urge*, like, and not be able to resist?" Tim said, making all the girls look at him with surprise. He truly was a Kung Fu Monk.

"What? No, of course it wouldn't, you bender!" Ian said. Benson's face changed a bit, like he was getting it. Richie looked like he always looked. I'd no idea if he was getting anything. Either from this conversation, or off Marian, to be honest. Jury was still out on them.

"Well then, how is it gay?" said Portia, giving Ian all the time he needed to answer her, but he couldn't, and I did a mental *phew* that everyone had forgotten about asking me whether I preferred *oysters or snails*, at least for another while, anyway.

*****

I could hear music coming from Richie's room when I went out to get us some ice. I leaned against the door to listen. It was *Comfortably Numb.* Uncle Frank was mad into Pink Floyd, especially The Wall. I knocked, hopefully loud enough for him to hear.

"Yeah?" He opened the door a small bit and looked out the gap, smoke coming out his nostrils like a dragon.

"*Hello! Hello, hello. Is there anybody in there?*" I said, cos I was hilarious.

"Very good, come on in, girl." Frank had a book in his hand.

"Are you *reading*, is it? At a music festival, like? You swot, you,' I said, sitting down on the edge of the bed.

"Ah yeah, have ye read this one yet, Kweev? Got great reviews, it did." He held it up so I could see the cover.

"Trainspotting? Eggghhh."

"Didn't like it, no? I'm enjoying it now, I have to say." He offered me his joint, but I shook my head. Wasn't falling for that one again. I could smell from here that it was his crazy Skunk stuff from yesterday. *Je n'en veux pas, Oncle François.*

"Ah, I tried reading it, Frank. Couldn't get into it," I said, having a nose around to see how messy Richie's room was. It was pretty tidy, maybe Mar had cleaned it when she came in here earlier with him. I wouldn't have put it past her.

"Was it all the Scotch language, like? Takes a bit of getting used to all right, says you."

"Eh, kind of. I just didn't like his writing style. All the slang and the colloquialisms and the bad grammar. Tenses all over the place, too. And like, it's just a book about people doing drugs, or people describing being on drugs. There's no like…plot." I'd given up about four chapters in.

"Ah, there's more to it than that, like. Ye should give it another go. They're making a film of it and all, like."

"Maybe I'll just wait for that, then." The guitar solo was on now, that was the best bit.

"Yeah, shur. Anyway, I'm glad you popped in to see me. Cos, here." He handed me over a pouch of tobacco.

"I don't smoke rollies, Frank. But I can give it to Ian if it's going spare, cheers." I'd no idea how anyone smoked them. It was like smoking bits of beard.

"Pfffft! Open it up and have a look, before you start giving it away, girl."

"Ooooh! Are these all for me, yeah?" the pouch was full of pills. The ones with the cute little bird on them, and the right coloured speckles, of course. The good shit.

"Hahaha, go'way ou'r that. They're for all of ye, for later, so's ye don't have to come find me, yeah?" He picked up his book again and got comfy against the pillow on Richie's bed.

"Sound, Frank. So, what, do I hold on to them? Will I bring them with me?" I wasn't sure that would be a good idea.

"Jesus, no. Take them in there, get everyone to take one with them now, in the pocket or back the neck, it's up to ye. If there's any left leave them here. You don't wanna be walking around with a load of yokes on you, Caoimhe. That's only asking for trouble," he said, as if we hadn't met him walking out the Cork road with a fucking schoolbag full of them. He was a gas man, altogether.

*****

"So what is actually going on with you two, or should I not ask, chickee?" Bríd was in my room while I had a quick shower and put some new clothes on. Portia and Marian were gone to their room to change. The men of the tribe were in 213, discussing politics, the stock market, and fine dining, probably.

"With me and Li- with me and Portia?" I came out of the steaming hot bathroom, wearing a big towel around me, because I had towels now.

"Yeah. She's... quite something, isn't she?" said my new blue-haired cartoon friend. I'd figured out who she reminded me of in the dress and the white stockings. Princess from Battle of the Planets. All she needed was a cape and a helmet. No one understood who I meant, except Benson and Frank, so it must have been a cartoon that only me and current geriatrics had watched, as children.

"Ah, so are you, babe." I pulled my knickers – they definitely weren't panties, although they did come from America - up, under the towel, then put my arms through the bra, fixed it at the front, and turned my back towards her. "Do the honours there, Princess, *s'il te plaît*." I wondered what time it was, but it wouldn't be that useful to know. The set times at this thing weren't being followed to the letter or anything. Blur would probably be on later than they were supposed to be.

"I'll stop asking, then. All done!" Bríd said, finally getting the snaps lined up straight and the clasp fastened. I'd forgotten I was asking someone on yokes to do something that needed a bit of dexterity. I could barely press the lift button last night, and that was literally just a button.

"I'm matching you tonight. Well I'm matching your hair, anyway," I said, changing the subject.

"Matching it?" Bríd couldn't stop checking herself out in the mirror, it was double-adorable. She was like someone who had been Cinderella'd by a Sex-Godmother.

"Yup, look!" I put down my outfit on the bed for her to see. There was the baby blue mohair crop top with cap sleeves that I'd got in London, and my amazing, tailored, red tartan golf pants that went with pretty much everything I owned, including my new hair.

"Coooooool," she said, running her fingers through the material of the top, which made me do it too. It was nice. Like touching grass that was made of wool, my brain decided.

"*You're* cool," I said, pulling the top on over my head. I wanted a fag now, but I always wanted a fag. They'd be the death of me.

"Not as cool as you," she said, wandering over to my row of assorted feetwears. "Size are you, chickee?"

"Four, usually. Five, sometimes." Five, most of the time, but I lived in hope that I'd one day find the perfect diet to lose stubborn foot weight, and all my Size Fours would fit without crippling me.

"Can I try these silver ones, yeah? They're only about three inches, aren't they? I could manage them, I'd say,

Kweev," she said, somewhere behind me. I'd stuck my head down between the bed and the radiator to look for matches or a lighter.

"Yeah, take whatever you like, babe – what's mine is yours. Except the wedge ones on the end - I'm having those. Or the green patent ones, they're nearly broke, I dunno why I even brought them. Or my Docs, I was wearing them all day yesterday, they're manky. Anything else, though. You're grand." My fingers finally touched the matchbox they'd been looking for, down in the dark. I'd have this fag now, then I'd put my trousers on. I wouldn't have a cup of tea, but I'd definitely think about leaving the house. PARKLIFE!

*****

"Oh. My. GOD! Who are you, and what have you done with my Bríd?" We ran into Ciara in the underground car park, outside the lift, when we were leaving. She had the Zachary boyperson in tow. Good looking fella, all the same. Very tanned and tall, but tall in a skinny way, like my old friend Nick Cave.

"I know!" Bríd said, after she stopped hugging her. "I'm like a whoooooole different me, aren't I?" I'd given them all their rations of speckled doves, but no one had taken another one, yet. We were way too up on the first ones already.

"You're like a shiny sherbet shex-pot," Ciara said. She still hadn't even saluted me, but she hadn't saluted any of the rest of them either, so.

"Once again, thank you. Thank you both. So much!" Benson said, into my ear.

"No need to thank us, B. You're the one who *fucked* the girl-next-doorness out of her," I said, which made Bríd laugh, but he didn't really get it.

"And you!" Ciara said, finally acknowledging my existence. "Look at you, being all furry!" She had a good old grope of my top, which I tried to pretend was no big deal, but I'd missed her touching me. I'd missed her, full stop.

"Yeah I'm like the porno version of Cookie Monster," I said, even though Cookie Monster was a totally different shade of blue. Details, though. Details didn't matter anymore. Not on Christmas.

"You're something, all right," she said, giving me a smile and flashing those witchy eyes again. Fuck!

"This is Zach, by the way, for those of you who haven't had the pleasure." Ciara pointed at him with her thumb, and various people made various noises or said hi or nodded.

"Zach, yeah?" I said, offering a hand, which he took and shook. "Where's Screech, then? Or A.C. Slater? Are you going to score with Kelly Kapowski tonight, or have you got your eye on some other stone cold fox, Zach?" I was officially an absolute gowl now.

"Heh." he said, and then he said no more. I'd destroyed the lovely friendly atmosphere, clearly. Well done, Caoimhe!

"Anyhooch! Ummmm, I've to go slip into something much less comfortable, so we'll follow you lot on in a bit, yeah? Brìd, is my suitcase above, yeah?" Ciara said, already heading for the lift, with poor Zach, who probably thought I was some kind of psychopath now – especially if he'd never seen Saved by the Bell.

"It is, yeah. I left it in room 213, like you said to, the door's not locked. You sure you don't want us to wait for you? It's no bother, chickee," Brìd said, as if she was going to be the one driving the van. Room 213 was Ian's room. Hmmm.

"Oh no, thank you, but no. I've no idea how long we're going to be, you know the way it is, honey."

"Okay, cool. We'll see you there, then, yeah? Love youuuuuu!" Brìd said, blowing her a kiss. I was just standing there, wondering what exactly was gonna take them so long up there, but it was probably literally that she had to take a shower, dry her hair, do her face, and get dressed, so I told my stupid brain to shush.

"Ciara?" I said, remembering something.

"Yes, love?" She was regarding me again.

"Here," I said, putting my palm into hers, and discreetly passing her two pills, like a bona fide street hustler off a movie. "For you and Zach, for later," I whispered into her ear, the closeness of her face bringing back some very recent, very nice memories.

"*C'est parfait, merci!*" she said, giving me a soft peck on the cheek that made my heart go a little dizzy. I had no idea what was going on in my life anymore, really I didn't. I went back to the others, and we started walking to wherever Benson had parked this time. Portia was beside me.

"Oh, you looooooove her," she said, giving me a little dig in the ribs with an elbow. She'd put on these tiny red denim hotpants, with white, big-hole fishnets underneath. They looked great with her skin colour.

"I do not!"

"Yeah you do, cupcake. You love her the *most*." Instead of wearing a proper top, she'd got two thin, *bandeau* boob tube things, and worn them diagonally across each other, like an X. It looked amazing. Only Portia could pull something like that off. It suited her small boobs. Made them very hard not to stare at, for me anyway.

"Shush!" I said, sparking up a fag, cos it had been literally minutes since my last one.

"You love her the *most*, you love her *on toast*, you love her more than a big Sunday *roast*..."

"Hahaaah! Stop, I'm gonna die!" I'd laughed halfway through inhaling the fag and given myself the hiccups.

"If you die, you'll just come back and love her as a *ghost*," Portia said, beaming at me now. She was so sound on top of everything else. The hotness, the dress sense, the incredible poetry skills.

"Right, get in, you *gowls*," said Ian, because me and Portia were the only ones still outside B's Mystery Machine. I wondered which one out of the Scooby Doo gang I would be, and I settled on Fred, because I liked his kerchief thing.

"Hey, egg fu yung?" said Marian, once we were inside.

"Yes, shepherd's pie?" said Portia, sitting down on the floor, since all the actual seats were taken.

"When you picked out this yoke for me upstairs, you forgot one important thing, honey." Marian was wearing a ridiculous black minidress – it had a high neck and no sleeves, and the hem of it barely covered her arse.

"And what was that, pickle?" Portia had magicked a bottle of water from somewhere. She took a swig and gave it over to me.

"That I might have to sit down at some point, love." She was pulling the edges of it down her thighs, but there really wasn't much for her to pull. It was like trying to divide by zero, poor girl.

"True, true. I can see your fallopian tubes from here, peanut."

"Ah well, I'll be standing up again in a bit," said Mar, pulling her feet closer to preserve what was left of her modesty. Her legs were bare – all golden and shiny - and she'd gorgeous open-toed high heels, with roman straps, all the way up the calf. Richie's head had nearly fallen off when she came back down to us with Portia, earlier.

"Exactly, and then people will only be looking at your arse," I said, helpfully.

"Do want me to turn the van around so you can get some jeans, Mazz?" Benson said. I hadn't heard anyone call her that in so long that I'd forgotten it was her new, Dublin name, now.

"I do in my hole. Keep driving, B! Damon Albarn is expecting me, I can't be late!" She looked fantastic, really. A *bit* like a stripper, but like an expensive stripper, in a *classy* strip joint, so it was grand.

SEVENTEEN

"Giiiiiirls! My gorgeous girls! Oh my word, will you look at all of ye!" said Brian's Aisling, coming over to us in the backstage bit. I'd been right about the set times. The Beautiful South were still on, so we went out the back for a drink at the free bar. The crowd outside were chanting "We want Blur! We want Blur!" so Paul Heaton and friends would probably pack it in soon and go for a drink at the free bar too.

"Aisling!" Bríd said, giving her a massive hug.

"Brid! Oh God, I didn't recognise you with the blue hair! And with the, well, all of this. God, that feels amazing! What is it, rubber?" Aisling was having a fair old grope of the dress and the stockings. She must have been plastered. She was normally... not like this.

"It's latex! Which *is* rubber, yes, I think? Yeah, of course it is, duh! I borrowed it off Caoimhe, like. Look at you, though! You're dolled up to the nines, like, Ash. Looking fierce glam altogether, honey. You've pulled out all the stops tonight, you're like Jackie Kennedy, I swear!"

"Ah thanks, I'm not, but thanks. Caoimhe! I *love* your outfit! Come heeeeeere to me!" She swallowed me up in a big hug, and then started molesting my fancy wool top. She was wearing a lovely navy-blue dress – off both shoulders and sleeveless. She could have walked straight out of a cocktail party. Or straight into one.

"Aisling, you haven't met the girls yet, have you? This

is Marian. She's Richie's, uh – she's an old friend of Richie's," Bríd said, bringing them together.

"Howrya?" said Mar, who had no idea who this one was at all.

"Hi! I'm Aisling, my fella is sort of the manager of these lot. Well, of some of them, anyway. You're beautiful! Marian, was it yeah? And look at this dress! Jaysus I'd love to have the figure to get away with something like that, fair play to you," she said, as if she'd never seen herself in the mirror before.

"Ah thanks, you're looking lovely yourself, Marian said, stepping back so the other new one could have an introduction.

"Hi, Aisling! I'm Portia. Like the sports car." She put her hand on Aisling's bare shoulder and pulled her in, kissing her on both cheeks. That girl was an enigma wrapped in a fucking riddle.

"Oh *gosh*, look at you! You're so beautiful and Chinese and thin and petite and did I say Chinese? I did. But anyway, look at this! How did you get those things to stay on you?" She was touching one half of Portia's amazing, gravity-defying X top.

"Oh I stick it to me with wig tape," Portia said, answering the question that I hadn't even thought of until Aisling brought it up.

"Wow! That's so clever, I must remember that. It looks so sexy though. Cos it's covering everything, but it isn't at the same time. Like, if I go here," Aisling bent down and put her face between Portia's arm and her ribcage, "I can sort of see all your boob, but not really?" What the *hell* was she on tonight, like? Mad out, altogether.

"Hah! There really isn't enough boob there for anyone to see anything, but yeah."

"No! No, don't be silly… Portia, wasn't it? You're beautiful, and so is *all* of your body. Never put yourself down, Portia. None of the rest of ye either, girls! There's enough people in this world who'll be quite happy to put us down, we don't need to give them any help. And like I said, your boobs are gorgeous. Your boobs are *perfect!*" She looked a bit crazy now, but in a lovely, fun sort of way. She was a champion Irish Dancer – and she used to do ballet - so she'd the sort of legs ZZ Top might write a song about. Brian was punching way above his weight there, and he knew it, too.

"Thanks, I'll let them know you said that, when they get here," said Portia, moving back so she was touching off me again.

"You'll let who know?" Aisling said, puzzled.

"Aisling… have you taken some *Ecstasy* tonight, babe?" Bríd said, maneuvering so she could see her pupils. That was a ridiculous thing to ask. Easy knowing Bríd had gone to Scoil Carmel and not Laurel Hill, I thought, because if she'd ever been in a classroom with Aisling Flanagan she'd know that taking-

"Yes! Yes I have, Bríd, love. Why? Was I not supposed to? Come here again and let me feel that dress, will you? I'm like addicted to it or something, girls. Ohhhh, it's SO GOOD to see ye all!" Aisling put one arm around Bríd's shoulder and then stretched her other one out so that me, Mar, and Portia could crowd in and have a big pilled-up group hug. On stage, Blur started up *Tracy Jacks*, and we all screamed like thirteen-year-olds at a Take That concert, and made our way out into the real crowd, full of real people.

*****

"He's a very beautiful man, isn't he, Caoimhe?" said Speckled Dove Tim, in a relatively heterosexual way, pointing at the big screen. Drug Tim was a superior creature compared with Drunk Tim. Probably because drugs were so superior to drink, I thought. Well, this drug was, definitely.

"You're right, there. I've always been more of an Alex girl, but you can't argue with that bone structure, Tim. Or that lovely hair." I hadn't recognised the second song they'd played, it might have been a new one, but they were starting up *Sunday Sunday* now, from Modern Life is Rubbish, and everyone in the crowd knew it, so Tim and me grabbed onto each other and onto the crowd around us and pogoed away like there was no tomorrow. Eventually we pogoed into Niall, who was looking kind of shifty, but you probably had to look shifty if you wanted people to ask you for drugs, so.

"Timbo! Shoxy Lady! Fancy seeing ye here!"

"Not if I see you first!" I said, quite inexplicably, even to me.

"What? Here, have ye met Brillo's missus yet tonight, lads?" Niall had a smile on his face that could only mean one thing.

"Oh Niall! You didn't! So it was you???" I hadn't thought to ask her where she'd got the pill, I was still so shocked that she was on one. She was around, somewhere, with Portia and the rest. We were all around, somewhere.

"What? You're saying it like I spiked her or something. She wanted to take it. I gave her one of the good ones, as well – the ones we're on." He was trying to keep his voice down while shouting, it didn't really work.

"Oh, she just came up with the idea out of the blue, did she?"

"She did! She's a dark horse, that one, Caoimhe. You'll have to keep an eye on her tonight, like."

"We literally *will* have to, thanks to you, you big PUSHER, you!" I said, laughing my head off now. I was sooo-ooo fucked, in a good way. Blur were playing *Chemical World* now, which was apt, although *She's So High* might have been even… *apter*? I'd no idea they were this good, live. They were blowing the roof off, even though there wasn't one.

"Pusher! Hah! I didn't even charge her, like. By the way, I'll keep an eye on her myself, if you want. She's *such* a rrrrr-riiiiide, isn't she? Fucking hell, the legs on her, man. And the rest. I dunno how Brillo does it, Kweev."

"It's his natural charm," I said, not quite sure that was it. He was very decisive, mind. Some girls liked that, or so people told me. I preferred a nice arse, myself.

"He's probably *hanged* like a donkey," said Niall, which wasn't an image I wanted in my head, but thankfully a *speak of the devil* moment happened, and Drug Aisling appeared behind Drug Tim. She had the rest of our Vajayjay Community with her too. Apart from Ciara, who was bringing her vajayjay here later, I hoped. *End of a Century* started then, and I let the girls grab me up and drag me off towards the front of the crowd, for some more pogoing, garment-feeling, and general loved-up lushness.

*****

"They put on a mad show, don't they, boy? Fair play to them. Yer man Albarn is full of beans, like. I wasn't expecting all that bouncing around on stage," Frank said. He'd got a taxi, somehow, on the Saturday night of the Féile. Probably his Cork accent, opening doors. Or maybe he was in the Freemasons.

"What were you expecting?" I said. Blur's music was pretty bouncy in general. The earlier stuff was kind of Shoegazer, but these days they were all *STREETS-LIKE-A-JUNGLE*, or *PARKLIFE*. Music you couldn't help but bop to.

"Ah, like the other lads. Oasis. I went to see them last year. Yer man Liam just stood there with his hands behind his back. He didn't even take off his coat, like."

"I guess they're *real* rock and roll, Frank. They're too cool to be doing things like... moving," I said. I wasn't a fan. I only liked *Married with Children* off their album. Me and Niall had a great harmony worked out for it, whenever there was an acoustic jam. Didn't like any of the big singles. Their B-sides were better, half the time, I thought.

"Yeah, shur. Or maybe he was just a bit chilly that night," Frank said. "Right, mind yourself, I'll be back in two shakes." He was looking over at one of the security guys – a short, round, bald guy. I wondered what was up for a second, then yer man gave Frank a wave, and Frank waved back, saying, "That's Billy Higgins, I went to school with him, boy. Small world, yeah?" I was going to point out that they weren't after spotting each other on the street in New York, or Shanghai, so it wasn't really the world that was small, it was Munster, but he was already gone. Vamoosed.

"Where do you keep disappearing to, jellybean?" Portia was behind me, sliding her hands around my waist and locking her fingers in case I might escape again.

"Oh, hey! Dunno, I'm just mingling." *Single and ready to mingle.* Not that I was single, or anything. Even though I actually was, technically. Was I, though? Fucked if I know, these days, I thought.

"It's hardly mingling if you're only talking to Uncle Frank, blossom. Is he okay?" Her arms were so thin, but if you watched them move, or if she was gripping onto something, you could see lots of little muscles, especially her upper arms – she was really *toned*, that was the word.

"He's grand, shur. Frank is just Frank. Hey, Ling, do you do lots of riding?"

"Don't believe everything you read in the papers, sugarplum. I was just bringing that man his newspaper in the morning. And then my clothes were blown off. By a hurricane. And then I tripped over his dog. And landed on his penis. Could happen to any of us."

"Shut up, you gombeen. I meant do you ride horses?"

"Oh! Yeah, I do. I love it. How did you know, pudding? Do I smell of stables or something?" She sniffed herself, behind me.

"Hah! No, I was looking at your arms and all the muscles, and I thought they looked like horse rider arms." Blaithnead O'Reilly in school had arms like that, although she'd a face to match them.

"Well, aren't you quite the little observer, Lieutenant Colombo?" She squeezed me tight around the middle. Those arms were dead strong, when she needed them to be.

"I'm not just a pretty face, Xû Ling." I had a very good bottom as well, especially in these pants.

"Oh, I'm aware, cherry tart. What's that line again?"

"Line?" I pictured us doing cocaine together in a bathroom. When was that? I'd lost all sense of time, now.

"Yeah, from the song." She'd come around the front to face me. Damon was talking away up on stage, between the songs. Everyone around us was listening to him, the atmosphere was great, even if it wasn't quite a marquee full of pills and thrills.

"What song?" Her rigout was amazing, all the same. Wig tape - I'd never heard that trick before, but it was a diamond. It'd be brilliant for keeping your knockers from falling out if you had a dress on that you couldn't wear a bra with. She owned lots of wigs, so she might have enough of it that I could borrow some off her.

"Your song!"

"What, by Elton John?" She probably meant the bit about forgetting if my eyes were green or blue. Although maybe not, since she thought they were chocolate Minstrels.

"No! *Your* song! A song *you* wrote, marshmallow," she

said, touching my stomach. I pulled my muscles in, half instinctively, and half in case touching my bloaty tum had made her think about marshmallows.

"Ah! Which song? Which line?" Always great to meet a fan. Her fishnets were immense (and lush, and sickening), I thought, looking at them. They fit so well on her. I'd bought ones before that were too tight, and they looked *uafásach*, like my giant thighs were joints of pork for the Sunday dinner.

"Dunno what it's called, sorry, but the line goes something like… Lately I've been flirting with Death, but Death's no good at reading signs…"

"Death thinks we're platonic buddies, Death pops round for chats and wine." It was from *But Not in That Way*, which was going to be on our album.

"Haha, yeah. I like that one. You're funny," she said, arms around my shoulders now. She moved in for the kiss and I didn't react until her mouth was already on mine. Everything froze when our lips came together. Couldn't even hear the music, let alone the crowd. I had my eyes closed, as well as my mouth. I only wanted to change one of those things.

"Aaaaand, relax!" she said, breaking away before I had a chance to make any decisions.

"Oof. I'm a lot of things right now, Ling, but relaxed isn't one of them. How did you hear that song anyway? It's not on the EP. It's not a B-side on anything either."

"Oh, Mazz has a bootleg of one of your gigs, she loaned it to me so I could tape it, but she didn't write down the song names for me, cos she's a lazy cow," she said, arms still around me, moving her hips side to side, same as I was. Her eyes were still wowing me, like beautiful emerald kaleidoscopes. Or maybe *jade* kaleidoscopes, considering.

"A bootleg! Jesus, maybe we really *are* a big deal, eh?"

"Awww, you'll always be a big deal to me, snookums," she said, looking me in the eyes. I stared back and marvelled at how a bunch of words could have such an instant, warming, uplifting effect on me, and then I remembered I was on a fuckload of drugs.

"Thanks, Ling. I won't forget you when I'm rich and famous," I said, squeezing her cheek like she had done to Tim earlier. I wanted to pull her face in close again and have another little kiss, but I didn't. It felt like we were at the *playing with fire* stage now, and if we weren't careful, someone definitely would be able to do us for it.

"You're already rich, bonbon. And you'll have forgotten *my* sorry ass by Tuesday." She was smiling, but there was a tiny sadness hidden behind it.

"I'll never forget an ass like this, Ling-Ling," I said, grabbing a handful of denim, skin, and fishnet.

"Fucking right, you won't. But, darling?" She followed my hand with hers, and linked fingers with me again.

"Yaw?" I needed water; my bottle was empty. New gum, too, if there was any going spare.

"I'm *loving* you calling me Ling, but I'm gonna have to draw the line at *Ling-Ling*, okay? I'm Chinese, babe. I'm not a fucking panda." She was brilliant, I loved her; I wanted to be able to keep her.

*****

"Am I supposed to be taking this personally, pecan pie?" said Portia, when we saw Ciara arrive, a little later on.

"The dress?" I said, but of course she meant the dress. Ciara was wearing an absolutely stunning Chinese-style frock. High neck, with a collar, no sleeves, knee-length, and it looked like she'd had it tailor-fitted. Purple silk, with gold designs of little birds and Oriental fans, and other things. It was enough to take the actual breath out of your lungs.

"The dress!" said Portia. "Don't get me wrong, I'm not offended about her stealing my culture or anything, Caoimhe." She hardly ever called me by my name. I almost forgot it *was* my name, when I was with her.

"You're not?" I didn't know how these things worked; I was definitely too white to understand stuff like that.

"No! Shur, I'm Irish, shur. Shurrrrrr! No, I'm, like, offended cos she looks better in it than I ever would, the cow. It's mainly cos she has tits, and I don't, but still." She was smiling, that was good, at least.

"Ah stop, you gowl. You'd look good in anything, Ling. You're literally just wearing two bits of random cloth now, and you still look like every boy's wet dream."

"Like every boy's wet dream! Haha! I'll take it. Still, she looks double-triple hot. I've *no* chance with you now."

"What?" I looked at her now, forgetting Ciara and her dress for a minute.

"I'm joking, kitten. I never had a chance with you."

"Here now, hang on one minute," I said, grabbing both her hands, and pulling her nearer. I was trying to find the right words.

"It's fine, poodle. I don't want to get stuck in some big love triangle anyway. Too much drama. And, like I said – you're into her brain, not her bra. I don't even own a bra. And, more importantly, she's your friend, *she* lives where *you* live. I'm just a footnote in this little weekend adventure of yours. I'll be ancient history soon." She was still smiling, but it didn't make me not want to smother her in a hug and make the ouches go away. This was all so confusing.

"How about we just forget all that, yeah, and have a

great time?" I said, because that was exactly what I wanted to do. We were all too loved-up for any of that stuff. I was higher than I'd ever felt in my life, and even if I had missed Ciara, I wasn't in any hurry to not be in Portia's company. But then, maybe that wasn't my choice to make.

"That, my love, is the best idea anyone has ever had. Let's go over to the circle of ladyness, and do things that ladies do, whatever those might be." She took my hand, and then our faces were close again. I took a big breath through my nose, like a High Diver getting ready to go off the edge of the board, then I gave her the briefest, softest, tiniest of kisses on her lips, before we walked over to rejoin the gang.

*****

"You see, it's like, I dunno how to put it exactly, sorry girls. I'm soooo *mashed*, sorry! Anyway, what was I saying?" Aisling was holding court in the Circle of Ladyness when we arrived.

"About our clothes, chickee," said Bríd. I was already used to her looking like this now. It was still Bríd, just a different level of her. Like a bonus round.

"Oh yes, yeah. Oh look, we've the whole set again now, bitches. Welcome back, you two!" Aisling Flanagan calling people bitches as a term of endearment was going to take a little bit more getting used to than Bríd having blue hair and sex-clothes.

"Cheers, dears. Ciara, I LOVE the dress, babe. It's fucking lush to the power of fifty!" Portia said, mildly surprising me, but not too much, because she was genuinely lovely as a person, and she was also full of drugs. She was next to Ciara now, touching the hem of her garment, quite literally.

"Oh, you do? Thank GOD for that, like! I was worried that you might – ah, I was a little bit-"

"No need to be a little bit anything, push pop. You look

double-fantastic. I absolutely covet everything about this. Is it real silk?" She was fondling every part of the thing now; you'd swear she was Aisling Flanagan or something. It was nice, though. I wanted these two to get on with each other, and I'd been afraid that they wouldn't.

"Push pop, hah! I love this girl, Caoimhe. Where did you find her at all?" Ciara said, motioning at me to come over to them.

"It was me who found her, actually, Portia said, twiddling the hair at the side of my forehead. "Practically stalked her, backstage, I did. Anyway, we're being rude, Aisling. Carry on!" I was standing with a Ciara on one side of me and a Portia on the other, so I'd probably wake up any moment now, in the back of the minibus, after Frank's weed.

"No, you're grand. I was listening to the story, like. I love listening to stories. I love *telling* stories too. I just love *talking*, especially tonight! Anyway, what I was saying was – like, when I see all of ye here tonight – all these strong, intelligent, funny, beautiful, SEXY women – I'm so proud, like. I'm so proud to know ye, girls. Even the ones of ye I only met tonight, yeah? Portia, Marian – the two of ye are only fucking stunning, brilliant, lovely girls, if ye don't mind me saying so. Hang on, fuck, that was a big one. What are they called again, Bríd?" She had a glug of water while she waited for the answer. It was fascinating seeing her like this. I felt like I was watching a David Attenborough documentary, about swotty girls taking their first ever yokes.

"Rushes?" Bríd was as amused as me, but we were laughing in a *kind* way, I thought; we weren't being sneery at her or anything.

"Yeah, rushes. Fuck me, I can't believe I never tried this stuff before. I've wasted my life, girls, hahaha! Anyway!"

"Anyway!" said Portia, and I felt her hand on the small of my back, doing swirly things with her thumb.

"Anyway..." said Ciara, the other side of me. I was suddenly aware that it was *her* thumb doing the swirling, not Portia's. Oh boy.

"Anyway, girls – my point is, I was blown away by all your outfits tonight, and I just wanted to say to ye that I think you're all amazing, and stunning, and that one day, hopefully soon, hopefully before we're all too old to appreciate it, women like us will be able to go out on the town dressed in whatever we want, without anyone *judging* us yeah? Men *or* women judging us, I mean. We'll wear what the fuck we like - rubber dresses, or tiny shorts, or two pieces of cloth stuck onto our boobs with double-sided Sellotape, or... I don't really know how to describe your frock, Marian babe, other than it's sensational, and okay, I can pretty much see your front bottom from here, but-"

"FRONT BOTTOM!" Bríd shrieked, and everyone went into convulsions, even Marian, who had closed her legs so quickly her thighs made a slap you could hear over the music.

"Ah now, I didn't mean anything bad, lads, or Marian. You've nothing to be ashamed of, yeah?"

"Yeah, you've a lovely looking front bum, Mazz," Portia said, setting us all off again.

"She does! I mean, I'm sure you do, Marian. I haven't my glasses with me, so it was a bit of a blur. Hah! A *Blur*! Get it? But yeah, shur all of ours are lovely in their own way, whatever size or shape they are. Whether it's a big one or a small one, a peach or a... pumpkin, an *innie* or an *outie*-"

"An innie or an outie!!!" Ciara said, nearly falling over with the laughter. Aisling waited for her to finish, all polite like.

"Yeah, you know what I mean, like – you've all been in the changing rooms after hockey, yeah? We've all had a look, haven't we? No? Maybe just me, then. Forget I said that, hahahaha! *Abort! Abort!* Anyway, it's the same with every bit of our bodies, girls. Yeah, Portia? Do you hear me now, there, gorgeous? Yeah, you *are* perfect, just the way God made you."

"I'm pretty sure it was the devil who made that one," said Marian, giving Portia a wink. I'd have to have such a massive catch up with her later. Or tomorrow. Both were equally possible.

"Either way, says you. She's gorgeous. Ye're all gorgeous. And clever, and unique, and *powerful*, ladies. We *are* powerful, even if the patriarchy tries to keep us down, yeah?"

"Fuck the patriarchy!" Bríd said, punching the air.

"FUCK THE PATRIARCHY!" we all said, getting some mad looks from the people around us at the concert we'd forgotten we were at.

"Is it called the patriarchy because your special holy man, *Saint* Patrick started it? I don't know a lot about Western, Christian culture, sorry," Portia said, making everyone stop what they were doing and look at her with varying expressions from confusion to outright pity. She let it carry on for a few seconds, then she shouted, "I'M FROM DÚN LAOIGHRE, YOU FUCKING RACISTS!" and everyone collapsed laughing again. This day, or this night, was just getting better and better. It was incredible, considering the absolute doom that it started with. I couldn't even remember what that was about now, until I clocked Ciara beside me looking all puppy dog eyes at me, and I remembered. Portia's hand (it was definitely her hand this time) was doing nonchalant finger arcs across the material of my pants, specifically on the top part of my bum. I was incredibly sensitive around there, even when I wasn't swimming in chemicals. I didn't know which of them to look at, but then Blur started playing the start of *Badhead*, so we all turned towards the stage and the big screens, and it was dancing time again. What a life we led.

*****

"Oooooh, it's the slow set, ladies. Pick a partner, quick! A *woman* partner!" Aisling said, when *To The End* started. I loved this one, it was pretty.

"A woman partner?" Bríd said, smiling. Tom Baker was in my head now, saying "*You have a WOMAN partner, m'lord!*"

"Yes! Fuck the patriarchy, babe," said Aisling, sidling up to her and assuming the position. That was the first pairing decided, anyway. I panicked a tiny bit, thinking of the possible permutations from the ones of us who were left. Did I have a mock slow dance with Portia now? Or was it my chance to grab Ciara, and finally get some time to talk to her? Find out the things that had been bugging me? Have *a moment* with her? Fix things? But what about Portia? How would she-

"May I have this dance, madam?" Marian was in front of me, suddenly, looking all beautiful, and golden, and perfect, and back in my life again.

"I'd be a fool to refuse such a kind offer, good sir," I said. That solved that dilemma, anyway. I looked beside me and saw Ciara and Portia already all up in each other's personal spaces and moving to the music, so that was sorted as well. Damon started singing. A little hoarse, after shouting his way through the louder songs earlier, but he still had the voice of a mock-Cockney angel.

"Soooo, having a good weekend then, Shaughnessy? Do anything nice?" said Mar, flashing her perfect pearlies at me. She was too Hollywood-looking for real life. She belonged up on a big screen.

"It's been okay so far," I said. My arms were around her neck, hers were down behind my back. She felt very warm against me, but I must have as well. Being out in the open air wasn't as cooling as it should have been, because we were surrounded by the heat of tens of thousands of other bodies.

"Yeah, I have to say I'm not hating it too much either, chick. I've missed you, by the way, you know? It's been waaaaaay too long. I'm so happy you're here!" She pulled me in a little tighter. We were moving in a tiny circle, but I wasn't sure which of us was supposed to be *leading*, if there was such a thing as leading in this sort of crude, school disco version of dancing. It was hardly Strictly Ballroom.

"Yeah, me too. I can't believe it's been so long. There's so much I want to tell you, like. And so much I want to ask you. It's just... it's so great to see you again. God, I'm really *mashed*, as Aisling Flanagan over there would say, like." I put my head on her shoulder and took a giant breath of fresh air, mixed with yummy Marian-smells.

"Haha! She's a scream, that one. She's definitely the designated yapper tonight, like, God bless her."

"The what, now?" I looked beyond and saw Portia and Ciara dancing away, foreheads pressed, looking deep in conversation, but occasionally breaking into laughs. It made my heart go double-fuzzy, looking at them. I wasn't jealous, I was whatever the opposite of jealous was, and I didn't know if there was a word for that. I'd ask Tim later, once we'd stopped eschewing oppressive males. Or Richie, because he'd got into Trinity, to do English, although he didn't really like mentioning it.

"Oh just, when people are on yokes, there's always one person who ends up doing all the talking, all night. All night, like. Until they're the last man standing - or woman." Marian took her arms off me for a second, I wasn't sure why. This song was absolute paradise – I was back in Heaven, or some new version of it. I felt a million times nice. Nice to the power of ten trillion.

"I see. I don't think we had one of those last night," I said. She reached behind her neck and tapped on the back of my hands. The song was still going. We weren't finished our dance. "Everyone just kind of took turns, talking?" I was probably remembering it wrong. Maybe *I'd* been the yapper, and no one had told me.

"Ah, a genuine democracy. Quite rare in the world of yokes and yoking! Um, I'm acting like a weirdo, sorry. Can you just switch the *hand situations* with me? Let me go up here and you go the other way, like I was doing on you?" she said, already moving my hands down behind her, and putting hers around my neck.

"Okay, happier now, chick?" I said, wondering how this was any better, or any worse.

"Yes! Now do me a favour and hold onto the bottom of my dress, yeah? Batten down my hatches for me, Caoimhe. I'm getting a bit para in this fucking rigout."

"Why, what's happened, babe?" I said, doing what she'd asked. There wasn't much material to work with, but I had her covered, quite literally.

"Oh, the usual. Men, looking. Men, staring. Men, saying things." She rolled her eyes. It was weird being this close to her but having such a different dynamic with her than I would with Portia, or with Ciara even. There was nothing flirty about it, in the slightest. It was a different kind of nice. It felt right, cos she was my Marian from when I was small. She wasn't a sexual being. *Not yet anyway.* Shut up, brain, you whore.

"Men, eh? Who needs 'em?!" I said. The song was nearly over now.

"Well, unfortunately for me, I do. Sometimes, anyway. Not all of the times. Not now. Fuck the patriarchy!" said Mar, as the music finished.

"Yeah, fuck 'em," I said, still attached to her, lazily dancing in our circle. I looked at Ciara and Portia again, they'd unhooked from each other, and Portia was inspecting the Chinese dress again, in a very flirty, fondly way, I thought. Aisling and Bríd came over to us, arms around each other's waists, mouths chewing animatedly, their looks contrasting so drastically that they sort of complemented one another, in a weird way.

"Well, thank you for the pleasure of that dance, young lady," Marian said, taking her arms off my neck, but not away completely, just moving them down so that we were mirroring one another. I leaned back so I could take in all of her lush, sickening, double-pretty face.

"The pleasure was all mine, Mr. Darcy," I said.

"Well now you've got me thinking about Ray D'arcy from The Den," she said, as we turned around to go back to the Clitoral Council.

"What, sexually?"

"Ray is always sexual, honey. I think it's the puppets."

"You're not wrong, there," I said, picturing the very handsome, tanned Ray, lying down - naked except for a strategically placed Zig and Zag covering his unmentionables – like that old Cosmo photoshoot of Ian McShane off Lovejoy with a sausage dog sitting on his lap. Thankfully I hadn't pictured Dustin the Turkey down there instead. That would have been obscene.

*****

"Bonjour!" Ciara said, coming my way during the next song, with a Portia attached to her.

"Fancy meeting you here," I said, regarding her. "Where's your *boyfriend* got to, then?" I added, out of absolutely nowhere. Portia gave me a *what the fuck are you doing?* look, but her guess was as good as mine.

"Heh. My *boyfriend*. You're silly. I'm in love with this

top, where did you steal it from?" She was fingering my mohair now, and not making eye contact.

"Uh, I got it in London, it's Vivienne Westwood, I think." *Think*, my arse. I knew exactly what it was, but it was so disgustingly expensive I was almost ashamed to own it.

"Wow! How the other half live," Ciara said, clearly meaning nothing by it, but I'd managed to rub myself up the wrong way now, somehow, and I couldn't shake it off.

"Heh. You can have it if you like. It'll probably fit you," I said, but not in a friendly way, in a *complete gowl* way. The hell was wrong with me?

"I, uh-" She stopped talking and looked at me.

"What would everyone say to a lovely big joint?" Portia said, putting her face between ours, and an arm over each of our shoulders.

"Oooooh! Can I try some?" said Aisling, joining the huddle.

"You can try anything you like tonight, rosebud," Portia said, blowing her a kiss. I was calming down now, thank Christ. I had no idea where that attack of the grumps had come from.

"Except heroin," Ciara said. "Do you have skins and all that, Portia?"

"No, I thought one of you might, sorry." They were walking together, side by side. I was all alone in the world, now. Served me right.

"Hey, you! Do you have cigarette rolling papers?" said Aisling, to some random crowd guy. He was taken aback for a second, then he got a good look it her, and a wankerish smile crept onto his face.

"I might do. What's in it for me, love?" He literally licked his lips when he said it, like a sort of human Pepé Le

Pew.

"A kick in the fucking balls, if you don't scram, squire," said a very familiar man's voice.

"Brillo!" said one of the girls, probably Bríd. Definitely wasn't Marian, as she'd just sprinted off to the toilets, possibly for a discreet puke, since weeing was off the table for the foreseeable future. Or maybe all the talk of a naked Ray D'Arcy had got her all hot under the collar. Both were equally possible.

"Hey, Brian! How's the form, Maurice?" I said.

"I'm good, Shox. What's going on here, like? Have they been looking after you, Ash, love? Or are they leading you astray?" he said, laughing the laugh of a man who clearly had no idea what he was in for tonight. *Girls and Boys* started then, to the loudest cheers of the night so far. I was grabbed on either side by female arms and dragged up to have a pogo. One set of arms was Ciara's, which was a big relief. I hadn't made her hate me yet, with my stupid paranoid nonsense. The night was still young, mind.

*****

"Right so, tell me again. Who do I have to kill?" Brian was over by the beer tent thing with me. I'd passed on having some of the joint, so that I could take him for a chat. I was basically the Mother Theresa of the Circle of Ladyness.

"No one, Brian! She's fine, honestly. She's better than fine, like. She's having a great time." I was having a fag; that was almost as good as a real smoke, for now.

"Yeah. You *say* that, Maurice, but she's clearly off her face on something. Drugs, like. *My* Aisling. On drugs. I never thought I'd see the-"

"She took *one* pill, Brian. You'd swear she was smoking crack, the way you're carrying on." I avoided rolling my eyes at him, cos I was trying to win him around, but it was a struggle not to.

"Carrying on, says you. I'm just – I'm not happy, yeah?" He had his arms folded no, like a dad having a passive-aggressive strop at your mum while still looking at the soccer on the telly.

"Not happy about---?" The fag tasted great; I couldn't remember when my last one was.

"Happy about *her*, doing *that*, with – which of ye put her up to it, like? She's not like ye lot, Caoimhe. She's dead quiet, shur. She's a-"

"She's not quiet at all; she has no trouble putting you in your place half the time, you big galoot. And she's more like us than you'd think, Bri, and not in a bad way, either. She's absolutely sound out, and she's just letting her hair down, for God's sake. How many years was she up in Laurel Hill, with a fucking stick up her arse, studying away like a mad woman? Not even going out to the pub at the weekend during the school year? You know yourself, like. She was bound to go wild someday. It's only natural."

"Drugs aren't natural, though, Caoimhe." His face was starting to look a bit punchable now, even on these yokes. I needed to channel my inner Kung Fu Monk Tim and become serene.

"What are they, so?"

"They're – they're… chemicals, like. Mind-altering chemicals, like. They're dangerous."

"You're literally drinking alcohol, Brian. How is that not a mind-altering chemical?" This time I did roll my eyes.

"Ah, shur don't give me that shite. Beer is different. Beer comes from… from the earth, like."

"Where do drugs come from then, the Moon?" It was hard to get through to him, he was a fifty-year-old trapped in an eighteen-year-old's body, sometimes.

"Feck off, you know what I mean."

"I do, and you're wrong. Anyway, look – she's taken it now, of her own free will, and she's having a great night. Time of her life. And it's not going to affect you, in a bad way. Unless you *make* it affect you in a bad way, Brian." Blur finished *Country House*, the new one they were having the battle with Oasis over, and started another one. *Bank Holiday*, it sounded like. I was missing all the dancing and pogoing, but it couldn't be helped.

"What do you mean, Shox?"

"I mean that you know Aisling. You know how bloody independent, and strong-willed, and... *feministy* she is, right?"

"Tell me about it..." I'd got a smile out of him at least, this was progress.

"Okay so, then you know that the worst thing you could do tonight is try to tell her you don't approve of what she's doing – what she's doing *with her own body*, remember? – she's an automatic robot woman, and all that jazz."

"Heh, yeah, I suppose..." Another smile, we were getting there, slowly.

"So the best thing you can do now, is go back over, and just soak up all the big mad lovey-dovey feelings she has and let her hug the fuck out of you and tell you how you're the best boyfriend in the world, and how she loves you forever, and how you're the best at riding, and other random, assorted praise. You *love* praise, Brian."

"I, ah, I'm not averse to it, all the same, you're right there."

"Good! And listen, if all the yapping gets a bit too much for you, shur just leave her with us to mind for a bit, and then later – this is the best bit, by the way, I saved it for last..."

"What's this now?" He was suddenly all ears, bless.

"Well, when we do give her back, Brian, she's going to be so fucking horny that you'll have to put on a pot of strong coffee if you want to keep up with her, like."

"Go on..." His pupils were dilating now, and the only drug *he* was up on was Guinness.

"Like you wouldn't believe, love. And it won't be just normal sex she'll be wanting either, Bri."

"No?" He looked halfway between very interested and slightly scared, now.

"God, no. She's gonna want the filth. She's got no inhibitions tonight. You're gonna be getting begged to do stuff to her that you didn't even know was physically possible, babe. Some of it won't even be legal in Ireland. You're going to wish you had two dicks."

"Jaysus, and this... this pill will make her that way?" He was leaning in now, like I was telling him his fortune, which I sort of was.

"Brian, she's already that way, trust me. This pill will just allow her to feel good enough about herself, and to feel comfortable enough in front of you, to *show* you that she's that way. Multiple times tonight. And probably again, in the morning."

"Well holy God, maybe I've ah, misjudged this whole drugs thing, yeah? You live and learn," he said, taking my arm and pointing us back in the direction of the girls. My work here was done.

"Happens to the best of us, Boxer." I threw that last bit in as a treat for him, since it was Christmas.

"*Boxer*, hah? Finally!" he said, chuckling away. He was all right, Brian, all the same. I let go of his arm before we got to them, just in case Aisling got the wrong idea and decided to claw my fucking eyes out.

*****

"Awww, this is it, I think. This is the end, apple jack. Well, the end of Blur, anyway. We still have The Orb to come, and *Little Fluffy Clouds*, and pill number 2." Portia and me had drifted away from the main group by the time Blur played *This is a Low*. Seemed like a strange tune to finish on, but then again it was one where everyone swayed together and held up their lighters, so maybe it was actually ideal.

"Awww. They were great though, all the same. Yay to Orbs and clouds and pills, though. I've had *so* much fun today, Ling, and it's mostly been because of you." I was still noticeably buzzing on the first pill, and maybe on a tiny bit more coke that no one else saw either of us bog-snorkeling, so you couldn't do us for it.

"Yeah. This whole day has been great, hasn't it?" She was sitting up on a low wall bit, over where the terraces started. I had my back to her, standing between her legs, getting a shoulder and back rub that was much needed and felt like double-heaven.

"Has it really only been one day, though?" I said, feeling like I'd been awake for a week, all of a sudden. Not that I was tired, or anything.

"Us knowing each other? Yep. Not even a full one, either. I only met you in the afternoon, after your little acoustic gig, plum pudding." She was massaging my scalp now, and it wasn't even my birthday.

"Wow. Feels like I've known you a million years, slush puppy," I said, pushing myself back into her, and squeezing her thighs on both sides. Her skin felt lovely and cool to touch, in between all the fishnet strings, even though neither of us were feeling the cold properly, yet.

"Same, pop tart. I really loved that song you did." She was making fireworks go off in my brain and the rest of me with the scalp massage. It was something I didn't know I needed until I was actually having it. I loved discovering stuff like that.

"The Nine Inch Nails one?" I'd enjoyed playing that, even if it had made me a little teary. Best part was shouting the chords at the poor lads from Revelino, like I was some insane orchestra conductor.

"Naw, I loved that too, peach, but I meant the Joni one."

"Oh yeah. Yeah I love her. She was like my whole life when I was about 13 and full of angst and blackheads.

"Same, pop tart." Ugh, I adored her even more now.

"So we've known each other, what? Less than... *ten* hours, maybe?" There was no waaaaay that could be true. No one could understand me this well in that amount of time. No one could understand my *scalp* this well, let alone my whole being. Then again, I'd told her hardly anything about myself – about my life, and all the mental things that had happened to me last year, so maybe she didn't really know me. She did, though. She just lacked some details, and details didn't matter at Christmas.

"Yep, it's been a whirlwind, darling. Ooh, hang on, wait until you feel *this*, toffee pop." She pushed her thumbs into the skin under the backs of my ears – held the pressure, hard, for a few seconds, then released it. My eyes went dark, then bright again. My head suddenly felt like it weighed nothing and was going to float off.

"Whoa! What the hell was that???" I said, almost unable to handle the lovely, floaty, helium-headed feeling.

"Hah! Just a little trick I know," she said. I felt her thumbs on the same places again, but this time there was no pressure, just soothing rubs.

"What trick is it, though?" I said, noticing the thumbs where gone now, and had been replaced by soft lips, kissing where she'd pushed the magic, invisible buttons.

"You don't want me to bore you with the details, trust me." I felt her face in the back of my hair, inhaling my inherent Caoimheness.

"Well, now I definitely want you to bore me with the details!" I leaned back into her in a stretchy, feline way, pressing my cheek against hers. My toes were curling from the loveliness of it all.

"Okay, fine! I cut off the circulation in your arteries for a couple of seconds, and then I let the blood flow again. I *almost* made you pass out, but I *didn't* make you pass out. Your brain assumed I *was* going to, so it sent a shot of adrenaline or euphoria or something - to wake you back up, and that's why your head went all OOOOOH. See? Explaining it ruins the magic. No one needs to see how the sausage gets made, sausage."

"True, true. It was amazing though. You'll have to teach me how to do it, so I can return the favour, Ling." I'd probably mess it up and accidentally kill her, knowing me, but I liked learning new skills, so.

"Maybe I will, bubble tea. Maybe I will." She was turning me around to face her now, her small hands on my furry shoulders.

"What's the plan, strawberry flan?" I asked, delighted with myself for thinking of that one.

"Heeee! I dunno. I think I was gonna kiss you?" she said, hopping off the wall so we were face to face again.

"Whoa! A proper kiss? They *can* do you for that, Ling," I said, getting the quivers, like a bowl of Chivers.

"Is this a proper kiss?" she said, leaning in and planting a slightly open-mouthed one on me.

"Felt *almost* proper, I think. Let me have a look." I wiped my lip and pretended to study the evidence on my fingertip.

"Think they could do us for it? How about this one?" She gave me a similar, lazy kiss, but this time she put enough pressure that it parted my lips, and without thinking about it, I ran my tongue across the width of her smile, sliding over her lovely, polished teeth. Our mouths were half open, and now her tongue was touching mine. The tip of it slipping under, then over me. Dipping into the pools of wet, soaking it up, and leaving her own in its place. Pressing down on me, massaging me, reeling me back into her mouth, where it was warm and close, and it tasted of her.

I forgot any notions of restraint or caution and completely let go, pushing my thigh into the space between her legs, grinding her against the little wall in a rhythm that was in perfect time with our kisses. The soft, slow sensation of tongues tangling contrasting crazily with the bruising urgency of lips smashing into teeth and fingernails raking over scalp and skin.

It was no wonder we didn't realise we were being watched, until we opened our eyes and saw her standing there, in her lovely Chinese dress. Purple silk, with gold designs of little birds, and Oriental fans, and other things.

"Ciara," I said. It was the best I could come up with on such short notice.

"Aaaah, *just the girl!*" Portia said, making a beeline for her. I didn't have time to process what was happening yet, I just stared.

"I am?" Ciara said, slightly confused, until Portia's mouth was already on hers. I stared even more, because words were out of the question now. Ciara closed her eyes, and their heads both tilted, and then it was a proper, proper kiss. Nothing one sided about it. There were definitely two people in this tango. When they finally came apart I was still too shell-shocked to move or to say anything. Portia linked one of Ciara's arms and then came and did the same to me.

"Now!!! Let's go take *lots* more drugs and have *lots* more fun and make this a weekend we'll *never* forget, yeah, muffins? One to tell the grandkids about," she said, practically dragging us along, she was walking so fast. I wasn't looking at Ciara yet, and she wasn't looking at me. I had no idea what had just happened. I wasn't sure anyone did, apart from Portia. This was her world, and the rest of us were apparently just living in it. *C'est la Ling.*

EIGHTEEN

"What's the difference between The Orb and Orbital, then?" I asked, when I'd recovered my tongue from the cat, and we were back in the safe, loving embrace of the *Coterie du Clitoris*.

"I'm not sure. One of them is dance music and the other one is trance music – chillout, comedown stuff, yeah?" said shiny sherbet shex-pot Bríd. I wondered where her Benson was. Probably off somewhere indulging his secret drinking habit, which I kept forgetting about and remembering again.

"That sounds pretty specific, darling. How exactly is that being not sure?" Ciara said. I still hadn't looked her in the eye, let alone discussed anything. Was there anything to even discuss though? Or had Portia the genius managed to cancel out my little transgression by jumping in and transgressing the face off *her*, too? I had no idea.

"Because I don't know which one does what, you see – I don't know if these lot are the chillout ones or if it's the fellas on tomorrow night." Bríd took a fag out of my box, put it in her mouth, spotted me gawking at her in disbelief, took it back out, passed it to Ciara, and shook her head, saying to herself, "Silly Bríd... you don't smoke!"

"You definitely don't smoke, Bríd! Bad for you! Bad kitty!" said Aisling, giving her a smack on her rubber-coated bum. It made a brilliant noise, like whacking a balloon.

"Ouch! That hurt! *Do it again! Please!*" said Bríd, laughing.

"Kinky," said Marian, appearing beside me. I threw my arm around her shoulder and squished her in close.

"Hey, Collins. How's your arse? Chilly?"

"Hey, Shaughnessy. My arse is grand. Getting an auld Moon-tan, it is. So are we all gonna take another one of these things, yeah? What time is it at all?"

"No idea, love," I said, still looking at my wrist though, in case the Watch Fairy had visited.

"Will you be okay to play your gig in the morning if you do another one, chick?" Ciara said. I didn't answer her immediately because I assumed she was talking to someone else, because why would she ever talk to me again, after what I-

"She'll be GRAAAAAND, wontcha, Kweev? You bloody beautiful, sexy, furry, sexy rock star, you!" said Aisling, stepping into the space in front of me and going straight for the mohair with her fingers. She was like a crackhead for sensory delights, tonight.

"Am, yeah. I'll be okay. I think?" I had flat-out forgotten we were playing tomorrow. Or that we were playing this festival at all. Or that I was in a band. I'd be okay, though. Some sleep would be got. Maybe. If not, I'd just Jim Morrison my way through it. Hopefully without dying in a bath afterwards.

"Okay, girls, *women*, aaaand everyone in between. It's time. Come close. Gather!" said Portia. We got in a huddle around her, everyone holding onto someone else, like we were in a rugby scrum, but without all the heaving, or the scrotums.

"What are we gonna dedicate this one to, girls?" said Aisling, who should definitely not, under any circumstances, have been taking a second E, but any bit of reason or sensibility had left all our brains a good while ago.

"To questionable life choices!" I said, since pretty much all of mine this weekend had been.

"Perfect," Portia said. "Who has the water?" She opened her hand, took one of the two pills that were in it, and gave it to Aisling. Everyone else already had one, from when I'd doled them out earlier.

"Thanks, angel!" Aisling necked the yoke and followed it down with a swig of Ballygowan, like it was second nature to her. Amazing.

"My pleasure, fruit gum. Okay then, what was it?" I looked really closely at her hair. If it was a wig, it was a fucking good one. It wasn't, though. I'd felt her scalp through it, lots of times. I wanted to feel it again, but I could wait.

"Poor life decisions?" Ciara said, next to me. She smelled of CK One and vanilla again, but no Black Jacks.

"Questionable," I corrected her, gently, because I'd definitely used up all my *being a gowl to her* chances tonight. I got my turn on the water and swallowed down my pill fast, because I didn't want it touching my tongue and giving me that yucky, hairspray aftertaste.

"To questionable life decisions!!!" Aisling said, because even though Portia was kind of our leader tonight, Aisling had that whole Mallory Towers Prefect/Class Captain/Head Girl vibe going on.

"TO QUESTIONABLE LIFE DECISIONS!!!" we all shouted, then the huddle became a hug, the Orb started up their first tune, and the stage went blue and pink and purple. The colours spilled out into the crowd and moved over everyone's faces. I was holding my breath, staring at the hypnotic prettiness. I felt fingers on my shoulder – rubbing first, then massaging. I looked beside me and saw it was Ciara, so I stared at her hypnotic prettiness instead for a while. Portia was on her other side, smoking a rollie. Portia didn't smoke though, so it must have been a joint. Mmmmm, a joint. The pink light from the stage was suddenly directly on the three of us and on no one else, which I took as a sign from God. A sign of what, I didn't know yet. He was always moving in mysterious ways, that fella.

*****

"So then, what's the story, coco pop?" Portia said, when we'd done another one of our disappearing acts, this time into the middle of the crowd, which was as big as it had been for the Prodigy. Not because the Orb were as popular, more because everyone was still on one high or another, and nobody wanted to go home just yet.

"Which story?" There had been a lot of stories this weekend, and we still had another day left of it. And two whole nights.

"You know… the story. With *the girl?*" She was facing me, while walking backwards, her fingers hooked into my belt loops. She was somehow not banging into anyone either. Vampire magic.

"Which girl? You?" I said. The lights were different colours now, they changed every time the songs did, not that I could tell one Orb song from another.

"Hah! No, the imposter Chinese, not the real deal, petal." She stopped her backwards walk quite abruptly, making me crash into her. I wasn't sure if that was deliberate, but I didn't mind.

"Ciara? I dunno. You tell me? You've snogged her more recently than I have," I said, but not in a gowlish way, hopefully. We were lovely and close to each other now. I ran my fingers down the side of her arm and back up again. She had such amazing skin, all over her.

"Hah, I was just thinking on my feet, pudding."

"Looked like more than *thinking*, from where I was standing." I thought about them kissing and I wasn't even jealous – of either of them. It wasn't painful to watch, it was just sort of... *new*? But I was on a fuckload of happy drugs. If they eloped together in the morning and left me forever, I'd probably feel differently. I was stroking her side now, in between the criss-cross things. There wasn't a pick on her, but she wasn't an *unwell* kind of skinny. It was just right. To my eyes, at least. But my eyes were the only ones that mattered in this moment.

"Oh well, what can I say, possum?"

"You don't have to say anything, Ling. Just stand there and look pretty." I noticed that my wandering fingers had wandered onto the side of her braless boob, and my wondering brain wasn't sure if I should leave them there or take them away.

"Careful now, honey pie. A few inches to the right and they'll definitely be able to do you for it." She had a look in her eyes that I was starting to know very well. It was rarely followed by anything other than us getting into a whole heap of delicious trouble.

"My right or yours?" I said, finally deciding to remove the hand. It wasn't that I didn't want to leave it there; more that I realised that there was just as much fun in the *not doing* as there was in the doing. That was starting to be a theme, this weekend.

"Heheh. What were we talking about again?" Her hand was on my face, stroking me with the tip of her thumb. Felt nice, but then everything felt nice when she did it

"The girl. Or the girls – you included."

"It's nice to be included, I think." Her face was all earnest and sincere again. I loved when she dropped the Portia act and was just Ling, in my presence. Made me feel double-triple special.

"I can't not include you – you're fucking amazing. You're wonderful. You're the best," I said, remembering to breathe, finally.

"Heh. Still *second* best though, right?"

"Nope," I said, because she wasn't.

"*First* best?" Her fingers were in my hair, over my ear. My head tilted into them, and she scritched me on my scalp with her incredible nails.

"Nope," I said, because she wasn't that, either.

"You gonna explain, lemon slice?" She straightened herself up a bit and brought her face closer so she could fix me with her starry gaze.

"Can't," I said, because I couldn't.

"Okay..." The starry eyes went slightly sad. She took her hand off me, and her body language changed. I needed to say something, quickly.

"What I mean is, I can't explain things I don't understand myself, yeah? I can't explain my feelings, because my feelings are very, very new to me. But I can explain that I like you. That... I like you tonnes and tonnes already, even though I've barely met you. I barely know you. But I love what I do know of you. You're so cool and effortless and mysterious. And like, on top of all that, you're the sexiest, hottest, most gorgeous woman I've ever seen in real life – honestly, like. You're so *delicious*. I haven't met all the billion Chinese people in the world, but I bet you're the prettiest one. You're Canton-easy on the eyes, Ling. You're like, *Chairman Wow...*"

"Hahaaaaaah! Keep going, keep going!" She'd been smiling, listening to me, but that last bit had got a proper laugh, so I was delighted with myself.

"Honestly, it's not just your face or your body or your clothes – it's your... *attitude*. Your confidence, which isn't even the right word for what you have. You're not confident – you just *lack* a lack of confidence. You're not insecure – you're ... *outsecure*! But then, sometimes, you let your mask slip, and I see that on the inside you're really human and vulnerable and real, and it makes me want to protect you and make sure no one ever hurts you. You're not semi-precious, Ling. You're *fully* precious. So stop thinking you're second best, to anyone, ever. Okay, I'm done now." I took a deep breath or three and lit up a Marlboro Light.

"Thank you," she said, taking my hand that didn't have a fag in it, and then we looked up at all the lovely lights for a while together, and listened to the song about fluffy clouds that was the only one any of us knew by The Orb.

*****

"Ah now, you're just talking shit, love. No offence." Ian was being his usual charming self, despite his bloodstream being filled with double the regulation amount of *joy-joy feelings*.

"I'm talking sense, honey. And you know it," said Aisling, giving me a wink and a mwah when she saw us come back.

"What's Ian wrong about this time, eh?" I said, taking a joint off Niall. All the boys were back now, if you didn't count Brian or Frank.

"She's saying Live Through This is better than Nevermind, for fuck's sake," Ian said. It was amazing how we girls had gone out of our ways to look so fab and over the top and *occasiony* tonight, and these fellas had basically put on whatever looked like it needed the least ironing, and then not even ironed it. Bloody patriarchy.

"Well obviously it is. What's your point?" He'd find

no ally in me. I adored Courtney, and I wanted to have her smack-addled babies.

"Pffffft! Ye know nothing about music, like." Ian swiped the joint out of my paw and took a lungful.

"Who is *ye*? Do you mean women?" Aisling said, wild-eyed, but still smiling, because it was very, very hard to be cross on these magic beans.

"No! I just meant, uhhhh." He either didn't know what he meant, or he'd just had a massive rush which made him not care anymore. Both were equally possible.

"Yeeeeeah. Exactly. Look, here - Nevermind was catchy and easy to listen to and full of hits - and it was obviously a *seminal* record, the way it like, broke Grunge into the mainstream. Changed the whole scene, they did. But it's still overproduced pop-punk compared to Pretty on the Inside, or Live Through This. Bleach is a waaay more *authentic* record than Nevermind. Kurt didn't even like Nevermind. Listen to *Radio Friendly Unit Shifter* off In Utero. Or just listen to any interview where they let him say what he really thought." Aisling took the joint and had a pull, because having pulls on joints was something she did now. She was still somehow really articulate and on the ball, fair play. I was just trying not to snigger at the word *seminal*, because I was twelve years old.

"Yeah, but Live Through This has catchy songs on it too, like?" Richie said. I looked over and gave Mar a smile, as I hadn't seen her in tens of minutes, probably.

"It does, but that's good songwriting, though. All good albums have catchy songs on them. Even like, Pink Floyd, or something. *Money* is catchy as anything. *Another Brick in the Wall* was on Top of the Pops!" I said, chipping in as the resident lyricist here.

"So how is that different to writing *Smells Like Teen Spirit*, or *Lithium*?" Ian said. He was less angry sounding now;

it had definitely been a big rush. He was *ag mionghaire go mór.*

"It's not!" Aisling said. "My point is that Live Through This is just as full of catchy songs and great hooks as Nevermind, it's just that it still has... balls, and sincerity, and rawness. It feels *real*. You can relate to the emotions in it, like. That album tears me to pieces and puts me back together again, Ian. Nevermind... does not. You understand me, don't you, Shocks?" Who *was* this shit-cool bitch and where had she hidden Aisling Flanagan's corpse?

"I do, I do. Like, *Doll Parts* and *Jennifer's Body* and *Miss World* – they're all guaranteed hits, in my mind, anyway. But they're not the be all and end all. The real album is all the rawer, more meaningful songs, like-"

"Like *Asking For It*," said Ciara, because Ciara was here now, plus a Zachary.

"Yeah, that's sooooo good. *Credit in the Straight World*, or *Plump*, or that one at the end that has two different names?" Bríd meant *Rock Star*, or *Olympia*, depending on when you'd bought your copy of the CD, cos there was a mistake on the earlier ones. I knew this fact. I was dead clever sometimes.

"WHEN I WENT TO SCHOOOOOL!" I belted out, in my best Courtney voice.

"IN OLYMPIAAAAA-AH-AH-AH-AH!" sang everyone in our circle who was born without a willy, and then we carried on with the whole song, and forgot about silly arguments with silly boys, cos we were right anyway, and also cos it didn't matter.

*****

"So, um, I have a favour to ask, Bríd said, a bit later. We were walk-dancing through the crowd with no aim, just seeing where the night and the vibes took us.

"Shoot!" She could have anything she wanted, as long

as it wasn't unreasonable, like one of my kidneys. Even then, I had two.

"Can I hold onto this outfit tonight? Til the morning?"

"Course you can, sweets. You're not gonna sleep in it, are you? You'll boil to death, like."

"Sleep in it? Jesus, no. I just wanted to, well, I was going to take it off for sleep." She was very chewy now, I wondered if I was as bad, but then I remembered I didn't care.

"Oh, and put it back on in the morning, yeah?" I got her, now.

"Yeah. Just for a bit, like." She was smirking, but not looking at me.

"Just for a bit of COCK, more like. You fffffilth!" I'd remembered the Fat Dick Fairy.

"Am not," she said, not exactly protesting too much.

"So are. Naw, you're grand. I won't be needing it back soon or anything, I'll be wearing a different thing on stage." I didn't know what yet, but it would be something different, definitely.

"Sound. And I'll eh, get it dry cleaned for you, is that what it needs?"

"Pffffft, *dry-cleaned*. What are you like at all? Just turn it inside out and wipe all the semen off with a J-Cloth. That'll do me, sugarplum," I said, lighting up yet another ciggie.

"You're terrible, Muriel!" she said, slapping me on the back of the wrong hand and almost getting fag-burnt. We were miles from everyone else now, we might need to set off a flare gun for them to find us. The music was very trippy and trancey and hypnotic, but there were still plenty of beats under it all, so it was grand.

*****

"I mean honestly, it's not even all their fault," Aisling said, when we'd found the rest of Team Uterus. "The perving, I mean. The actual sexual harassment is definitely their fault, but the other stuff isn't. Maybe."

"What makes you say that, then?" said Marian, whose arse getting pinched by a random man had started this whole discussion, as far as I could tell.

"Well it's just constantly rammed down their throats all their lives, and down ours, obviously. This – this objectification, this seeing us as things first, and people second. Marian, you're a film student, have you ever read any Laura Mulvey?"

"I don't think so, Ash. What things has she written?" said *my* childhood friend Marian, who apparently told complete strangers what she was doing in university before she told me. I could have huffed!

"Oh lots of stuff, but the big one is Visual Pleasure and Narrative Cinema, from the 70s it is, I think. It's quite old, anyway. It's the one where she talks about the importance of the Male Gaze?"

"Bit sexist. The female gays are just as important," I said, because I was hilarious.

"Hah! No, she was talking about how in cinema, because the whole business is dominated by men, from the producer, through the director, down to the camera guy, the way women are portrayed is primarily through a male, heterosexual lens. Like, they're sexualised even in non-sexual situations, and in sexual situations, they're downright exploited, you know?" Aisling had a joint again. She probably knew how to roll them now. She was probably growing her own plants.

"Right, and so men, they…" I couldn't think of how to word the question, so I just took the joint from her instead.

"They grow up thinking it's normal. They watch all these sex comedies like Porky's or Revenge of the Nerds or whatever, where behaviour that's basically criminal is passed off as just, *boys being boys*?"

"Yeah, we never get the excuse of girls being girls, do we?" Ciara said, beside me, taking the next go off the spliff.

"That's because when boys are being boys, they're being awful. But when girls are being girls, we're awesome, like!" Bríd said, and everyone nodded and smiled and agreed, even though that was total bullshit, and any of us who had ever gone to an all-girls school (and that was all of us, except maybe Portia, who hadn't told me where she'd gone to school yet, but had probably told Aisling Flanagan, like) could attest to that.

"Possibly," Aisling said, winking at her. "Anyway, so the normalisation of all this exploitation and objectification makes it almost socially acceptable for men to harass us and grope us or just to go all *scoptophile*."

"Scopto-what?" Ciara said. She had Portia on her other side, so she was in an Us Sandwich, lucky her.

"It just means getting pleasure from looking at stuff, or at people, or at people doing stuff. Freud was always going on about it," I said. I knew things!

"Yep. Gold star for Shocks! You look *so amazing* by the way, Caoimhe, babe. I just want to… ooooooh, squeeze every bit of you, like!" She reached her hand out and did a grabbing gesture, but I was too far away for her to molest this time. "Anyway! Yes, um, I mean, in layman's language I just meant like, those creepy starer guys. Or the guys who spend all their time looking at porno mags and blue movies, and never talk to women in real life, so their image of us is all warped and detached from reality, and stuff. Those guys don't know how to interact with us properly – they've spent too long seeing us as like… walking *fuckholes* with no autonomy or agency, because that's what we *are*, in the media they're consuming. It's scary. Guys like that can end up being *very* dangerous, like. Guys like that can end up being Ted Bundy." She paused the lecture to horse down most of a bottle of water in one go. I said a silent prayer for her vital organs.

"The male gaze," I said, to no one in particular. I was always gazing at women and their womanly parts. That was probably grand, though. I probably wasn't a scoptophile, or a Ted Bundy. Or a male gay.

"Yeah, actually Shocks, that reminds me of in Philosophy when we did Sartre, remember?" Aisling talking about us being back in school together suddenly made my brain aware of how insane it was that she was standing here with me in the middle of what might as well be a rave, off her face on recreational pharmaceuticals. What a life she led, now.

"Oh yeah! The gaze - *Le regard!* From... Being and Nothingness, was it?" I said, cos I was literally dead clever, sometimes. I'd got six As in my Mock Leaving Cert and everything. I didn't talk about it much, though. I wasn't Richie.

"Yeah, well remembered. God, I loved that class, Caoimhe. It was so fucking *interesting*, and we didn't have to do it *as Gaeilge* either."

"Yeah, it was brilliant. I love me a bit of Jean-Paul, all the same," I said. I liked all the Jean-Pauls, to be honest. Sartre, Gaultier, Belmondo, Van Damme – all the important ones, anyway.

"I'm more of a Camus girl, really," said Aisling, gazing into space beyond us. She was in *my* year all through secondary school, but she'd actually known Áine better than she knew me, because they did hockey together. Poor Áine. She'd have loved seeing Aisling Flanagan on yokes.

"What are ye ladies nattering about then?" said Ian, breaking our sacred circle without asking.

"Shoes!" I said, lighting up another Marlboro.

"Makeup!" said Marian, fixing her ever-rising hemline again.

"Vaginal discharge!" shouted Aisling, pretty much into Ian's face, which thankfully made him wander off again, before we had to tie him to a stake and sacrifice him to Penthesilea.

*****

"Hang on, speak of the devil, here she comes," Ciara said. We'd been sitting down for a quick leg-rest and a fag, in a patch of grass that had no one dancing on or near it. We'd barely talked since sitting down - not for any *bad* reason, we were just sort of taking in the atmosphere and the lights and sounds together. It was a comfortable silence. I liked those ones. It was only broken when I'd wondered aloud where the other woman in my life had disappeared to this time.

"Hello again, beauties!" Portia said, diving down onto the grass and then rolling over on her back so she was lying between us.

"Welcome back... you." I was going to call her Ling, but it felt weird with someone else here, even if that someone else was Ciara.

"How many people are in Menswear?" she said to neither of us in particular.

"What, the band, or..."

"Yeah, the band, pudding." She wrapped her arm around my knee, and then did the same to Ciara. The Us Sandwich, with a different filling this time.

"Five, I think," said Ciara, reaching out her arm to put it on my back. This was all getting very cosy. I liked it.

"Right, well three of them have already propositioned me sexually this evening, so I suppose I should try and go for the full set," said Portia, as if it was the smallest deal ever, that sort of thing happening to you.

"You might as well," I said, not at all worried that she might take any of them up on it.

"Indeed. Anyway, Ciara!"

"Yes, darling?"

"Why were you snogging that Zach guy earlier on?"

"What?" said Ciara, stubbing out her fag in the grass.

"What?" I said. My fag didn't need stubbing out yet, so my *what* was less cinematic.

"You, and young Zachary. Playing tonsil hockey, by the bleachers." She said American words for things sometimes, it was very her. "I thought he was gay?"

"He is!!!" said Ciara, smiling in the way you do just before a laugh escapes.

"He is?" I said. I'd heard the rumours, to be fair. Still though.

"YES!" they both said.

"Why were you shifting him, then?" I said, more curious than anything. I didn't feel jealous. Not now I knew he was batting for the other side, anyway. The male gays.

"Haha! I dunno. We were just wrecked, and chatting about how I was the last girl he was with before he realised he wasn't bi, he was 100% gay. And whatever way the conversation went, he ended up suggesting I snog him, to see would it turn him half-straight again."

"Like a really fucked up Disney fairytale," said Portia, and the three of us giggled.

"And did it work?" I said, feeling all relieved for some reason or other.

"Nah, I'm apparently not hot enough to cure gays,

lads." Ciara opened her fag box and offered one to me. They were nearly all gone, but I still took one, cos it was Christmas.

"Ah you are," I said, "You just need to apply yourself a bit more." I gave her a wink and got a smile in return. I felt so good now, I didn't want it to stop, ever.

"So, you're able to turn boys queer, but you're not able to turn them back again. Well, petal. That's half a superpower, at least," said Portia, running a hand through her hair in a way that was a little more than just friendly. I wasn't sure how it made me feel until she ran her other hand up my thigh and only stopped a few millimeters short of my actual vajayjay, and then I immediately didn't mind her touching Ciara's hair, one bit. It was funny how stuff like that worked. I wondered what was next.

"Guys!!! Have any of ye seen Bríd? I think she's missing. I can't find her anywhere, and it's not like she's hard to spot in those clothes, and that wig," said a big, deep, Benson voice from up in the sky, above us. Apparently, *this* was what was next, damn it.

"I think I saw her by the bar a while ago, pear drop. Two seconds, and we'll come help you look," said Portia, deftly detaching herself from Ciara's hair and my leg, and pulling us both up with her to join the search party.

*****

"Bríd? BRÍD!" I was on my own. We'd decided that splitting up was the best way to look for her, but it was still weird being by myself in this crowd now. It wasn't like the marquee; it was a different vibe here. A lot more drunk people. A lot more groups of just fellas. All the more reason to find Bríd quickly, I thought.

"Sorry, hello? Hello?" I tapped a girl on the shoulder.

"HI!" she said, very hyper and pissed, but very friendly as well.

"Hi, I'm looking for my friend, have you seen her? She has a luminous pink, rubber dress on, and she has blue hair?" I realised how bizarre it sounded once it came out of my mouth.

"Luminous pink? Blue hair? Hang on and I ask the girls for yous now, love." She had a Dublin accent, or somewhere close to Dublin, anyway. I didn't know all the accents, just the major ones. The other girls listened while she told them my description. I was feeling the cold for the first time tonight, but I was still whizzing. Hadn't even got to the peaky bit of pill number two yet, I didn't think.

"Okay, Aoife is the only one who saw her, love. Tell her there, Aoife, go on!"

"Ah yeah, I definitely saw someone in a pink dress, ah, I thought her hair was purple, but yiz know how it is. Can't see fucking nothing properly with all these lights going on." This one, Aoife, had a proper Dub accent, like Dustin the Turkey. The way she said "purple" was incredible. *Pooor-pal*. She was dressed like a real raver chick. Hotpants, belly top, fuck-me-boots. High ponytail, hoop earrings, fake tan, fake lashes, and that magical thing people did with liner pencil, lipstick, and gloss that made their lips look twice as full as they actually were. She'd probably been in the tent thing all day, then migrated up here for The Orb. None of them looked like Blur fans to me, but I was probably just being gowlish.

"And when was that, babe? Where?" I'd struck gold already, this was gonna take no time at all, the gods were smiling at me.

"Ah, only a small while ago. Up there." She pointed *oop deyr* for me, and I saw she meant the fence where the backstage gate was. Of course! We hadn't even thought of looking there, back when we were deciding who would look where.

"Oh, you're such a star, Aoife. Thanks so much!" I gave her a big loved-up hug. She had an absolute bang of perfume off her, but it was a really nice scent, not *whore's boudoir* material.

"No probs, love. Listen, is it tomorrow yeez are playing or what?" she said, breaking away from my violently affectionate embrace. She had great cheekbones. She'd done some sort of shading with bronzer to make them stand out, but they'd been good to begin with. I'd love to have been that skillful at makeup, but it always felt like too much work.

"Pardon?" She'd lost me. The other girls were all closer to us now, listening in.

"The band, like. Yous are Kweeva Shox, like, yeah? Off Crane?"

"Oh! Oh, yeah, I am. Sorry!" Always great to meet a fan.

"Yis don't sound too sure, wha? Do yiz want to check your ID or something, to make sure yous are her?" She'd a great smile too, this Aoife one. They were all quite young, as far as I could tell, through the makeup and in this light. Fourteen or fifteen. I wasn't going to festivals when I was fourteen, fair play.

"Ah no, I definitely am. Listen, I'll give you a shout out from the stage, yeah? Aoife what, was it?" I probably wouldn't remember, but maybe I'd write it on my arm or something, later.

"Aoife O'Connor! Aw, thanks. Me brother - me younger brother, like – he'll be dead jealous of me, he will. He thinks you're an absolute screw, so he does. I'd say he pulls the fucking wire off himself every night, thinking about yous. No offence."

"None taken! He's clearly a man of taste, Aoife darling. Okay, I have to go find this poor woman before she gets killed to death by murderers. Enjoy the rest of yeer night, girls. Love ye all!" I gave them a big wave and multiple blown kisses and started towards the gate. The crowd got denser the closer you got to the stage. I could have done with Portia's vampire powers now, but she'd volunteered to look for Bríd over by the beer tent area, so I was *sans* her for a little while, at least. Hopefully just for a little while, I didn't like being *sans* her for long.

*****

"THERE YOU ARE!" I screamed, when I finally found her, standing side-stage, looking at the Orb, or looking at their big laser light machine, more specifically. Maybe that was the actual Orb, and the two guys were just its human slaves? We'd literally never find out. Bríd turned her head and smiled.

"Hello, chickee. Isn't it beautiful? Where's everyone else?" She looked absolutely spaced out. If I didn't already know she was on drugs, I'd have suspected her of being on drugs.

"They're all looking for you, you gombeen," I said, wrapping her around the waist from the back, since she hadn't turned around properly to greet me.

"That's silly. I'm not *missing*. I'm right here," she said, squeezing my hands.

"Well, we didn't know that, did we?" I said, detaching myself a bit from her, because my stomach was sticking to the rubberiness of her back.

"I suppose... Look at the lights though, Caoimhe. It's like... galaxies or something, isn't it? It's like heaven. I'm sooooooo good, right now. I don't ever wanna be... not this good, you know what I mean?" More hand squeezing, harder this time.

"I know exactly what you mean, chicken. It's immense. This is the best time, ever. It's lush as fuck."

My nose was getting tickled from the fibres in the wig. It wasn't real hair – synthetic stuff. Little bits of it stood up on their own, from the static electricity. My furry top and her rubber dress were probably causing it – like when you rubbed a balloon on your jumper. I could probably pick her up and stick her to the ceiling now, I thought, and I giggled to myself, picturing it.

"What's so funny, gorgeous?" She turned on the spot to face me. She looked extra other-worldly now, with her blue hair getting backlit by the humming, throbbing, artificial nebula on stage behind her. My eyes took a Polaroid of her and put it in the back of my mind to look at, another day.

"Everything. Everything is funny, and everything is gorgeous. Especially you, Brigid. Now let's get you back to the gang, before they have to send out a search party for me, too."

*****

"Oh my God! Oh my God! Oh. My. GOD!!!!!" Marian was having a religious experience when we got back to where everyone had agreed to meet. All eyes were on her, and on Brian, for some reason. So much so that they hadn't even noticed I'd found Bríd, the ungrateful wretches.

"How in the name of all that is – where did you fecking pop out of, Cuz?" Brian said, looking at her in disbelief. I had no idea what was going on. No one was filling me in yet, either.

"I've been here all day!!! When did – why are you – how…" Marian looked like she was going to faint. I grabbed Richie and pulled him into me.

"What's this? I don't get it?"

"Oh, like, Marian is Brillo's first cousin. They're both Collinses. But like, she didn't know he was our manager or anything. She didn't know he was here, she – I mean, *I knew* that they were cousins, but like-"

"You knew??? Why didn't you tell me this?"

"When?"

"Like, ever?" I was talking to him, but my eyes were still on the family reunion. Small world, eh? Even smaller Munster.

"I didn't even know ye knew each other before until ye told me today, like. Why would I be telling you that Brillo is cousins with some girl I was going out with a million years ago, Kweev? When would that come up in conversation?" He had a point.

"True. But, like, today? Why didn't you say anything about this all day? Why didn't you tell Mar that her cousin was here, and bring her over to him? Why didn't you tell Ais-"

"I've been a bit busy, like, Caoimhe. I've been a bit *preoccupied* today, you know?" Richie still hadn't noticed Bríd. No one had. Everyone wasn't back from the search yet, I didn't think. I couldn't see Ian or Tim or Benson. Definitely couldn't see Portia.

"Preoccupied?"

"Yeah, with the whole thing of *the love of my life* appearing out of nowhere and wanting to spend all this time with me and hang around with me and talk to me and touch me all nice and shift me and tell me all these lovely things and say she wants to come sleep in my room tonight and-"

"Okay, okay. I get ya, Rich. I get it. Preoccupied." He'd said they shifted already. Of course they had though, she was already talking to me about shagging him tomorrow morning, for fuck's sake. I'd just missed witnessing the kissing. Probably happened on one of the million times I'd snuck off with Portia to not-touch her boob, or to let her chew on my earring. He'd called her the love of his life, too, which made my heart do a little chemically enhanced flutter, whether he was being serious or not. The love of his life and his band manager were hugging it out now, and Aisling had joined the hug too.

"Bríd's here!!!" shouted someone, and everyone who wasn't in the triple hugfest turned around to look over our way.

"Hello! I am heeeeeere," said Bríd, and then she shrieked with the shock as Benson lifted her up from behind, then he yelped with the pain when she toppled over backwards and flattened him into the grass with her big rubber bum. The Collins cousins and the future Mrs. Collins broke up their clinch, and Marian and Aisling ran over to dive on top of the fallen lovers, all of them laughing like hyenas.

"Where's your *giiiiiirlfriend* gone anyway, Shaughnessy?" said a voice beside me. It was Ciara, but she wasn't being gowlish, she'd a big mad smile on her face.

"Was gonna ask you the same thing, pudding. Will we go hunt her down?" I said, taking her hand and joining our fingers. We hadn't talked about anything tonight – anything serious, anyway. Last night and this morning felt like a million years ago now. Maybe we'd talk later. Or maybe we wouldn't. Both were equally possible.

"Nah, let's just plonk ourselves down here, Kweev. She knows where we're at. If we go looking for her, we'll probably get lost ourselves, honey. Fag?" She took the plastic off a brand new twenty box of B&H and yoinked out the gold paper bit.

"Actually, that is a much smarter idea. The fag, and the staying put. Two smart ideas," I said, waiting for her to do the Lucky Cigarette thing before I took mine.

"Not just a pretty face, me." She lit up hers and moved the flickering match nearer to me, her hand around it to stop the breeze.

"You've a pretty lots of things, chick," I said, having another look at the amazing Chinese dress and its amazing contents.

"Yeaaaaah, I know," she said, and we sat our arses down on the grass, still holding hands. Listening to the rest of them talk, but saying nothing ourselves, because comfortable silences were lush.

*****

Portia still hadn't come back by the time the Orb finished. Neither had Frank and Niall, but I didn't care as much about that. I wasn't worried about them, and I didn't *need* their physical presence in the way I needed hers.

"When was the last time you spoke to her, honey?" Ciara said. She was hugging herself to stop the chilliness, because the temperature had really dropped in the last half hour or so.

"Same time you did. Remember? Just before we all split up."

"Who are you talking about?" said Marian, coming over to us now, with Richie. He'd given her his tracksuit top, like a fella giving his suit jacket to his date after the Debs, it was dead cute. Although, cos of the shortness of her dress, and the... *longness* of Richie's top, it looked like she was wearing nothing under it except her strappy shoes. Which was also cute, but more in a Flashdance way than a Pretty in Pink way.

"Portia," I said. "I can't find her anywhere, babe. I'm getting worried." I looked around and saw that almost all of us were here. We were going to get a lift back in Benson's van. Brian and Aisling were coming too, for a small while, he'd said. For as long as she bloody felt like, she'd corrected him.

"Oh, she's gone back to Jury's already, honey." Marian was chilly, even with the extra top; I could hear her teeth chattering. Bríd was the luckiest of us all, cos she was probably still boiling in that rubber thing, underwear or no underwear.

"She has? With who?" I suddenly pictured her being shagged by three to five members of Menswear, so I just as quickly unpictured it.

"Uh, I dunno. By herself, I think?"

"But... how do you know that's where she's gone, sweetie?" I said. I wanted a tracksuit top too, now. Maybe Niall still had that cardigan? Although he was on the missing list too, damn it.

"She came back and asked to borrow my key to our room, just after we all split up to go look for Bríd? I thought it was strange, cos she has her own key, but she must have lost it or something. I didn't get a chance to ask her, cos she was acting like it was urgent – like she was in a real hurry? She looked a bit panicky, now I'm thinking back on it, babe. I'm sorry, I was actually going to say something about it earlier, but then that whole mad thing happened with Brian, and after that, and I just forgot?"

"Right, so," Richie said, giving the love of his life a big warm squeeze-hug from the side, "if she's already *in* Jury's and we're *going* to Jury's, then… why don't we all just get in the van and-"

"*Go* to Jury's?" Ciara said, already heading in the general direction of *outta here*, and pulling me with her by the hand.

"Sounds great to me," I said, feeling very relieved that my Ling wasn't missing or dead, and trying not to picture her back in Jury's having a torrid, incestuous gangbang with The Kelly Family.

NINETEEN

"Ah now, you *are*. Like peas in a pod, the two of you. You'd make a lovely couple," Aisling said, when we were en route to the hotel. Brian had drunk lots of mind-altering Guinness and didn't want to risk the Blackboard Jungle minibus (or his girlfriend's life, although he hadn't said that, I'd just inferred it), so the two of them were in the van with us.

"Fuck off!" said Ciara, rolling her eyes.

"We're nothing like each other!" I said, although I wasn't sure that was true. We'd the same sense of humour, definitely.

"We're like chalk and cheese!" Ciara said.

"We're like a dichotomy!" I said, although I wasn't 100% sure that was what that word meant, because my brain was watery.

"Ye're like a dyke *something*, definitely," said Ian.

"Do you want some acid, Ciara?" said Benson.

"To throw in his fucking face? Yes please," she said, because she was hilarious, just like me.

"Haha! No, seriously. Do either of ye want a tab?" he said, still keeping his eyes on the road, because we'd made him promise not to kill us, earlier.

"Candy-flipping, like?" Ciara said, but I didn't know what that was.

"I don't know what that is," I said.

"Ooooooh, it's like when you take acid and Ecstasy together, chickee. It's really good. You're supposed to drop the acid first and then the E, but I don't think it matters, really," Bríd said, leaning over the headrest of the passenger seat, still blue-haired and spaced-out looking.

"Is *that* what's wrong with you?" I said, not meaning it in a gowlish way or anything. She'd been acting quite strange since I'd rescued her from The Orb and their magic hypnosis machine.

"What? Am I candy-flipping? Well, yeah. Why aren't you, anyway?"

"Why aren't I what?"

"Well, B gave Portia a couple of tabs for you and Ciara, so I thought you'd taken them, no?"

"No!" said Ciara, and I shook my head to agree, if that was something that was possible to do. "No, what happened was Portia came and found us, she was there for like two seconds, and then-"

"Yeah, then I came along and told them you were missing, and then Portia disappeared herself, so they never actually got them, Bríd," explained Benson. "So do ye two want one now, or…?"

"Go on, so," Ciara said.

"I dunno, B. Is it really strong, or intense or something? I've to get some sleep at some point, cos I've to sing tomorrow, and my voice is already gonna be wrecked from smoking and talking all day," I said, which was remarkably sensible for me, but it was true, so.

"Nooooo, it's really mellow, honestly," Richie said. Richie got bad trips from smoking hash, so he was actually the best person here to gauge the strength of it, I thought.

"Yeah, honey. You know me, I'm no good with psychedelics either and this is just very mild, and warm, and fuzzy," Marian said, as if I'd been taking drugs with her for years or something. Last time I'd talked to her I still secretly owned three Barbie dolls.

"Okay, cool. Who else is on them? Ian?"

"Yup." He gave me a thumbs up. I hadn't forgotten the dyke comment, his shins were mine in a little while.

"Aisling?" Surely this would be her limit. Although maybe not, since all bets were off, and it was also Christmas.

"No, honey, I'm sticking to what I've already had, I'm feeling good enough, don't want to push it by tripping the light fandango. Also, I was thinking about later, and you know, *the sex*. I don't want that to be all weird, for me, or for Brian." She squeezed his knee in that cute way that made you envy people who were in relationships, a bit, sometimes. "But it's *my* decision and mine alone, don't worry, ladies. I don't give *this* cunt a say in what I put into my own body!"

"Aisling Mary Elizabeth *Mastrantonio* Flanagan!!! Language, please!" I said, laughing so much my belly started to hurt.

"I'm on the LSD as well, Caoimhe," said lovely Tim, who I'd missed the most today, while we'd been sequestered voluntarily in the Village of Vadge.

"Yeah, babe? How you finding it?" I said, wondering if any of us would ever truly get to know this enigmatic young man.

"It's grand, Caoimhe. It's not like you'd imagine or like you hear about. I'm not having big hallucinations or wanting to jump off a building to see if I can fly. It's more like, just, the edges of stuff have become blurred – undefined…"

"The edges of what, honey?"

"Oh, just like, you know... the edges of a table. Or of the floor. Or of *reality*."

"Okay! Okay! We're here, ladies and gents!" Benson stopped the van and killed the engine.

"Thanks, Benson!" said everyone, including Benson himself, which somehow didn't feel weird at all. What a life we led.

*****

"Oh God, that's brilliant, Ciara. Don't stop. Don't ever stop." Marian had taken off her strappy shoes when we got settled in Room 213, and Ciara was massaging her sore calves, where the string bits had dug into her over the day. We still had no Portia. She wasn't up in their room when we checked, but her stuff was all still there, so at least she hadn't done a runner or anything. Marian had said not to worry, that she'd appear in a bit, with some mad story about where she'd been. I was still a bit worried, but there wasn't much we could do, except wait.

"Wait until she gets to your feet, Mar. You'll need to have a fag afterwards, I swear," I said, remembering the going over she'd given me during the Prodigy.

"I don't remember volunteering to do the feet," said Ciara.

"Ah, don't worry Ceer, you're grand," said Mar, wiggling her toes, either from the relief of taking the shoes off, or from the sheer pleasure of the leg rub she was getting.

"I can give it a go, if you want?" I said. I'd never done it to anyone before, but how hard could it be?

"Ah, I don't want ye to go to any bother for me, lads," Marian said, in that way you said it when you'd quite like someone to go to some bother for you, if they didn't mind.

"No bother at all," I said, one of her feet already in my

hands.

"Oh, you're an angel," she said, already making appreciative noises at my rookie foot-pummeling efforts. It was pretty simple to do. I just used my thumbs to push against the skin and tried to find where the muscles were all taut, and then sort of crunch them. It was the same as massaging someone's back, and I'd done a fair few of those last night and today.

"Just lie back there on Richie's lap, and we'll have you fixed in no time, Ciara said.

"Teamwork!" I said, remembering I had some Vaseline Intensive Care body lotion in my handbag. I paused a second, got it out, squirted some on my palm.

"What are you… OOOH!!!" Marian almost had a seizure when she felt the cold cream on her hot feet. I rubbed it into the ball and the heel, and anywhere else the skin was a bit hard. The smell of it was gorgeous – much better than the slight whiff of shoe sweat that was there before, anyway.

"None of the rest of you get any ideas now, yeah?" Ciara said, taking a bit of the moisturiser off me to rub into Mar's sore calves. "Anyone else wants me and Kweev to do them, it's twenty quid."

"Each!" I said, in case they thought we came cheap.

"A BARGAIN!" Marian said, and the three of us laughed. It was actually no bother at all – it was nice to be touching someone's skin, and it was lovely to be doing something for someone. Apparently, you got a kick out of altruism when you were on Es. I hadn't come up on the LSD yet at all. I wasn't sure I'd notice it when I did, since I'd had two incredibly strong pills, and the acid was supposed to be so mild.

"It's okay that I have the horn watching this, isn't it?" said Trippy Tim, with his usual Timlike honesty.

"Whatever floats your boat, boy who I barely know!"

said Marian.

"Yeah, Tim. Horn away. You're the only man here who can, so it would almost be rude *not* to have an erection, I think," said Ciara.

"Are you one of those strange guys who finds feet erotic then, Tim?" I said. I'd met one or two of them in my life. They terrified me.

"No. I just find three really beautiful women touching each other with slippery hands very erotic," said Tim, which was fair enough.

"Don't we all, Timbo. Don't we all," said Ciara, giving me a wink.

"Do I not get any say in this?" Richie said, giving Tim slight evils across the room.

"Nope. It's Marian's feet, her choice, Richard!" said Aisling, who was still with us, entwined in poor, very not-drugged Brian on the carpet near the door. They were a cute pair, in all fairness. They were a good match, without being anything alike. That worked, sometimes. Me and Jon were a bit like that. I closed my eyes and shook the Etch-a-Sketch which held the picture of that memory, until it was just formless, meaningless powder in the bottom of the frame again. Fuck, that's the acid kicking in, I thought. Oh boy.

"My feet, my choice, Tim's langer, his choice, fuck the patriarchy!" said Marian, doing the raised fist thing, which I was pretty sure was for Black Power, but I didn't correct her, because fuck it, solidarity to everyone.

"Bríd! Are you okay?" I asked, because she looked miles away, mentally. Like she was having an out of body experience.

"Huh? Yeah, I'm fantastic, chickee. I'm just watching the breathing. It's so cool…"

"The breathing…? Anyone?" I said, switching feet now, and putting more gloop on my fingers, much to Mar's delight. She probably wasn't going to let us stop. She'd probably get a twenty and stick it down my knickers in a minute.

"The carpet, the wallpaper, any surface really. They look like they're breathing, when you're tripping," Benson said. That deep voice coming out of his very non-threatening face was always a surprise when you forgot that was how he sounded.

"Sounds… well, trippy," I said. It was grand, though. Breathing carpets, I could handle. If the loo seat grew teeth and tried to bite my arse off though, I might feel less okay.

"Yeah, it's just… cool. It's all cool. I'm cool. You're cool. You're all cool," said Ian, sounding incredibly mellow.

"Ye're all mad, is what ye are," said poor Brian, and I gave him a very convincing pretend lunatic smile, just to keep things interesting.

*****

"What's yours then, Mister B?" said Marian, a little later. We were doing a survey of *what's the best song ever?*

"Probably something from Vera Lynn," said Ciara. She was sitting in front of me, nestled between my thighs. Still no sign of the other one. I was trying not to worry about her. The carpet was gently inhaling and exhaling, but I hadn't been to check on the toilet seat yet.

"Fuck off!" said Benson, smiling. He was well used to it by now.

"How much older are you than Bríd, Benson?" Aisling said. She was in the same position with Brian as Ciara was with me, so I guessed that meant I was the fella in our scenario. I was literally the one wearing the trousers, so.

"About ten years," Bríd said. She didn't look *embar-*

rassed, she just looked tired of always discussing it, I thought.

"That's nothing, really," Aisling said, still full of surprises.

"It isn't?" said Brian, behind her. I still couldn't get over him being Mar's cousin. It was six degrees of separation all over the shop.

"Nah. She can go out with who she wants, Brian. You're very mature, so you're grand for me. But I'd probably be going out with an older fella, if we weren't together."

"You would?" I said.

"How much older?" Brian looked a bit worried, behind her.

"I don't know, lover. He's only hypothetical. I can't cut him in half and count the rings, if he doesn't exist. But I've always liked older men. I just never did anything about it. You're like the first boy I've even been able to *tell* my Mum and Dad about, and that's just cos I knew you'd get on with my father, over the rugby and all the other things ye have in common, you old codger. I knew he'd trust you with me, as if it's even any of his bloody business what I do, dear. Anyway, what I'm saying is, people are attracted to who they're attracted to, tis none of anyone else's business, as long as it's legal, and no one is getting harmed."

"That's true," I said, although I wasn't thinking about age differences when I said it. Still, I would be less gowlish to the two of them from now on about it, I decided.

"*Another Girl, Another Planet*," said Benson, confusing us all for a second. "by the Only Ones."

"Oh! The song, right. Yeah, that's a good one, B. When is it from? When did it come out?" I said. Dave Fanning was always playing it, but I'd never seen the video, so I couldn't tell how old it was from the fashions or the hair, like you normally would.

"Ah, 1978, I think?" said Benson.

"Really???" Ian said. Tim hadn't said anything for a while, but he was still here, still conscious, and probably still erect.

"Wow! I was only one year old, then. A little baby!" said Ciara.

"What age were *you* when it came out, Benson? 21, was it? Did they play it at your birthday party, yeah? When you were blindfolded on a chair, sucking 21 dicks in a row?" I said, already forgetting my pledge to be less gowlish.

*****

"Well, she's definitely not under there," I said, taking my head out from under the big double bed in Marian and Portia's room, upstairs.

"Ah, well. We had to make sure, shur." Marian had wanted to come up and get changed into something else, so I said I'd come with her.

"I hope she's okay," I said, sitting down on the mattress. I might have been imagining it, but their bed felt a lot softer than mine. I'd been sitting on a hard floor for ages though, so everything probably felt soft compared with that.

"Ah, she'll be grand. She can look after herself, Caoimhe. She's a black belt in Kung Fu, like." Marian was already dressless and scouring her suitcase for pyjamas or something similar. I was averting my Female Gaze, because I was a gentlewoman.

"Is she really?" I pictured Portia in my head, dispatching baddies with a single kick, and speaking dubbed English. This acid was great for imagining stuff vividly. You just had to make sure you only imagined nice things. I was staying the fuck away from all matters Áine or Jon, that was for sure.

"Noooooo! You fucking racist. She's from Dún

Laoighre." Marian held up an emerald green tank top vest thing against herself for my approval. I nodded, cos it was gorgeous, and the colour was lovely with her skin and her hair.

"Hah, yeah. You got me. Is there a pants to go with that, then?" I said, undoing her bra for her with my eyes closed, because it was easier than trying to look at it. My eye jitters were mixing with the *everything is breathing* effect. I got it open on my first try, thanks to imagining Obi Wan in my head, telling me to use The Force.

"Ohhhhh, thanks. Release the Krakens, like. Jeeeesus, that's better." She slipped the vest thing over her head and spun around to face me again. A tiny bit too fast, because I saw her have a little wobble for a second, but she was grand, then. "Pants? There's a shorts for them. Come here and I show you. Whatcha think?" She held up a pair of matching colour shorts, same kind of ribbed cotton material, with white piping on them, that reminded me of soccer ones from the 80s. That's what they looked like – sexy soccer pants.

"They're gorgeous, Mar. Jesus you'll have to take me under your wing and teach me some style tricks, all the same. Everything you own is dead chic. Even your PJs."

"Ah now, you're too nice. And anyway, you're the one who's a style icon, according to the Clare Echo, Richie tells me."

"Yeah, but I can't carry that burden alone, babe. Maybe we'll have a word with Brian and see will he hire you as my stylist, yeah?"

"You know, I could almost see myself doing that. In another life. Are you gonna look at my fanny if I take off my knickers in front of you, now that you're a big lesbian, Kweev?"

"Hahahaaaah! No. I'm not. You gowl," I said.

"Why not? Something wrong with my fanny, is there?"

"Well, I wasn't gonna say anything, but..." I took a fag out, cos I hadn't had one in literally thousands of seconds.

"Fuck off, you'll make it paranoid now," she said, losing the knickers and stepping into the shorts. She looked much cuter and way sexier in this outfit than she had in the stripper dress, I thought. Pair of knee socks was all it needed, and they'd have her in FHM or Loaded, no bother. Maybe I should be *her* stylist.

"Like Richie after three pulls on a joint," I said, getting the giggles again. Whatever about breathing carpets, this acid stuff was very gigglesome. Like that Squidgy Black hash we sometimes got.

"God, please stop making me imagine Richie as my vagina, or my vagina as Richie, Kweev. I'm way too... *vivid* at the minute. I can literally see that in my head."

"Aaaagh! So can I, now!" I said, linking arms with her on the side I was smoking, and finding her mouth with my fag. She took a long pull and exhaled. The smoke looked all weird and trippy and pretty and purple, in the light of the hallway outside.

"If I walk into that room and Richie South has a fanny instead of a head, I'm walking straight back out again and getting a taxi to Dublin."

"We can split the fare," I said, hoping we didn't run into any rock stars between now and the second floor, because three to five members of Menswear mightn't be able to resist young Collins in that little rigout.

*****

"Boys, boys, boys! And man, sorry Benson. Let me... let me, as the oldest of the women here – Portia's older, but she's fucked off back to Hong Kong or something – Let me just say, that ye're all worrying about fuck all, basically." Marian was standing up in the middle of the room, with everyone around her. She was quite tiny without shoes.

"Yeah, guys. The only people I ever hear talking about big dicks are you men," said Ciara. "And it's nearly always straight men, which makes even less sense." She'd agreed with me about Mar's outfit being sexier than the dress, so maybe we weren't that chalky cheesy after all.

"Yeah, but I keep hearing that it matters, like. *Size...*" Ian said. He was feeling the material of his corduroy pants in a strange, intense way, but hopefully that was an LSD thing, and not some mating ritual.

"It does and it doesn't, sweetie. Every girl is different. There's no accounting for taste. Like, every dick has its *perfect* fit, somewhere out there, but we're very stretchy – we can make a whole baby come out of there when we need to, remember? Saying that, what *all* of you consistently fail to realise though, is that the fella attached to the willy matters *way* more to us than the actual willy," said Aisling Flanagan, who had apparently met other willies before Brian's, it seemed.

"That does actually make sense, I suppose," said Tim, the One-eyed King of the Willies.

"I'm not so sure," said Richie, who had started this whole conversation off a little earlier on, talking about some porn movie he'd watched that starred a fella called Long Dong Silver, which had made me giggle for far longer than was necessary or appropriate.

"Richard South. Or, The Beautiful South, as I like to call you," said Marian, dropping down on her hands and knees in front of him.

"The Beautiful South!" Bríd said, still looking all rubbery and colourful in Benson's lap. Everyone laughed again, even though we'd already laughed when Mar said it. It was that kind of night.

"Anyhoo, Rich. Look at me now. Look in my eyes, there's a good boy. You know… you know when you smoke normal sized fags, right? And then one day you decide to buy superking ones?"

"Uh, yeah…" he said, not looking at her eyes, just gawping down her top, but he was probably allowed to. Her boobs looked incredible in it, even without a bra. I might have hated her if I didn't love her so much.

"My face is up here, South. Focus! Anyway, yes. So, now you're smoking the superkings, you know how they look massive in your fingers for the first few days? Like they're too big, and they don't belong there?"

"Yeah, kind of. No, yeah, I do. I remember now." Richie didn't smoke anymore, so it was probably not the best analogy, I thought.

"Okay, good. Well, that feeling doesn't – didn't last forever, right?" She came off her knees and sat down properly in front of him, probably because she'd realised she had her shorts-clad arse pointed in Ian's direction, like a female baboon *presenting* to her mate in a David Attenborough programme. My imagination was way, way too vivid now.

"How do you mean?"

"I mean that, after a bit, the big fag just looks - and feels – normal. Like, cos they're the size you smoke, now?", said Mar, motioning at me to throw her a ciggie, because talking about fags always made you want one.

"I get you," said Richie, looking enviably at her light up in the way ex-smokers always did when they'd had a few pints. Or a fuckload of drugs.

"But then, if you decide to go back on the shorter fags, what do they look like, or feel like, to you?" She lit up her smoke, which was one of my normal sized ones, not a Long Dong Silver one.

"Tiny!" he said, looking like he was close to getting it.

"But then, after a while, *those ones* feel normal, because they're the ones you smoke now, and you're used to them," Ian said, finishing the story for Marian, and for everyone else. She turned around and smiled at him.

"This guy, he gets it, see?" she said, then turning back to Richie, "Feel a bit better now, gorgeous?"

"Well, kind of," he said, reaching out to pull all her tanned, blonde, emerald-coated lushness a bit closer to him. "Except now I've a movie in my head of you smoking Superkings with your fanny, and I can't make it go away."

"You're not the only one," said Tim, and everyone laughed, and I wondered where Portia was, or where Niall and Frank were, because all three of them had been AWOL for hours now.

*****

So, is it going to be your first time having sex? Tomorrow, I mean?" I said to Marian, when we'd gone to the toilet to see if we could beat the pills and manage a sneaky trickle. She was going first, but failing, so far.

"No, I've definitely had sex before, babe. Full frontal heterosexual intercourse. Penis entering vagina, like in the biology book in school." She stood up, gave herself a cursory wipe, and let me have the vacant throne. I was struggling with the button fly on my golf pants, though, so I couldn't sit down just yet. It was a combination of my stupid drug-fingers, and the pants being extra tight from all the bloat.

"Hahaha! You know what I meant. Your first time with Richie, like." Still couldn't get the bottom three buttons open.

"Here, let me try, honey. Um, yeah. First time with the Richster. Exciting!" She got one open straight away, but the next one was proving more of a challenge.

"That's mad, like. So, back in what, 1991, were you…"

"A virgin? Yeah, of course I was, Caoimhe. What do you take me for, some kind of - *There!* Success!" She got the last one undone and I nearly gave myself carpet burns on my thighs, I ripped the trousers down so quickly.

"THANK YOU! I might just… wait a second, here it comes." It didn't come. Although a small fart did, which caused the briefest of awkward silences, then we both burst out laughing, because farts were hilarious.

"Pardon you, milady."

"I could have done that with the pants still on, like. What a waste. Anyway, so. You never had sex with Richie, *back in the day*, as the kids say? Actually though, speaking of kids, that's why you didn't, isn't it?" I stood up reluctantly and wondered would the buttons be easier to do up than they were to open. We'd soon find out.

"I don't follow you, sugar. We going back outside, yeah?"

"Once I get these fucking things done up again," I said, wishing it was later, or that we were going back into an empty room, so I could just take the pants off and be done with them. My knickers were way too *skimpy* today to be parading around in though. Especially with a very drunk, very undrugged Brian Collins in the audience.

"Here I'll do them. Tell me again now? What were you saying?" She was a star. There was a really familiar smell off her. Took me a second to realise it was just the stuff we'd rubbed on her feet and legs, earlier. My hands smelled of it too, that's why it was so familiar, duh.

"Oh, I was just gonna say that I understand now why you didn't go the whole way with Richie back then, like." She'd already done me up, apart from the easy top button. I might have to get Brian to hire her after all. As my Lady in

Waiting, maybe.

"And why was that?" She fastened the last one and we were ready to motor.

"Because you didn't want to go to prison for sexing a child," I said, cos I was hilarious.

*****

"Right so, ye degenerates. We're off to the B&B. Taxi is outside. Thanks for having us, it's been… an experience," Brian said, standing by the door with his Aisling. They'd stayed ages with us, fair play to them, especially to him.

"Wait until I get you back there, *stud*. Then you'll have a real experience," said End of the Movie Edition Sandra Dee, or as we knew her, Aisling.

"Promises, promises, Flanagan. Anyway, the rest of ye? The ones in the actual band, I mean. Get some sleep, please, all right? Oh, and when that Niall finally gets here, one of ye kick him up the hole for me, yeah?" He had the big awkward looking mobile phone in his hand – he'd used it to call the cab.

"We will, Brian. Have a… *nice* night now, the two of ye," I said, mildly jealous that they were off to have sex, but not that jealous, because it was sex involving Brian, and that'd be like shagging your cousin or something. That'd be like Marian shagging him.

"So long! Fair well! Auf wiedersehen, adieu!" sang Aisling, sounding like her old Head Girl self for a second again

"To screw, and screw, and screw and screw and screw-ew!" I sang back, cos I was hilarious. I felt Ciara's arm around my waist, and I squooched into her.

"Night night, Brian. Night night, Aisling. Make sure you take precautions," said Tim, very smiley-looking now.

"I'll precaution you in a minute, squire," said Brian, and then they were gone.

"Soooooo," I said, looking at the remaining gang. "What are we doing? Early night, is it?" It was long past early, unless you meant the early hours of the morning.

"Ehhhhhhhh!" Bríd said, yawning with the whole top half of her pink rubber body.

"That's probably my cue, guys. The van-bed is calling," Benson said, standing up and and pulling her to her feet.

"I'm going to go to my room and listen to The Doors, with no clothes on, and pretend I'm in the desert," said Tim, making it sound almost tempting to join him. I didn't want him to poke me in the eye with his rigid mickey though, so I'd pass.

"Right, okay. Richie, come with me, we're gonna make sweet, sweet love. Can I scab a few fags off ye, lads? If it's not too cheeky?" said Marian. Richie looked a bit scared, but he got up with her.

"You know I can't – I mean, the pills, like. You know-" He stopped, because he'd forgot how to sentence properly.

"Your tongue still works, doesn't it, Rich?" Ciara said, making me feel a little feeling. The room looked very weird now. Fuzzy around the edges, as Tim had described it earlier.

"It works very, very well, if I'm remembering right, Ciara. Ooh, thanks, darlings!" Marian said, picking up the trove of donated fags we'd all put on the carpet by her feet. The two of them left without wasting any more time. I was dead excited for her - and for him too - about to be cunnilingually reunited with the actual love of his life. I hoped it all went brilliantly for them, I really did.

"You two going to fuck off then?" Ian said, meaning me and Ciara. I was about to get cross with him, then I realised it was his room we'd all been in, so he couldn't actually go to sleep unless we did fuck off.

"How shall we fuck off, oh Lord?" said Ciara. We still

had no Portia – or Niall, or Frank - but I couldn't stay up any longer, I was running on fumes now. Whatever it was about the candy-flipping thing, it seemed to have taken the wide-awake energy part away from the pills, and replaced it with a kind of mellow, relaxed, sluggish vibe. But the happy part was still there, so it was grand.

"Night night, Ian baby, you big angry teddy bear," I said, giving him a surprise peck on the cheek, and dragging Ciara out the door with me.

"Right, so!" she said, when we were out in the hall.

"Right so," I said. I had no idea what was going to happen now. This wasn't the plan, during the day. There hadn't been a plan. I suddenly felt very overwhelmed and confused and unsure and vulnerable, and I didn't know if all that was real, or drugs, or –

"Now! Missy. We… we probably have lots of things to talk about. And I'm sure you think you have lots to say to me, for some reason that you think is a good reason, but…"

"But?" She was making me anxious already, I didn't like it.

"BUT. I dunno about you, but I'm tired, in a nice way. And I'm really, really fucked, also in a nice way. So… if I'm coming in there with you, there has to be some rules. Okay?"

"Okay. What are the rules?" I wasn't sure I liked where this was going, but on the other hand she was here, she was with me, and she was coming into the room with me. I liked all of those things. Maybe the rules would be okay too?

"Oh, baby. Don't look so serious. It's okay." She came closer to me and touched my face. I took a deep breath and reached for my fags.

"I'm…"

"Nope. Don't have a fag yet, save it. I have this!" she

held up a joint. I hadn't had any hash in hours, or if I had, I'd forgotten about it.

"Wow. You're the bestest," I said, opening up the door to my room.

"I know," she said, walking towards the bed, but stopping before she got to it. "Pull this down for me?" She pointed at the zipper on the back of the neck of her Chinese dress. I still hadn't heard any of the rules but having to keep our clothes on was apparently not one of them, so hooray for that.

I unzipped her slowly and carefully, in case it might get stuck on the way down. The gradual reveal of her bra strap first, then the back of her extremely pretty knickers, felt like the most erotic thing ever, for some reason. Felt like I was watching it happen in a movie, instead of real life. Then the dress was on the floor, and she was stepping out of it, and turning around to face me.

"Little overdressed, aren't you?" she said, putting the joint in her mouth, unlit.

"You might have to help me with some buttons," I said, striking a match and watching the yellow catchlights glimmer in those intoxicating amethyst eyes of hers. Oh boy.

TWENTY

"Those knickers are *ridiculous*, Caoimhe. What's the style of them called? Where are they out of?" We were sitting on the bed, sharing Ciara's delicious joint. Well, *she* was sitting, up on two pillows. I was lying on my front, deliberately, because my knickers were *ridiculous*, and I wanted her to see my arse in them.

"They're Brazilian," I said, delighted that my cunning arse plan had worked.

"What, like, from Brazil?"

"No! Although they're from America, so close enough. They're Victoria's Secret, the whole set is, obviously." I turned on my side, to show her the bra, even though she'd seen it already.

"So, what's the Brazilian part about? I thought Brazilian women wore like tiny G-strings?"

"They do, I think. On the beach, anyway. But this cut is like the shape of a thong, and then it's like they put... extra *knickersness* at the top of the bum part? So, it's less *thongy*, but it's still *good-arsey*?" An A, I got in my pre-Leaving English. An A+, technically. Over 90%.

"It's absolutely *good-arsey*, babe. Well done, Brazil. And Victoria, as well, with all her secrets. This stuff goes reeeeally well with the acid, doesn't it?" She took a long drag and passed me the smoke.

"What do you mean *this stuff*? Is it different stuff? Wait, it's not from Frank, is it?!" I took it out of my mouth, in a panic.

"No! No, it's that squishy black Moroccan stuff. Benson gave it to me. It's niiiiiice." She got down from her pillow seat and slid down the sheet, so we were side by side. I came off my stomach, so I was facing her.

"Hello," I said.

"Hoi," she said, in a silly voice that sounded very cute.

"Squidgy Black gives me the mega-giggles, Ciara. You'd better be very unfunny from here on in, yeah? Or I'll die laughing, and they'll have to put that in the obituary." This was gorgeous, lying like this, looking at her face, and looking at anything else I wanted to, too. Her bra, and everything in it, was making for particularly good viewing. Two thumbs up, from my inner Siskel and Ebert.

"Okay, I will *not* be funny then. I'll put that on the list of rules," she said, miming a notebook and a pencil.

"Oh yeah, the rules," I said, remembering. "What *are* tonight's rules, then?" I hoped they weren't awful rules. I didn't like awful things; I was funny like that.

"Oh, there are only two rules." She took a last hit off the joint and held it in, handing me the roach, because I was near the ashtray.

"Only two?" This sounded promising.

"Bwhaaaaah!" She let all the smoke out into the air above us, instead of my face. "Sorry. Yeah, the first rule is, no discussing anything."

"No discussing anything? So, like, we can't talk? At all?" That sounded not so promising.

"No, you goon! Just like, no serious talks. No heavy chats. No getting into stuff. No talking about hypothetical situations, in the future or whatever. Oh, and no talking about last night." She reached over and grabbed my shoulder, using it to pull herself across the sheet to be closer to me. Her legs touched mine, and I immediately felt a bit more awake.

"What, like ever?" I said, tentatively reaching a hand out and stroking the skin on the top of her arm. She was very, very warm to the touch, but she felt silky, not clammy or *damp*.

"Noooooo! Just not tonight. Leave it for another day. My head is too full of drugs and tiredness and madness. I can't be getting all… whatever. Is that okay?" She ran her fingers really lightly from my hip, down my thigh, and stopped at my knee.

"It's probably the sensible choice," I said, thinking about all the millions of things I wanted to say to her and to ask her, and how they'd probably ruin the fuck out of this moment - whatever this moment was.

"Good. I'm glad. I'm glad you agree." She hooked her hand behind my knee and lifted my leg a small bit, sliding her thigh into the gap, so we were as close as we could physically be. Well, almost as close. I tried to make words come out of my mouth, and it eventually happened.

"W-what was the second rule?" I said, pretty much prepared to accept anything at this point. I moved her head up so I could get an arm under her neck and pull her in closer to my face.

"Second rule is, no funny business," she said, which made no sense to me at all.

"No funny business?" I said, running my other hand through her lovely, silky hair.

"Yep. No monkey business. No fooling around. None of that. No soup for you!"

"So, we just, what? Go to sleep now?" I said, immensely

confused, because I could definitely feel someone's thigh pressing into my vajayjay, and there was no one else in the bed except her.

"Yeah, that'd be the sensible choice, wouldn't it? But no. We can just hang here, and be all close, and talk," she said. She smelled edible. Not the vanilla or the CK One, or anything else like that. Just the smell of utter Ciaraness off her.

"In our underwear?" I said. Our bras were touching. I wasn't squished into her enough for there to be skin on skin boobular contact or anything, but it still felt very close and nice.

"What do you normally sleep in, a raincoat?"

"Haha! Good point. No, I just… no, you're right. So, we just lie here, and hang, and be close, and talk." It didn't sound terrible. Well, unless she did another runner. I thought of Portia again. Everyone did runners from me these days. It was very in vogue.

"Yeah. Enjoy each other's company. Like we used – I mean, like we always do," she said, smiling again.

"We don't always do it in our underwear, though." I'd known her nearly a year and this was the most undressed I've ever seen her, even including last night.

"Well maybe that was our mistake all along, haha."

"True. Everything is better in fancy undies, I reckon. But definitely no funny business?"

"Definitely not. We'll just… refrain," she said, giving me a wink, which could have meant anything, really. Probably not anything I'd have liked it to mean, mind.

"Refrain?" What a nice sounding word for a terrible thing, I thought.

"Yeah. Refrain. Let's just enjoy tonight – or what's left of it - and each other, without making things complicated.

We can pretend we're real Catholics, or something. For now."

"So, not forever?" Not forever sounded better than forever.

"Maybe not forever." She was still close to me, she hadn't moved away, physically. But...

"Okay. I get you. I mean, I don't really get you, but I'm listening."

"Thanks. Hey. You excited about tomorrow?" Her hand was on my side now. I moved my elbow over it, thinking maybe that might keep it where it was.

"Tomorrow?"

"Yeah! Playing Féile 95! Or did you forget?" That smile again. I loved that smile, and those perfectly sized teeth.

"I do actually keep forgetting, honestly! And then I remember again, like. It's crazy, because it should be the most important thing happening this weekend, and it is, kind of. But lots of other things have happened – or are happening. And they're not like, more important – but some of them feel just as important, you know?" I wasn't sure if I was getting my point across. Mainly because I wasn't sure what my point was.

"I think I do, yeah." Her hand was on my hip now, at the side of my ridiculous knickers. The ones that had no sexual power over her, apparently. Damn you, Victoria, and all your secrets.

"I mean, once it's actually happening, and we're side stage, and they call out our names, them it's gonna be like... woo! But until then, it..."

"It won't feel real?" She took her leg out from me for a second, gave it a stretch, then put it back where it was. I was glad she was being this physically close with me, even if we had to... refrain. It felt better than rejection, at least. Even if I was still feeling a little rejected.

"Exactly. You'll be fine. You'll be better than fine, you'll be brilliant. You're Kweeva Shox, remember? She's a superstar." She smiled again and moved the top half of her closer to me. Maybe this whole refraining thing wasn't so bad at all.

"She's a superstar who's probably coming down from those two Es now," I said, suddenly coming over all strange and empty.

"I have something for that – for a little later, chick. But for now, I have this." She rolled away from me, and I immediately felt abandoned. She went down her side of the bed for something. My skin got colder without her. I wanted to reach out for her. But then she was back. With another joint of Squidgy Black goodness and, more importantly, a big glass of water.

*****

The second joint was a good idea, because the more we smoked, the easier coming down would be, Ciara said, and I didn't fancy any sort of horrible comedown. She also said she had sleeping tablets, off Benson (who else?), if we needed them. I was sort of interested in seeing what would happen if we stayed awake a little longer, mind.

"Where do you think she went to, though, like? The whole asking Marian for the key thing was the weirdest bit, wasn't it? Because she didn't even come back here. It's so bizarre, like." Ciara was talking about Portia. Apparently, this was a discussion which was allowed.

"Well, she didn't come back here as far as we know, anyway," I said. We were sitting side by side at the end of the bed, getting some cool breeze from the open window. The air felt all gorgeous and goosebumpy on my bare skin.

"What do you mean, sweets?" She passed me the joint, and the water. Her hand was quite high up on my inner thigh, not doing anything, just existing there.

"I mean what if she came back, and then left again?" I had my arm around her waist, with my thumb inside the elastic of her knickers, also not doing anything, also just existing there. Just existing was kind of hot, it turned out. Wasn't technically funny business either, since no one had stopped me.

"But she hasn't taken anything, has she? Marian said all her stuff is still there. She didn't even take like a change of clothes."

"Hmmmmm. True." I had the last bit of the joint, trying to get all the Squidgy goodness out of it before it died forever.

"Don't worry, anyway. She'll turn up, eventually. Your new Chinese girlfriend."

"She's not my girlfriend, Ciara; Chinese or otherwise." I stubbed out the roach, already sad to see it leave.

"She's not?" Ciara sounded genuinely surprised.

"I have literally kissed that girl – properly kissed, I mean – as many times as you have, Ceer. About 30 seconds before you did. And that was it." I suddenly felt the need to lie back and stretch my whole body out, so I did.

"Get OUT of here!" Ciara said, following my lead, and lying back too.

"Not even kidding. It's true," I said, turning lazily on my side to face her, and she did the same, like we were two sides of a mirror.

"Wow... I thought – I mean, I assumed, well-"

"Ciara?" I put my finger on her lips and pressed them closed. "First rule, no discussing things."

"Mhmmm!" Her eyes went all big, and they looked extra pretty in the light pouring in the open window from the street outside. Her whole face looked extra pretty. I really wanted to kiss her.

"Second rule, no funny business?" she said, taking my fingers off her lips, with a smile, and holding onto them.

"Whatcha thinking?" I said, sensing a change in her. Maybe what I'd said about Portia had got her thinking she had me all wrong. But did she? I did like Portia, and I had been flirting with her. I wasn't going to lie to her about that just to get her to lift her silly rule or whatever. I wasn't like that. At least I hoped not. No, if she asked me more about it I'd just be honest with her, I decided.

"Oh, lots of things, you know."

"I don't unless you tell me, babe." I was getting physically hot in the not nice way now. There were no covers to take off, though. The only way to get cooler would be to untangle our legs, and I didn't want to do that either. Just in case they didn't end up tangled again.

"I'd tell you if I understood any of it myself, chick. Or maybe I wouldn't, cos first rule, and all that."

"That rule sucks."

"You leave my rule alone!" She pushed me in the chest, but playfully.

"Okay, it doesn't suck… as much as the second rule!" I stuck my tongue out at her, and she laughed, thankfully.

"I'm only doing it for my own good. And for your own good, babe. For our… brains and stuff." She reached across and took my hand, and it was like a shot of niceness right in my heart.

"Whatever you think is best, Ciara," I said, linking fingers with her while the swelling in my heart got bigger.

"Mmmmm." She closed her eyes, but it wasn't in a sleepy way.

"Now what are you thinking?" I said, still mashing her paw and never wanting to let go.

"I'm thinking lots of things, none of them very sensible, madam." She opened her eyes again and I swore they flashed at me in the dark. Might have been the LSD, though. At least her eyes weren't breathing. Touch wood.

"When were we ever sensible?" I said, willing her to come closer to me than she already was. I didn't care about overheating now.

"We've had our sensible moments! Probably apart, and never together, bit still!" She was playing with my hair again. One of my brand new Top Ten things I enjoyed.

"Apart, they were sensible gals, but together, they were Nothing but Trouble!" I said, in my best Movie Trailer Guy voice, which wasn't a very good one, but it was my best, so.

"We're terrible, Muriel."

"We're the worst. But also, the best," I said.

"We really, really are," she said, then she let out a long, loud sigh, that was somewhere between a yawn and a lament.

"You okay?" I said, studying her face for anything I could read.

"Hah! Who knows? It's been a strange weekend. It might even get stranger." She came away from me and sat up, facing me. I didn't want to feel awkward or silly, so I sat up too.

"You sure you're okay, Ciara?"

"Mmmmm, I think so, yes. Come here, you," she said, putting her arms out. What was this, now?

"Nah, *you* come *here*."

"Fine!" she said, moving towards me until she was

right next to my face.

"Hello again," I said, appreciating the closeness, and the boob squishing. I was easily pleased tonight.

"I'm bored of refraining now." She put her arms around me and pushed her chest into mine a bit harder.

"Oh, you are, are you? Well maybe I *like* refraining, now? Maybe I've become accustomed to it? Maybe I looo-ooove it, yeah?" I pushed back against her, suddenly noticing how strong she was.

"Well then, this is going to be awkward," she said, and now I was on my back, with her full weight on me. Things had suddenly taken a turn for the rough, in a good way. I was finding out all sorts of things about myself this weekend, to put it mildly.

"This is more like restraining than refraining, honey," I said, feeling a bit helpless under her, but in a good way.

"It is, isn't it? Sorry I'll refrain from restraining you, then." She rolled us so we were on our sides again, legs tangling and rubbing on places where it felt nice for legs to rub. Fuck, this felt good.

"To be honest, I kind of liked it. You're a lot stronger than you-" I lost my train of thought when I felt her touch on me. Not doing anything, just there, existing.

"You okay, beautiful?"

"Uhhhhh, your hand is on my *vulva*, sir!" I said, because that word was never not hilarious.

"It's clearly not. It's on your knickers, see?" She moved her body out of the way and nodded down to the scene of the crime.

"The knickers is where the vulva LIVES, Ciara! That's his HOUSE!"

"Hahaaah! His house!" Ciara laughed so hard she fell

off me, and my vulva. I reached out to grab her, so she didn't fall off the bed as well.

"Come back, you fooool," I said, pulling her up on top of me again, staring into my eyes, breathing heavy. Mouth close enough for me to kiss.

"Hello again," I said.

"Hoi. Sorry I touched your *vulv*, Kweev." She put her fingers in my hair in that way she knew I liked.

"It's grand. I've ruined everything again now though, haven't I? I am become Kweeva, destroyer of shags," I said, doing a frown.

"Nooooo! Don't be an eejit. I'm the one who has been fucking with your head, really." She leaned down and kissed my forehead, then my giant nose, then my chin. Then both my cheeks. Then my nose again. Maybe she liked it?

"Nah, you haven't. You probably thought *I* was fucking with *your* head all day today, like – but I didn't mean to be," I said, wondering what all that flirty Portia stuff must have looked like to her, and suddenly feeling like a right shithead. She was lovely, she didn't deserve me hurting her, even if I hadn't been doing it deliberately.

"I was a little confused, yeah. Then I was *really* confused when the hot Chinese girl snogged me."

"Yeah, that was a fucking head-wreck, all right," I said, half smiling, half cringing.

"I dunno, I kind of liked it."

"Yeah, I noticed," I said, smiling to let her know I wasn't being gowlish.

"Was it horrible, like? To see, I mean? I dunno. I..."

"Nah, it wasn't bad. It was kind of hot, to be honest. Kind of."

"Hey. Caoimhe, honey? Listen, I'm sorry that I-"

"Ciara?" I put my fingers against her lips. I moved her hair out of the way with my other hand, so I could look at that face. She was so, so, utterly, utterly gorgeous. I *was* a bit *Head Over Feet* for her, Portia was right.

"Yeah?"

"First rule, no discussing anything!" I pulled her face in and kissed her, properly this time. For a long time, cos I had a lot of kissing her properly to catch up on. It was just as good as I remembered. It was actually even better.

"Second rule – second rule appears to have been cancelled, for now," she said, when we finally stopped, then she immediately kissed me back, for even longer. Things got very *torrid*. There may even have been some boob squeezing. We had a lot of catching up to do. I was fading a bit, and I could feel the comedown on its way. We'd probably started the proper funny business way too late. I tried not to yawn, but there was definitely one in the post.

"Third rule, I love you," I said, because it was fine to say that, since it was true, I said it all the time, in a *non-gay* way, so you totally couldn't do me for it.

"Fourth rule, I love you more," she said, moving beside me so she could lay her head on my chest and get her hair stroked. Bliss and heaven. I was definitely coming down, though. There was no escaping it.

"Will we maybe be sensible Sallies and take those sleeping tablets, Ciara?" I said, not sure I wanted to be a sensible Sally – I still had two or three pills in my tobacco pouch - but really conscious of the fact that I had the biggest gig of my life in a few hours, and it wasn't just me I'd be letting down if I was shite.

"Oh. Okay, yeah, you're actually right. Cos you've to sing and stuff, tomorrow. Shit, I've been really selfish, haven't

I, keeping you up?"

"God no, don't be silly, chick. This idiot makes her own questionable life choices. You're grand." I scooped her up for a very booby clinch, and then turned to see where the ciggies were. Under the pillow, it turned out.

"We having a fag?" Ciara sat up as well. Her hair was all messy, but it just made her look ten times sexier. I really needed to lie down and close my eyes, but nicotine didn't care about your wants or needs, unless you wanted or needed nicotine.

"Yes! Fag, sleeping tablet, water, big snuggle, and hopefully sleep. That would be perfect, please." I found the box and gave her over one.

"Mmmhmmm, yes. Snuggles and sleeps, please. No more 'scussions. Just snuggles and sleeps" she said.

"I have to warn you though, my snuggles are very erotic." I lit up the fag and it tasted about as good as any fag ever had. I'd been a fool to even consider not having it.

"Oh, so are mine," she said, squeezing my calf so hard I felt the knotty muscles crunching under skin.

"Cool. Oh, and I kiss a lot in my sleep, too. Sleep Kissing, my doctor calls it. So, you should probably not leave your lips unguarded tonight."

"I do a similar thing, but it's fingering. Sleep Fingering, my doctor calls it. So, *you* should probably not leave *your* lips unguarded either tonight," she said, cos she was hilarious.

The end of her lit fag looked crazy in the almost dark, like a tiny sun, orbiting her fingers. I was definitely still tripping a bit, but at least the toilet seat hadn't eaten me. Every cloud. Still no Portia, but maybe she *had* come home since, and just went to bed? I had no idea what time it was. I necked the sleeping pill and waited for Ciara to finish her fag, so we could drift off together in blissful snuggles and all would be right with the world. And I was playing Féile 95 in the afternoon. Life could have been a lot worse, really.

*****

"Ciara?" Nothing.

"Ciara!" Maybe I should nudge her, I thought. So I did.

"Ciara?" Still nothing.

"Ciara, are you still awake?"

"No," said Ciara, awakely.

"Me neither. Why didn't the sleeping tablets work, Ciara?" I was definitely not asleep. I wasn't really awake, either. I felt like I was in a deep, dark cave or something, it was hard to describe. I was conscious but it felt like a lucid dream, or sleep paralysis, or one of those ones where you are fully sure that you're awake and in the real world, but you're actually asleep, because you wake up from it. I'd read loads about all that stuff once in a book I got from the library. The worst part had been the bit about the Shadow People.

"They did, you're asleep. I'm asleep. We're *all* asleep," said Ciara, awakely.

"I'm not convinced. Where are you? Why are you far away? Come to me, please. Come to me and be to... be on... just, uhhh." My brain was as melted as the rest of me.

"I'm here now, sorry!" She scooched across and found me in the dark, all soft skin and nice smells and silky hair. I inhaled her like a bouquet of roses. It felt like I hadn't seen her in years.

"What's happened, why do I feel so melty and *malleable*, Ciara? I mean it's nice. It's not... unpleasant. But it's not sleep either." It felt like the air was dense and heavy around me. Like there was a glitch in gravity. Like treading water in a pool of glue. None of it felt disturbing, it just felt like unreal reality. Blurred edges, like Tim had said.

"Yeah, I think what's happened here is that we took too many drugs, and they interfered with each other, like? So, parts of them didn't work properly? So, the sleeping tablet we took, the Flunitrazepam?"

"Floooooooneytrazzzzepammmm" I said, finding the word hysterical for some reason. My bones felt like jelly, but in a nice way.

"That's the one. Well, it sends your body and your brain to sleep, but because we've taken so much other stuff today, I think it missed out on the brain part, or something. Cos my body is like soup right now, chick." She was very close up to me now, it felt great. It felt extra great because of whatever the fuck this flooney floozy stuff was doing to me. I felt extremely comfy. That was the word. Comfy.

"Do you feel comfy?" I said, reaching out and pulling her in as close as possible. It was too dark to see anything – the window was closed now, and we'd fixed the curtains earlier to block out all the streetlights – but I felt her legs slide into mine and slip between each other, and our arms wrap around our middles. Her being here made everything feel okay, despite all the weirdness.

"I feel so comfy, yeah," Ciara said.

It didn't feel real – it was like experiencing it third hand, somehow. Like living a story someone was telling to you. That made no sense – none of it made any sense. But it was comfy. And close.

"Do you feel close? Ciara? Ciara, do you feel close to me? Do you feel-"

"I feel so close, yeah," she said, in a whisper that was right inside my ear, so it was a whisper, but it was loud at the same time. My bones felt so melty that it was hard to tell whose limbs were whose in the fleshy tangle of us on the mattress. It didn't matter though. It felt ideal. I liked that idea

– being so close with someone that you were practically the one entity. Like you were sharing DNA.

"Caoimhe?" Her voice sounded far away now, even though she was so near me. So close to me.

"Yes babe?" I open my eyes to see if I could find her in the dark, but then something changed. My skin got colder, there were fewer legs and arms and…

"I think I need to be sick." She was already out of bed and halfway to the en suite. The light came on and took all the mysterious magic away, and it was just a normal hotel room again, in Cork City, with someone having an attack of the gawks in the jacks. What a life we led.

ACT 2 – SUNDAY SUNDAY

TWENTY-ONE

I woke up alone for the second time in as many days. *Sans* Ciara Slattery for the second time in as many days. In the depths of chemically induced depression for the second time in as many days. At least no one was banging down the door, though. I lay there for a while, frozen. The new curtain setup was doing a brilliant job of keeping the sunlight out, but it was obviously morning, from all the noise and traffic outside.

Last night hadn't gone perfectly or anything – all that stuff with rules, and no discussing anything – that had been stressful. But we'd sorted it, I thought. There had been lots of kisses and groping. Friday night hadn't had any groping. I could at least tick that off my list of *Bisexual Things I've Done*. I thought of Portia, then I stopped thinking of her, cos even if she had come back, I'd seemingly hitched my wagon to Ciara now, only to have her abandon me again. I was terrible with women already, and I'd only been trying them out for a couple of days. Someone needed to bring me a Tim Wheeler, quickly, and sit him on my face. Wait, no, that wasn't how it worked! Being a half-gay had already made me unable to heterosex correctly. I was doomed. I wanted to get up and open the curtains, except that would have involved getting up, or opening the curtains, neither of which I wanted to do. Perhaps I could just lie there until I died of starvation or something. That sounded better. I needed a fag.

That whole thing with the sleeping tablets had been mental. I still felt a bit melty, but I felt rotten all over, inside and out, so that was the least of my worries. Portia was gone. Ciara was gone. Áine was gone. Jon – I snapped out of that train of thought, because it felt like I was going down the water slide in Salthill, but not in a fun way. There was no lovely, heated pool at the bottom of this mental descent. It was probably lava, instead. Lava with human faeces in it. So, not that dissimilar to the pool in Salthill, really.

I looked for my fags under the pillow, and when they weren't there, I looked under the other three pillows. Gone. Probably Ciara who took them, along with every towel in the bathroom, and my poor heart. Had she planned this all along? To punish me, for ignoring her all day, and running off with an Asian supermodel, and doing blow in toilets without her, and having my nipple almost touched and my knickers almost breathed on, by the same Asian supermodel? She wouldn't have been too out of line for that, really. I had been kind of a dickhead. But she had too. She had run off with my towel, and probably had wild, animal, heterosexual intercourse with Ian, and with her gay ex-boyfriend too, and all sorts of other things I had no proof of and had just invented in my head in that way I had of wildly speculating and jumping to conclusions instead of just asking people what was going on. I couldn't ask her though – she hadn't been around to ask. And, when she was, well I'd just sort of forgotten to. But, later on, when we'd ended up in my room, she'd done that whole stupid "no discussions" rule. Although near the end she had actually tried to explain something or other and I'd shushed her and ate the face off her instead. I hated when I argued with myself and lost like this. No wonder I'd never made the debating team in Laurel Hill. The bathroom door opened, and Ciara walked out, all wet and shiny and wrapped in fresh white towels.

"Morning, Baby Dykeling! Sleep as terribly as I did?" I tried responding to her, but my brain seemed to have forgotten how to mouth.

*****

"Honestly, it was such a long day, I'd forgotten about that whole thing by the time we ended up in yours again. I'm really sorry I didn't just explain when I saw you next! You're mental, by the way, though." Ciara was on the bed with me now, having a delicious fag and a cuppa and being generally lovely.

"I am?" I was, obviously, but still. Not allowed to actually say it to me!

"Well, yeah. I know I was kind of rude disappearing, but as I said, I needed a shower, you had no towels, Ian was the first person who opened up when I knocked. And by the time I'd had my shower and listened to all his comedowny sob stories about the breakup with Sarah, I was exhausted and so was he. Closed my eyes for 40 winks, didn't wake up until the afternoon. It was literally that simple, but instead of just walking up to me and asking me, you did a Caoimhe."

"And how does one *do a Caoimhe*, exactly?" I said, sipping my surprisingly nice black tea.

"I dunno yet, I've only had the shift and got a bit of tit off her, so far," said Ciara, cos she was hilarious.

"So far, eh? So, there'll be more?" I said, very glad we were talking again, and even more glad we were flirting again.

"Stop trying to wife me up already on this, the third day of your Great Minge Odyssey, you lunatic. Have you never met me before, like? Do I ever have a boyfriend? Or a girlfriend?"

"Great Minge Odyssey!!! And er, no. You don't ever have one, do you? A boyfriend, I mean. Girlfriends you could be having in secret, like the secretive secret-keeper you are!"

"Well, I'm sorry I can't be like you, dear. Parading your personal harem of catwalk models from every corner of the globe for all to see."

"Hey, now! Don't be mean. I let you have a go on my Chinese one and everything. I'm a *sharer*, is what I am." We'd go and see what the scala was with regards to Portia and the other two missing persons in a bit. After I had a shower, maybe. Or after I had a Ciara. Both were equally possible, with any luck.

"Good kisser, that one. Smelled amazing, too. You know how to pick them, I'll give you that, Baby D. What's on the menu today for you, then? A Filipino maid? An Amazon warrior? East German bodybuilder?" Ciara was one of the only people I knew who could make you like her more by slagging you off. It was a gift.

"I was thinking of sticking to 100% homegrown today, chick," I said, twiddling the bit of wet hair that had fallen down out of her head towel.

"I was born in Camden though, so that's me out of the picture. And my mum's English, so I can't even claim the heritage. I'm a stinking mungrel." She took her hair out of the towel for a second to redo the wrap, and I was treated to a whole heap of gorgeous smells. Reminded me that I probably smelled like a bin full of scraped-off anchovies, though, so a shower was definitely necessary before I even thought about anything else.

"Oh well, we had a good run, anyway, I said, patting her on her knee. "I'm going to hop in the shower quickly, if you haven't STOLEN all my towels again, okay?"

"Okay, chick. Go forth and… ah, cleanify." She leaned in and gave me a peck on the cheek that made me forget the hammer-babies in my skull for a few seconds. It was going to be a brilliant day; I could feel it in my bones.

"Miss you already," I said, in a silly American accent, because only Yanks said things like that.

"Enjoy. Don't be too long, mind."

"No?" I'd been planning on staying in for a lengthy, intense scrubathon to rid my body of all these toxins and possible evil spirits. I opened the bathroom door. It was still steamy inside, and my face got wet immediately.

"Well, you can take your time if you like, Baby D. But I'll be getting dressed soon, and once I'm dressed, I'm dressed."

"Oh."

"So, if you want to have any chance of kissing me on my *front bottom*, make it quick, yeah?"

"I'll make it lickety-split!" I said, because I was hilarious, too.

*****

My last-minute decision to not walk out of the bathroom completely naked turned out to be a wise one, since the first person I saw was Uncle Frank, not Ciara. I was still wearing a little too little for his uncle's gaze, but the second he saw me he got up and said:

"Sorry, Caoimhe, I'll go outside now and let you get dressed. Ciara will ah, fill you in." Well yeah, I'd been hoping she might, Frank. Just not in the way *you* mean, I thought.

"Okay, Frank. Is everything… never mind, shoo now. Good Uncle. Scram." I locked the door after he'd gone, just in case anyone else decided they wanted to come in and ruin this leg of my Great Minge Odyssey. It was such a disgusting word, *minge*; that was why it was so hilarious.

"Hey." Ciara was standing in front of me now, dressed. I hadn't even been that long! But she'd probably had to put stuff on quickly, when Frank came a-calling. She was wearing a pair of PJ bottoms and a t-shirt, both belonging to me, so she wasn't really *that* dressed. I could probably *un*dress her in a flash, I thought. Lickety-split, even.

"Hello! I thought I was kissing your front bottom or something?" I said. I hadn't really thought it – I knew she was just being flirty. I wouldn't have known where to start, and I definitely wouldn't be doing *that* for the first time while sober and hungover. Baby steps, for Baby D.

"My front bum can wait, sweetie. You can meet her later. We have a problem, now. We have more than one problem. How quickly can you get dressed and stuff?" Her face was 100% business, 0% barbecue. Oh dear.

"Can I leave this thing on my head, or do we need to actually leave the building? What's this all about?" I said, trying to remember which drawer I'd commandeered for *knickerseses*.

"I'm honestly not sure, myself. Frank was a bit babbly, I couldn't follow him at all, there. Something about Portia, and maybe Niall? He's a bit hyper. Doesn't look like he's had a wink of sleep. We'll find out in a minute. We're only going into Ian's; you can leave the wrap on. Just get dressed, I'll wait in there." She pointed at the bathroom door.

"Eh, you don't have to," I said, although I was secretly happy she'd suggested it, for reasons I didn't quite understand myself yet.

"Ah, I do. I'll be fine. I'll have a fag." She moved her face near mine, but instead of going for my mouth, she ducked at the last second and kissed me near my collarbone, which was way better. If we were in a Hollywood movie, I'd have spontaneously dropped my towel, and we'd have got it on right there on the dressing table. She'd also have been a man, though, so it was probably better that we were in real life instead.

*****

"Right, so we're all basically fucked then, yeah? Nice," I said, after we'd heard the whole story from Frank, a little while later. I was walking down to the hotel café with Ciara, to get something foodish inside us before we decided on doing literally anything else. I'd had the fastest blow-dry known to man, and Ciara had put on some tackies, she was still in my t-shirt and Pyjammie bottoms. Brian would be here in a bit, knowing absolutely nothing yet, and I couldn't face him without some fried egg sandwiches in my poor famished stomach.

"Doesn't look good, no. For Frank, or for Niall. Or for ye, either, cos..."

"Cos we can't play the gig if we don't have a bassist, yep. Fuckety fuck fuck FUCK!" I said, almost crushing her linked arm with the frustrated squeezing.

"I know, honey. I know. Let's get feeded first, and then everything might be a little clearer. Or not." Ciara picked us up a wooden tray and we joined the line of hungry hotel guests.

"Both aren't equally possible," I said, seeing a man in the queue ask for fried eggs with his breakfast and be given them, so things were already looking up, kind of.

*****

"What I don't understand is why Niall is still in jail and Frank is out, free. I mean Frank was the one dealing," I said, devouring my cappuccino before it had a chance to cool. The egg sandwiches were already in my belly; they'd barely touched the sides, going down.

"Well, it was just luck, wasn't it? Frank was sold out of his, and Niall still had some. So, when the cops arrested them it was Niall who was the most fucked. Frank said – you mightn't have heard this bit, cos Ian was talking to you, I think – he says that all he had was an empty pouch, but there was dust off pills in it, and the Drug Squad guy literally did the movie thing where he dipped his finger in and licked it, and that was enough to bring him in too, like. It's crazy, all of this. It's surreal."

"It really is. And did he – Frank says that he told Niall to say nothing at all, yeah? Til he gets a solicitor, is it?" I lit up a fag and gave one to my new wife who probably didn't want to be my new wife, but that was a dilemma for later.

"I think so. But like, Niall's not eighteen yet, is he?"

"Am, I'm not sure? He mustn't be, like. There would have been a party or a night out or something. We'd remember it." I mightn't have remembered the specifics of the night out, but I'd remember if there had been one, definitely, I thought.

"True, so he probably isn't. And that means they can't talk to him without a parent, is it? I only know stuff from films and TV, and none of them are about Irish *legal things*, so." She shrugged, and so did I.

"Well, I should know, considering what Dad does, like. I don't though, sorry."

"Well, if he literally has said nothing, they won't even know he's underage though, will they?"

"You're right. And like, he's probably shitting himself over all this, so the last thing he'd want to do is have them ring his mum or dad, right?"

"Right. But then, we don't know anything, really. We dunno how he's feeling. Didn't Frank say they didn't even bring either of them in for questioning until eight this morning, because they were both too wrecked to interview last night? They let them sleep it off, in the cells, he said. Well, interview Niall, anyway. They just let Frank go, shur. Waste of time, fingerprinting him and filling out all that paperwork, when they couldn't actually charge him with something, I suppose? But Niall... Niall's not so lucky." Ciara was drinking more tea. Her cup was made of glass. She'd left the teabag in. It was weird being able to see it through the side of the cup. I felt like a bit of a scoptophile.

"Fuuuuck. That's so grim, and scary. I can't imagine what he's going through, like. The silly, silly boy." I was picturing him now, in some cell last night, off his face, too. No music. No hash for the comedown. *Very* grim.

"Yeah. Silly, silly Niall. But there's nothing we can do to change what happened now, Kweev. Nothing at all. And as for Portia, well..."

"Fuck. Yeah. What do you think?" I knew what I thought, and none of it was good. I wanted to hear her thoughts on it, though.

"What do I think of which? Her coming back to the hotel and stealing the bag of drugs? Frank being stupid enough to let her keep them in her room when he'd only known her five minutes – just because she was belonging to Marian and Marian sort of belongs to Richie?"

"Either," I said. "Both?" I couldn't believe that we'd been duped like that. I didn't want to believe it, because it didn't make sense. Or maybe it just didn't make sense to my ego – because I thought I genuinely liked her, and that she liked me too, genuinely. But had she duped us, from the start, deliberately? It wasn't as if she could have planned it. Sure, she knew that her pal Marian used to be friends with me, and used to go out with Richie, but she couldn't have known anything about the drugs or about Frank. So, it must have been a spontaneous, opportunist thing.

Whatever it was, she was gone, and so were the drugs. Frank hadn't paid for them up front. He had to sell them and bring a massive cut back to some absolute gangsters down in the Island Field, wherever the hell that was. And now he couldn't. He didn't have the cash from the sales he'd already made either, because that had been in the bag too.

How could anyone be that stupid, to get taken in so easily by a pretty face and a hot body? But then again, so had I, so I supposed that made me just as stupid, really. I wasn't going to get my throat cut for ever setting foot in Limerick again, mind. Frank was a dead man walking. It was very, very grim.

He had given Marian the third degree so much in Ian's room earlier that Richie had to step in and tell him to cool it. Then he'd taken her back upstairs to the room they'd shared last night. Apparently, they'd been interrupted mid-shag by Frank opening the door with the key Portia had given him (so he could go in and out during the day and get more pills). Hopefully they'd immediately got undressed and started riding each other again once they got back up there, because it would be nice to know *everything* wasn't fucking ruined today.

I realised I hadn't been listening to Ciara at all, and now she'd finished talking and was looking at me as if I should answer her, so I just took her hand and said,

"We're so fucking fucked, babe. Let's go get a drink," because I couldn't face Brian Collins while my bloodstream was this devoid of gin.

*****

We were still in the hotel bar when we spotted a familiar pair skulking in.

"Marian! Richie! Over here!" I shouted. Marian gave us a sheepish look, and Richie waved. He said something in her ear, and she walked over to our table. She didn't look well. Not in an ill way. Just in a... *different* way.

"Sit down, gorgeous. What's wrong?" I said, sliding over in the boothy snuggy thing so she could fit beside me.

"What's wrong? Really?" She gave me a look that made me regret opening my idiot mouth.

"Sorry, Mar. I know. I'm sorry. Look, if it's worth anything, they probably all hate my guts, since I'm the one who introduced her to the group, like," I said, wanting to put an arm around her, but afraid of the invisible barbs that were surrounding her.

"Can we just... please?"

"Talk about something else?" Ciara said, from the other side of me.

"Thank you, yes." Mar gave us a weak smile, then opened a box of fags. She was definitely back on them now, poor girl. She offered us one and Ciara said no thanks, but I didn't, cos she owed me about 37 of them from yesterday, not that I was counting.

"Consider it done, love. So... moving on swiftly, what was Richie like in bed, then?" I said, hoping this wasn't also something we couldn't talk about, or we'd run out of things really quickly.

"Ah, he was like... he was a bit like the boy who used to spend an hour rubbing himself off me on my bed or on the couch, four years ago – except it was *real* sex this time, obviously. And probably not for an hour. Not an hour in one go, anyway, you know how it is. It was really great though, and lovely, and special, and maybe a little rough? But that's exactly what I like – all that pinching and pulling and getting thrown around a bit - and he hadn't forgotten that about me, and that was sweet as well. It was like, so familiar being with him, but so new as well, just cos."

"Sounds like bliss," I said. "And Jesus, who would be wanting an hour of dick up you, non-stop? At least pause halfway for a fag and a can of Fanta," I said, and the other two nodded.

"I prefer my hour to be mostly kissing, bit of groping, a couple of nice fingery orgasms – mouthy ones if I'm in the right mood. Just pop the dick in near the end and let him go wild for five or ten minutes, like, godhelpus." Ciara said, sounding very specific altogether. Somewhere in Limerick, a boy's nose was probably itching.

"Yeah, like. By that point they've earned it, shur. Poor lambs." Marian was smiling now; things were looking up already now. Kind of.

"Bríd says Mr. Benson d'be banging away for *more* an hour, *at least*, every time. Auld fellas last a lot longer. Probably because they've worn all the sensitivity away. Like when you get those pencils with the rubber on top and you use the rubber too much." Ciara said, laughing.

"Jesus. And what's she doing during that? Knitting?" I said. Sounded like a lot of hard work to me. For Benson, and for poor Bríd's vajayjay.

"No, she loves it, she says. She says he knows loads of stuff. Like hitting her g-spot, apparently."

"*Hitting* it? With what, like, a mallet?" I said. My gin and tonic was nearly finished already.

"With his eraser-top penis, I'd imagine. There's a few angles that work, definitely. Or, you know, if you get on top and lean back a bit?" said Ciara, demonstrating it for those who mightn't know what leaning back looked like. She was on the Black Jack leg openers again. I liked the smell. I wanted to taste it – from her mouth, not from the glass – but I was pretty sure you couldn't do lesbian things in straight people pubs. I'd never seen any of it in my many years of straight people pub-going, anyway.

"Gross!" I said, because there'd be no penises allowed on my Great Minge Odyssey. I really had to stop saying that – even in my head.

"Ah, G-spots aren't gross," said Marian. Richie was finally here with their drinks. He didn't know where to sit, since there wasn't any more room on our snuggy boothy bench, so he plonked himself down in the chair opposite us.

"What's this now?" he said. He looked very well. He would, though. He was living the dream at the moment. Meeting his first love again and getting all up inside her heart and her vajayjay. He had a pint of cider. Marian was on the Southern Comfort again, I could smell the sweetness of it from her glass, and from her mouth.

"This thing," Marian said, making a *come-hither* gesture at him. "Remember I showed you?"

"Oh right, yeah. The choongum," Richie said, which he was going to absolutely have to elucidate on, or there'd be trouble.

"Richie thinks it feels like dried chewing gum, stuck to a path. My G-spot, I mean. When he touches it with his fingers, like? How romantic is that? Hahaaaah!" It was great to see her smiling again and hear her laughing. I gave her a squeeze on the thigh, but in a sort of manly way, so she didn't think it was a lesbian squeeze.

"Chewing gum on a path. Jesus, Richie. You're lucky you're good at riding her," Ciara said, sliding her arm down behind where my back met my bum, and I squooched into her a bit more.

"I'm good at riding her?" He seemed surprised by the news.

"Eh, you're all right, like. Seven out of ten, maybe. *Must ride harder.*" Marian tried to keep her face straight, but she didn't last. She reached out a hand to him and he gave it a squeeze. Awww.

"Best shag she's had in the last ten years, she told us," I said, immediately regretting it once I'd subtracted ten from her age in my head.

"Ruined her for other men, you have, Richard," said

Ciara. "You melt the chewing gum on her little path like it's the hottest day in August - that's what she told us, anyway."

"CIARA!" said Mar, frisbeeing a beermat at her head, but missing.

"Cool..." Richie said, leaning back a little bit in the chair and looking across at her, and somewhere inside my heart I felt a little pang for him, because I could tell he was falling right back in love with her, and that it would probably end in tears.

*****

"I will, I will, I will, shur. Look, I'm gonna see what I can do, and if not, then I'll see you when you – what? I don't know, Seamus. Shur, fecking, they're all scattered around the place now, and I haven't even two hours to... what? Okay. Yeah, hang on. Hang on, I can see her now. And Ringo. What? The youngfella of the Souths, sorry. I will. Okay, Seamus. Okay. Sorry again. I know. I know, shur. Pffft. Yeah. Okay, boss. Talk to you then." Brian was on his Zack Morris phone when he found us. He was doing that thing where he looked at you while talking and used his eyebrows to communicate. The eyebrows so far had said "There you are! Hello. I'm talking to someone now, but in a second I'm going to shout at you," as far as I could tell with my limited fluency in eyebrow language.

"Brillo! How's the form?" said Richie, turning around to face him.

"The form, Richie? How's the form, says you? Well, you tell me, Maurice. I'm just after being on the phone there, trying to fucking salvage yeer musical careers, listening to a fella who's spent tens of thousands of his own money on ye - believing in ye, booking studios for ye, getting records pressed and posters printed and whatever – and I'd to tell him that he's wasted his money, cos ye can't play the festival now, and ye won't get the TV coverage or the nice articles in the papers. That the only articles in the papers will be about that big galoot getting himself arrested for selling E tablets. That I can't even find ye all to bring ye together and have a meeting about what we're gonna do now. That the whole thing is FUBAR. How do you think the form is, squire?" I'd never seen Brian lose his temper properly before, but this was pretty close.

"Brillo, it's not my fucking fault, man. I didn't do anything. I wasn't selling-" Richie spotted the barman looking over, so he quietened his voice a bit, "I wasn't the one selling yokes, or giving him yokes to sell. I'm as pissed off as you are, sham. But what can you do, like?" He shrugged, and took a sip of his second, or maybe his third pint of cider.

"Brian, honey. Sit down a minute with us, yeah?" Marian said, nodding at the empty chair next to Rich. I wondered for a second why she seemed so familiar with him when she spoke to him, but then I remembered the whole *cousins* thing. Duh!

"I can't, Mar. I've to… I have to try and get a – I don't know what I have to try and do, yet. But I can't do *nothing*. I…" He gripped onto the back of the chair and his knuckles went white, like he was on a rollercoaster. We were were all on a rollercoaster though, kind of, I thought. And we hadn't even visited Tim's fairground. I stood up.

"Sit down for two seconds, Brian, you'll feel better. I'll get you a drink, yeah?"

"I don't want a drink, Caoimhe!" he said, but he sat down anyway.

"Yeah, you do, love. Guinness, isn't it?" I went past behind his chair and touched him on his shoulders. He was more tense than a tent full of pillheads. I started unknotting him out of sheer instinct.

"I don't want a – oh God, that's good, Kweev. Jesus,

you're like a pro. Jeeeeeesus, yeah. A Guinness, so. Just the one. Can't hurt, I suppose."

"Exactly," I said, massaging him some more. "Oh hi, love. Can you stick on a pint there, for this lovely, hardworking, stressed out man?" I said, to the barman, who'd come over to collect our empties. He nodded at me, not needing to say anything else. "A pint" when you said it to a barman meant a Guinness. Everyone knew that.

"And a small Jameson's. Neat, on the rocks," Brian said, before yer man was out of earshot.

"He means a large," I said, because fuck it, it was Christmas, even if it was starting to feel like the worst Christmas ever.

*****

"Right, so. *Options*, boys and girls. Give me options." Brian was slightly calmer after his double whiskey and his massage, but only relatively.

"Options liiiiike?" said Richie. He'd switched seats with Ciara so me and him could face Brian. Then I'd swapped places with him, cos otherwise I'd be the one having to publicly molest Marian every five seconds, and I had enough women in my life already.

"Liiiike, who else out of ye can play the bass, Maurice? Think!" Brian had a Guinness moustache, but I couldn't be arsed telling him about it. Made him look like a baby in a highchair eating yoghurt. A very hairy baby.

"Well, I can't," Richie said, shrugging.

"Well, I assumed that, Ringo. I wasn't talking about you; I meant the *musicians*." Brian must have heard my brain, because he wiped the baby yoghurt off his top lip. With a paper napkin, as well. Not with his sleeve, like a normal person.

"Fuck off, Brillo."

"I'll fuck off when ye give me a solution, squire. The clock is ticking, yeah?" he pointed at his Tag Heuer, but I couldn't see what the time was from this angle.

"Well, I can't play the bass anyway, sorry Brian." My fingers were too puny for the strings. Niall's were like butcher's sausages.

"But you can play the guitar! I see you play the guitar all the time!" he said. He was even less of a musician than Richie. He didn't know anything about anything.

"I see you cycling a bike all the time, Brian. Doesn't mean you'd know how to ride a unicycle if I gave you one," I said, drinking some of my cider, which was weird, since I was on G&Ts.

"Give me my fucking pint back, you scobe!" said Richie, solving that mystery, at least.

"Yeah, but if you gave me a unicycle, I'd at least *try* getting up on it, shur." Brian wasn't getting me at all.

"And you'd fall on your arse," Ciara said, next to him. I gave her a smile. At least that part of my life wasn't fucked. Yet, anyway. Give it time.

"But I'd get back up on it and learn how, like!"

"And how long would that fucking take, Bri? Is it more time or less time than it would take me to learn how to play the bass? Because we haven't time for either, according to you," I said, getting annoyed with him now. I went to have another sip of cider, but Richie slapped my hand and took the glass off me. "Ow!!!" I rubbed the stinging away. Assault, that was. Definitely could do him for it.

"Get your own, you gowlawalla!!!"

"You get your own! You...*big bitch*!" I said.

"Big bitch!" Marian said, laughing and giving him a

cuddle, when I was the one who actually needed consoling, with my critically injured hand.

"Okay, anyway, back to the matter in hand, folks – what about Hurley?"

"Ian?" Richie said. I wanted a cider now, but I'd have to get up and get it, and that would involve actually getting up, and I didn't want a cider that much.

"No, Rich. Red Hurley, from the Eurovision, in 1976. The mam at home loves him, shur," said Brian, all sarcastic.

"Ian can't play the bass," I said. "And even if he could, who would play guitar then?"

"You, maybe?" Brian didn't have an Aisling with him this morning. I smiled to myself, remembering how mad she'd been last night, and how brilliant and sound, too. I loved her now, it was like we'd got a brand-new friend out of someone who'd already existed before.

"Brian, I can't play lead. I can play lead about as much as I can play bass. Which is, not at all. I sing, in case you haven't noticed. I sing, and I play acoustic, and-"

"Okay! So how about doing that, Kweev?!" Brian looked like a cartoon lightbulb had switched on over his head.

"How about doing what?" I still had some gin and tonic left in my glass, I'd just forgotten to move it across the table when I'd swapped with Richie. I finished it in one gulp, put the lemon slice in my mouth and bit down. No idea why. Immediately regretted it. "Bleuuuurgh! That's rotten!"

"Whats ro- never mind. What I'm saying is, why I don't I tell them there's been a change of plan, and you're gonna get an auld stool, and sit up and do a few numbers by yourself? Unplugged, Maurice. Like on *the MTV*?" He said the last bit like a Da. Or like in that Dire Straits song.

"Will you fucking STOP, like?!" I said, spitting my

lemon slice into the ashtray.

"What? It's a fucking better idea than the *nothing* the rest of ye have come up with!" said Brian, pushing the ashtray as far away from him as he could without knocking it off the table altogether.

"Are you SERIOUS, Brian?" I said, lighting up a fag from the stress of even thinking about it.

"I am, yeah. Why?" No one else was saying anything, they were all just staring at us now.

"First off, I'd shit myself getting up there in front of a load of people, Brian." None of these goons understood the whole *introvert* thing about me.

"You get up in front of crowds all the time, what are you on about, Maurice?" He was doing the wafting thing with my fag smoke, like a prick.

"That's different, though," said Ciara. Finally, someone understood.

"How is it different?" said Brian. He went to drink the end of his pint, but it was Guinness, so it had gone manky.

"Because when I go up there with the band, I'm with the band, Brian. I'm... not like, Caoimhe. I'm Kweeva," I said, realising that those two things sounded exactly the same, but it wasn't like I had a pen and paper to show him.

"I don't get it," he said, turning to the bar to tell yer man to stick another one on for him.

"I don't expect you to, Brian. I'm just saying I'd feel... naked, like." I'd done the thing backstage yesterday, but that was different. There was a band, I was doing covers, and no one had come over a PA announcing me as Kweeva Shox, or anything. I'd done it for fun, cos I wanted to, and I didn't *have* to do it. There had been no... pressure.

"Well, I'm not asking you to do it naked, Kweev," he

said, although he probably would, if he thought he'd get away with it.

"Look, anyway, it doesn't matter. I'm not doing a set without the lads, Brian."

"Well, you don't have a choice!"

"Oh, I do have a choice, Brian. I always have a choice. And I choose *no*." He had no clue how catastrophic it would be if I went up there instead of Crane, and it was just me on the TV, not the rest of them. Ian would just leave. I'd no doubt about that. I was the last one to join the band he'd started, but I was constantly being made the focus of everything, instead of them, or him. I couldn't even argue with him about that, it was true. Me doing this would be the last straw, I thought.

"What about Tim?" Ciara said, coming to my rescue like the angel she was.

"What about him?" I said, realising I hadn't seen him since last night. He hadn't been in Ian's when Frank was telling us all the bad news. Why was that, I wondered now?

"Yeah, Timbo is a musical genius, like. He can nearly play the drums better than me, sham. He plays guitar, he plays the accordion, he plays the violin as well, shur. I bet he can play the bass, Brillo. I bet he's such a fucking brainbox he could pick the thing up and play along with us just by listening. Why don't we ask him? Have we time still, like?"

"Not *too much* time, Maurice," Brian said, flashing the famous watch at him. "But if we get a fecking move on, we might just be back in business, says you."

Richie was right. Tim could probably play any instrument. He was like Phil Collins, or something. He'd be able to play a bass. He didn't have puny fingers, he was a piano guy, they had the best fingers. We just had to go find him, ask him, grab Niall's guitar, and grab Ian as well. Everything was going to be okay. Everything was going to be grand.

TWENTY-TWO

"Tim? Tim, are you in there? Tim!!!" I could hear music from inside the room, but no one was answering.

"Will we just go in?" Ciara said, next to me.

"What if he's dead, lads?" Richie said, not helping.

"Stop that, he's not dead," said Marian.

"TIM! OPEN THE FUCKING DOOR NOW, OR I'M GONNA KICK IT DOWN!" Brian was in no mood for barbecues. Still no answer.

"It's probably open," I said, trying the handle. It was. I pushed the door in. It was dark, but not fully. The curtains were closed, but there were candles everywhere, at different degrees of being burnt down.

"Where the fuck did he get candles?" Richie whispered.

"Candle shop, probably," I whispered back. There was no sign of Tim that I could see. Just his bed - which was bare except for the sheet - and a pile of pillows and a quilt in the corner.

"Why are we whispering?" Marian said, whispering.

"TIM! SHOW YOURSELF!" Brian was in no mood for whispering.

"I think he's gone," said Ciara. But where to? None of us had seen him all morning. The pile of stuff in the corner suddenly stood up.

"JESUS!" said Marian, grabbing onto me.

"What the fuck is that???" Richie said, sounding like he was in a horror movie. The music in the background wasn't helping. *The End*, by The Doors, it was.

"It's... it's Tim," said Ciara, pointing at the living quilt, which now had a face. A human face, thankfully.

"Tim!!!" I said. He looked at me with the strangest expression, and then the living quilt with a face had two hands, and two arms.

"Jesus, fuck!" said Richie, when the quilt fell down and we all saw that Tim was completely bollock naked underneath.

"God bless us and save us..." said Marian, looking directly at Tim's uncovered penis and balls, which we all were looking at, now. Even the lads.

"Welcome," said Tim, not moving. His arms were outstretched, like he was on a crucifix. The candlelight made him look like a statue in a church, to me. It was all a bit biblical.

"Tim, put some clothes on, for fuck's sake, you steamer!" Richie was making a point of covering his eyes, but they weren't really covered. He was still looking.

"Clothes... hahah. I don't have any need for clothes, Richard. I'm not of your realm anymore. Your... primitive, material world. I've seen things. I've seen everything." He was talking very strangely. Like an actor. Or a preacher, maybe.

"Yeah babe, we've seen everything too, so you can put it away now, yeah?" I said, cos I was hilarious.

"I have no need for your modesty or your shame, Caoimhe. I'm moving on a higher plane, now. I don't feel those baser things. The flesh is transient. Pain is imaginary. Death is an illusion." He smiled, but it wasn't at any of us. It was a smile for him.

"Your mickey isn't an illusion Tim, and I'm not imagining looking at it. Cop on!" said Brian.

"Why have you all come to me? Is it for answers?" Tim said, putting his arms down now, but not putting his meat and two veg away.

"Kind of?" I said, thinking that we were technically looking for him to answer "Yes" to the question "Can you play the bass guitar?"

"Answer me this, Tim. What the fuck sort of drugs are you on?" Brian said.

"*Drugs* is such a simple, human word," said Tim, doing the smile again.

"Well, I'm a simple human, Tim. Apologies for that. Now what is it you've taken? Do we need to call you an ambulance or something?" An ambulance! Brian really had no clue about anything drug related. You couldn't OD on acid. Well, you could, but it didn't kill you. It just made you insane, like that guy from Fleetwood Mac, or that other guy, from Pink Floyd. Tim was in no danger. Apart from possibly turning into a nutcase for the rest of his life, obviously.

"What is it you people want, that you've come and disturbed my meditation? I was on the Astral Plane. I was communing with the Godhead, I was-"

"You were lying on the ground in a duvet with your bollocks out, Tim. You're not the Dali Lama," said Ciara, making me giggle.

"When the doors of perception have been cleansed, everything will appear to man as it is – infinite," said Tim, doing the praying thing with his hands, and bowing his head, serenely.

"That's just something Val Kilmer said in a film, Tim. We can all do that. *You can be my wingman anytime.* See?" said Marian, picking up one of the candles, and putting it back down again quickly, because Tim literally snarled at her.

"I think he's gone feral," I said, to Ciara, squeezing her hand. Our chances of having a bass player for the set were starting to look a bit slim.

"Tim, pal? Have you had some sleep, no? Any at all?" said Richie. None of us had moved any closer to our naked friend since he became naked. We were even less likely to now, since the snarling.

"Sleep is for the people whose eyes are not open!" said Tim, following it with a really creepy laugh that echoed all around the room.

"Well, duh!" said Ciara. *The End* had finished, so there was no music anymore. The music was over, and the lights were turned out.

"Tim, love. How many of those acid tabs did you actually take?" I said. I could see some bits of cling film on the dressing table, but there were no tiny squares of paper in them anymore.

"The answer to your question is meaningless in my state of being, Caoimhe O'Shaughnessy." His head was still bowed, his hands still joined, his willy still hanging free.

"Okay, but just humour me, yeah?", I said. I wanted to spark up a fag, but I wasn't sure smoking was allowed in Tantric Tim's Temple of Todgers.

"I took..." he held out his hand and counted on his fingers. "One, two, three, four... *all!*"

"All?" said Richie.

"All what?" said Brian. Maybe we could teach *him* to play the bass? He had massive fingers.

"All of the tabs!" Tim said, laughing that laugh again. "They are within me! And I am within them. I am one, with Source. I am eternal, Brian. I am majesty. I am-"

"You're a fucking looper," said Richie, shaking his head in despair.

"Come on, let's go, before I fecking murder him," said Brian. Time for plan B, or plan C, or whichever one we were up to now. I suddenly had a brainwave, as we were leaving. A plan, that might just work, I thought. I needed to get to get to a phone, first.

*****

"Hello?"

"Hello, is that you, Caoimhe?" said my mother. The reception was awful on Brian's stupid mobile.

"It is, yeah. Is Dad there, Mum? I need to-"

"How are *you* doing, Mammy? Keeping well? Sorry I haven't called all weekend." Mum was being an arse. I didn't have time for this, now.

"Stop being an arse, Mum. I don't have time for this, now." I needed Dad. Or, more specifically, I needed his special solicitor help, and hopefully one of his special solicitor contacts in Cork, so we could spring poor Niall from the joint.

"Don't call me an... *arse*, Caoimhe Colette O'Shaughnessy. I am still your mother, you know. You still live under my roof..."

"Yeah, well, not for – look, can you please just put Dad on to me? I'm on a mobile phone here, it's probably costing a bomb." I didn't care how much it was costing. I wasn't paying for it. Neither was Brian. It was all taken care of by Seamus, who probably hated us now, anyway. Hanged for a sheep, and all that jazz.

"A mobile, is it now? Well, well. How the other half live,

says you. What did you want to speak to your father about, then?"

"It doesn't matter! Can I just-"

"Caoimhe, have you been drinking? At this hour of the day?"

"NO!" YES!!!

"Hmmmm. You know I said to your father that it was a bad idea letting you go down there to that thing on your own, Caoimhe. I've read all sorts of things in the paper about this... Féile thing. The Bishop was saying-"

"The BISHOP? Really, Mum? Since when do you give a fff- since when do you care what the Bishop thinks? You haven't been to mass since my Confirmation." None of this was getting me any closer to talking to Dad. This woman was a fucking nightmare. I should buy him some tickets to the Ukraine for his birthday, I thought.

"Since your Confirmation, tut, really? I go to mass all the- well, I went for – anyway, tell me you're okay, yeah? Caoimhe? Please?"

"I'm fine, Mum. Can you just put-"

"You haven't been offered any drugs or anything, have you?"

"What? Drugs, Mum? What do you think this is, Woodstock?" If she only knew the half of it.

"No need to be smart, Caoimhe. That's your father's side of the family, where you got that mouth. Definitely didn't come from me."

"Okay, Mum." I was going to hang up on her in a second, although I didn't know how you hung up a mobile. Or how you hanged up one.

"And no one has tried to touch you, inappropriately?"

"Chance would be a fine thing!"

"Pardon?"

"Nothing, Mum. Can I please talk to Dad, now? It's kind of urgent." That was the understatement of the century.

"Urgent? Caoimhe, you're not in any trouble, are you? You know you can talk to me, just as much as you can talk to your father. I mean, really, you should be able to talk to me much easier, but-"

"MUM! PLEASE!"

"Okay! Okay, okay. Listen, I can't actually put you on to your father right now…"

"WHY THE FU- Why not, Mum?" My knuckles were doing the rollercoaster thing now, around the edge of the phone.

"Well, because he's not here, dear."

"Well, where is he?" She could have told me this at the start, the stupid woman.

"Where is he ever, Caoimhe? At the office, doing some extra work, for someone important. Never occurs to him that there's someone important right here, at home, you know? Or more than one important person, when you're here. Of course, there used to be more of us. But …" She trailed off, like she always did when the subject turned to my dead sister. She was seeing a counsellor, still. I stopped going to mine after two weeks. Didn't see the point of it. Just some person in a chair asking me how stuff made me feel. Fuck that for a game of hockey.

"I know, Mum, I know. Sorry. Can you give me his office number, then? So I can call him there? Please?"

"Okay, it's changed since last month, Caoimhe – something about putting in a new computerised system, for routing calls? To be honest I wasn't really paying attention when he told me about it, you know how he gets. But I do have it written down somewhere. Let me just find it, yeah?"

"Okay, Mum. Thank you." This was not good at all. Trying to get through to Dad at work was like ringing in to the radio station to win concert tickets. It was always engaged. It was just the luck of the draw if you ever actually got through. It was a Sunday though – that might give me better odds in the draw, hopefully, I thought.

"Okay, I have it now. Have you something to write it down with?"

"No Mum, but I have a really good memory." I did when I was sober, anyway.

"Okay, if you're sure. It's ahhh, O-six-one, obviously…"

"Obviously. What's next?" I was going to have to repeat the number in my head until I could grab a pen.

"Seven one…" I could hear next door's dog, Buster, barking behind her, it sounded like she was in the garden, so she must have picked up the cordless when I rang.

"Seven one, yeah." I drank some of my pint of water. It had ice and lemon in it, because I was fancy.

"Six three…" More woof woofs in the background. Buster was getting old, for a dog, but he was still fit and healthy enough to be a pain in the arse, especially if you had a hangover.

"Six… three. Yuh?" I wanted to spark up a fag, but I knew she'd hear the match being struck, and start giving out to me for it, so I left it.

"Five two. Say it back to me now?"

"Seven one, six three, five two." *Seven one, six three, five two. Seven one, six three, five two.*

"With the O-six-one, remember. Because you're in Cork, yeah? You'll need to put the whole thing in, yes?"

"Yeah, I know." I wasn't going to bother telling her that you had to put the area code in all the time on a mobile, like Brian had told me earlier, because it wasn't important, and because I wanted her to fuck off and let me ring Dad.

"Great, and listen, you'll be back tomorrow afternoon, right?"

"Yeah, Mum. Afternoon, maybe a bit earlier, depending. Why, like?" I had no clue when we'd be heading off, just that we had to get out of the hotel rooms by eleven.

"Oh, nothing. I just need to – your father and I have some news for you…"

"Some news?" I didn't like the sound of that. Maybe they were splitting up. Maybe she was pregnant. Ughhhhhhh, Mum and Dad riding each other.

"Yeah, look, I shouldn't have said anything, Caoimhe. Just mind yourself today and tonight, and get yourself home safe, and we'll have a chat then, just the three of us."

"A chat about-"

"Bye now, love. Bye." The phone clicked off on her end, but my end was still live. I found the red button for hanging up, listened for a dial tone, and regurgitated the numbers in my head onto the big, stiff, clumsy keys. Brian would be back soon to see how I got on, and to make sure I hadn't done a runner with his Motorola.

The line on the other end actually rang, three times. I was going to get through, first time! A recorded voice told me my call was important – that'd be the new system, then - and a very scratchy recording of one of Vivaldi's *Four Seasons* played. *Spring*, maybe, at a guess. Tim would have been able to tell me which one, I thought. Then I remembered Tim was the Lizard King now, so he'd probably just tell me that all seasons were transient, while I tried not to stare at his genitals.

*****

"What's that? Vivaldi is it?" said Richie, walking past the table I was sitting at with the phone, waiting. I'd found out a way to put it on speaker, so I didn't drive myself insane with it up to my ear, listening to the same bit of hold music over and over.

"Yeah, actually!" That boy was full of surprises. "Which season is it? Spring?"

"How would I know? I'm not a steamer," he said, wandering off again. I was going to say something after him, but someone picked up on the other end.

"Shaughnessy and Partners International, Limerick office, Cliona speaking, how may I help?" I grabbed the phone and shoved it up to my face.

"Uh, hello!" I wondered how long I'd been sitting there waiting. It only felt like about eight hours.

"Hello?" Cliona Davis had been about three years ahead of me in school. She was doing Law out in UL, that's where Dad met her, and gave her the part-time job. Full time in the summer.

"Hey, Cli! It's Caoimhe, is Dad around?" If she told me he was in a meeting I was just going to smash my pint glass and slit my throat with the broken pieces.

"Heeeeeey, gorgeous! Hey, I thought you were playing the Féile this weekend, rock chick? Today, isn't it?"

"Uh, yeah. That's the plan, anyway." The plan that was completely FUBAR, obviously. "I just need a word with himself for two secs. Please tell me he's there, and he's not busy!"

"Haha! No, he's definitely here, and he's *always* busy. But he's never too busy for you, honey." What an outright lie that was, I thought, but it sounded nice, anyway.

"Ah I know, shur. Wrapped around my finger, says you." My water was finished. I'd had four fags since they'd put me on hold, and my throat was parched. Maybe if I snapped my fingers a waiter would arrive. Doubtful though, since I wasn't in a restaurant. Or in a cartoon.

"Daddy's girl, yep. Aren't we all, Caoimhe? Aren't we just? Oh! Speak of a queer and one will appear, huh? Just walked in the door, he did, babe."

"Brilliant," I said. I could hear her talking to Dad, with her hand over the mouthpiece, then a different voice came on.

"Hello, sweetheart. Are you okay? Nothing's happened, has it? Where are you? Still in Cork?" Dad sounded tired, but he always did. It was his own fault, working all those hours when he definitely didn't have to.

"I'm okay, Daddy. I'm good! Nothing's happened, don't worry. Well, nothing has happened *to me*, anyway. I… need your help."

I stopped, so I could get the story right in my head. No matter how right I got it though, I'd still have to tell him what Niall had been arrested for – otherwise he wouldn't be able to help us - and once I did that, things wouldn't ever be quite the same between us. He'd already had to listen to the police tell him about all the stuff Áine had taken the night she died, on top of hearing about everything else that had happened to her. He didn't have a clue that I was as bad as her for drugs – probably worse than her, nowadays anyway.

I could lie to him all I wanted about how it was only Niall messing around with drugs, or how it was just some of the others, not me, but even if he believed me, I'd still feel awful. So, I wasn't going to lie to him. He didn't deserve that from me. That said, if he didn't fucking ask me, I wasn't gonna tell him, either. That wouldn't really be lying. It wouldn't even be a *white* lie. It'd be me getting off on a technicality, like some of his dodgy criminal clients. Couldn't do me for it.

*****

"Right. What's the story, Maurice? Are we back in business, or what?" Brian had been hovering around me like a vulture for the last few minutes of the call with Dad. The nervous energy coming off him was nearly making my hair stand on end.

"Well, there's good news and bad news," I said, lighting up another fag and immediately regretting it, cos I was still desperately in need of liquids.

"Gimme the bad news first, then. Let me have it, says you."

"Okay well the bad news is he won't be out in time to play, Brian. It's not possible. You're gonna have to tell them we can't do it." There was no point on sugar-coating it for him.

"Fuck! Why's that?" He stood up from the chair, and looked over at the bar, bit there was no one serving.

"Well, it's a longish story, but basically, Dad's friend Charles – the solicitor – he's based in Cork all right, but he won't be free for another hour at the very least. He's the only one Dad can think of that's near, so he's the best option we've got, Bri. For Niall, I mean." We weren't playing today. That was 100% definite, now. I had already thought we weren't playing, but it hadn't hit me yet. Not until the chat with Dad. Not until I said it out loud, to Brian, just then. My heart was sinking further by the second. I felt like crying, but I didn't, as well. Probably the lack of serotonin.

"Ah, Jaysus, that's rough. But listen, thanks for trying anyway like, Caoimhe. I know it wasn't – I know it was no walk in the park or anything, having to tell the auld fella all the details, Maurice. Especially since you weren't even asking for you, like. You were just being, well... thanks, anyway." He looked very down; more down than I probably did. He was probably thinking of having to ring Seamus though, and get a bollocking, or worse.

"It's grand, Brian. Twas no bother, like. Any of ye would've done the same for me, I hope." Dad hadn't asked me anything about if I was taking drugs, so I didn't have to lie to him. I didn't know if him not asking me was a good thing or a bad thing, really though. It was something I'd think about later on, mind. Not now.

"Hah! You hope, anyway, says you. So, what was the good news?"

"Sorry?" I was looking over to the table where the rest of them were. Bríd and Benson had shown up while I was gone. She wasn't still wearing my dress or the blue wig, so I had to readjust my brain to realise it was her.

"You said there was good news? As well as bad news?" Brian finally caught the barman's eye and signalled for another pint. No sign of Aisling yet. Maybe he'd murdered her, and he was trying to get as many Guinness into him as possible before the Gards turned up.

"Oh sorry, yes. The good news is Dad says that Charles specialises in stuff like this, and as long as Niall didn't have too many pills on him, he'll probably get let off with a Caution. No proper charges, or criminal record?" I didn't know how many he'd had on him last night, and neither did Frank, unfortunately.

"How is that good news for *me*, Maurice? Gig's ruined now, whole fecking weekend's ruined too. I don't give a fiddler's fart if he rots in there, he's no use to me now, shur." The barman came over and put a pint down in front of him. "Oh, cheers bud, what's the damage, again? Oh yeah, three-fifty, wasn't it? How could I forget that, like? I'll be keeping the glass for that price, Maurice. And a few of these ashtrays, go on with ya!". He probably wasn't being serious about not caring about Niall, but then again he might have been, too.

Both were equally possible.

*****

"How bad a stain is it? And how the hell can you... I'm not even sure I want to know, Bríd," I said, wondering what chemicals were inside Benson that he could manage to ruin a latex dress simply by having sex with her while she was wearing it.

"I don't know. I just... it was fine, when we – it was okay, when I had it on. Then, when I was getting changed, there was all this... purpleness on the pink." She shrugged. Benson didn't say anything, he just looked guilty.

"What part of the dress was this purpleness on, then?" said Ciara, stubbing out her B&H.

"Ah, around the... front." Bríd waved her fingers across her chest. I kind of wanted to see it, because it was bloody expensive and probably ruined now, forever. I also didn't want to see it though, because bleurgh.

"Fired a warning shot across her bow, did you, shipmate? Aaaarrrrr!" Richie said. He was still drinking cider. Wasn't like there was any reason to stay sober now. He'd be doing no drumming today.

"Richie!" said Marian, slapping his leg. She did it like a reflex now. She probably didn't care what he'd said. It was just their *thing*, already. He said something inappropriate - she whacked him. They were such the instant couple.

"He didn't!" said Bríd. "Okay, he might have, but that still doesn't explain the stain – colour of it, like." Benson still wasn't saying anything. He looked a bit tired. Probably from all the ejaculating.

"Purple spunk," said Brian. He hadn't phoned the Féile people to tell them we were a no show yet. He had better do it soon, I thought, or our name would be mud around these parts. Although it would be anyway, soon.

"Twas far from purple spunk ye were reared," Ciara said.

"No, he didn't rear her, he just came all over her tits," said Mar.

"Marian!" said Richie, slapping her on the leg. The circle was complete. The student had become the master. The barman was drying some pint glasses while pretending not to listen to us.

"Barney the Dinosaur," I said, having a sip of my fresh G&T.

"What about him?" Ciara said, squeezing my leg under the table. That was our *thing*, possibly.

"No, I was just trying to think of someone who would have purple spunk."

"Apart from Benson, obviously," said Brian, looking at his phone but still not pressing any buttons.

"Obviously," I said. "Where's Ian, by the way?" I knew where Tim was, and obviously where Niall was. We were missing a band member here though.

"He's in his room, playing Smiths songs on his acoustic and staring at the wall," said Benson, who hadn't lost the power of speech after all.

"Why don't you ask *him* to do a set on his own, Brian?" I said, not serious or anything.

"Cos he can't sing a note, Kweev. You've heard him, he's worse than that poor lad Eric off the DTs." I hadn't heard that name in ages. They had split up, supposedly. Something to do with getting beaten by a better group in a Battle of the Bands last year, I heard. Poor misfortunes.

"Yeah, true. He hasn't really got the stage presence either, no offence to him," said Ciara, because it was true.

"He's no Kweeva Shox, that's for sure," Brian said, looking at me, with hope in his eyes.

"Stop looking at me with hope in your eyes, Brian. I'm not doing it!" I said, lighting up my five millionth fag of the day.

"Ah, twas worth a try, says you," he said, picking up the Motorola again. "I suppose I'd better get this over with, yeah? Face the fecking music, and all that, Maurice."

"Yeah, I suppose you'll have to, Brian. Oh, here's your better half," I said, spotting Aisling coming in the door, looking sickeningly fab altogether. "How did ye get on last night, by the way? You haven't said a word about it, you sly dog."

"Last night? Hang on, it's ringing," he said, pretending he didn't know what I was on about.

"The sex, Brian. The intercourse. The rumpy-pumpy. The riding." They'd either gone back and she'd gone all Two Moon Junction and Nine and a Half Weeks on him, or they'd passed out exhausted and done nothing. Both were equally possible.

"Ah, now, Caoimhe. A gentleman never kisses and tells."

TWENTY-THREE

"He put it up my arse, like. I *asked* him to, and he did it. And I *liked* it, Caoimhe! What have you people turned me into at all?" Aisling was in the toilets with me – the hotel bar ones. We were both back in the land of regular weeing today, thank Christ. I spent my life in toilets with women, these days, it seemed. It was a strange, new, pine-fresh existence.

"Up the bum, like? Jesus, Aisling. Didn't it hurt?" It was a risky conversation to be having between public cubicles, but at least there were only the two in there, so there was no chance of anyone being in a third one, taking notes.

"Not really, no."

"What do you mean, not really?" I'd never had the displeasure, myself. Just a handful of near misses. Aisling Flanagan had pulled ahead of me in the sexual experiences race. Or the heterosexual experiences one, anyway. What a life we led.

"Well like, it hurt a bit, even with lots of that *jelly* stuff we were using. But the way I was last night, on those pills, literally everything felt good, you know? Any touch or feel or kiss or whatever, so… even the stuff that kind of hurt, it kind of hurt in a good way?"

"Fucking hell. You're a braver woman than me, like. Fair play, Ash." I tried not to picture Brian Collins bashing away at her back entrance, but the image was there now, damn it.

"Nah, not really. See, I've a theory." She flushed her loo, but she didn't sound like she was getting up or coming out yet.

"A theory?" I flushed as well, and I also didn't get up, because I wasn't in any hurry to get back in there. In there was where all the reality was. I wasn't too keen on the reality right now. It was too depressing.

"Yeah, it's like… hang on, are you finished in there?"

"Yeah. I guess so…"

"Okay, hold on and I come in and join you." She clicked her lock open, and I stood up to let her in. She was wearing a very non-her outfit today. Tight, black, fake leather pants, and a red silky-looking top that was very plungey and booby, without being cleavagey.

"Wilkommen!" I said, making room for her to stand in with me.

"Howdy," she said. She had mad big heeled shoes on too, same colour as the top. She couldn't quite manage in them yet, but she was learning fast.

"Where did you get your top, and the pants, babe? They're beeeauuutiful." Looked like Penney's, maybe, I thought.

"These? Penney's! Dirt cheap, as well. I went on a bit of a shopping trip earlier, while himself was busy doing… whatever he was doing, with you lot." She hadn't much done with her face, but it was still a lot of makeup compared to how she normally looked in the daytime. Or how she used to look in school, which was wearing none at all.

"You did well for yourself. Those pants are amazing, especially with your legs. And the top…"

"I know, it's very low, isn't it? What's that cut called, the zig-zag thing? You know all this stuff, don't you, Caoimhe?"

"Haha, I do. It's called a *surplice* neck. They're normally not that deep, like. And if they are, it's more flat-chesty ones who wear them, you know who I mean – Hollywood skinnies." Mum owned a clothes shop in town, and she used to be a dressmaker, so I *did* actually know these things. I was dead clever, sometimes.

"Yeah, definitely. Well, I'm not a Hollywood skinny myself, Kweev – far from it, like. But I'm not flat-chested either, so it's grand." Far from it, my arse, I thought – she was *lithe* all over, with her ballerina legs and her Riverdance bum. She was wearing a bra underneath the top, but it was a plunge one, so it made her look like she had magical boobs which stayed there on their own – didn't even need some of Portia's magic wig tape. I immediately put Portia out of my head, just because.

"You're definitely not flat, Ash, no. What was this theory of yours, anyway?" I'd almost forgotten, in all the commotion.

"Oh yeah! Well, it's only a new theory, like. I only came up with it last night, after the…"

"After the buggery, yes."

"The unholy sodomy I'm going straight to hell for, yeah." She did the sign of the cross on herself. "Anyways, my theory is – well, *I* think I've *quite* a tight, you know…" She pointed vadgeward.

"Front bottom," I said, speaking to her in her native tongue. I'd no idea where this was going, but I was enjoying it, all the same. I loved New Aisling. She didn't even need the Es anymore, it seemed. She was out of her shell forever, now. Out and proud.

"Haha! I'll never live that one down, will I? But yeah, *that*. I mean obviously I've only had Brian inside it, no one else..."

"Really?" I said, pretending to be surprised, because it felt like the right thing to do.

"Yes, really. But anyways, him and me, it's a very *snug fit*, and I don't think he's like massive or anything. He's like..." she did an estimatey measurey thing between her fingers, and I nodded, even though it wasn't that detailed a description – just the length. "And sometimes *that* hurts me, if we've rushed the sex part a bit, yeah? Do you follow me?" She was big into eye contact, I noticed. It made you feel like you were special when she talked to you.

"Yeah, I know what you mean," I said, because I knew what she meant. A dick in you when you hadn't summoned up the necessary amount of *gloop* first could be quite a squeaky affair. A little chafey.

"So, my theory is, if you've a very tight hoo-hoo-"

"*Hoo-hoo!*" I said, laughing. It made her vagina sound like Al Pacino.

"Yes! Anyways, if that's tight, shur your arse isn't much different then, really?"

"Well, in some ways, yeah," I said, because my vagina did many neat tricks, but shitting wasn't one of them.

"In some ways, yeah. But I mean, in that specific way. As a... *prospective thoroughfare*, Caoimhe."

"Hahaaaaaaah!" She was gas, I loved her.

"So, my theory is..."

"Your theory is that girls who say they wouldn't let someone do them up the bum cos it would hurt too much must have enormous, baggy vajayjays? Is that what you're accusing me of having, Aisling? A fanny like a burst couch?" I'd stolen that one off Niall, but he was in jail now, so he couldn't do me for it.

"Hahahaha! Caoimhe! No!!! No. But like, yeah - if the shoe fits. You burst couch-fannied whore, you." She'd a lovely, filthy laugh when she was being a *cailín dána*, I noticed.

"I can assure you my hoo-hoo is very petite, Aisling. It's like mouse's ear. You can have a check if you like," I said, hoping she wouldn't take me up on the offer – we'd corrupted her enough already for one weekend, for fuck's sake. I remembered I still had some of Portia's coke in my handbag, which was technically *my* coke now, after all the stealing and the absconding she'd done. No, though. No more tainting the soul of poor Aisling Flanagan. At least not until after we'd had lunch, anyway, cos I was starving again.

*****

"Well? What did they say?" I asked Brian, when we got back to the table. Ciara gave me a strange look when I sat down, but I was probably imagining it. *American Pie* was playing on the jukebox. The value for money crowd must have been in. Eight minutes for 20p.

"Well, they were a bit annoyed, cos they've no one to open now, squire. But yer man said they could just tell the next lot to go on earlier, and play a few extra songs, if they have them, so they'll be grand."

"That's good, so. Isn't it?" I said. I didn't know what I'd been expecting to happen, really. I hadn't thought about it properly.

"Well, yeah. Except now ye'll probably never get another gig off MCD, and ye won't be asked back to this next year, and the word will get around that ye're unreliable and that'll affect all yeer future bookings, and if that happens ye'll struggle to get any gigs when ye're trying to promote the new album, so that'll probably have to be delayed as well. But, other than all that, yeah, ye're probably grand, Maurice."

"Well, fuck me pink," I said. I was stealing that for

good, now. Portia was gone; she couldn't do me for it.

"Jeeeesus. When you put it like that, Brillo, it's fierce fucking depressing, isn't it?" said Rich.

"Will we head over anyway and watch the show?" said Ciara. I nodded, because her and Bríd and Benson weren't in the band, and they'd paid for tickets to this thing. Wasn't fair to make them miss it just because we were all suicidal.

"Yeah, shur. Might as well get a few free drinks before they tell the barmen to stop serving us and throw us out," said Richie, standing up. I hadn't even thought of that possibility, damn it.

"It's lovely again outside, lads. Will we walk, yeah?" said Bríd, linking arms with her boyfriend, or *Purple Rain*, as I called him now – ruiner of my £300 latex dress.

"A walk would be lovely, ladies," said Aisling, still tottering a little in her new heels. *Vincent* came on the jukebox, next – definitely a Don McLean fan hiding in the bar somewhere.

"Nah, fuck that, I'm taking the minibus," said Brian, who was probably shattered from all the sodomising last night.

"Lads, I'm so sorry for you all, like. And for you, Brian. You've worked hard for this as well. You've worked very hard," Aisling said, giving him a lovely girlfriendy cuddle.

"Ahhhhh, shur, what can you do? That's the way it is. What does yer man say to Jack Nicholson at the end of that film, lads? After yer one he's trying to save from her Da gets shot, and the Da is gonna get away with everything evil he did to her, and Jack can't do anything about it?"

"Forget it, Jake. It's Chinatown," I said, delighted with myself for knowing what film he was on about, and even more delighted with myself for getting the answer before Marian did. I was dead cleverer than Film Studies students, sometimes.

*****

"So, what was all that about, then?" Ciara said, once we were on our way. Me and her were at least a half hour behind the rest of them, because I'd insisted on getting changed and she'd insisted on agreeing with me. We'd just put on a couple of light, summery dresses and our Converse, cos it was absolutely boiling out. We were kind of matching; it was dead cute.

"What was all what about?" I said, lighting up a Marlboro. There had been lot of things. Maybe she meant the Chinatown quote. She'd have to be more specific.

"You, in the toilet, with Aisling. What was that, another notch on the belt for you on your odyssey?"

"Huh?" I looked at her to see was she being serious. I couldn't tell. There was a smile there, but it wasn't necessarily a happy one.

"Sorry. It's hard to keep up with you, that's all. It's me, then it's the Chinese girl, then it's me again, now it's-"

"Now it's nobody! I mean, now it's... I was just in the toilet. Going to the toilet, you know? Like people do, in toilets." Where the fuck had all this come out of?

"Hmmm, okay. Cool." She wasn't looking at me anymore now. I didn't like it.

"Is there something wrong, Ciara? Did I do - are you *cross* with me?" There was an ouch in my chest again, and it wasn't from the fags.

"No. No, I'm not cross with you, Caoimhe." Still no eye contact, just looking ahead, walking.

"Then what is it, Ceer? Are you *jealous*, or something?" I said it and I immediately knew it was the wrong thing. She looked at me now, but it wasn't a good look.

"Hah! *Jealous*. Why? Were you *trying* to make me jealous? Was that the plan?" I didn't like this new look on her face at all. Not one bit. I was suddenly very glad the others weren't around to hear us like this.

"No! I wasn't! We just went to the bathroom, and then we got talking, and…"

"Was that what you were doing all day yesterday then, yeah? With Portia? Trying to make me jealous? Like we were on an episode of Home and Away, or something?" She was smiling now, but it wasn't a friendly smile. I didn't like it. I didn't like any of this, I wanted it to stop.

"No! I wasn't at all. I wasn't even thinking about you, I-"

"Well, that I can believe."

"What do you mean??? Look, Ciara, you're the one who's all – *let's not do this, let's not get too serious, I never have boyfriends or girlfriends, don't go past my Rubicon* - and all that. I'm the one who really wants to – who really wants *you*, I mean." I couldn't find the right words. I felt like I was going to cry.

"You've chosen a pretty cavalier way of showing it, Kweev. No offence."

"Gah!!! I don't understand this! I don't understand you, sometimes, I – I'm sorry, okay? I'm sorry." My palms were really sweaty.

"What are you sorry for now?" She was regarding me again. Jean-Paul Sartre would have loved her.

"I don't know," I said, because I sort of didn't.

"Well then."

"Well then, what?" I fucking hated this. We were gone all funny with each other again and I hadn't even seen it coming, so I wasn't able to stop it happening. I didn't like this new, complicated version of us. I just wanted it to be simple again.

"Well then don't say you're sorry if you don't mean it, because that kind of sorry is meaningless, yeah?" She stopped at some traffic lights to wait for the green man.

"I'm sorry. I mean – I'm sorry for saying sorry when I didn't mean – Ciara, I don't wanna fight with you!"

"We're not fighting, Caoimhe."

"We aren't?" I was very confused. I lit a new fag off the end of the other one. This was stressing me the fuck out; I didn't need any more stress today.

"No. I don't think so, anyway. We're just – I don't know what we're doing, Caoimhe. Maybe we should just stop."

"Stop seeing each other???" *No! Don't do this! Not now!*

"We're not *seeing* each other, Caoimhe. There you go again, like. I just meant maybe we should stop talking about all this, because we're going around in circles, yeah?" The green man came on and she walked across without waiting to see was I coming with her. Although of course I was; where else would I go?

"Are we not?"

"What, seeing each other? I don't – How could we be seeing each other? You're not even – you only just decided that you like – whatever this is you're going through, it's brand new. And anyway, you definitely didn't think we were seeing each other yesterday, when you were hanging out of that other one all day, until she did a runner, and then you were hanging out of me again. Did you?"

"Did I what?" My chest was entirely made of ouch now, and it was spreading. My face was scarlet, I knew that without having to look in a mirror.

"Did you think I was your... *girlfriend* when you were

spending the whole day ignoring me and doing... whatever the hell *all that* was, with your new gal pal? It's a simple question, Caoimhe." She'd stopped walking now and turned around to look at me.

"No!!! I was like really upset that you were gone in the morning, and I was missing you, and I was worried about where you'd gone! I was confused, and I wanted to talk to you, and I wanted everything to be okay between us."

"Sooooo, what – you decided the best thing to do about all that would be to... hook up with some complete stranger and go do coke with her in the loos, yeah?" She was looking at me all incredulous, and what really annoyed me was that she had a point.

"Ugh, it wasn't like that. I mean, it was. But it wasn't that simple either, Ceer."

"None of this is simple, is it?" she said, shrugging her shoulders and starting to walk again.

"No, but I don't – I'm sorry!!!"

"There's no need to be sorry, Caoimhe."

"There is! I upset you, or something, and I don't want to upset you. I don't want you to be cross at me, Ciara. Not ever!" I wished she'd just stop walking and hug me or something. I wasn't able for all this, not today.

"You haven't upset me, Kweev. You just... you *frustrate* me. The way you're so intense, and hopelessly gooshy one moment, and then you're off on some mad lesbian festival adventure, and then when your other options run out – literally ran out, she did, with all Frank's drugs, by the way – you're all schmoozing up to me like none of that happened. And I wasn't *jealous*, Caoimhe. I don't own you – I've no right to be possessive of you. But I'm allowed to feel a bit shit over being treated like a consolation prize, yeah?" She looked cross. She was cross. And she was absolutely right, she deserved to be cross. I felt so awful.

"I'm so sorry, Ciara. You're right. I didn't – I'm just… I am sorry. For treating you like that, really I am." We were at the stadium entrance.

"Okay. That sorry you're allowed, since you actually fucking know what you're saying it for. I just… let's stop talking, yeah?" She wasn't looking at me. I wasn't sure I wanted her to, in case I saw something in her eyes that ripped me to shreds.

"What, stop talking forever?" I said, in a mild panic.

"We'd have to sew your fucking mouth up first, for that to be possible," she said, but with a nice smile this time, and I got such a huge, full body feeling of relief from seeing it, that it made me a little scared. Scared of how one person could have that much control over my emotions. Scared of what would happen if I let that person fully into my heart. Scared of how I'd feel if they ever broke it.

*****

"This is the magazine you want me to be in, is it, Brian?" I said, holding up the August issue of Loaded I'd found on the bar when I went up for a drink.

"That's the one, yeah. Classy enough, is it?"

"Well, I dunno about classy, but they've definitely got good taste in singers, so I'll be in good company anyway," I said. Kylie was on the cover, in a swimsuit. She was inside as well, in several swimsuits. It said "The Swimsuit Issue" on the front, so there was definitely a theme.

"Will you be in a swimsuit then, yeah?" Richie said, leering over Marian's shoulder at the Princess of Pop herself.

"Her issue wouldn't be out until Christmas, so she probably wouldn't be in a swimsuit, no," said Brian, who knew lots about these things, or didn't have a clue about them and was just winging it. Both were equally possible.

"Maybe you'll be in a Christmas swimsuit?" said Mar, turning the page to another picture of tiny Kylie in another tiny bikini. She was exquisite. Her hair was brunette, not red, in these photos, so they must have been taken a while back. It didn't look like a wig. She had it backcombed and lacquered on top, 1960s style. Every hairstyle looked good on her though, she was something else.

"Or Christmas underwear," I said, making a face, cos that'd be red, and most red underwear was rank. It was the sort of underwear a fella would buy you, if he didn't know anything about buying underwear. Which was most fellas, in fairness.

"Or a sexy Santa suit, maybe. Without the beard, though. That'd just be confusing," Marian said. "She's so tiny and petite, isn't she?"

"She is! I was standing across from her on the stage on Friday, and-"

"Were you??? Did ye meet her?" Marian hadn't met us until yesterday; I'd kind of forgotten that. It felt like she'd been with us the whole time.

"Nah, we didn't get to talk to her at all. I was raging, like. I met Nick Cave, though. Twice!"

"Yeah, he was staying on our floor, they said, but we didn't run into him, or into Kylie," It was weird hearing her say "we", when I knew who she meant. No one had brought Portia up in a while, but it was going to happen. We couldn't avoid it.

"Yeah, he assured me she didn't stay over that night, and that she wasn't staying with him, but I don't think I believed him," I said. The Kylie photos were finished now, I had no need for Loaded magazine anymore. It'd be cool though, if I did the shoot, cos then I could say I'd been in the same magazine as her. We'd be like Magazine Buddies, or something. Not that I'd being the shoot now though, since our entire careers were over, probably.

"Yeah, I think he was probably just being discreet," Aisling said, beside me on my other side.

"Like your Brian was, when I asked him about you and last night's shenanigans," I said, pushing the magazine over past Mar and into Richie's greedy, perverted paws.

"Was he? Awwww! Thanks, Briany-Bri!" Aisling said, in his direction.

"What do you mean, thanks? Thanks for what?" He was on the Guinness again, but he always was on the Guinness, a creature of habit.

"She means thanks for not telling everyone about the arse sex," I said, way too loud, and then I dragged her off with me before all the questions started.

*****

"What do I do again, sorry?" Aisling held the spoon of cocaine in front of her face, studying it like we were back in Ms. Carty's Chemistry class.

"Ah, you put it right up under this fellow here," I pointed at her nostril. "Then you put your finger over that fellow there, to shut it off," I pointed at her other one. "And then you just SNEEP it into you."

"SNEEP!" she said, trying not to spill any of the precious powder when she laughed, like she was in some sort of deviant egg and spoon race.

"Sneep it up your smellhole," I said. I was dead poetic, sometimes.

"Okay, down the hatch! Or... up the hatch?" She did as I'd instructed, getting it absolutely spot-on first time, like a good little Head Girl.

"It's good for what ails ya," I said, taking back my spoon and putting it away in my bag, since dresses never had pockets, thanks to the patriarchy.

"It's certainly, uh, something. And what will this do to me, then?" She sniffed an extra sniff and ran her tongue across her teeth in a way that was slightly distracting. Quiet, brain!

"Oh, I dunno. It just makes you feel good, really."

"Well, I can't really say no to that," she said, smiling. She was wearing a little eyeshadow, and some mascara, but no eyeliner. Lots of foundation, but no lipstick. It worked fine enough, but it still made me want to sit her down and finish her off, so to speak. Quiet, brain!

"You *should* say no to it, Aisling. Just say no! What would Brian Collins think at all?"

"Ah, I think I'm well past shocking that fella now, in fairness. And anyway, I'm a strong, independent, autonomous female woman, or something." We were sharing a cubicle, for obvious, necessary reasons. I'd thought I heard someone come in to the one next to us, but there was no noise now, so they were either gone already, or they were staying very silent, so they could hear everything we said. Maybe I should tell Aisling about the paranoia, I thought. Maybe not, though.

"Yeah, that's true. So, is he the reason you've like, changed?"

"Changed? This weekend, you mean?"

"Well, yeah. But, no. I mean, over the last few months, like. You've been coming out to the pub and just socialising more. I don't remember you doing that a lot, before." I didn't remember her doing it at all, really.

"Oh. No, I mean I'm nearly with Brian two years now, so… it's not him. Well, he *is* kind part of it, but it's more *me*."

She sniffed again. I could see her face changing ever so gradually as the effects of the coke went through her; it was fascinating to look at.

"Feeling it a bit, yeah?" *I* definitely was, but I was well used to it. She was having yet another first, out of many firsts, this weekend.

"Just a bit, yeah! Woo!" she reached over and squeezed my forearm, then kept holding it. "Anyway, what-what I was saying was… it's not Brian. It's more that I'm eighteen now, and I had like a really strict, really religious upbringing, Kweev. My parents literally waited until the day of my eighteenth before even slightly treating me like an adult." She looked somewhere between sad and cross, but it wasn't directed at me, at least.

"Yeah, you're like a Mormon or something, aren't you?" I was pretty sure that was it. Almost 100% sure.

"A Mormon??? Haha, no! You eejit!" She took her hand off my arm and slapped me on the chest with it, as if we'd suddenly become two rugby lads.

"Ouch! Sorry, okay. A Jehovah's Witness?" It was one of those types of things, definitely. Or maybe a B'hai, whatever that was. I was no longer 100% sure. Of anything.

"Again, no!" She slapped the other side of my chest now. I was going to have to remind her that I was a girl in a minute, before she ended up trying to knee me in the balls or give me a wedgie.

"Okay, okay! What *are* you, then?" I wanted a fag. Needed one, really, but I didn't want to be puffing fumes into her face, even if she probably deserved it now, for all the assaulting me.

"I'm not anything!" She went to slap me again, but I grabbed her wrist, which made her do a little face at me, then I pushed her arm down so her hand went on my hip.

"Well… what *were* you, then?" I said. Her hand moved from my hip, around the back of me, and we were suddenly very close. "Hello," I said. Definitely needed a fag.

"How'rya?" she said, giving me another funny look – I didn't know what sort of funny it was though. I wasn't fluent in her face, yet.

"Grand, I am. So, are you gonna tell me what fecking cult you were in, or am I gonna have to choke it out of you, Aisling?" I held my hands up to her throat, messing. Then I put my arms around her waist, because it felt like the right thing to do – in a comfy way, not anything else. It couldn't be anything else, because she was Aisling Flanagan, from school. Aisling from my Philosophy class. Aisling the ballerina, with the endless legs and the great bum. Quiet, brain!

"Haha! Wait, are you trying to seduce me, Mrs. Robinson?" She did her cailín dána laugh again.

"Pffft, you should be so lucky," I said, feeling extremely warm all of a sudden. "Do you mind if I smoke?"

"What? Before or after?" she said, putting her other arm around me, so now we were practically dancing, except we weren't moving, and there wasn't any music.

"Haha! You're brilliant, Legs. Can I keep you?" I said, wondering if this version of Aisling would turn back into a pumpkin when Féile 95 was finished. It would be awful if she did.

"Legs! I like it! You couldn't afford me, honey," she said, motioning to me to give her a fag, which I did, for some reason.

"I literally *could* afford you. My family's loaded," I said, lighting the cigarette for her, putting it between her lips, and marvelling at how she didn't do the movie thing of coughing her lungs up on the first pull.

"Fine then," she said, taking another drag and blowing

it out her nose, like she'd been smoking for decades. "But you have to give me back to Brian at the weekends."

"Every other weekend," I said, wondering if we should go back out now, in case Ciara was thinking stuff about me again. She was outside in the main stadium though, talking with Alleged Homosexual Zachary, so she probably didn't even know where I was. Or care where I was. She *hates* me now, probably, I thought.

"You drive a hard bargain, Shocks, but it's a deal," she said, flashing me another one of her new Bad Girl Aisling smiles. "Please tell me you still have some gum, by the way. Himself will fucking brain me if I come back smelling like an ashtray." Apparently, her strong independent robot female autonomy didn't stretch to being allowed to smoke by her boyfriend.

"I do of course, Legs. Hang on two shakes, now." I looked in my handbag for them and came across the pouch with the three Es in it. Possibly the only ones still in existence, thanks to Portia the thief, thieving Frank's bag (and possibly my heart). What would I do with them? Who would I give one to, if anyone? We'd soon find out, I guessed. I found the Wrigley's and took two out, because my mouth tasted a bit rank, and I was standing very close to Aisling, even if I wasn't going to seduce her.

"Cheers! So, will we go back out, or do you want to…" Her chewing immediately made me think about last night, and her on pills. Maybe I'd give *her* one of my secret extra pills. She probably deserved it most.

"Do I want to… what?" I said, my brain full of lots of things I wanted to do, and none of them were "go back out".

"Have another little SNEEP!" she said, all flashy-eyed and lip-licky and flesh-squeezy. We'd created a monster. But she was a lovely monster, so it was grand.

"You do not know the meaning of pacing yourself, do you, Legs?" I said, taking out the stuff with an air of mock reluctance.

"Ah, fuck pacing ourselves, Caoimhe. Shur it's Christmas," she said, having a little check to make sure she wasn't falling out of her precariously booby Penney's top. Probably another first for her, out of many firsts, this weekend.

*****

"So, who was that one you were going out with before, Brillo?" Richie said. He'd got a round in for everyone, including the two of us who'd been in the toilets. Sound man, even if they were free.

"Before when?" said Brian, finishing the end of one Guinness before he started on the new one.

"Like, last year, or whenever. About the time I joined this thing."

"What, last summer?" Aisling said, giving him the confused eyes.

"Yeah, last summer. Last… July, maybe. This was before he was going with you, like," Richie said. Marian was in the loo; we'd passed her on our way back.

"That's not right," I said. He'd got me a gin and tonic, but I'd have loved a cider with ice. I'd get one of them too, I decided. It wasn't like he'd be offended. He hadn't paid for them. Well, hopefully he hadn't.

"Why isn't it right? It's just a fact. He was going out with someone last year. I just wanted to know what her name was, like?"

"Her name was Aisling," I said, lighting up a cigarette.

"No, you fucking eejit. That's Aisling, there," said Richie, pointing at her.

"That's me, yep," she said, sipping her vodka and Diet

Coke.

"I know!!!" he said. "But what was the other one's name?"

"AISLING!!!" said Brian, Bríd, and me, all together.

"So, you went out with two birds called Aisling, one after the other?" Richie said. I looked over at Benson. He was totally lost, but that was natural – he was new to the group.

"No, I went out with one bird, called Aisling, Richie. This bird, here." Brian pointed at her.

"Stop calling her a bird, Brian!" I said, just to stir the shit.

"That's not the same bird!" Richie said. Marian was back now; she must have pissed standing up or something.

"Stop calling me a bird, Richie!" said Aisling, looking bemused by the whole conversation.

"Look, Richie, you fucking half-wit. That's Aisling Flanagan, yeah? The same Aisling Flanagan I've been going out with for nearly two years, now-"

"Anniversary coming up. Not dropping any hints, or anything, I'd just like to point out that I like emeralds better than diamonds," Aisling said. I nodded at her, cos emeralds were way nicer than diamonds. Sapphires were, too.

"Your Emerald anniversary is after 55 years together, so you'll be waiting a while, Ash," said Bríd, because she knew lots of things.

"55 years? You'd get less for murder!" said Brian, and then his phone rang. "Hello? Oh right, how's yourself? Yeah? Hahaaah, you're some man, all the same. Herself? No, she's here in front of me; you're in luck. Okay. Okay so, well I'll hand you over now, squire." He handed it over my say, mouthing the words *your da* at me.

"Hello, Caoimhe?"

"Hey… Dad." I was suddenly very aware of how much I'd had to drink.

"Hey, love. How are you feeling? You weren't able to reschedule your concert, no?"

"My concert?"

"I- I'm sorry, your gig."

"Our set," I said, but I was just being gowlish.

"Oh, okay. I'm sorry, Caoimhe, I'm not very hip, as you know yourself."

"Ah, you're grand, Dad. You can leave the *being hip* to us young cats, like." He was making me want to give him a hug now, the silly old fool.

"Okay, I will so. I'll stick to my Hank Marvin, heh heh heh."

"Christ, I'm Hank Marvin myself actually, now that you mention it." I'd totally forgotten to raid the buffet when we arrived, and now my stomach was doing that thing where it suddenly remembers you're hungry and it won't let you rest until you give it cake.

"I don't understand you, dear. Anyway, I'm just calling to say that he's at the Garda station now, and-"

"Ooh, your solicitor friend?!" This was good news. Too late to save our set or our careers, but I really wanted Niall out of there.

"Charles, yes. And, from what he's told me, I think he can get that boy out today."

"Today? When, today?" Any time would be good enough, but I'd no idea where they were holding Niall – if he was still in the single cell where he'd slept, which would be fine. Or if they'd moved him into some holding pen like in the movies, and he was getting traded for packs of cigarettes by tattooed Mexican fellas.

"Could be this evening, could be within the hour. It all depends on the evidence; do you understand me?"

"Of course, Dad. Of course. Look, thank you so much for this, Dad. I know it's been – I know I screwed up."

"Ah, you didn't really, darling." He sounded nice and sincere, but I knew he was disappointed in me today, and it hurt.

"I did, Dad. I screwed up. Doesn't matter if it was my fault or not, I still had to call you to ask you this favour. So, in my mind, that was me screwing up. Do you get me? Do you know what I mean, like? Do *you* understand *me*?" God, I sounded coked up. I hoped to Jesus he wasn't hip enough to know what that sounded like.

"Of course, Caoimhe. Of course."

"Oh, and Dad?"

"Yes, darling?"

"Thanks in advance for not telling Mum what this was about, yeah?"

"Hah! All right. What do you suggest I tell her you called about, when she asks, though?"

"Just tell her I got myself in trouble and I needed money for the boat to England, like."

"Caoimhe!!! You're too much, you are. Too much. Where did we find you at all? Hehehe. Oh, speaking of your mother, when you come home tomorrow, she and I need-"

"- to talk to me about something. Yes, I heard. Sounds very ominous, Dad. Should I be worried?" I wondered if he was going to tell me more than she would; not that she'd told me anything at all.

"Well, I'd like to say no – to reassure you, Caoimhe. But, well it's complicated, and neither of us know how you're going to react to this… news, so the best thing to do is to wait until you're here in person, yeah?"

"I don't feel very reassured, Dad."

"Ah, don't worry, darling. Okay, I have to go now – busy, busy, busy. Work, work, work. I've given Charles the number of Brian's phone, so hopefully you'll hear from him soon. I'll see you tomorrow. Love you, bye!"

"Love you too, Dad," I said, but he was already gone.

"You tell your dad you love him?" Richie said, making a disgusted face at me.

"Of course I do. Don't you tell Mick you love him, no? Does he not tell you the same?"

"He's my Da, Caoimhe. We're not *riding* each other."

TWENTY-FOUR

"Right. Say that again to me, because I'm not sure I believed it the first time, Benson."

"Um, the guy said Menswear have been delayed – on the road here – and that they'll be playing later than they're supposed to. After Dodgy, probably. Maybe later than that," he said, giving me a *don't shoot the messenger* face. He dressed strangely, this boy-man of Bríd's. Like someone who researched hippies or surfers in the Encyclopedia Britannica and went to expensive clothes shops to kit himself out like them.

"So, they just get to... come along later, but we get told to fuck off?" I was livid. Who the hell did they think they were? I could hum like two of their songs. They were very good songs, but still. And how could they be *on the road*? They were *here* yesterday, trying to have sex with Portia – unless that had been a lie. It probably had been. She was the villain of the piece today, so her whole backstory could be rewritten in our heads. Couldn't do us for it.

"Looks like it, yeah. Bummer," he said – in an Encyclopedia Britannica Surfer way, not a casually homophobic one.

"It's not a bummer, it's an injustice!" said Bríd, because she was sound, even if she had ruined my dress by wearing it while acting as a moving spunk target for B.

"An absolute injustice," I said. We were up at the side stage, listening to Schtum, who I didn't really know, but they were good. Northern Irish, heavy guitars, but different from

Ash, or Therapy? They just sounded like themselves. I liked them. They deserved to be in front of a bigger crowd than this.

"They're the flavour of the month, Maurice. The next big thing," said Brian, meaning Menswear. He wasn't helping.

"I thought *we* were the next big thing," I said, pouting like a moody teenager, although I was technically still a teenager, and I *was* feeling very moody, so you couldn't do me for it.

"Ah, ye are. In this country. But they had A&R guys from six different record companies at their showcase gig, Caoimhe. There was a bidding war for them, backstage – I read about it in Melody Maker, Maurice. They're a marketing wet dream, like. Five good looking lads, Britpop sound, fashionably dressed, mad drinkers and womanisers. It's like if you made Take That out of Oasis," Brian said, making me think he should be managing them instead of us.

"How many A&R people were at our showcase gig, then?" I said, remembering no such event, but that wasn't unusual.

"Ah, just the girl from Crabtree, like."

"Oh."

"And she was only there because the whole gig was set up specially for her to watch us."

"Oh. Yeah, that's ringing a bell, all right."

"And that only happened because Seamus knows your Da. He pulled a few strings for ye, Mr. Shox did. He's a diamond geezer, your auld fella, in fairness."

"Yeah, Brian. I get it now." It wasn't a fact I liked thinking about or telling people about. It made it sound like we were shite and only had a record contract because my Daddy fixed it for us.

"Ah but, listen – pulling strings will only get you so far, Maurice. The fact is, ye were brilliant that night, and they'd no choice except to sign ye before any of the big labels came sniffing around ye. Twas your Da doing Seamus a favour, really. Not the other way around," said Brian, not only suddenly knowing exactly the right thing to say, but also putting a very out of character arm around my shoulder and giving me a small squeeze. Arse sex had changed him, for the better.

"Hey Aisling, I'm having him every other weekend, okay? For the sake of my poor, fragile ego," I said. She laughed, knowingly. He smiled, knowing nothingly. Schtum were finished, so we gave them a big clap and a cheer. My best friends Revelino were up next. I wondered where Ciara was, then I stopped wondering, because unlike Brian, she wasn't good for my poor fragile ego at all, at the moment.

"Right, Shox. You're coming with me," said a Thomondgatey voice, behind me.

"Why am I coming with you, Richie? *Where* am I coming with you?" I turned around, and he was at the bottom of the steps, making eye contact with my stomach.

"It's a surprise," he said, taking me by the waist and lifting me down off the stage, like your dad would if you were up on a wall. I was either after losing a few pounds, or he had started pumping iron on the sly, I thought. He'd got fierce strong altogether.

"Ooh! I *hate* surprises! Thanks! What is it? Heroin?" I felt all funny when he put me down, mainly because Marian was looking straight at me, and she wasn't exactly smiling. Thankfully she didn't snarl, though.

"If I told you, it wouldn't be a surprise, sham," he said, giving his Mar a little wave goodbye, so she wasn't coming with us, apparently. She looked at me again, but now it was with a grin, so I was probably grand.

"Definitely heroin then, yeah? I'll start looking for a good vein, cheers."

*****

"Wow, Richie. A *chip shop*," I said, sounding all sarcastic, when he took his hands off my eyes. I was absolutely starving though, so it wasn't that bad a surprise.

"Not *just* a chip shop, like," he said, as if I should be noticing something else about the place. We'd walked outside the stadium, and across the road. He'd only started covering my eyes about two minutes ago, so I hadn't been expecting to see the Statue of Liberty or the glass pyramid of the Louvre when he uncovered them, or anything.

"A *fish* and chip shop?" I said, looking at the posters on the wall that showed all their value combo meals.

"No, you spastic!"

"RICHIE!" I slapped him on the arm, because it was nearer than his thigh, and also his thigh was Marian's now, and I didn't want to be a homewrecker.

"Sorry! I forgot the rule!" he said, actually looking sorry for once.

"You're okay. It's been a stressful day; I'll let it go," I said.

The *rule* he was talking about was *my* rule. My auntie Caroline had a baby last year – Madeleine, she was called – and the baby had Down's Syndrome. Such a gorgeous, happy child. We all doted on her and spoiled her rotten with cuddles and presents. It was only after she was born that I realised how many times a day all the lads, me included, called each other handicaps and spas, and retards, and other things like that. And now I couldn't hear any of it without feeling really bad for poor baby Maddie. So, one night, when I was suitably plastered, I stood up on a table and told them all about Caroline, and Madeleine, and about how using that sort of language was not on, and totally lousy, and they all agreed to try and cut it out for good – in front of me, at least. They didn't always remember, but about 95% of the time, they were good.

"Caoimhe are you even listening to me or are you away with the fairies again?" said a Richie-shaped voice.

"What? Of course I was listening to you," I said, lying.

"Grand, so. So you want a cod and chips, yeah? My treat, obviously." Richie had some notes in his hand, thumbing through them.

"Ah, is there anything else? No, wait, I'm just being a gowl, give me the cod and chips, then. Loads of salt and vinegar, like. LOADS, now, Richie. Tell them loads, for me." Chip shop people usually didn't understand how much I meant by *loads*. I meant LOADS.

"Loads. I know, Caoimhe. LOOOOOOOAAADS."

*****

"These are the best fucking chips I've ever tasted, Richie. I'm not exaggerating, like. They're fucking Michelin starred chips, they are. What did they put in them? Heroin, is it?" I couldn't get the food down me fast enough – my belly was acting like we'd just got the first good batch of spuds after the Famine. I'd probably eat the paper bag when I ran out of chips. The fish was already in my belly.

"You're obsessed with heroin, Caoimhe. Don't ever be trying it or anything, yeah? You'd probably end up loving it too much, sham. I don't want to have to lock you in a wardrobe or something."

"No, it's grand. No fear of me and the old heroin, Rich. As long as you keep feeding me these chips, like. Hey! Excuse me? Why are yeer chips so lovely?" I said to the friendly looking foreign fella who was clearing the table next to ours.

"It is because we put so much *heroin* in them, lady.

Makes them very, very *extra* tasty. Secret ingredient, yes? Shhhhhh!" he said, chuckling to himself and walking off. He'd heard me say the thing about heroin a minute ago, I thought. Hopefully he had, anyway.

"Right, are you ready for your *real* surprise, then?" Richie said, squashing his empty chip bag in his fist, and taking a noisy slurp of his Diet Coke through the straw.

"Wait, so this wasn't the surprise?" I was finished mine too, but I was scrabbling around hopefully in the bottom of the vinegar-soaked bag for any rogue chiplets that might be hiding.

"Since when is a bag of chips a surprise, Caoimhe?" He stood up with our tray and all our rubbish, looking for a bin, because Marie South had raised him well.

"Well, maybe when they're full of smack," I said, already missing them being in my gob. "So… what comes next, Mr. Mysterio?" I said, walking over with him to the swing bin where you emptied the tray into the hatch and then left it up top to be collected. He put the whole lot, tray included, through the hatch.

"Cuntfuckbollocks anyway! That wasn't right, was it?" He did the sort of face a three-year-old did when they shit their nappy before getting all the way to the potty, or the big boy toilet.

"Nobody saw anything, Rich. Just keep walking and act cool. Can't do you for it." I linked his arm, because he was my Chip Daddy now.

"Okay, anyway, it's through here," he said, walking us into a different part of the shop, behind the bin he'd just abused and abandoned.

"What's in here, I don't- OOH!!! RICHIE SOUTH, THIS IS THE BEST SURPRISE EVER!!!" I looked around at all the arcade games and nearly had a stroke trying to decide which one we should play first.

*****

"Which one is this? Is this a new one?" We were at the big, sit-down Street Fighter II machine, finally, after all the horrible kids had fucked off from it.

"It's Super Street Fighter II: The New Challengers," said Richie, helpfully pointing at the writing above the screen that said exactly that, duh. We'd played Daytona a few times – I came second twice, and he won once. Then we'd gone on Lethal Enforcers, but my gun – the SEXIST pink one – was faulty; the trajectory was all off, so I got frustrated with it and stopped.

"And what's special about it?" I put in a 50p so we could play one on one. "Is it faster or something?"

"No, it's slower than Turbo, actually." He hit the 1UP button and waited for me to hit my 2UP, which I did. All the characters came up – loads of them.

"Wait, can I play as ALL of these, Rich?"

"Yep. That's what's special about it. You don't have to unlock any of 'em. You can play as the bosses, or you-"

"Richie! I can pick Cammy!!!"

"Yep. You can play as any of 'em. Like I said, it's-"

"Cammy, Richie! I can be Kylie Minogue! In a beret! With pigtails!" What a life we led.

"Oh yeah, she was her, in that film, like. Fucking awful, that was, sham. It was shit even for a Van Damme film, and that's saying something."

"Kylie is never awful, Richie. Kylie makes everything better!" I moved the cursor over to Cammy and boinked the button. "Hold on, who are you gonna be, Rich?"

"I'm gonna be Guile, like. I knows all his moves – I have

Turbo on the Super Nintendo at home."

"Heh, Super Nintendo. You fucking loser, you. Anyway, look, why don't you be Chun Li, Rich?" I squeezed his thigh, which probably confused him, since women usually punched him on it, these days.

"Why? Why would I pick her? She's handic- she's shite, like."

"Is not! She's brilliant. She does that helicopter spin kick thing, and she's really fast at punching." I used to use her all the time, until I switched to Ken, who was really boring, but him and Ryu were the easiest ones to finish the game with, cos they were a good match for anyone.

"Nah, I'll stick to my-"

"PLEASE, RICHIE! Be Chun Li! For meeeeee?" I gave him my best cutesy sexpot face.

"That doesn't work on me, Caoimhe. You can't like, manipulate me." I was really starting to suspect he simply didn't think I was attractive. The *cheek* of it, like.

"I'm not trying to!" I was definitely trying to.

"Good, cos it isn't gonna work. Why do you want me to be her, anyway? Do you just want me to be a Chinese girl so you can beat me up – beat me up using Kylie Minogue – and you can pretend you're beating up Portia?"

"NO!!!" Yes. Exactly that, yes.

"I don't believe you." He gave me a rare Richie smile. He wasn't a miserable git, or anything. He just had one of those faces that always looked pissed off. It was probably the overbite. His top lip was a bit Simpsons charactery, especially from the side.

"Awwww, Richie! I'll be your best fwiend!" I said, squeezing his leg again. It was safe to do that, because he never, ever reacted all sleazily to it. Not when I did it, anyway, cos he thought I was a fucking munter, clearly.

"*Awww Richie*, nothing! I don't want to be a part of your weird lesbian voodoo rituals, Kweev," he said, making me chuckle. The way he said everything with a straight face made it funnier, for some reason. Tim was like that, except Tim didn't know he was being funny, usually.

"But, but, but … you're supposed to be giving me a special *tweat*!" I wished I'd worn something more sexual now. This gorgeous shift dress with the Peter Pan collar was no use when trying to manipulate normal red-blooded men like him. It lacked the visible boob flesh. It only impressed women, and gays, and those rare, more sophisticated men you'd occasionally meet, who were probably just secret gays.

"I wasn't giving you a *treat*; I was giving you a surprise. And you're having it, right now, love. Don't be ungrateful!" He was a tough nut to crack.

"I'll tell you secret things Marian said to us – *sexual* things. Nice, sexual things, about you.

"Chun Li, you said, was it?" He moved the flashy thing onto her and boinked the button. Round One! FIGHT!

*****

"Why don't you be *my* boyfriend?" I said to Richie, during our fourth match. I'd let him stop playing as Chun Li after the first three, once I'd got my frustrations about Portia out of me.

"Stop trying to put me off, you gowl. I'm beating you fair and square!" He was Guile now, obviously. I was Ken – because Cammy was cool and she was Kylie, but I didn't know how to *haduken* the living fuck out of someone with her, so she had to go.

"I'm not trying to put you off, I'm very serious!" I said, definitely trying to put him off and not at all serious.

"Don't be a fucking idiot. Why would you want to go out with me, like?" He did his signature throw thing and killed me to death. End of round one, damn it.

"Awww, Rich. Don't be so hard on yourself. Shur aren't you lovely altogether – the girls are always after you." I pinned him in the corner and did the shin kicks on him until he went dizzy.

"Fuck! Stop doing that to me, you prick! And I'm not being hard on myself – I didn't mean it like that. I just literally meant why would *you* want to go out with *me*? What have we in common? Ah FUCK!" My Ken gave his dizzy Guile a massive *SHORYUKEN!* and it was lights out.

"What do we have in common? We've loads in common, Rich. Final round! FIGHT!"

"Like – hang on. For fuck's sake, stop pushing me into the corner, you coward – like what, exactly?"

"We both like video games!" I was massacring him in the shins again, but he was good at the blocking. I was just waiting for his hand to get tired so I could do the old *tatsumaki* hurricane kick and it would be all over for poor Guile.

"That's one thing, like. Hah, fucking eat shit!" He'd done a Flash Kick and got out of the corner, somehow.

"You jammy bastard, you. We've more in common than that, Richie. I'm sure we do." I had no idea why I was pushing it; I didn't want to go out with Richie South in the slightest. He belonged to Marian, anyway.

"What, like that we both love vaginas, is it?" He had me now, I'd almost no energy left, and he was doing Sonic Booms over and over again. All I could do was jump them.

"Very good. But yeah, I guess. What about the band?"

"What about it, like? Stay still so I can kill you, will you?"

"No, shag off, I want to win. I mean we have the band in common, you dickhead." I had a plan. For the game, not for dating Richie, mind.

"Yeah, while we still have a band. We'll probably be fucking spli- NO! HOW DID YOU DO THAT, YOU PRICK?!" My Ken did a forward flip over his fireball and hit him with a *haduken* on landing. Lights out, Guile. Goodnight, Vienna.

"I'm the fucking queen of Street Fighter, that's how," I said, leaning back to savour the victory, then having a mini heart attack when I remembered the seat had no back, so I was leaning into nothing, except a potential broken neck.

*****

"Feel better now?" Richie said, when we finally headed back to Páirc Uí Chaoimh, the rest of them, and reality. The noise from the band on stage spilling out into the street was really cool, but it made me feel a bit sad knowing that it wouldn't be the noise of us any time today, or ever.

"I feel *so* much better, thank you! It was the best surprise! And they were the best chips, too. *You're* the best, Richie." I gave him a hug that went on a bit too long and a kiss on the cheek that went on for just the right amount of time.

"Ah, no probs, Kweev. I thought it might cheer you up. And me, too." He handed me a small bottle of Martell that had only a little drunk out of it, so far.

"Ooh! Where were you hiding that? Up your arse?" I unscrewed the top and took a swig. It was lovely and chocolatey tasting. I really liked cognac, although it was nicer with coke. The mixer, not the drug, although it was nicer with that, too.

"Yeah, that's the best way to get it to room temperature," he said, taking it back off me.

"I can keep it up my front bottom if you want, Rich. Then it'll be womb temperature."

"You're disgusting, you know that?"

"Yup. So what are we doing now?" I said, stopping outside the dance tent, and wondering if there would be a crowd in there, this early.

"Going back to my mis- going back to the lads?" He took another drink and handed it over again.

"Hah! You nearly said your missus. You're in looooove with her, aren't you?" The second swig was even better than the first, cos I was used to the taste now.

"I was in love with her a long time ago, Kweev. And when she went away, I hadn't talked to her in about two weeks – after we broke up, cos we didn't have a very nice break up…" He looked a little sad.

"Oh. I'm sorry, Rich." I wanted to ask him the details, but he'd tell me if he wanted to tell me, I thought. No need to pry.

"Nah, it's fine. We had one last, lovely chat, the day she left. I got to say goodbye, at least – and it was a million years ago, I'm a different person now, but…"

"A little of you is the same person, right? And a little of her too, is it? The bits of ye that still love each other?" I sparked up a fag. The music inside the marquee was sounding more and more tempting. I still had coke and speed. I still had three pills too, and Richie had shot up to Number One, in the chart of people who deserved one off me, *so to speak*.

"Something like that, yeah. But I don't know. This weekend, it's all very unreal. There's drink and drugs and all the craziness. Maybe we just feel so intense and happy cos we know it can't last. Maybe that's why it feels like more." He didn't look sad anymore, but he did look a bit serious. He took another drink of the cognac, and it was a long one this time.

"Like a holiday romance," I said, not just meaning him and Mar. My weekend had felt a bit like that, too, only way more complicated than his.

"Exactly. And we're both on the rebound, so. But Caoimhe?"

"Yes, honey?"

"Knowing all that stuff doesn't stop me wondering if *some* of it is real. Like, it doesn't stop me wondering if me and her could *work*, out there, in the real world?" he pointed into Cork City, de facto capital of the real world.

"Yeah, I know, Rich. But you need to be careful as well, babe," I said, fully aware that I was being the most romantically reckless person on Earth this weekend. But then maybe that was why I was warning him.

"I know, I know. I mean, she lives in Dublin. But so would I, if I actually went to Trinity, you know?"

"What, and give up the band?" I'd hate the band if Richie wasn't in it. He was probably my favourite one, and he was… well, he was a guy who saw me being sad and stressed and took me out for chips and Streetfighter, without wanting a thing in return. Couldn't be not having that guy in my life.

"No! I mean, I don't know…" He handed me the bottle again, we were really polishing it off between us, fair play.

"What don't you know?" I took a long gulp and enjoyed the warm shivers off it.

"I don't know how long we're still going to have a band, after today," he said. Then he took my arm and we walked back in, to find the lads, and the ladies, and his missus who wasn't really his missus, and my missus who wasn't my missus at all.

*****

"Well? Did you enjoy your chips and video games, babe?" said Marian, coming into the toilets when I was fixing my makeup.

"I did! So much, like. It was very sweet of him, Mar. I'm so touched."

"Not too touched, I hope," she said, giving me a slightly evil look.

"What? Noooooo! I didn't- I wouldn't-"

"I'm joking, Caoimhe! Stop!" she was laughing, thank God. I was riddled with the paranoia; all of it drug induced. I needed to cut right down on the old cocaine, starting today.

"Your outfit is amazing, Mar. What's that colour called again? Coral?" She had a spaghetti string vest on and a pair of pedal pushers that were the same shade. A white belt as well, to break up the colour at the waist; she was no slouch in the fashion stakes, as my Mum would say.

"*Coral* is a better name for it yeah, definitely. I was calling it pinky-peach," she said, rolling her eyes. "Hey, darling… do you have any, eh…" she put a knuckle against her nostril and sniffed.

"I might do, possibly." I wasn't sure which type of sniffy stuff she meant, but I had some of both on me, in fairness. I was the Pablo Escobar of Cork City this weekend. Well, I was now that Frank had to retire, anyway.

"Fancy paying me back for Richie's kindness, yeah?" she said, opening the cubicle door and pulling me in before I had time to say yes or no.

"That would only work if ye were an item, Mar," I said, locking the door behind me. "Do you ever wear a fucking bra, by the way?"

"Haha! I do! I was wearing one last night, with the black dress – you took it off me, remember?" she said, almost looking self-conscious for a second, but it passed. I'd completely forgotten realeasing her Krakens until she mentioned it. All these drugs were giving me short term memory loss, definitely. I got out the coke and the spoon.

"Not gonna answer the Richie question then?" I said, remembering that me and him had got on so well and had such a laugh playing Streetfighter II that I'd actually not had to tell him any Marian secrets. He'd been swindled and he hadn't even noticed, poor sod.

"No comment!" she said, but she'd definitely talk to me about it sometime later. Especially now she'd noticed how good a friend Richie considered me. She'd probably think I was the best one to talk to, because of that. She still hadn't talked about Portia, and I was going to be the one she wanted to spill to over that, too, I thought.

"Okay, we'll leave it there, then. Except for me saying that he's lovely, and he's sweet, and he's obviously mad about you, so pleeeease be careful with his poor little Richie heart, Mar?" I wasn't sure if it was out of line for me to say that, but it was said now, so.

"Oh I absolutely am being careful with it, and I absolutely will be, Caoimhe. I promise. And careful with *my* heart, too. I have to be." She looked very sincere; I believed her.

"That's all I needed to hear. Now, you want some of this, or have you changed your mind and chosen a life of purity?" I held out a big, heaped spoon of powder, and she moved her face towards it. She took it all into her with one fell SNEEP, and I loaded another one up for me, because cutting down on the old cocaine could wait until tomorrow. Monday was a better day for turning over a new leaf, anyway. Even if it *was* a Bank Holiday.

*****

"Ooh! You're back!" Aisling said, dancing over to me in her new trousers that must have been like a steam room in this weather.

"I always come back," I said. "I'm like a cold sore."

"Haha! Do you want to go out and see the bands?

Dodgy are on next. I fucking hate them, but their music sort of goes with the weather." She had a cocktail of some sort. A pale green thing, that looked like it was mostly ice. She put the straw off it into my mouth and I took a slurp.

"Mmmmm, brain freeze. Minty, as well? What's this one?"

"A mojito, darling. It's mo-jostly Bacardi. I got him to put a lot of it in there. I think he likes me." She nodded over at my favourite barman, who still didn't have a name.

"Careful now, he's probably just trying to get you drunk, chick."

"Well then, he's succeeding. Where's the guitar guy? Did we not bring him?"

"Ian? No, I think we forgot. He's probably better off where he is," I lied, trying not to picture his swinging feet when we came back later and found him hanging from the rafters. He'd be fine, though. Those rooms didn't have any rafters.

"Hmmmm. And Brian says Tim has turned into a weird naked Indian? I didn't really understand him, to be honest. He says a lot of strange things, Brian. Sometimes you just have to smile and nod; that's what I do."

"You haven't seen Wayne's World 2?" I caught the eye of the nameless barkeep and pointed at the Bulmer's tap, then the ice bucket, and gave him an air kiss.

"I haven't even seen Wayne's World 1, babe. The video recorder is banned in my house. Because of Jehovah," she said, messing with me.

"I'll have to take you under my wing and teach you the ways of the Outsiders, Rachel Lapp," I said, even though that film was actually about Amish people, not Jehovah's Witnesses. Potato tomato, though.

"I think you've taught me enough bad habits, Caoimhe O'Shaughnessy," she said, sounding like a Head Girl again.

"Plenty of time left in the day to teach you some more," I said, taking my pint of icy cider and gulping some down.

"Promises, promises, Shaughnessy," she said, because everyone was borrowing everyone else's catchphrases this weekend. Couldn't do us for it.

"If it's good enough for you, it's goooood enough for meeeeee!" Bríd sang, getting the words arseways. I hadn't seen her come over. She was looking very non-cartoony and not at all like a French spacewoman; we'd have to fix that later.

"Bríd! Benson!" said Aisling, coming over to dole out some big smooshy hugs. Everyone who wasn't in the band was coping fine, thank God. It was only the rest of us who were suicidal, or in denial, or chanting naked. I thought about Ciara, and where she'd got to, then I stopped thinking about it, because there was no point.

*****

"I'm literally only watching this so that if anyone asks me later what Dodgy were like, I can shrug and say, *Good Enough*, I just thought I'd make that clear," I said, to nobody, because nobody was listening to me.

"Do you think Menswear will be on next?" said Richie – my only true friend left in the world, and my partner in a future Lavender Marriage.

"Fuck Menswear!" I said, getting one or two evil looks from the indie teenybopper girls around us. I'd be stabbed to death soon, if I wasn't careful. The Dodgy man on stage finished up their Dodgy song, and everyone around us cheered like mad things. I wasn't feeling it, myself.

"It'll be okay, Kweev. We'll be grand," said Richie, giving me a small hug around the shoulders, even though he secretly didn't want it to be okay or grand. He wanted us to split up, so he could go off and be a child prodigy at Trinity College, and live in Dublin full-time, and touch Marian's delicious choongum in the evenings. I knew his game.

"Hey! Hey, people! How you all doing? Just to let all you Menswear fans out there know – they've been delayed, they've been even more delayed, but they'll be here!" said the Dodgy man. The crowd of indie teenyboppers screamed with hormonal delight around us, making my ears ring.

"They're telling – the guys are telling me, now – that it's The Wildhearts up next, then Galliano. And, after that, FINALLY, the one and only Menswear, so sit tight, guys! Sit tight, and jump around!" Dodgy man started up *Staying Out for the Summer*, and the crowd went mental again. I threw my hands up in the air to show my absolute rage and frustration at the injustice and unfairness of it all, but nobody noticed; they probably thought I just really liked *Staying Out for the Summer*. I walked off, away from everyone, because my head needed some serious straightening out. Or, if that didn't work, some serious fucking up. Both were equally possible.

*****

"So, then. Mister Barman, my old pal, my good buddy. What's ah, what's your name?" I was backstage again, mainly because none of the rest of our lot were.

"My name?" he said, taking a freshly cut slice of lemon and dropping it into the large gin and tonic he was making me.

"Yeah, your name. It's like a word that your parents think of when they see you as a baby," I said, staring at the drink to make it be ready quicker.

"I know what a – it's Yuri."

"Yuri? Like yer man who went into space? Are you Russian, Yuri? You're not fucking rushin' with that drink, like." I was basically the new Bill Hicks; God rest his soul.

"What? No... *Ruaraidh*." He handed me over the glass, although he probably didn't want to, anymore.

"Cheers. Your name is Rory? Well what's the story, Rory?" I said, sinking half the thing in one gulp.

"No, it's *Ruaraidh*. R-u-a-r-a-i-d-h." He wasn't exactly warming to me, this Yuri fella, I thought. The Russians were a cold people, though.

"Well, then. What's the *stuaraidh*, Ruaraidh?" I said, cos I was hilarious, despite the poor reviews.

"Brilliant. I've to go serve someone else now, Caoimhe. See you later," said Yuri/Rory/Ruaraidh, then he walked about five feet down the end of the bar and just stood there, not serving anyone. *Everyone I know, goes away, in the eeee-eeend.*

*****

"Right, and how much is the smaller one, then? No, not that small – the other one. That one. Yeah, the middle sized one."

"That's nine pounds?" said the shopkeeper guy. I'd gone over the road to get a bottle of cognac to drown my sorrows with. I could have just stayed at the bar and ordered double after double – for free – but I wanted to laze on the grass and drink, and I also didn't want Yuaraidh thinking I was an alco or something. I'd an image to maintain.

"Cool, give me that, then. Aaaaaand this," I put the two litre of Diet Coke on the counter, "and twenty Marlboro Lights, aaaaaand, what are those weird looking fags, there? Gowlwashes, is it? Fags you can wash your gowl with?" He didn't think it was funny, but he was a Pakistani or something similar, and they probably didn't say "gowl" over there.

"Gauloises, yes?" he said, taking down the pack and

showing it to me.

"Yeah. What you said. I'll have those too, for Ian. He likes weird fags; they might cheer him up." I wanted to get something nice for Richie, but I couldn't think of anything he liked, apart from video games and Marian, so.

"Okay, lady, is that all?"

"What do you mean is that all, it's loads, shur!" I said, opening my purse to find the right amount of money, even though I didn't know what it was, yet.

"I mean does madam need anything else?"

"Do I need anything else? Jesus, how long have you got, eh?" I wondered if Menswear had shown up yet, or were they just going to saunter on stage halfway through the Stone Roses later on and start playing *Daydreamer*. The shopkeeper ignored what I'd said and started tapping things into his till.

"That will be, altogether…"

"Here, keep the change," I said, handing him a twenty pound note, which was way too much, but fuck it, it was Christmas.

*****

I found the perfect spot, backstage, away from all signs of civilisation, and from any chance of accidentally having to run into my friends. I stretched out as much as I could on the warm grass, put my handbag under my head as a crappy pillow, and poured out a big glass of the very strong mixture of cognac and Diet Coke that I'd made in the bathroom – I'd poured out a third of the coke and filled the rest up with Hennessy. It was quite literally a recipe for disaster, at that ratio. I was just lighting up the first fag of the new box – sun beating down on my bare legs, muffled sound of The Wildhearts coming from the back of the stage, all being almost right with the world – and then an American voice came out of nowhere above my face:

"Whoa, honey. Looks like you've had a rough day. Mind if I sit for a bit?"

"No, of course not. More the merrier," I said, although I meant exactly the opposite of all that, because whoever the fuck she was, I'd have much preferred that she *did not* sit for a bit. I'd have much preferred that she spontaneously combusted and left me to my cognac, my fag, and my misery. But you couldn't say stuff like that to people. It'd be rude. *American woman, stay away from me-eeeee.*

TWENTY-FIVE

"So... the *harsh* reality of this... situation is, you've missed your spot, you can't get a new spot, it doesn't matter anyway because your guitarist is still in jail-"

"Bassist," I said, as if it mattered.

"Sorry, your bassist, Neil?"

"Niall," I said, as if it mattered. I was still lying on the grass, drinking my drink and smoking my fags. American Woman was sitting up, near my head. I couldn't see her face properly, because the sun was right behind her head, and I didn't have any shades on, so I was mostly keeping my eyes closed, when I wasn't squinting at her.

"Niall, right. Caoimhe, Niall... *So Irish.* I love you guys. I love this country. I used to live here, you know. In the Eighties? In Drogheda? Anyway, Niall is in jail, and the keyboards guy, Tim?" She pronounced Drogheda better than, well, better than people from Drogheda would. That was the worst accent in Ireland, including Cavan. It sounded like a Scottish person having a stroke.

"Yep, Tim," I said.

"Tim has crossed over to the other realm, psychedelically. Oh, and Ian – the *guitarist* guitarist – is in the Bad Place, mentally." She was older than me – in her thirties, maybe. She had blonde, messy hair, and a funny nose. A different kind of funny to mine, but still funny. The rest of her upper face was covered in giant, Jackie O sunglasses. She had nice lips, and her teeth were American white – way whiter than mine.

"That's about the size of it, yeah." I didn't know her name. She might have said it, at the start, but I was terrible at noticing things like that, and anyway, I'd been praying she caught fire at the time, so you couldn't do me for it.

"That's a pretty rough day, all right, honey. I'd be hitting the bottle too," she said, giving me a smile with her American mouth. She had a cool voice, like a kind of hippy Earth mother from the movies. She was really friendly and kind, too. I almost regretted wishing her a fiery death now.

"You're telling me," I said, drinking straight from the bottle, as the glass was pointless now; there wasn't any ice left in it.

"But the drummer, Richie. He's still good? He's the one who took you on a special trip. Is he a… is he boyfriend material, then?"

"Richie? Naaaaah. He doesn't fancy me. And I don't fancy him, either. And he's with Marian, as well. She's the most beautiful girl in the world. I couldn't compete with that, even if I wanted to, like." I wanted to say her name, the American Woman, but I couldn't just ask her what it was, now. Not if she'd already told me it. That'd be mortifying.

"Oh, I'm sure she's not perfect. Nobody's perfect, Caoimhe." I liked how she said my name. All drawly, like "Kweee-eeee-vaw."

"True, but she's as close as you can get. She's all natural blonde, and golden skin, and she's got the *perfect* body. Boobs like you can't even imagine, legs up to her neck. Everything about her is top notch." I wasn't exaggerating. Mar was sickening, in the good way. But also a little bit in the bad way, maybe.

"Maybe *she's* boyfriend material then, yeah?" American Woman flashed me a smile. It was weird when people smiled, and you couldn't see their eyes. Or when their eyes were covered in giant black oval things that made them look like a fly. That was even weirder.

"Haha! No, she doesn't swing that way, unfortunately," I said, like some sort of vaginal veteran, and not the actual Baby Dykeling that I was.

"And you do?" She said it in a matter-of-fact way, not a judgmental one. Americans were probably different, though. More open minded. Apart from the Bibley ones, anyway.

"Lately, yeah. Lately that's the only way I've been swinging." Swinging and missing, mostly, I thought.

"Interesting! I'm happy for you. And is there a girl? A special one, I mean?" She smoked, which was strange to see an American doing. But we were backstage, so she probably had some connection to one of the bands, and rock and roll people all smoked, even the American ones.

"Yeah. Well, there was actually two special ones, but one of them ran away, with all the – um, she's not here anymore. It's just the other one. And I've probably fucked that up now, so..." I didn't know if I had or I hadn't, but everything felt like it was gone to shit today, so that might as well have, too.

"Fucked it up beyond all repair, or..."

"Well, I dunno if it's FUBAR quite yet. But I've definitely been an idiot, more than once this weekend, and it's all kind of shitty right now. But that's *my* fault. *I made my bed, I'll lie in it*," I said, singing the last bit, just because.

"You're Miss World, somebody kill you?" She had a great laugh; it was all throaty.

"Exactly!" This chick understood me. And she was familiar with the classics, too. She could stay.

"So where is she now? This special girl, I mean. She

gone as well? Or is she still kicking around here somewhere?" She leaned down to light my fag for me and I got a better look at her face for a second. She suddenly looked very familiar, especially the nose, but I couldn't quite place her. Being absolutely shitfaced wasn't exactly helping my memory, either.

"She's out the front somewhere, with her ex-boyfriend," I said, taking a long drag.

"Oh. That doesn't sound good," said Miss Familiar Face.

"No, he's gay now," I said, realising how ridiculous all of this must sound.

"He's gay??? What a life you lead, honey."

"I say that all the time!!! Well, in my head, anyway, like."

"Heh. Well it's true. So, what's the other thing?"

"What's what other thing?" I said, having another slurp of my concoction. It was starting to taste rank now, because the sun was making it go warm, and the fizz was almost gone.

"Oh, I just... I see *pain* in you that's much bigger than just a missed gig, or a broken heart. I'm like – I have a pain like that, so I can see it in other people, sometimes? You lost someone, right? Someone died?"

"Wow, you *are* good," I said, swallowing, even though there wasn't anything in my mouth anymore.

"Oh you have no idea, baby girl. So, spill? You don't have to if you don't want to. But I've got this feeling – this *kismet*, yeah? – Feels like I was *destined* to meet you today, and I was meant to help you? So, if I can?" She gave me another smile, and it was almost on the tip of my tongue – where I knew her face from. I put it to the side for a second, took another drag on my ciggie, then I told this nice stranger all about Jon Musgrave, about my sister Áine, and about how I ended up joining Crane, becoming almost famous, and how I came to Cork to play in a music festival but ended up experiencing *so much more* – pretty much everything except actually *playing* at a music festival.

*****

"Wow. That's a hell of a story, Caoimhe." American Woman had stayed quiet all the way through my insane, meandering ramblings, but it had still felt a bit like a therapist session, because of me lying down, eyes closed for most of it – half from the sun, half because I was so fucking wasted now – and her sitting up, nodding occasionally.

"I wish it *was* just a story, though. Instead of being my actual life." I stubbed my fag out halfway before the end, because I'd been chain-smoking, and my lungs felt like they were churning butter.

"Yeah, that's true. I mean, I'm so sorry you had to go through all that, but look at you now, honey. You're…"

"Drunk in a field, recovering from shitloads of drugs?" I said, because it was true.

"Haha! That too, but no. You're stronger." I liked her accent. It made words sound cool, like in a movie.

"I am?" I was *not*.

"You're still here, aren't you?"

"Barely," I said, taking another sip of the lukewarm rankness, because the fags had made me parched. Water was what I really needed.

"Don't be so hard on yourself. When I lost, well, when my husband died, I went crazy."

"Your husband?"

"Well, yeah…"

"How did he… if you don't mind me asking?" I wasn't

sure if it was okay, but then I'd just spilled my actual guts to her, and I didn't even know her name, so.

"Heh. You're cute. *If you don't mind me asking...*" I still couldn't see her face properly, and trying to look was giving me a migraine, so I stopped doing it.

"I'm sorry," I said. I'd probably pried too much. I did that a lot.

"No need to be sorry, I just thought you would- I thought everybody – well, maybe not. Okay, well my guy, he was in a lot of pain. Physical, mental, there was so much of it, and he found it so hard to talk about, or to deal with it. So, one day, he just checked out, you know?" She sounded really sad. I wondered how long ago it was, because she was still pretty young. Younger than most widows, anyway. Not younger than me, but I wasn't technically a widow, really.

"Checked out?" I said, being very careful not to go too far with the prying this time.

"You really don't – heh. Yeah, he took his own life. I didn't know. For days. He was just gone. And then one day, I found out, well. That he was really gone."

"Oh. I'm so sorry." Why didn't I know her name, damn it?!

"Yeah, it was hard, honey. Especially with all the – especially when it was so public, and out there, and… But it was more than a year ago now, and I'm stronger every day. And I have our daughter, and she has his beautiful face. So he's with me, all the time. I see him in her, I feel him in me, and all around me." She sounded sad again, but of course she was. It was an awful thing to have happened to her, especially with a kid.

"That's something good at least, I guess?" I said. I was suddenly aware of how drunk I must sound. It felt kind of rude – trying to be sympathetic to someone, when you sounded like a mad pirate off a movie or something. She didn't seem to mind, though. I was going to ask her something else, when Aisling Flanagan appeared out of thin air.

"CAOIMHE!!! Oh my God, there you are! I've found you. Quickly, you have to-" she lost the flow of whatever she was saying when she spotted my American Woman.

"Hi there," said my new friend, to my old friend. Aisling looked like she'd seen every ghost in the history of ghosts.

"Oh my God. Oh my God, it's really you, isn't it? Oh Jesus, I'm so- I'm like your biggest fan. Jesus, I'm shaking! I LOVE YOU!!! Eeeeeeeeee!" She looked like she was going to collapse and die. I was enormously confused. I needed to sit up, but I couldn't quite manage it.

"Um, thank you. Nice to be appreciated. Nice to be recognised, too, hehehe," said my American Woman, turning to me and winking. I was definitely sitting up, now.

"Jesus fucking Christ," I said, when it finally dawned on me who I'd been speaking to all along.

"Oh, wow, - this is just… eeeeeee! Um, anyway, sorry! *Focus, Aisling, focus!* Ahhhhh, CAOIMHE!"

"YES???" I was going to wake up in the back of the minibus any minute now.

"They've given ye the slot!"

"Which slot?" I said, trying to get my shit together but really failing. My head was absolutely spinning, and I was about one stray burp away from puking up all the Hennessy, Diet Coke, Martell, chips, and fish.

"Menswear's slot! They can't make it! They – the promoters, they want you guys to do it instead!!!"

"What??? But what about Niall?"

"He's been released! Brian is driving over to pick him

up now!" Aisling still looked like she was going to have a heart attack, and I'd probably join her in a minute. It was all too crazy, even for this weekend.

"But Tim!? And Ian?" We still needed them, and at least one of them was currently orbiting the moon.

"We're going to go get them now!!! That's why we need you!!!" Aisling was pulling me up by my shoulders, completely oblivious to how much she was risking getting vommed on.

"Why me???" I managed to get up, just about.

"Because I dunno, cos Richie said you'll know how to get Tim back to normal, or something. Can we discuss it on the way? We have like twenty-five minutes!!!"

"Okay!!! Okay, I'm coming. Hang on one second, though." I dropped down onto the ground again, on my knees, and put out my arms. "Thank you! For the chat, and the help, and the being nice to me. Can I have a hug?"

"You're totally welcome, baby girl. Come here and get some of this." I got wrapped up in her hug for a few lovely seconds. I couldn't believe this was happening. I wanted to pinch myself, but my hands were all full of actual Courtney Love, so I couldn't. "There you are, that's better, honey. Now, go get your band together, get yourself back here, and give these *motherfuckers* a show they'll never forget!"

I stood up, but I might as well have floated. I *knew* that nose was familiar. Aisling was already breaking into a dash, so I did too. Twenty-five minutes didn't sound like a lot. We'd make it, though. We *had* to make it. Kismet, all over the shop.

*****

"How could you not know it was her?" Richie said. We were in Benson's van, running red lights and breaking inner city speed limits.

"I just... it was sunny! She had big glasses on! I don't know!" No wonder she'd sounded all funny when I didn't know how her husband died. If I hadn't been so drunk right now, I'd have been mortified.

"Remind me never to call you as an eyewitness if I'm up for murder," Bríd said, because they were all having a go, now.

"I should have hugged her, too. Why didn't I hug her, Caoimhe? Why didn't you tell me to hug her?" Aisling was still in a bit of a daze, poor thing.

"I didn't know I had – Benson, are we there yet?" His Encyclopaedia Britannica hippy van was cool, but it lacked the ability to see out of the sides. There were windows, but he had curtains over them, and I was too lazy and drunk to stand up and open them.

"We just came into the car park, we've got plenty of time," he said, lying about the second bit. It took ten minutes to get here, and it would take ten minutes to get back. That didn't leave a lot of minutes out of twenty-five.

"Okay, cool! Now, listen up," I said, because I had a drunken plan. It wasn't a *good* drunken plan, but it was some words in my brain that knew how to come out of my mouth, and that was the best we had right now.

"Listening!" said Aisling, looking all business and no barbecue. Head Girl mode engaged.

"Benson and Richie, ye need to get Tim's big stupid keyboard and case and bring them down here."

"What about Ian?" said Richie.

"You also have to get big stupid Ian and his guitars and cases down here, okay?"

"Okay, that's doable. What are ye gonna do?" B said, turning off the engine and opening his door.

"Us ladies are gonna bag ourselves a Weird Naked Tim," I said.

"By fair means or foul," Marian said, hopping down out of the van, with Richie's help.

"I might have to hold you to that, Mar," I said. Hers was going to be the least physically demanding part of my plan, but probably the most important. I'd explain more to them on the way to the room, once Richie was out of the way.

"We'll try to take him alive, but I'm not making any promises," said Aisling, lighting up a fag that she definitely hadn't got off me, the cailín dána. We were already in the lift.

*****

"Okay, people. Prepare yourself now, for the madness and the nakedness. We're going in." I pushed Tim's thankfully unlocked door and we entered his spooky room. *Heroin*, by the Velvet Underground was playing, which did not help settle me.

"Tim?" said Bríd.

"Tim, dear! Come out, we have good news!" Aisling said, still puffing on the fag she wasn't supposed to be having.

"He's gone again," I said, then there was a horror movie door creak, and our keyboard player emerged from the big wardrobe in the corner.

"News is a construct of the cloistered mind," he said, still very naked.

"Shut up, Tim. We've got the spot. The gig. We're playing!" I said, maintaining steady eye contact, even though his eyes were anything but steady. They were darting around the candlelit room, probably seeing ghosts that weren't there, or ghosts that *were* there. Both were equally possible.

"I don't need to *play*, Caoimhe. I don't need your childish games. I don't need anything, or anyone. I am... complete."

"He's completely mental," Aisling whispered to me, stubbing her fag out in the waxy bit of one of Tim's candles, because she couldn't have it in her hand when she did the thing I wanted her to do. Good thinking out of her.

"Stick to the plan," I said, nodding to where I needed her to go.

"Tim, it's okay – we understand you; we really do. We just – we just need your help," said Marian, standing in front of him, with me and Bríd on either side of her. Aisling was in position, bending down behind him, trying desperately to ignore his naked arsehole.

"You need my guidance?" said Tim, looking more interested now.

"Kind of," she said.

"She needs you to look at something for her, Tim," I said, double checking that the bathroom door was open.

"I can do that. My eyes have been opened. The scales have been lifted from me. I see everything, with a new light, and understanding."

"Yeah, but have you seen *these*?" said Marian, flipping her top up and showing him the wonders beneath. Tim's very open eyes suddenly got even more open, as did his mouth.

"NOW!" I said, and me and Bríd rushed him, grabbing onto one arm each and gripping tight. Aisling wrapped his ankles with both her arms like she was playing on the wing for Garryowen, then she lifted him up, so he was horizontal between the three of us.

"Marian! Shower!" I shouted, not sure how long we could hold him up for; he was heavier than he looked. She sprinted into the en suite and turned on the water.

"WHAT ARE YOU-"

"Shut up, nature boy, we're fixing you!" said Aisling, moving quickly across the room after Bríd and me, until we were at the open glass door of the shower.

"One! Two! Threeeeee!" we all said, except Marian, who was busy putting her tits away. She'd taken one for the team today. Her sacrifice wouldn't be forgotten.

"How much time have we got?" I said, asking none of them in particular. Tim was writhing like a jellyfish under the steamy water, but he wasn't trying to escape.

"Not enough!" said Aisling. "TURN THE COLD ON!"

"Grab some towels there, Bríd. I'll go find him some clothes," I said, trying to ignore the screams.

"Ooh, I like this one, turn it up," said Marian, because *Perfect Day* was on the CD player now. Apt, really, as it was turning out to be quite a perfect day after all. Well, except if you were Tim. Or Frank. Or Niall. Still though.

*****

"I saw your girlfriend's breasts," said Tim, back in the van, still quite wet, but pretty much back to normal, thankfully.

"Shut up, Tim!" said Richie, too far away to punch him.

"Yeah, shut up, Tim," said Aisling. "She's not his girlfriend." She was no longer smoking. She'd robbed some more chewing gum off me, to cover up her sins.

"Shut up, Aisling," said Richie. Marian gave his leg a squeeze, and he cheered up, slightly.

"How come he got to see tits, and I just got shouted at?" said Ian, who was also back to his normal self, although it was harder to tell with him, cos he was such a fucking gowl.

"Because you don't deserve them," I said. He had a really cool top on. A blue Adidas one, with yellow stripes and piping. The yellow was a particularly lovely shade – like buttercup flowers.

"Nobody deserves them!" Richie said, scowling at everyone, but mainly at Tim and Ian.

"I didn't even see them," I said, because it was true. I deliberately hadn't looked, cos I was a gentlewoman, and I was too busy grabbing Weird Naked Tim anyway.

"You can have a look at them later, honey," Marian said, giving me a wink.

"Can I really?" I said, lighting a cigarette. We'd been moving for at least five minutes now, but I didn't know how fast or how far.

"Nope!" she said, crossing her arms and sticking out her tongue at me.

"Speaking of boobs, where's Ciara? Did any of ye tell her that the gig is back on?" said Benson, not looking back, eyes still on the road.

"Why did speaking about boobs remind you of *her*?" Bríd asked, too far away to punch him.

"She's out watching the bands, with *Zachary*. She's gonna see us when we get on stage. *If* we get on stage, that is. What's the time? Benson? How close are we?" I said, starting to get really anxious now. My head was still drunk and dizzy, and I felt a bit vomity. All that running around and carrying a whole human boy into the shower had not helped at all.

"Shhhh! Calm down. I'll get us there. I promise," said B, but I didn't believe him – promise or no promise.

"Is there any word about Niall?" Bríd said, opening a can of Budweiser. The smell of it, even from as far away as she was, made me want to spew. I felt like I was seasick, and the way Benson was driving wasn't making my ship any steadier.

"How would there be any word? Carrier pigeon? Smoke signals?" Ian was definitely back to his worst. We didn't have to worry about him anymore.

"I don't – shut up, Ian. No wonder no one wants to show you their tits," she said, drinking some more of her disgusting lager as we went around another bend, and everyone tried not to fall off their seats.

"I'm gonna puke," I said, and then I puked, because I was true to my word, if nothing else.

"CAOIMHE!!!" said Tim, diving out of the way before he got covered in the contents of my stomach. Everyone else made various noises and cries of disgust. I was just really impressed that I hadn't got any on my dress or my Converse. Chucking up on my Chucks would have been poetry, mind.

"You're cleaning that up, Shox!" shouted Benson, from the front.

"Fuck you, B. We'll call it quits for you ruining my dress with your ancient wizard spunk!" I said, and he shut up then.

"We're here!" Aisling said, pointing towards the front and the big Páirc Uí Chaoimh out the window.

"YES! WE MADE IT!" said Tim, as if he wasn't the main reason we almost hadn't.

"Okay, go go go! And don't slip on the vomit!" I said, stepping carefully over the mess of my own making, marvelling at how there were always diced carrots in it, no matter if you'd eaten them or not that day.

*****

"Go go go!" I said, shouting at everyone around me, as we got through the backstage fence gate thing and were almost at the steps. Some MCD guy got in my way, and I had to stop running – which was good, because I had the lungs of a sixty year old and I was about to drop dead.

"You're late," he said, showing me his watch.

"They're still playing!" I said, hands on my knees, trying to steal some breath out of the air around me.

"They're still playing because you're late," he said, like some sort of wise, annoying Yoda cunt.

"Okay," I said. I wanted a fag. That would be the best thing to fix the shortness of breath – suffocating myself with toxic fumes.

"Are we all here?" Richie said, holding some drumsticks. I couldn't remember him having them in the van, but he must have.

"We're missing one of us," Tim said. His keyboard case was a lot thicker than the guitar cases, because it had the stand in it too, folded up.

"Who are you missing? I thought you said you had everyone now. That's what your manager told me. Listen, if ye don't have the full band-"

"We have a full band, we're all here," I lied. Where the hell was Brian? They were going to cancel us again, and then I might have to kill someone, or just burst out crying.

"You sure?" he said, looking around at all of us, trying to figure out who wasn't there. Luckily we weren't famous enough for him to know how many of us were supposed to be here.

"Is this the face of someone who lies to figures of authority?" I said, pointing at myself.

"Ummmm, okay then, they're finished now. You got fifteen minutes to set up, try and get it done in ten, yeah?"

"So that we have time for an extra song?" said Ian, picking up his two cases to take them up the steps.

"Nope," said the guy from MCD, them he walked away without explaining any further, the prick.

"Right then," I said, still feeling vomity and lightheaded, but taking charge regardless, because no one else seemed to be. "Let's get set up, and if we're lucky, Brian and Niall will be back before we start the first one." I nodded at the Wildhearts as they came down the steps and walked past us. They were all kind of old, and very rockerish.

"Okay, grand. I'll go check out the kit," said Richie. All the earlier bands were using Dodgy's drums. You were supposed to supply your own cymbals and bass pedal, he said to me earlier, but he'd asked the guy from my best friends Revelino for a loan of his ones.

"I'll go set up," said Tim. He still looked slightly mystical and away with the fairies, but he had clothes on, and he was here; that was enough for me.

"Yeah, whatever," Ian said, trudging up the steps after him.

"Any chance you have a secret mobile phone on you that you can call your beau with?" I said to Aisling, suddenly aware that I was gasping for some water.

"Not even a pager, sorry," she said. She was going to be a doctor, so she probably would have one, one day.

"Want us to go have a look out for them?" Bríd said? She meant her, Mar, and Benson, but he wasn't back yet from parking the van somewhere.

"Nah, a watched pot never boils, like. Why don't you go find Ciara, see if she's – oh wait, no. She's with that guy, and he doesn't have a pass, never mind it."

"Yeah. I'm gonna go out there anyway, though. It'll be cooler to watch ye from the real crowd. If B comes back here, tell him that's where I am, chickee. Break a leg, yeah?" She gave me a big hug and she went off, so it was just me and Mar and Aisling now.

"Suppose you two want to go out there as well, yeah?" I said. I needed that water, quickly, before it was too late. The bar wasn't far, I could make it there and back in time.

"Yeah, I think so. We'll come back in when you're finished though. To give you champagne and throw flowers at you," Aisling said, squeezing my hand.

"Fine, then! ABANDON ME, like everyone else does!" I said, doing an offended face, then we had one big squooshy hug between the three of us. I watched them go, then I looked at the stage, with the lads all up there, and I got a little nervous and excited. Water first, then I'd go check out the mic, and then Niall would definitely arrive on time, and everything would go absolutely brilliantly. Or he wouldn't arrive at all, and everything would go to absolute shit. Both were equally possible.

*****

Walking out onto the stage was mental. There was a much bigger crowd now than there would have been for our actual slot, but that wasn't necessarily a good thing, because they weren't here to see us. No one whooped or cheered when I walked across, even with my very obvious hair. There was so little reaction that I changed direction and went over to Richie behind the drums instead of going to the mic stand. I felt tiny, all of a sudden. Insignificant, like I was nothing. It wasn't a great start. Richie stopped kicking his borrowed bass pedal and laid off hitting the cymbals, when he saw my face.

"What's wrong, sham?"

"I dunno... I feel like – like I shouldn't be here," I said.

"Fuck off back to the hotel then," Ian said, not helping, because I wasn't in the mood to tolerate his alleged humour.

"Shut up, Ian, or I'll box the head off you," Richie said, in his most Thomondgatey voice. Ian rolled his eyes and went back to making guitar tuning noises. I looked over at Tim, who was already fully set up. He gave me a wave, and a weird grin that made me wonder was he still mental, even after we'd held him down and showered the madness out of him.

"I feel like an imposter, Rich. I feel like all these people are gonna look at me and think, who does this bitch think she is?" I didn't turn around to look at them when I mentioned them. I was sort of frozen, I couldn't turn around even if I wanted to. We hadn't played to a crowd that size before. And it was in the daytime, so you couldn't avoid seeing them. They were very *there*.

"Ah, that's normal Caoimhe. Shur everyone is like that, sometimes." Richie was very good at being a friend. He'd probably make a great boyfriend, really, if he wasn't such a homosexual when it came to finding me attractive.

"Thanks, Rich. I'm sorry we had to use your Marian's boobs to capture Tim and save him from the madness. I'll show you mine if you like, to make up for it."

"Don't be disgusting, Caoimhe. I don't want to see your tits."

"Thanks, Rich." Such a gent.

"Go do your one-two, one-two thing, Kweev. It'll make you feel better, I promise."

"Right, five minutes, Crane!" shouted a clipboard girl from the side of the stage. No Niall yet, but they didn't know we were waiting for him. His bass was here, in a stand. I wondered if I could learn how to play it in five minutes.

"He's not coming!" Ian said, wandering past me, trailing a purple guitar lead behind him. Niall banged some more on the drums, which didn't help with my nerves at all. The crowd were getting bored. They'd be shouting at us soon. Where the fuck were Brian and Niall, though? I got to the mic and picked it up, deliberately not looking at the crowd. There were one or two sleazy wolf whistles, so at least my status as a piece of meat was still good.

"One-two! One-two-one. One-two!" It was incredibly loud, but of course it would be. It was a big stadium, the noise had to travel really far, even if it was only about half full.

"Two minutes, Crane!" said clipboard girl. Fuuuuuuuuck. We weren't going to make it. Two minutes. 120 seconds. Not even that, because it was already counting down. I looked around at the others. They all looked sheepish, except Tim, who was staring into space and grinning like an idiot. The two minutes were up now. No one had said they were, but they had to be. It was game over. We were done. I wanted to cry, or to vomit again. Both were equally possible. A voice came over the PA and made me jump.

"Okay, guys and girls. As you know, we've had a few changes to the lineup today. Menswear SADLY will not be able to get here in time to play..." A massive section of the crowd started booing and jeering, and the blood in my veins went all chilly, because even though they weren't, it felt like those boos were for us.

"I know, I know! We're so sorry, guys and girls. Especially to those of you who came from as far away as England to see the boys. One or two of you from as far as the USA!" Oh fucking Jesus, we were dead. The Menswear superfans were going to literally kill us, figuratively speaking.

"But! It's not all bad news! We've got one of the best new bands in Ireland to take their place!" Please stop saying we're taking their place. No one can take their place. Please stop, disembodied voice guy.

"All the way from LIMERICK CITY!!!" Oh God.

"Is it the Cranberries?" shouted some little fucker in the front row, and everyone heard him.

"Haha, not quite!" Disembodied PA guy had heard him too, apparently. "But no, maybe even BETTER than that..." Jesus Christ please stop saying things, sir.

"Please put your hands together, Páirc Uí Chaoimh, and give a big Feile welcome, to CRAAAAAAANE!!!" The crowd made a noise that was about 20% clapping, 80% *who the fuck are Crane?*

"Hello Páirc Uí Chaoimh!!!" I shouted down the mic, just to banish the lack of clapping or enthusiasm. They didn't exactly scream back at me.

"Hello Féile 95!!!" I shouted, which made even less sense than saying hello to a GAA stadium. The shout back was better this time, louder. We still had no bassist. I was literally just stalling until they figured us out and banned us for life.

"Have we got anybody here from Cork?" There were bound to be some, in fairness. Big cheer back. Now we were cooking with… something.

"Have we anyone here from LIMERICK?" I said, and the shout was surprisingly big, too. A lot of people here were clearly liars, but it was all good for me.

"And is anyone here from DUBLIN???" This time the response was a mixture of Dubs cheering and everyone who wasn't from Dublin hissing and booing.

"Well, FUCK OFF HOME, THEN!" I shouted, and that got the biggest cheer so far. I'd robbed the whole routine from the singer off the Sultans of Ping, but they weren't playing this thing, so he couldn't do me for it.

I'd run out of stalling tactics, I was either going to have to start up a song without a bassist, or feign a massive heart attack and get taken off on a stretcher by the St John's Ambulance paramedics I could see down by the crash barriers. I looked into the crowd to see if I could see any of the lads, but it was too sunny, and they were too far away. I literally couldn't spot Courtney Love when she was sitting next to my head, talking to me, though. There was some feedback from a speaker or from another mic. I put my fingers in my ears to stop it zapping my brain. We were fucked. Every second I stood there in front of all those people, saying nothing and playing nothing, felt like an hour. The other mic, wherever it was, made the feedback sound again, and then someone's voice came over the PA.

"Rubber inner tubes? I barely touched her! Thank you, I'm here all week." I knew that voice. I turned around and saw our giant ginger Chewbacca, alive and well, standing by the backup mic stand, bass guitar strapped to him, with a smile as wide as the Shannon estuary. Ian started the guitar intro for *Season of the Witch*. Two bars later, Niall's bass came in. Two bars after that, and I put the mic to my lips.

"*Ah, when I look out, my wind-eau. Many sights, to see-ee-eee. And when I look in my wind-eau. So many different, people to be-eeee.*"

We'd done it. We'd made it. We were literally playing Féile 95, in front of more people than we'd ever played to before – regardless of how that had come to be. The sun was shining, the boys sounded great, and I suddenly didn't feel like an imposter anymore. I didn't feel insignificant or small, up on stage. I felt like Kweeva Shox, and I felt like I fucking *belonged* here. What a life we led.

TWENTY-SIX

"*M*ust be the season of the wiiiiiiiiiiitch, yeahhh!*"* I finished the song on my knees, front of stage, the crowd having sung the chorus with me for about ten extra refrains, which wasn't unusual. That was kind of the reason we started putting it in the set; it was so catchy that even if they didn't know it, they knew it by the time we finished it. Ian and Richie were still going, because a rock and roll ending was kind of compulsory in front of a crowd this big. I picked my exhausted drunk self up off the floor.

"Thank you! Thanks! Wow! *Fuck* me *pink*." I looked out at all the happy, drunk, sunburned Irish faces. They looked pretty into it. The Menswear fanlings were probably already in the toilets, slashing their wrists, poor loves. "This next one is…" Fuck, I didn't know what the next one was – a combination of being plastered and not having a piece of paper by my feet with the song order written on it. Niall played a few notes behind me, but then he stopped. Richie shouted "*Deep Breaths*!" and Niall went again, this time with the real intro. After a bar or two the drums kicked in, then a blast of organ from Tim. He'd done a completely new solo for *Season of the Witch*, but it was all in tune and it was the right length, so it was grand. I listened for my cue.

"*Easy go, easy come. I'm sensitive, you are numb. Your eyes are closed, but I can't see. Nothing here is healing me.*" Ian's distortion pedal ripped through the speakers and Tim's keyboard switched over to high-pitched violin synth sounds.

"*Friends are here, I'm not alone. Sympathy comes down a phone. You'll be okay, it's not the end. Living is the best revenge.*" Ian's pedal shut off, and he switched to lead, because the chorus on this one was much quieter than the verses.

"*They told me I should take things slow, but really how slow can I go? They said that I should take deep breaths, but you're not breathing, really. You're not breathing freely. You're not breathing, really. You're not breathing freely.*"

Ian's pedal kicked in again, and I rushed along the stage, high on the adrenaline. It wasn't even a happy song – I'd written it about something awful – but that didn't matter now. I stopped running just in time for the next cue.

"*Grab your friends, pour the drinks. See how high that we can sink. Toasting what you might have been. We'll never know, it's such a sin.*" Just one verse this time before the chorus, and this time the chorus had a screaming bit at the end, like Kim from the Muffs, or my new Auntie, Courtney Love might do. Hopefully my poor fragile throat would survive it enough to be able to sing the final verses. Or to sing the rest of our set.

I was close enough to the crowd to notice one or two people singing along, which was mental, although it wasn't that mental, because we'd got into the Top Ten with this one.

"*They told me I should take things slow, but really how slow can I go? They said that I should take deep breaths, but you're not breathing, really. You're not breathing freely. You're not breathing, really. You're not breathing freely. You're not freely breathing, YOU'RE NOT REALLY BREATHIIIIIIIIIIINGG-GGG, YEAAAAAAHHHH!!!!*"

Tim went back to the big organ sounds, and Ian started his solo. I never knew what to do during guitar solos. I spotted a big Marshall amp that was get-up-onable, and I got up on it. Ian was hitting every note perfectly, and it was amazing hearing it this loud – from both the amps pointing out at Páirc Uí Chaoimh and the monitors scattered all over the floor. I wanted a drink of some sort, but we didn't have any lackeys to bring me one. Solo was nearly over anyway; I'd get one after the song. I hopped down from my perch and walked over to Niall, because I'd missed seeing his silly face all of today.

"If they ask, say I'm fine. Another night, another line. Anything to pause the pain. Bedside vigil, graveyard rain." Sometimes I forgot how personal these lyrics were, until I heard myself singing them out loud. To most people listening though, they were probably quite vague. I was on my knees again now, for the old *Deep Breaths* switcheroo. After this much quieter verse, the last chorus got very loud.

"Pat my back and say you're proud. Take my life and live it loud. Don't forget to have your fun. He'd want you to mooove on. Move on. Move on. Move ooooooonnnn." I leapt to my feet as the guitar kicked back in, with Ian's heaviest pedal.

"They told me I should take things slow, but really how slow can I go? They said that I should take deep breaths, but you're not breathing, really. You're not breathing freely. You're not breathing, really. You're not breathing freely. YOURE NOT FREELY BREATHING! YOU'RE NOT REALLY BREATHING! YOU'RE NOT BREATHING FREELY! YOU'RE NOT BREATHING, REALLY! YOURE. NOT. REALLY. BREATHIIIIIIIIIIINGGGGG, YEAAAAAAHHHH!!!!" I was on my back, lying down, having a bit of a Jim Morrison writhe, while the rest of them did another rock and roll finish. I wasn't as out of control as I was pretending to be, though. You could tell by the way I was carefully angling my body, so the crowd weren't able to see up my dress. Couldn't have someone taking a sly photograph of my hoo-hoo. Not on Jesus's special day.

"Okay, this next one's called *Quiet Pleas*," I said, looking at the sheet of paper I'd nicked off Niall, because he didn't deserve to have it, what with all the delaying he'd caused, and the general criminal behaviour. I liked the title – I liked wordplay. Wasn't my title, it was Richie's, but he probably also liked wordplay, because he'd got into Trinity College to do English, or so the whispers went.

"I wanna dedicate this to all the ladies here who've ever been in love…" A few cheers from the crowd, a few groans.

"…with a fucking *psychopath!*" Much more cheering, and a bit of applause, too. I looked around to find Ian's eyes, because this one needed us both to start at the same time, like *Basket Case*. Richie tapped us in with his sticks, and off we went.

"*You're a maniac, but you're not on the floor. You do all your maniac-ing outside my door. I shot five or six bullets, and I'm not even sorry. You're a punk feeling lucky, I'm Debbie Harry.*" Tim was on guitar instead of keyboards for this one, because it was heavy and fast, and Ian played really cool lead all the way through.

"*You're the class clown, I'm the teacher's pet. You're a French peasant, I'm Marie Antoinette. You're a flat Pepsi, I'm Bacardi and Coke. I'm the Queen of Everything, you're a fucking joke.*" This song was pretty vicious. The guy it was about had probably never heard it. Hopefully he would, someday, though. Chorus!

"*I've told you once, I've told you fifty times, but nothing sticks. How do I show you that I'm interested in other p…eople? I've tried everything – the soft approach, the short sharp shock. Why can't you understand I no longer enjoy your c…ompany?*" God, I was hilarious, all the same. Time for another guitar solo and a much-deserved sit down on the giant Marshall amp. I liked the way the massive, hummy vibrations off it felt. It was basically the most sex I'd had all weekend.

*****

"How was prison, anyway?" I said to Niall, in between songs, when I went over to steal water off him.

"I wasn't in prison," he said, pushing my mic away from our faces with his giant fingers, so the crowd couldn't be part of our conversation.

"Jail, then. Tomayto potahto." He didn't actually have water, he just had random pints on top of his amp, so I'd taken a Bulmer's. Rank, warmish, but better than the literally nothing I'd had five seconds ago, so.

"I wasn't in jail, either. I thought your dad was a lawyer, for fuck's sake."

"Solicitor, actually," I said, although I didn't think there was any difference.

"Potato, tomato. Actually, speaking of lawyers, and your dad, can you-"

"Hold that thought, big boy. We're back," I said, seeing Tim had put away the Fender and was behind the keyboards again, ready to motor. I put the mic back up to my mouth and started back towards my adoring public.

"Uhhhh, sorry about that. This one's called *Cervix Charge*." Tim started the plinky plunky piano intro that always fooled people into thinking this one was going to be a slowie.

"*I'm not really sure about, the things I cannot do without, I miss when you're not next to me, it's nothing more than sex to me, this thing...*" Ian came in with one heavy chord and let it ring out.

"*Weeeeee. Haaaaave.*" Niall's bass started up – the same note as Ian, repeated, then a different note, also repeated. Ian came back with some choppy guitar. It all sounded a bit *Psycho Killer*, but not quite, so David Byrne couldn't do us for it. Tim's piano got more frantic, and Richie finally came in with a beat that was so full it was like several rolls stitched together. I bounced up and down on the spot, waiting to come in again.

"*Maybe it's not love and maybe it's not even liiiiike, oh. Sometimes I wanna kill you boy, you make me fucking psyyyyyy-cho!*" I always did a crazy face for that part, even when there weren't any cameras on me – which was all the time, really. Except for right now.

"*All the ways you touch – you're in my body, on my mind. Feeling you, you're filling me – my thoughts get left behind.*" This one wasn't about anyone in particular. I just wrote the words one day when I had a massive horn. That occasional, rare type of horn when you start sizing up root vegetables in the fridge. We'd all been there at some point.

"*Don't whisper sweet nothings, I've heard them all before, boy. Just pull my hair and give me bruises from the floor, boy. Don't ask me nice – just push me up against that wall. Don't take my number and pretend you're gonna call.*" This song didn't really have a chorus, it was all about the mad guitar and piano solo in the middle. Ian had written the tune – I only added the lyrics. That was probably why they were so graphically about lady-sex. Just to annoy him. They were starting their bit now, so I put my mic in its stand and lit up a fag.

There was a small gap between the edge of the stage and the barriers that had nothing in it, apart from a few random cables, and one fat security guy who was way down the other end. I wondered if I should do a Bono at Live Aid. I decided I definitely should, because fuck it, it was Christmas – even if the poor Ethiopian fellas didn't know it was. I hopped down, and the people up the front started screaming and waving at me. This was the life! Still keeping half an eye on the fat controller, I ran across the gap and threw myself into a wall of arms and hugs. It was like the exact opposite of a good time if you were the famously introverted Caoimhe O'Shaughnessy, but I was the famously famous Kweeva Shox now, so it was grand. Some of the hugging was turning a bit tit-gropey now, so I made sure to keep moving. The band were still belting out the solo above and behind me, so I had plenty of time, yet. I spotted a lad smoking a joint, bold as brass, and made my way over to him, quickly.

"Hi!" I said, wishing I'd brought the mic with me now. He regarded me, Sartrely.

"Hey there." English accent. Maybe he was a Menswear fan. He seemed a bit old for that, though. And a bit male. I grabbed the yoke out of his mouth, because I was a cheeky little scamp.

"Oi!" he said, but he was smiling. Easier to ask for forgiveness than permission, I thought.

"Won't be a sec," I said, taking a massive drag. The crowd gave a big cheer, even the ones way down the back, and I didn't understand why until I looked where Mr. English Guy was pointing, and I saw that I was on the big screen. Whoops.

"Smile, we're on Cannabis Camera," I said, because I was hilarious.

"Oh that's not cannabis," he said, doing a face. He was correct, too. It didn't taste like any hash I'd ever smoked. It didn't even taste like Frank's weird weed.

"What is it, then?" I spotted the fat security guy coming towards us, and I wasn't sure if it was because I was off the stage, or because I had been up on the big screens, and the TV cameras too, probably, smoking a big load of...

"Opium!" he said, as if that was a normal thing to come out of anyone's mouth in a GAA field in Cork.

"OPIUM???"

"Yeah. Mixed with a bit of tobacco, mate. I'm not insane," said the clearly insane man. Fat controller was almost next to us now; he really did not move fast.

"Are you Dorian Gray? Is this Victorian London? Am I a Chinese sailor?" I said, shoving the thing back into his hand so that the chubby fella couldn't do me for it. I wasn't phoning Dad twice in one day to get someone out of jail.

"What's going on here then?" said the fat controller.

"A rock concert!" I said, swerving away from him and making a jump at the stage. I pulled myself up first time and rolled over on my side, like Nancy Sinatra in that weird video clip of her singing *My Baby Shot Me Down* on a TV programme that I'd seen once. The solo was pretty much finished, I just had to sing the last part, which wasn't a chorus and wasn't a verse, it was just some words. I got to the stand just in time.

"Woo!" I said, taking the mic out and running back to the front of the stage, and the sea of lovely drunken faces.

"*I'm into you, you're into me, I come with you, you come with me, I'm into you, you're inside me, I come with you, you come in me, I'm underneath and you're on top, let's switch around, let's never stop, I'm feeling you, you're feeling me, I'm feeling you, you're filling me, I'm good inside, cos you're inside, I'm satisfied, think I just died, oh what a... riiiiiiiiide.*" I took a bow and spun around to make the rest of them take one too, even though it wasn't our last song. Or maybe it might be, if the fat controller told the clipboard girl that I'd been smoking heroin joints with filthy English immigrants. What a life we led.

*****

"Okaaaaaaaay! How's everyone doing? You all right?" I was sitting on the amp again. Creature of habit. The crowd were saying things back, but I was fucked if I could hear any of them individually, so it wasn't really a conversation.

"Just time for one more quick one and then wrap it up!" shouted clipboard girl, but I pretended not to hear her. We'd done another three after *Cervix Charge*, so we'd had a good innings, in fairness. I was fucking exhausted, as well.

"Everyone had a good weekend, yeah?" They shouted a thousand things back, but I decided to take all of those things collectively as a yes. I was only talking to them because Niall was fixing a string he'd broken during the last song – *Future Ex*. Usually there would have been a spare bass for him to just pick up, but no one had been kind enough to leave one lying around.

"I've had a pretty strange one myself, to be honest. But it's been pretty good, really. We, ah – we had a few problems. Especially today, like. Niall was in prison up until about 20 minutes ago. That's Niall, there." I pointed over at him and he gave me a face that said *please stop pointing at me, we are literally on TV and my mother is going to watch this tomorrow*, so I stopped pointing at him.

"Or maybe that isn't him? Both are equally possible. Anyway, yeah. We're gonna finish with someone else's song now. It's ah… it's a Cranberries one. Yeah. So that lad from earlier will be fucking delighted, I'd say. Uh, this one isn't actually on any of their albums yet, so it's kind of an exclusive. I don't have permission to play it or anything, but like me and Dolores are like this," I did the universal finger gesture for being *like this* with someone, "so she'll probably be grand with it." She probably would not, I thought, especially if it ended up on RTÉ. "And, even if she isn't, shur it's easier to ask for forgiveness than for permission. A great man taught me that lesson, guys. When he tried to put his – well, we'll skip over that bit, like. Anyway, Niall, who I showed you earlier – or *did* I? – he's gonna do backing vocals for this, so whenever you're ready there, Nailer."

"I'm good to go, Foxy Shoxy," Niall said, into his mic.

"Rapid altogether," I said, hopping down off my favourite amplifier. "Thanks for having us, Páirc Uí Chaoimh, yeah? And sorry we were so late, and that we aren't Menswear." I wondered if I should go stand next to Niall for this one, but I decided against it, cos it was our last song, so I wanted to go right to the edge of the stage and see all the faces, one last time.

"This one's for anyone who's missing someone this weekend. Whether they're gone forever, or they're far away, or even if they're with you now – cos I think it's possible to be miles away from someone who's right beside you, and sometimes that's your fault, not theirs." I stopped my drunken, opium-tinged, sentimental babbling, Niall and me did our *doobie-dah*s, and I tried to get all the way through the song without any tears. I almost managed it, too.

*****

"Oh my God, you were amazing! That was the best gig of all time!!!" said Aisling, mauling me at the side stage when I tottered off. The rest of them were there as well, they must have rushed through the gate while we were finishing *When You're Gone*. Even Ciara, sans the passless Zach, although she was farther away, and not trying to maul me, unfortunately.

"Uh, thanks. Where's my champagne and flowers, though?" I said, unhooking myself from her grip.

"Oh. Well, here." She showed me one of her hands, it was full of daisies.

"Ooooh! I was only joking, but thank you! We can make daisy chains!" I didn't know how to make daisy chains, but I was a quick learner.

"We totally can. And, Brian? Where are you, love?" She looked behind her.

"Here! Here! Coming through." He barged his way in past the others and handed me a quite big bottle of Moët & Chandon.

"You're fucking joking me! Hooray!" I said, taking it off him. A bucket of ice would be needed, but the thought was the thing.

"Well done, Maurice. You surprised me. Ye all did. Fair

play," he said, putting his arm around Aisling's waist in a nice, boyfriendy way that made her squooch into him.

"Will we get down off here, then?" I said. Galliano were already on stage, so we weren't in anyone's way, but I needed to sit, even if it was only my arse on some grass. The weather hadn't broken once all weekend, so the ground was still sittable.

"Yeah, let's move to the VIP lounge, squires," said Brian, putting his other arm around my waist, in a not-boyfriendy way, this time. By the VIP lounge he just meant the grass near the bar, but still.

"Well done, chickee," Bríd said, when we came past her and B. Ciara didn't say anything, but she was all smiles, so I smiled back at her. Maybe everything was going to be okay. I doubted it, but still.

"Have we got everyone then?" I said, looking around and doing a mental head count. Everyone except Frank, who I hadn't seen since this morning. I suddenly got a very bad feeling about him, but it wasn't there for long.

"We haven't got everyone, no." Marian was drinking a mojito now, too. Aisling must have got her into them. "We're missing at least one drummer!"

"Oh. Richie! RICHIE!!!" I couldn't see him anywhere.

"He's probably dead," said Ian, not helping.

"Have you ever considered a career in Not Being a Twat, Ian?" Mar said, punching him on the shoulder. His top was still lovely, mind. I coveted it, as a Chinese girl I used to know would have put it.

"Hang on, I'll go check up here," I said, untangling myself from the Brian and Aisling threesome. I walked up the steps, just as Galliano started their first tune. They were dancy, hip-hoppy. I wouldn't have guessed it from their name. Richie was there, all right. Standing on the edge of the stage, looking down at the crowd.

"There you are! What's the matter, pudding? Still a bit shell shocked from watching my incredible performance?" I put my arm around his shoulder, because he was my Chip Daddy now; we were quite close.

"I'm not a pudding, Caoimhe. Come here to me. Do you see that as well, or have I gone fucking mad, sham?" He pointed down at part of the crowd, about three rows back from the barriers.

"What am I supposed to be looking at here, sausage?" I was following his fingers with my eyes, but it was so sunny out there that everything had a haze over it, so it was hard.

"I'm not a sausage, Caoimhe. There, look. Next to the guy with the purple jacket, see?"

"Ummmm, yes! I do see! It's Uncle Frank!" I said, delighted that he'd seen our gig, and also that he hadn't *hunged* himself from all the stress and despair. *He* had a backstage pass, though. Why hadn't he come back with the rest of them?

"Yeah, I know that, sham. But who's that next to him? Who's he talking to, like?" He pointed again, but I was already looking at her.

"Oh. Oh my God, Richie. That is quite literally your mum."

******

"Well now, is this how the other half live?" said Marie, when me, Richie, and Frank brought her through the gate. I'd got her a pass from clipboard girl, who was actually really sound, it turned out. Or maybe she just fancied me, like all women did now. All women except Richie.

"Don't get too excited, Mam. We're literally going to be sitting on the ground. It's like posh Bush Drinking," said

Richie.

"I don't know what Bush Drinking is, Richie. I'm not down with the kids anymore," she said, although she was down with the kids enough to know the phrase *down with the kids*, so.

"Ye probably called it Cave Drinking when ye were young, Mam. Cos it was caveman days, like."

"He gets his sense of humour from his father's side, Caoimhe. That's why he doesn't have one. Your dress is gorgeous, by the way. Pure mod altogether. Not sure about wearing sneakers with it now, but I guess you're the rock and roll star, so you'd know better than me." Marie was gas, she'd come to lots of our gigs, usually with her fella. This had been a surprise, though. I felt lousy about it as well, cos she'd obviously been here all afternoon, thinking we were on early.

"Ah, I'm not a rock and roll star that long, Mrs. South. I'm still learning the ropes." We were here now, in the circle of... Crane & Associates. The others spotted us, one by one, and gave us waves and smiles.

"Well! Here ye all are, yeah? All the usual suspects, says you. And is that... surely it isn't... RICHIE! YOU DIDN'T TELL ME-"

"Howrya, Marie? Long time no see, wha?" Marian said, hopping up and running over to give her a hug. I'd forgotten that they'd know each other. It was a lovely moment, although Richie's mum did look a bit like she was gonna faint, for a second.

"Oh, wow! Well now, stand back there and let me have a look at you properly, Marian Collins. Jeeeeesus, aren't you after growing up to be some stunner altogether? I mean, Jesus, you were always the most *beautiful* girl, but... wow. The one that got away, hah? You fecking eejit, Rich," she said, thumping him on the arm, which made everyone giggle.

"I didn't dump her or anything! She dumped me!" he said, making a meal out of the punch from a tiny, five foot nothing mother of two in her forties.

"For a good reason!" Marian said, making me instantly curious and making Richie go scarlet.

"Ah shur, that's all water under the bridge now, says you. What brings you here anyway, Marian? After all these years, like. Four years, is it? Jesus, time flies, like." Marie drank wine, I remembered that. I'd get her some in a minute, or she could have some of my Moët once it was chilled.

"She couldn't resist the raw sexual magnetism of your son any longer, Marie. She was crying herself to sleep every time she heard him drumming on the radio," Bríd said.

"Jesus, if you're going to lie to me, at least make it believable, girls," said Marie, which was probably a fiercer dig than the one she'd given Rich on his arm.

"Mam! You're supposed to be on my side!" he said. Marian walked over to him and gave him a little smooch on the lips, and he instantly stopped caring about anything.

"Well now. Maybe it wasn't such a lie after all," said Marie, giving Marian a look I couldn't decipher, but it felt like they'd shared similar looks in the past. Mad to think these people I knew had a history together that I'd never heard about before.

"Don't worry, Mammy South. I'm only borrowing him for the weekend," said Marian, draping her arm around Mammy South's pride and joy.

"Well make sure ye borrow some *protection*, Marian Collins, cos I don't want to be meeting you again in nine months, and you turning me into *Granny* South before my time," said Marie, making both of them feel about fourteen in an instant.

"Ye can borrow some off me," said Benson, which was

a surprise, as latex and his spunk weren't known to mix well.

"It's weird hearing you talk about Richie as a sexual being, Marie – stop it!" I said, getting a thankful nod from my Chip Daddy. "I assumed you still thought he was blowing his nose on the sheets."

"Hahaaaaah! Oh, Caoimhe, you're something else, you are. Blowing his nose on the sheets! I mean, if he was blowing his nose on them, someone needs to explain the four hundred used tissues under his bed to me. Anyway! Where can I get a drink around these parts, and how much are they going to rob my purse for it?"

"The bar is open, Mrs. S," I said, linking her arm to bring her over.

"Well I'd hope it is, Caoimhe. It's only the afternoon. I know we're in Cork, but still."

"No, Marie. It's an Open Bar." Yuri/Rory/Ruaraidh was serving, I noticed. That poor fucker never had a day off. Or a break.

"Oh, it is, is it? Like at a wedding?" She had tiny feet, I noticed, looking down at her shoes. They went with the tiny rest of her.

"Like at a millionaire's wedding, maybe." I hadn't been to too many receptions since I started drinking, but I didn't remember the bar being free at any of them.

"Oh no, Caoimhe, love. The millionaires wouldn't have a free bar. The millionaires would make everyone pay for their drinks. That's how they're fecking millionaires, says you," she said, getting Yuri's attention before I did. "Large glass of white wine, please, love. And what are you having yourself, Miss Rock and Roll?"

"I'm grand for now, Marie. I'm taking it easy for a bit. Watching my figure, like," I lied, thinking it was about time I popped to the loo again. I hadn't powdered my nose in ages.

*****

"So now, tell me again, was Niall really in jail or were ye just having a mess?" said Marie, once we were all back together. All of us except Ciara. I'd given her a spare pass to go out and give to Zach, because I was sound out.

"Yes," said Ian, making Bríd give him a kick in the shin.

"Yes to what, love?"

"Yes, I was only messing!" I said, giving Ian another kick in the shin, but with my eyes.

"I was just helping the police with their enquiries, Mrs. South," Niall said, not helping.

"They're only pulling your leg, Mam," said her pride and joy. I noticed he wasn't smoking in front of her, which was sweet, but then I remembered he didn't smoke anymore, which made it less impressive.

"I dunno what to make of ye, sometimes, I don't, boys and girls. Full of secrets, ye are, I think. Especially you, Richard South." She gave him a sly look, with a helping of Mammy Look on the side.

"What did I do, sham?" He looked very aggrieved, the poor misfortune.

"Don't say that word, Richie, you know I hate it. You'll have them thinking you were dragged up, not brought up, I swear. And anyway, *what did I do*, he says, like butter wouldn't melt. How long has this thing been going on, eh?" She pointed down at where Richie and Mar's hands were clasped. "When were you planning on telling your poor old mother about it? Never, was it?"

"There's nothing to tell!" he said, still stuck onto her like a barnacle on... another barnacle.

"Nothing to tell... pfffft!" I said, giving him a more Mammy Look than she had.

"Caoimhe fancies girls now," Marian said, throwing me under the bus to save her own skin.

"Is that right, Caoimhe?" said Marie, forgetting the whore who stole her son, for a second.

"I – well I, I dunno. Maybe?"

"Ah shur, it's hardly a shocker now, is it?" she said, lighting up a Rothman's. The bang off them was something fierce altogether. They'd put hairs on your chest, although probably on the inside of it. Hairs in your lungs.

"What's that supposed to mean???" Why was no one ever surprised about this? Why did no one ever go, *a lesbian? Surely not youuuuu?*

"Oh I didn't mean anything bad by it, lovely. I'm just saying, with some people you just *know*. Look at Richie, shur."

"I'm not a lesbian!!!" he said, opening up a can of Scrumpy Jack. I'd no idea where he'd got that from.

"Ah now, you *are* really fond of vaginas," said Mar, squeezing the hand of his that was surgically attached to her.

"I'm only fond of yours," he said, making everyone around them want to vomit.

"Richard South! Please! Don't say *vagina* in front of your mother," Marie said, but she was laughing. He hadn't actually said vagina either, so she couldn't do him for it.

"What do you mean anyway, Marie? Did you think Rich was gay?" said Tim, who I'd again forgotten existed, and who I couldn't really look at anymore without picturing his willy.

"Ah, no. Not really. He was a very sensitive child though. Very artistic. And the soft voice, as well. So sometimes I did maybe wonder about him."

"Mam! I wasn't a steamer child!"

"Don't say that word, Richard. You know I hate it."

"Yeah, RICHIE!" said Marian, slapping him on the leg, to get her fix of Richie leg-slapping.

"Ouch!!!" Poor Rich was getting it from all angles.

"So when did you decide he wasn't a ste- he wasn't gay, Marie?" said Ian. I still wanted that Adidas top; I was going to have to steal it when he wasn't looking. I'd wait until he took it off first, mind.

"Well, I didn't have to decide, really," she said, finishing her big glass of wine. I'd pop the champers open in a minute and save her having to get up for a refill.

"How was that?" I said, lighting up a Marlboro, because I'd just remembered that Marie wasn't *my* mother, so it was grand to smoke in front of her.

"Well, because before he'd had a chance to even grow his first little short and curlies, didn't some *tramp* of an older woman move into the house next door to us and take away his innocence, lads. He didn't have a chance. She was like one of them Sirens in the old stories, calling the sailors to their deaths on the rocks." Marie was doing a serious face now, so she had everyone's attention.

"Sorry, what?" I said. I couldn't really process what she was saying. I didn't know poor Richie had been… touched by some woman as a kid. That sounded awful. And why was-

"I'm so sorry, Richie. I'd no idea," said Aisling.

"Yeah, Jesus. That's grim," said Tim.

"I don't know what to say, Rich," Bríd said, looking distraught. "I really don't."

"Oh, Richie…" said Ciara, giving him sad eyes.

"Lads, she's talking about *me* you fucking eejits. The *faces* on ye, like. And feck off you, Marie. You should be thanking me, for making a man out of him, with all my womanly charms," said Marian, then everyone else in the circle stopped looking horrified, and burst out laughing.

*****

"Right, so. And what do you do, Benson? When you're not hanging around the rock concerts with teenagers, I mean. Have you a job, or?" Marie had got herself some more wine. She was being collected by her friend in a while – the friend who gave her the lift up. We'd asked her to stay and watch the Stone Roses, but she'd never heard of them, and anyway, she had to go to work at the restaurant tonight.

"He's drawing the pension, Marie," said Ciara, who was back now, with her boyfriend who wasn't her boyfriend.

"Ah now, he's not that old," said Marie.

"Compared to you, maybe," said Richie.

"I'm still a young woman, Richard South. Life begins at 40, did you not know that?"

"I think you look fabulous, Mrs. South – for your age I mean," said Tim, not exactly helping.

"Stop trying to get off with Richie's mum," said Ian, making Richie do a disgusted face.

"Ah now, he's not my type, lads. No offence, Tim," said Marie, lighting up another horribly strong-smelling fag.

"No one is your type, Mam, stop! You're too old to be having sex!"

"She is not, Richie. She's in the prime of her life. And anyway, this isn't telling us what Benson does for a job," said Aisling, which was true – the second part, at least.

"Yes, Benson – what kind of a fecking name is that, honestly – tell us!" Marie said, leaning towards him to get the lowdown.

"Uh, I work in sales," he said, not looking at any of us.

"What do you sell? Used cars? Double glazing? Your

arse down the docks?" said Ian, lighting up one of his Gowl Washes.

"Jesus will ye all leave him alone, like?" Bríd said, looking half-serious.

"I'll leave him alone when he leaves my clothes alone with his-" I stopped when I saw Marie was looking at me and listening. That wasn't a conversation I wanted to have with her. Although she was a mum, so maybe she'd know some foolproof olden days methods for getting spunk out of a rubber dress.

"We don't even know if that was my fault!" said Benson, which was news to me.

"Who else's fault could it be? Did a load of sailors on Shore Leave pop into your van and ejaculate all over Bríd while you were out having a morning wee?" I said, immediately forgetting that I didn't want to be having this conversation.

"CAOIMHE!" said Richie.

"Don't be shouting at me, Richie. My bodily fluids don't ruin clothes!" I said, although some of my knickers might have told him a different story.

"I don't know what this is about, boys and girls, and I'm not sure I want to know," Marie said, drinking down some more wine.

"I second that emotion," said Zachary. I didn't like him. I didn't know him or anything, but still. No one was allowed to kiss my Ciara this weekend, except me. And maybe Portia – but I hadn't authorised that, and anyway, she couldn't kiss her anymore; she was a fugitive from justice.

"I sell insurance," Benson said. I'd forgotten we were talking about that.

"Wow, that's quite interesting!" said Marian, on possibly her third mojito since we'd sat down. Everyone was on the booze today, probably because we had no drugs. Well, *they* had no drugs.

"Is it?" said B, smiling a little now.

"NOPE!" said Mar, and everyone laughed at poor Benson again. It wasn't easy being him around our lot, but he got to have full sexual intercourse with a teenager out of it, so he couldn't complain.

"Is it life insurance you do? I might have a word with you in a bit so, if it is?" Marie said, not joking this time.

"Why would you need life insurance, Mam? You're not gonna die," said Richie, looking slightly worried.

"Shur we all have to die sometime, Maurice," said Brian, rejoining us after his trip to point Percy at the porcelain, as he called it. That wasn't even his worst one. I once heard him say "Just going to go drop the kids off at the pool", and that would stay with me until my grave.

"Some of us sooner than others," said Frank, which were literally the first words out of him since he came backstage, the depressing bastard.

"Ah, cheer up, Frank. Might never happen, says you," Marie said, immediately creating the most awkward silence of the weekend so far.

TWENTY-SEVEN

"So, then. Which one are you spotting? Is that what ye say now these days, yeah? Spotting? Or is that one out of date already, Caoimhe? It's hard to keep up!" I'd taken Marie to the toilets. Not to do cocaine with her, or to play Can't Do Me. Just for a wee, like normal folk did in toilets.

"It is, yeah. What do you mean, though?" I was at the mirror, fixing my sweaty face. It was mad that I'd had a load of sexy outfits delivered to Cork, but I'd ended up doing the gig dressed as boring old Caoimhe O'Shaughnessy. Brian hadn't given out to me for it yet, though – for not *maintaining my image* – so it was grand.

"I *mean* which one of the girls do you have your eye on? Or is it someone else?" She was still in the cubicle, I was trying to ignore the sounds, in case she was dropping the kids off at the pool.

"Oh! No, I dunno. No one special, Marie." I spent half my life lying to Richie's mum, for some reason. Well, half of my life today, anyway.

"So it's Ciara then, yeah?"

"Fuck me pink! How did you know that, Marie?" Maybe she was secretly on Es, and she had the telepathy.

"Ah, women's intuition, love. And a mother's intuition, too. I see how you looks at her when she's talking. Like a little lost puppy. So, does she not… like girls too?" Marie flushed, and came out of the cubicle.

"Ahhhhh, she does, Marie. Between you and me, I mean. I don't want to be reading people behind their backs, like." My mascara was blobby. I'd have to wipe it off and start again. I was still exhausted. I needed more heroin chips, to counteract all the booze. And the heroin.

"Oh, of course, no. My lips are sealed, Caoimhe. So she likes girls, but she doesn't like *you* that way, is it? I'd say that's fierce hard, like. Cos, if you're... that way, it's probably hard enough to find anyone else who's that way too. So when you do find one, and you like her, and she doesn't-"

"No, she does like me back, Marie." I dotted the foundation onto my forehead, cheeks and chin.

"Oh, right, so. And that boy... what's his name, Zachary? The queer fella," she said, meaning queer in a non-homosexual way.

"Yeah, good old Zach," I said. The fucking twat.

"He's getting – he's in yeer way, is he? Or in *your* way, anyway." Marie was checking her own make-up in the mirror now, but it was immaculate, cos she hadn't just played a musical festival while on cocaine and smack.

"Well, only logistically speaking, Marie," I said, rubbing in the last of my Maybelline.

"Logistically? Does he drive a truck or something?"

"Haha! No, I mean he's not her boyfriend – he's actually gay, would you believe..."

"Ah. That explains it."

"Explains what?" I took out my lippy and lefty-looseyed it. It smelled like wet crayons, but it was a lovely shade – fuchsia.

"Explains why he seems so gay, Caoimhe, no offence to him. He's like auld Larry Grayson, he is. Shut that door!"

"Heh, yeah." I didn't know who Larry Grayson was.

Benson would. Benson probably had all his albums. On vinyl.

"So if he's gay, and she's gay-"

"I think she's bi, Marie," I said, although in the year I'd known her I hadn't seen her kiss a single boy. She had exes though. Non-gay ones, and everything.

"Bisexual, yes. And is that what you are now, or are you still deciding?" I loved how she was talking to me about it like it was no big deal or anything. I wondered would she have been the same if Richie had been holding hands with Zachary when she arrived today. We'd literally never find out.

"I'm still uh, I dunno, Marie. One step at a time, says you. I just... I just wish it was easier, you know? I wish everything wasn't so complicated. It wasn't before – when we were just pals. But now..." My make-up was done; I was more than mortal man deserved, again. Or mortal woman.

"Shur that's *everything* though, Caoimhe. Doesn't matter if you're in love with a man, or a woman, or a herd of goats – it's never easy. But shur, we get on with it, and we survive, and at some point, it all works out. Even if it doesn't work out the way we planned in the first place, yeah?" She was probably talking about her marriage breaking up, and her ending up with the new fella. She was still with him now, so that was something that worked out, I thought. For her, anyway. Not for poor Mick.

"So I should just..."

"Calm down, take it easy, and shur whatever happens, happens, love." She gave me a hug around the shoulder that felt more *girl pal* than Mammy, cos she was one of my girl pals now.

"*Que sera, sera*," I said, walking out with her.

"*What will be, will be!* I used to sing that to Richie when he was a baby, you know?"

"And didn't he turn out grand," I said, squinting when the sun hit my eyes.

"Well. So far, anyway," said my new girl pal, chuckling away. "We'll see, says you. We'll see."

I suddenly had a really rotten feeling in my stomach – not an illness feeling, more the sort you get when something awful happens, or when something awful is *going* to happen. Richie was outside the toilets, waiting for us. I was going to say something smart to him about not worrying that I was stealing his mother, but then I saw his face, and how white it was, even with the sunburn.

"Frank's after hanging himself," he said, and the rotten feeling in my guts became a rotten feeling everywhere else, too.

*****

"Jesus fucking Christ, Rich. You could have told us the bit about him not being dead, first. You should have led with that piece of information, instead of giving us a heart attack." We were still standing outside the toilets – all of us – watching the St. John's guys bring Frank out on a stretcher. I needed a drink, but all I had was the bottle of champagne, and that would have been very inappropriate in the circumstances. The popping noise wouldn't have gone down well at all.

"I didn't think I – I said he hung himself, like."

"Hanged himself," said Tim, not helping.

"I'll fucking box the jaw off you in a second, Tim," Richie said, looking like he might just do it, as well.

"Language, Richie..." said his mother, who was holding onto me still, for moral support.

"Look, can we all just shut up a second, yeah? Is he unconscious, or..." said Ciara. Her Zachary was the one who'd found him. Frank had got up on one of the toilet seats and looped his belt around a pipe up above, according to Zach. I was shaking just thinking of it, so it must have been terrifying for him, actually seeing it.

"I think he's awake now," Marie said, looking over. Frank had an oxygen mask on, and his eyes were open, but only barely. What an idiot. What a stupid, stupid idiot, I thought. But then, I wasn't him. I didn't know what he'd been feeling. He'd told us how fucked he was, but I'd just assumed he'd figure a way out of it. Or that we'd figure a way out of it, for him. Turned out he didn't fancy sticking around to see if it would happen.

"Is there someone we should ring, for him?" said Marie, cos she was one of the only proper adults here, thinking proper adult thoughts.

"There's Marie, but I don't know her number or anything," Ciara said, meaning the other Marie – the one who owned the house where Frank and Harta lived.

"Or his sister," I said. I did know Jon's mother's number, because it was Jon's number too. I really didn't fancy ringing her up to tell her about this, though. She already thought Frank was the black sheep of their lot. This wasn't going to make her think any better of him. Well, not if she found out *why* he'd done it, anyway.

"Why would he do this, lads? I know he has the auld depression and everything, godhelpus, and he was a bit down earlier when I was talking to him before yeer show. But like, he's usually grand. He's usually…"

"Ah, it's complicated, Mam. I'll tell you some other time, yeah?" said Richie, almost reversing roles with her, cos it was usually your mum who said she'd tell you things later – or when you were older, but never followed through with it.

"I don't like secrets, Richie. Secrets make me worried.

About you – about all of ye." Marie had the full Mammy Face on now.

"It's not really a secret, Marie. It's more a private matter – I don't think Frank would want us talking about it, you know?" said Bríd. It was a lie, but it was a white one; and a good one.

"Well I don't know the secret either, Marie, for some reason. So you're in good company, at least," said Brian.

"Me neither, love. We should just leave it though, yeah? The main thing is he's okay. Or he's going to be okay, yeah? I hope he is, anyway," said Aisling, who absolutely *did* know the secret, but still.

"Yeah, thank God you went in there when you did, Zach. Kismet, it must have been," I said. He just nodded at me. He was probably still in shock.

"Sorry lads, I need to get some details off ye, for the hospital, yeah?" said the St. John's Ambulance lady. She was really tiny – she looked younger than most of us.

"Is he going to be okay?" I said. I wondered if I should go to the hospital with him, or would it be too much to cope with, emotionally.

"He'll be fine, please God. He didn't exactly know what he was doing, so... so there were no bones broken, and very little asphyxiation. He's lucky your friend came along when he did, though. You probably saved his life, honey," she said, to Zachary. Again, all he could do was nod, poor fucker. Ciara was minding him, though. She was the best candidate for that job.

"Listen, I can give you his name and address," said Bríd.

"That's a start, anyway. Come over to me and we'll get the form. Now, the ambulance will be here in a minute. There's probably room for one other person, if one of ye wants to go to the hospital with him?"

"I'll go, shur," said Marie, making everyone look at her.

"Mam, why would you go?" said Richie. "You're not his family or anything, sham."

"Yeah well, there's no one here now who *is* his family, Rich. So I'll have to do." I immediately thought of Jon when she said that, of course. Whether she'd meant it like that or not.

"You've work tonight, Mam!" said Richie.

"Ah, not until about ten, Rich. I can go over for a while, just to make sure he's okay, yeah?" Marie and Frank got on great, probably cos he was nearer her age than he was our ages. Or maybe he wasn't. I couldn't be bothered doing mental arithmetic now, I'd enough on my plate.

"I can go," I said. I didn't mind, really. Well, I did – but if it was only for a small while I wouldn't mind *too* much.

"You, *madam*, are the last person who should be going," said Marie, giving me a girl pal squeeze, or a Mammy one. Both were equally possible.

"Why is that?" I thought I was the perfect person to go. We were practically related, after all.

"Because you've had enough stress and sadness with that family to last you a lifetime, Caoimhe. Let someone else do the heavy lifting this time, yeah?" said Ciara, and some of them nodded or made agreeing noises.

"I don't get it?" said Marian.

"She means Jon, and what happened last year," said Richie.

"What about it?" She looked lost, but obviously she would, because she wouldn't have had a clue who Jon was.

"Well, cos Frank is his uncle, and Caoimhe…" he looked at me to see if it was okay to carry on.

"Caoimhe...?"

"Jon is Caoimhe's fella. Sorry, he *was* Caoimhe's fella," said Marie. The *was* part made me a little ouchy, but that wasn't her fault.

"My Jon, like? Jon Musgrave?" said Marian, looking no less confused than a minute ago.

"What do you mean, *your* Jon?" I said, the hackles going up on my neck. My Jon wasn't her Jon. What was she on about at all?

"My – *our* old friend, Jon. Jonathan Musgrave, from Thomondgate. *He* was your boyfriend?" Her old friend? This weekend got stranger and stranger as it went on.

"Uh, yes? How do you think I met all this lot, like? Why do you think I'm in the band?" I said, lighting up a much-needed fag. It did actually make sense when I thought about it – Jon was Richie's best friend, so of course she'd have known him, back then. Especially since she lived in Crossroads. But her being Richie's ex was a thing I only knew since yesterday, so it wasn't like I'd had time to consider any of this stuff before. Couldn't do me for it.

"And he was going out with you when he-" She stopped before she said it outright. People often did that, as if somehow the avoiding saying it might make it not have happened. I was used to it by now, though. It had been a whole year.

"Yeah, he was. Have I not told you all this already?" said Richie, who clearly hadn't told her a fucking thing.

"Nope. You don't tell me *nothing*, Richie South. You're *useless*, you are," she said, lighting up one herself, so she could take on board the newest plot twist in a weekend full of plot twists. What a fucking life we led, seriously.

*****

"Why are ye always going on about feminism anyway,

like? Don't ye have enough rights now, or what?" said Richie to Aisling, a while later, after we'd seen Marie and poor Frank off.

"Enough rights?" Bríd said.

"Well thanks for giving us the vote, Richie, yeah? That was sound of you," said Ciara. I really wanted to talk to her, but I needed to get her on her own, first. Maybe I could bribe her with some cocaine. I really was the Pablo Escobar of Cork City now.

"See? Ye've the vote, ye can work, ye can take the pill, ye can have abortions-"

"No we can't!" I said. I put my hand on the bottle in the ice bucket. All the ice was nearly melted now, so the champagne was bound to be cold enough.

"Ye can if ye go to England," said Benson. I wondered if he'd ever taken a girl to England for one. He was old enough, he might have taken two or three girls, over the years. Or not, since his purple spunk was probably incapable of creating life.

"That's not the same thing!" said Ciara, glaring at him.

"Okay, but everything else, like. Ye've it good now. I dunno what ye're complaining about, like," Richie said, making me wish his mother was still here, to sort him out. Marian was gone to the loo again; that was probably why he was being so brave now.

"We've it good??? Tell me, Richie – this morning, when you got up, yeah?" Aisling said. Brian was still here with us. I'd to slap her hand earlier when she reached over for a fag out of Marian's pack, the drunken eejit.

"Yeah?"

"What did you do? Brush your teeth? Have a shower? Get dressed?" She only had ice left in her mojito, but she was still slurping away at it.

"Yeah," he said again, although I wasn't sure how much I believed him, apart from the getting dressed bit.

"And then, tell me – did you have to sit down for nearly an hour and PAINT YOUR FUCKING HEAD, just so people won't be asking you if you're sick all day?"

"What? No…"

"Well then, sit the fuck down and shut the fuck up," said Aisling pointing a patriarchy-destroying finger at him, making all the girls laugh, and some of the boys too.

"But… I am sitting down," he said, looking perplexed.

"Then shut the fuck up twice," said Bríd, reaching over to the bottle of Moët and rubbing her finger down the side of it. "This ready yet, Kweev?"

"I think so, but there's not gonna be much of it to go around," I said. It was a big bottle, but it wasn't *that* big.

"There will be if we only give a glass to everyone who has a vagina," said Aisling.

"Well Tim's in luck then," Niall said, but he didn't get as big a laugh as he expected, since he was mostly talking to people who had seen Tim naked today and could testify that he definitely didn't have a vagina.

*****

"What *is* our plan, anyway?" I said, once the champagne had been poured into some plastic party cups I'd got from Yuaraidh.

"Elastica?" Aisling said, taking a cup.

"Carl Cox, Laurent Garnier, Chemical Brothers?" said Ciara, which was also a good suggestion, except we had no Es. Well, not enough for all of us, anyway. I had three pills, but I wasn't Jesus – I couldn't make them stretch to feed the five thousand. Or even just the five girls. I had speed and coke left. Maybe I could do some mental arithmetic in a bit.

"Dress Up Bríd Part 2: The Revenge?" Bríd said, hopeful sounding.

"We're doing that anyway, sugar. When we go back to get changed for the Stone Roses." I definitely needed to change. The sleeves on my dress were like sweat traps; I was wringing.

"What are we toasting to, lads?" Marian said, holding her cup up.

"To Frank's speedy recovery, I think," I said. Marie had Brian's mobile number with her, she was going to call later with an update.

"And to Zach, for finding him in time," said Ciara. She had a point. I got another cup off the stack.

"Zach? Zachary? Zachariah?" I said, until he finally turned around and acknowledged me.

"Yeah?" He was terrified of me, a bit. I couldn't remember why now, but he was probably right to be.

"You've been made an honorary girl for this toast – here, have some champagne."

"Is this a trick? Is there poison in this, Ciara?" he said, holding the cup like it was full of acid, and not the sort of acid that made you get naked and listen to The Doors, either.

"No, I think you're fine, Zach. We're just showing our appreciation for you saving Frank. Take it quick, before she changes her mind." They were talking about me like I wasn't standing right there between them. Delightful.

"Oh okay, then. Thanks, Kweeva Shox," he said, smiling.

"You're welcome!" I said, stepping back so we had a circle of people again. A circle of friends, like in the book. Except none of us were that bitch Nan Mahon, hopefully.

"To Frank and a speedy recovery, the fucking eejit!" I said. "Oh, and to Zach, the hero of today!"

"To Frank and Zach!" said everyone, including Zach, the absolute narcissist.

"God, that's actually nice!" I said, looking at the remainder of it in my cup after I'd had a decent gulp. I loved the way champagne felt on your tongue, even if it did give you breath like dog shit after a few glasses.

"Why wouldn't it be nice? It's champagne..." said Ciara, then they all looked at me.

"Yeah, but it's-" I was about to say it was *only* Moët & Chandon, and then I remembered that Aisling and Brian had bought it for me, and that none of these people were as rich as my family or had a father who was a wine expert, and that if I'd carried on with that sentence everyone there would think I was a complete twat – so I rerouted my mouth and said "it's usually only this nice when you're drinking it in France!", which only made me sound like half a complete twat, so it was grand.

"Well, Cork must be the new Paris, then," said Marian.

"Vive la Cork!" said Zachary, our honorary woman.

"Vive la Páirc Uí Chaoimh!" said Ciara, who I still hadn't cornered for a chat.

"Viva la Caoimhe!" I said, because I was an absolute narcissist, sometimes.

*****

"You okay, babe?" Marian said. We were over by the side stage, waiting for Elastica to start.

"Me? I've no fucking idea. How about you?" I said. It felt like the day had been around twelve hours long already. Us playing the gig and Frank having his little mishap were only about an hour apart. Portia was still somewhere out there, absconding with all the drugs. Turned out Marian and my/her Jon had been best friends way back in the 80s, or whenever it was. My head was going to explode with all these things. What if there were more to come? I wasn't sure I'd be able to take it.

"I'm really, really sorry," she said.

"Sorry for what, Mar?" Maybe it was her who spunked on my dress. It was always the ones you suspected least.

"Well, it's all my fault, isn't it? I'm such a shit. It's all my fault. All of it." She looked sad, and a bit drunk, but mostly sad.

"What is? What happened to Frank?" That couldn't be what she meant. I was being stupid now.

"Yeah. If I hadn't come along – if I didn't bring Portia, then…"

"Marian, don't be stupid. I was the one who brought Portia into… into our weekend. You just sort of tagged along, like."

"No you didn't. She went looking for you, remember? And she found you. That was because of me. I wanted to see Richie, and to see you. We tried getting backstage, she was the only one who was able to sneak in. But if it wasn't for me, she wouldn't have come talk to you, you know? She was only talking to you for me. I wanted to get backstage so I could see you, and see Rich. It's all my stupid fault…"

"But you told me that she had a thing for me, or something?" Her story was full of holes already, and I was Hercule Poirot.

"Shit! I did, didn't I?" She was definitely leaning more towards drunk than sad now, the big eejit.

"So was that not true then, or what?" If Portia *didn't*

have a thing for me, then she'd either developed one extremely quickly, or she was just an excellent actress. Both were equally possible.

"No, it *was*! It is? It was! I don't know! I was just trying to say sorry, anyway, Kweev. Sorry."

"Mar, if I give you a big hug will you shut up about all this and just chill and relax and enjoy the rest of this night for me?" I said, putting my arms out. I had no fight with her. They weren't my drugs, and she couldn't blame herself for Frank, either. That was ridiculous. He was a grown man. He made his own choices, no matter how stupid they were.

"I might, yeah. Thanks, Caoimhe. Love you. I'm so glad I got to meet you again, even if I did ruin everything and nearly kill Fra-"

"Come here, you big silly fool." I squished her in really tight and inhaled her lovely, clean, Timotei shampoo smell.

"Stop enjoying my tits on the sly, you bender," she murmured, romanti-drunkly into my shoulder.

"I don't even like your tits; they're all wonky, like your stupid, wonky face," I whispered back, lovingly. I was really glad I'd met her again too, even if she was going to break my Chip Daddy's heart and leave me to pick up the pieces after she was gone. Elastica started up their first song, *Line Up*. I liked that one, but I liked all their songs, so.

*****

"Where's Benson gone, Bríd?" I said. Elastica were great, so far. Kind of moody and grumpy, but Aisling said we women didn't owe men arbitrary smiles, so maybe they'd heard one of her lectures.

"Ah, he doesn't really know any Elastica."

"What an old philistine. The cheek of him!" I said. B could go to hell.

"So he's walking to the hotel to get the van and bring it back here for us."

"What a strapping young hero! We should get more champagne, just for him!" I'd always liked that fella.

"I know! Means we can go back during Paul Weller, get ready-"

"Get *you* ready, is it?" Justine Frischmann was way more feminine looking in real life. She still had the boyish hair, but her face was very womanly. Big Julia Roberts lips, and very pretty eyes. No wonder Liam Gallagher wanted to steal her off Damon.

"Haha, yes please!"

"And where's your Richie gone?" I said, poking Marian in the shoulder a bit too hard.

"Ow! Stop it! He's, ah, gone to the toilet with Ian, I think." Elastica started up *Rockunroll*. They apparently liked wordplay too.

"At least it's not with Zachary," I said, as if all gay people did was take straight people into toilets and try to get sexual with them. Wouldn't catch me doing such a thing, obviously.

"Be nice, you! Zach saved Frank. He's an honorary woman tonight," said Mar, poking me back.

"Maybe you should take him into the Ladies with you then. Show him your wonky tits as a reward," I said, poking her again.

"Stop flirting with me, Caoimhe. I'm not one of your front-bumchums."

"Pah. If I was flirting with you you'd know all about it." She absolutely would not. I probably wouldn't even know about it. Still though.

"Who's flirting with whom, now?" said Ciara, coming

up the steps behind us. She was good at grammaring correctly. Maybe she'd been in the toilets too, I thought. It seemed to be where all the cool kids hung out. So to speak.

"Caoimhe is trying to get off with me," said Marian. She was either spending a fortune on cocktails, or Richie was getting them at the bar for her on the sly by doing an impression of a man who actually drank mojitos. Both were equally possible.

"Yeah, she does that. Gotta watch out for this one," said Ciara, making me feel awful immediately, then she looked right into my eyes with her gorgeous purple peepers and ran her finger across my cheek, stopping at my lips, which made me feel something else, altogether.

"Back off, all of ye. This one's mine!" Aisling was behind me, putting her arms around my waist, which at least broke the weird tension between me and Ciara.

"Hello, lover. You need me for something?" I said, knowing fully well what it was she needed me for.

"I need you for *everything*, baby. Toilets?" she said, starting to push me there before I had a chance to answer.

"If Richie and Ian's cubicle is rocking, don't go a knocking!" said Bríd, getting a poke in the arm for it off Marian. Justine and the girls started up another one. It sounded like *Hold Me Now*. Their one, not the Thompson Twins one; that would have been weird. Or maybe quite good.

*****

"Christ, I've been waiting ages for you to give me one. Thank you!" Aisling said, once we were safely inside the loos and away from her boyfriend.

"My pleasure," I said. "But you really can't make a habit of this, Aisling." I sounded like I was her mum or something now.

"All right, Mum! I know, I know. It's addictive." She took a long drag. She already had lungs of steel. Maybe people like her who were incredibly fit from dancing and hockey were better at smoking than unfit druggies like me? Stranger things had happened.

"It's addictive like you have no idea." I couldn't remember when I'd even started smoking. Probably when I was about thirteen. Probably stole one of Marian Collins' ones, when she wasn't looking. Poetic, really, since she'd stolen about 37 of mine yesterday, not that I was counting.

"I'll stop doing it after this weekend, Mum. I swear on the holy bible, like." She probably had lots of bibles, from being a Jehovah's Mormon.

"You'd better," I said. "Or I'll tan your behind, young lady."

"Promises, promises, O'Shaughnesy." Such a cailín dána. I still wanted to do her makeup for her. I'd pounce on her when Dress Up Bríd 2 was happening and everyone else was getting dolled up, I decided. Then it would feel natural, and not like I was criticising her or something.

"You coming back to the hotel?" I said, fiddling with her hair again. It was very fiddlewithable.

"What, right now? At least let me finish my fag, you nympho."

"Haha! Fuck off, no I meant are you coming back in a bit with all the girls, to get ready and stuff? You weren't with us last night, when we did Bríd. It was great, you'd have enjoyed it." We'd only met Ecstasy Aisling after the big makeover. Or at least that was how my brain was remembering it, anyway.

"You *did* her? How many of ye did her, Caoimhe? All at the same time, or did ye take turns?"

"Stop it! You know what I mean!" This was way more

like flirting than someone poking you in the arm. Ciara Slattery would have been outraged.

"Clearly, I don't know what you mean, Kweev. You might have to show me." Her top was still intact, and her magical boobs were still sitting symmetrically. She was a natural at public boobery, after so many years of dressing a bit Mary Poppins. That was exactly who she'd been like – Mary Poppins. Incredibly pretty, but too prim and proper to be sexy. Unless you were Fred the chimney sweep, obviously.

"I'll show you the back of my hand in a minute if you're not careful!"

"Will you? Oooh!" Her and Brian definitely did the smacking her bum thing, I reckoned. Strong, feministy girls like her were always a bit *spank me* in the bedroom – for the sheer contrastiness of it all. I read it in a book once, so it was definitely true. It was a fiction book, by Harold Robbins, but still.

"Shut up, Legs; you little minx. So, will you come or not?" I said, immediately regretting the choice of words.

"Depends on how many of ye are doing me. How many were doing Bríd?"

"AISLING!"

"Sorry! Yeah, I'll tag along, that would be great."

"Brilliant! All the girls, just. We'll let the smelly boys stay here and be smelly." Brian might want to stay for Paul Weller. He seemed the Paul Weller fan type. A bit of Dad Rock. Niall liked The Jam, so he'd definitely be staying for Paul. Having no drugs was sort of liberating, when it came to making plans for the evening. But it was also kind of shit, so.

"Except Zachary?" she said, finishing her fag before I'd finished mine. Hopefully I still had some Wrigley's.

"Do we have to?" We probably would have to, if Ciara

came. She was minding him. She hadn't been at Dress Up Bríd 1 last night, I remembered, so he hadn't been an issue.

"What have you got against that poor boy? He might even come in useful, you know?"

"How?" I couldn't think of a use for him, apart from finding people hanging themselves in toilets, and that wasn't going to happen again tonight. *Touch wood.*

"Cos he's gay. They're really good at clothes and stuff."

"Wow. The stereotypes!"

"Haha, sorry! You have my permission to spank me for that." She turned a little and stuck out her Riverdance bum.

"You should be so lucky, mate. Anyway, I don't think he *will* be any good at stuff like that. Not yet. He's only *recently gay*, as far as I know." I wasn't sure how recent. I hadn't looked him up in the Encyclopaedia Britannica.

"Well then, you two should get on like a house on fire," said an cailín dána.

"That's it. That's the last straw. Bend over while I go fetch my paddle," I said.

"Give me six of the best! I deserve it!" she said, making me wonder if the Jehovah's Mormons were into corporal punishment, and if that was where she'd got her kinky side from.

*****

"Okay, now we have no boys?" I said, when we got back from our smoke, and from me not spanking Aisling Flanagan.

"Yeah, they're gone to the tent, to see Carl Cox, or Laurence Garnier," said Marian. I didn't correct her about poor Laurent. I wasn't Tim.

"What, without any drugs?" I said. That sounded awful. And scary.

"Yeah... they're all a bit pissed though, so they don't care," said Ciara. Zachary seemed to be gone too, which meant I could finally get her alone for my important chat. Knowing this made me immediately forget all the things I'd been planning to say to her, which was just typical. Maybe the important chat could wait.

"Even Richie is gone?" I said, poking Mar in the arm, because she loved that.

"He's his own person, Caoimhe. He can do what he wants!" she said, not poking me back.

"You've literally arranged an exact time and place to meet him later, haven't you?" said Ciara, doing one of her faces that was somewhere between smug and very kissable, although the second part probably wasn't noticeable to everyone. I needed a drink. Or maybe something stronger.

"We may have, we may not have!" said Mar, poking Ciara now. She was poke mad, that one.

"Shhhh, listen!" said Bríd, because Elastica were starting up *Car Song*, another good one. All the rest of the band were just wearing t-shirts, but Justine had made an effort, with a black halter top. She'd nice arms. They looked good when she was rocking out on the guitar. Reminded me of someone else with skinny arms that were full of little muscles, but there was no point thinking about her anymore, she was gone. *Everyone I know, goes away, in the eeeeeend.*

"Have you got something special in your bag for me?" Ciara said, whispering into my ear. Her breath was all hot and filled with recent memories.

"Is that a euphemism?" I said, cos I was hilarious.

"Shhhhhh, let's disappear for a minute – come help me powder my nose," she said, still into my ear, making me feel all funny in my tummy.

"I've just come back!" I said, not protesting too much,

though. Now I could have the important chat with her. I'd remembered most of the points I was going to make. I could wing it after that. I was glad I hadn't paid for a ticket to this thing, because I'd probably seen more of the toilets than the actual bands.

*****

"God, that's good. Thanks!" Ciara said, after she'd sneeped a spoonful of my rapidly depleting stash up her greedy smellhole.

"Glad to be of service. I am Cork City's Pablo Escobar, after all," I said, scooping some more out for myself.

"Is he the soccer player? The one who got shot after he scored the own goal?" she said. No one ever knew who I meant by Pablo Escobar. Probably because none of them had read their dad's copy of *Kings of Cocaine* when they were far too young to be reading it, like I had.

"Close enough, Ciara. Close enough." Same country, at least. And almost the same name.

"So, did you want to talk to me, or something?" she said, regarding me in a very regardy way, even for her.

"What? No!" What? Yes!

"Oh. My mistake, then. Sorry." She gave me an *I don't believe you* look, and lit up a fag, making me want one too.

"What mistake was this?" I sniffed the delicious cocaine up and my nose welcomed it back, like an old friend, or a prodigal son.

"I just caught you looking at me a few times, and I thought you were wanting to tell me something, or say something. Maybe I was wrong, though." *Caught you!* Looking at her was a crime now, apparently.

"Well, I. I dunno, Ceer. It's been a long day," I said, sounding even more resigned than I actually was.

"It's been a *crazy* day." She took another drag on her fag and I couldn't resist any longer, so I took mine out and lit up.

"Just a bit. You coming back to the hotel?" Zach was gone off to be an honorary boy again, now, so I didn't have to worry about whether he was coming with us or not.

"What, now? Jesus, let me finish my fag first, you hussy!" She gave me a smile with her perfectly sized teeth. Were we flirting again? Probably not.

"No, I meant to do Bríd!"

"You're doing Bríd now? I can't keep up!"

"CIARA!!!" She was very annoying, sometimes.

"Sorry! I'm very annoying sometimes, aren't I?" Another smile. I'd never get annoyed with her smile, at least.

"You're grand," I said. I wanted to touch her. To touch her anywhere, really. And to be touched. What had I been planning on saying to her that was so important? The words had fallen out of my brain the second we closed the cubicle door.

"Hey." She put her hand on my waist, by the hip. I felt like I'd been given an electric shock, but in a good way.

"Hoi," I said, putting my own hand down to touch hers.

"Are you okay?" Her eyes were kind now.

"About what?" There were far too many different things to be okay or not okay about.

"About Frank." Oh. *That*.

"Oh. *That*. Yeah, I dunno. I'm trying not to think about it, you know? Until Marie rings, anyway." I realised then that Brian wasn't with us anymore, so he wouldn't be around when she called. He wouldn't have gone to the marquee with them though, he must be somewhere else, I thought. I'd ask Ash when we went back.

"Probably for the best, yeah." My hand was still on her hand, but it wasn't progressing to anything more. I wondered if I should just take it away, before it got awkward.

"I'm sorry for earlier," she said. Her other hand went to my opposite hip, and I got a nice feeling in my chest that wasn't just a cocaine one. I took a deep breath, and wished we were on pills, so I'd appreciate deep breaths more.

"Forget about it. You were right, I'm mental."

"You're not mental, Caoimhe." She touched the hair by my temple, and one of her fingers brushed the skin on my face.

"I think we should leave that for the medical professionals to decide, Ciara," I said, looking into her pretty eyes again.

"Okay, you're a little deranged. But I like deranged." Her face was almost close enough for me to kiss, but was that what she wanted? Someone call Phil Collins, cos I'm in the *Land of Confusion*, I thought.

"Thanks, I think?" I walked my fingers up her side, and it felt achingly familiar. We were so close, all I had to do was lean in and-

"Will we get back out there, yeah?" she said, stamping on my poor heart with her Converse All-Stars. "Or else we'll miss *Waking Up!*"

"Yeah, definitely." If we were in a romantic movie, I would have said some amazing line about missing waking up with her. But we weren't in a romantic movie, we were in a toilet. And anyway, I didn't know what waking up with her felt like – she kept fucking off while I was still asleep.

TWENTY-EIGHT

The mood in the van to the hotel was different. I couldn't quite put my finger on why it was different, but it was. Different from last night, definitely. No one was on ecstasy, was probably the reason. It was a much more downbeat vibe; you could feel it in the air. Booze was such a rubbish buzz compared with yokes. You could only drink so much before you got tired and depressed – especially on the third day of burning every end of your candles. I thought about Tim's candles, and then about Tim's penis. Some things you could never unsee.

"You know when this is all over?" said Aisling, who was sitting on the van floor with me, being my van floor buddy.

"What, life?" I said. I only had four fags left, I'd have to get some in the machine in the hotel.

"No, silly! This weekend," she said. Her fake leather pants made a squeaking sound that I mistook for a fart, until it made the exact same sound again, a second or two later. No two farts were that alike.

"Oh, I see. What about it?" I turned to look at her. She had a curious expression on her face. I wasn't sure what it meant yet.

"Will you be my friend, and stuff?"

"I am your friend, honey!"

"Ah, you're not, really. I mean – I know you, and you

know me, cause of all this stuff here, and Brian. And we know each other from school, kind of. But, I mean, we weren't *friends*." She looked somewhere between sad and adorable. I wanted to pick her up like a baby and rock her until the bads went away.

"Oh, Aisling…"

"No, it's okay. Like, I wouldn't have expected to be friends with you or anything. You're really cool and stuff…"

"I am not. I'm an eejit, really," I said. I wasn't cool. I just did cool things. That didn't make me cool. Although maybe it did, to other people. It was impossible for me to know, since I wasn't other people.

"You're not. You're really cool. To me, anyway. Maybe once I get to know you better, I'll see the eejit inside, though," she said, looking even more adorable now.

"I'd like that!" I said, throwing an arm around her because she looked like she needed some serious hugging.

"Good. So you'll be my friend then? My *real* friend?"

"Of course!" I wanted to spend loads of time with her from now on. She was much cooler than me, she just didn't know it yet.

"Real friends – talking on the phone, going shopping together, going for lunches…"

"Aisling, I'm a massive introvert, I'd hate all those things. They'd suck the life force out of me," I said, trying not to crush her dreams too hard.

"Well thank fuck for that, I'd hate them too. I was just testing you, like. Will we just go for nice walks together, and cook meals at home for each other, and watch movies in our bedrooms instead?" She put her arm around me too now, so we were van floor huggy buddies.

"Now you're talking my language," I said. "I mean we

can totally go out on the tear and stuff, too. I'm fine with all that as long as I'm shitfaced."

"Okay, we'll do that too, then."

"We'll do everything! Hooray!" I said. My mood was lifting already, I really hoped there wasn't another twist coming in this weekend. If Aisling turned out to be an android like Ian Holm's character in Alien, I'd be very disappointed.

"Well not *everything* everything, mind," she said, mysteriously. She took a fag off me, cos we were Brianless for a while.

"No?" If she couldn't do some things because she was an android like Lance Henriksen's character in Aliens, I'd be very disappointed.

"Well, yeah. No fingering and no lickouts." I *knew* she was going to say something like that, but it still made me laugh, regardless.

"Boooooo! Hissssss!" I said, absolutely 100% not picturing either of those things in my coked-up mind, because I was a gentlewoman.

"Okay, not until I'm single again then," she said, definitely only joking, but still.

*****

"All righty, then! Are we gonna cheer up, or will I just turn the van around and drive back to Limerick?" Benson had turned into a dad. We were heading into the underground car park, and no one had said anything in a while. It was like a comedown, but we weren't coming down from anything. Except maybe the high of performing, or all the alcohol we'd been drinking since some time in the morning, or a big whack off an opium joint, or various bumps of cocaine – although Aisling wasn't coming down from hers. She was so new to it that she was still flying. She just had no one to be flying with. I felt like I was made of rocks.

"Shut up, Benson," said Ciara, because we all were thinking it, but she was the only one who could be arsed saying it. We needed a boost. We needed a reason to be cheerful. We needed a schoolbag full of ecstasy tablets.

"Okay, I'll shut up then," he said, not even sounding pissed off. I was starting to like him, all the same. You never saw him giving Bríd evil looks or dragging her away from us for some tense argument. And she seemed very happy with him, in a *content* way – it wasn't one of those horribly intense things that burned bright and turned to ashes quickly. I'd give him the benefit of the doubt from now on, I decided. I'd be nicer to him. I'd treat him a little kinder.

"So, are you still letting Bríd borrow another one of your sexy outfits for tonight, Kweev?" he said, parking the van. Half of them only realised we were at the hotel when the engine stopped, they were so immersed in drudginess.

"Not if it's gonna end up festooned with your technicolour cock-yoghurt, you sex case." My truce with him had been short and unmemorable, but at least I'd got a laugh out of this miserable bunch.

*****

"The Stone Roses, though. We're going to get to see them live. Think about that, like! When was the last time they played Ireland? Have they ever played Ireland?" Benson was still trying to get us going and enthusiastic and happy. I felt like I wanted to go to sleep, although the cocaine wasn't going to let me any time soon, so I'd just end up lying in bed, thinking a billion thoughts, and feeling fidgety.

"Don't know, don't care," I said. I didn't even have the will to make a joke about him being old enough to remember the last time they played. I was that bad.

"Come on, ladies. Let's uh… oh, I dunno." Aisling didn't look tired or anything, but everyone else's downer mood seemed to be draining the enthusiasm out of her too.

"Bríd, do you wanna go get those outfits from my room, then?" I hadn't the enthusiasm to even look for my key. She could just kick the door down if she wanted them.

"Ugh, I dunno, Kweev. I mean I tried them all on last night, and ye all saw them." She didn't sound arsed. Dress Up Bríd Part 2 was looking unlikely.

"I didn't," said Aisling, not protesting too much, though.

"Me neither," said Ciara, sounding even less arsed than Bríd.

"We seriously need to put on some music," said Marian, which was a good idea, but I couldn't think of a single song that would get me in the mood for... anything. Maybe Benson should have driven us back to Limerick when he'd threatened to. At least my own bed was there.

"Where's the CD player? Or is there one?" said Aisling.

"It's in Tim's room, remember?" I said, remembering *Heroin*, and The Doors, and Tim's genitals. It was like having flashbacks to Vietnam.

"Where's the CDs?" said Marian. "Good CDs, I mean. Not stuff that'll make us go mad and get naked."

"I'm fine with you all getting naked. Might cheer things up," said Benson, who had developed a death wish, apparently. If looks could make noises, the ones we all threw him would have sounded like a nest of vipers, hissing.

"Portia had a wallet thing," I said, wondering if she'd taken that too, as well as Frank's bag, and his reasons for living.

"That's in my room," said Marian. "So are the wigs, if anyone wants a wig?"

"Is there a wig that'll make me not want to curl up and

die?" I said, realising I'd forgotten to get fags, and now I'd have to go out to the hall and get in the lift.

"There's a blonde one. Blondes have more fun, I heard," said Bríd, looking like fun was some foreign country she'd never visited.

"Do we?" said Marian, taking out a new twenty box of fags, at least 36 of which belonged to me. Not that I was counting.

"What's *wrong* with us???" said Ciara, having a yawn, which made everyone else yawn too.

"I don't know," said Marian. "I was fine until near the end of Elastica, then I just came over all... bleh."

"It's like Friday and Saturday were the buzz, and tonight is the big, harsh comedown," said Ciara. Her eyes didn't even look purple anymore. That was one of the signs of the apocalypse, probably.

"I need a shower," I said, not wanting to move, let alone get wet and have to make myself dry again.

"Go have one then, chickee," said Bríd. Benson had given up already. He was just sitting on the floor next to her, staring at nothing.

"Don't feel like it," I said. I had the three pills, still. I could go into the toilet and neck them all at the same time. And have the rest of the cocaine. And some speed. And then overdose and die, with any luck. There was a knock on Ian's door. It didn't register with most of us at first, because we weren't expecting anyone to arrive, and it was a bit late for the maids to change the beds or anything.

"Did everyone else hear that?" Aisling said, still looking really alert, compared with the rest of us, which wouldn't be difficult. The knock came again, louder this time.

"Someone gonna open it?" I said, definitely not volunteering.

"WHO IS IT?" shouted Ciara, way too loud for any of our fragile dispositions.

"DELIVERY!" said the woman's voice on the other side of the door.

"Did we order food?" Bríd said. Benson shook his head.

"WHAT DELIVERY?" Ciara screamed, even louder than the last time.

"Delivery! Open up!" said the woman, which felt odd. There was something peculiar going on. But I wasn't going to turn down a free takeaway, cos I was suddenly starving again.

"Open the door, Benson!" I said, because if we had to have a man here, we might as well make use of him to scare off murderers.

"Okay, okay." He stood up slowly and went over. We all sat silently, moving our necks to follow him, dying to see what might happen next. He turned the knob and pulled the door inward. I wondered if it was pizza, or chips, or-

"Okay, which one of you *fuckers* ordered a Chinese?" said Portia, stepping over the threshold. She was wearing a baby blue Oasis t-shirt over last night's denim hotpants, although she had tackies on instead of heels, so she looked much tinier. Most importantly, she had a bag on her shoulder – it was Frank's bag, and it did *not* look empty.

*****

"But how the fuck did you get on the ferry, without a passport?" Marian said, a little later, when Portia was telling us her tale. We had got the important stuff out of the way, first. Namely, everyone necking one of the precious speckled doves. Then she'd perched on Ian's bed and started from the beginning. She'd been wandering through the crowd, looking for Bríd, when we all split up. She'd started coming up on the acid Benson had given her, when she witnessed the whole thing with Niall and Frank and the Drug Squad. She'd panicked, kicked off her shoes, and ran all the way to the hotel to get the drugs, because they were in her room, and she was terrified that the police were going to find out about them. So even though she didn't really have a plan, she grabbed the bag and put on some sneakers and got the hell out of there. She'd been walking aimlessly up the road when a bus stopped, and the driver started talking to her. It was the Menswear tour bus. They'd invited her on, and that was when her mental adventure had begun.

"You don't need a passport for the boat," B said. He'd probably know, as he drove, and he was old, and he'd been across the water for all those abortions, I thought.

"Yeah, but you have to check in or something, don't you? So you can pay, or show your ticket?" I'd only been on that ferry crossing to England once, with school, and I remember vaguely having to show someone a ticket at some point.

"Oh, we didn't have the tickets, pudding – not until later, anyway. I didn't even know we were on the ferry until the waves started making the floor of the bus all wobbly, and even then, I just thought the acid was a bit strong!" It was amazing to have her here with us. It hadn't even been a long time; it was just I'd assumed I'd never see her again. So, seeing her now, so unexpectedly, was like coming up on an E. Although I'd be doing that too, soon enough. What a life we led.

"So, you were just in the bus, hanging with the Menswear lads, driving to Wexford..." Ciara said.

"Well I didn't know where we were driving *to*, sugarplum. I couldn't even look and see road signs – the whole thing is converted inside. Blacked out windows, no bus seats, just couches and chairs and bean bags, like a big, double-long living room. I just was glad that I was safe from the cops!" She laughed, and it was great to hear that again too.

"So did you have sex with the whole band?" said Benson, tactful as ever.

"What? No, they were all really sweet, B. Gentlemen, all of them. They absolutely double-love a fucking drink – that's not some image made up by their record company, trust me. But they were quadruple-cool with me. A few of them chatted me up at the Féile thing, yeah, but that was all bravado, I think. They didn't do anything like that when I was their actual *guest*. I felt triple-safe, there was no fear of me, as you white people say."

"Even though they kidnapped you and took you to England," said Aisling, smoking a fag she'd robbed off Mar.

"Wales!" said Portia. "Beautiful place, apparently. Not that we saw much of it, cupcake."

"You didn't?" I said. I was trying to do the timeline in my head, but I didn't know how long it took to drive to Rosslare from Cork, because I didn't drive. They must have sailed in the early hours of the morning, and got there when the sun came up, because the sun came up pretty early this time of year.

"No, cos we had to come back almost as soon as we arrived – well, a few hours later, anyway, lemon slice. Love your dress, by the way – it's lush. You'll have to tell me about it later – and about your gig that I missed by being such a double-douche, sorry."

"Ah, you're grand. You didn't miss much, Ling," I lied, whitely. So what parts of Wales did you actually see?" I'd called her the thing while other people were around, but no one had noticed, so it was fine, probably.

"Ah, I saw the sky, the ground, some hills, and then mainly the inside of a pub in Fishguard called The Boar's

Head. They do very nice food, actually. You should pop in if you're ever there. Tell them Portia recommended the lasagne."

"I'll make a note of it," I said. We hadn't told her about Frank, yet. I wondered how we were going to bring it up without devastating her. She thought she was doing the right thing, last night. And she'd kind of indirectly got us our slot, by taking Menswear to the actual United Kingdom for a booze cruise, even if it hadn't been her idea. And she had brought back all the drugs and all Frank's money. It felt like it would be the shittiest thing in the world to lay that guilt on her now. Maybe we'd tell her tomorrow.

"Can I carry on telling this story later, possums? I really need a shower and a change of knickers and a big hug, not necessarily in that order. I assume we're going back for the Roses?" Portia hopped down off the bed, and I noticed again how teeny she was without her stilt shoes.

"We are! And we're actually going to enjoy it now, thanks to you! C'meeeeeere!" said Aisling, giving her the big hug she'd requested. They broke apart after a bit and instinctively put their arms out to usher the rest of us in for one big group cuddle. Even Benson, who was definitely not an honorary girl, but he had a van, so it was best to keep him sweet.

*****

"Oh, perfect. Turn that up, Ceer." We were in my room, sitting on the bed, waiting for Portia to finish her shower. I'd found a local radio station that played all indie and alternative tunes. That was what I felt like listening to now, not dancey stuff. I'd probably feel differently when I came up on my yoke, though. The Stone Roses were yoke music, though. Especially *Fool's Gold*. They'd been around during the golden age of yokes – at the Hacienda, in Manchester. I knew things!

"Absolutely!" she said, turning the volume up full

blast. It was *Cannonball*, by the Breeders. Possibly the greatest guitar song ever created by woman, man, or herd of goats. The bathroom door clicked, and out came Portia, holding a face towel over the breasts she claimed not to have, and wearing a spectacular pair of knickers.

"A hundred and fifty dollars. Frederick's of Hollywood," she said.

"Sorry, what?" I said, transfixed by the knickerage now. They were a sort of yellow colour that was almost amber. They were even more *ridiculous* than my Brazilian ones, and I'd only seen the front, so far. They were half sheer, half embroidered, and they fit her like they'd been painted on.

"My paaaaanties, dear. I assume that's what you're both gawping at, and not just my fortune cookie." She grabbed the top she'd laid out and pulled it on, dropping the towel as she did it. It was like that magic trick where the guy pulled the tablecloth off, and all the crockery stayed where it was.

"Fortune cookie!" I said, cracking up. It was *so good* to have her back.

"Is there a wise saying inside it?" said Ciara.

"That's for me to know and you to find out, custard cream." She pulled on a pair of amazing blue-green silky flares that sparkled when you looked at them, and the best knickers in history were gone from our sight.

"Promises, promises… uh." Ciara didn't know her surname. Only I was privy to that sort of information, because I was special.

"Xû!" said Portia, doing up her flies. Apparently, I wasn't that special anymore.

"Gesundheit!" I said, because I was hilarious. Her top was cool – just a white cotton sleeveless thing, with a high neck, but it had four diagonal rips across it, like she'd had a run-in with Freddy Krueger.

"Very good," she said, winking at me. Ciara just looked confused. "Who's going next in there, or are you going in together, you lovers?"

"Uh…" I didn't look at Ciara, there was already enough awkwardness in the room to power a small African village for the best part of a year.

"I don't think that works in real life, really – it's just a movie thing," Ciara said, giving my thigh a little squeech that relieved most of the tension, thank God.

"Yeah," I said. "In real life it'd just be a load of soap in your eyes and things accidentally going in the wrong hole," I said, not sure if I was making things better or worse.

"There are no wrong holes, cupcake," Portia said, picking up the highest platform shoes ever created by man, woman, or herd of goats. "There are only wrong lovers."

"Thanks, Come-fucious," said Ciara, grabbing a towel and fresh undies off the bed next to me, so she was going next, apparently. I lit up the last fag in my box, and patted the mattress beside me, cos I wanted some lovely Portianess before I went for my scrub.

"A hundred and fifty dollars for a pair of knick-knicks, Ling? Rrrrreally?" I brushed her fringe out of her eyes in quite a practical, non-flirty way, although it still felt a bit illicit, with my missus who wasn't my missus in the shower next to us.

"Well, I don't wear bras, so I can afford to splash out on the bottom bits, kitten." She stroked my cheek in a way that made me feel a bit like an actual kitten. Or maybe a sex kitten. I immediately felt all tingly. I'd missed her, and this.

"Speaking of splashing out, if I paid that much for a pair of knickers, I'd have to train myself to never have discharge again," I said, immediately killing the mood, because I was become Kweeva, Destroyer of Shags.

*****

When I finally got in the shower it was glorious. I left Portia and Ciara to catch up, or to play Can't Do Me, or to vigorously sixty-nine each other – whatever they decided was best. I'd already decided what to wear – inspired by Portia's thrown-together outfit. My white denim shorts, and a band t-shirt, plus some strappy shoes. That would be perfect. The water felt incredible on my skin. Whether it was the temperature, the pressure, or what, I didn't know. I'd been standing there for five minutes before I remembered I needed to wash myself as well. I put some shampoo in my hair and lathered it up. That felt brilliant too. The texture of the suds on my fingers; the scraping of my nails on the scalp, the little ouch in the roots when I pulled the length out until it squeaked. It was like a sensory overload. I turned around to rinse it out and the trickle of hot water down my spine and over my bum was like a waterfall of niceness. I was hot and chilly at the same time. I stepped out of the stream to put conditioner in, and I could feel every individual droplet roll down my body like they were someone's fingers trailing over me. It was bizarre. This was truly the greatest shower ever had by man, woman, or herd of goats. I stepped towards the nozzle again and the spray on my face felt like being kissed by angels. I moved a little to let the full blast hit my chest and *that* was a whole new experience. I moved back again, inch by inch, so the jet stream hit new bits of me. My rib cage, my belly, and then… well, when the water hit the entrance to Vajayjay Valley, it became incredibly clear that I was coming right up on my pill.

"Oh, wow…"

I put my forearm under the water, and it was the same amazing feeling. On my arm! The least erogenous of the appendages.

"Fucking hell."

I could feel every individual drop as it hit the skin and rolled off. I angled myself so the water hit me on the thigh, now.

"Fuck. Me. PINK."

"Are you okay in there, honey? It was Ciara, outside the door. I switched the water off for a second so I could hear her.

"Yeah! I'm, um, fine. Why?" My body already missed the delicious, prickly stream of warm, wet micro-massages.

"Oh, nothing. You were just... shouting stuff."

"What? Was I saying those things out loud?" I'd been in my own little world – I'd forgotten about the existence of other humans, or that they had ears.

"Very out loud, yes." Ciara sounded much happier. Maybe she was coming up too, or maybe it was from the vigorous sixty-nineing. Both were equally possible. I turned the shower back on, and it went cold for a couple of seconds, so I got a blast of icy spray right on the boobs.

"JEEEEEESUS! That's so good!" The cold was even better than the warm, almost. I needed to remember this whole phenomenon for the next time I took yokes, definitely. I needed to tell everyone else about it too. Maybe I could write a book about it? I'd be a *billionaire*, probably.

"What's *so good*, pudding?" Portia, this time. "You're not flicking your bean in there, are you? Want us to come give you a hand?"

"Ah, no. I'm not flicking my – I'm just really coming up. On the yoke. And the shower feels really nice. It's all... ffffffffffsssss – it's all... so... *nice*." The water was warm again, and I'd found the little flicky switch on the shower head to change it from a wide spray to a narrow jet. Oh boy.

"Ah, yeah. That'll do it all right. Well when I'm dressed,

I'm dressed, so I'm not getting in there with you, sorry," said Ciara, laughing. I wondered what it would feel like being in here with your clothes still on. Probably brilliant, since everything felt brilliant.

"And I definitely would, lemon slice, but it's not the movies, so I'd just get soap in my eyes, and an accidental fist up my arse," said Portia.

"Yeah, and none of us wants to have to explain that to the nurses in A&E, Ling. I have to rinse this conditioner out anyway, but tell me – is this shower head fixed to the wall, or does it come off so you can move it around?"

"Fixed to the wall," said both of them, at the same time, and with the same disappointed tone.

"Right, I'll be out in a minute then," I said, equally disappointed. Maybe it was for the best, mind, or I might have spent the whole night in the shower, blasting my bean, and poor little Ian Brown would be raging that I stood him up.

*****

"Jesus, Bríd! I didn't recognise you!" I said, when we got back in to 213. She had her hair hidden in a wig again – this time it was red – the auburn kind – in an Uma Thurman length bob.

"You look like an assassin. A sexy assassin, who assassinates men. With sex," said Ciara, who was probably definitely up on her yoke now, from the sounds of that.

"Is it a bit too much?" said Bríd, as if that concept even existed anymore.

"No!" said Portia. "Where did you get the catsuit??? You look like Bridget Fonda. Bríd Ó Fondah, maybe."

"Haha! Bríd Ó Fondah. No, that's another Kweeva Shox original," I said. It was very cool, all the same. Sheer flesh coloured nylon, covered in black fishnet. There were magic blurry bits to hide your nipples, and the knickers area was opaque, so it probably wasn't breaking any indecency laws. The wig really went with it, though. All she needed was a gun. Or maybe a samurai sword.

"Your dress is so beautiful, Ciara," said Aisling. It really was – a light blue, knee-length thing, with a deep neckline, and beautiful patterns of birds and orchids all over it. It looked sort of Japanese. She was single-handedly representing the Far East this weekend, one dress at a time.

"Thanks! Look at you though, all Hollywood; where did you get that?"

"Oh, this is Bríd's! She's got clothes going spare, since she took up the Sex Assassin life." It was a simple looking navy blue, short bandage dress – sleeveless and strapless, but she had the legs to make it look like Billy Joel might try to marry her if she wandered into his petrol station.

"Sorry to interrupt this episode of Head 2 Toe, ladies, but I have an announcement," said Benson, who I'd forgotten was still with us.

"Inviting us to your 50th birthday, are you?" I said.

"Are there 50 blow jobs at that one, or is it like birthday candles, where you stop after you're about 30?" said Ciara.

"Firstly, fuck off, both of you. Secondly, I'm only just coming up on this E, so my willy still works…"

"Congratulations, Benson!" said Aisling, giving him a friendly pat on the shoulder.

"Is he going to suggest a reverse gang bang? Because I'd just like to say up front – I'm about 70% not willing to do that," said Portia, intriguingly.

"He's saying that we're going next door for a few minutes," said Bríd. "So I can assassinate him with my vajayjay."

"Oh!" said everyone.

"Okay, but be quick, cos Stone Roses!" I said, suddenly remembering the Stone Roses existed.

"He's never quick, remember?" Ciara said, making B give Bríd a look, but he could hardly be mad at her – she'd given him great reviews.

"Speaking of quick – everyone come here, quick," said Portia, so we did.

"What's going on, China Doll. We doing a prayer circle?" I said. She smelled so great; I couldn't believe I'd gone almost whole rotation of the Earth without smelling her.

Nope, we're double-dropping!" She opened her hand and revealed a multitude of speckled doves.

"Are we? What's that then?" I said, taking a pill off her, since everyone else was.

"Well it's the third day on these, so they mightn't be as strong or last as long, so…" Portia popped hers in her gob.

"So we drop another one while we're coming up on the first one, and Bob's your lobster," said Bríd, which wasn't as scientific as her usual explanations, but I got the gist.

"It's only my second day!" said Legs, the cailín dána, necking hers anyway, because she was the most hardcore bitch I'd ever met.

"Right, we're off, see you in a while," said Bríd, blowing us all kisses as B dragged her off for a good seeing-to.

"Oh, and if any of ye want to come in and watch, it's ten quid each," he said, making the money gesture with his thumb and finger.

"BENSON!!!" said Bríd.

"What???"

"That's degrading to me!"

"Fine then," he said, shrugging. "Twenty quid each."

"That's more like it," she said, and then they were gone.

"We're going to listen to them, right?" said Aisling, lighting up yet another cigarette despite not being a smoker.

"Oh, 100%," said Ciara. "If they *didn't* want us to listen, they'd have gone to a room that wasn't right next to us, like."

"Perverts, the two of them," I said, "Sickening, deviant perverts. Hey, does that thing from the movies with the glass tumbler against the wall actually work?"

*****

"The start of this is like the start of *Rebel Girl*," said Aisling. "By Bikini Kill?" We were in the van, en route to Páirc Uí Chaoimh, listening to *I Am the Resurrection* on the CD player.

"It does, yeah! And *All Along the Watchtower* as well," I said. "I love that you're into cool music, Legs."

"Ah, you only think it's cool because it's the same music you're into, Arse." Hopefully that wasn't my new nickname from her. It wasn't the same as calling someone Legs. I didn't want people thinking she thought I was an arse.

"That's true, but still. I didn't know you listened-"

"You didn't know I listened to *music*, Kweev?" She gave me a funny look. I hoped I hadn't offended her.

"No, I just – I mean, in school and stuff, to look at you, well-"

"Nerdy unpopular girls have bedrooms too, Kweev," she said, offering me a chewing gum like the lifesaver she was. "And we have walls full of posters, and CD players full of songs, and hearts full of dreams."

"Stop making me love you more than I already do, Legs. I might just burst, with all the love," I said. Double-dropping was the greatest invention known to man, woman, or herd of goats.

"If you think you love me now, wait until you taste my delicious Arrabiata," she said, reminding me of our impending future best friendship.

"Well I've never heard it called that before, but I'm sure it's very tasty, dear," I said, cos I was hilarious.

*****

"How married are you to this t-shirt, sausage?" Portia was touching the material of my Rolling Stones tee – the one with the Sticky Fingers mouth. We were almost at the stadium. *Shoot You Down* was on the CD player – I loved that one. I loved all that album, really. Everyone did.

"What do you mean? Do you want it?" She could have it if she wanted. She could have what was underneath it too. Quiet, brain!

"No!!! I just am, I got you something, chocolate chip." She was holding a plastic bag. I'd seen her with it earlier, but I'd forgotten to ask her about it.

"A present? For meeeee?" Everyone was watching us, I noticed. Must have been nothing good on telly.

"Yeah, just a little thing, cream bun. But hopefully a special one. I got it for you when I was in Wales. I saw it in a gift shop, and I thought it was very you."

"Well now I'm intrigued." I felt touched – both that she had thought of me to bring me home a present, and that she thought she knew me enough to pick something I'd like.

"You're a Size 8, yeah?" She went into the bag to get the thing, which was apparently clothes, going by that important clue.

"Keep your voice down, Ling. These bitches hate me enough already as it is!"

"Haha, no one hates you, Kweeva Shox. You're Kweeva

Shox. Anyway, here, look!" She held up the thing. It was a t-shirt. A gorgeous shade of purple, in the ringer style (I remembered what it was called now) with a white collar and white sleeve bands. In the middle was a painting of a half a lemon, and a lemon slice.

"Oh, it's PERFECT!" I said, not exaggerating. If it didn't fit me, I was going to get on the ferry to Wales myself and get the next size up.

"It is, isn't it? Because you love lemon slices, and you *are* a lemon slice. And you love things that are purple, too." She pointed at the streaks in her hair, at the purple strappy heels she'd nudged me towards wearing earlier (I knew why, now!) and then at Ciara's eyes, which surprised her a bit, from the expression she made.

"This is all very true, thank you!" I said, giving her a big Irish hug on her tiny Chinese body.

"Try it on!" Ciara said. Everyone else said similar things, so I had to obey.

"Okay, wish me luck that I'm still a Size 8, lads," I said, as if I *wanted* them all to hate me or something. I whipped off the Stones one and replaced it with my new special present from my new special friend.

"Perfect fit!" said Marian. She'd been quiet on the drive over. Probably missing Richie, the poor sap. She was wearing cool indie clothes tonight. A black pinafore dress with a ribbed white top under it, and knee-high oxblood Docs. She was so pretty she could dress down and still look like she was doing a magazine shoot about dressing down. She looked like a proper rock star's girlfriend, but then she was, for now anyway.

"Best present ever, Portia," Aisling said, giving her a hug. I was old enough to remember a time when Portia didn't do hugs or handshakes. It had been quite the journey, watching her grow so much since… yesterday afternoon. The van stopped; we were here. I looked around at them all and thought about how much I loved them right now. I had a strong feeling that this was going to be a weekend I'd never, ever forget. None of us would. Heaven *was* a place on Earth, but that place wasn't on any map. It was wherever you happened to be, if you were there with the best people you knew.

TWENTY-NINE

We'd managed to get there for the start. *I Wanna Be Adored*. First song on the first album, and the first song they played in their set tonight. Hearing the bass line build up as we made our way through all the people felt like we were living the opening scene of a movie, even if it was actually almost the closing scene of Féile 95, and our incredible weekend, and my mad bisexual adventure.

Portia was back with us, and she was safe and good and not the villain of the piece anymore. Frank was alive and, hopefully, okay. Marian and Richie had found each other in a field in Cork, by a mixture of fate and strange coincidences. John Squire's lovely, melodic lead guitar rang out over the park – tens of thousands of people in various states of intoxication and joy, moving their bodies and nodding their heads along with every note on an invisible tablature. The atmosphere was so incredible you could almost see it in the air around us, like a lovely, welcoming fog that you just wanted to lose yourself in forever.

Aisling was beside me, gripping on tight to my arm as we meandered towards the big screens and the stage, smiling at strangers and passing good vibes between ourselves and anyone we brushed against – it felt like we were ants passing new knowledge to the rest of the colony by rubbing our feelers together. She'd had a mad adventure too, and we were going to be great pals after all this was over. I couldn't wait. I had so few real friends – it was something you only ever realised whenever school ended for the summer, and the amount of people in your day to day life dropped dramatically, because they were no longer forced to be in a building with you for seven hours a day. When school was over forever, you had to fill those gaps with new college buddies or work colleagues, but it was the same deal, really. They weren't your real friends. Your real friends were the ones who wanted to be around you when there was no reason except to be around you. When you found people like that, you held onto them for good. I held onto Aisling now, and my heart swelled up with a mixture of actual love and feeling-exaggerating chemicals. There was just about enough room in there for both.

"This is very... peopley, isn't it?" Aisling said. I wondered if she hated crowds as much as I did, and if she didn't really mind them when she was off her face, like I didn't.

"There's certainly a lot of... folks," I said, regarding all the random faces and limbs that made up the collective entity of good times and happy feelings. We were part of it, but we were our own separate thing too. I wondered where the boys were, and if we'd even find them in this crowd. We probably would though, because they were part of our separate thing – even Ian, who was a gowl for 99% of his waking life. And because Richie and Marian could probably sniff each other out like a Great White smelling a drop of blood in a thousand miles of water.

"It's the Stone Roses! Hooray!" said Ciara, who was linking arms with Portia now. They'd probably bonded during their *soixante-neuf* earlier.

"Apart from Reni, said Benson, who had managed to cut his sex time down from the regulation *at least an hour* to about six minutes, earlier, not that anyone was timing them with a stopwatch or anything. Faster Benson Sex equalled a very screamy Bríd, we'd learned, through the thin hotel room walls. No purple spunk damage to my catsuit as far as I could make out, though. I'd wondered how they'd even managed it, with her in that getup, but then I remembered that there were snaps on the crotch, for when you needed the loo. The fact that B's sweaty, 1960s penis had been going in and out through that magic weeing hatch was enough for me to decide I could never wear it again, so she could have it as a gift, now. It would save me the hassle of having to burn it.

"Apart from Reni," I said, because their drummer had quit – I'd read that somewhere, or else someone had told me. Possibly someone who was Benson.

"I want a Richie. Get me a Richie, please." Marian had no one linking her or holding her hand – she was the odd one out, it was lousy. I pulled her over to my side that didn't have an Aisling on it and grabbed as much of her as I could.

"If you build it, he will come," I said, loving the feel of her hair on my skin and all the gorgeous scents of her when she leaned her head into my neck.

"I want him to come now, though," she said, taking out a fag box and offering us both one.

"He'll find you, Mar. He has to. He's your destiny and stuff," Aisling said, swiping a ciggie like a *cailín dána*.

"Yeah, he's your swan," I said, because swans mated for life. Everyone knew that. They could also break your arm with their wings. Everyone knew that, too.

"*You're the swan that I want. You are the swan I want,*" she sang, her face cheering up again. What a *ridiculous* smile.

"*Ooh! Ooh! Oooooh!*" me and Aisling sang back, because we knew all the cool music.

*****

"No, sorry. I have a boyfriend," I said to the random man who had decided to interrupt my perfect, heavenly night to chat me up.

"Oh, right so. He's a lucky man!" said the boy person, then he left.

"You don't have a boyfriend," Aisling said, looking confused and lovely at the same time.

"Yeah, but you know… the thing," I said.

"What's *the thing*?" she said, clearly not knowing about the thing.

"Boys fuck off quicker if you tell them you're taken," said Portia, also looking lovely, but not confused. She knew about the thing. "It's like they respect another man's property more than they respect a woman having her own free will. It's double-cuntish of them."

"Exactly. If you tell them you're just not interested, they take it one of two ways, Legs. Either *really* personally – cos how dare you not find them delightful, or something…"

"Or they take your polite *no* as a soft *maybe*, and they just think it's up to them to persist a bit more. Or, worse, they think you not wanting to be with them is a problem they need to solve, and we all know how men are such natural problem solvers," said Ciara, looking lovely too, and also very booby. Looking at Ciara's cleavage when I was on yokes was like gargling champagne with my eyes – in a good way.

"They're not, though, are they?" I said. I usually went to my mum when I had a problem. Well, unless it was a legal problem, and that had literally only happened for the first time today.

"No, they just think they are," said Ciara, turning around to look up at the stage, so I was no longer hypnotised by her swollen, creamy-skinned front bumps. I was dead poetic, sometimes.

"Fucking eejits," said Aisling, pulling up the top part of her borrowed Bríd dress, because gravity had been up to his old tricks while she was dancing.

"Hey, Ling..." I said, having her full attention now Ciara was watching John Squire absolutely wailing on the guitar during Waterfall.

"Yes, lemon lumps?" she said, looking at my chest and then at my face.

"Lemon lumps! No, what I was going to say was, I just realised the craziest part of your Wales story, Ling."

"What was that?" She was doing a little dance while she spoke. Barely moving overall, but also definitely moving every part of her, really sensually and sexily. It was a dance that someone who never felt self-conscious would do, but that was her – she was outsecure.

"Well the fact that you accidentally smuggled enough drugs to put you behind bars for twenty years into one country, and then back again to another country."

"I KNOW, cupcake! I kept thinking about it – I was quintuple-paranoid! The boys showed me a hatch thing in the floor of the bus, under the carpet, where they kept their weed, but I was like, no thanks."

"Why no thanks?" said Ciara, who was back, and had brought the twins with her. I was never going to be able to fancy boys again, I thought. Although I still fancied Tim Wheeler, and he'd have looked really silly with tits.

"Because I thought if we were unlucky enough to be met by some sniffer dogs, that hatch would be the first place they'd sniff out, see?"

"Not just a pretty face, are you?" said Ciara, kissing her on the cheek in a long, smoochy way that seemed new, to me anyway.

"Nope. I've also got a *lovely* little box," said Portia, giving her a kiss back on her cheek.

"Oh, we're aware," said Ciara.

"We've seen the goods," I said, remembering her fortune cookie in its $150 wrapper.

"Well, now I feel left out," said Aisling, messing. She passed me a lit fag and I didn't even query where she'd produced it from. We were long past that, now.

"We'll send you a postcard from it," said Ciara, and I laughed, even though I didn't really get the joke.

"You're ridiculous looking, though, Ling," I said. "You don't even look human."

"Is that supposed to be a compliment, or should I be offended?" said Portia, pretending to look confused.

"It's definitely a compliment," Ciara said, getting all touchy feely with her. "Like, I was looking at you after your shower, and you were standing up straight, but it looked like you were leaning forward, if that makes sense?" It did not make sense.

"Elucidate, please," I said. The Roses were doing Ten Storey Love song, one of the best ones off the new album, I thought. Ian's voice was... not good tonight, but no one seemed to mind, so it was grand.

"Okay. Like, I have a *tummy* – shut up, you bitches, this isn't me fishing for compliments – and when I'm looking at myself in the mirror, sometimes I lean my top half forward, and it makes my stomach look smaller, and my waist and my hips look better – you know what I mean?"

"A bit, yeah," I said. I did things to make my elephant thighs look less elephanty or my beak nose look less beaky, but it was all the same thing, really.

"Okay, well this one," she put her arm around Portia and pulled her nearer to her. "This one just looks like that, naturally. Like, you have no tummy. I don't know where you keep your organs. Your intestines must be the length of *one* sausage. Where's your liver? In your handbag?" We all laughed, even Portia, which was the important bit. Otherwise it would have felt mean.

"I ate it, with some Fava beans, and a niiiice Chiaaaaanti," she said, and we all did the noise with our mouths, because it was compulsory. I looked around, sensing a presence, and there were the boys.

*****

"Wow, this is the best t-shirt in the world!" Ian said, feeling me all over said t-shirt, but not in a weird way and not on the boobs, so I didn't have to headbutt him for it.

"Er, thanks? Yours is much nicer, though. I *covet* the fuck out of it." I didn't feel his t-shirt up. Looking at it was enough, and I didn't want him to think I was trying to ride him.

"Naaaah, mine is shit. Yours is lovely. It *feels* lovely too. You're lovely, Caoimhe. Did I ever tell you that – how lovely you are?" He was creeping me out with how nice he was being. The Stone Roses were playing *Daybreak*, off the new one. I didn't love it, but it was kind of funky and it made you want to boogie a bit.

"Er, thanks again. Hang on a second," I looked into his eyes, in a non-romantic way, I hoped. "Are you on yokes???"

"I am!" he said, laughing a big smiley laugh, and smiling a big laughy smile.

"How??? We have the Es!"

"We have the Es, too, Caoimhe. We have loads of Es. Cos of Tim!" He was dancing now; I didn't like it. It was like he'd been possessed by some friendly, happy demon.

"Tim?"

"Tim is a DJ now," said Marian, appearing next to me. She'd found her swan. He was also off his face, from the looks of him. The plot was getting really thick.

"Elucidate, PLEASE!" I said. The Stone Roses were between songs, and I could hear a little better.

"Timbo knows Carl Cox, apparently. Something to do with when we played in Camden with the Cranberries. I don't remember the whole story, like. But anyway, he gets chatting to Carl, down in the tent, and next thing we know, Tim is on the decks, mixing tunes. In front of Carl Cox's crowd! And everyone who was there to see the Chemical Brothers too," said Niall, who I'd forgotten was out of chokey.

"What a plot twist!!! And what, did Carl Cox give ye a load of yokes, then?" This weekend just got madder and madder. The Roses started up a new song. It was just a load of weird noises first, then I realised it was *Breaking into Heaven*.

"Nah, I don't think Carl does drugs. We got the yokes off Tim's groupies," said Ian, still feeling my t-shirt, still not doing it in a way that deserved a slap, yet.

"Tim has groupies?" I said. I was surrounded by the boys, plus a Marian, now. My girlies had floated off to the side, somewhere.

"See for yourself, said Zachary, the final piece of the boy puzzle, if you didn't count Brian or Benson. I'd no idea where Brian was; Aisling hadn't even said. I looked at where Zach was pointing, and there he was – Tim, holding court, surrounded by what was definitely young Aoife and her gang of junior rave chicks.

"I know them!" I said, pointing. "They found Bríd for us! Kind of!" Young Aoife saw me pointing and waved over at me, so I waved at her to come here.

"Kweeva Shox! How's the form, like?" she said, like we were old friends. She was dressed in even less tonight. All tits and legs, like you dressed in the early days of discovering you had tits and legs, and what power they had over silly boys.

"I'm grand! You look SO gorgeous!" I suddenly became

aware of how much I was chewing and sucking in breaths. Double-dropping was good, but double-dropping was *strong*. That was another reason she looked so good. Everyone just looked extra-fuckable tonight. I couldn't see a single flaw in anyone. Ian Brown started singing again. It was still bad, but at least it wasn't one where he had to strain to hit the notes.

"Awwww, thanks. I tries me best, like. Your Tim is a fucking deadly DJ, wha? Me girls are all over him – they'll be fucking tearing each other's hair out over him in a minute, like." I loved her accent, it made everything sound like Fair City. Well, like the characters on Fair City who were working class, anyway – and the actors who were pretending to be.

"Well now, I'm sure he's loving that," I said, finding Tim's new status as a sex god to jailbait Dublin ravers just about the funniest thing that had happened all weekend. I'd definitely have to warn him later though. We didn't want him to end up doing a Rob Lowe. That publicity definitely wouldn't be good publicity.

"Ah, yous know yourself, Kweeva. I'm sure all the lads are trying to ride yous tonight. Love the top, man. Is that – is that like a Stone Roses one, yeah? Cos of the lemons? They loves the lemons, don't they?" She pointed at a guy walking past in a Roses t-shirt – a print of the first album cover, with all the spattered paint, and the lemon slice.

"Ah, it's not, actually, Eef. But I suppose it could be, yeah?" She smelled of the nice perfume again. Her face was a lot prettier tonight. She'd given herself a make-under and worn a lot less slap. I was trying not to look at her boobs, because I wasn't sure if it was legal to, and I didn't want to do a Rob Lowe, either.

"Shur go with the flow, wha?" She'd a great smile. And gorgeous lips, too. Quiet, Rob Lowe brain!

"That's all we can do, yeah? So do I get a hug, or am I chewing a brick?" I said, suddenly feeling devoid of huggage.

"Course you can, Shoxer – hop on, like," she said, diving into me and letting me wrap my arms around her. The whole *not wearing many clothes* thing she was doing made it an extra-good hug, because touching skin on yokes was amazing, but touching skin while double-dropping was double-amazing. I finally unhugged her, but we kept an arm each around one another's waists while we looked up at the Roses finishing *Breaking into Heaven*, and I wondered if she'd let me join her cool raver chick gang or was I too ancient already to qualify.

*****

"Ash, babe? Where's your Brian?" I said. The Stone Roses were taking a little break while the roadies put together a different set-up. It looked like they were switching to unplugged for a bit. Oasis did that. I remembered watching them on TV last year and Noel sitting down on a stool and singing *Married with Children* instead of Liam, and *Half the World Away*, which was a B-side, but it was my favourite of theirs.

"Oh they said he went to the hospital," she said, puffing on yet another fag. First thing I was going to do in our new best friendship was get her off the ciggies. And me off them too, although probably not.

"Fuck! Has something happened to Frank?" I did not need this. We hadn't even told Portia. Luckily, she'd fucked off to the bog when the lads arrived, so I'd been able to swear them all to secrecy, for tonight, at least.

"Noooooo! No, lovely Marie, who I love, by the way – she rang him and said Frank was doing well, but that she really had to go, and Brian said he didn't like Paul Weller that much, so he'd swing by there and bring Frank a few things. Toothbrush and toothpaste, a few magazines, some bars of chocolate."

"He's such a surprising guy, your fella is, Legs. You

chose well there." My heart was going to burst with the sweetness of it all.

"I know! Why do you think I keep him around, babe?"

"Cos he fucks you up the arse and it only hurts a little and you definitely like being hurt, a little?" I said, regarding her.

"The cheek of you, Caoimhe Colette O'Shaughnessy! But yeah. All of that, too." She'd a gorgeous smile. She'd a gorgeous everything. I stole a little look down at her legs. They were like the legs a statue would have, only they weren't cold when you touched them. Not that I'd touched them, ever.

"Hang on, one second," I said, squatting down by her feet. I put a hand on her ankle and ran my fingers all the way up to the hem of the dress, standing up as I went. "Okay, I'm done now, sorry."

"Okaaaay. And what was that?" She didn't look cross or anything, just mildly perplexed.

"I just wanted to feel your leg," I said, because that was literally all there was to it. Couldn't do me for it.

"That's a fair enough explanation, my new best friend. Feel it any time you like. Well, any time tonight, anyway. Not like, when we're at mass with my parents." She was smiling so hard I was worried the corners of her mouth might rip, but in a good way.

"I'm going to mass with your parents now, am I? That feels like a big step," I said, wondering if she actually still did go to mass. I hadn't gone voluntarily since I was eleven.

"Well that'll come after a good while in our relationship, Kweev. Don't get worried, or anything." The Roses were playing *Your Star Will Shine*. I knew it off the album, but also from the B-side of *Love Spreads*, cos we'd all bought *Love Spreads* the day it came out.

"After the fingering but before the lickouts, yeah?" I said.

"Something like that," she said, not looking at me. She put her hand out and placed it on my actual boob, without any warning. I held my breath and swallowed all the chewing gum spit I'd been hoarding in my mouth. She moved her fingers around sofly in a circle, then took the hand away. I breathed out, a little gaspy.

"Okaaaaay. And what was that?" I said, hearing my heart pounding in my chest, despite Ian Brown's best efforts above us.

"I just wanted to feel your boob," she said. "Or *any* boob, really. But yours were the closest."

"Well that's a fair enough explanation, my new best friend," I said, and then *Tightrope* started, and we both cheered at the stage, which put an end to whatever the fuck *all that* was, thank Christ. What a life we led.

*****

"Look at her, like. Just *look* at her, Caoimhe. Look at how amazing she is, like. Look at the way she laughs, and the way she moves, and the way she wears her clothes, sham." Richie was particularly loved up tonight. Probably a mixture of whatever pills he'd got off Tim's Army of Whorelets, and the fact that he was *Head Over Feet* for the Collins girl.

"I'm aware of her, Rich." Marian was a little bit away from us, having an animated conversation with Aoife. It seemed to be about clothes, since they kept pointing at each other's.

"Yeah, I know, like. I was aware of her too – a long time ago. And she was great then, don't be getting me wrong, sham. It's just now, like – now she's a whole load more... great. She's *perfect* – and not just the way she looks. She's sound too. And she's funny." He shook his head.

"She's not too good for you, Richie," I said, touching his arm.

"What?"

"You're just as great as she is. Maybe even greater. *She* didn't buy me chips or find me a pretend arcade." He didn't look like the male version of how hot she was or anything – he wasn't some tall, tanned, muscle-bound Adonis, but that meant nothing. She was fairly *Head Over Feet* for him too. That was more important than any of that other stuff. He needed to start being more confident and less insecure though, or he'd never hold onto a girl like that.

"Why was it a pretend arcade?" He wasn't looking at me – he was still transfixed by Mar's greatness – but if he had been, he'd have been looking at me funny.

"Cos it didn't smell like a real arcade. I love the smell of arcades. That one just smelled like, well, chips."

"You're so strange, you know that?"

"Yup." I didn't care if he thought I was; he couldn't take away my love of arcade smells. I'd always have that. The Roses were playing *Tears*, from The Second Coming. What a tune it was.

"You're lucky you're such a ride, cos otherwise you'd just be a freak." He gave me a smile when he said it, so I couldn't justify headbutting him. Also, he'd called me a ride, and he'd never done that before. He'd be feeling the tit off me next – it was all the rage around these parts.

"A sexual freak?" I said, although I wasn't one of those, either. Unless you counted the gayness. Gayness wasn't freaky, though. Putting a chair leg up your arse – that would be sexually freaky.

"Don't know. I've never had sex with you," he said, going back to regarding the love of his life, with her perfect face and her perfect body and her perfect everything.

"And you never will, with that attitude, Richie."

"What attitude?" he was looking at me again now, but without the smile.

"The attitude of never wanting to have sex with me." His immunity to my vajayjay was an insult to beak-nosed, elephant-thighed rides, everywhere.

"Oh, right. No, I would probably have sex with you, Caoimhe. Actually I definitely would."

"You would? Cheers, Rich." I didn't want him to, I just didn't want him to not want to.

"I didn't say I'd enjoy it," he said, swerving his ribs out of the way of my swinging elbow.

"Fuck off, you'd love it." I took out a fag and lit it. I didn't know where the box had come from, it was just in my bag.

"I doubt it. You'd just be sucking my nipples and trying to finger my arsehole like it was a fanny, sham."

"Yeah, and you'd love that too." I tried to get the image out of my mind, but it was there now. I could almost smell it.

"I'd probably love it if *she* did it, in fairness," he said, nodding at the girl who was better than me in literally every way. She saw us and waved.

"I can believe it, Rich. Tell me something about her that's *not* perfect, go on. Tell me she's terrible at blowjobs. Just humour me. Please!"

"Nah, she's good at that. Ye all think ye are, though."

"We all think we are what?" He'd lost me for a second.

"Well, tell me – how good do you think you are at giving blowjobs?"

"Me? Brilliant!" I'd literally never had any complaints.

"Exactly. And where did you get that notion?" He was

looking at me again now, because apparently this was an important topic.

"I got it from all the boys I've ever, well, you know – I got it from what they said to me, afterwards. And obviously from the fact that they all…"

"Spunked off?"

"Well, I was gonna say came, but yes!" I'd never failed. He was a fool to doubt my mouth, young South. I was dead poetic, sometimes.

"Do you know how bad at sucking a dick you'd have to be for a boy to *not* spunk off, Kweev?"

"Huh?"

"Exactly. We're not ye, Caoimhe. We're not complicated machines when it comes to that stuff. We spend most of the time *trying* not to come. Ye're the opposite. And another thing…"

"There's another thing?" I didn't want to know more facts, I wanted to go back to that happy, ignorant time, when I was World Blowjob Champion of Ireland.

"Yes! The other reason ye all think ye're amazing at it is because we *tell* ye ye're amazing at it."

"So?" How else were we supposed to find out?

"So, of course we tell ye that. We *like* getting blowjobs, Caoimhe. We love it. If we told ye that ye were crap at it, how many more blowjobs would ye give us?"

"Uh, none." Damn him and his facts. I preferred him when all he gave me was chips.

"And if we told ye that yeer crappy blowjobs were the best blowjobs we'd ever had, how many blowjobs would we get off ye?" He said "blowjobs" funny. Like *blawjabs*

"Loads and loads?" I hated Chip Daddy now. I was

never going to give him a blawjab, ever.

"Exactly!" he said, looking smugger than a very smug thing. The drums for *I Am the Resurrection* started, so it was good that this conversation was over. The six minute guitar solo *demanded* that we all stood around, legs apart, air-guitaring every single movement of finger on fretboard, as was the custom.

"Exactly? Exactly what?" said Marian, who'd come over without either of us noticing.

"Oh, Richie was just telling me how bad you are at giving blowjobs," I said, dancing away to my girlies and letting him pick the fucking bones out of that one.

*****

"So did everyone like *interrogate* Mazz about me when you thought I'd stolen Frank's bag and his money and... where's Frank, by the way, lemon slice? I feel like I need to see him, face to face, so he can thank me, or slap my arse, or whatever it is that the situation calls for." Portia and me had wandered off together after the six minute solo that seemed to last sixteen minutes.

"That's a lot of questions, Ling. Your pants are sickening, by the way. They're like what the Little Mermaid would wear to a disco – when she had legs, like." I was gonna do everything I could to not answer at least one of those questions. I could distract her by talking about her trousers.

"And yet, no answers. What are you hiding from me, cream cake?" She regarded me with that lovely face which never got uninteresting to look at. I'd missed it. I'd miss it even more tomorrow, when it had to go away.

"Um, well actually it was only Frank who had a go at her, Ling. In the morning. He was really stressed, as you'd imagine. He was just all, where does she live, how long have you known her, what's her telephone number in Dublin, where would she have gone – all that stuff."

"Oh. Poor Mazz. And what did she say?" She was playing with my hair again, and doing finger things on my neck, which felt double-nice; either because I was double-dropping, or because I was double-happy to have her back.

"She just, uh... oh, keep doing that, please – she said she's known you for yonks, that you're really honest, that you're a nice person, and you're not a thief, like. You're sweet and you're really loyal, and you'd never do anything like that. Especially not without telling her. She said she was worried about you. Then Richie stepped in and told Frank to leave her alone, cos he loooooves her."

"Aw. I'm triple-touched. She's right. I just – I wasn't exactly thinking straight, you know? And it wasn't like I could leave her a note or something, pudding. I was double-sure the police were going to search that room – or all the rooms. I couldn't just be like, "I have taken the drugs somewhere safe. Meet me under the tree where we first saw the full moon. Lots of love, Xú Ling!", could I? And anyway, I didn't have a pen."

"You could have written it on the wall, in lipstick, like a serial killer," I said. My fingers were in the rips on her top, touching all the lovely-feeling bare skin around her collarbone, and besides. I'd started doing it without thinking; it was instinct.

"Or on the bathroom mirror with my finger, so she only saw it after the steam from the shower fogged it up. You having a nice time there, sausage?"

"Where?"

"Fingering my slit, dear."

"Haha! Sorry!" She made it sound about fourteen times more intrusive than it was, so I stopped.

"Oh, I didn't say stop."

"Yeah, well I'm going to, anyway. Always leave 'em wanting more, yeah? So, you and Ciara are bonding, I see?" I lit up a Marlboro Light. I almost offered her one, then I remembered she didn't smoke. We had a few of them in the group now. Her, B, Richie, Tim, Bríd. They'd be outnumbering us cool smokers soon. Maybe I should encourage Aisling to go full time, to bolster our ranks.

"Bonding? Are you jealous, lover? I haven't been fingering *her* slit, don't worry."

"Oh, I wasn't worried, Ling." I definitely had been a bit worried.

"Good. And how about you?" She was feeling up my new t-shirt now in a very non-Ian way, but I didn't want to headbutt her for it, and if she strayed into boob territory, I'd probably allow it.

"How about me?" *Love Spreads* was playing, and everyone was going mental to the *let me put you in the picture* part, but we were way over at the side, so no one was in any danger of accidentally moshing us to death.

"Last night – with Ciara. Any slit-fingering of note occur between the happy couple?"

"Ah, I don't think so. Not unless it happened when I was asleep." Last night felt like a thousand years ago. I had to double-check in my head that Ciara had even been with me. Short term memory. Too many drugs. Bleurgh.

"Yeah, in your sleep doesn't count. I prefer to be conscious when I'm getting vagined. It's one of my very few rules in the bedroom." She was definitely straying into boob territory, but only for a second at a time, before taking her fingers elsewhere. My skin was about 80% goosebumps now.

"What are your other bedroom rules, then?" She'd forgotten about Frank, for now. My breasts were doing the Lord's work, clearly.

"I'll let you know next time we're in one," she said, somehow finding exactly where my nipple was, behind my bra, and giving it the smallest of pinches through the fabric. The 80% goosebumps shot straight to 100. John Squire was playing another solo on stage. I had no idea what me and Portia were playing, but I liked it, so far.

*****

"Where did you two *sssssluts* disappear to, then?'" Ciara said, putting out her arms and taking the two of us into one big hug. Our three faces were right next to each other. I had to focus and unfocus my jittery eyes until I could see properly.

"Caoimhe was fingering my slit," Portia said. We were all so close that I could feel it in my face when either of them smiled.

"And who'd blame her, shur?" Ciara's purple eyes were almost all pupils now. They looked like two beautiful solar eclipses, in a faraway galaxy where their suns were different colours to our one.

"Isn't a jury in the land that'd convict her, vanilla slice" said Portia, whose eyes were faraway galaxies all by themselves.

"I didn't actually-" I couldn't finish my sentence, because Ciara's lips got in the way. Soft, long, smoochy. Another *not quite but almost* type kiss, which I didn't mind one bit. She broke off from me and gave me a flash of perfectly sized teeth, then her lips were on Portia's – a little less soft, a little less long, but still very smoochy. I was back to 100% on the goosebumps scale.

"You good?" Ciara said. None of us had made any effort to detach from the smoochy triangle. I wondered if anyone was looking at us, then I realised I didn't care.

"You know at the seaside, sometimes – or it might be at a carnival – where they have that Test Your Strength machine? With the big mallet? And people come up and hit the rubber button thing, and there's this gauge or meter, and it goes up the harder you hit, until someone hits it so hard it rings the big bell at the top?" I said.

"I can picture it, pudding." Portia smelled like apple shampoo, and caramel lip balm, and Juicy Fruit gum

"I know the one, yep." Ciara smelled like CK One, and ice-cream, and Doublemint.

"Well that rubber button thing is basically me right now. And that bell is gonna get rung any minute." I said, giving each of their bums a squeeze, because fuck it, it was Christmas.

"I know exactly what you mean," Portia said, finally breaking the hug, which was fine, because I desperately needed a fag.

"Ding, ding, ding!" Ciara said, grinning a big loved-up grin, and offering me a delicious B&H. The Stone Roses had just finished *Good Times* up on stage, but it felt like the good times down here were only starting. *Driving South* came next, and I wondered how long there was left of the set, and if we were going to stay to see Orbital, or if we'd just go back to Jury's and carry on the party there, and if Aisling was going to come with us, or if Tim was going to bring his underage entourage, and then a big wave of pure, unadulterated pleasure went through me, so I stopped wondering about future stuff and just appreciated the now for a bit.

*****

"Right, right, right! Everyone shut up a second, and someone tell me what's the matter?" The Stone Roses were finished. They'd played *Made of Stone* at the end, and we'd all got up dancing. It was fantastic. If we hadn't already been stood up, we'd have given them a standing ovation. There was drama now, though, and I didn't know why.

"Tim's girls are after inviting some scumbag back to Jury's with us; or he's after inviting himself," said Niall, doing a big involuntary ecstasy smile while telling me something that definitely wasn't funny.

"Wait, Tim's girls? Why are they inviting people back to our hotel? They aren't even – who invited *them* back to our hotel?" I said. Bríd and B were back. I wondered where they'd been.

"Ah, I think *we* might have," said Ian, not specifying who he meant by we, but definitely meaning everyone in our group with a penis who didn't already have a girlfriend.

"Well that was clever," I said, meaning the opposite.

"Who is the scumbag and why does he want to come to our hotel?" Ciara said, doing her serious voice, which made her sound like a teacher. A sexy teacher, who made you stay after class, and – quiet, brain!

"He's one of their boyfriends, I think – or he thinks he's her boyfriend, anyway. I'm not sure she agrees," Niall said, sparking up a huge joint, as if he hadn't been arrested and thrown in jail last night for drug offences in this very field.

"Well why doesn't he just fuck off to his own hotel with her?" I said. I was cross now, more than anything else. My perfect night and perfect weekend were being spoiled by some unknown goon.

"I dunno. He's a dealer, see. He's the one who – he's where the girls got the Es from, so like, he thinks he's entitled to go where the party is. You know what they're like," Ian said, taking the joint off Niall.

"I know what *who* is like?" I had better be next on that thing, I thought. I couldn't remember the last time I'd had a toke. I only realised how much I wanted one when I saw it in Niall's mouth.

"Dealers. Scumbags. I dunno," Ian said, taking a last

drag, then handing it to Aisling, who didn't even smoke gear. Although from the way she immediately horsed it into her the second she got it, I might have been wrong.

"Where is this cunt, sham?" Richie said. At least *he* didn't smoke hash. I'd be ahead of him in the queue for it, anyway. Unless he suddenly changed his mind about it, to spite me.

"Over there, talking to Tim," said Niall, pointing. Timbo was in a circle of scantily clad teenagers, facing off with the poster child for crime. He had all the standard accoutrements – baggy jeans, gold chain, puffy jacket, the whitest tackies known to man, woman, or herd of goats. Head shaved into an undercut and tied up at the top and back – that one was very Dublin Scum. The fashion hadn't reached our local scum in Limerick yet.

"Right. I'll be back in a minute, love," said Richie, kissing his one true *amour*. As we watched him walk over, I could have sworn he got about a foot taller. His body language changed completely – there was a swagger to him, and his footsteps looked very deliberate.

"What is he going to do?" Mar whispered, to me.

"I dunno, but it's kind of exciting!" Ciara said, looking like she would have enjoyed a carton of cinema popcorn to eat while watching this. I had the joint now, and I was keeping it. We saw Richie reach the circle of junior ravers, and they parted to let him through. He tapped Tim on the shoulder and said something to him, which made him walk away, over to my good friend Aoife O'Connor. Now Rich was face to face with the Scum King. We couldn't hear what they were saying, but just watching their mannerisms was gripping enough. The guy was all posturing and head flicks. Richie was more elaborate hand gestures, and terrifying smiles.

"I can't watch, but I can't look away, either!" Portia said, resting her lovely chin on my shoulder.

"Richie is going to get murdered, lads," Ian said, not helping.

"Nah, Richie could take that little fuckbag," Marian said, wildly overestimating the fighting pedigree of our drummer, in my opinion.

"Wait! Something's happening!" said Ciara. Richie was offering a hand to the guy – in friendship, it looked like. The guy wasn't offering one back. Richie shrugged, and put his hand away.

"Something *isn't* happening, apparently," I said, not helping. I smoked the J down to the roach, burning my fingertips a little, but I didn't care. I had more important things to be concentrating on.

"Hold on, who is he pointing at?" Portia said, meaning the Dealer guy. We looked over to see, but he could have been pointing at anyone in our group, really. The guy put his hand back down and leaned in close to Richie, saying something.

"What's he saying?" Marian said, as if I had dog's ears, or something. We saw Richie do a smile that was anything but genuine, friendly, or even an ecstasy grin.

"I can't take this!" Ciara said, on the opposite side of me to Portia, so I was the meat in the Us Sandwich now. I couldn't look away. The guy was smiling back at Rich. Then he was laughing. Then Richie raised his arm up and cracked the guy in the temple with a lightning quick elbow, instantly flooring him. He went down like a bag of spuds and didn't move.

"FUCK ME PINK!" I said, my heart going a thousand miles a second inside my poor little chest. Richie walked back to us without even stopping to check if his opponent was still alive. I suddenly remembered him telling me that he'd done kickboxing or Muy Thai, or something like that, when he was younger. He apparently hadn't forgotten the moves.

"I think I just came," Marian whispered, looking at Richie with brand new eyes.

"I should probably go start up the van, guys," said Benson, and he was right. We'd have to see Orbital some other time. Fellas like that guy never went anywhere by themselves – even if they were hard as fuck, they always had back up, just in case. There would be a gang of them, and they'd come looking for Richie when they found out what had happened. We needed to vamoose, pronto.

"What the fuck did he say to you that made you do that, kid?" Niall said, squeezing Richie on the shoulder.

"He was talking shit about my woman, Nailer. Can't be letting anyone get away with that, sham. Chalk it down," said Richie, taking Mar's hand, and following Benson to the exit, like the rest of us were. Brian Collins appeared out of the crowd in front of us, gave us various head-nodding or eyebrow-raising salutes, then linked arms with his Aisling, who 100% smelled like fags and hash, but he didn't say anything to her about them, because he was a surprising guy, her fella, and she'd chosen well there.

THIRTY

"Last night in Heaven, guys," I said, walking into Room 213 after Ian opened it for us. I had a Portia in one hand and a Ciara in the other. Us Sandwiches, all over the shop.

"It's only Jury's Hotel, Caoimhe. Calm down," said Niall, who clearly hadn't heard my speech about how Heaven is wherever you are when you're with the best people, mainly because that speech had been in my head.

"It's not the location that counts, it's the company," said Ciara, E-telepathying me.

"Speaking of which, lock that door, yeah? I don't want us having any more company than this," said Marian, who knew that even her street fighter boyfriend couldn't hold off a whole gang of scumbags – scumbags who would know exactly what hotel we were in, once their unconscious friend woke up.

"We're not all here, though," I said, remembering that Aisling had gone with Brian in the minibus, but they were definitely coming up here for a while, she'd promised.

"They can knock, we'll hear them," Marian said, and I nodded, because that was fair enough.

"Put on the radio, someone!" Bríd the sex assassin was looking fidgety, holding onto her B.

"I'll get some CDs if you like, buttercup." Portia's shiny trousers looked extra shiny under this room's lights, for some reason. I was mesmerised by them. I wished I'd seen them when I was on acid, but then we hadn't had a Portia at all when we were taking that stuff, I remembered.

"Where are they, up in your room?" I said. I wanted a fag, but I couldn't see an ashtray anywhere. I also didn't have any hands free.

"Yeah, unless one of you stole them, pudding." She took her fingers out of mine, but only for a second, then put them back in a slightly rearranged way that made them fit comfier.

"I'd never steal from you, Ling," I said, resting my head on her shoulder and taking in the lovely scent of her.

"Well..." said Ciara, the other side of me. I wanted to sit down, but Bríd, Benson, Marian, and Richie had already stolen the bed, and three of us weren't going to fit on an armchair.

"I was just *minding* that cocaine for her!" I said, realising what she meant, now.

"Were you minding it up your nose, pudding?" said Portia, not looking pissed off or anything, thank God. I'd only taken it because I thought she was an evil thief. She couldn't really do me for it.

"Yeah, sort of. And up some other people's noses too. I'm not a greedy glutton!" I said, giving her shoulder a little gnaw, because apparently, I was a mouse now.

"It's fine, pumpkin. Nice to know I could bring some joy to people, even when I wasn't here. Will I go get the music then, or?"

"No," I said, doing a pretend grumpy face.

"Why not, sausage?" Her face was turned to me, up close to mine. She was stroking my cheek with her free hand, and it was so nice, I almost forgot the other people were there.

"Because she's not letting you out of her sight again, in case you run away to Wales, said Ciara, putting her head close to me on the other side, so I could feel her breath on my neck. Oh boy.

"Fair enough, lemon slice. I'll stick to you like glue, then," Portia said, walking over to the corner of the room to sit on the floor, and taking the two of us with her – hand in hand, like one of those chains of paper men we used to make in Junior Infants.

*****

"You guys spend far too much time worrying about things you can't change, or things that don't matter." Portia was doing the thing again – where she spoke to the whole room about a subject, and everyone listened to her. She was full of wisdom, and not just the stuff in her fortune cookie.

"How can you say that baldness doesn't matter?" said Niall, who was standing up, for some reason. "I mean, it mightn't matter to you, cos you're never gonna go bald…"

"She might. If she gets cancer," said Ian, not helping.

"Thanks, Ian. Lovely thought," said Ciara. I'd got her to light up a fag in her free hand and we were sharing it between our mouths, like we were Siamese twins. Slightly unhygienic, but I was always swapping saliva with her, so it was grand.

"Yeah, and anyway I won't, because Chinese people can't get cancer; we're like sharks," Portia said, possibly telling an untruth, although I couldn't check; I didn't have an Encyclopaedia Britannica handy.

"Why doesn't it matter, though?" asked Benson, who was clearly someone who'd have to worry about this stuff a lot sooner than the rest of the boys, what with him being elderly.

"Because," Portia said, shifting herself on the floor beside me to get a little more comfortable. "Because if you're handsome and lush and you lose your hair, sausage, you'll still be a handsome, lush bald man, yeah?"

"I guess so," Benson said, and most of everyone else nodded or agreed.

"But if you're already fuck-ugly, then your hair was doing absolutely nothing to make you better looking – unless you'd literally brushed it down over your face, like Cousin Itt – ergo, if you lose your hair, you're still fuck-ugly. So, it doesn't matter!" Portia unclasped herself from my hand again and moved me, so I was holding her around her waist, which was fine by me, as Ciara was still Siamesing the fag into my mouth, so I didn't need those fingers anyway.

"Thank you, Portia," said Niall, sounding less than pleased.

"Thank *me*?" She regarded him with a very regardy stare.

"Yeah, thank you. Thank you for stopping me being insecure about whether or not I'm going bald. Now I'm just going to be insecure about whether or not I'm fuck-ugly, so."

"Glad to be of service, ginger snaps." That was my favourite Portiaism – when she did a bespoke term of endearment, just for you. Made you feel a little special.

"You're not fuck-ugly, Nailer," I said, giving him a sympathetic smile.

"Thanks, Kweev." He gave me a thumbs-up that didn't seem very sincere.

"Yeah, you're more *can't-get-a-fuck*-ugly, said Ciara, because she was hilarious, and cruel, but mostly hilarious.

*****

"Well this should be interesting," Ciara said.

"I don't understand, why is it such a big deal?" said Portia, reminding me that she not only didn't know Brian that well, she also hadn't been here last night, when he'd been the only straight one in the room, and his normally straight missus had been on her first drugs ever.

"Brian has never even smoked a joint, Ling. This is definitely a big deal." Aisling had arrived about a half hour after the rest of us, with a Special Announcement for the class. She'd managed to convince her boyfriend to drop an actual ecstasy tablet – so that he'd be included in this one last farewell night of pilled-up, loved-up craziness. No one could believe her at first, and now we were all watching him like hawks, to see when he came up – as if it was going to be some dramatic, An American Werewolf in London style transformation, instead of just his pupils getting bigger, him chewing like a maniac, and going around telling everyone he loved them.

"Okay, yeah. Can ye all stop looking at me now, please. I'm anxious enough as it is, thinking about how I'm going to die of drugs. Has anyone water? Do I need to drink lots of water?" Poor Brian was in for a massive shock to the system in about ten minutes time, but he was going to love it, and he was already around the best people for it.

"No. Don't drink too much water, Brian," I said, remembering Brid's science lesson.

"Why not???" He looked very confused. Ian threw him over a bottle of Ballygowan, or possibly a Ballygowan bottle full of tap water – it hardly mattered.

"All your organs will fail, and you'll die," said Brid, helpfully.

"WHAT? How much is too much?" He put the bottle down, untouched.

"You'll know when you've had too much, don't worry,"

I said, wondering if there was more water where that bottle had come from.

"How will I know?"

"Because your organs will fail," said Ciara.

"And you'll die," I said, finally spotting the stash of waters on the floor beside the bed.

"Right, enough of this now, lads," Aisling said, giving us all her Head Girl face. "Or I'll take him back to the B&B with me right now, and ye'll never know what it's like to see your favourite Brillo on Es."

"Sorry, Aisling!" said Bríd.

"Sorry Brian!" I said, because she was right; we were being gowlish to him.

"What did you just call me?" Brian said, to Aisling, but she ignored him.

*****

"Hey, what happens when one of us wants to go for a wee?" I said, to my two fellow Siamese triplets, a little later on. We hadn't broken apart once yet. Any time we needed something, like water, or a beer, we got the others to throw it to us.

"Why would one of us need a wee?" Ciara said, giving me one of her withering looks – I hadn't seen one of those in ages.

"Oh yeah. I'm a fucking idiot, sometimes." I was also dead clever sometimes, though, so it balanced out.

"You're a pretty idiot," she said. Ciara had called me pretty on Friday night as well – before everything went weird. I only remembered it because no one ever called me pretty. They called me hot, or a ride, or sexy, so I couldn't exactly complain – that would be gowlish. But I *wanted* to be called pretty. So it was lovely.

"You're preeeeeeetty!" sang Portia, taking my fingers in hers again.

"Pretty vaaaaaacant!" I sang back, and I looked over at Niall, because he loved the Sex Pistols, and I knew he'd have a big happy head on him when he heard us singing that, because he was easily pleased, godhelpus.

*****

"I've just remembered something," Niall said, plonking himself down in front of the three of us.

"What's that, ginger nuts?" I said, which kind of worked, since they were a type of biscuit, as well as his testicles. Ciara had a fit of giggles beside me – must have been the drugs, cos I wasn't *that* hilarious.

"You've touched my penis now, and you can't ever say that you haven't," he said, delighted with himself.

"You touched his what, now?" said Portia, because she hadn't been with us on Friday.

"It's a long story," Ciara said, rolling her eyes.

"It wasn't a long penis," I said, cos I was hilarious.

"Ah, here! You can't judge me on the way it was during pilly willy. That's not fair. I want a retrial!"

"I'll see when I can fit you in," I said, because the hilarity never stopped with me.

"What's it like right now, Niall? Any life in the old dog?" Ciara said, reaching over and rubbing his cords in the part where a penis might reside.

"Dead again," he said, looking forlorn.

"How about now?" Ciara said, taking his hand and putting it on her boob. We were clearly at that bit of the night where inhibitions were gone right out the window.

"Nope. But thanks. I'm putting that carefully away in

the wank bank, for later," he said.

"Pffft. Fill your boots," Ciara said, not giving a fiddler's. I wondered how many of them wanked about us, or about me. Probably all of them. Except Richie, obviously.

"Richie!!!"

"WHAT?" He was still over on the bed, enveloped in the Collins girl.

"Have you ever had a wank about me?" I said, making the others stop their conversations and listen up.

"Don't be disgusting, Caoimhe," he said, predictably enough.

"How about me?" Ciara said. I looked at Mar to see just how uncomfortable this conversation was making her, but she was on yokes, so the answer was not at all.

"Yeah, you've had plenty of wanks about Caoimhe, sham," said Richie, because he was hilarious, even if he did have terrible taste in women.

"Have you ever had a wank about *me*, Caoimhe?" said Marian, who'd decided just listening to the conversation wasn't enough.

"Nope, sorry," I said, pretty sure that I was telling the truth.

"Why not???"

"Because, you conceited bitch, the last time I knew you I was about 13 or something!" I was only joking about her being conceited. She really wasn't. She was very humble for someone who perpetually looked like she'd just wandered off a catwalk.

"You weren't strumming your banjo yet when you were 13?" said Portia, regarding me with something between curiosity and pity.

"I was! Just... not about girls, yet!" I said, trying to defend my wanking honour.

"Ah, I see," said Ciara, who had apparently been flicking her bean to ladies since she was knee high to a grasshopper. Eight years old, she'd said – although that was when she started fancying them. She probably didn't start the other thing until she was much older. Or she did. Both were equally possible.

"I'll have a wank about you next week, Mar. Is that okay, love?" I said, nodding at Ciara to spark us up another fag. I wanted water too; I'd get Portia to open one in a minute and put it in my mouth. It was great, this – like having slaves, but without all the racism.

"That's perfect, babe. And when you're finished, write me a letter about what you were thinking about during it, yeah? Since I'm so *conceited*, and all?" Oh God. I'd offended her.

"I'M SORRY I CALLED YOU CONCEITED, MAR, YOU'RE THE LEAST CONCEITED PERSON I KNOW!!!" I'd have got up to hug her, but I was a bit conjoined at the moment.

"Apology accepted, honey. But I still want the letter, yeah?" She gave me a nice wink, which calmed me a bit.

"I'm only sending it if Richie sends me a similar one," I said.

"Okay, Kweev. I'll have a wank about Marian and then I'll write you a letter about it, sham." Marian collapsed with the giggles beside him.

"I hate you, Chip Daddy!" I said, but I loved him, really. I loved all of them right now, even Ian, so I was definitely on drugs.

*****

"So, ah... this is quite different, Maurice," said the

newly yoked-up Brian, when he came over to have an audience with the Three Wise Rides, as only I called us, and only in my head. His pupils were like big shiny black buttons, and his jaw was going so fast it was like someone had started it up with a ripcord.

"Different from what, bean bag?" Portia said, possibly implying that she ate soft furnishings, as well as flowers.

"Different from *not* being on drugs," he said, which was technically very true.

"Good different or bad different?" I said, hoping it was the first one.

"Oh, it's very good, Maurice. I'm feeling all sorts of mad things – but they're good mad things. It's like – I dunno how to describe it as good as someone like you would, Caoimhe – you're very good with words, cos of being into the songwriting and all that. Actually, I was meaning to tell you how good your lyrics are – they're really clever, squire. They're not just a load of meaningless words put to music, you know – there's some thought gone into them, definitely, fair play to you, all the same. You're some woman altogether. You're very strong, too – with all you're after going through since last year, kid. There's no one I know who'd have handled all that, no one at all. You're a fierce auld warrior of a woman altogether. And my missus is mad about you too; says she's going to be your new best friend when ye get home. Says she can't wait, Maurice. What was I talking about again, girls?"

"No idea, Brian, but come here and have a big hug, will you? From your three favourite women, apart from Legs, obviously." We'd found the Designated Yapper tonight, definitely. But it was his first time in a weekend full of firsts, so we couldn't do him for it. I was about to say something else to him, when there was a knock on the door, and all of us froze.

"Shhhhhhh! And turn the music down!" said Marian. Lousy, as it was *Time of the Season*, by the Zombies, and I loved that one, it was my Mum's favourite song.

"Who the fuck could that be?" I said.

"It's the scumbags!" said Niall.

"It can't be," Ciara said. "I told yer one at reception that there were a load of scumbags around tonight, and to watch out for anyone trying to get in, and she said thanks for the heads up, and she wouldn't let anyone get in the lift or go up the stairs if they didn't have a key, so…" The knocking happened again, louder this time. Then someone outside the door spoke.

"Hello?" It was a man's voice. Couldn't tell much more about it though; not from just one word. He spoke again.

"Hello? Will ye let me in?"

"No!!! Go away, scumbags!!!" I shouted, sounding very much every inch as rich and Castletroyish as I was. Not exactly intimidating. I'd leave that to Richie.

"Scumbags? Who's a scumbag?" said the scumbag. I could hear other voices behind him as well. They'd brought a gang. We were all dead. What a horrible way to end such a wonderful weekend – getting actually murdered to death.

"YOU ARE!" screamed Marian. "JUST FUCK OFF AND LEAVE US ALONE, OR WE'RE CALLING THE GARDS!"

"Jesus Christ, fine! I'll just go around, then!" said the scumbag, and nobody understood what he meant. There was a sound of people leaving, then another sound, nearer. In Room 212. They'd got into Tim's room! He must have left his door unlocked, the fool. I turned around to shout at him about it, but he wasn't here. The adjoining door opened, and we all held our breath, bracing ourselves for the horde of scumbags that was about to breach our lovely, loved-up commune in Room 213.

"What the hell was all that about? Why didn't ye just

let me in?" said Tim, looking at us all with something between bewilderment and disgust. I suddenly realised that he hadn't come back with us in either Benson's van or the Blackboard Jungle bus, and that he was so quiet normally that none of us had even noticed he wasn't here. Poor Tim!

"All right, Limerick bredrens? Where's da fookin' liquor at, wha?" said Aoife O'Connor, following Tim into the room with her posse of questionably-aged cutesters, so at least we had enough people to have a proper party now. Marian clicked the radio back on, and it was playing *Turn! Turn! Turn!* by The Byrds, so she immediately turn, turn, turned the dial to a local dance music station, just in case these kids might think we weren't down with them.

"Will we drop number three then?" said Portia, which sounded like a fine idea, and so that's what we did. There was nothing important we needed to be straight for in the morning, it was our last night in Heaven – our last night with Portia, and Marian too – and, on top of all that, it was Christmas, so fuck it.

******

"Yeah, Daz is a fookin' spanner, like. Fookin' hate him. Was fookin' deloited when youses man fookin' knocked him out. Fair play. One elbow in his fookin' head – gone. Are yis three having a good one, anyway?" The blonde girl kneeling down in front of us was *extraordinary* looking. She made Marian look like a bowl of Pedigree Chum, no offence to Mar. Obviously the Es were making her look *much* better than normal, but that was irrelevant, since the way she looked now was the only way any of us had ever seen her look.

"I'm sorry if I'm being a bit forward or rude, petal, but how the *hell* are you so *god damn* gorgeous?" said Portia, speaking for all of us.

"Yeah, like, what planet are you even from?" I said. She was very tanned, and very thin, but she had an arse that would make grown men weep, and a pair of boobs that made you want to stick your face in them and suffocate yourself to death.

"I can't even process what I'm looking at, seriously," Ciara whispered, although it was a terrible whisper, because everyone heard it.

"Wha? Ah lads, yis are too much, like. Cheers, though. Smoke on tha?" She pointed at the joint in Ciara's hand. I was supposed to be next, but I didn't care. This golden-skinned goddess could have it. She'd earned it, just by letting us look at her incredible face.

"Of course!" Ciara said, practically jamming it into her hand.

"Sorry, what was your name again, pudding?" said Portia, squeezing my hand so hard she might as well have been giving birth. I was looking at the girl's legs now. She even had gorgeous calves, and I'd never thought that about anyone before. I took a big, deep, loved-up breath and popped in some fresh gum.

"Suzie!" said Suzie, looking at us a bit funny with her face that was probably a veteran of launching thousands of ships at a time.

"And what age are you, Suzie?" I said, suddenly overcome with a rare bout of sense.

"Ahhhhhh, my real age, like?" she still had the joint; no one had asked for it back, we were too preoccupied.

"That would be the best one, love, yes," said Ciara, sitting back a bit, and giving her spine a stretch. We'd have to get up and walk around soon, or we'd be destroyed with cramps.

"Um, I'm fifteen," said Suzie, immediately changing the atmosphere of the group.

"Fifteen…" Portia said, shaking her 21-year-old head. I felt mildly sick. Ciara sparked up a fag.

"Well, fourteen, but I'm nearly fifteen!" Suzie said, oblivious to anything that was happening, which was for the best, really.

"Okay, Suzie. Well it was lovely to meet you, anyway!" I said, getting my hands free and giving her a very chaste hug, making sure I didn't accidentally touch any fourteen, nearly fifteen-year-old tits or arses in the process. The other two gave her a hug each too, and up she stood.

"Okay. Cool. See yis later, girls, yeah? Do yis want the joint back or wha?" She was quite tall for a child, really.

"No, keep it!" said all three of us, in perfect harmony, and then she was gone, taking her very handsome calves with her.

"Well, we're all going to hell," I said, not looking at either of them.

"Prison first, then hell," said Ciara, holding the fag to my lips so I could have a much needed drag.

"We're on pills – you see the beauty in everyone on pills, they can't do us for it," said Portia, opening a new stick of Juicy Fruit and making me immediately want to taste it off her mouth.

"At least me and her are technically still seventeen, Ling. You're the one who's gonna get the chair for this," I said, but she was right. Everyone looked gorgeous on yokes. I'd sort of fancied Niall a bit earlier; that was how strong these fecking things were.

*****

"Where did Zachary go, Ceer?" I said. The Three Wise Rides were in Tim's room now. We'd gone to stretch the legs, but Mar was still paranoid about Daz and his army of scumbags tracking us down, so she wouldn't let us outside the three middle rooms.

"Oh, he pulled, earlier. So he took that guy back to his place."

"Aw, that's nice," I said. I'd not noticed him not being around either, as well as not noticing Tim not being around, so I'd been pretty rubbish at noticing stuff tonight.

"Was the other boy on pills too?" said Portia. We were all standing up, despite there being an actual bed there. But we needed it, after all that floor-sitting. I wondered if we could figure out a way to all simultaneously give each other back massages, but there was only three of us – not quite enough people to make a human circle.

"I don't know, to be honest. Why?" Ciara read my mind again, turned me around by the shoulders, and immediately went to work on my poor back. I gave her a groan by way of thanks. I couldn't do words properly while she was doing this to me.

"Oh, I was just thinking about pilly willy, and how it worked with gay guys, cupcake. Like, two of you there in the bed – loved-up and ready to go – and no one's dicks working at all. What a bummer, pardon the expression."

"Yeah! I've never thought… about it like that, no… but… I guess they'd just do other… stuff," said Ciara. Her voice was all funny. I didn't realise why until I spotted the three of us in the mirror and saw that Portia was doing her while she was doing me, *so to speak*.

"Other stuff like what?" said Portia. I felt sorry for her now, having no one to massage her while the two of us were getting all the lovely relief.

"Sixty-nineing each other's arseholes?" I said, just as Niall walked into the room. He turned around and walked straight back out again, without a word, so he'd definitely heard me, godhelpus.

*****

"Right, are we done?" Ciara said, finishing with my back, because Portia had finished with hers, apparently. I felt completely uncramped and unknotted. It was another Heaven, in a weekend of Heavens.

"Ah, yeah. But what about you, Ling? Do you not want a massage?"

"Ah, not right now, lemon slice. Right now, I just really fancy a drink. Vodka and Coke, maybe? Can we manage that?" She took my hand and Ciara's so that now she was the meat in the Us Sandwich.

"I think we have both of those out there, but maybe not ice," Ciara said. I wanted a G&T, but there was not a single lemon slice in our whole three rooms, unless you counted me and my lovely new t-shirt.

"Oh, and me and Ciara will definitely do you later; we'll do you twice, one after the other, yeah? Or at the same time?" I felt so guilty about us having massages and her having none.

"That's the dream all right, pudding. That's the dream."

******

We were back outside, in the party. Portia had her vodka; I had my gin. Richie had used his kickboxing skills to brave the hallway and get us ice, and the underage children were all helping to polish off our spirits and leftover cans. They loved Richie the fighting god almost as much as they loved Tim the DJing god, much to Marian's slightly snarly amusement.

"No having sexual relations of any kind with these girls, please, Tim. Definitely not that Suzie, anyway. And possibly not Aoife. Or just not any of them, to be safe. We've had enough of this band in jail for one day, thank you very much." I was putting my foot down, in lieu of our actual manager, who wasn't fit for purpose tonight.

"But Suzie is the best one! I'd *never* get a woman like that in real life. This is like my only chance. It's not fair!" Tim said, pouting.

"She's not a woman, Tim. She's a child," said Ciara, who was sticking to water, but at least it was iced water, now.

"She doesn't look like a child," he said, nodding over at the Lolita of the Liffey, who was talking animatedly to a very pilled-up Brian Collins. What a life he was leading tonight.

"Tell it to the judge," said Portia, still looking amazing despite possibly not having slept in two days.

"But I'm actually eighteen, girls," Tim said, looking like he'd found a loophole.

"That's not how it works, Tim. You're not trying to buy a bottle of Buckfast in Fine Wines!!! It doesn't matter how old *you* are – well, it does, but definitely not in that way!" I raised my hand and did a fake slap in his direction, but he didn't even flinch. Serene Buddhist monk training, probably.

"Fine, I won't have sex with any children then, MUM!" he said, with a shoulder roll and a sigh that made him seem even younger than the girls we were forbidding him to shag. Men! There was no need for them, honestly.

*****

"Did I imagine it or did your Niall guy walk in when we were having our *massage a trois* earlier, lemon puff?"

"No, that actually happened," I said," smiling at the image of his face.

"Did it? I didn't see him," said Ciara. She was having a fag, over by one of the only two ashtrays that seemed to exist at our impromptu disco.

"You were too busy writhing with pleasure, vanilla pop," said Portia, who was rolling a joint for us. I couldn't remember seeing her do that before, so it was probably another first in a weekend of firsts.

"True. And he just walked in, yeah?"

"Yeah, and he walked straight back out again," I said, lighting up a fag myself, since we were here. It was a good spot for people-watching, in this corner. You could see all the action.

"Lucky we weren't all getting it on, then," Ciara said, blowing a perfect smoke ring. I'd forgotten she could do that – it was such a cool skill. Impressed the chicks, anyway, if I was anything to go by.

"Well…," said Portia. "If we had been getting it on, it would have been really lucky for him." She lifted up the papers and gave them a long, slow lick. She was doing a thing with the end of her tongue that made sure she never ran out of saliva along the way, so she was able to do the whole length in one, uninterrupted movement. It was a little breathtaking to look at.

"Watching you do that makes me feel it might have been lucky for us too," I said, apparently out loud.

"Caoimhe!" said Ciara, laughing and nudging me in the ribs.

"Like you weren't thinking it too, love," I said, nudging her back. I wasn't sure what I was up to yet, but I was definitely up to something.

"Fine. Fine, I was," she said, slipping her arm around my waist and giving me a long overdue squooch.

"What can I say, possums – I have a very talented mouth," said Portia, holding up the perfect looking cone for our approval.

"Definitely!" said me and Ciara at the exact same time, which made us look at each other in surprise, and then all three of us laughed, because everything was funny now, and everything was brilliant, too.

*****

"You okay, blue eyes?" I said to Richie, when I found him *sans Marian*, for once. I was sans the other two as well, because I wanted a stroll around and neither of them fancied it, so we had to break up the sacred triangle, temporarily.

"Me? I'm fine, sham. I'm good – buzzing away."

"But?" There was something definitely up with him, under the surface. I could tell, because of the E-telepathy.

"Ahhhh, it's complicated." He was looking across the room, at everyone doing their things. Niall was chatting up Suzie. I didn't need to warn him to not have sex with her – he had no chance, there. I could tell a mile away from her body language. Ian was deep in conversation with another one of the Dub girls – Alyssa. She was sixteen going on seventeen, like the song, so we couldn't do him for it, and neither could the Gards, probably.

"Everything is complicated, Rich. We're all complicated. But we're all simple as well, you know?" I put my arm around his waist and squooched him in a platonic way. Not that he'd ever consider anything I did to be non-platonic. I could be giving him an actual *blawjab* and he'd still think I was just being weird.

"I'm not simple! I got into-"

"Trinity College to do English, yes dear. You've mentioned it once or twice." Niall was really trying all his best moves over there now, but he wasn't on home turf, in a filthy carpark, so he was against difficult odds.

"Exactly. No, what I'm saying is, it's complicated, the thing that's wrong with me. It's not easy to explain. And some of it I can never explain. Some of it I can never tell anyone. Especially not you, some of it. And especially not Marian, some other parts of it." He was making no sense now.

"You're making no sense now, Rich." What were these things he could never tell me, I wondered? Or the other things he couldn't tell Mar?

"I've said too much already, sorry." That didn't sound very reassuring. I wanted to know, now. But maybe I didn't, too? This was all a bit heavy to try and process after three pills.

"Are you sad that Marian will be leaving tomorrow?" I said, changing the subject, although not exactly onto something nicer.

"Ah, well yeah. I mean I'm not sad – it's fucking impossible to be sad right now, sham. I'm flying. But, tomorrow, I will be." He did one of those brave, sad smiles that broke your heart to look at. I loved him so much, the poor sod.

"I know, Rich. But here's something that'll cheer you up," I said, sparking up my quadrillionth cigarette of the weekend.

"What's that now, Foxy Shoxy?"

"Tomorrow morning you can ride the absolute hole off her. As many times as you're able to manage. You can ride her from every angle known to man, woman, or herd of goats, and there'll be nobody banging down your door to interrupt you!"

"You know what? You're right, sham. That does cheer me up. Thanks, Kweev." He gave me a squooch back, also platonically.

"And I'll tell you something else, Rich," I said, remembering an important fact.

"What's that, then?"

"Even though she knows I was joking earlier about you saying she gives bad blowjobs, I can absolutely guarantee you as a fellow woman that, the first blowjob you get off her tomorrow morning is going to be the best blowjob she's ever given in her life."

"Is it?" Now he looked double-cheered up, as my Chinese girlfriend would say.

"Trust me, Rich. She's going to suck your dick like she's having an epileptic fit while bobbing for apples. She's going to suck it like she's been rescued from drowning and your dick is the first bit of air she can get into her lungs. She's gonna-" Richie put his hand over my mouth and instantly cut off my words.

"There you are, lover! What have you two been up to, then?" said Marian, giving me a slightly strange look on account of her fella apparently gagging me with his hand.

"Nothing, really," said Richie, subtly unhanding me.

"He was just… counting my mouths!" I said, making a very swift exit and heading back to my delicious Us Sandwich.

*****

"Can I have everyone's attention, please?" I said, over the noise of the dance music on the radio. I got no one's attention. Everyone was having too much of a good time to listen to me.

"Are you trying to do a poignant speech?" said Ciara, still being sensible and drinking water. Maybe she was pregnant. I definitely wasn't the father though, so it was grand.

"These kids don't need poignant speeches. They only need two things – discipline, and the Bible!" said Marian.

"They're getting busy living, Mar. Hopefully we'll get through the night without any of them getting busy dying."

"Where did you appear from, Benson?" I said, noticing him in our presence for the first time in literally a million years, figuratively.

"I was, uh, in Richie's room, with Bríd. He donated it to a good cause."

"What good cause was it, Help the Aged?" I said, cos I was hilarious.

"Are you staying in there – overnight, I mean?" Portia said, fondling another vodka and Coke with her mouth.

"I think so. Marian said Richie is staying in her room, I think?" Benson was drinking Heineken from a bottle, which was very him. Apart from the fact that he didn't drink, obviously.

"You mean in the room she's sharing with me, broad bean? The room I half paid for? Well... that's going to be a tight squeeze." The sarcastic version of Portia was kind of sexy.

"I'm sure we'll find somewhere for you, P," said Ciara, turning down the fag I was offering her. Definitely pregnant. I'd have to buy a new hat for the christening.

"You don't have a room, Slattery. You don't even have a van. Kweeva Shox has the only room. Kweeva Shox has all the power!" I said, throwing my arms around her and hugging her into me tight, just in case she thought I was being gowlish.

"First you get the room, then you get the power, then you get de weeeemin," said Portia, my new homeless friend.

"Hey, have any of yis any skins or wha?" said a raver girl who none of us noticed approaching our group, so she'd probably just dropped down from the ceiling. She was a fabulous looking thing, even at this hour of the night, godhelpus.

They'd all been using Niall's bathroom to redo their

make-up. The maids in the morning were probably going to think he was a secret transvestite. He was still chatting to the Suzie one, but their dynamic had completely changed. He no longer looked like he was trying to pull her, and she no longer looked like she was terrified of him. They had a buddy vibe going on now, sitting on the floor in his room. Perhaps he was mentoring her. Teaching her the ways of the giant ginger.

"Here you go, you little scamp!" said Portia, handing over a packet of King Size silver Rizla, and ruffling the little raver girl's meticulously lacquered hair in a way that would have got her a stabbing in different circumstances.

"Tanks very mooch, Mrs. Chinee. Sound, yis are. Koneechy-wah!" She spun around on her giant heels and went back to the swarm.

"*All right, all right, all right.* That's what I love about these secondary school girls, Caoimhe." Benson said, talking into my ear, with a friendly hand on my shoulder. "I get older. They stay the saaaaame age."

"Benson, you're lucky I've seen that film, or I'd probably think that was the creepiest thing you've ever said."

"What film is that?" he said, walking away with an enigmatic smirk, back out to Richie's room, to clean up the blood and dispose of Bríd's corpse, probably.

*****

"Aisling!" I said, grabbing my new future best friend as she went past.

"Oh. Hello!" Her eyes were completely black now, not an iris to be seen. It was kind of beautiful, in the way a possessed, satanic cat from a Japanese cartoon might be beautiful.

"How is Brian holding up?" I hadn't seen him in a bit, and I wasn't sure I wanted to, as he'd probably burn the ear off me for forty minutes, talking about how groovy the curtains felt, godhelpus.

"He's GREAT! I think I might have converted him, Kweev." She was bopping away on the spot, but I wasn't sure it was in time to the music in the room.

"Converted him to what, though?" I said, spotting him across the room. He was dancing with one of the strumplings – in a sort of Dirty Dancing/Lambada way."

"I dunno. Into something better?" she said, looking over too, but not giving a shite, apparently.

"You not all jealous of that, and stuff?" I said. It was hard to be jealous while on three Es, but sometimes nature found a way.

"That??? Pffft! Nope. First of all, I have a better arse than her, even if she is about TWELVE, like." She wasn't twelve, but still.

"That you do. That you definitely do," I said, looking down at the bum in question.

"And anyway, Portia said to me that you shouldn't ever be jealous of your fella flirting with anyone."

"She did?"

"Yeah. She said, as long as he's good at it, anyway. If he's good at it, and it's only harmless flirting, shur that makes you look good to other women – according to her, anyway. But, if he's really shit at it, and he's fucking embarrassing himself, well-" She took a drink of her water, and offered it to me, but I shook my head, cos I was grand.

"If he's shit at it, then it makes you look bad to other women, cos they think you're voluntarily going out with a man who can't even flirt properly," I said, sort of getting it now.

"Exactimundo, dude," said Aisling, because she was a Teenage Mutant Hero Turtle now, apparently. We looked over at poor Brian again, who was having his crotch area chamoised by the mini-skirted bum of a Dublin raver girl. Definitely a first for him, in a weekend of firsts.

*****

"Have yis any more water?" said Suzie, squatting down in front of me a little later, resting her folded arms on my knees. She hadn't got any less pretty in her absence.

"I do, yeah, here." I handed her a Ballygowan bottle full of tap water from the fresh ice bucket. Richie had gone out three times already, and returned three times without being murdered, so he was on a winning streak, definitely.

"Ah, sound. Your Niall – Nailer, wha? He's lovely, isn't he?" She drank half the bottle in a single gulp, and I could almost see it replenishing her little life force in front of my eyes.

"He's all right, yeah. Did he tell you about his time in the Big House?" Of course he had. That would have been his big conversation starter all night – especially with these streetwise little drug urchins.

"Yeah – arrested for dealing. Fookin' cops, like. They never gives us a fookin' break, wha?"

"Yeahhhh. The bloody Man – always trying to keep us down. So, ah, you're getting on with Niall, then? You two are looking very close there," I said. A bit too close, I thought. They weren't doing anything, but the night was young, and so was she. Too young.

"Ah yeah, he's sound out. Big gentle giant, wha? And yanno – all the fellas are usually trynta fookin' get up on me, especially when I'm wearing this sorta shit, and when everyone's on the old disco biscuits, yeah? But yer man Nailer is different, Shoxy. He's a gentleman, like. He's lookin' after me. I think he might be a queer like, but shur that's fine. Love is love, Shox. Let sleeping dogs be bygones, wha? Catch yis later anyways, chick. Tanks for the wawturr." She stood up and took herself away across the floor, shaking her thang and wobbling her wares.

"Was that our favourite womanchild?" Ciara said, arriving back from a makeup detour with Portia in hand.

"The Suzester? Yeah. She's so attractive that she's after turning Niall into a homosexual, apparently," I said, getting myself a water now, because I was suddenly gasping.

"That's a very particular skill set, muffin," said Portia, sliding in next to me on the floor with her shiny pants and her Juicy Fruit mouth and her hair that smelled so nice you wanted to climb inside it and go for a snooze.

*****

"Right!!! Turn the music off there, Ash, thanks." Brian Collins was standing on a chair, and somehow keeping his balance. Aisling did as he said, and suddenly all the beats and bass were sucked out of the room like a backdraft in that film about firemen. Backdraft, it was called. I knew things! Everyone made noises of disapproval when the song stopped, but Head Girl shushed them, and they somehow all obeyed her.

"Excellent, thanks. Listen – people of Cork. Well, people of Limerick, really. And all the young Doooobs, as well. I just want to say…"

"SPEECH!" shouted someone, and I almost got jealous, since no one had wanted a speech off me, earlier.

"No speech, no. I just wanted to say… I've had a brilliant auld weekend, with all of ye. Old friends, new friends. Chinese friends, as well." He was smiling like an idiot, but it was nice.

"And long-lost cousins!" said Marian, over on the bed, entangled in the South boy.

"Well, yeah. You too, Mar. Anyway, I just wanted to say

– well done to the boys and girl from Crane – ye nearly didn't make it up on stage, but by Christ once ye did, it was worth it, Maurice. Blew Páirc Uí Chaoimh away – they didn't know what hit them at all, Shoxy. I'm pure proud of the lot of ye – even you, Nailer, you fecking criminal."

"Nailer! Nailer! Nailer!" shouted Suzie, who was now sitting on Niall's lap, but there was no fear of her getting poked by an erection, since his willy no longer worked, and since he was an out and proud gay man, now.

"Indeed, Suzie. Look after him for us, you. We don't need to lose him twice in one weekend. Anyway, so... I've never done this, ah, these pill things before, lads and ladettes, and I was a bit iffy about taking one tonight. But, thanks to the most gorgeous woman in the world..."

"Hey! Don't drag me into this!" I said, cos I was hilarious.

"Fuck off, Shox. Anyway, thanks to the lovely and fragrant Aisling – the absolute love of my life, Maurice – I've changed my tune a bit, to put it mildly. I can see now what ye all see in these... things. So, am, what I'm saying is..." He'd lost his train of thought, because the lovely and fragrant Aisling was standing behind him, giving him an impromptu thigh massage.

"What he's saying is," Aisling took the invisible mic off him, and he sort of collapsed downwards into a sitting position. "...that drugs are good, and they have absolutely no negative consequences, so everyone enjoy what's left of the night, and please don't steal anything!" That last bit was definitely aimed at all the young Dooobs.

"Bravo!" I said, starting the clap, and everyone joined in, apart from Bríd and Benson, who were probably already naked in Richie's room, although she'd probably kept the wig on, as a treat.

*****

"Why are we in here? What about everyone else?" I said, when we got to my room. I had loads of things I wanted to say to loads of people, still. I wanted to ask Richie what he meant by all that stuff earlier. I wanted to ask Marian about Richie, and her intentions with my Chip Daddy. I wanted to ask Niall if he was gay now, and if he had only converted to gayness so that Suzie the Wunderkind would sleep in his room with him tonight. Everyone was gone now, though. And so was the music.

"We're in here because the last two nights, we left it so late to go to bed, that we were completely shattered, and heading for a comedown, and our heads were all over the place, and-"

"I get it, yeah," I said, putting my fingers on Ciara's lovely lips to politely shush her. "But why is Portia here?" She'd come in with us, but she was in the en suite now – doing whatever she was doing.

"Because I belong here, lemon slice," she said, coming out the bathroom door behind us. I turned to look at her.

"I think you forgot to put your trousers back on, Ling." Frederick from Hollywood's greatest artistic achievement was on full display, instantly drawing my eyes to her lower half.

"What's she going to do, wear trousers in bed?" Ciara said, turning her back and motioning to me to unzip her.

"Hmmm, true," I said, undoing the zip with only a little trouble, relatively speaking. My eyes were fully jittered, and my fingers weren't communicating brilliantly with my brain anymore.

"Unless you don't want me in your bed, cupcake?" Portia was behind me now, touching my hips. I could feel the heat of her against me. A dressless Ciara turned around to face me, and it was suddenly the best version of the Us Sandwich we'd had all weekend. I couldn't breathe, let alone say something smart or witty.

"Are you getting this, or will I?" she said, over my shoulder, to Portia.

"I'll do this bit." Portia's hands came around my front and undid the button and the zipper on my denim shorts.

"And I'll do this bit?" Ciara said, gently taking my wrists and lifting my arms up, before taking my t-shirt off. I still couldn't breathe or speak. I felt Portia below, yoinking my shorts down to the ankles, and I stepped out of them.

"That's better," Ciara said, moving herself into me so that our skin was touching all the way down our bodies. Portia pushed herself into me from behind, and the Us Sandwich was more tightly packed than it had ever been.

"Has she gone mute, vanilla slice?" said a Portia voice from behind me.

"Give her a minute, she's adjusting," said Ciara, moving her face past mine, and planting a long, wet, smoochy kiss on the lips of the girl who was bringing up my rear, so to speak. Oh boy.

"I'm grand," I said, words finally escaping my mouth and sounding immediately strange to me – like they were someone else's. Every part of me was boiling hot, and I wasn't sure it was from the drugs.

"She's grand," Ciara said, coming back a bit so she could look at my face, and then giving me a long, wet smoochy kiss as well, because it was only fair.

"She'll survive," said Portia, turning me on the spot and pushing her mouth into mine, because if she didn't give me a long, wet, smoochy kiss, the universe would have been thrown out of balance altogether. Ciara moved in behind me and I felt her teeth scrape on the skin of my shoulder and her fingers making feather-light swirls on my bum. All the times during the weekend when I thought I'd been in Heaven had apparently been false alarms. This was the real deal. Portia took her mouth away for a second or two, and I didn't even have time to miss it before it was back again – firmer this time, open too. The taste of Juicy Fruit, and her, mixed in my mouth for the first time in quite a while, and it was very welcome back. When we broke apart, I felt like I'd been physically and emotionally winded – in a good way. Ciara moved me a little and I moved a little too, and then the two of them were the ones swapping chewing gum flavours. It was incredibly nice, just watching them. I could have watched them do that all night and been about 90% satisfied. When they eventually stopped, none of us said a word, we just grabbed whatever hand was near us, and glided across the floor until we were on the bed. Ciara picked up a joint off the bedside locker, and I nodded at her, because although all this was the greatest thing that had ever happened to man, woman, or herd of goats, it was also incredibly intense, so a nice relaxing joint would be the perfect punctuation. Not a full stop, obviously. Just a semi-colon, until we were ready to start the next clause.

*****

"You're very quiet, cupcake. You're not coming down, are you?" said Portia, after we'd finished the joint. I was lying back, with her on my left and Ciara on my right. I wasn't coming down, and I wasn't being quiet, either. I was just… taking everything in.

"She's grand, apparently. Weren't you listening when she said she was grand?" Ciara said, smiling at Portia, then at me. She trailed her fingers down me, from the underwire of my bra, to the elastic of my knickers, and then left her hand there. I was on my best behaviour, determined not to become Kweeva, Destroyer of Shags now.

"Cool, cool. As long as she's... grand." Portia's fingers were on me too now, but she was running them over the material of my bra, at the bit where the skin met the little embroidered flowers. We were getting well past Can't Do Me for It territory, but that was fine by me.

"Let me see how grand you are, Caoimhe," Ciara said, moving her face closer, and turning my head towards her. I looked in her eyes for a second, and then they were closed, so I closed mine. The kiss was lovely – all wet and slow and full of touching tongues and bitten bottom lips. Portia slid in at the other side, moving my hair out of the way and replacing it with the softest, warmest neck kisses. Someone's hand was on my boob now, and I didn't know whose. I could have opened my eyes to see, but that seemed like less fun. Fingers trailed and scraped across my belly, and then even lower. My stomach muscles went tight, and it left a gap between elastic and skin that someone immediately took advantage of – not that I was being taken advantage of, or anything. I put my hand behind my head to feel for Portia's face, and when I found it, I broke off from Ciara and switched to her. Ciara spooned in behind me and even with my eyes closed I could tell *these* hands on my boobs now were hers. They'd visited that region before, however briefly, and it was nice to have them back.

I still wasn't in any way sure about how to do things with girls, but tonight felt different. Tonight felt like I couldn't do wrong by anyone, as long as I just followed my instincts and did what came naturally. Even then, I was letting these two do all the leading. It wasn't exactly a burden, being sexually pampered and spoiled like this. It was Heaven, times twenty. I put my hand up inside Portia's rippy top, and despite rumours to the contrary, those were definitely boobs I'd found. All small and firm and lovely to touch, just like the rest of her. Ciara was doing extremely teasy, slightly tickly things with her fingertips under the waistband of my knickers. I wasn't sure if all the teasing was deliberate, or if she was just going kind of slow with me, but either way it got a bit too much to bear, so I reached down and took her hand, pushing it a little farther down, and a lot firmer onto me. She froze for a second, probably not sure if I had been telling her to stop, or what. Then she relaxed a little, and I felt her fingers find all the good bits of me, and when she started working her magic, it was so perfect and organic, it almost felt like I was doing it myself. I wanted to kiss her while she did it, but then I'd have to take myself away from Portia and her delicious tasting mouth, and her boobs which seemed to be very much enjoying my discovering them. What a life we led.

*****

"We're just never going to sleep, are we?" I said, absolutely devouring a Marlboro Light after yet another gorgeously exhausting round of rotating kisses, many-handed feel-ups, and exponential wetness. The whole room absolutely smelled of *fucking*, but in a good way. That smell was never bad if you were one of the ones doing the fucking, I found.

"Oh I'm sure we will, kitten," said Portia, not smoking, unless you counted how smoking hot she was in those knickers, which had somehow stayed on during our repeated sexual melees.

"Yeah. On Tuesday, probably," Ciara said. She was smoking, and also smoking hot, although her knickers had gone AWOL. They were probably tangled up in the sheet somewhere, as knickers usually were, whenever they tried to escape. She wasn't covering herself up or anything, like a Bond girl would. We were way past being embarrassed or coy around each other, now – all three of us.

"Tuesday sounds grand," I said, because everything sounded grand, tonight. I put my fag out and had a sneaky stretch, getting all the muscles unknotted, ready for whatever these two were going to spring on me next.

"Tuesday sounds absolutely grand indeed," said Ciara's voice, which was now coming from somewhere a bit farther down our bed.

"What are you up to, Slattery?" I said, seeing her purple eyes peeking up at me from down between my thighs. My knickers had not gone AWOL yet, even if my bra had been kind of ripped off by two sex-crazed women earlier.

"Never you mind. Keep your eyes on the road, Shaughnessy," she said.

"Or keep your eyes on me, lemon slice," said Portia, taking my jaw in her hand and turning me in for a kiss. I forgot about what Ciara was up to for a few seconds and just fell into the delicious Lingness of her; swapping tastes between our mouths, feeling her hands on me, knowing just how and where to touch me, and when to not stop. I was so distracted by it all that it took my brain a little while to process the other thing when it happened. The feeling of Ciara's wonderfully familiar mouth on me, while I lost myself in Ling's lovely, deep kisses – that was a first, in a weekend of firsts. Mad the way I'd spent the last few days driving myself crazy over which of these two beautiful, incredible women I wanted to be with. Turned out, both were equally possible.

EPILOGUE – BANK HOLIDAY

"What in the name of God happened here?" said the first voice I heard on Monday morning; definitely not Portia's or Ciara's. Those two were just as surprised and woken up by it as I had been. I looked down in panic and was glad to see we'd got the top sheet pulled up over us. It had been way too hot for the quilt, even as mostly naked as we were.

"Oh, good morning, Tim," I said, thinking he'd actually have been fine to see me naked, as I owed him some nudity, godhelpus.

"Hello, cupcake. Have a nice night?" Portia sat up and stretched. She still had her ripped top on; nobody had, well, ripped it off her in all of last night's commotion. I suddenly became aware that our room probably still smelled of fucking – it didn't smell like it to us, because we'd been acclimatised. But to someone just walking in, like Tim, it must have been wall-to-wall vagina. Oh well.

"Not as nice a night as you, obviously," he said, still not explaining why he was here, or why he'd forgotten the concept of knocking.

"No gangbang with the sexy kids, then?" said Ciara, spooning into my back a bit so she could use me as a boob shield in Tim's presence.

"Ye said I wasn't allowed to!!!" he said, looking very wounded altogether.

"Ooh, what's this then? *Menage a trollop*?" said Nail, because apparently we were an exhibit at some sort of Amsterdam Sex Museum, now.

"Shut up, pretend gay man. Where's little Suzie? You didn't murder her, did you? Murdering women is a form of abuse, Niall." Ciara was trying to find something under the covers, possibly her bra. I'd been the one who took that off, but I was fucked if I knew where I'd put it. It was probably hanging from the light fitting.

"I'm here, wha? Oh. Are yis all lesbians, then? I knew there was something a little funny about yis. Love is love, though. Do yis want me to hop in too?" said Suzie, looking about ten years younger than she had last night, because it was daylight, and we weren't off our actual tits anymore.

"NOOOOOOO" said all three of us girls, in unison.

"YEAAAAAH!" said Niall and Tim.

"GET OUT, ALL OF YE NOW!" I said, because I needed to get up and have a wee and I was wearing nothing under this sheet.

"Fine, fine. See you later," Niall said, heading out.

"Have a nice orgy, wha!" said Suzie, following him like a lost puppy. Tim hadn't moved.

"What's wrong, Tim?" Ciara said, giving up on the bra search but leaving her hand down there, because it had landed on my bum at some point.

"I just... everyone is a lesbian now, girls. It must be all the rage. No wonder I can't get a girlfriend. It's not fair."

"None of us are lesbians, Tim. That's not why you don't have a girlfriend, don't worry." My voice went all funny at the end, because Ciara's fingers had got bored where they were, and started moving to more interesting places.

"Oh. So I might still have a chance with one of ye, then?" He looked a little cheered up, godhelpus.

"Nope!" we all said, in unison again. Ciara's fingers

were knocking on a particular door and if she was a little more persistent and if Tim took the hint and fucked off, she might be granted entrance, for a little while, at least.

"Unfair!" said poor Tim, looking resigned. He still hadn't mentioned the smell. There mustn't have been one at all, because Niall would have immediately said it. He was tactless and disgusting; pretend gay or no pretend gay.

"The greatest injustice of our time," said Portia, rolling onto her front and having a stretch. My hand strayed across to her, under the sheet, and found the small of her back. We didn't have to be out of here until eleven. It definitely wasn't eleven yet. Shenanigans were possibly on the menu.

"Yep. But shur, what can you do?" he said, shrugging his shoulders and looking ready to leave. Finally!

"Forget it, Jake. It's Vaginatown," I said, and we all laughed, even Tim, who then left us in peace so we could have a morning of sleepy, sloppy, lazy kisses, and hopefully a lot more. I arched myself a little to accommodate Ciara's very patient hand, then I pulled Portia across to me, because I'd done lots of amazing new things last night, but there was one I desperately wanted to cross off the list, and I couldn't do it without her… assistance.

*****

"Okay, ladies and gents! Everyone who has to say their goodbyes, say their goodbyes. Everyone else, climb aboard." We were all at the minibus, getting ready to leave. Frank was still at the hospital, so Bríd and Benson were going to pick him up on their way. Better, really, since Portia still knew nothing about what had happened him, and telling her now would be… well, lousy. Richie and Marian were over at a wall, too far away for us to eavesdrop on them. That was better too, though; I didn't want any more reasons to potentially burst into tears – I was already devastated to be losing her and Portia.

"You have my number, lemon slice?" She was so pretty, even after not sleeping for three days, and staying up all night with me and Ciara. Maybe she actually was a vampire? Would explain a lot.

"I do. You have mine?" Dublin wasn't that far away – we'd be up there lots with the band, or with radio and TV, hopefully. I'd definitely see her again. Or she could come stay with me – my house had loads of room, and my mum would absolutely love her, cos she was so exotic and interesting, and Mum loved exotic, interesting things – although that might not stress to having a daughter who fancied girls, just yet, so the treehouse might have to become our rendezvous point, for future lesnanigans.

"I'm gonna get it tattooed on the back of my hand, pudding," she said.

"So... do we?"

"Have a goodbye kiss, and is it allowed to be a proper one?" Ciara said, appearing beside me like a genie, without the puff of smoke.

"Allowed? Who's going to disallow it, vanilla pop? The Pope? The bishops? Gay Byrne?" She gave Ciara a proper, full-on, tonsil-tickling tour de force of a kiss goodbye.

"That was practically pornography, Maurice," said Brian, who was supposed to be getting the minibus ready.

"Don't be vile, Brian. No one forced you to watch," said Aisling, who I was very glad had not turned into a pumpkin this morning. We'd met her after we checked out earlier, and she was full of funny stories about Brian last night, full of curiosity about what we'd got up to in my room, and just full of lovely Aislingness in general.

"What can I say, possums – I have a very talented mouth," said Portia, then she grabbed me and did the same. The kiss felt even better than it looked; when it was over, I was genuinely light-headed.

"Wow, I can still taste myself on you, cupcake," she whispered in my ear, which really didn't help with the light-headedness.

"Come see me soon, Ling?" I said, trying not to get too emotional, although I probably didn't have enough serotonin to get emotional.

"Come and see *us* soon!" Ciara said, which sounded even better, to be honest. My head immediately started playing little mini-movies of last night, and they weren't the PG-13 kind.

"Wild horses couldn't stop me, muffins. One more hug for moi, please, yes?" We double-triple-obliged her and held on for as long as was physically possible, plus a little bit more.

"Why do you call her *Ling* all the time, Caoimhe?" Tim said. He and Niall and Ian had already seen the raver kids off, earlier. I hadn't been there, I'd been busy eating fortune cookies and whatnot, but I was sure it had been an emotional affair. Niall and Ian were in with Bríd and Benson – we were a split group for the journey home, just to make it more interesting, and to give B and B some company on the long drive.

"It's short for cunnilingus," I said, because I was hilarious. Richie was making his way slowly back to us while Portia made her way slowly over to Marian. We'd already had our Mar goodbyes a little earlier and I'd got her number too, so this weekend had given us so much more than great memories or new experiences. It was going to live on in the new friendships, or in the old ones that were rekindled.

"Are you okay, blue eyes?" I put an arm around Richie because he looked ready to cry, poor thing.

"I will be, Kweev. I will be, in a while. Here, Mar said to give these to you, like. She's gonna give up again today – new week, new start, she said, so." He handed me a box of B&H

with barely any taken out of it.

"Ooh! Sound of her, Rich. Nice one." Might go some way to paying off the 34 she still owed me, not that I was counting.

"Right! Hear that sound? That's an engine, Maurices and Mauricettes! It's the sound that means: Get in!" said Brian, and so, reluctantly, we did.

*****

"What you thinking about?" Ciara said, about an hour into the journey home. She was lying into me, all lazy and cute. I was definitely the designated big spoon in this thing we had or didn't have – whatever it was or wasn't. I was taller, so it made sense.

"Mmmmm, lots of things," I said, because it was true. The happy vibe of last night and this morning was fighting with the sad one of having to say goodbye to people, and somewhere in the middle, a bunch of chemicals were telling me that I actually had no emotions anymore, so everything was pointless and futile.

"I hope I'm one of them," she said, which was kind of surprising. Flirty Ciara was someone I knew, and Sexy Ciara was someone I'd been getting to know a lot recently. Lovey-dovey Ciara was new, though. Especially when I couldn't blame it on pills.

"Always," I said, fussing with the hair on top of her head, and kissing the bit of scalp that was visible at her crown.

"Mmmmm. I wish you had your own place. Or I had my own." She found my hand and linked fingers with me.

"Why's that?" I said. I did want to get a flat, but there was the small problem of a steady income. Dad basically refilled my savings account any time I emptied it, without ever asking questions – hence why I was able to keep up a frankly impressive drug habit, and why I already knew what cocaine felt like before I'd met my equally loaded Chinese wife – but a rent cheque seemed a bit different from that. Or maybe it wasn't. I could always just ask him. One of the advantages of being the surviving child in a family where one of the children had died suddenly and tragically was that your parents were very reluctant to say no to you. Just in case it turned out to be the last thing they ever said to you, I guessed.

"Oh, just because we wouldn't have to say goodbye this morning, that's all," she said, squeezing my hand again, and making me feel all warm inside.

"I can meet you tonight?" I hadn't exactly got plans. I never had plans, unless it included the band, or people I didn't really like dragging me out to things I didn't really want to go to. Hence why I got shitfaced all the time. That was going to change now, though. I'd be spending much more time with Ciara, and with Aisling too. I could just be sober and enjoy my life properly. But also occasionally get fucked up with either of them, or both of them. It was going to be the best of both worlds; I couldn't wait.

"Oh, I'd love that, but I think I'm going to be asleep from about an hour after we get to Limerick, until possibly Wednesday. I was just saying I'd rather it was me sleeping next to you."

"You're going to make me diabetic with all this sweetness, if you're not careful, you two cuties," said Aisling, who I had totally forgotten was sitting opposite us.

"Hah! Sorry, we'll try and rein in the sweetness, then," I said, slightly mortified, but only slightly. I looked over at poor Richie, who looked a bit like he was going to a funeral, or coming from a funeral, or preparing for his own funeral, and I felt awful for him.

"Hey, Richie!" said Brian, from the driver's seat.

"What?" How one syllable could convey that much pain I had no idea.

"Someone on the phone for you!" said Brian. Tim was holding the Motorola, and he passed it over to a very suspicious looking Rich.

"Brillo if this is a wind-up, I'm gonna tell you now, I'm in no mood, and I- Hello? Oh. Hi! How are you? You what? No, I'm – services place? With the shops? Yeah, I think we might be. Can she drop you there, and we'll wait? Yeah? Do you mind, sham? No? Okay. What? Brillo says? He says we'll be there in – okay, so. No. No, sorry, I just cant believe it. No! No, I'm delighted, sham. Wow. Okay. Okay, I'll just… what? Yeah. Yeah, she will and all. Haha! Okay. Okay, look, I'll see you in a bit? Right. Yeah, me neither. Bye."

"The fuck was all that about, Rich?" said Ciara, because everyone else was thinking it.

"That was Marian, like. She's getting Portia to drive her to the big services place, remember the one from Friday, like? They're about fifteen minutes behind us, at the rate Portia's hammering it, anyway. She's gonna come stay for a couple of weeks." He was as excited as a child on Christmas Eve who still believes in Santa, godhelpus.

"Portia drives?" I said. I didn't know this fact. In fairness though, I didn't even know what she did for a living – I hadn't asked her, it hadn't been that sort of relationship, or that sort of weekend.

"Yeah, why do you think I drove to that place back there, where her and Marian left us, Maurice? That was the repair garage. She left it in there on Friday, for a bit of a tune-up or something? New tyres, I think it was. Did she not tell ye?" said Brian, who apparently had a different relationship with Portia than I did.

"Yeah, she has a very fast Mercedes sports car," Tim

said. "She barely uses it though, because she's away so much with work, doing the whole air hostess thing." Maybe it had been that sort of weekend, after all?

"She's not an air hostess, she's a flight attendant!" said Aisling, who also knew everything about my Chinese wife that I didn't.

"Did you know she drives, or that she has a Mercedes, or that she's an air – a flight attendant?" I said to Ciara, quietly.

"Nope, I knew none of those things," she said.

"How could ye both spend so much time with her and not know anything about her?" Tim said, apparently disgusted at our lack of small talk skills.

"Probably because we were too busy SITTING ON HER FACE, Tim!" I said, which wasn't precisely true, but still hilarious.

*****

"So then, if ye're quite finished there, lads?" said Brian, in the direction of the pile of snogging flesh that used to be Richie and Marian. I'd no idea why they were all over each other – they'd only parted about 90 minutes ago, and she was coming home with us to Limerick, not leaving us again. We'd seen Portia again, briefly, but she didn't get out of the car, because she didn't do Second Goodbyes, apparently, and she had to get back to Dublin, for work. Possibly as a flight attendant. Possibly as an exotic dancer. Both were equally possible.

"Sorry, Brian. Yes?" said Mar, wiping the Richie slobber off her poor, perfect face.

"Where are you planning on staying? My folks will be delighted to see you, but I dunno about a bedroom or anything, Maurice. There's a spare room, but since the brother moved out, it's where the Da does all his model trains, squire.

He's been obsessed with the things, since the Ma gave up riding him, I'd say."

"You could stay with me, but I've no double bed, so." Richie shrugged his shoulders. Maybe Mick had a double, and he'd swap with them, so he could sleep in Richie's room, and hear them riding all night. I severely doubted every part of that scenario, though, so maybe not.

"Just come stay at mine," I said. "Mum and Dad already know you, so it won't be awkward, and they won't dream of saying no, like." It would only be for a week or two. She wasn't running away from Dublin or quitting UCD or anything. Just an impromptu holiday with her one true love. A very, very impromptu one. She must have had a big, romance movie-style moment of indecision. It was dead dramaticute.

"That's a great idea, Caoimhe. Are you sure they won't mind? I don't want to be any trouble, babe." She hadn't got many clothes with her, but we were the same size, boobs notwithstanding, and there was always Penney's.

"Won't be a bother, chick. Be great to have you there. I've missed you." It'd be really cool, apart from all the parts that would bring up horrible Áine memories, but most of our memories of Áine weren't horrible at all, so maybe the good ones would outweigh the bad.

"Will you come to my house today first though, for a while? And get the bus up to Castletroy later?" said poor Richie, terrified he was going to miss out on some precious hours with the actual love of his actual life, godhelpus.

"COURSE I WILL, SHNOOKUMZZZZZ!" she said, grabbing him by the chin and shaking his little face, which made us all giggle, even though none of us had any emotions left.

*****

"Okay, this is me, thanks!" said Ciara, when we got to Kileely, after dropping Love's Young Dream off in Crossroads so they could surprise Richie's dad.

"Am I coming out with you?" I asked, suddenly very unsure of myself, and of what I was supposed to be to her. Hardly the best choice of words, either.

"If you like," she said, stepping out of the minibus and helping me down after her. I'd been here before, at her house. It was a grim looking street, but the house itself was lovely.

"Um, I'd invite you in, but…"

"You don't love me?" Quiet, brain!

"Hahah!!! Of course I love you, you gombeen. No, I was gonna say, I'd invite you in, but your parents want you back early today, remember? Cos they have news for you?" She made a face that said she was wondering if the news of my parents having news for me was also news to me. She was kind of right.

"OH YEAH! I knew there was something I was fucking forgetting about. Thank you!" I lunged at her to kiss her and her eyes went massive like a cartoon, and she swerved a bit, so my kiss hit her on the cheek.

"Sorry!" she said, giving me a very nice squooch that stopped all the mad doubts that had popped into my head.

"No lesbian kisses in public in Kileely, right?" I said, feeling like a big sillyhead again.

"Yeah, I'd leave it out, to be honest."

"Not ready for that kind of thing here, no?" I said, as if my mother would be throwing garden parties to celebrate the fact that I now enjoy vaginas.

"I don't think IRELAND is ready for it yet, babe." She had a hat on now. One of those Donny Osmond caps. It was the cutest thing I'd ever seen in my life, and I'd seen a baby panda.

"Yeah, but their kids are gonna love it," I said, giving

her one last massive hug, and then hopping back on the bus to go home and face the news, whatever that might be.

*****

Mum and Dad both standing in the hallway when I came through the door did not fill me with hope that the news was going to be good news. She didn't look pregnant, at least. That was good. He looked a little pregnant, but that was down to too many business lunches and a fondness for the black stuff. I looked at them, and they looked at me. There were no formalities. No one asked me if I had a nice trip, or a good gig, or if I had gone down on any decent looking Chinese girls. They were all business, no barbecue today, my Mater and Pater.

"Well. Okay, there's no easy way to say thing, Caoimhe, so we're just going to tell you. Okay, love?" said Dad. He was usually the Good Cop in these scenarios.

"Listen, honey – it's about Jon," Mum said, making literally no sense. What was about Jon? Which Jon? *The* Jon? It had to be *the* Jon, otherwise they'd have specified, like with a surname or something. I was head-babbling now. I looked at Dad again.

"What about him, Dad?" What could they possibly have to tell me about Jon that I didn't already know, and why was it so urgent and dramatic that they were making this much of a song and dance about it? Unless…

"He's come out of the coma, love," said Dad. The room around me got a bit wobbly. Reminded me of the breathing floors on acid.

"He's off life support," Mum said, with a weird, half-smile. That stupid fucking song was in my head now, the Jon song, from the night we met, and from the Battle of the Bands – *Sweetness Follows*.

"He's actually talking, honey," said Dad. None of this

was real. I was gonna wake up in the back of the minibus in a minute, after Frank's weird joint.

"He's been asking to see you," said Mum. I was probably supposed to react; to say something back. I was probably supposed to get emotional, but I had no emotions left, so I just said the first thing that came into my head, but I said it from the heart.

"Fuck... me...pink."

I lit up a fag in front of them too, because fuck it, it was Christmas.

AFTERWORD

That was all right, wasn't it? I'm assuming it was, otherwise why would you have read this far? Anyway, I hope you enjoyed this one, and I hope you'll enjoy the next one (What Do I Do Now?) even more. I am writing them using a new, top secret system that involves all sorts of complicated bells and whistles and trade secrets, but all you need to know about it is that it works, and it works well, and it's very quick. Now, if you'll excuse me, I have to get back to writing 4,000 words a day, underwater, while playing the kazoo.

All the best,
Mister West

Printed in Great Britain
by Amazon